I0824358

The Street Gypsies

Glendell Latham

The Street Gypsies
Published through Lulu Press, Inc.

This is a work of fiction. Names, characters, places, and incidents are the product of the author's imagination or are used fictitiously. Any resemblance to actual persons, living or dead, events, or locales is entirely coincidental.

Interior Book Design and Layout by
www.integrativeink.com

ISBN: 978-0-6151-4205-0

Dedicated to
my mother, Alberta
and all my relatives.
Thanks for your love, wisdom and courage.

TABLE OF CONTENTS

PRELUDE V

CHAPTER 1 HUSTLER'S PARADISE 1

CHAPTER 2 SWEET SURVIVOR 114

CHAPTER 3 RING STING 211

CHAPTER 4 COLLEGE FRESHMAN 286

CHAPTER 5 ABSTINENT LOVE 421

CHAPTER 6 THE STREET GYPSIES ENDING 572

Prelude

"The Street Gypsies" written by Glen Latham is a fascinating submission of original fiction based on a true story. The author characterizes it as about eighty percent true; the remainder being fictionalized only enough to develop the story and carry it to it's logical conclusion. Surrounded by insidious depravity and moral bankruptcy, the central character, Jack Rollins refuses to cross the line and lose himself in this depraved environment. He manages to maintain a semblance of character; even though he struggles with his own immense faults. He finds it not within himself to commit the acts of atrocious behavior he often witnesses. Introducing the reader to Mr. Rollins in 1975, the author successfully conveys the atmosphere he inhabits. Granting access to a world precious few ever witness, the author vividly portrays the diseased environment far too many allow themselves to wallow. Most in Mr. Rollins' community find it necessary to rely on public assistance and illegal schemes. Presenting harrowing adventures and unsavory but, colorful characters provides the foundation from which the author constructs this gritty and riveting tale which possesses many of the same elements often associated with classic works of the same genre.

Composed in captivating narrative and compelling dialogue, the story flows at a brisk pace. The plot contains more than a few strategically placed, unexpected twists which should maintain the reader's interest throughout. The characters are developed and presented in a multi-dimensional fashion revealing the intricacies of their unique personalities and individual agendas. The author's highly descriptive style of writing combined with a keen attention to detail could further enhance the appeal of this work. In addition, the author effectively manages to avoid artificially padding the work with superfluous material and unnecessary characters; thereby keeping the focus directed toward the primary storyline. He navigates the plot to a well-conceived conclusion; this may leave the reader with the sense of time well invested in the reading of this intriguing story.

CHAPTER 1
HUSTLER'S PARADISE

In 1975 on the northside of Chicago in the heart of Uptown stood the notorious Malden Arms. 4727 North Malden. It stood ominously among the two and three-flat apartment buildings near Lawrence Avenue in this adventurous neighborhood; a drab apartment-hotel that was a haven to various colorful street characters in the area such as; Big Red, Flukie, Motic, Saheeve and Patch-eye Slim who were the more notable in a society of free spirits---street hustlers extraordinaire; dope dealers, gamblers, pimps, prostitutes, thieves and con artists who lived in the "Arms" as it was called, with some of the down-trodden who were not hustlers; just poor souls trying to survive. Most all of them, the hustlers and non-hustlers alike, paid their rent with money from social security, disability or general assistance checks. These street hustlers lived for the exhilaration of high-risk hustling and getting high----the game was religion and the streets were church. They were urban nomads, living from place-to-place like gypsies----they were Street Gypsies. The life was fast and hard. The hatching of nefarious hustling schemes was the order of the day----running game. Success was paramount for survival. Jail and death were all part of the life.

Jack Rollins was an impetuous, whimsical street hustler. He was intelligent, loyal and generous. He was defiant and somewhat unconventional; even for the crazy life he was living. In spite of his recklessness and thievery, there was a good heart. Jack, for all of the cunning and savvy that he had gained in his few years on the streets, was sometimes just as naïve; perhaps, because he was not capable of the viciousness that some of his fellow hustlers were. He had seen some set up their so-called friends to be robbed just to get a hit of dope. He had seen others taken in out of the cold only to steal from those who had sheltered them. He had seen men try to steal their friend's woman while the friend was in jail. Jack was well aware of how things went in the streets and he was no saint himself. He had committed his share of gratuitous wrongs. But, he seemed to operate out of his own set of principles and codes of decency. He could not muster up very much cruelty, even when urged on by others. Jack refused to cross the line into absolute depravity. His mission seemed more rooted in survival.

1975 was a wild year in Uptown for Jack Rollins. He had moved into the Malden Arms during the Fall, more than a year after losing his job. The apartments were small kitchenettes with a stove, bed, bathroom and closet.

At the beginning of last year, there had been many problems at the State Office of Employment Security. People's unemployment compensation checks had been held up for months. No one was receiving them. There was a near-riot at a downtown unemployment office where Jack had gone. People were standing on top of tables. Jack remembered a man standing on top of a table and shouting "I want to get hold of a supervisor!" Jack finally began to receive his unemployment checks in the spring last year. But, after a year, it had run out without him finding another job. Soon, Jack had no money and nowhere to stay. He had lived in the streets, literally, for most of the summer this year because he had gotten evicted out of his bachelor apartment at 4848 North Winthrop; a more civilized venue suitable for family living where he had first moved into Uptown. Finally, after several trips during the late summer to the Aid office, he had gotten a steady monthly check coming so he could have the apartment at the Arms. He tried to settle into the kitchenette apartment as best he could with very little money. He had gotten that first big check from the Aid office and after paying the rent, went on a get-high spree that left him broke, as usual. But, this was the usual routine. It was the way Jack and all of the other street hustlers lived; from day-to-day; moment-to-moment; the future and the past meant nothing; right now was all that mattered.

Jack was able to retrieve clothes he left at his friend "Willie-the-Weep's" room at the YMCA on Hermitage and Wilson and take them back to The Arms. The clothes had been there since the middle of spring because Jack had nowhere else to keep them. Besides, The Weep was his drinking buddy and they had shared many a day hustling for drinks together. Weep even sneaked Jack in to crash in his room a few times.

It was a sunny day in late September, 1975. Jack slept most of the day after another wild night of drinking. He finally woke up, showered and dressed. He locked his door and left his apartment at about 5:30pm. He was walking down the hall, heading for the stairwell when an elderly man with a cane passed him on his left heading in the opposite direction. Two men who seemed to be together passed him, as well, going in the same direction behind the old man. As Jack neared the stairwell, he could hear dialogue between the old man and the two men. "Hey, Marty…how ya' doin'?" Jack could hear one of the men say to the elderly man just before he pulled the stairwell door open to walk down. Jack could hear the old man saying something just as he entered the stairwell. When Jack reached the lobby, he walked over to the public phone in the far right corner.

When the hustling was not so good and he was broke, Jack would ask Pretty Willie to front him some dope to sell. In the past, he had gotten small amounts of heroin on consignment from him. This was something that Jack preferred not to do. He did not like the haggling with the dope-fiend clientele or the risk of getting stuck-up. He only asked for small amounts of the good heroin that Pretty Willie would have so that he could sell it quickly and make a small profit by stretching it slightly. He would pay Pretty Willie back after selling out. Pretty Willie knew that Jack was a good hustler so, he fronted him. Jack knew that it took a while before the word would spread about anyone who was working alone selling dope out on the streets; and it was usually not long afterward that they would be stuck up. So, he would have sold those small amounts of heroin too quickly for the stickup artists to draw a bead on him. For these reasons, selling dope was a last resort and he did it only once in a great while.

He was calling Pretty Willie now so that he could front him again. "Hello" a male voice greeted on the phone. "Hey…who is this?" Jack asked. "This L'il Jake"...who you want?" the voice replied. "Hey, man….I need to holla' at Pretty Willie" Jack said. "He ain't here…he won't be back until later on" L'il Jake replied. "How much later, man?" Jack asked, as he began to feel a little bit of frustration from what L'il Jake had said. L'il Jake began saying something on the phone to Jack when, suddenly, Jack felt a tug at the elbow of his sport jacket. It startled him somewhat and interrupted his listening to L'il Jake. "Here ya' go, bro'" a man's voice said. Jack turned around to see that it was one of the two men he had just seen not more than a few minutes ago in the third floor hallway. "Hey, check this, man,"..."bro-man, check this here!" the gritty looking character said to Jack while his partner stood behind him several feet away. Jack thought they wanted to buy dope from him; perhaps, sent by some of the fiends he had sold heroin to in the Arms recently. "I don't have nothin', man!" Jack said as he turned back around to continue his phone conversation. "Bro'…bro'….check this, man…look!" the man insisted as he tugged at Jack's sleeve once again. "Hold it a minute, L'il Jake" Jack said into the phone as he turned around with an annoyed expression to face the man. "Hey, bro'…this yours" the man said as he nudged Jack's elbow with his hand. Jack looked down to see a crisp twenty dollar bill half-folded in the man's hand. "I know you seen that" the man said. Jack paused with the phone in his hand, puzzled at what was going on. Seeing that Jack was hesitating, the man grabbed his left hand and forced the twenty dollar bill into it. "You alright, bro'"…you didn't see nothin'…okay?" The man said to Jack as he backed away and turned to his buddy. "He's cool, man....let's ride!" the stranger said. With that, they both walked out of the front entrance in a hurry looking wild-eyed, anxious and suspicious. Jack just stood dazed as he watched the two men disappear through the front entrance door. "I don't know what kinda' bullshit is goin' on" he thought "but this shit is alright whenever you can get paid for just standin' around" He snapped out of his daze as the voice could be heard on the phone. "Hey, guy...hey, guy" L'il Jake's voice repeated over the phone. "Aw…hey, L'il Jake…I'll try to catch Pretty Willie a little later" Jack said still somewhat mystified by the incident that had just occurred while he gazed at the new twenty dollar bill in his hand.

He hung the phone up and decided he would head over to the poolroom on the corner of Lawrence and Winthrop and cop a taste at Saxony Liquors on the way there. When Jack stopped at Saxony, the owner, "Nick the Greek" was waiting on customers. "Pint 'o Dimitri', Nick" Jack said, smiling as he gave the crisp new twenty a spirited slap across the palm of one hand as he held it in the other. Jack had counted his money when he woke up this morning. He had $3.27 in his pocket. He was just happy to have lucked up on the twenty dollars. He didn't know why he received it. But, he was not going to "look a gift horse in the mouth" He really didn't give a damn what the reason was. He would just buy the drink and forget about it. He decided that he would sit in the poolroom and nurse the drink he bought and hang around and see what was happening out in the streets. It just seemed like something good always came his way when he was high and his inhibitions were non-existent.

On an average day, he would just hang around the poolroom hanging out with any of the regulars who happened to be around. They would usually ante-up on one drink after another; a fifth of "Rose" or a half or whole pint of cheap vodka, depending on how much change they could scrape up. No one worked. Most everyone hustled. This was the life that so many of them had fallen into. Working a steady job for these Street Gypsies never even came to mind. It was so far out of the realm of how they lived; stealing, conning, lying and cheating was the rule. Most of them had a regular general assistance, social security, disability or some other check coming in steadily to keep a place to stay. The check paid the rent and they hustled for everything else. A hustler could make it as long as he had a place. If he didn't have his own place, he had to "carry a stick" which made his life much harder because he would have to scuffle to survive in the streets with nowhere to stay. Otherwise, he would have to find someone who would let him stay with them. Then, he would have to live by their rules. A Street Gypsy's life was not an easy one. But, was the way he or she chose to live. It was complete freedom of the mind, body and spirit. You did whatever you wanted. You kept your own hours of how late you stayed up and when you went to bed. You spoke a language that only street hustlers understood. You lived in a society of undesirables and misfits; everything centered on getting high and hustling for a living; you ran a lot of risk living this way; you had to deal with the plain clothes, plain car detectives known to Street Gypsies as "The Slick Boys" These cops were always hassling Street Gypsies on the streets with stops and searches; sooner or later a Street Gypsy made enemies in the streets; usually over money or drugs; they found themselves taking all kinds of risks trying to hustle. Street Gypsies did retail boosting; selling drugs; break-ins; conning and most anything else they could get away with to make money.

Good things happened sometimes when they were high. But, other times the worst things would happen, too. Sometimes, the street life was fatal; like the time the Jamaican hustler, Raul was chased by the police and died from falling on the third rail at the Wilson Street elevated train tracks. He got himself good and high and busted out a retail display window on the street and stole merchandise right out of the window. He was feeling so good from his high, until he didn't even run---he just walked as he looked for a place to hide. But, the police started chasing him before he got there. He tried to escape by running along the L tracks and slipped and fell on the third rail where he was electrocuted.

Jack paid "Nick the Greek" for the pint of vodka and continued eastward on Lawrence Avenue toward the Aragon Poolroom He passed the entrance of the Aragon Ballroom where there was a lot of activity going on inside in preparation for the next big music concert that was advertised on the huge marquee that hung over the entranceway. "Journey Sept 24-25" it read in big letters outlined by the flashing bulbs that could be seen from far away. He passed the A&W burger joint next door to the poolroom that was owned and operated by one his fences, John and his wife Marcie. It was Friday and already the hustle and bustle of the crowd that got off work the earliest had begun to fill up the small carry-out restaurant. On Fridays, people usually had more money and most ate out or just picked up something on the way home. The sound of frying burgers and the smells of the restaurant food wafting out to the street were so familiar to Jack. He began to get that feeling of anticipation and excitement that he always got on days like this. Especially in the late-afternoon-early-evenings on the weekends when the sun was going down and turning orange with its mild glare that cast over the streets; bringing a feeling of exuberance that made him feel even more alive.

This was Jack's paradise; this corner; this street and everything that went on around it. This was where and how he lived and hustled--his "hustler's paradise" He walked up to the double-glass doors of the poolroom entrance and swung one of the doors open effortlessly as he had done a thousand times before and easily as he breathed the air. His eyes darted around the room as he gauged the level of activity inside and looked for familiar faces. Some of the local regulars were already unwinding from work with a spirited pool game as they traded the usual good natured bragging and taunts mixed in with hoots and laughter. Jack was feeling low-key right now, even a little mellow.

He had settled into his crib over at the Arms and that was what really had him at ease. Because he had "carried a stick" all during the summer, he had almost lived in and around the poolroom during that time. Now, it really felt relaxing that it was no longer a struggle for him. He could go home and lay his head down and have some peace-of-mind and privacy. He could shower and wear clean clothes on a regular basis. He could do all of that and yet, he was only a few blocks away from his favorite spot, The Corner. Jack looked around the poolroom. There were a few games going but, the poolroom didn't get full until another hour-and-a-half later at around seven-thirty. The patrons would file in over that time until the action reached a fever pitch when the place was crowded. Jack loved the crowd and the noise and the loud bragging that was a regular part of the poolroom on Friday and Saturday nights.

Like most any street hustler, Jack was always looking to make money--- to make a hustle. Jack did not shoot pool because he used most all of his money for drinking and because he did not seem to have the patience. He had hung around the poolroom over the last two years using it as an anchor for most of his hustling activities. If he had gone into a retail store on Wilson Avenue and boosted something or conned for any kind of merchandise, he would sell it to any one of the several fences he knew in the radius of two blocks from the poolroom. He had sold plenty of merchandise to John, the owner of the A&W burger joint next door and to "Nick the Greek", the owner of Saxony Liquors; and Stan, the owner of The Green Mill and to Sharon and her husband, the owners of Sharon's bar across the street; or to Jose, the owner of the Aragon or to his managers and workers or to any of the people in the bars or on the streets who might be interested in what he had to sell. He had sold overcoats, battery chargers or blue jeans stolen from Goldblatts a block away on Broadway; or ladies lingerie that he had stolen on several occasions from

Jupiters, the five-and-dime store at the corner of Leland and Broadway; or the boom-boxes, radios, tape recorders and small TVs he got from the audio store next to the Green Mill Cocktail Lounge. Jack had become so good at this kind of hustling because of how well he dealt with the fences and the way that he gave them the utmost respect while persuading them with his style of talk. He was good at being charming and he used that skill with them; but, he maintained a degree of trust with them by dealing honestly with his hot merchandise. He would never sell them bad merchandise or make a promise about it that was not true. He knew that trust was all he had to work with when dealing with his fences and he protected it no matter what. Jack had gotten so good until other hustlers would bring their merchandise to him because of all the connections he had with his fences and the rapport he maintained with them. Now-a-days, Jack could just sit in the poolroom and not have to run up and down the streets to make money. Other hustlers brought their merchandise to him because it was quicker and easier than trying to sell it themselves. When they did, Jack would feel a cheap sense of loftiness and credibility when they would come around the poolroom and reverently solicit him to sell their wares. They didn't have the connections with fences nor the knack for selling that Jack did; and, of course, they had to give Jack a fair cut if he sold anything for them; and if they didn't, he had gotten his off the top, anyway.

Jack sat in his favorite spot at the seat in the far left corner from the entrance door. There, he could survey everything that went on around the poolroom; who came in; who left out and when people outside passed by the stretch of the poolroom window facing Lawrence Avenue. This way, he could see people he was avoiding before they saw him. Carlos was at the poolroom counter checking in customers tonight. He was the son of Jose, the owner of the Aragon. He was rarely there during the week. He was only seen on the busier nights on the weekends when receipts were heaviest. He had come to accept Jack as a fixture around the poolroom. Jack respected Carlos because he never gave him a hard time. Carlos kind of liked Jack because of the excitement he sometimes generated around the poolroom that entertained Carlos and his workers at the poolroom counter.

Finally, some familiar faces entered the poolroom. Fuzzy and Woody. They came through the entrance door with Fuzzy's familiar voice chattering away loudly. Jack could tell that Fuzzy was already high. He could hear the slurring in his speech. Jack knew their routine because six months after he moved into the 4848 high-rise, he met Fuzzy. They shared some drinks and hung out together for several months before Jack had become so scandalous. Since then, they had drifted apart and Jack had not visited Fuzzy's home. He knew Fuzzy and Woody's routine. On Friday nights, when they got paid, they would meet up at Fuzzy's place on the fifth floor of the high-rise on the corner of Gunnison Street and Sheridan Road, a couple of blocks from the poolroom. They would have their packaged liquor that they picked up on the way. They would drink and socialize there for a couple of hours before heading for the poolroom. Fuzzy and Woody worked steady jobs. Their lifestyle was very different from Jack's. They did not steal or do any of the kind of hustling that Jack did. They had witnessed what Jack did in the streets. They watched him selling all kinds of stolen merchandise around the poolroom. They watched him get into fights and get arrested. All of this made them not trust Jack. Jack knew this but, he didn't care what they thought of him. He didn't care for their square style of living, anyway. "Bunch o' lame-ass shit" he would say of the way Fuzzy and Woody carried on. The two were the best of friends and Jack didn't have anything against Fuzzy. But, he did have some resentment toward Woody.

A little more than a year ago, Woody somehow, wound up sharing Jack's apartment with him on the third floor at 4848. Jack had started getting his unemployment checks back then and he needed a roommate to help with the rent. Woody stayed for three months without paying; all the while promising to pay what he owed in rent to Jack when his unemployment checks would start coming in. When the first check finally did come, Woody had them going to Fuzzy's house while he lived at Jack's. He left Jack's apartment the day he got the first check and never told Jack about getting it and never paid him a dime. That pissed Jack off. He and Woody had words and nearly came to blows. But, they never fought because Fuzzy and some other mutual friends jumped between them and made them promise not to fight. Jack tried to let it go because he was going through so much at the time with trying to keep his apartment. That experience hardened Jack quite a bit. What Woody had done was low-down, he thought.

Jack vowed that he would never be taken advantage of like that again. The experience seemed to serve as some kind of initiation into the Street Gypsy life.

Jack decided that it was time to get mellow so, he headed for the back of the poolroom to the men's restroom. He went into a stall and pulled out the pint of vodka and slowly began to sip on it, pursing his lips, bracing himself for the bitter, burning taste that he had experienced so many times before. "Hummph!" he groaned as the burning vodka went down his throat. He took another good hit before returning to his seat in the corner at the front window. He sat peacefully watching the poolroom activity and listening to the buzz of bravado from the growing crowd of pool patrons; occasionally looking out of the window to see the pedestrian traffic on the streets become more lively as the night wore on. Jack had no idea what he would be getting into tonight. There was nothing planned; no business to take care of. He would just be spontaneous to what ever came his way tonight. He would take advantage of whatever situation arose to put money in his pocket. He was constantly hustling because his general assistance check was strictly for his rent and there was never anything left except the food stamps. He sometimes sold some of those within a few days of receiving them.

Almost an hour had passed since Jack entered the pool room. Since that time, a steady stream of patrons had come in with the earliest arrivals just starting to leave. Some were regular patrons that Jack really never knew who came from nearby neighborhoods. Some were from other parts of town, stopping on their way home to relax with a few games. Others were neighborhood regulars whom Jack had a nodding acquaintance with; and usually, there were the regulars from Fuzzy and Woody's group of working friends. They all knew Jack and he was on speaking terms with all of them. But, Jack rarely carried on conversations of much length or depth with any of them. Jack knew that they thought they were more decent than he was because they worked every day and had money most of the time; unlike Jack who didn't work; was sometimes broke and was always getting into some kind of trouble while he hustled in the streets.

Finally, one of Jack's best friends, Coley came through the door. Jack watched him from a distance as he walked through the entrance door and continued straight ahead to the group with Woody and two other players shooting pool across the room from Jack. Coley sat down next to Fuzzy and Jack could see them meet and exchange greetings and start casual small talk; smiling broadly as they both watched the players maneuvering around the pool table in front of them. Jack couldn't hear what they were saying above the chatter in the long, stretching room. So, he decided to walk over and talk to his friend. He felt much more comfortable with Coley because they got high together on drinking and Ts and Blues and they hung out together and occasionally plotted together on one money-making scheme or another. Coley was not only his friend but, somewhat of a mentor because he was about fourteen years older than Jack--almost forty. He was one of the few people on the streets and around the neighborhood whose advice Jack listened to. Coley admired Jack because he was a young man who, despite his scandalous ways, had some redeeming qualities. Coley was surprised that he could trust Jack as much as he could. He always teased Jack and was amused by his wild and crazy exploits; how he was involved in one mad scheme after another. One day, while a group of the regulars were gathered up on the side of Frances' Tavern, Coley said something to them about Jack while Jack stood there listening. "The rougher it gets, the better he likes it" Coley said. The words struck Jack in an odd way. He had never thought about himself in that way. But, he had to admit that it had a ring of truth to it. This insane street life had led him to this. He had adapted to the madness of the streets in order to survive. The more civilized part of him had gradually disappeared over time because of the brutal conditioning of the streets and the things he did to survive in them. When Coley said those words about him, Jack took them in and ruminated momentarily. But, after that moment, he accepted it as valid with the same calloused indifference as all the other truths about himself---it didn't matter. He had to keep on doing what he had to do.

"Hey, Coley….what's happ'nin', brotha'!" Jack greeted Coley. "What's goin' on, fool!" Coley replied with a broad grin as he turned to give Jack a soul handshake. "What you up to, man?...I know you got some shit up ya' sleeves…you might as well tell me all about it" Coley said, playfully. "Naw, brother-man…I cain't kill nothin' and won't nothin' die!" Jack joked with a chuckle and smile. “Damn, Jack…that’s a boss sport coat you got there, man….you tryin’ to get clean on us out here, huh?” Coley teased as he looked over and admired the navy-colored sport jacket that Jack was wearing. “Yea, Coley….now that a brotha’ got a place to lay his head, he can try to get a little sporty…you dig?” Jack replied with a slightly pursed upper lip to emphasize the pride he felt in how he was now dressing better. “You wanna get up on a taste, Jack?” Coley asked. “Don’t worry ‘bout it, baby…got a taste right here” Jack replied. “What you got, Jack?” Coley asked “Treat me, man…treat me!” Jack replied in a lyrical tone. It was an inside joke that Coley and all the others that Jack drank with understood. It was a play on the name of the Dimitri vodka. It came about one day when Robert Lee, in his usual joking manner, asked Mae, as she returned from the liquor store to “Treat me to Dimitri” in front of a small group hanging around the front entrance of the Tower building. The whole crowd had a big laugh at the play on words and they all began to use the catchy phrase from that day on. The two men walked to the men’s restroom in the back of the poolroom to drink the vodka that Jack had stuffed in his inside sport jacket. They did not say much as they traded the bottle between themselves a couple of times; each man making his own grimacing reaction to the taste of the cheap vodka.

“What you been up to Coley?…I ain’t been seein’ you on the scene lately” Jack inquired as the two men walked past the pool games on the way back to the front. “Aw, shit, man…I’m always gettin’ static from my old lady, Shirley…she always naggin’ me to do somethin’ more main-stream…but, I always tell her, baby…I‘m a hustler…have been most of my life..I can work a job for a little while, but, sooner or later…I get to itchin’ for the street life…I just cain’t help it…it’s in my blood!” “Yea” Jack said with a sigh of agreement. “You have had quite a hustlin’ career…pimpin’…sellin’ drugs…gettin’ paid from every which-way…I can believe it’s in your blood, man…sho’‘nough!” “…but you know what?…I can see her point when you consider she is about to finish college...seems like you and her are in two different worlds” Jack said, adding his analysis to the topic. “Yea, but..you know what?…we ain’t in so different-a-worlds as you might think…when a woman decides to be with a man, it don’t matter what he’s doin’ or what she’s doin…once she makes up her mind to be with you…don't matter!" Coley philosophized as he emphasized the "don't matter" "Besides…I been carryin' my weight with her for quite a while now…we been together for over three years now and I bought most all the furniture…I bought that car for her and put a down payment on it that damn-near paid for it…she only had to pay a small note on it for a few months after that…all from hustlin'…no job!" Coley bragged.

Jack and Coley stopped near the pool table where Coley and Fuzzy had first met a little earlier. The game was in high gear. They sat in the two seats next to Fuzzy. "Big-time Jack…what's goin' on, man!" Fuzzy greeted rather loudly. Jack could feel the energy generated from Fuzzy's high. Everybody liked Fuzzy---even Jack despite the fact that Fuzzy's best friend was that jive-ass Woody who had played on Jack over a year ago. "Hey Fuzz…what's poppin', man!" Jack replied in his usual upbeat manner. Together, the three of them sat at the Winthrop-side poolroom window in front of the game that Woody was playing with two other friends. They traded comments about whatever came to mind; occasionally bursting out in unison with hearty laughter.

This was the way most Friday nights went and this was why Jack loved these fun-filled evenings so much; the laughter and excitement; the banter and camaraderie; the crowded pool room buzzing with activity---this was what he truly enjoyed. He could have a good time and it seemed that he was much more care-free than he was during the dead weekdays when nothing was going on. Besides, on the weekends there was more money floating around and that seemed to create a lot more joy in the atmosphere. The bar would start to get crowded at Sharon's across the street; over on Broadway, two blocks west, the Green Mill faithful would pack the house; the small bar section inside Saxony Liquors would have a good crowd on Friday nights and the take-out would be non-stop. Of, course, one of the best things about these nights was that they were good hustling nights. Just like any other Street Gypsy, Jack loved these nights because money could be made faster and easier.

The banter had subsided between the three men when a stranger, a white man of about medium height, not quite six feet walked close to the group sitting in a row on the plastic seats in front of the Winthrop-side window. He stopped within a few feet of Jack who sat on the end seat. The stranger scanned the pool room with an expression on his face that said he was looking for something or someone. As he paused, all three men took note of his presence and could tell that he was about to say what was on his mind. Then, he looked straight at Jack "Hey, my man…how ya' doin'?" he greeted. "What's goin' on, guy?" Jack responded with an anticipating expression. After that, the stranger leaned over and lower, then squatted down about a couple of feet from Jack. "Hey, my man…you know where I can score some good weed?" he asked almost in a whisper. After he spoke, Jack looked over to Coley and said "be cool for a minute, Coley" and walked a couple of steps to the other side of the stranger and turned back to him and gave a little beckoning flip of his hand and at the same time mumbled "follow me" The stranger followed Jack to the vestibule between the front entrance double doors and the single inside door. Jack never liked to be seen outside talking to white dudes about copping drugs because the "Slick Boys" would pass by in their unmarked cars, see them talking and turn around and sneak up on them, jump out of their cars and start searching and harassing both of them. He had learned from experience to stay out of sight. Jack stopped and stepped to one side to allow room for people to come in and out. "How much weed you tryin' to get, my man? Jack asked very business-like as he turned to face the man. "I don't know, man…it depends on how good it is" the stranger replied very casually. "Well, I'll tell ya'….dude got some fire over there in the courtway" Jack said in a tantalizingly rhythmic tone. The stranger paused as he looked out of the window to the corner directly across from where they stood. He could not see the courtway from where he was standing. But, Jack knew he was probably familiar with where it was. "Is it good, though, is what I'm sayin'" the stranger said plain and simple and very relaxed. "Hey, I cain't make no guarantees, my man…cause I haven't had any for a little while…but, last time I copped…it was bumpin'" Jack said, going into his sales pitch. "…and I'll tell ya'…he don't mess with nothin' that ain't kickin'…dig what I'm sayin' player?" Jack said spiritedly as he raised the tone of his pitch, sounding as hip as he could. "Aw, man…check this…speak o' the devil!" Jack said emphatically. "Look over there, man…" Jack said to the stranger. "What?" The stranger replied. "See them two studs right there?.." Jack said as he pointed from inside the double doors "They come over to the weed man and cop every Friday evenin'" Jack said as he started his usual gestures and motions when he was into his hustling and conning mode. "You see…now, they fucked up offa' that weed….they comin' from visitin' this chick in the courtway….the chick went two doors over and copped from the weed man…they laid at her crib and got bent offa' that weed…I'll tell ya', man…them boys is wrecked!" look at 'em…they cain't hardly stand up…and they don't hardly do no drankin'…just that weed!" The stranger was so affected by Jack's gestures and sales pitch until his next words were "Will you cop for me?" Jack stopped talking after the stranger spoke. He stood looking at him for a long moment and just grinned.

Inwardly, it was a smile of satisfaction for Jack that he had his "mojo workin" and could affect a person in a way to make himself some money. "Okay…okay….I'll cop for you, my man…no problem…only one thing, though…" Jack said calm and deliberately. "What is it?" the stranger asked quickly with a slight furrowing of his forehead "Can you look out for me?" Jack asked in a peaceful, almost polite tone "What you want, man?…joints?…some dollars?.. …name it…I'll throw a little somethin' your way...no problem, long as you cop and the weed is good and it's a fair amount for the money" the stranger said showing a little anxiousness in his now excited eyes. Jack and the stranger huddled up in the corner of the vestibule as the stranger counted money for the weed into Jack's hands. Jack looked around and paused anytime someone walked past. He walked across the street to the courtway. He was gone about ten minutes before he returned to the poolroom vestibule where the stranger was waiting. "Hey, guy…let's go to one of the stalls in the back so you can check it out, okay?" Jack said. The stranger didn't say a word but, turned around to the inside single door and walked through it and headed for the men's restroom with Jack following close behind.

Jack and the stranger entered one of the stalls and the stranger opened the package that Jack gave him and sniffed. He inspected it by pouring a little of it out and spreading it in his palm. He quickly rolled a joint, lighting it to take a couple of tokes. He handed it to Jack after his second toke. Jack was not a weed smoker but, he took two small hits, making the usual sucking noise with his lips to appear that he was really into it. The aroma was strong and rich as it wafted with the smoke into the stale restroom air. “Hey, my man…this shit is alright!” the stranger said after breathing out the last toke and showing a faint smile of satisfaction on his face. He cut the smile short because he knew it would affect how he compensated his runner, Jack. He probably had strangers cop for him many times before and knew that, in the end, he had to pay something to the runner. But, he didn’t want what he paid to be measured by his show of satisfaction.

“Here you go, my man…how’s that?” the stranger said as he handed Jack a five dollar bill. “Aw, this cool, man…this is cool…but…check this here…Jack started. “I like to get high too, man…can I get a joint or two outa ‘ya?….I’m ‘sposta’ meet my little honey tonight and a coupla’ joints sho’ ‘nough would top it off!…my money’s a little short right now” Jack said to the stranger as he was up close to his face talking low and soft in his conning voice. “Come on, player...it ain’t gonna hurt you with all that weed you got …and it’s fire, too!” Jack added turning up the persuasion and adding the facial expressions to go with it. “Okay, man…alright..you got somethin’ to put it in?” the stranger asked. “Hey…I got somethin’ right here” Jack announced as he reached to the inside pocket of his sport jacket and pulled out the pint of vodka. “I’ll just take the skirt offa’ this bitch!” he said, half-mumbling as he concentrated on pulling the brown paper bag from the bottle and placing the bottle back in his inside pocket and then spreading the bag flat before he began tearing a section of paper from it. “Yeah…this’ll do the trick, baby!” Jack said, talking aloud to himself. After he had the section of paper spread flat in his hand, he walked back to the stranger who had backed out of the stall and was standing just outside the half-opened stall door. Jack just paused for a few seconds then said “Get on back in here!” “You don’t want these chumps to see you with no weed!....they will beg the draws offa’ yo’ ass, man!…get on back in here!” Jack admonished the stranger as he reached out and pulled him by his wrist back into the stall. “…and lock the door, man!” Jack directed after the stranger was completely inside the stall. The stranger seemed slightly unnerved by Jack’s aggressive, savvy style. He reached slowly into the side pocket of his thin blue jean jacket and pulled the nicely wrapped small manilla bag out and held it close as he aimed the flap of the open bag to the spread-open piece of paper. “Treat me right, player…treat me right.. I'll cop for you anytime you come through…don't never worry about it…" Jack went on; adding all the persuasive little catch-phrases he could in the few seconds before the weed began to pour out onto the piece of paper. "Hey…there you go" the stranger said after pouring what he felt was two joints worth of weed. "Come on, dude…touch me up just a little bit mo', man!" Jack urged before the stranger could pull the envelope of weed back. "Don't be scared to drop it…go 'head…" "Alright..I think that oughta' do you good" the stranger interrupted before Jack got carried away. "Okay" Jack shot back very quickly, as if to acknowledge that he had been pressing the stranger too much for his weed. "Ok, bro, thanks…I sho' 'nough 'preciate it…my little honey gon' love me for this here…mercy!" Jack said excitedly with a gleeful grin. He folded the paper bag around the small mound of weed inside and tucked it away in his right lower jacket pocket. The stranger had quickly pulled the bag away, closed and wrapped it and stuffed it back in his blue jean jacket pocket. "I got to get going, my man…alright?" the stranger said. "OK, guy…be smooth, now" Jack said as he watched the stranger walk through the restroom entrance door to leave.

Jack walked back into the noisy poolroom to hear the tune "Tear the Roof Off the Sucker" by the Parliament blaring over the audio system. He could feel the rhythm take hold of him and his joy was boosted as the tune played "we gonna turn this mother out…..we gonna turn this mother out!" the lyrics blared. After several steps from the restroom, he did a little diddy of a step to the tune with his "James Brown" slide at the end. He was feeling good. Jack walked back near the front to where Fuzzy and Coley were still sitting in front of the pool game where Woody was playing.

"What you beat that white boy out of?" Coley quizzed with a low snicker. "I didn't beat him outa' nothin" Jack replied innocently …."I went and copped for him…but, check this…while we was standin' in the doorway up there…hehehehe..I seen Buster and Jo-Jo crossin' the street out there…with their alcoholic asses….Hehehe…they was comin' from the courtway….hehehehe…and I told dude..hahaha….that they was weed smokers…hehehe..hahaha….and they was bent…hahahaha…offa' that weed..hahaha..when they really drunk offa' that wine…he saw how high they was…hahaha…and his eyes popped out…hahahehe…he wanted me to hurry up and…hahaha.. cop some o' that weed…hahahaha…Jack said as he laughed heartily at the thought of his little con. "Coley began to snicker along with Jack. "You just tickled to death, ain't you, Jack?" Coley asked. "That shit *is* funny, man…you got all kinda' shit up ya' sleeves, don't you'?" Coley chided as they both laughed and snickered. "But, you *are* right, Jack..them fools do get so wasted until their asses…hehehe..are draggin' the ground…hahahahaha…Coley admitted as the two men continued to laughed.

Their laughter finally subsided. They sat for a while watching Woody's pool game kind of absent-mindedly when they simultaneously turned their heads toward the pool room entrance as the door swung open. They saw Blane and TJ coming through the door; two hustlers from the low-end down around Irving Park Road. Although they were the same type of small-time hustlers as Jack, they were not nearly as good. They walked into the pool room looking wide-eyed and gazing all around as if they were looking for something. Jack recognized that look right away. He knew that they had something they were looking to sell. He kept his eyes on them; watching them stride in nice and easy as they looked all around for prospects to buy whatever it was they were trying to sell. They were not carrying anything in their hands; no big, bulky item to sell, which was good, he thought. In Jack's experience of hustling in the streets, he preferred not to carry around large or bulky items that could be seen from a distance because they drew too much attention from the police and other people. It was too obvious and people knew too much of your business right away by observing your wares. Whenever he had bulky items to sell, he always put them in a bag or covered them so that people could not see them. But, sometimes that's what small-time hustling involved. If you didn't have anything else to sell, you never passed up an opportunity to make money. You tried to sell it, whatever it was. Besides, Jack kept his hustling small-time for a reason. He had heard of too many other hustlers committing big robberies or even hurt or kill someone for money and get caught and get big time in jail. That was not his style and he did not take those kinds of chances because he did not want to serve any big time. Besides, he could not bring himself to hurt people for money. His style involved conning more than anything;

along with a little boosting and anything else that did not involve stick-ups or hurting people. He had done days and weeks in jail. He had done a month just once and that's the way he wanted to keep it. He knew he was not the type to do hard time. He did fairly well at staying out of jail, usually going only for overnight stays in the local jails at the Foster street station, or the Town Hall station down on Halsted and Addison.

Jack had already prepared in his mind what he would say to these two lame, so-called hustlers. He knew that they would hang around in his stomping ground around the neighborhood and pool room, trying to sell what they had themselves; talking to the pool players and people in the streets. Usually, if it was something that was worth anything, Jack knew that the average person in the pool room and most people around the area did not have the money to buy the merchandise. Jack could tell by the look on Blane and TJ's faces and the way they were acting, that they had something really worth selling. Jack knew that the people who would most likely buy their merchandise were his fences. They were not the average people. They had money. Jack watched the two men start from one pool table across the large room. He saw Blane approach one of the three players and speak briefly to him as he held that "hustler's" expression on his face. Jack watched him turn his back and huddle up a little close to show the man something he had in his hand as they both looked down at the item. Jack just sat and watched. He knew it was some small item, perhaps, a ring or some other piece of jewelry. He would be surprised if Blane and TJ could sell the item to anyone who was in the pool room right now. Jack knew exactly how this kind of hustling went. He knew they were asking the wrong people; that eventually, they would grow weary of asking and come to him in a round-about way and ask him to help them sell the item. He had prepared himself and was ready. Whenever either of the two men scanned the room for prospects and saw Jack, Jack would pretend that he was not looking and did not see them; that he was unconcerned and uninterested. But, this was how he made his money on a good hustling night; a few dollars from the stranger looking for weed on top of the weed he had already skimmed from the bag before he gave it to him; plus the three joints he got out of him; two that were given to him by the stranger and one from the little bit extra that he talked him out of; now, maybe he could make a sale of some other hustler's merchandise as he had done more times than he could count.

Jack watched Blane and TJ move through the room from table-to-table, trying to sell the item; trying to stay low-key; talking very discreetly to each person. About twenty minutes had passed and Jack could see the frustration begin to wear on the two men. Jack knew that this was as far north as these two usually came. He knew that they had probably already hit all the hotspots along the way; Sheridan Liquors, the Boozery, the Green Mill. He knew, too, that they did not go into Sharon's place across the street because it was a hillbilly kind of bar and they did not like the atmosphere. That never really mattered to Jack. He would sell to anyone who wanted to buy and he was bold enough to go anywhere to do it.

Finally, Jack could see out of the corner of his eye, TJ whispering something to Blane who had possession of the item, and cutting his eyes across the room in the direction where Jack was sitting. Jack could see, too, out of the corner of his eye, the two men walking very casually toward him. He could see Blane split with TJ and walk toward the front of the poolroom and sit in a seat in front of the long window facing Lawrence Avenue. At the same time, he could see TJ continue toward him. Just as TJ had come within a few feet of him, Jack looked up from where he sat and acted surprised "Aw, hey…what's happ'nin', TJ?" he greeted. "Brotha' Jack…what's goin' on, man?" TJ responded trying to act non-chalant as the two men engaged in a soul handshake. "Thangs jumpin' 'round here tonight, huh?" TJ said with a broad smile as he made a quick, short scanning motion of his head to give his words effect. "It's like this every Friday night" Jack responded very casually as he braced himself mentally for the conversation he knew was soon to come. "Makin' any money tonight, Jack?" TJ asked with genuine curiosity. "So far, some two's and fews but, the night's still young" Jack replied. "Hey…check this…me 'n Blane got a cold piece…a watch with a gem in it that we tryin' to off" TJ finally said. "Aw, yea?" Jack responded trying to act surprised. "What you tryin' to get for it?" Jack inquired. "Hey…step over here with me to where Blane is 'cause he's holdin' the piece and you can look at it" TJ said. "Yea" Jack replied as the two of them walked slowly over to where Blane sat. "Let him check that piece" TJ said to Blane after stopping a couple of feet in front of him with Jack standing a short distance behind TJ. “Hey, bro’” Blane greeted. “Alright, now” Jack responded. “Yea..” Blane said as he rose quickly from his seat and made a broad stretching motion of his arms to expel the weariness he was feeling. “…let’s step over in the corner back here and you can look at it” Blane continued as he began to walk to the far corner of the room. After the men stopped and were facing the corner, Blane pulled out a royal blue velvet case and opened it, extending his arm out so Jack could get a better view. After he opened it, Jack saw a watch with the word “Movado” leaping out from the inside of the case cover. It was a quality man’s watch with a sapphire gem in the noon position and a black face in a gold casing. “Yea, man…that’s a cold piece…fourteen karat gold casing….nice gem…Movado…yeah…sharp piece….sho’ ’nough sharp” Jack commented in a low tone as he concentrated on the watch’s features. “I’d say it retails from about three to three-fifty” Jack said confidently. “Out here on the street …you probably ain’t gonna’ get no more that a note-and-a-half for it” ya’ dig?” Jack said, demonstrating his hustling knowledge. “Well..if we could get about one-seventy, that would be straight” Blane said. “That’s possible, but, I don’t know” Jack responded. “The way you do it..you ask for two-hundred and then go down ten-at-a-time from there..‘cause I know…you ain’t gonna get over one-fifty for it….you got to make it a real bargain for the buyer” Jack explained. “Alright, I’ll tell you what…you know some folks around this way that might wanna’ knock this piece…I know you got some fences you dealin’ with around here, right?” TJ surmised. “Oh, fa’ sho’…I can go right next door to see the owner of the Aragon…I done sold him a lota’ shit before.... he ain’t always around but, I know he’s there tonight” Jack went on. “Okay, brotha’ Jack…see what you can do, man” Blane cut in showing a little weariness as he handed the velvet case to Jack. “We’ll wait right here” he added. With that, Jack walked toward the front door and exited. The two men could see him walking outside along the stretch of the pool room window heading west to the Aragon entrance next door.

“Hey, Rodrigo…what’s happ’nin’, my man….I need to see Jose” Jack said after he had walked through one of the four sets of tinted glass double-doors that spread across the entrance and were part of the alluring décor of the impressive Aragon. Jack stood out in the middle of the cavernous, dimly lit lobby a few yards from the custodian's office in front of him. Rodrigo, the custodial manager stood behind the half-door to his well lit office. "He is down the hall in another office…I can call him on the phone...what's going on?" Rodrigo said. "Hey Rodrigo…I got a beautiful piece of merchandise here, my man..you need to check it out" Jack said as he moved with a slight bouncing motion and spoke with a tone of excitement and a broad smile on his face. "Let me see" Rodrigo said.

Rodrigo and all the workers inside the Aragon had come to know Jack fairly well over the last couple of years. They had seen all kinds of merchandise that he had tried to sell them---from car batteries to jewelry. Jack had impressed his style upon them with his loose way of cracking jokes; sometimes crying the blues and other times dispensing his irrepressible logic; but, always being passionate in the delivery of his sales pitch; no doubt urged on by his desperate need to survive in the unforgiving streets of Uptown.

Jack went into his sport jacket pocket and produced the velvet box. "This is a very nice Movado man's wrist watch with a beautiful gem…check it out" Jack said as he handed it to Rodrigo. When Rodrigo had began to see Jack coming into the Aragon trying to sell stuff almost two years ago, he was skeptical of buying anything. But, when some of his workers bought from Jack and seemed very happy with the price they paid for very good merchandise and then the big boss and owner, Jose bought from Jack and seemed to think nothing of it, that's when Rodrigo began to give Jack a little respect and buy from him, as well. "Hey, Amigo…this watch does look very good" Rodrigo commented as he continued to inspect it in the opened velvet case. "I sure would buy it if I didn't already have a couple of nice dress watches…my daughter just bought me a very nice, expensive one for my birthday about three months ago" ….this is very good…someone will buy…what are you asking?" Rodrigo inquired. "All I'm askin' is one-ninety" Jack responded with an inflection that hinted that the watch was much more expensive. "This sells in the stores from about three-fifty to a little over four hundred…and I believe this particular model may be a little higher than similar models" Jack said, going into his sales pitch mode of sounding very astute. It was part of his sales talk to sound as knowledgeable as he could as well as to baffle and bullshit his prospects. "Ok…hey..I'll phone down the hall to where Jose is so he can step down and take a look" Rodrigo said as he stepped over to the phone sitting on his desk and began to dial the black rotary phone. "Yea...Jose…can you come down here a minute...I want you to see something..okay..alright" "He'll be here in about five minutes…okay?" Rodrigo said. "Thanks, Rodrigo…'preciate it, man" Jack replied. Rodrigo went back to looking at his workers' schedule while Jack just occupied himself by singing little tunes soft and low to entertain himself until Jose arrived.

"Que Pasa, amigo?" Jose greeted as he walked toward Jack from the long, wide stretch of lobby. They shook hands. Jose looked like the refined gentleman that he was who was classy and rich enough to own the Aragon. He wore a fine pair of bone-colored linen slacks and a very nice summer shirt with a pair of expensive casual shoes to match. He wore an expensive gold watch and rings. "How ya' doin', my friend?" Jack greeted Jose with the utmost respect. "I am fine…what can I do for you, my friend?" Jose asked politely. "I want you to take a look at this and see if you would be interested" Jack said as he took the velvet case out of his pocket and handed it to Jose. Jose looked at it for a long moment, then took his glasses from his shirt pocket and looked closer. "Very nice….no problems with this, right?" Jose asked, referring to the condition of the watch. "Oh, no…it's brand new…the warrantee is right there in the case" Jack replied. "What are you asking, my friend?" Jose inquired. "Well, I'll tell you, Jose…I am asking less that half the value and I am sure a man like yourself knows the value" Jack said, cleaning up his speech a bit from the street language as he did whenever he was speaking to his most worthy fences. "Okay…how much?" Jose finally asked. "One-ninety" Jack replied. "Jose paused for a moment and thought; being the shrewd business man that he was, he spoke. "I'll tell you…come down a little on the price and you have a deal…this is new, you are in luck, Amigo…I need to give someone a gift…what do you say?" Jose offered. "Okay…how about one eighty…naw…one-seventy-five for you, Jose" Jack responded. "It's a deal" Jose said with a smile as he stuck out his hand and they shook. Jack responded with a smile of relief because Jose did not always buy. Many times before he had graciously declined. Jack, of course, never took it personally because he understood and always thanked Jose for his time.

"Jose.." Jack started "…I have to go back to the pool room to speak briefly to someone…could you hold onto that until I come back?" Jack asked politely. "I'll tell you what" Jose spoke "I will leave it here with Rodrigo until you return…meanwhile, I will go to get the money and return shortly..okay?" Jose replied. "Okay…that's fine…I'll be right back" Jack said. Jose handed the case to Rodrigo who sat it on his office desk as Jack turned and headed back outside to the poolroom.

A moment later, Jack entered the pool room and burst through the entrance door. Blane and TJ were sitting near the far corner where Jack had first sat. Upon seeing Jack enter, the two men rose from their seats with a look of anticipation as Jack strolled toward them. "What's goin' down?" Blane asked anxiously. "Here's the deal…" Jack started "…I asked him for one-eighty …but, he didn't wanna pay that much…after he said that, I started tellin' him about the quality and how it sells in the store for three to three-fifty…he wouldn't go for that….then I pointed out that he got a warrantee and everythang…he wants it, though…'cause he said he needs it to give as a gift…he's talkin' 'bout one-fifty, man…and that's all he'll go…." Blane and TJ paused and each man was silent as they looked at each other with an expression that asked if the other wanted to accept the offer. "You know, the more you get, the more we can kick you down, right?" Blane advised Jack. "Yea… fa' sho'…you know I know that…we have done business before and y'all kicked me down proper, man…he is a business man, though and he knows us hustlers out here ain't gonna' turn that kinda' money down…'specially a bill and-a-half!" Jack said. "That's cool" Blane said firmly…Handle ya' business, man…go on…get the money!" he relented. "Yea…go 'head, Jack…I'm tired o' stompin' 'round, anyway" TJ chimed. Jack disappeared through the entrance doors. He returned a few minutes later. The three men walked over to the far left corner of the pool room and huddled for a short moment. Jack handed Blane the money. "Jack, you alright, bro'…you sold that piece in fifteen minutes and we been messin' around almost three hours" Blane said as he took the half-folded bills from Jack and gave back a crisp twenty dollar bill. "Yea, man…my dogs is barkin' from all this walkin' we been doin'…I'm sho''nough glad we ran into you!" TJ confessed. "That's straight, ain't it?" Blane asked Jack. "Oh yea, brotha' Blane…sho' you right…this'll work…right on!"

Jack responded with embellished enthusiasm. "Shoot…after all this runnin' around, I need to get myself right…let's ride, TJ!" Blane said. The men took turns giving Jack a parting soul hand shake. "Later, player!" Blane said to Jack as both men strolled toward the front entrance with much more energy than they had coming in. Jack just stood and watched as they exited the door. After they were gone, a faint smile slowly spread across his face. "Hustler's paradise, baby…and the night is still young!" he thought gleefully.

Jack continued to hang around the pool room well into the night; drinking; having lively conversations with the patrons; joking around; going in and out of the pool room and out onto Lawrence Avenue; occasionally speaking with people he knew and sometimes people he did not know. He hung with his buddy Coley all night long; taking a couple of short trips down to Saxony Liquors to buy bottles of vodka; hitting on any unescorted, fine ladies that he happen to see along the way. He and Coley bullshitted the night away laughing and joking up and down the streets and acting crazy. This was the routine that he had for the last couple of years; making money hustling and living carefree.

The night sky was clear and the neon lights up and down the streets shone especially bright in the crisp air. Jack relished the excitement that nights like this brought to the strip. The bustling of well-dressed people out for a good time; the neighborhood regulars spread out around the corners, up and down the streets in little cliques of gatherings that shifted throughout the night with each little group gaining new ones from the other groups; usually coming together over their 40 ounces of Schlitz Malt Liquor; six packs; weed; wine or other liquor; the buzzing of the group chatter and laughter filled the atmosphere with liveliness.

Finally, Jack and Coley sat down on the concrete ledge in front of the parking garage next door to Saxony Liquors. They had begun to feel a little weary from the night of fun. This was a favorite spot of Jack's and many of the neighborhood drinkers like him. They could sit on the ledge where most of the interesting traffic passed by; watching the activity in the streets; joking; debating and making comments about the goings-on.

Meanwhile, a short distance up the street, groups of young fans of the rock band Journey had begun to line up in the alley on the west side of the Lawrence Avenue L station. This was what happened whenever one of the popular rock bands played at the Aragon on the weekends. It was always a two-day set and the fans would start camping out on Thursday night for the Friday and Saturday afternoon and evening shows just to be among the first into the theatre. They would wear the band's t-shirts with their old tattered jeans and come with all their friends and revel the whole time; drinking their favorite beer by the case; sleeping on blankets and sleeping bags around the clock until the big moment came when the entrance doors of the Aragon opened for the first show.

"Hey, Jack…look down there…there yo' money is for tomorrow" Coley said to Jack with lazy-drunken, half-slurred speech. "Yeah, I see 'em down there…I'll be ready for their asses tomorrow" Jack replied a bit more soberly. Jack knew exactly what Coley was talking about. Jack often sold fake hashish to the suburban crowd that came into Chicago in throngs on the weekends when any one of the big rock bands played the Aragon. It was a formula that he had gotten from "White Boy Silver" about a year-and-a-half ago. "Silver" was an old-time hippie who occasionally hung around the neighborhood with the "brothers" buying drugs and getting high. He was such a regular that hardly anyone paid attention to the fact that he was white. He was himself, the ultimate Street Gypsy. He drifted from place-to-place, getting high wherever and however he could. No one ever knew exactly where he got the recipe for the concoction that the fake hashish was made of; ground sage mixed with dark cooking syrup; when mixed just right and baked to a desired texture in the oven, it looked and smelled just like hashish. Jack used the formula every once-in-a-while. He would go and make a batch shortly before a big rock concert was to play. He would carry several pieces with him and he would just hang around the Aragon, mixing and mingling and being as discreet as he could while he tried to sell the phony hashish. His tactic was to go and buy a bag or a bunch of joints from the best weed man in the neighborhood; usually, Joe in the courtway who had been selling in the neighborhood for years. He would roll it all up into joints and start selling to the concert crowd before the show. The joints were very good so, they gained him the trust he needed to sell his phony hashish. Jack would not sell the phony hashish to anyone who was stone cold sober. He would sell to the concert crowd because almost every single one of them was already high and that way, they could not really tell if the hashish was getting them high or not. He sold several pieces most of the time; getting ten to twenty dollars for a piece, depending on it's size and how good his sales pitch was. But, he knew he couldn't wear that hustle out."

Yea, brotha' Coley… I got to get paid tomorrow….I'm gonna' buy my shit early tomorrow….bake it up and serve it up to them chumps" Jack said sluggishly. "You gonna be bakin' some cookies tomorrow, huh?" Coley said smiling and humoring himself with the thought of Jack's scandalous, conniving ways. "Sho' ya' right…I'm gon' be clean tomorrow….'bout two hours before the show, I'm gonna' be buzzin', too" Jack said with drunken bravado. "Just be careful out here tomorrow….don't get ya' ass busted" Coley warned. "Coley…I have done this shit many times, as you know…I ain't about to get knocked for sellin' that shit… I know how to play it…now…have you ever known me to get knocked?...huh?...huh? Jack asked with a drunken slur. "Naw…I haven't but, there's always a first time, Jack…don't overload ya' ass, now…be cool out here…that's all I'm sayin'.." Coley responded emphatically.

"Hey, look what the damn wind blew in…look who's comin'" Jack said as he turned his head westward up Lawrence Avenue and focused into the distance. "Who, man?" Coley asked. "My mella…Willie-the-Weep" Jack said, grinning broadly. "Yea…with his country ass" Coley said with cutting sarcasm. "Hey, man…the brotha' is alright with me…I don't give a damn how country he is…I see he done stopped down by Saxony…let me step that way and see what this fool is up to" Jack said as he raised up from his seat on the ledge, smiling as he peered down the street. "Go 'head, see what ya' boy is doin'" Coley said with a tone of indifference. "I'll be back in a few, Coley" Jack said as he began to step away heading west toward where Willie-the-Weep stood near the front entrance of the liquor store. "My, man Weep….what you doin', bro'?" Jack greeted in a joyous tone of fellowship.

"Hey, brotha' Jack…what's goin' on, man?" the Weep responded. Before anything else could be said, The Weep asked a man passing by for some change. The man stopped and spoke to The Weep in words that were vague and that The Weep could not understand. Jack stayed where he was as The Weep had stepped several feet away to come closer to where the man stood. "Do-you-have-any-change?" The Weep asked again of the man, patronizing him because he realized that he did not speak very good English and was some kind of foreigner. The man spoke to The Weep, uttering, again, some indistinguishable phrase. "Hey, bro'…I cain't make out what you sayin'…see…do you have any spare change?" The Weep gestured to the man as he spread his palm open to show a few coins. "I am 'ze police!" the man uttered sternly as he waved his open hand in front of The Weep with a shooing motion. "Hey, man..you don't have to git all worked up..I jes' axed you for some change!" The Weep responded in his usual southern drawl. "I am 'ze Police!" the man said once again with a noticeable slavic accent even more emphatically as he stepped menacingly toward The Weep. "Hey, now, back yo' crazy ass up offa' me…or I'll put one o' these African soup bones on ya'!" The Weep warned as he braced himself with a defensive stance and shook his balled fist near his face to show the stranger. Jack noticed the way that the man had stepped closer to his friend and feeling good as he did, stepped several feet closer to impose his presence upon the man. "Hey, watch it, now!" Jack warned the stranger as he stared him down.

The strange man looked at Jack wide-eyed for a moment then, turned away murmuring a stream of phrases in a foreign, slavic tongue; intermittently punctuating them loudly with angry sounding words. He walked hurriedly out into the streets near the crosswalk where Lawrence Avenue and Broadway met. He turned his head south then, north looking up and down Broadway frantically as the busy Friday night traffic streamed past him from each direction. Finally, he began to wave his right hand high into the air at a Chicago police paddy wagon in the middle of making a left turn from Lawrence Avenue onto Broadway heading north. The driver noticed his frantic waving and stopped at the curb on Broadway just a few feet north of the intersection.

The two policemen were very slow getting out. They walked over to the man standing on the northeast corner near the rear of the paddy wagon. Jack and The Weep stood in place watching what was going on. "Aw, shit…Jack, you ain't got no warrants do, you?..cause this som' bitch done called the po'lice…"The Weep said somewhat nervously in a near-whisper. "Naw…Weep…I'm alright…just be cool" Jack said in a tone just as low. After a moment or so of standing there talking to the police, Jack and Weep could see the man pointing in their direction. Soon after, the two burly cops walked toward them. "Good evening, gentlemen…what's going on here?" the cop walking in front asked. "Nothin' officer…we jes' standin' out here gettin' some air" The Weep said sheepishly. "We couldn't quite understand this gentleman here completely but, he seems to be saying that you guys are bothering him or done something to him…now ….what's the story?" the cop said firmly. "Officer…I swear…we ain't bothered him at all…to tell the truth…I was jes' short a little change for a drink and I axed him when he was passin' by could I get about twenty cents from him…that's all…then, he started gettin' all excited and then he said he was the po' lice" The Weep explained. The cop who had spoken paused for a moment to digest what had been said. Then, he looked at his partner for a quiet moment as if they were speaking with their facial expressions. Without saying a word, the cop walked back several feet to the strange man and spoke. "You said you are the police?" the cop asked. "Yes!" the man said quickly with a hint of uneasiness. Made more curious by the response, the policeman stepped closer and asked to see the man's ID. The stranger took his wallet out and several moments passed as he pulled identification pieces from his wallet. The big, burly cop looked at each piece and continued to press the stranger for more. After a few minutes had passed, the cop finally spoke again. "Where are you the police at?" he asked the man. "Downtown!" the man said with the same distinct slavic accent. The two cops huddled for a moment. The other cop went to the paddy wagon with a piece of the man's ID in his hand. He sat in the car and appeared to be busy with an ID check. "Gentlemen…don't go anywhere…we need to check a few things out" the first cop said to Jack and The Weep. After that, he walked over to the stranger and told him to "wait right there…we'll give your ID back in a few minutes" Jack and Weep stood silently as the cop waited alongside them. After about five more minutes, the cop in the wagon opened the door and exited the paddy wagon walking deliberately toward his partner. They huddled close again as the cop from the wagon held a lone piece of the stranger's ID in his hand as he was saying something to his partner. The big cop who did all of the talking turned to the stranger and asked him again. “You say you are a policeman?” “Yes!” the man said again. “You’re not!” the cop shot back, pausing afterward. “Why are you saying you are the police?” the cop demanded. The man just stared quietly into the cop’s face. “Alright…let’s go…get in the wagon….you cannot go around impersonating a police officer, you understand?” the cop said. With that, the policeman who had done the ID check clicked a set of handcuffs onto the wrist of the strange man before he knew it. Jack’s heart began to race because he just knew that he and The Weep were next. The strange man began to plead in his foreign tongue, occasionally mixing in a few English words as the two policemen escorted him from either side with his hands cuffed behind his back. He tried to resist--stopping his steps and leaning back with mild resistance. “Come on…let’s go…don’t mess around!” the first cop said as he felt the feeble resistance in the man’s body as he held his left arm.

Just as the two cops were forcing the man forward, grabbing his arms on either side, a man dressed in African garb stepped in front of them in passing and bumped into the handcuffed stranger. He backed away then, tried to step around the two cops again but, this time he bumped into the bigger cop. “Watch it, sir…can you move back, please” the cop asked, with a tone of exasperation. “I want to go!” the African man said with a thick accent as he tried to step around again, bumping into the other policeman. He was accompanied by another man dressed much like himself. “Ninataka-enye-pita!” the first African man said. “What did you say?” the bigger cop said, sounding offended by what the African man had said. The words were not distinguishable to Jack or the Weep. The African man finally passed to the other side of the two cops and the stranger and said something else in his native tongue as he gestured angrily with a wave of his hands high in the air, seemingly in disgust. The bigger policeman took offense to the man’s gestures and started after him as his partner had just put the handcuffed man in the paddy wagon, closed the rear door and walked back quickly to back him up. “What the hell are you talking about?…you tryin’ to be some kinda’ smart-ass?...come here!” the cop said as he rushed over to confront the African man who had stopped in his tracks and turned to face the policeman. “What do you wish?” the African man said with an accent and a hint of defiance as the bigger policeman walked up close to him and they came face-to-face. “What do I wish?…what do I wish?…let’s go!” the big policeman said angrily as he grabbed the man by his arm with his partner grabbing the other and they hustled the man toward the rear paddy wagon door.

The Weep and Jack stood still several yards away near the Saxony Liquors entrance. They gazed in disbelief at what was happening before their eyes. They watched as the two policemen cuffed the African man and opened the rear paddy wagon door and shoved him inside and locked the door. They jumped into the wagon and sped off. Jack and The Weep paused for a moment and looked at each other wide-eyed. They burst out together in laughter. “Did you see that shit, Jack?” The Weep howled with laughter. Jack began to snicker, still holding the amazed expression on his face. “Hehehahaha!” Jack began to laugh out loud. After laughing for a while, Jack spoke.. “I’ll be damned!…Weep…that is the damndest shit I ever seen!....that fool tried to get us locked up and got locked up his damned self!” “Whooohahahaha” Jack howled. “Yea…with his Daffy Duck ass…shouldna’ been fuckin’ ‘round talkin’ ‘bout he’s the po’ lice!...then, to top it off, the African dude come by talkin’ his shit…showin’ off and his l’il monkey-shines got his ass locked up, too!” hahahahaha…” The Weep cackled.

Scattered rays of sunshine peeped through the slightly tattered shade covering the window and gently warmed Jack’s face as he slept on the mattress of the Murphy bed in his kitchenette apartment. His eyes suddenly sprang open. Several minutes passed while he lay quietly before he felt a slight swimming sensation in his head as he became more conscious. It was the same old dried out, half-alive, spent feeling that he sometimes had when he awoke from a wild night of drinking and carousing. It gave him a somber, empty state of mind. It was that familiar, crazy feeling that he dreaded so much. It was the down-side of drinking, having fun and feeling so alive when he was high. He hated facing the morning because of it. His thoughts turned next to how to get rid of the feeling. Suddenly, he remembered that he had taken the last pint bottle home in his jacket! He remembered the weight of it in his pocket from last night. But, did he still have it? Was there anything left? He dragged his seemingly dead weight up from the bed and stepped over to the little sofa-chair on the other side of the bed where his sport jacket lay. He grabbed it and felt the pocket---there it was! It felt like the pint-size bottle. His awareness leaped to another level of consciousness with a sense of relief. He rumpled the jacket to find the pocket it was in and snatched the bottle out. His eyes focused on the liquid sloshing inside. "Thank God" he thought to himself…"I'm straight!" The bottle was about two-thirds full; enough to straighten out his jangling nerves so he could function and start his day. He sat back down on the edge of the bed with the bottle in his hand. He paused for a moment before quickly turning the bottle up to his mouth for a few seconds, guzzling down some of the burning liquid. He gulped and grimaced as the warm feeling started down his gut. He cleared his throat with a man-sized grunt. "Now, to get myself together" he thought. Jack rummaged around for the few bath towels he had and headed into the shower. He was fully dressed in about twenty minutes. He made his bed and checked his drag in the mirror; then counted his money. He still had enough to get the stuff he needed for the hashish and enough change left to keep him nice and mellow while he did his hustling.

After showering and dressing, he went downstairs and was walking through the lobby when he overheard the desk clerk talking to one of the tenants. "Yea…they knocked ol' Marty in the head and took his whole damn soc' secur'ty check yesterday…damn shame 'ol feller like that got to get robbed 'n carryin' on right here in the place where he stays…there's some crazy-ass folks 'round here messin' with people" the clerk said to the tenant with a noticeable southern drawl. Jack paused on his way outside and acted as though he was straightening his clothes up. "Marty…Marty…didn't I hear one of them two studs that passed me in the hallway yesterday say Marty to that old man?" he thought. Jack continued walking out of the lobby, still thinking about what he just heard and suddenly it came to him…that twenty....the old grizzled dude…they robbed the old man!" he thought. Jack dwelled on the thought a little while longer. He realized that the strange man who had given him the twenty dollar bill had given it to him to keep him quiet. "Slick-ass" he thought.

The truth was that it was a rather clever move because, now Jack was overhearing what had happened and he certainly did not want to be a part of it by telling anything. He wouldn't tell on another hustler, anyway. He would just stay out of it. That was the way hustlers operated. You didn't "trick" on another hustler, no matter what his method was. It was none of his business. It was the code of the streets.

Jack felt fresh from his shower and began to get that frisky feeling from the drinking that he did when he first woke up. He had the bottle with him in the back pocket of his khaki pants wrapped in a paper bag. He left his room and walked south on Malden Avenue, heading to one of the neighborhood grocery stores on Wilson Avenue two blocks away. He would get the ground sage and dark cooking syrup that he needed to make the hashish – or at least what passed for it. He finally arrived at the corner of Malden and Wilson where the Private Eye pizza joint and the Wilson Liquor store stood prominently on the southeast corner next to one another. He also saw a few of the local regulars milling around the liquor store near the alley. Jack was familiar with their routine because it was the same as his had been most of the summer---stay out all night getting high until daylight. Then, wait until the liquor stores opened in the morning. If you were broke or were short on a drink, you stood around panhandling until you had enough to buy one. It was all part of the reckless, mindless way that Street Gypsies lived-----without a care.

A wave of gratitude passed over Jack that he was not out there with them; staying out all night because of not having anywhere to lay his head. He was grateful that, at least for now---he did not have to do those things. He knew all too well how it felt to get high throughout the night then, because all the take-out liquor joints closed by 2am---you started getting sober after that time---drifting aimlessly around the streets in the meantime. He had gotten enough sleep last night and felt pretty good.

Jack stopped on the northeast corner for a moment and after he had seen the few people hanging around the Wilson Liquor store, he realized he did not want to go near them. They all knew him and he had drank with each of them at one time or another. Right now, he did not have time to fool around with them. He knew himself. If he stopped and talked with them, they would ask him for change on a drink and he would end up drinking with them. He needed to go ahead and get the stuff for the hashish. If he stopped, he would not get the hash done like he wanted and his hustling plans would go awry. He realized, too that he probably could get the sage at the little neighborhood store there a few doors west from the corner but, he figured that they might not have the dark cooking syrup and if they did, they would charge too much for it. Before any of the group across the street could draw a bead on him and recognize him standing on the corner, he dashed across the street, crossing Malden and heading west on Wilson to go to the Butera Super Market on Clark and Wilson about three blocks away. Jack found the sage and the cooking syrup there, bought it and took a different route back to avoid the drinkers around the liquor store on Wilson. He drank from the bottle that he still had in his back pocket as he walked back to his apartment at the Malden Arms.

When he got back, he found a bowl in the apartment to mix the sage and syrup concoction; pouring the entire large can of sage into the bowl then, mixing in the dark syrup little-by-little to get just the right texture. Then, he spread the mixture out on a baking sheet like cookies. He lit the oven of the old stove and started the baking. He opened the lone window near his bed and stuffed a bed sheet under his front door to minimize the smell from escaping out into the hallway and drawing curiosity from his neighbors or the building personnel. As his money-making concoction baked, Jack turned on his radio and grabbed the bottle out of his back pocket. He took a sip and laid back on his elbows on the Murphy bed, listening to his favorite rhythm and blues radio station as several lively tunes played and the D.J. chattered away; keeping him company while he was alone in the apartment tending to the hash mix in the oven. He felt relaxed, grooving to the music as the sunshine glowed outside his window as he felt the effects of both lifting his spirit.

Jack loved these moments. They allowed him to forget about the mess that his life really was. He didn't understand exactly how he wound up living this way---it was not his plan. But, he did not know how to change it. He loved this Street Gypsy life and he hated it at the same time. He had to face the fact that he fit right into it. He didn't have a girlfriend or a wife or any kids. He did not stay in contact with his mother or father or his one brother and one sister.

His father had kicked him out of the house five years ago and he had been on his own ever since. In the first few years, he had lost a couple of good jobs because he could not separate having fun from his responsibility of getting to work every day. The weekends lapsed over into absences from work on the weekdays.

That was several years ago and for the last two years, he had tried to get a steady job; going to the employment office at The Center on Montrose a few times a week with no luck. Now, none of that mattered to Jack at all. He just lived from day-to-day in the streets he had come to know as his home. He needed to be carefree and live this way. He didn't know why---he just did. But, deep down inside he felt a sense of hope that one day, things would change---somehow.

Jack had tended to the baking hash-mix for about forty-five minutes when he checked it and finally decided that it was ready. He turned the oven off and sat the whole baking sheet of the mix on the top of the stove to cool off. After about twenty minutes, the big chunk on the baking sheet was cool enough. Jack broke the solid chunk up into pieces and before he would wrap each piece in aluminum foil like he always did, he would scrape the side of the hash that was in contact with the baking sheet on concrete in the streets somewhere to give it a look and texture that seemed more natural because it looked like it was baked on that side. He went into the bathroom and did a little extra grooming. He put on a different jacket that was the top part of a leisure suit. It matched the khakis he had on and he liked the way it looked on him. He put on a dab of English Leather cologne and started out of the door.

It was almost noon when Jack arrived at the corner of Lawrence and Broadway; long before the 4pm Journey show at the Aragon. He could see the show crowd gathered at the alley on the west side of the Lawrence Avenue L stop. The crowd was big for the concert that did not start for another four hours. Before he could start selling to them, Jack knew he had to go and cop some more weed because he gave away some of what he had to his friend, Coley last night and sold the rest. He passed Saxony where some of the fans were traipsing back and forth, buying liquor in the one block area between the liquor store and the group lined up for the show at the alley on the north side of Lawrence. He crossed over to the south side of Lawrence and headed east and then turned right at Winthrop and went into the courtway. He spent ten dollars on a bag of weed and came back to the Spanish-owned grocery store across from the Aragon to buy some rolling papers.

Jack did not see any of his drinking crowd anywhere around The Corner. Most Saturdays, somebody would be hanging around. But, none of the regulars was anywhere in sight. After he copped the weed and bought the papers, Jack had to go back home to "roll-up" so that he could pitch the weed to the concert crowd ahead of the hashish. He went back home and took a half-hour to roll about sixteen joints. He sipped on his bottle of vodka the whole time. He left his apartment and now, it was almost 1pm in the afternoon when he arrived back near Saxony Liquors. He had killed the vodka and, now he needed to buy another to keep himself in the right mood. He bought a half-pint this time and stepped into the little breezeway between Saxony liquors and the parking facility and took a couple of good hits. He was ready. He came out making comments to anyone that was from the concert crowd.

"Hey, folks…ready for the concert? "Yea…rock on, baby..rock on!""" You ain't ready for the concert unless you got some 'o this weed, good people….check it out…come on down…the price is right..…hey sweet thang..I got that weed…come on, now…don't pass it up..I got them joints, people…got these joints" Jack was barking up and down the street as he looked around the street for the cops. Some of the concertgoers would stop and ask about the weed with some passing because they wanted a bag instead of joints. A few times within the first half-hour, Jack got several concertgoers who wanted joints and he would take them into his drinking spot in the breezeway between Saxony and the parking facility to make the sales where he would pitch his hash with two takers out of about five weed sales. He made about fifty dollars from the hashish fairly quick. Jack knew that the concertgoers that he sold the joints to were going back to the group and sharing the good, quality weed that he was selling them. He was careful to only push the hashish after he had sold a few joints. His plan was working like a charm. In between sales, Jack was drinking from his bottle, occasionally ducking into the breezeway. Now, he had that feeling that he was always looking for---he was "buzzin'" real good and feeling free as he moved back and forth in the same two-block area between Broadway and Winthrop on Lawrence Avenue; having fun talking to the concertgoers as he pitched his wares and laughing and joking up-and-down the street;

occasionally stopping for brief periods to talk with some of the neighborhood regulars and have a drink or two with them as he made his hustles. Meanwhile, the streets became livelier as the afternoon wore on. The practice sessions could be heard out on the streets from the band Journey inside the Aragon. The revelry of the partying fans escalated outside, the closer the time came to the first of two shows at 4pm. Jack continued to traipse up and down the streets, pitching joints and hashish to the concert crowd as he continued to find a customer here and there. He was steadily making money and if a concertgoer seemed as though he was sober, he only pitched the joints of weed.

"Hey, there, player…you look like you feelin' mighty fine…you ready to rock, baby?" Jack asked a young man standing in front of the parking facility near the liquor store. The man stood in one place and seemed to be swaying slightly from his high, smiling to himself. "Journey rocks!….I said…Journey rocks!" "Can I get five on that, my man…give me five" the young man said to Jack, mildly slurring his speech as he stumbled over to Jack, red-eyed with a wide, euphoric grin. He slapped the open palm Jack had extended. "Hey, man..I got that hash, my man…got that hash…check it out, it's real good…don't pass it up!" Jack urged in a near-whisper as he clasped his palm around the man's hand and pulled him up close. "Hey, my man...I ain't got but a coupla' pieces left..I'll give you a deal…alright?" Jack said, seizing the opportunity as he could see that his prospect was in the kind of condition he liked for his hash customers to be. Jack went into his jacket pocket and pulled out one of the chunks wrapped in aluminum foil and held it low in his open palm close in front of him as he scanned the immediate vicinity. "See there…better get it while the gettin' is good…I already sold most of it…I just wanna sell what I got left and go home, man" Jack said, saying whatever came to mind to help his sales pitch. "Hey, man…that's hash you got there?" the man asked as he gazed down at it. "It's..good?..really good? The young man asked. "You wanna see?…you wanna check it out?…come on!" Jack said as he turned and took a few steps in the opposite direction that the man was facing. Jack had taken three steps but, the concert fan did not follow. Jack re-traced his steps. "Come on, man what you doin'?" Jack urged as he turned around again and started walking. The man did not say anything but, just followed behind Jack looking a bit lost. “Don’t worry, man…I promise to give you a fair price…they call me good deal O’Neal… Jack said, again saying whatever came to mind. “Oh, yea?” the concert fan mumbled as he tried to keep pace with Jack who was stepping lively. Jack led the man into his “office” in the breezeway. The breezeway was perfect because it was narrow and it was dim going in; but, a faint light from a street light shown in the back and the little space barely could be seen from the street. “Here…check it out” Jack urged as he pulled a hash pipe out of his pocket to let the prospect test a sample. Jack knew that the man was already pretty high; that the smell and taste would sell him on the hash. “Here, man…I’m fixin’ you up..see” Jack said as he opened the aluminum foil and let the man see him break a piece off. After breaking the sample piece off, Jack held it under the man’s nose. “See….smell it” Jack said as he moved the piece back and forth underneath the man’s nose. “Now…” Jack started as he put the sample piece in the pipe. He pulled out a cigarette lighter and took his time to light the pipe. “…go ahead and toke, man” Jack said after he handed the man the lit pipe. The stranger made a sucking noise as he took a deep toke from the pipe. He held it in for a moment, then made the usual sounds exhaling. He was quiet as he breathed deeply in and out, then took another deep toke with a loud sucking noise. “Hey…pretty good, my man…pretty good” the young prospect said as he nodded his head up and down slightly.

Jack was elated to hear what he just said and immediately the wheels in his head began to turn. I told you…see…see what I mean?” Jack said with a sense of pride that his prospect was impressed. “Hey…I’ll give you a damned good deal on the last two pieces I got….see” Jack said as he went into his pocket and pulled out two chunks wrapped in foil. “Look at that…you see about how many grams that is, right, man?” Jack asked holding the pieces out in his open palm. “Yea…how much?” the stranger asked. “You got about sixty dollars worth right there for thirty-five…you cain’t beat it…that’s a deal anywhere you go….in fact…that’s a hell of a deal, and you know it!” Jack preached on. “Ok, dude…I admit…it’s a deal…I can’t pass it up…my buddies’ eyes are gonna pop out when I show ‘em what I got for this price..far out, dude!” the man said while slowly going into his front pocket. Jack froze with anticipation as he watched the stranger go into his back pocket as he swayed ever-so-slightly from his high. An eternity seemed to pass as he took his time slowly fishing into his pocket before he produced a wad of money from a long bill fold. Jack was startled. He could see a thick wad with a fifty on the outside. The man began to fumble with the bills, seeming to struggle as he concentrated on his counting. He held the bills low to his side as he leaned back up against a metal rail on the side of the breezeway. Jack began to get anxious, hoping that the man would hurry before some of his buddies found him. He was not so worried about the police because he knew it was hard to see into the narrow space from outside. The man spread the money out in his hand but, was still fumbling. Jack grew more anxious and finally stepped over close to him and opened his hand to show the man the two pieces of hash.

"Look here, man…we got to hurry up and finish this deal…I see a guy comin' that wanted to buy this from me and he wanted to get it too cheap…don't look behind you, he's comin' this way…here…this is yours…see" Jack said as he took the liberty to open the flap of the top right pocket on the man's jean jacket and stuffed the two pieces in. "Now…we got to hurry… here he comes…this is mine…see..this is what I'm gettin'…see…I'll just take these thirty dollars….that's cool…forget about the other five, my man" Jack said, talking fast and behaving anxiously while he reached into the spread out wad of bills in the man's hand and took a ten and a twenty next to one another with his right hand. At that precise moment, while his right hand was blocking the view, he used two fingers of his left hand to quickly slide out a fifty next to the fifty on the outside of the wad. He did not choose the fifty on the outside because he knew that the man would feel it sliding in his hand. After pulling the ten and the twenty dollar bills from the wad, Jack held them up to the stranger's face to show him and, at the same time, block his view as he balled the fifty up and slyly slipped it into his left front pants pocket. "Be cool now, guy…enjoy the show…don't let that hash get you too high, now..that's some fire..be careful" Jack said as he backed away from the stranger grinning and patting him on his shoulder before he turned away and started walking at a hectic pace to separate himself from the man as soon as he could.

He wanted to lose himself as quickly as possible in the crowd of concert revelers and other people out on the streets. "Alright, dude…cool, man…right on" the stranger replied lazily as he leaned back against the rail and stuffed his money back into his billfold while Jack faded into the sidewalk traffic. Jack continued to walk hurriedly, heading east on Lawrence Avenue, crossing Winthrop. He was looking to get away from the area where he was hawking his hash and weed so that he could be alone to count his money and relax for a while. He was pretty high, too and he didn't want to start getting careless hustling out in the streets. He had gotten busted several times in the past by getting too high and too reckless and he did not want to end up in jail.

As he crossed Winthrop, a voice yelled out to him…"Hey, Jack…where, ya goin', brotha'?" Jack turned to look back and could see his friends, Jabo, Larry and Michael Carlton standing on the Winthrop side of Frances' Tavern where he could not have seen them as he headed east on Lawrence until he got to Winthrop. Frances' Tavern stood on the Southwest corner of Lawrence Avenue and Winthrop. He stopped in the middle of the street to turn around and walk back to where they stood. "Hey…what y'all up to?" Jack said quickly, masking the slight anxiousness he was feeling. "Hey, my main man, brotha' Jack!" the old timer Jabo said flashing his characteristically broad smile. "We just tastin', man…you want a hit o' this vodka?" he asked Jack. "Naw…I'm cool…I got a little taste right here myself" Jack said as he casually went into his back pocket and pulled up his half-pint bottle and took a sip. Jack felt somewhat relieved that they had stopped him. He needed to slow down and relax. Stopping to "shoot the breeze" with them was right on time.

"Hey, Mike…I haven't seen you in a long time,…where you been, man?" Jack asked curiously. "I been around…just been layin' low" Mike replied very blase. "Where you at now, Mike?" Jack inquired. "I'm up on Kenmore…at Foster" Mike answered. Jack had known Mike for many years back to when they were young kids living in Cabrini-Green. For that reason, the two men felt a sort of kinship. He was never real tight with Mike but, they would drink together and hang out whenever they ran into one another in the Uptown area. Jack and the men stood out on the sidewalk talking, debating, laughing and joking for a while. As they did, Jack could see across the street the reveling concert crowd disappearing into the entrance of the Aragon for the 4pm show. He felt even more relieved because now, he would not be tempted to continue his hustle while he was feeling a little too high.

"So, what brings you down here on my end, brotha' Mike?" Jack asked. "Aw…hey, man…I met this snow chick earlier…she's inside Frances' right now" Mike said to Jack as he made a motion of his head toward the wall of Frances' tavern. "Why you out here with us and not in there with her?" Jack asked inquisitively. "Is she a dog, Mike?" Jack added with a humored expression beginning to spread across his face as he anticipated Mike's answer. "Naw, man" Mike replied. Jabo and Larry had drifted a few yards away, embroiled in some other topic of conversation as Jack and Mike stood close while they spoke. "How she look then, Mike?" Jack asked with a puzzled curiosity "Go look for yourself…she's sittin' at the bar havin' a beer.…she is the brunette chick in the blue jean outfit" Mike said with a tone of indifference.

"Alright, brotha-man…I think I *will* check her out" Jack said as he began to step away as Mike leaned non-chalantly against the wall they were standing in front of. Jack straightened his posture a bit as he looked back at Mike with a mixed expression of curiosity and befuddlement. Jack almost never sat at the bar in Frances' Tavern. He just wanted to get a look at the woman that Mike had met to see how lucky or unlucky he was in meeting her. So, he just walked in and headed straight for the restroom in the back. As he walked in, he glanced quickly to his right at the woman sitting on the third bar stool. Just as he was about to pass her, he could see her out of the corner of his eye as she turned her head slightly to cast a momentary glance in his direction while she was saying something to a woman seated on the bar stool next to her. His immediate sense was that she couldn't really look as good as the impression he had gotten from his quick glance. Jack made his stop in the men's rest room and checked his appearance in the mirror before he stepped back out of the restroom door to walk out. Now, his curiosity was piqued even more. He had to get a better look at this woman to see did he really see what he first saw. He walked the path from the restroom that passed the patrons on bar stools to his left and the booths of patrons on the right that led to the tavern exit. There was a fair crowd in Frances' small tavern of about a dozen bar stools and there was a low buzz of conversations. Jack was about to pass the brunette-headed woman again when she swirled around on the bar stool from speaking to the woman on her right to speak to the older man on the bar stool to her left. At that precise moment, her eyes met Jack's and she held her gaze a little long and Jack could read a bold look of interest in her eyes. A flash of excitement passed through Jack like electricity because she *did* look as good as his first glance had told him. He also noted that she was shapely by the form fitting pants of her jean outfit. He knew right away that he liked her looks. He could see intelligence in her face. The overall sense of her had him very aroused. Jack was puzzled by Mike's seeming lack of interest in a fairly attractive woman. He paused just inside the entrance door momentarily to think of how he was going to play it off. He did not want Mike to know that he was interested in *his* woman. He never liked doing that. It was not his style. The code in the streets amongst Street Gypsies, when it came to women, was "get your own" You didn't steal another man's woman unless he was your enemy or you had differences and were trying to get back at him. If he was your friend, you did not try to make a play for his woman. Jack felt a sense of excitement with his interest in this strange woman. He decided right then-and-there to go ahead and "let it all hang out" Ask Mike was he interested in the woman or did he plan to do anything with her---and if not---let him know up front that he was interested.

Jack walked back outside to Winthrop where he and Mike were talking. Mike was still there in the same spot—standing there alone---looking as though he was just mellow and enjoying his high. "Hey, brotha', Mike…that's your girl?" Jack asked with a note of seriousness in his tone as soon he was close enough to be heard. "Not really, man…I met her earlier this afternoon up the street at Saxony…we talked for about an hour and then we went to my crib" Mike explained. "So, then what, Mike?…did ya' bone her or what?" Jack pressed on. "I wanted to, man but, I was too high…I think she's a freak…said she's in college…she needs a man…likes black men" Mike said with short pauses between broken sentences. "Damn, Mike…" Jack started ""….she looks nice, man….you gonna' deal with her?" Jack asked, tempering his tone to just the right degree as he treated his exchange with Mike ever-so delicately. "Hey, Jack…she's alright…I ain't that crazy about white chicks, man…I don't feel like messin' around with her right now" Mike said with a tone of indifference. "You sho' you don't wanna do nothin' with her, Mike?" Jack asked again, pressing the issue. "Naw, man…you wanna deal with her?…be my motherfuckin' guest" Mike said in his usual tone when he felt irritated or was expressing his displeasure about something. Jack knew Mike and he knew that he meant what he was saying. He had heard enough and felt a sense of relief that he did not have to go against the unwritten code that Street Gypsies lived by. He felt a sense of excitement at the same time. "Hey, brotha' Mike…introduce me, then, man…I don't wanna go in Frances' and just start rappin' to her and she don't have a clue who the hell I am…can you do that much for a brotha'?…I swear, Mike…I won't bother you no more after that…cool?" Jack asked using his best, most delicate and persuasive tone.

Mike was leaning with his upper back against the wall and after a momentary pause, sprang up from the wall and said "Okay..come on" and started to walk the few yards toward Lawrence Avenue to the entrance of Frances' Tavern. Mike led Jack inside and just as he opened the entrance door, they could hear arguing …"That's bullshit!…you shoulda' counted the money after I gave it to you!" Sol, Frances' brother yelled at her as they stood near one another behind the bar. "I told you not to do that shit time-and-time-and-time again!" Frances barked back at Sol. "Kiss my fuckin' ass!…you hear me!…kiss my ass!…you want me to do everything around here…then you wanna' accuse me of cheatin' ya'…I'm sick o' this shit…I can go home…I don't have to take this!" Sol raged on. "You need to get those damned glasses I told you to get…you won't get your glasses…that's where the hell all my damned money is disappearing to around here…you can't fuckin' see..you're miscounting the money and you won't do nothin' about it!" Frances fired back.

Meanwhile, some of the patrons grinned and others smiled while a few snickered but, most ignored them as Frances and Sol carried on their argument. It was nothing new to the people who lived around and patronized Francis' Tavern. Frances and her brother Sol fought like cats and dogs; often times cussing each other in front of the patrons. They needed each other to run the tavern but, could not work an entire shift at the bar together without a big blowout. Frances had to be around her late-fifties, early sixties and Sol was a few years younger. He hardly spoke any time other than when he was having a big argument with his sister. He walked with a limping motion from an old World War two injury and spoke with a mild speech impediment. Together, they were a fixture around the neighborhood. They were people who had been raised in their homeland in the Ukraine but, had come to America as young adults. Everyone knew them and protected them because of their attachment to Frances Tavern and the familiarity of them being part of the neighborhood. They lived in a two-flat they owned together in a Ukrainian neighborhood several miles northwest of where the tavern was.

Mike stepped over to the brunette-headed woman still sitting at the bar and began to say a few words to her, holding his head close to her's as they spoke because of the loudness of Frances and Sol's arguing. They took turns talking into each other's ear. Finally, Mike turned to Jack standing a few feet behind him, waiting as patiently as he could. Mike stretched his arm out with a flat palm to point to Jack "Tina, this is a good friend of mine, Jack…he lives around this way" he said as he looked at Jack and moved to one side of her to allow their introduction. The brunette-headed woman smiled pleasantly as she extended her hand to Jack and Jack took her hand and held it in both of his, gently clasping one open palm on the top and the other on the bottom of her hand for a long moment. He smiled his best smile at her and said "It is my, pleasure…I'm pleased to meet you" trying to sound as gentlemanly as he could and to hide some of his rough edges. "I'll buy beers for all of us and we can sit at a booth…is that cool with you, Tina…Mike?" Jack asked both politely as he could. "I'd like that…thank you" the woman said as she held her gaze. "Cool" Mike mumbled. Jack paid for the beers and they found an open booth at the back of the tavern.

Jack couldn't have been more pleased at how things were developing. He felt encouraged by the vibes that he was getting from this strange woman. The desire that he was feeling for her had put him in a charming, witty mood. He had not felt this way in quite some time. What he felt was more than a sexual desire. Somehow, a little random romance seemed to be just the remedy for his soul right now. He had enjoyed the times that he had in recent months with a few fairly desirable women. But, they were women he had met roaming the streets of Uptown who traveled in the same circles that he did. They were encounters of necessity that left him feeling nothing more. This woman had that something that made him want her.

They all sat and talked about any and everything; laughing and joking the whole time. Jack made several flirtatious comments to Tina, keeping them subtle enough so as not to offend his friend, Mike. Even though Mike had told him that he didn't have an interest in her, it would not have been righteous of Jack to "front" Mike off. A lot of things that went on between Street Gypsies went unsaid. Sometimes, "one man's meat was another man's poison" Even if a man didn't want a woman, you didn't make him look bad by making a play for her right in front of him or other people who knew the situation. Mike was loose and feeling good. He engaged in the conversation with occasional low-key laughter and short quips; but, seemed insulated and oblivious to the undercurrent of mutual interest between Jack and his new acquaintance.

"Hey, y'all…I got to make it to the crib…I'm gettin' sleepy…I cain't hang no more" Mike said to Jack and Tina. "Mike…what's wrong, man?…you *that* sleepy? Jack asked. "High *and* sleepy, brotha'…I need to lay down for a while…I'm gone, y'all…be cool" Mike replied as he began to rise from the booth. "You want us to walk you home, Mike?…if you're too high, man, you oughta' let us see you get home alright, brotha'?" Jack replied, turning his attention to his old buddy with genuine concern. "Yea…I want to see that you get home okay, Mike" Tina added. "Naw…that's okay…don't spoil ya' good times on account o' me…I'll be alright…I can make it by myself" Mike said with a hint of manly pride. " Mike…at least let us get you a cab, …don't go out there and pass out somewhere….I want you to get home" Tina pleaded. "Hahaha….ahahaha.. whoowee!…Mike laughed. "Come on, now…be serious…ain't no cab gonna' stop for *me* out here on Lawrence….besides…I only live up on Foster, four blocks away…by the time you flag down a cab, I'll be home already….."Mike reasoned with conviction, invoking the cynical sentiments and reality that most black men understood well.

"Why *wouldn't* a cab stop for you Mike?" Tina asked innocently. aaaahaha ….hahahahaha" Both men burst out in laughter.

"Hehehehehahaha....they continued......Whooowweee!.... You know somethin', Tina...you are funny as hell...you know...the latest statistics say eighty-five percent of the black male population don't know what the inside of a cab looks like and the other fifteen percent only know 'cause they're cab drivers...can you dig that?..hehehe.."Jack snickered. "I got tears comin' out of my eyes" Mike said, trying to let his amused laughter subside as he wiped the thin streams of laughing tears from his cheeks. "Tina, that woke me up, sho-nough!" Mike quiped. "I don't understand...what's so funny?" Tina asked with a puzzled, innocent look on her face as she turned to one, then the other of the two men. "Tina...cabs don't like to stop for us colored fellas...it's as simple as that" Jack said with a straight face. "I'm sorry...I know there is a lot of prejudice out there" Tina said. "Well...hey....let me get goin'...I'll take a cab...it's cool" Mike said more seriously.

The three of them gathered themselves and walked out of Frances' Tavern. Sol and Frances had stopped arguing by that time and the place had returned to the normal hum of conversations "I got an idea, Tina...would you flag a cab for Mike?.... alright?...they'll stop for a fine woman like you..." Jack said before he realized what he had said. Tina looked at Jack with a sweet, glowing smile as they were walking along the sidewalk in front of Frances' Tavern. She seemed very pleased with those words and the fact that Jack had revealed what he was thinking. He had hinted around at the booth in Frances' but, had not said anything quite so forward until now. "I'm a fine woman, huh?" she said still smiling with an aroused, warm expression that pierced Jack through-and-through. "Oh, yes...fine" Jack finally let out after a slight pause while he looked her straight in the eyes. From that point, they walked alongside each other holding a gaze for a long moment with Mike walking along on the other side of Jack, separated by about a yard where he was not privy to the warm exchange between the two.

After Tina waited for a cab to flag while the three of them milled around near Frances', they decided to walk two blocks west to the corner of Lawrence and Broadway to have a better chance at her catching a cab for Mike. Finally, a cab was seen in the distance south of them on Broadway heading north toward the group as they stood on the southeast corner of Broadway and

Lawrence. Tina waved at the cab as it drew nearer in the stream of northbound traffic. The cab stopped and she opened the rear passenger door and turned and beckoned to Mike. "Mike…come on….here you go..'"" "Are you going to come back out?" Tina asked after Mike walked up to her and was standing in front of the open cab door. "I don't know….maybe…" Mike responded wearily. "You can call me if you want…okay?" Tina added. Mike just shook his head up-and-down slightly to acknowledge what she had said. Meanwhile, Jack walked up to the cab front passenger side and said "Here's the fare…take care o' my boy…" as he reached in and handed the driver a five dollar bill. Mike entered the cab. Tina closed the door and the cab sped away.

At last----this was the moment that Jack had hoped for---alone with this sexy, strange woman. He cherished his friendship with Mike. But, he was glad that he had cleared the way to get close to her as well as his conscience. He paused and looked her up and down while she was still watching the cab speed off; all in a quick couple of seconds. She was attractive and he wondered how Mike could not be really attracted to her just because of her color. As far as Jack was concerned, there was plenty to like about her; from her openness and nice personality to her apparent intelligence; her good looks and that shapely body---and just as important, she was not prejudiced---she liked black men. Jack never understood all of this racial stuff about segregation---limiting your choices, that many people practiced. Many seemed to behave as if it was illegal to be with someone of a different race or culture. He didn't go along with it and was not going to let society or anyone dictate what he could or could not do. He was going to do whatever he wanted. How could he pass up such a woman because of color?

"So….what should we do now?" Tina asked with a smile and an expression on her face that held a hint of anticipation. "Let's hang out, baby…keep the good times rollin'" Jack said as he tried to suppress the excitement he was feeling because he knew it didn't look cool. "Tell ya' what….let's go catch the show over at the Green Mill across the street over there" Jack suggested as he pointed across to the northwest corner of the intersection. "You know what…it seems crowded and noisy over there from what I can see and hear…can we go somewhere that's more quiet so we can talk and get to know something about one another?" Tina said in a reasoning tone. Jack paused for a brief moment. That was very thoughtful of her and even more encouraging than he expected, he thought. “You, know what, girl?…I like that idea…you are on the ball…why didn’t I think of that?...you hungry?…we can go over to the Delmar across the street and I’ll treat you to dinner… I’m kinda’ hungry and I know you haven’t had dinner, either…how about it?” Jack offered. “You know what, boy?…you’re on the ball…I like that” Tina said as she patted him jokingly on the back. “Alright, you got me…damn…that was a good imitation of me…” Jack said as he was caught off-guard and now was even more impressed with her spontaneous sense of humor. “Just start stepping it off to the restaurant, young man” Tina continued to joke. The two of them walked casually across Lawrence after getting the green light and entered the restaurant. It was about 9:30pm and they sat, ordered, ate and talked.

“So…Jack…what do you do?” Tina asked as the two ate. “Uh…what was that?” Jack asked, feeling a little caught off-guard again. “What do you do?…what kind of job do you have?” Tina reiterated. “Oh…uhh…I’m a street hustler” he said point-blank. “A street hustler?…what does that mean, exactly?” Tina asked. “Well…I had a little bad luck when I got laid off from my job with Michelin Tire over two years ago…and as you know, the economy has been bad for a while now….I just haven’t been able to find any real work since then” Jack responded. “So, I have to make money in the streets while I’m still lookin’ for a job” Jack explained. “Wow…so, where do you go to look?” She asked. “I go to the State employment office over on Montrose and Hazel…been goin’ there ever since I got laid off…it’s a joke…they don’t have any jobs, I have only gone on about four interviews in a year…I’ve had my employment card stamped so many times until they had to staple another piece of card to it….my extended unemployment ran out about a year ago” Jack said as he opened up and told her things that were going on with him that he had almost forgotten himself. He seemed to be cleaning up his speech a little bit, as he tried to make a better impression. It had been quite some time since he had articulated his circumstances and an even longer time since anyone had cared to ask. He was enjoying the interest she was showing. It seemed more like a real heart-to-heart conversation that was not about drinking or drugs or telling lies or bragging or about trying to make a dollar like so many conversations he had in his daily life in the streets of Uptown that seemed to always have forward-looking, ulterior motives of survival. It was a refreshingly pleasant change from the fierce grind of the streets. "...Yea, baby…I'm on my own out here" Jack added after a long pause. "You don't have any family in town?" Tina asked with a probing, squinting of her face that shown genuine concern. "Oh…I have family…we just don't seem to be too close…I left home about five years ago…the old man kicked my ass out 'cause I lost my job…we didn't get along, anyway…we were never close…we really don't know each other" Jack said matter-of-factly. "Hmmm…that's too bad…what about your mother, brothers…sisters…Tina continued. "I was close with my mother…I love my mother…I have one younger brother…he's way younger by about eight years…my sister is a few years older…Jack said. "Well…where do they live?" Tina asked. "In Chicago…I think" Jack said. "What?...you don't know where they live?" Tina asked almost in shock. "Well…the last I knew, my father and brother lived in the same house my dad kicked me out of…. on the far Southside of Chicago" Jack said. "Well…what about your mother and sister?" Tina asked. "My mother and father were in the process of divorcin' the last I heard" Jack said. "My mother moved out almost a year after I left…I don't know where she lives…my sister got married and lives on the Southside somewhere with her husband…so…I don't know where she moved to… I don't know if my father and brother are still there…I haven't seen any of them in about three years" Jack explained. "Why, Jack?" Tina asked in amazement of Jack's story of his broken family relations. "Well, it doesn't seem to matter…nobody cares about anybody…so, I haven't kept in contact…why should I?" Jack said flippantly, trying to hide the pain he had suppressed for so long. "Anyway...I don't want to talk about it…it's depressing….what about you?...I don't know much about you…tell me about yourself" Jack said, sounding more upbeat and relieved that he had changed the subject.

Tina paused for a long moment, trying to change her state of mind from Jack's wrenching revelations to focus on herself. Her expression suddenly went from serious to a smile. "Oh…okay…uh…yea…well..fortunately, my parents are still together…they live in a nice little section of Evanston…they are public high school teachers….they love it…I have one younger sister who is a junior in high school and she will be following me into college in a couple of years" Tina started. "Yea…that's all cool and everything…" Jack cut in as soon as she spoke her last word "…but what about you…you…that's what I'm interested in knowin' about…come on with it, girl" Jack said, smiling broadly. He felt that this was the meat of their acquaintance; that this sexy, attractive woman that he had become so enamored with so soon, he would now begin to know who the person was behind such an alluring presence. Tina paused again, slightly blushing at Jack openly expressing his interest in her. "Well…I'm about to finish college…I'm going to start my last semester next week and finish in December this year…" she said. "Okay, baby that's cool…what about what makes you happy…what makes you smile…what makes you feel good inside…what are your hobbies…likes and dislikes…that's what I'm talkin' about….for instance…you seem to like black men…that's obvious…how did you come to be that way….tell me…"" Jack cut in again.

"Well…I have been attracted to black men since I was about thirteen toward the end of grade school…I remember having this crush on this one black boy in my class…no one ever knew it….our schools were pretty well mixed…I just thought he was the cutest boy and he was smart…most of all, he was very nice to me…especially nice…I think he may have had a crush on me, too….I have been curious ever since and I had my first date with a black guy from my college in my sophmore year a couple of years ago. I've dated a couple of others since and I enjoyed it…anyway…I dared not tell anyone…my parents would not have cared because they have always been liberal and they believe in the public schools where they teach and they believe in integration…they want to make the schools the best they could be and they dedicate themselves to that …anyway…I didn't listen to some whites…just one or two kids back in school who would say something mean about blacks…and an adult or two that I have overheard saying something cruel about blacks…I believe and I know from my own experience that we are all just people" Tina went on. "Okay, sugar…that's cool…that's all nice and everything…you seem very sweet and it looks like your folks raised you right…but…you know what?…I'm sort of a bad boy…a character…at least that's what a lot of folks think about me around this way…'cause I hustle in the streets and I might do some shady things…but, you know what else?" Jack said with a smile on his face that shown a hint of mischief. “What?” Tina asked. “I’m really a nice guy and I sho’ ’nough’ like what I see in front of me….you look goodna’ guv ’ment check” Jack stated boldly. Tina did not say anything right away but, responded with a broad, warm smile. “I guess that’s a compliment…I’ve never heard that one before…thank you” she finally said, still smiling.

“Now, Tina…one other thing…what’s happ’nin’ with you and my man, Mike?…I know he told me you two just met a few hours before I met you…anything goin’ on between you two?” Jack asked with focused curiosity. “Well…I wish I knew…we started off talking over at the Saxony bar next door…we had a few drinks…he seemed a little tipsy…we did go to his place for a little bit…we messed around for a minute…he nodded out for about a half-hour...I told him I wanted to have some fun, not watch him sleep so, we came back out…he seemed like a nice guy…a nice-looking man…tall…clean shaven… friendly…but, somewhere along the line, he lost his enthusiasm…I’m not sure if he really ever had any…I know more about you than I do about him right now…that’s it” Tina explained with a shrug of her shoulders. “So…you felt like he kinda’ blew you off? ….’cause I know ladies dig it when a man don’t pay ‘em no mind…understand me?” Jack said, secretly fishing for what, if any attraction Tina may have had to Mike and how he matched up. “Nooo…don’t be so sure of that…Mike seems like a nice guy but, he was a little too low-key for me…you seem a lot more spirited” Tina admitted, perhaps, not purposely. “Uh-huh” Jack uttered then paused as he began to feel that his fishing was paying off. “So…you kinda’ sayin’ you and me…we can hang?” Jack asked. “Yea…we can hang” Tina said assuringly. “Look, here, sweetie…you got a boy friend?…cause you actin’ like you don’t…what’s the deal?” Jack asked. “Oh…well…I’ve been really tied up with trying to finish school in the last two semesters or so…I haven’t really had a steady boyfriend…I just come out a couple of weekends a month to have a good time…maybe meet somebody nice to date…but, nothing serious until I’m done with school” Tina said. “So…you sayin’ all that to say you ain’t got no main squeeze right now…am I callin’ it right?” Jack inquired. “Yea…you’re right…that’s it” Tina admitted. “You know what?…she started. “….I like things, too” again playing on imitating Jack. “Like what?” Jack asked. “You think about it…you can figure that one out” she responded with a glimmer in her eyes and a smile that said she was having fun. “Now…what about you?…you haven’t said whether or not you have a girlfriend…do you?” Tina asked. “Baby, baby, baby….I’m just out here…I’m talkin’ to you, ain’t I?…I don’t have no girl right now…straight up” Jack said cool and casually. The two laughed at the romantic tit-for-tat game they were playing to feel each other out----but, it was a standoff---at least for now. “Hey…the food was pretty good…thanks for dinner” Tina said. “Aw, sugar it was my pleasure…without a doubt” Jack said, feeling a little more relaxed and open and allowing a glimpse of the real street character that he was.

“Tina…I got another good idea…” Jack started. “Wow…you keep coming up with these brilliant ideas…I’m getting excited” Tina joked with a big smile. “Okay….what’s on your mind?” she said more pointedly at the end of her smile. “Well…there’s a disco called The Machine….it’s a little bit out of this area up on Sheridan and Lunt…the place grooves…I’m tellin’ ya’….we’ll have a good time…we can work off this food on the dance floor… can you dig that?” Jack said with a big smile. “Sounds good to me….let’s go” Tina said with an excited smile. The two rose slowly from the table. Jack paid the check and left a tip.

Tina caught the cab just as she had done for Mike and after a short cab ride, they were at the Machine a few miles north of Lawrence where they had first met. The place had various shades of blue décor on the outside. There was the usual crowd of dressed-to-kill discoers hanging out, spread out along the sidewalk near the club entrance. Jack had been to the club several times in the last couple of years since it had opened. His life seemed to have become one big party in that time. So, he had become more familiar with places like the Machine around town and knew what each one was like. Tina seemed impressed with the atmosphere on the outside of the club as she looked around at the sharply dressed patrons in their disco outfits. “Nice…” she commented as they walked up to the club entrance from the cab. She also noted that the crowd was mixed with blacks and whites as well as others. After Jack paid their admission and they were inside, she seemed to get a relaxed vibe from the atmosphere and she could feel the excitement taking hold. It was crowded. The dim lighting inside was cleverly arranged with the same blue patterns as the outside with three big, round disco floors evenly spaced and people dancing energetically to the rhythm of the driving beat. It was deliriously noisy. "Let's have a drink and check things out…then, we can get out on the dance floor in a little while…is that cool?" Jack said almost shouting over the noise near Tina's ear. "Okay, let's find a seat and order" Tina replied almost shouting, as well while they both looked around for seats. They sat and Jack ordered drinks. They sat very comfortably in a booth in front of one of the disco floors as a few rows of comfortable booths were near each disco floor where patrons could be spectators to the dancing or just rest after coming off the floor themselves. Their drinks came and Jack and Tina sat and watched the excitement on the floor in front of them, occasionally smiling to each other whenever some clever dance move was made by any of the dancers.

During that time, while he sipped on his drink, Jack was thinking about Tina and the sense of her that he had gotten so far. She had a pleasant disposition and yet there was a mysterious fearlessness about her; a sense of adventure that she possessed that made him curious and excited. Why would a college girl like herself go into a neighborhood that was mostly black and just hang out as though it was no big deal, he thought. He admired her courage and unassuming attitude. He felt very comfortable with her. She was a self-respecting woman. But, he could tell by her last forward statement about "I like things, too" that she could be bold, as well; and seemed self-assured in what she said. He had decided that she was different from most any other woman he had met--black or white. He decided to put his arm along the back of the booth and around her shoulders. He did and she just smiled pleasantly and continued to watch the disco floor and sip her drink. Jack was pleased with her reaction and he could feel a smile inside.

Finally, they had finished their drinks, and being the high-spirited fellow that he was, Jack leaned over to Tina and said "Let's get down, baby….let's hit the floor!" when he heard one of his favorite Earth, Wind and Fire tunes, "Reasons" begin to pulsate over the audio system. Tina fixed her small purse to one of her blue-jeans belt loops and they moved with excitement to the disco floor. Jack moved to the groove of the music and seemed happy and lost in the fun. Tina focused on moving with Jack to the rhythm, smiling the whole while at Jack's antics as he began to clown on the dance floor. He was feeling good and loose from the strong rum in the mixed drink that he had when they first came in. They continued to dance as they moved to the music with smiling faces. It went on for another half-hour as they had an occasional slower song in-between when they were able to dance close and catch their breath. Finally, they sat again and ordered another drink. "You're not bad at all on the dance floor" Tina complimented Jack. "Thanks…hey, sugar…I was checkin' ya' moves …you was shakin' it pretty good out there yourself….you sure you ain't part black?" Jack teased. "No…I am *not* part black" Tina said smiling and giving Jack a playful slap on his arm as it laid on the table where they were sitting. "Let's slow it down a little, sweetie…I need to rest for a while" Jack admitted. "Yea…I want to relax, too" Tina chimed in. They talked for a while, commenting on little things they had done on the dance floor and which songs they enjoyed dancing to the most. After he had begun to feel rested, Jack's thoughts turned to Tina and how he had enjoyed the way she moved on the dance floor. It increased his desire even more to get close to her. "Hey, it's almost one…I think that was my last dance, baby…that's it for me" Jack said with a tone of resignation. "Me, too" Tina said. There was a long awkward silence as the two just sat and looked at one another.

"So…you got somewhere you gota' be today?" Jack asked Tina. "No, not really" Tina replied. Jack began to think about how to do what he had in mind. He needed to proceed cautiously. He felt somewhat hesitant. But, he had decided to go after what he wanted. "Well….you wanna hang with me or are you goin' home?" he asked knowing that what he was leading up to depended on her answer. "I can hang…it's not that late" she replied. "Cool, baby…let's catch a cab back down my way, then" Jack announced. "Okay" Tina replied. They caught a cab in front of the Machine and after a nice, easy ride with the windows down and the clear night breeze blowing through the cab, they were in front of the Malden Arms where Jack lived. It was dark in front of the building and Tina leaned out to look at the front of the building, scanning it briefly with mild curiosity. "This is it?" she asked after the cab stopped. "Yea…this is us" Jack replied as he pulled some bills out of his pocket and paid the cab driver. They got out and walked to the entrance. "Let's walk up the stairs…the elevators are always pretty slow" Jack said, thinking that he did not want to be embarrassed by what they may have seen in the elevator on a Saturday night. He knew that many of the residents in the building got "blasted" on the weekends and there was a good chance that evidence of somebody's high might end up on the elevator floor as he had come to expect. "How far up are you, Jack?" Tina asked without much concern. "Third floor, babe…the flights are short…you'll see" Jack assured. As they walked up the stairwell, they came upon a couple of the more hardcore characters who passed them going down the stairs. They both turned and gazed at Tina with lustful approval without saying a word.

They were finally inside his apartment and Jack felt that stir of excitement rising inside. He was extremely courteous, asking for Tina's jacket and hanging it up with care; asking her did she want something to drink. Jack partially undressed leaving on his pants, undershirt and socks. Tina took off her jacket and shoes. They began to talk the kind of late-night talk that people often do after coming in from partying all night. The conversation was lively and relaxed with laughs and giggles. They were finally laying side-by-side on the bed after an hour or so of conversation when Jack made his move. He rolled over on his side facing Tina and they began to kiss---gently at first, then with passion as they both undressed and got underneath the bed spread. The passion grew and became more intense and took flight into an erotic symphony with a shuddering crescendo.

Sunday mornings were always subdued in the Malden Arms because many of the residents were quiet and spent from their wild weekends. It was quiet in the building and outside. Jack awakened first. He looked over at Tina and could see her sweet face; eyes shut, breathing easy and gently; sleeping quietly. He had not had such sweet company in all the few months he had lived in the Arms. It gave him a warm feeling inside as though he had somehow come closer to the center of normalcy for this time he was spending with this woman. She was a normal person; the likes of which was rare in the world he lived. She was not a dope-fiend or a street-walker or a dope dealer or a street hustler or any of the street types that existed in his world. He wondered, too just what she saw in a fellow like himself. He knew that he was not so bad a person----yet, nothing near the normal person that she was. He wondered right then, what forces could possibly have brought them together. He decided that it was an extraordinary encounter only because of the person that she was because most women of her type would not have much to do with Jack. Although he resembled a normal person on the outside; being a fairly good-looking man and dressing with style---it was his circumstances and his street persona that would have repelled them at the outset. He had decided that it took an exceptional person who did not have the usual fear and apprehension to see beyond the surface of what they saw of him.

He lay in the bed feeling a light haze of sleepiness in his head that felt relaxed. He did not feel the usual way that he felt after most nights in the streets. Perhaps, because he did not continue to drink from bottles throughout the night as he was accustomed to doing. He did not drink so much because he was with Tina, it occurred to him. He lay awake for a little while and faded back to sleep. He awakened again from that deeper sleep and it took a short while before he regained full awareness and remembered that he had been with Tina. He looked over once again and could see her still sleeping peacefully. He went to the bathroom and brushed his teeth and rinsed with mouthwash; took a shower and came back out. Tina was sitting up in bed.

"Good morning, Mister All Night" Tina said with a pleasant smile on her face. "Good morning, Miss Freaky Thang" Jack joked with a grin as he stuck his tongue out slightly in a playful expression. "Uhmmm…I haven't had that much fun in a while" Tina said with a broad smile. "You are some kinda' woman, girl…I thought *I* was supposed to be the one wearin' people out" Jack said, still smiling. Tina rose from the bed and embraced Jack with a warm hug. "I need to freshen up with a shower…you got towels for me?" Tina asked. "Oh, yea, babe…let me get a face and dry towel for you" Jack said as he went over to the dresser drawers and pulled them out and handed them to Tina. She showered and they milled around the room talking about different things as Tina began to dress while Jack finished dressing. "How ya' feelin', sugar?…I'm goin' downstairs to the desk clerk…he bootlegs drinks on Sunday mornings…you want anything?" Jack asked. "I don't really need anything, Jack…you can go for yourself if you want" Tina responded. Jack paused for a moment then said "Ahh…I really could use a beer to clear the cobwebs out…it won't take but a few minutes for me to run down…you'll be alright if I leave you for a few minutes…huh?" Jack asked. "I'm fine, Jack…go ahead" Tina urged. Jack went out of the door, locked it and went downstairs. He was gone not more than five minutes before he was coming back through the apartment door. He had a fair sized brown paper bag with him. "What did you do…buy him out?" Tina joked. "Naw..I just bought a few beers….I'll just have one for now…you sure you don't want one?…they're really cold" Jack offered. "Okay…I'll take one" Tina responded, perhaps wanting to make Jack feel more comfortable by not having him drink alone. "Say…is that restaurant we were at last night still open?…I'd like to stop there for breakfast, then I have to head home on the L train at the Lawrence stop" Tina said. "I'll treat you to breakfast…I know you need some energy after last night" Tina teased. "You sho' 'nough got that right!" Jack responded, smiling at Tina. They sat on the edge of the bed side-by-side after Tina was fully dressed and began to kiss again; laying back on the bed for one more deep, passionate kiss. They both sat up with hazy eyes and heaving mildly to recover from the ecstasy of the moment.

They walked the short distance to the Delmar restaurant on the northeast corner of Broadway and Lawrence and entered the restaurant. It was shortly past 11am. It was a partly cloudy day that seemed sullen and in tune with the mood of Sundays like this one when everything had quieted and the lively Saturday night had merged into the peacefulness of a lazy Sunday morning. They ordered, ate breakfast and talked. Tina and Jack seemed to talk with easy, relaxed, flowing conversation; as though they had connected and had known one another much longer than one night; a little laughter and a quip or two kept the mood upbeat. "So…when am I gonna' see you again, babe?" Jack asked. "I don't know…it depends….school…you know what I told you…it's gonna keep me busy" Tina said. "You can call me…here" She said as she took one of the restaurant napkins and wrote her telephone number on it and handed it to Jack. "Now, don't just stuff it in your pocket and lose it or use it without thinking and mess the number up…write it down on paper soon as you can" she said with a tone of serious admonition. "Okay…I'll write it down" Jack replied compliantly. "Can anybody call you at your place?" Tina inquired. "Oh, yea…you can call the desk clerk and they will take a message …only thing is, though…I don't remember the number" Jack said. "I'll give it to you the first time I call you…alright, sugar?" Jack said as he spoke real nice to let her know that his interest in her was still strong and he wanted to stay in contact and see her again. Tina stared at Jack for a long moment as though she was pondering something. "Wow…you don't have a job and you make your money in the streets…I don't know what it is about you, Jack….must be something" she said almost hypnotically, as though she was giving deeper thought about the choices she was now making. "Jack, I really have had a great time with you…you were much more of a gentleman than I expected…somehow, we get along fine" Tina said in a heartfelt, sincere tone. "….not to mention your erotic skills…can you dig me, baby!" she said, adding the last little phrase to imitate Jack as she giggled and smiled playfully while saying it. "Yea…I think you was tryin' to kill me, girl…first, you have me dancin' all night on the dance floor then, you schemed your way up into my crib and tried to break a brotha' down…you a rough woman…you know that?" Jack laughed teasingly while dispensing his brand of street humor. "Whaaat!" Tina gasped with feigned outrage and trying to hold back a smile as she stood up, grabbed a spoon and pecked him on the top of his head with it while Jack continued to laugh out loud. It was his way of being himself in a light-hearted, good-natured kind of way. It was the way he talked when he really felt comfortable with someone. He could feel it inside. It was rare when he felt this way and when he did, it usually put him in a much happier mood. It was such a nice change from the usual hardened frame of mind that the streets demanded of him. "Jack…from the moment I first saw you at that tavern on the corner, I knew you wanted to get close to me….you couldn't hide it…I was scheming to get into your place?…your imagination is running wild!" Tina said, still trying to hold back a smile and keep as straight a face as she could.

"Okay, Jack…walk me to the L stop, alright?" Tina said in a tone that let Jack know she was nurturing the connection that they had. "Yea, baby…sure…I guess it's that time, huh?" Jack replied with a hint of resignation that it was time to part with Tina. They left the restaurant with Tina paying the bill and tipping. "Thanks for breakfast, baby…to tell you the truth…I cain't remember *ever* havin' a woman pay for my meal…sisters ain't gonna' do it.. hahaha…sho''nough…a brotha' ain't gonna' get *nothin'* outa' them…they will be lookin' for you to buy *them* a meal and anything else they can get out of you…I hate to say…I love them sisters but, they are *haaarrd* on a brotha'…I guess a woman like ya' self comes from a whole different background where you ain't tryin' to play on a man all the time…am I right or am I wrong?" Jack asked in a lively, rejuvenated tone. "We have our ways…we just don't do it quite the same way" Tina replied. They walked very slowly for a while without saying much when finally, Tina grabbed Jack's hand and they began to hold hands. The streets matched the partly cloudy day with the stillness in the atmosphere and very few people seen on the streets along with the light vehicle traffic. The surrounding peacefulness also seemed to be in tune with the quiet, romantic mood of Jack and Tina at that moment. Tina paid two fares at the CTA ticket booth so she and Jack could have a little more time together and together, they climbed the long, empty stairs to the platform, stealing a couple of passionate kisses along the way. After reaching the platform, they chatted for a while and it occurred to Jack during that exchange that he and Tina talked like true friends---he felt a sense of authenticity from it all---he had a close relationship with some of his street buddies but, it was not the same. This was outside the realm of the madness he endured on a daily basis—it felt good---and real.

Finally, the train was coming for Tina to get to Evanston, and while it was still in the distance, the two shared another kiss. The train arrived and Jack said "Bye, baby…I'll call you" "You'd better…you don't want me to break you down, do you?" Tina teased as she boarded and after she was on, looked out of the car window and waved with a sweet smile to Jack as the train pulled away. Jack went back to his place and fell asleep.

Jack awakened to see the red letters of the time on his clock-radio sitting on the dresser jump out at him in the dark room. 5:44pm it read. He felt groggy but, refreshed from the sleep he had. He remembered coming back home after walking Tina to the L and taking off his clothes to go to bed because he felt spent; not just from his late-night tryst but, from the days-on--end of non-stop drinking and carousing that was his usual routine. This was the first lull in quite a while and it had all come down on him in this one quiet Sunday afternoon. He was glad to have rested. But, now, the magic of his night with Tina had worn off and he was alone again. It came to him as he sat up on the edge of his bed thinking, that he was a person who was alone and he could not decide if he was lonely. He had never *felt* lonely before. But, somehow the notion of loneliness was in his head at this moment. He wondered where it had come from. Was it because he felt truly connected to someone last night for the first time in a very long time? He realized that what was different last night, was that he had trusted for the first time in quite a while. Usually, Jack trusted no one. He was never treated well growing up and that was where it all started something deep inside reminded him. Tina never judged him; never made any assumptions about him. She allowed his interaction to speak for itself. She had not prejudged him. For that reason, he felt relaxed with her and opened up. He could be himself; be funny; say what was on his mind. Jack didn't even trust his closest friends like Melvin and Coley. They were fiends and opportunists who would take advantage of him whenever the chance presented itself. Jack knew how fiends operated; how they thought; what motivated them; he was one of them and he would do the same to them if the chance came about. This was how it was in the streets amongst Gypsies because money was hard to come by when you lived this way. You scrapped and connived in a cut-throat society of liars and thieves to get what you wanted. Getting high was the primary motivation.

Finally, he decided that he was not going to stay inside for the rest of the evening. He needed some human interaction and decided to dress and go outside to see what was going on. Jack freshened up and decided to go to the Wilson-Malden corner where the Wilson Liquor store was. He would not show himself on Lawrence Avenue today; even though he had kept his hashish sales to the concert crowd only. He knew it was not a good idea to go back the very next day to where he had beat people out of money. He left out of his apartment and walked through the eerie silence in the drab lobby of the Arms. He could see a couple of the residents loitering and looking lonely and somber with nothing to do. After walking through the entrance to the outside, he turned left and strode south on Malden.

He arrived at the northeast corner of Wilson and Malden. When he turned left to head east on Wilson, he immediately saw three older men, perhaps ten to fifteen years older than himself, sitting on concrete steps directly across from the Wilson Liquor store. They were huddled together, passing around a large bottle of liquor as they sat, talked and drank. He recognized them all from around the neighborhood; but, noticed right away that two of them were the gritty dude who gave him the twenty dollar bill the other day and his buddy. “Hey, my man….what’s happ’nin’, bro?” the “gritty” one spoke out to Jack after he turned his head slightly to his right to see Jack approaching. “Ain’t nothin’ goin’ on, my man…say…ain’t you the stud who gave me that package?” Jack asked the “gritty” one. “Yea, bro-man…that was me… now, you did understand what the deal was, didn’t you?” The stranger asked. “Hey…well…I didn’t know right then but, I figured it out a little later on” Jack replied. “Yea…I fig’ ‘ud that…yea…naw, bro..I wasn’t just handin’out money for the hell of it…that was your cut for stayin’ cool…that’s what them Italian mafia in the flicks call….hush money…hehehehe” the stranger said as he chuckled and slapped hands to give five with his accomplice who was sitting right next to him. They all chorused in with agreement after he made that statement by laughing and saying “Yea...you got that right…hush yo’ mouth money” and “Right on…shut-the-fuck-up money!…hahhaha” and they all seemed tickled by the shared quip. “Hey, my man…I’ll tell you…that double-saw sho’ ‘nough’ came in handy, ‘cause I was short at the time” Jack admitted as he grinned good-naturedly at the thought of that fortunate moment. “What’s ya’ name, brotha-man?” Jack asked as he began to feel a sense of fellowship from the stranger and his group and extended his hand to him for a shake. The stranger extended his hand and they shook. “They call me “Mo”…”Motic” the stranger said with a sense of sinister pride. Jack shook with the others “Obie” one said “Julius” the other said. “I could see you was a player, bro-man…we know’d you’d reca’’nize a hustler doin’ his thang…we was makin’ money when you seen us up in the Arms over there and we cain’t afford to have nobody trickin’ on us…that’s how we play it…twenty dollars ain’t nothin’ to keep from gettin’ twenty years” Motic said again as he slowly began to chuckle after he realized the double-entendre and leaned slightly to his left and cut his eyes without turning his head and said “Y’all hear what I said?…y’all dig that?” to the others sitting behind and beside him as he continued to chuckle. The others let out low, easy laughter and said in agreement “Hell yea…I’ll give up twenty dollars to keep from doin' all that time" and "You know it…you got to know how to play this thang out here" After the spirited exchange between them subsided, Jack said "Man…that was a clever move…I really didn't see nothin' but it woulda' been insurance if I did…seein' as how I didn't know y'all and y'all didn't know me…but...I ain't the type to trick…I'm a hustler myself..I do thangs that I wouldn't want no tricks to see" "Yea…I see you dress like a player…hey…you want a taste?" Motic said as he extended the large pint bottle of liquor to Jack "Naw…that's cool, Motic…I was gonna get myself a taste a little later on…thanks, anyway" Jack replied. "You welcomed, now…we don't care nothin' 'bout this shit, man…we shares our drinks…just don't ask for none 'o my… "hair-on" and we cool" The stranger said, getting tickled with himself with that last phrase and again, turning with a broad smile to his cohorts for approval and extending his hand to the closest one for another "five" hand slap. "Fuck you, Mo" Obie, the closest one said as he playfully slapped Motic's hand away rather than slapping "five" "…you better give me some o' yo' "hair-on" and that "blow" and any other kinda' high you got, nigga'… far back as we go and all the shit we been through together...damn right" Obie said facetiously as he feigned disapproval of Motic's statement. "Motic just let out another chuckle and then turned somewhat serious as he turned to Jack. " See…these ain't just my hustlin' buddies…these is my home-boys…we all from Memphis..we hustlers…killers, man….you don't wanna' cross neither one 'o these players…they may laugh and joke with ya'…but, they don't play…cross 'em and I'd leave town if I was you…understand me?…know what I'm sayin?" Motic said to Jack in a blustery manner. " I hear...ya', bro'…I hear ya' Jack said in agreement, not really being all that impressed. While he knew this was probably true and that they were a ruthless bunch---he had struck a chord with them and they all had the same understanding. Jack knew how the game went---he knew not to cross the regulars out here in the streets---you only played on the marks and not other hustlers. "Yea, bro'…we gambles, stick-up, sell dope, pimp hoes…it don't matter..we do it all" Motic went on in a boisterous manner. This was the usual kind of talk that Jack would hear all around the circles he traveled in Uptown. It seemed that there were very few who didn't try to impress people from their mouth---that is building themselves up through mere talk. It was common and he was used to hearing it. It was not really his style but, whenever he found himself doing it---it was for some reason other than trying to impress. It was usually because he was setting up some mark to rip him off while he was hustling. Doing it just to impress was pointless as far as Jack was concerned. If it didn't make him any money---then he didn't give a damn about it.

Jack continued his street corner "bullshittin" with Motic and his group when his friend Sandy appeared across the street. She was one of the neighborhood women that he had made friends with almost from the beginning when he moved into Uptown. She was a woman about ten years older than Jack. She was one of his drinking buddies. Sandra had two little boys; little David who was about four years old and Gerald who was about six years old. The boys' fathers were two different men who were regulars in the neighborhood. Little David was "Old Man" Dave's son and little Gerald was Coley's son; and because she had a son by his close friend, Coley, Jack called her his "play sister-in-law" She occasionally talked about a grown daughter that Jack had never seen who lived in another part of Chicago. Sandra was a rather plain-looking woman. She possessed a great spirit and was a funny and fun-loving person who loved to laugh. She was a very good piano player and played at church services at the Leland Baptist Church at Leland and Winthrop. Jack did not quite understand how she drank so much and attended church. But, she was his friend; like family; so, he did not care what she did and did not try to judge her. Jack and Sandra had shared many a laugh and quite a few drinks together. Whenever they saw one another, each knew that there was a good time in store. Occasionally, the three of them, Coley, Jack and Sandra would drink together if Sandra had someone to watch the kids, like Becky, who lived with her much younger boyfriend, Roosevelt. They lived in the huge apartment building that took up the area from the northwest corner of Winthrop and Leland back to the alley on it's west side. Their apartment was situated right over the Leland Baptist Church and it was convenient for the baby-sitting arrangement that Sandra had with Becky. Becky loved children and babysat without pay for the sheer joy of having the little boys around. She loved them and would occasionally help Sandra out with money for the two boys.

As soon as he spotted her across the street at the opposite corner, Jack said to the group

"Hey, fellas…there goes some 'o my people…I need to holla' at her….I'll check y'all later" With that, he strolled across the street, smiling as he walked toward Sandra and her two little boys. "Hey, woman…what you up to?" Jack greeted her. "Hey, Jack" Sandra replied with her usual broad smile. "I'm headed to church… I wish I had time to get me a little taste 'cause these little rascals been gettin' on my nerves all this mornin'….I'll be glad when I get over there and hand they little butts over to Becky for a while" Sandra said in her characteristically plaintive tone. "What you doin'?….why don't you walk me on over there and if I see you when I get out, I'll buy us a taste…alright?" Sandra offered. "Sho' 'nough, sister-in-law….you know that ain't no problem" Jack said with a tiny bit of reluctance because he didn't really want to go that way. But, he decided to go ahead with Sandra and just not go up on Lawrence Avenue and to stay around Leland Avenue. He knew that it was very unlikely that he would run into some of his hash customers and he knew, too that because of the way he played his game by only selling to those that seemed to be already high; that he had little to worry about. But still, he operated this way as a matter of routine. Because it seemed to assure that there were no confrontations with unhappy hash customers.

They walked and talked as they guided the two boys along the way, alternately carrying them across big streets and allowing them to walk when it was safe on the sidewalks. Their chat was occasionally punctuated with laughter, as always. These little get-togethers always seemed to lift the spirit of each of them. They seemed to understand each other just as most friends who had made such an amiable connection often did. Finally, they arrived in front of the church on Leland. "Okay, now Jack…I'll be lookin' for you when I get outa' church…don't go nowhere…okay?" Sandra said, sounding hopeful that Jack would submit to her request. "I'll be out here….just look around…you'll see me…" Jack said, avoiding a firm commitment. "Alright, then…good....'cause I want to get mellow when I come out…I'll see you later…I got to get them up to Becky's before I go in the church…she gon' keep 'em 'til tomorrow mornin'…I'll be free the rest of the night…hallelujah!" Sandra said with a broad smile as she entered the stairwell next to the church entrance to climb the stairs to Becky and Roosevelt's apartment.

Jack stood momentarily in front of the church entrance after she and the kids were gone. He began to see a couple of parked cars on the block with people emerging from them. They were church-goers coming for the Sunday service. Jack decided to go to the corner, away from the church's entrance lest anyone mistook him for someone who wanted to go inside. Besides, he did not feel like having to speak and say hello to the church-goers who would soon be crossing his path to enter the church. He knew from experience that when they spoke to him, they would throw in a "praise God" or a "bless you, brother" which was fine and good. But, he felt a mild uneasiness from such piety because it was a rebuke to how he was now living his life.

He stood on the northwest corner of Winthrop and Leland and looked north to see that the streets were mostly empty. In the distance, the Aragon stood still and silent with remnants of trash littering the area around it from the people traffic and revelry that had ensued the night before. The day was still partly cloudy and it was early evening. Jack could feel the subdued mood in the air that he knew so well of these quiet Sunday evenings. They were quiet for most people but, not for Gypsies like Jack who had no obligations on Monday mornings and did not have any particular direction nor any orderliness in their lives to maintain. Gypsies did not live by the same clock, schedule or beliefs that normal people did---almost everything they did was spontaneous.

As Jack was gazing up Winthrop street, he could see in the distance on the southwest corner of Winthrop and Lawrence, two male figures suddenly appear after turning the corner at Frances' Tavern. They were directly in his line-of-sight on the same side of the street and heading in his direction. A moment passed before his sight adjusted to see that it was his hustling buddy Melvin and J.T., one of his very best friends who grew up with Jack in Cabrini-Green. J.T. and Jack had known each other since their teens when Jack and J.T.'s older brother, Matt were best friends. They meet as young boys around the age of twelve in the Cabrini-Green housing projects. They started out together hustling with their wagons; pulling groceries for the customers at the neighborhood grocery store. The store was eventually burned down during the riots of the late-sixties. Jack and Matt continued to be close friends on through their teens and early adulthood. Jack had come to be considered as one of the family. J.T. 's first name was "James" He had earned the name "J.T. Silk" several years ago from his days as a pimp around the near-north area near Cabrini-Green where he grew up. J.T. was always well groomed. He was a sharp dresser and smooth hustler. He carried himself with a regal bearing----easy, charming and charismatic with an air of supreme confidence. He knew how to make people like him and many did. They admired his easy, flamboyant style as a pace-setting hustler on the scene. He was respected because he was smart and tough. Having grown up in Cabrini-Green where he became a good fighter. He was a proud person and did not take bullshit from anyone. Having grown up poor in a large family in Cabrini, he burned with ambition and saw the hustler's life as a shortcut to his dreams. Jack had met Melvin shortly after he moved into the 4848 Winthrop apartment high-rise. Melvin lived on the ninth floor. Jack once stayed on the third floor. Eventually, Jack, Melvin and J.T. began to hang out together in Uptown. Jack lost his job about a year after moving in. He began to collect unemployment and had a lot of idle time back then. He became acquainted with Melvin and some of his other Vietnam buddies who lived in the building. He met Fuzzy and Woody and many others during that time. As Jack became more acquainted with Melvin and his group, he began to pick up some of their bad habits. As he became more-and-more frustrated with being out of work, Jack began to get high with Melvin's crowd; most of whom were "nam vets" with young families. As he got to know them, Jack was somewhat surprised that these men used heroin regularly and some were brazen in the things they did to get high. He began to pick up some of their street savvy and one thing led to another. Over the next year-and-a-half, it seemed that Jack's life and his personality had become profoundly altered. He had become someone else---he did not know who; but, it seemed he had embarked upon a whole strange, new world and the person he had become was new and strange, as well. He had come to have a life in the streets. He had become a Street Gypsy.

He could see Melvin carrying a brown paper bag and he knew that it was a drink. Jack was glad to see them because he felt better when any of the people that he associated with were around. Especially Street Gypsies like himself who got high. He did not like these Sunday evenings because they were dull and dead with not much activity or chance to make money. If he did not have any money left over from Saturday night, it made these Sundays harder to get through. Many a Sunday he passed the time just drifting around the streets; having a few drinks and sometimes getting high on the prescription drugs everyone in the streets called "Ts and Blues" The Ts were an orange pill for pain. The Blues were a drug for sinuses. When crushed to powder form and mixed with water, they produced a heroin-like high. Because of the cheap price of two dollars per pill for the Ts and one dollar for each Blue, they had become popular amongst the street crowd. Sometimes Jack would get real heroin. Jack waited at the corner as the two men fast approached him. He was feeling better already. "Road dog…"J.T." Silk…what's happ'nin, y'all?" Jack greeted enthusiastically. "Hey, Jack…what's to ya', brotha'" Melvin greeted, "Hey, now…brotha' Jack, my old home-boy….what you been up to, man?" J.T. Silk greeted as Jack took turns engaging in a soul handshake with each man. "Aw, man…I just got over this way…just hangin' right now" Jack replied. Without saying a word, Melvin handed Jack the brown paper bag with the pint bottle of liquor inside and Jack accepted it and took a drink. "Whooowee…damn…y'all drinkin' that Schnapps, huh?" Jack responded with a slight grimace as he negotiated the drink going down. "Silk…I ain't seen you in about two months, li'l brotha'…where you been hidin' out?" Jack inquired. "Well…you know…I moved out two months ago from them people I was stayin' with in 4848…I got my own place over on Irving and Sheridan…I been stayin' away from around here" J.T. Silk explained. "Aw, yea?…givin' this spot some "air", huh?" Jack surmised. "Pretty much" J.T. responded. "J.T. been rollin' pretty good, Jack…I run into him gettin' out of a cab up on Lawrence and Broadway…I said…hey, Silk…nigga, you ain't gonna' duck out on buyin' me a taste when you got money to pay cab fare…come on, now give it up!" Melvin said jokingly. "Yea…I felt sorry for his ass standin' out there on the corner by himself…Melvin…you *looked* like you was broke…you need to learn how to keep from lookin' broke, man and maybe people won't try to avoid you" J.T. teased, smiling broadly. They all had a good laugh from the banter.

This was how Jack and the group of Street Gypsies he called his friends carried on. There was always these high-spirited exchanges whenever they would meet-up after not having seen one another for a while. There was usually discussion centered on how each man was faring as far as his survival; what hustles they had made lately; little gossip about what other members of the loosely connected association of street characters were doing; or what had happened to them or to other people they knew in the streets. This was what Jack enjoyed the most---these little get-togethers when he felt connected. It did not seem to bother Jack when he was alone, doing his own thing for long stretches of time; but, he felt somewhat comforted that he was part of something and belonged somewhere, however dubious.

There was also this underlying anti-social philosophy these men shared that went unsaid; the notion of living free and easy without having to account to anyone by working a job. It was about how being a black man in America affected their sense of manhood; their personal freedom and how they had to account for being black in little ways in society; how they could not go into a store and be treated like a valued customer but, rather as a suspect; never being given the benefit of the doubt; how they could not understand why it was so hard to get hired. It was about how the police always seemed to view them as criminals rather than citizens. How trying to fit into the larger society and still having self-respect had compromised their sense of who they were; it was too uncomfortable; too complex; too difficult; too much of a strain to try to assimilate; and so, there was this defiance; this discord in their souls; this cry to be completely free from those demands; because sentiment never seemed to be on their side; this was what brought many of them to this way of life---a lifestyle as self-destructive as it was liberating.

"Silk…you still ain't said what brought you back this way, man…what's poppin?" Jack inquired. "Aw…man…I came to pick up some stuff o' mine that I left with them people I was stayin' with…I owed one of 'em some money…so I got to straighten my bill, then I can get my shit" J.T. explained. "So when you gonna' take care o' business?" Melvin cut in. "I wanted to get me a bump before I go to get my stuff" J.T. explained. That admission was music to Melvin's ears. "I know where you can cop" Melvin shot back quickly. "Slow ya' role, Road Dog…slow ya' role…we'll do somethin'…be cool….I called this guy Ralph, the one I owe the money and he said to meet him in front of 4848 around 9:30 when he gets in tonight…that's about two-and-a-half hours from now"

J.T. said as he looked at his watch. "So…we got to do somethin' before then 'cause I'm headed straight back home after we finish gettin' high" J.T. forewarned. "Silk…check this out, man…sho' 'nough…I know where you can get some fire over on Glenwood and Argyle…three or four can get high on a quarter bag…no bullshit…" Melvin went on with his fiendish overtures. Being the true fiend that he was, Melvin never missed an opportunity to get high and he had the gift-of-gab to put himself in position to get what he wanted. But, J.T. Silk was no easy mark. He was as street savvy as anyone; having been a true pimp at the top of his game, just a few years ago before his empire came tumbling down. He was shot over a bad drug deal by another associate in the game a few years ago; a major dope dealer that he once worked with by the name of Big Pete. He had matured considerably since that incident and had tempered his lifestyle to be far less risky He had maintained a much lower profile. "Alright…that sounds cool….but, how much *you* got on it…I ain't gonna spend all my money just gettin' people high…give me somethin' on it…'cause I can get high by myself, you know…I ain't got it like that" J.T. stated firmly. "Hey, Silk…I ain't got nothin' on it, man…I can just do the coppin'…that's all" Melvin admitted in a somewhat resigned tone. "Well…I guess that's worth somethin' but, I'll tell you what…I'm not spendin' no twenty-five dollars…I'll spend about fifteen…can I get somethin' for fifteen that will get more than one person high?" J.T. inquired. "Well…I'll tell ya', Silk…the best thing you can do is get two dime bags" Melvin offered. "Two dime bags, huh?" J.T. mumbled as he seemed to be thinking about the proposition intently. "Two dime bags?…I'll tell you what, Road Dog…I'll do a bag, but I'll give you half of the other bag…I need to take some home to my little woman..dig what I'm sayin'?" J.T. said. ….Yea…I guess that's cool since I ain''t got nothin' on it…I ain't got no choice…you holdin' the paper…so you callin' the shots, Silk" Melvin conceded. "Hey, y'all…I got a little paper, but… I ain't tryin' to get high like that tonight…I'll just hang….I'll buy the next drink since y'all got this taste already…cool?" Jack offered. "Yea, Jack…you know you're welcomed to hang…you my guy but…I just cain't get everybody high…I need to hold on to my little funds, ya' dig?…I need to have that money to pay Ralph so he can give me my little belongings that he's been holdin' for me" J.T. said, letting Jack know that he had not forgotten about him by explaining his money situation.

This was the way these conversations went amongst fiends. J.T. and Jack were not quite the fiends that Melvin was. They were known to be what Street Gypsies called "chippers" meaning that they did not want to go all out for drugs by being obsessed and getting high constantly and doing any and everything to get high on their favorite drug. Chippers would try to have the best of both worlds by getting high only occasionally to avoid all of the pitfalls that true fiends subjected themselves to. Chippers tried to maintain some level of sanity with getting high; trying to maintain what resembled a normal life while occasionally engaging in getting high on dope. True fiends could not be trusted what-so-ever---they would steal from their mothers and fathers, brothers and sisters and anyone who made themselves vulnerable. Often times, trading away all their worldly possessions for just "one more" Losing a place to stay; going to jail regularly. They were brazen in the risks they took in trying to get money to get high.

Melvin was not quite so bad---he had a wife and kids to consider. He had to at least maintain some level of civility and order in his behavior for their sake. But, it was a constant struggle for Melvin. He was often on bad terms with his wife who had to take care of the kids on her own because Melvin could not hold down a regular job. Fortunately for her and the kids, she had a very good job with the telephone company. She was decent and intelligent. She was far removed from the world that her husband lived in outside of their life at home. She was bewildered by her husbands behavior and in her moments of despair, would chalk it up to his stint in Vietnam; speculating that the experience had turned him into someone very different from the man she had been with since high school. On too many occasions, she had to cover for his transgressions; taking money from the family budget to bail him out of jail or giving him car fare to look for a job; still, like so many wives and mothers, she endured these difficulties in the name of family unity.

"Where is the spot we can cop, Road Dog?" J.T asked. "It's up on Glenwood and Argyle…..we can walk….it won't take that long" Melvin replied. "Alright….let's go, then" J.T. said. The three of them walked back north on Winthrop to Lawrence and turned west going to Broadway and then north to Argyle to go not much further west to the dope spot. It had begun to get dark as J.T. and Jack waited on the sidewalk outside of a well-kept three flat apartment building on the quiet street of Glenwood. Melvin had gotten the money from J.T. and gone into the building. After using the intercom, he was buzzed into the secured entrance door. After arriving at the apartment door, Melvin rapped on it lightly and waited for an answer. Almost thirty seconds passed before a deep male voice answered from inside----"Who is it?" the voice asked. "Road Dog" Melvin answered. "What's happ'nin'? the voice asked. "Two dimes" Melvin answered. "We ain't got no dimes...we just got rocks right now" the voice said. "Rocks?" Melvin asked. "Yea" the voice answered. "What's with the rocks, then?" Melvin inquired sounding puzzled. "The rocks is straight…it's fire….straight up" the voice said. "It's straight, huh?" Melvin asked as he began to ponder in his mind about this change in what the dealers were selling. "Can I get right with a double-saw worth?….'cause I been gettin' powder for the longest….I ain't never got no rocks from y'all" Melvin said, trying to probe deeper so that he could feel more secure about copping with J.T.'s money. "Ain't nothin' changed except the form….it's still fire….you wanna cop or what?" the voice asked with a tone of mild annoyance. "This ain't my money…I need to holla' at my man waitin' for me outside to see if he wanna' do this, 'cause I told him we was gettin' powder" Melvin explained. "Do what you gota' do….we ain't goin' nowhere" the voice said. "I'll be back in a few" Melvin said before he bounced down the stairs to go back out to the sidewalk. Melvin walked up close to J.T. standing on the sidewalk next to Jack. "Silk…guess what?…they ain't got no powder, man….they talkin' 'bout they just got rocks…I ain't never got no rocks from them before…I don't know" Melvin said, tailing off quietly at the end of what he said. He held an anticipating expression on his face for what J.T. would say. J.T. did not say anything right away but, paused momentarily to consider what Melvin said. "Everything you ever got from these people's been straight, right?" J.T. asked. "Yea.. no problems" Melvin responded.

"What can I get for twenty?" J.T. asked. "I asked him and he said. What you get is just as much and just as good as the powder….that's what you'll get" Melvin explained. "Fuck it…go ahead and cop" J.T. said, a bit exasperated with all of the back-and-forth negotiating. Melvin started back into the building and was buzzed in again. Jack and J.T.waited for his return. When he did, he opened his palm and showed J.T. the small nugget-sized object wrapped in foil. J.T. took control of it, peeled the foil open slightly and looked at it. It was the rich, dark-brown color that most fiends associated with good heroin. “Alright…I guess it’s okay….here..you hold it while we go back” J.T. said, being shrewd enough not to have possession of it in case they were stopped and searched by the police.

The three men stepped lively, walking at an anxious dope fiend pace back along the route they had come. They were walking south on Broadway approaching Lawrence Avenue when Melvin noticed the time on the flashing sign on the Uptown National Bank building. “7:54” it read. “Look, Silk…it’s eight o’ clock…you got plenty of time to get high and catch your guy to get your shit” Melvin said, hoping to settle J.T. down so that he did not have to be rushed later on when they were getting high. Melvin always liked to take his time getting high; savoring every moment until he reached that optimum stratosphere were he could not be reached by the outside world; where he could visit his uninhibited, worry-free, secret world of nirvana

They walked and talked. “Yea…that’s cool but, what about outfits and where are we gonna take off?” J.T. asked. ‘Y’all can take off at my spot” Jack offered. “Cool, Jack….right on, brotha’…I was wonderin’ where Melvin was gonna go for us to get high” J.T. said. “Where we gonna’ get some “fits” Road Dog?” J.T. asked Melvin. “Now, Silk…you oughta’ know me by now, brotha’…I got my shit with me…I’m *always* ready….ya’ dig” Melvin said with a big smile as he reached into his front pocket and pulled out a small oblong object wrapped in a small cloth bag that held two syringes. “Damn, Road Dog….you serious about gettin’ high, ain’t you?…you ain’t worried about gettin’ busted carryin’ that shit around?” J.T. Silk asked. “Worried for what?…it ain’t dope…what they gonna’ charge me with?…I always tell the po’lice that I’m diabetic…ain’t shit they can do….what they gonna’ charge me with?…dig what I’m sayin’?” Melvin responded with reckless disregard as he continued smiling. “Okay, Road Dog…long as you carryin’ it, I don’t give a damn…let’s go” Silk said. “We can head to the cooka’ now, baby…let’s ride, y’all!” Melvin said, grinning broadly. ”You live in the Arms, right, Jack?” Melvin asked Jack as he spoke with a tone of relief and gleeful anticipation. “Yea…y’all ready?” Jack asked “I’m gonna stop at Saxony and get that taste on the way…cool?" Jack added. "Yea…go ahead…cool" Silk and Melvin both chimed in. Jack stopped in Saxony Liquors and bought what they always drank when they would get high on dope….Richard's Wild Irish Rose---the street standard. It was the drink that most everyone drank because it was cheap and got you high quickly.

The men walked purposefully at the same accelerated pace as they headed toward Jack's place at the Arms. "Hey, Jack, you stayin' by yourself up in the "Arms?" J.T. Silk asked Jack as they hurried west on Lawrence Avenue, going one block before reaching Malden to make a left turn to go south. "Sho' 'nough, li'l brotha', I cain't play it no other way…I don't need nobody else up in there with me….I need my privacy, man….besides…I had enough o' carryin' that stick all summer long…couldn't hardly lay my head down…couldn't shower…I can do all that now and I intend for it to stay that way…I struggled too hard to get this little spot" Jack said with conviction as the three men approached the front entrance of the Arms. "Melvin…I know this is a silly question…but, did you bring a cooker with you?" J.T. asked somewhat amused already with the sly smile spreading over his face as he anticipated Melvin's reply. "You know I did…cain't get high right without one…got some cotton, too!" Melvin said spiritedly. J.T. could no longer hold himself as he burst out laughing. "Melvin…you crack me up…ain't got *no* money, but, you're carryin' around all that gear to get high!…hahahaha..you just *know* you are gonna get high somehow, someway…hahahaha.." He was always amused at Melvin's dope-fiend behavior and how far he would go to get high. Melvin just smiled and said "Hey…I like to get high…what can I say…" and shrugged J.T.'s remarks off because he didn't care and he knew that it really didn't make any difference to J.T. how he behaved as long as Melvin was useful enough to help him get high. Melvin couldn't see any difference between himself and anyone else who did what he did regardless of how seldom they did it. Even though he got high himself on occasion, just like Melvin, J.T. seemed to have a sense that being a chipper was better than being the full-blown fiend that Melvin was. J.T. had always maintained a sense of pride and while he chided Melvin good-naturedly, he was reminding himself at the same time that he did not want to go to those depths of losing his self-respect.

The three men walked through the front entrance door and passed through the dimly lit drabness of the lobby; passing the desk clerk area to enter the stairwell just behind it. They bounced up the three flights of stairs and were inside Jack's place. J.T. and Melvin made little scuffling noises as they arranged seats with one old table chair and the one beat-up sofa chair around Jack's dresser where Melvin began to lay out all of the get-high gear. Jack just sat back on the edge of his bed and watched as J.T. and Melvin huddled over the dresser with Melvin doing all of the preparing. Jack opened the drink that he bought from Saxony Liquors and began to sip. He was quiet and just leaned back on his elbows watching them. They were making small talk and had exchanged a few short comments when Melvin finally said

"Here we go…we'll find out what's to this shit, now" as he lit some matches underneath the aluminum bottle top with the paper piece taken out that was used as a cooker. He chipped off a piece of the dark brown, nugget-sized rock and placed it inside the cooker with a small amount of water in it; holding the edge of the cooker with his thumb and forefinger; carefully moving it ever-so-slightly back-and-forth to evenly heat it. Almost a minute had passed since Melvin began the heating when he said "What is that smell, Jack?...somethin' smells funny around here…" He made a couple of sniffing noises, sucking air into his nostrils to get a sense of what he was smelling while looking back at Jack with a curious expression on his face. "Damn….I smell it, too….what the fuck is that?" J.T. added looking puzzled himself as he rolled his eyes back-and-forth to gauge the smell. "Man…what the fuck is this!" Melvin said as he sat the cooker down on the dresser and jumped back a step. "Man…wha…damn..aw shit!! man…that's this rock, man…this ain't no dope…man…this is some shit!...sho-nough shit!" "Aw, hell naw!"…J.T. said with disgust as he leaned over slightly to the cooker that Melvin had laid down on the dresser. "Sho-in-the-fuck is!" he said. "Fuck this, Melvin…I want my money back!" "What kinda' bullshit you tryin' to pull, man?…huh?" J.T. said as his facial expression turned angry and he glared at Melvin with a piercing stare. "Hey., J.T…I swear, man…I didn't know they was gonna' give me somethin' bogus, man…man, this shit ain't never happened to me before since I been goin' to that spot…I swear, Silk..I didn't know, man...straight up!" Melvin pleaded. "Naw, Melvin…I know you wanna' get high pretty bad... but, you're playin' on the wrong people, my man.....that's why don't nobody wanna' fuck with you, see...see what I mean?" J.T. raged on. J.T. began to gather himself and step toward the apartment door, taking a couple of steps toward it as he chastised Melvin with short, disgusted comments. He paused between each couple of steps. "I'm sorry, Silk...I'll go back and try to get your money back...I'll go back right now!" Melvin pleaded on. "Melvin! "You know mothefuckers who are bold enough to pull some shit like this ain't gonna give you no money back!...that's the dope game when you're sellin!" "they're probably out of dope and just gave you that bullshittin-ass line about all-of-a-sudden havin' some rocks instead of powder and they took advantage..they played you..ya' dig!"...I know the game and I know what they call themselves doin'....remember, I've been in the dope game myself...it's played real dirty sometimes" J.T. continued. "J.T....you can believe what you want...but, I didn't know" Melvin said flatly. "Yea...I believe you, Melvin...I believe you...but, you still owe me, man...some money and a high...you owe me half the money and a good high..okay?...because you tore your drawers with me ...you understand?" J.T. said as he tried to let his anger subside, realizing that Melvin would go to quite some lengths to get high but, what had happened was extreme, even for him; that he had simply been "played" The two men continued to debate as they moved toward the door and opened it to leave, pausing in the doorway as they continued to argue.

Jack quietly watched them while lying back on his elbows on his bed with the pint bottle of Wild Irish Rose wine sitting on the floor near his feet. Finally, when he saw them step out into the hallway and stop, still arguing, he rose up from the bed and walked to the doorway quickly. "Hey, y'all...will somebody please take this shit outa' here?" he said. The two men paused after Jack had spoken. They looked at him, allowed what he said to register for a moment then, went back to arguing. They turned their backs to Jack and walked toward the stairwell, continuing their heated exchange. This was the kind of madness that fiends often endured. Whenever they ventured out to get high, there were risks of every kind. Quite often, the money to get high came about through "hard hustling" sometimes involving elaborate, risky schemes that could end up in jail and, at times, did. There was the chance that the dope they bought was stretched too far with by-products that rendered it impotent; leaving them with something almost worthless for their money. There was the rare chance, too of getting robbed by "stick-up artists" hanging around a dope spot because they knew people buying dope could not go to the police. Getting stopped and searched by the police was the usual risk that fiends ran but, worried about the least. With all these risks, it did not make sense to live this way. But, Street Gypsies were neither sane nor sensible. They were oblivious to any reasoning that said you can't do this or that. Their entire mind-set was based on defiance and unconventional means.

It was Monday morning and Jack had awakened to a partly cloudy day peeping at him from the light coming through his window with the torn window shades. He arose slowly from bed and could feel that usual dry feeling from the alcohol that he had consumed the night before. His mood was somber and this was usual, as well. He sat around for more than half an hour in bed, awake and just letting his mind wander. He always found the deadness of sober reality somewhat frightening and he was a little confused by the emptiness that he felt inside. He knew that the feeling would remain until he had once again put some alcohol, or something to change his mood, into his body. He looked over at the clock on his dresser. 9:27am, it read.

His thoughts slowly began to move forward and he thought about the day ahead of him. He felt that he would not go out drinking right away. He would shower and dress to go over to the employment office on Hazel and Montrose to at least try to get a job. He already knew that the chance of something encouraging happening was slight. He had been there every week at least once for over a year. Nothing had happened as far as a job. He just went through the usual routine. He would see a job counselor who would pull his file; sit him over at the microfiche machine and let him look for a job that way. Jack rarely saw anything that was open and if he did, he did not have car fare most of the time if the job was much of a distance from Uptown. Still, he persisted week-in and week-out; month-in and month-out until it had been almost a year-and-a-half since he began this routine. He held out hope that getting a job would put his life back on track. But, the economy had been bleak for the last several years and so was his future. He had really messed up a little over two years ago when he lost that good job with the tire company. It was the same baffling experience that he had a couple of times before that; making fairly decent money; buying nice clothes; getting situated in a nice little apartment and----bam! ----somehow, the foundation would fall out from under him because life had gotten too good. He could not stand success. He was baffled at his own behavior and why he always fell into this habit of self-defeat. He had tried-and-tried to piece this puzzling behavior of his together. But, he could never resolve it; never appreciate what he had enough to maintain it; perhaps, he hated himself. Was it that he didn't think he deserved a good life? Or was it the notion that living a good life and working hard to keep it was beyond his grasp? beyond his understanding? And each time he had gone through the cycle of achieving visible progress, he would sabotage himself at the worst possible times. He had studied this and ran this through his mind, it seemed, a thousand times, and he always came back to square one---he did not know---did not comprehend this perplexing dilemma.

He steadied himself in his mind to gather the will to rise out of this lethargic state of mind and body to shower and dress to head for the employment office. It was difficult to be dead sober and function for Jack without drinking. But, he could do it if he just didn't think about it. He would have a slight feeling of discomfort the whole time while he went about this simple task. But, he had vowed to himself that keeping this simple regimen of marching over to the State employment office once-a-week meant that he had not given his life up to this depraved existence. Sluggishly, he finally rose up from where he was sitting up in bed and walked over to the bathroom and walked up to the mirror. He looked at himself in the mirror, and saw the somber expression staring back at him. He slowly began the motions of preparing to shower and he went through the process mechanically until he found himself dressed and standing in the middle of his apartment without really remembering what he had done in the last moments. He was feeling a little spacey but, not really hungover. He started out of the front door and walked down the street north on Malden then, east on Lawrence until he had arrived at the building where the employment office was. He never could get there early; especially on Mondays----it was impossible. So, he never tried. The job situation had been so bad in recent years until the lines were long when the doors of the employment office opened at 8:30am Monday through Friday. But, the crowd had usually dissipated by the time Jack arrived and that was just the way he wanted it. He did not like just standing around in line feeling that slight jittery feeling that he always had after those wild weekends of drinking; at least not for long periods of time. He stood there quietly at the end of the line as he usually did and waited as the line inched forward; painfully slow as far as Jack was concerned. He began to feel that mild, edgy feeling that seemed to arise whenever he was standing still and quiet. It seemed worse when he was not doing anything; had no distractions to keep him from being aware of the annoying feeling. He knew that it was from the drinking and how poorly he treated himself; not eating properly. Oftentimes, having an alcohol breakfast and not eating until the hunger had become so pronounced until he was motivated to get something to eat. Jack smoked but, he did not smoke much until he began to drink. So, he could do without it for the time that he was not drinking.

As Jack stood in the line he looked to his left to see a board filled with flyers about out-dated day labor work, social programs and other announcements. He noticed one that was about enrolling in college "*Northeastern Illinois University: enroll now, attend the Community Center at 4414 N. Sheridan Road*". Jack looked at it and it prompted him to think of Tina and how she was making something of her life by going for her college degree. He looked at the poster again and continued to read on. "*financial aid available*" it read. The idea of attending began to emerge in his mind and he began to ponder the possibilities. He was standing in the same line that he had stood in so many times before; trying to get a job and nothing had happened in over a year. He thought back again to Tina and how much more mainstream and wholesome her life seemed compared to his own. He thought about how he lived his life by wit and whim in the streets of Uptown with no direction or future. He looked at the poster again and there was a phone number he memorized.

He stayed in line until his turn came and the job counselor called his name-- "Rollins!" He moved forward and began speaking to the job counselor as he went through the same routine that he knew so well until it had become second nature to him. He sat at the michrofiche machine with several of the films that the counselor had given him and he searched-and-searched. He wrote down some information about a job that he might call later on. The job position was really not something he was suited for and it was in a far away suburban town. But, these were the usual choices of scarce job listings that he found at the State office. He also wrote down the phone number that he had memorized for the college enrollment. He was leaving the employment office and was walking down the street while he thought more and more about the possibilty of his enrolling in college. It came to him that with no jobs to be had, this was his best option. It made all the sense in the world under his circumstances. He did not have a future, it seemed, and he needed to change the way he was living; have some structure in his life; some direction and purpose before this crazy street life had consumed him to the point of no return. He felt that every day that he lived this way, he was being conditioned more into it---becoming more used to it---accepting it more as part of himself and his existence---giving in to it little-by-little.

Jack began to feel a little hungry and he remembered to look into his pocket and count his money. As he strolled along Sheridan Road, headed back to Lawrence and Winthrop, he reached into his pocket and pulled out some bills and change----he counted-----twelve dollars and sixty-three cents. He began to think of how he would eat today and still have money for drinks. But, before he did any of that, he would call the college enrollment phone number and the job number that he had written down. He knew that he needed to do this now, before he had anything to drink because after he had begun to drink, it would not get done. He arrived at the corner of Winthrop and Leland and he decided right then that he needed to go into Jupiter; sort of a five-and-dime store at the corner of Broadway and Leland that sold all kinds of useful items cheap and buy an ink pen before he called these numbers. Because he knew he would likely need to write some information down during the calls. He went in to buy the ink pen and, as he did, he noticed the scarcity of employees in the store. Jack paid for the ink pen and headed for the outside pay phone at the E-Z-GO gas station at the corner of Lawrence and Winthrop. He used the phone to first, call the job number. He asked for the contact person who was the manager and said that he was interested in the job. He was told that the manager was not there at the moment and that the job was possibly filled at the end of last week. This was the same variety of responses that he got when contacting these jobs. The State employment office information always lagged behind the true status of these jobs. In his mind, Jack shrugged it off----"what else is new" he thought. He proceeded to call the college enrollment phone number and was met by the pleasant voice of a woman recruiter. She spoke well and cordially to Jack as she responded enthusiastically to his inquiry about enrollment. She asked him a series of questions about his education----"finished high school, and where?" she asked. "Yes…Waller High school" he responded. She went on to ask where he lived and if he was working. Jack answered those few questions and she encouraged him to come into the Uptown Center at 4414 N. Sheridan to speak to a recruiting counselor and fill out some papers. She said that if he filled out the papers soon, that he could very well start in the winter-spring trimester in January. Jack did not have to write anything down but, he began to feel encouraged and have a sense of hope.

He immediately thought about Tina and decided to call her right then while he was still at the phone to share the exciting news. He called the phone number and got her answering machine. "This is Tina, at the tone, please leave a message" it said. He left her a message that rambled on excitedly about his idea of enrolling in college and ended it with "I'm thinking about you---give me a call---later!" As Jack turned away from the phone, he was thinking that he really wanted to hear Tina's sweet, clear, calm voice. He not only wanted to tell her about his new prospect of enrolling in college, he just wanted to talk to her because he missed her. She had a steadying effect on him that seemed to relax him and give him this strange inner peace whenever he was communicating with her. With all of his business for the day done, his thoughts turned to what he would do next.

He looked up and down the streets. It was shortly after 11am and he did not see any of the usual crowd that he knew in the vicinity. He only saw Melvin on rare occasions, maybe once-a-week, or once every-other-week; usually in the evenings during the weekdays after his wife had arrived home from work and after he had dinner with his family. Melvin was a married man and because he was, he could not live in the streets and be the free spirit that Jack was. Jack did not see Coley or Jabo or Larry or even Cozell, the biggest drunk around the neighborhood who would usually be out by this time trying to scrounge up a drink. The streets had the usual Monday morning hustle-and-bustle traffic. There was nothing going on. Jack decided to go to the Delmar restaurant and get some breakfast to take care of his hunger before he began to drink. In his mind, he always conceded that drinking was a foregone conclusion. He did not have to ponder upon it to decide whether he would or not. He never thought about having to decide---he had no choice. Besides, what else was he to do at these moments living this Street Gypsy life. He went into the Delmar and had sausage and eggs. He took time to enjoy it. He paid $2.88 for the breakfast and left a fifty-cent tip. This was a big deal for Jack because he rarely sat down and had a decent breakfast. Normally, he would start drinking around noon-time and would not eat anything until much later.

He had this notion of taking better care of himself. Tina was foremost in his mind when he thought this way. He had begun to think of dressing better, as well. He hoped to continue seeing Tina. He had not thought much beyond that. He was keeping his hopes simple and not so ambitious. He was not a fool. He had experiences with women in the past where he had learned some valuable lessons; that a man would serve himself well to not put too much stock in a relationship with a woman; especially if she was desirable. He knew one thing about women----each of them knew just exactly how much attraction they had to a man. Because men would let them know in various ways just how attracted they were to them. If a woman was attractive, she played it for all it was worth. They seemed to not be attracted to men they knew they could get. They seemed more attracted to men that were a "challenge" that were a little out of their league--- a little out of reach. Jack had not been really hurt by a woman before. But, he had been disappointed by a woman on a couple of occasions in his life and he learned from the experiences and had become wiser; not making any commitments of the heart. Playing it "close to the chest" as it were by the Street Gypsy code. So, he knew just what kind of woman Tina was from the start. He understood his attraction to her in terms of the options that were available to him. He knew that other women played these seductive parlor games, always trying to get the upper hand with a man. If he was a fool, they would play him for all he was worth. These were the kinds of women that he had become accustomed to. His attraction to Tina was not just physical. But, was just as much about what kind of woman she was, as well. Her unassuming attitude was especially attractive because he knew she was not a “game player” as were most of the more appealing women that he knew around the area. He knew she was something rare----that he would not see in his environment ever at all. So, when he first laid eyes on her at Frances’ Tavern and had come to find that she was openly engaging----he understood the rarity of the opportunity. He also decided that at that time, his buddy, Mike Carlton was more than drunk. He was stupid to pass her up because she was white. Jack felt that he did not have time for the parlor game nonsense that so many of his brethren engaged in. He felt that a connection with a woman should be, ideally, a less contentious affair.

Jack was standing in front of the Delmar Restaurant where he had just walked out and peered east straight down Lawrence a short distance to see his buddy, Willie-the-Weep sitting on the concrete ledge where many of the drinkers always sat. It perked him up to see his friend and he began to walk toward him. “Hey Weep….what’s happ’nin’? Jack greeted. “Hey….my man, Jack…what’s to ya’ bro?” Weep responded with a broad smile. “What you up to Weep?” Jack asked. “Man, I’m short….help me out, Jack….you holdin’ anything?” The Weep asked in his southern twang. “What ya’ need?” Jack asked. “’Bout fifty cents for a pint and a dollar for a brick if you wanna’ go in” The Weep responded. “You need to get the shakes off, huh, Weep?” Jack asked, already knowing the answer. “Here ya’ go, brotha’, go ‘head and get the taste” Jack said after he reached in his pocket and handed him a dollar bill. “I’ll be right back” The Weep said as he nervously rose from the concrete ledge where he sat and began to stride anxiously in the direction that Jack had just come from toward Saxony Liquors. Jack sat patiently on the concrete ledge until The Weep returned. The Weep brought back a “brick” of Richards Wild Irish Rose wine. Jack and The Weep knew that they could not drink openly on the street during this time of day. So, they went into the alley next to the currency exchange a short distance east down the street and across to the other side of Lawrence Avenue. They found a spot at the back of the courtway building just off the alley across from the L tracks. They began to drink and make small talk. This was the way Jack passed his time;

drinking from bottles in the streets at different times with different people who were his friends all around the small area surrounding Lawrence and Winthrop. He and The Weep stood in the same spot joking, laughing and drinking for almost an hour when Jack began to feel high. His mind seemed to expand and become excitable. His inhibitions began to fall away from him and his speech became a little louder----he was feeling good. He was becoming restless, as well. He felt an urge for excitement and suddenly, it occurred to him to look into his pocket and count his money----seven dollars and sixty-seven cents. He was just about broke and the urge to hustle had come over him. He suddenly remembered the Jupiter store that he was in where he bought the ink pen earlier.

"Hey, Weep….check it out, man….I need to go and make some money, brotha'….I'll be back a little later" Jack announced. The Weep knew Jack well and he had a vague idea of what his intentions might be. The Weep was a much older man than Jack and he did not engage in the bold activities that Jack did. There was an understanding between them that went unsaid. After his announcement, Jack took off down the alley, going south which was a straight shot to the Jupiter store.

Jack arrived in front of the store and slowed down his pace; entering the store like a normal customer and going into the aisles. He walked around for a while, counting how many people were working inside and just as he had noted earlier, there were few people. It seemed they were short-handed compared to other times he had been inside the store. He went back to the ladies' lingerie section and looked around before he grabbed a couple bunches of ladies lingerie items and stuffed the thin, fine material down into his long socks and some down inside the side of his pants. He had on the thin leisure suit jacket and it covered up the slight bulge that could, otherwise be seen on the side of his pants. He grabbed a notebook to take to the counter and paid the thirty-five cents for it as he stood in line with other customers at the check-out line. He strolled out of the store with his purchase and his stolen merchandise.

He acted natural and walked around the corner to the right and turned left to go north up Winthrop. As soon as he turned the corner, he was met by a group of the regulars who lived in the block. Ella Mae, Anita, Dave, Cozell and Miss Jackson. They were all gathered together, talking as they stood and sat around the steps of the Winthrop-side entrance to the big apartment building that stood on the northwest corner of Leland and Winthrop. They were debating about something, as usual. They saw Jack and continued to carry on their conversation. After a couple of minutes passed, Jack walked back away from them a few yards and pulled out the wads of lingerie items from the side of his pants and his socks. He took the notebook item from the paper bag it was in and placed the big bunches of lingerie into the bag. He walked back the few yards and casually asked "Any o' you ladies wanna' buy some lingerie?" The women paused and fell quiet momentarily. "Lingerie?" Ella Mae asked. "Yea…check it out" Jack replied and he pulled out a handful of the garments to show them. When the women saw the lingerie was brand new with price tags still attached, all of them walked up closer to Jack and began to rummage through the handful of garments. "Oooh…this is *nice*, Jack…where you get this from?" Anita asked as she and Ella Mae looked through the garments. "Don't worry about where it come from…you don't wanna know, anyway" Jack said spiritedly. "OOooh, Jack…these *are* nice…" Ella Mae said. "These are just my size!" Anita announced. Jack pulled out more of the garments and the women began to compete over the items. "Jack, how much you want for these, these and this?" Ella Mae asked as she held several of the items out to Jack and began to pull money out of her jean pocket. Jack inspected the items she had in her hands. He added up the price tags. "Let's see…all of this would be thirty-eight dollars without tax…give me fifteen dollars….you gettin' a big discount today, baby…come on with it!' Jack said as he held his hands out for the money. Ella Mae gave him the fifteen dollars and quickly went back inside the apartment building entrance to put away her bargains. "I'll be right back" she said to the group. The other women haggled over the remaining bundles of lingerie and bought all of it from Jack and Jack had forty-five more dollars after it was done. As soon as Jack was paid the last money from the other women, he said "Hey y'all….I got some more stashed away….I'm goin' to get it right now!" he announced as he stepped away from them going back around the corner he had come from.

But, Jack did not have any more merchandise. He knew that everyone who was gathered around the steps just then had seen him make the money from the lingerie sale, and some of them were broke; and even if they were not broke, they knew he had money and they would begin to plot up on getting him to buy drinks for them or to borrow a few dollars. But, Jack had thought way ahead of them as he usually did. He was always one or two steps ahead of the game. He knew they were vultures who were broke more often than he was because they did not hustle in the ways that he did. They did not take the chances that he did; were not as wild, care-free and reckless as he was; and, so, it seemed to him, they were content to be broke; scrounging what they could here and there just as he had to do himself on occasion. The only difference was, that Jack did not like being broke and was restless whenever he did not have any money. He turned the corner and hurried out of site as he kept going across Broadway and onward several blocks further to another part of the area as he headed toward Wilson avenue; stepping lively in case any of the group that he had just left decided to follow behind him and tag along because he had money. This was how the game of survival was played in Uptown amongst Street Gypsies and the people they lived around. Money was always in short supply, and when a Street Gypsy had any, he lived it up, and at the same time, tried to stretch the windfall as far as possible. You did not let on how much money you had and if anyone drew a bead on you because they suspected that you had money to throw around; they played up to you in a friendly way to persuade you to share with them; mind games ensued and you fended them off by your wit or you just got away from them by making up some kind of lie; or you just slipped away without saying a word.

Jack arrived on the corner of Clifton and Montrose. There were just a few people around. He saw Annie, a woman who used to live on Winthrop where he just left. But, had moved to Clifton Street about six months ago. She was sitting on her back porch that faced Montrose Avenue where there was about thirty yards of empty lot space between her porch and the street. He spotted a couple of reefer dealers about a half block up the street on the opposite side. They were standing around and talking in front of the courtway building where they lived. He decided that he would go and visit with Annie and chat and flirt with her like he always did. Jack did not know why he liked to flirt with her because he was not attracted to her. She had a nice figure but, she was not especially good-looking by his standards and she spoke with a choppy kind of speech as though she may have had some kind of third-world accent. She had once mentioned having some Haitian or Jamaican ancestry. Jack liked her because she had this spirited enthusiasm and energy that seemed to lift him whenever he spoke with her. There was also something about how they interacted that made him feel free to flirt. He knew that when he flirted with her, it was all for fun and he enjoyed her reaction to his playful advances. He knew that although she verbally fended him off, she enjoyed his flirtatious ways. He walked over to stand in front of the porch to the left of her line-of-site. She was sitting in a chair just gazing out kind of absent-mindedly when she suddenly noticed Jack after he had spoken.

"Hey, Annie…what you doin', girl?" Jack greeted. "Hey, man…" Annie said with the same big, warm smile she always had whenever she ran into Jack. "What you doin'?….come on up" she offered. Jack walked up the short flights of stairs, smiling all the while. They greeted each other with broad smiles and a big hug and made small talk for a few moments before Annie asked "You got any money, Jack?…buy me a drink, okay?" "No problem…what you want, girl?" Jack responded calmly "No kiddin'?….you gonna' buy me a drink?…for real?" Annie asked again. "I said I would…what you want, now…I ain't gonna keep on askin' you" Jack insisted. "Alright…alright..I want some Seagrams gin…can you drink that with me, huh, Jack?" Annie asked politely. "Baby…I can drink whatever-the-hell you drink" Jack responded with a smile. "Okay…okay…'cause I could use a drink" Annie said with sincerity. "I'll be right back" Jack said. He walked back in the direction he had come from to Montrose Avenue and turned the corner going the one block east to the Tipaway bar. He was gone about ten minutes before he re-appeared and joined Annie on the porch.

They began to drink and talk when another woman came onto the porch from an apartment at the far end. She was slender and dark-brown complexioned and dressed casually as though she had been lounging at her apartment. She was, perhaps, ten years or so older than Jack and Annie. She walked over to join them. She began speaking with Annie and they talked like well-acquainted neighbors. Annie offered her one of the several paper cups that she brought out to the porch from her kitchen. "Aw, baby…I got somethin' to drink at my house that y'all might like…I'll go and get it" the woman said as she walked back down the long porch to her apartment. Jack had seen this woman around the neighborhood as he had so many other people. But, he was not acquainted with her at all. The impression that he got of her was that she was a person who liked to drink and who drank often, very much like himself. She returned after a few short minutes. "We gettin' ready to party, now, y'all…see what I got" she said, smiling broadly as she held up a quart of Jim Beam in a fancy glass decanter with a handle for Annie and Jack to see. Jack looked at the large container that was a few drinks short of being full. "You don't mess around, do you, miss lady?" Jack said. "Child, call me Virginia….that's my name….you know me…I've seen you around" she said matter-of-factly. "Yea…I've seen you comin' and goin' but, I never did meet you…my name is Jack" Jack responded as he extended his hand and he and Virginia shook hands "Okay, then, baby, help ya' self…pour your own poison, now…alright?" she said very cordially. "You don't have to ask me twice…I don't turn down nothin' but my collar, sho-nough!" Jack said as he seemed to open up to Virginia; grabbing a cup from the short stack of Annie's paper cups and reaching for the large whiskey container almost at the same time. He poured his drink. "Hey, y'all….I got to get somethin' else to liven thangs up…I'll be back" With that, Virginia hustled back down to her apartment and disappeared. Jack and Annie made small talk while Virginia was gone. "She wild about men…every man I know that look like anything, she come runnin' down here and start hangin' around" Annie said with an inflection of mild annoyance. "Well….she probably is a little lonely….she got a man?" Jack inquired. "she got some ol' bald head fool that come to visit her once in a while…but, I don't think he is her man….he look like he about ninety…he like her….but, she don't take him serious 'cause he cain't do what she want….he cain't do nothin' but talk…he always talkin' sexy to her but, cain't back it up" Annie explained. "Hmmm…" Jack responded kind of detached. "She don't look bad at all…I can tell she drinks a lot…she probably would look a lot better if she cut down on that drinkin' and fix herself up a little bit" Jack said. "She seem like she is a pretty cool ol' chick…she's friendly…sharin' her drinks and thangs" Jack added. "Oh, she is alright with me…I like her…I like her" Annie repeated to assure she was not bad-mouthing her neighbor. “She have been very nice to me…but, she gets on my nerves when she gets drunk…she always lookin’ for her some “mister big stuff” Annie said, letting out a light chuckle after she made the statement. “Hey ya’ll…looka’ here…y’all like the blues?….I got my music box right here” Virginia burst out almost startling Jack and Annie as she was already half-way down the porch on her way toward them. “Aw….hey…look out, now…party-time!” Jack said to show that he was in the spirit of things while he turned to Virginia and smiled. Virginia sat the radio down on a nearby wooden table next to the paper cups and plugged the long cord into a socket that was almost at the base of the brick wall outside of Annie’s apartment. “My baby don’t have to work…don’t have to rob and steal….”” the blues lyrics blared out after the music box was turned on. “Aw, shit, now!…that’s the sho-nough’ blues right there, y’all!” Virginia said excitedly. “I am a drivin’ wheel…”” Virginia sang along with the next verse while holding both of her arms straight up in the air above her head and snapping her fingers and closing her eyes with a soulful, immersed expression on her face. She did an easy, slow grind of her hips and turned her head from side-to-side as she stood in-between Jack and Annie seated in chairs on either side of her. “Honey, hush!” she said emphatically. “That’s what I need y’all..a man who-a’ pay my bills….give me what I need every night!” Virginia went on. “Yea…keep on wishin’, girl, keep on wishin’” Annie said with a note of cynical sarcasm. “Hey, woman…now why you soundin’ so negative about her findin’ a man, huh?” Jack asked with a tone of playful, mild admonishment. “’Cause ain’t no good men out here!” Annie shot back in her choppy sounding speech, seemingly cutting each word just short of it’s full pronunciation as she did whenever she expressed herself in an emotional, passionate way. “Now, see there, Annie…I been after you for over two years with your fine self and you won’t even give me a play” Jack said, playfully masking his insincerity “Aw, be quiet, Jack…you know you don’t mean what you say when you talk that mess to me” Annie challenged Jack. “Naw, sugar…you got me all wrong” Jack said, going into that strange mood that just seemed to come over him whenever he was speaking to Annie. He knew he was not sincere and was just having fun. But Annie seemed to respond in a way that seemed to spur him on with his little charade. “Baby… I been wantin' you for a long time" Jack said, going into his little act of speaking softly in his version of a sexy voice. "…and believe me…I want you bad!" Jack went on as he leaned his face forward and close to her's as though he wanted to kiss her. "Go 'head on, now, Jack…you know you like jivin' me…stop it, now!" Annie said gently placing her hand on Jack's chin and pushing his face back as she tried to look as serious as she could, suppressing the giggle that was trying to force it's way out. "Annie….I'm sorry, baby…I'm sorry…I just cain't help myself…you lookin' so good…I just wanna lick you everywhere" Jack went on in the same low voice as he continued his act. "Yea..right!" Annie said, rolling her eyes at Jack and pursing her lips with a playful, smirky defiance.

"What you say, man?…I heard that!" Virginia said, overhearing Jack's phony come-on and taking it to be real. Ummhumm!" I heard you say somethin' 'bout lickin' somethin'….what you gonna lick?" Virginia asked with curiosity, wedging herself into the exchange after the salacious comment. "Virginia…I been after this woman for two *long* years and she just don't wanna give a guy a play…what you think about that?" Jack said, plying his game of fun for all he could. "Baby…you like my friend, geetchy girl, huh?…you musta' done tapped her stuff before" Virginia said boldy, doing a little plying of her own of the sensual kind. "Naw…but, I sho-nough' would like to get next to this sweet thang" Jack said as he reached around Annie's waist and gently hugged her up to himself as she sat in the chair close to him. "Ja'aaack!...come on, now!" Annie said, playing her usual role of fending Jack off as she gently pushed him away again, with her left forearm. "Let's slip off into your place, Annie…come on, baby!" he half-whispered. Jack always pestered Annie in this way and despite the seemingly contentious interaction, they really liked and respected each other. But, Jack could never break her to the point of giving in to his fake advances. "I'll be right back" Annie said as she got up from her chair on the porch and opened the back door of her apartment and walked in. "She was gettin' hot, I can tell!" Virginia said. "You think so, Virginia?" Jack asked. "Oooh, yea, child!"…she want it, but, she scared for some reason…"Ooo....honey…look-a-here…your dick is hard!" and with that, she reached over and gave Jack's member, that was fully pronounced, a couple of firm squeezes. Jack was completely surprised, but, he just sat there and accepted Virginia's bold forwardness with cool indifference. He was also surprised that his pride-and-joy had announced itself to the extent that it was noticeable. He realized that he was so deep into his act of phony seduction with Annie until he had aroused himself. When the realization dawned on him, he laughed to himself with a low snicker at first with his shoulders jiggling with the laughter; then, he just burst out laughing… Hahahaha…hehehe…Aaaaww…shit!" Jack could tell that the Jim Beam that he had been drinking was taking effect. He was in a goofy, giddy, silly mood where he could easily laugh at himself.

You want somethin' to eat, Jack?…I got some collared greens, sweet potatoes and short ribs…you welcome to come on over and have some" Virginia offered. "Virginia …that's real nice of you but, I'm just not hungry right now…thanks, anyway" Jack responded. Jack was well aware of what Virginia was doing; trying to get him away from Annie and perhaps, arranging a subtle, easy seduction in the privacy of her apartment. Although Jack liked the idea of sex with a strange woman, he was not really attracted to Virginia. Even though there had been occasions when he had spontaneous encounters with women in the past and he was not averse to such endeavors, he did have a certain standard that he adhered to; and somehow, he was not moved by Virginia. He did think that she had a good heart.

He was thinking, too about Tina and how he was looking forward to seeing her again. At this moment, thinking of her seemed so surreal. He had not been thinking this way before meeting her. There had not been a reason to be thinking such tender thoughts of caring and longing for another person in Jack's life before now. He felt curiously odd in feeling this way at this time. He was not used to these thoughts.

"Hey, y'all…" Annie said as she walked through the back door of her apartment to return to the porch to join Jack and Virginia. As she returned, Jack snapped out of his daydream. The three continued their spirited talking and laughter as the blues playing on Virginia's music box added a festive atmosphere to their gathering on the porch. Finally, Jack had gotten fairly high and he had become restless. The surge of energy he was feeling gave him that usual anxious, excited state of mind that he seemed to get whenever he got this high. He felt bold, fearless, reckless---

-he wanted to move, walk; go here, there---roam around---he was in a wild and crazy mood.

"Hey, y'all…I got to go take care o' some business….dig?" Jack lied with a slight slurring. "Jack…Jack…sit down and keep us company…where you runnin' off to?….what business you got?….for real…what business?…huh?" Annie asked in the more choppy speech she would have after getting high. "Hey, baby…I enjoy y'all company but, I gots to handle my business..I cain't hang out with y'all all night…understand?" Jack said urged on by the anxiousness he was feeling. "Come here, Jack…I understand a man got to take care of his business, baby…come here and give Virginia a hug before you go…okay?" Virginia said dragging her speech and seeming affected as well by the drinking they had all done while they laughed and talked for the last couple of hours. Jack opened his arms wide to hug Virginia and as he hugged her, he could feel her hips grinding into his body. He laughed and said "okay, Virginia …alright.,.alright, now…you cool, baby…you cool" He got her message. But, he was not enticed.

The powerful urge for immediate excitement in the streets had become almost like an elixir in itself for Jack. He had become increasingly conditioned to this madness----the wild and reckless activity of roaming aimlessly about the streets. "Jack…when you gonna stop by again and see me?" Annie asked, speaking more seriously than she had earlier. She spoke in a way that said the tongue-in-cheek, playful exchange that they usually engaged in was off for now and she was speaking as the real friends they were. Jack was always touched by how Annie had come to be connected with him in this sincere way and how she had become one of a number of his friends and acquaintances around the streets of Uptown. This was important to him and it seemed that so many of the people that he gravitated to were people of his type; unattached; seemingly without family ties and living on their own. He valued these friendships because many-a-day, they were all he had. At times, when he could not raise a dollar, he could raise his spirit with these unconditional friendships. "Hey, baby…I'll see you around…whenever I get over this way, I'm gon' check you out….okay, sweetie…now, give me a hug so I can go" Jack said as he opened his arms again and gave Annie a firm, sincere hug. With that, he was on his way.

He headed north along the winding concrete pathway that passed along the east side of the Truman College building. After he arrived at Wilson Avenue where the entrance of the college was, he peered up the street to the east then, turned his head to the west to see what the late afternoon streets had to offer in the way of excitement. There were students hanging out in front of the college building and a steady flow of others entering and exiting the several doorways. The odd feeling came over him that the high he was feeling did not match this Monday afternoon mood of people soberly going about normal activities and living their normal lives. He was aware of it but, feeling as good as he did right now, he was insulated from any notion of caring about what people were doing around him.

He looked further west down Wilson Avenue and he could see in the distance, among the people moving about up and down the street, a walking figure that he recognized; the gait was distinctly familiar. He could see Sandy walking with her two little boys, moving with that motion that he knew so well. He started walking with an energetic pace toward her. She was walking westward away from Jack and he knew she was heading home. He caught up to her and as he came to walk along-side her on the sidewalk, he said, "Nice day, huh, miss" "Yessir, it is a very, ni….Jack!" maann…where you been!…I thought you was gonna hang around last night so we could have a drink and party a little bit…why you have me lookin' everywhere for you and you done forgot all about me…what you doin?" Sandy said after she had begun speaking before looking. "Hahahaha…hahaha!" Jack laughed, feeling especially frisky and playful. "Got ya'…didn't I, girl!" Hahahaha…"" Jack laughed. "You headed to the crib, girl?" Jack asked more sedately. "I'm pissed-off at Dave…that fool won't give me no money for his son…he talkin' 'bout that money he gave me the other day was all I had comin' for two more weeks…I cain't be tryin' to take care o' these boys with no help from their daddy" she lamented. "Hey, girl….I got you covered…don't worry….I'll be right back!" Jack headed into the Wilson Avenue liquor store that they had just passed. When he returned, he gave her a paper bag with a bottle in it. "This for me?" She asked as she took hold of the wrapped bottle in one hand. "Yea…that's you right there…and this, too" he said as he grabbed her other hand and pressed a tightly folded couple of bills into her hand. She opened her palm and unfolded the bills. "Fifteen dollars!...Jack, you cain't be givin' your money away like this!" Sandy said with a protesting tone. "Naw...naw...you better take that money or else we gonna' fall out, girl" Jack said insistently. "I love you, Jack...you always been good to me...I appreciate it 'cause I *did* need a little somethin' to tide me over 'til my check comes in a few days" Sandy said as she opened her arms wide and Jack walked into them to accept the hug she was giving him. "I cain't let my little guys down, right, Li'l Dave?" Jack said as he swept the little four-year-old up from walking on the sidewalk into his arms. "Hey, fella....you been takin' care of your mama, ain't you?" Jack playfully questioned the little boy in a playfully stern tone. Little Dave was quiet, and held the usual shy, blank expression that kids often had when suddenly queried about something. "You been takin' care of yo' mama, right...right, boy?" Jack went on as he held the little boy high up in his arms with the boys face close to his. Finally, little Dave shook his head up-and-down and said "yep" long after he had stopped shaking his head. Jack played with the boys along the way as he walked Sandy the short distance to her apartment building south of Wilson on Malden Avenue. As Jack played with the boys, he was out of balance and made the kind of jerky motions that people made when they were high. "Okay, Sandy...be cool, girl....I'll holla' at you" Jack said after they had arrived in front of the apartment building where Sandy lived. "I'll see you, Jack" Sandy said as she smiled at Jack, looking a lot more happy than when Jack had first seen her a short while earlier. "Thanks again" she said and hugged Jack again before disappearing through the entrance door of her apartment building with her two little boys.

Jack stood in front of the building, suddenly alone and still having the anxious feeling raging inside of him that he had when he left Annie and Virginia on the porch. He still felt the urge for some kind of excitement. He walked north on Malden back in the direction he had come from. He could feel the high carrying him down the street. He was gliding effortlessly as he walked along, stepping lively with exaggerated motion; feeling rather good about himself. He felt no inhibitions what-so-ever. He loved this bold, fearless feeling that being high gave him. He felt so confident---he was whatever he though he was; cool as he wanted to be. It was magical how he suddenly had no worries. He turned the corner at Wilson and Malden and began to walk down the street with the same energetic stride.

Suddenly, he heard a voice call out to him "Jack!..Jack!" He looked up and down the street and did not see anyone among the people walking on the sidewalk. "Jack!" The voice called out again and louder. Finally, Jack gained his bearings and located the voice. It was his old buddy Cooper. Cooper used to live in the Leland Avenue building that housed the Leland Baptist Church. He and his mother-in-law used to live next door to one another about a year ago. They had a lucrative "T's and Blues" business. His mother-in-law, Lorraine had a connection where she got those pills in large quantities. The pills were popular amongst the neighborhood fiends as well as those from all around. The family made plenty of money from selling them. At that time, Cooper and his family, including his in-laws were living high and were revered and envied by the neighborhood regulars because of their status of having what everyone wanted. It all stopped about a year ago because Lorraine's son, Percy got busted selling the pills to cops from a nearby apartment in the building. Cooper was in a car that was pulled over to the curb.

Jack walked over to the car smiling and bent over and stuck his head inside the open passenger-side window. "My man, Coop…what's goin' on, player?….I see you ridin' slick, brotha'…when you get this?" Jack inquired as he smiled broadly and gazed around at the interior of the 1971 Grand Prix Pontiac. "Hey, Jack…what ya' doin', bro'?" Cooper asked "Aw…hey…nothin' right now…just hangin'" Jack replied. "Get in!" Cooper said.

Cooper's fortunes had steadily declined since Percy got busted because the pills business had dried up and the connection had been lost. Jack had not known Cooper to have a car or anything of much value since then because he had fallen prey to the very pills he once sold. He was using them all the time now. He had not used them at all when he sold them. He had worn nice clothes back then; drove a nice car, and just drank a little beer and sipped a little of his favorite gin. His family had many things they wanted and everything they needed. But, that had all changed. His existence had become increasingly more desperate. He and his wife had been separated for nine months and were on the brink of divorce. Now, his existence was just as unstable as any of the other hustlers in the streets. He had become one of them and was reduced to the same "hard hustling" that many of the other fiends had been doing all along.

In the past year, as Cooper's fortunes declined, he and Jack had become "get-high" buddies. They had hung out together from time-to-time, occasionally hatching a hustling scheme and executing it together. They had become confidants for one another. Jack listened to Cooper lamenting his broken marriage and Cooper listened to Jack's issues of survival. Cooper did not live in the area anymore. Jack only saw him from time-to-time. Cooper had confided in Jack about nine months ago, around the time he had separated from his wife. It had been difficult being in the neighborhood, occasionally seeing his wife and kids and sometimes seeing her walking around with some other man. That was the main reason Cooper had disappeared from the neighborhood; returning only occasionally to catch up to some of his old friends and visit some of his old haunts. Jack opened the passenger-side door of the car and hopped in the seat before Cooper sped off. "So, what's poppin' brotha', Coop?….how you get to ridin' so slick, bro'?" Jack inquired. "Aw…hey…this here ain't my ride…I was gettin' high where I stay in Evanston…right around Howard…I was takin' off with this dude from around the way…a few blocks from me…we was at his crib and he got all fucked up…*too* damn high…he said he had to lay down…said go 'head keep the car a couple days if I wanted to…handed me the keys…here I am" Copper explained. "Sho-nough?" Jack responded. "What was y'all takin' off on?" Jack asked. "Some sho-nough horse, man…strong shit…it had me noddin' tough for a while…I told the stud…hey…I got to get me some air…that's when he tossed me the car keys" Cooper explained.

"You feel like hustlin', Jack?" Cooper asked, then paused, looking at Jack intently, waiting for his reply. "Hell yea…I made a little bit of a hustle earlier today…but, you know how that goes…I done spent most of that already…funds gettin' low" Jack said. "Alright, then, bro'…let's cruise for a while and see what we can get into" Cooper said, sounding committed and focused on the idea. "You holdin' any paper, Jack?" Cooper asked. "I got a little somethin' to keep us goin' until we can make us a decent sting" Jack said, sounding just as committed. It was now four-thirty in the afternoon and Jack and Cooper drove over to the Lake at Montrose Street and just sat and talked while parked in the car. "Coop…you still ain't got things straight with your ol' lady, huh?" Jack asked. "Naw…don't look like no good gonna' come outa' this, man…seem like ever since we started makin' that money with them pills startin' about three years ago….seem like we started driftin' apart' "When we didn't have money…man, it seemed like everything was cool…we was closer…when I made a little sting or got lucky gamblin'…which you know I only do once-in-a-blue-moon, I would come home to her….bring her a little nice gift, put somethin' in her pockets and we lay back and have a nice little talk late into the night before we got down…after the money started to rollin' in, look like everybody in the family got to bein' a big shot…Percy seemed like he changed…he started dressin' better and everything but, then he wasn't so nice to people no more…look like he got a little meaner and a little stuck-up, too…and his mama, Lorraine…my soon-to-be ex-mother-in-law, she used to not have *nothin!* ….used to borrow money from me all the time…and you know back then, I didn't have no money to give nobody…but, I gave her what I had, anyway and she was such a nice person back then, she would share with some of them other ladies that was her friends that had all o' them kids like she does and broke like her, too….but, now she thinks she is a gangster or somethin' 'cause she had her big ol' son, Percy and his just-as-big buddy, Guy out here sellin' "wolf tickets" and bein' "Flash Gordon" 'cause they was sellin' all them pills she was gettin' from her connect and makin' all o' that money…it's a shame the money changed us all for the worse" Cooper said with a deeply philosophical tone. "Yea, brotha' Coop….I remember all o' that back then…and you're right…Percy *did* start actin' all jive and everythang…I remember when he was broke, he didn't hardly have no clothes to wear…he was out here drinkin' with us…remember?....now, he dressin' a whole lot better….but, he still alright with me…I ain't never been the type to be hangin' around beggin' him and Guy…tryin' to get some free high…that's not me…so I don't blame them for feedin' these beggin-ass niggas with a long handle spoon…you dig?" Jack said with conviction. "I'm still keepin' my shit together, though" Cooper said, adding a note of positivity and a sense of hope to the conversation.

"Anyway, Jack…what the hell you been up to, man?" Cooper asked. ""'Aw…shit, Coop….things ain't as bad as they was earlier this year, man…I was carryin' a stick…naw….a forest this past summer…I was wild and shit was gettin' crazy…I was stayin' here and there…man….I was comin' close to either killin' myself or endin' up gettin' a lot o' time in jail….it was crazy, man…sho-nough!" Jack lamented. "But, now…things is a whole lot better….I got my own little spot at the Arms….I still go over to the Sallie thrift store over on Broadway and ask my girl, Ida for some fresh clothes for little or nothin'…and I ran into this sweet little snow chick on Saturday and we hit it right off….she's nice, too, man…we partied all night at the Machine…everywhere we went, motherfuckers' eyes was poppin' outa' their heads…I took her up in the Arms that same night and a couple o' them rough-hustlers was comin' down the stairs…maaann….I thought they was gonna twist their necks off starin' at her!" Jack bragged. "Damn, Jack…she was fine, huh?…I know y'all got busy, right?" Cooper inquired" "Yea…we got down…she was real cool…I like her a lot, man…she ain't like these 'hoes around here…always lookin' for a nigga' to give 'em somethin' Jack said. "Sound like you gettin' your shit together, brotha' Jack…if that girl is any good, hold on to her 'cause a good woman like that don't come along too often, dig?" Cooper said, intending to give Jack encouragement more than anything else.

"I wish I could say the same for me and my soon-to-be ex-wife…yeaaa….too, bad Ruthann broke bad on me…I'll tell ya', Jack…we broke up damn near a year ago….we had been together seven-and-a-half years, me and her…when I first met her, she was just a seventeen year-old girl and her family hadn't been too long come up to Chicago from the south… maybe three or four years before that…she didn't know *nothin'*…hadn't really been with no man 'til I come along…she was sweet, too, man…just like you was sayin' 'bout ya' snow girl….sweet and not all full o' games like these born-and-raised Chicago 'hoes….after we got together, wasn't nothin' she wouldn't do for me…she was in love, man…and I sho''nough loved her….still do…but, after a few years together, we had our first kid just before our three-year anniversary…I think I started strayin' while she was pregnant…I was stayin' out longer and longer at night…she caught me a couple of times hangin' with different chicks…she lost a lot of her trust and I guess some of her love for me, too…she believed in me until I started fuckin' up…takin' thangs for granted…but, I did straighten up when I seen how niggas that I knew musta' known she was my old lady tryin' to get next to her after the baby was born…one day this dude was tellin' me how good she looked to him and how he wanted to get next to her…you know she looks good…anyway, nigga' got through talkin' and I said…thanks for the compliment…that nigga's mouth flew wide open and I said yea…that's my old lady…he apologized all night while he was buyin' me all kinda' drinks…I took it as a compliment….but, I realized one thing at the same time…don't blow ya' good thang….through that guy I could see what I really had…I didn't fuck up no more but, she started kinda' flirtin' with some o' these guys after we started havin' that money when she was dressin' real good…feelin' a lot more confident about herself behind the dressin' up, too…I guess me bein' gone all the time 'cause that paper was burnin' a hole in my pocket didn't help matters, either" Cooper explained. Jack and Cooper talked a little while longer as they continued to confide in one another about their situations.

Finally, the two changed the conversation and their moods as they began brainstorming about ideas they had for making money that day. They decided to drive around to wherever their thoughts took them and make a hustle any place they thought they could. Each of the men knew that this kind of hustling was risky but, they were both high and buzzing pretty good so, they didn't worry about consequences---and besides, the way they were feeling right now, they were not worried about anything. It was all a part of the hustling routine; they needed the insulation of the false courage in those liquor bottles to pull off these rough-hustling escapades that they found themselves engaging in; randomly pursuing whatever opportunity that presented itself, where they would steal or con anything they could. Cooper pulled out of the parking spot at the drive along the lakefront and drove south on Marine Drive until he had reached Addison. He made a right turn onto Addison. He made a left onto Broadway and continued south until he had reached the 2900 block of Broadway. He was lucky enough to find a parking spot on Surf Street near where it intersected Broadway. "Why you stoppin' here, Coop?" Jack asked. "Cause there's a lot of little specialty shops around here where ain't nobody but one person in the stores….we could make a pretty good little sting around here if we play it off right….one of us pretend like we buyin' and keep 'em occupied and the other take whatever he can and slip back out…but, take a bag with you…don't be tryin' to walk around outside with the item in plain view because the "Slick Boys" *do* roll through once-in-a-while" Cooper explained. "Tell you what…go over to that hardware store and buy a bag from them…you can be the front man and I'll do the boostin'…cool?" Cooper offered. "Right on, brotha'…that'll work!" Jack agreed. Jack walked up to the hardware store and in less than five minutes, was returning with the bag in his hand. "Yea…that's cool, Jack…let me have that…I'll fold this bad boy up…let's ride…I'll follow you….remember…check the shops out, first…make sure ain't but one person in the store and pick a good store…don't go in no store that's got bullshit for sale…pick one that's got some shit we can sell real quick….you ready, brotha', Jack?…I know you're one of the best boosters around the 'hood, so I know you ain't gonna have no problem handlin' *this* role by lettin' *me* do the boostin'…right?" Cooper said. "You know me, Coop…nothin' else need-be-said, brotha'!" Jack said with a care-free, flippant attitude.

With that, they struck out walking along the beginning of the 2900 block of Broadway, heading north with Jack strolling casually several yards ahead of Cooper. Jack went into a couple of stores and came right back out. Then, he went another few doors further north and stopped and peered into a storefront window for a moment----finally, he walked inside and Cooper followed closely behind. When Cooper entered the store, he could see that it was a jewelry store, specializing in sterling silver and imitation design jewelry. Cooper mulled around the store, staying near the entrance as he pretended to be interested in the shop's wares. Meanwhile, further into the store, Jack was talking to the salesperson, who usually were the shop owners. He was making friendly small talk. The man spoke with the familiar lyrical lisp that Cooper had come to associate with being gay. He also wore very thick glasses and Cooper could not believe his luck with the obvious inference that this person did not have the best of eye-sight. "And what is this item here…what about this one?" Jack asked of the salesperson as they huddled over the glass case of silver design jewelry. "Oh…my dear…that…is an exquisite piece that is an exact copy of an eighteenth century piece….not many copies have been made since the turn of the century" the short man said as he beamed a big smile up into Jack's face "Wow…you seem to really know your stuff…you seem very well versed…my goodness" Jack complimented the man lavishly. "Oh, well…I *do* try to be as well informed as I can, you know" the man gushed. Meanwhile, Cooper was still meandering about in the background. The man looked his way, with a couple of quick glimpses but, he kept his attention on Jack who was doing a good acting job of feigning interest. "Yea…that's beautiful but…I'll tell you…this item over here has really caught my eye and I can hear it saying "buy me….buy me" Jack said playfully with an exaggerated smile into the man's face. He manipulated the man to look away from Cooper as the man leaned his head over to look into a different case of jewelry. Jack gave a hand signal behind his back to indicate to Cooper to make his move. "Oh…yea…hey…that looks like somethin' that my wife would love to have…my lord, your collection is simply fabulous!" Jack raved on, patronizing the man with his phony, psuedo-bourgeoise speech. "Look closer…can you tell me what that little crystal-looking part of this piece is….what is that?…it gives it such a nice, glowing feature…yes, indeed……marvelous!" Jack went on, attempting to further distract the salesperson from Cooper's presence. "How much?…I got to have that for my wife, Karen….listen…I need to cash a check real quick, just up the street here and I will be right back…no more than fifteen minutes…for sure…mister, please don't sell that piece…I'll be right back!" Jack said, playing his role to perfection. "Don't worry, sir…I will wait for you…no problem…go ahead" the store salesperson said, smiling broadly all the while.

Jack walked out of the store and looked around. He could see Cooper on the opposite side of the street heading back toward the car and peeking inside and running his hand inside the bag that Jack had bought from the hardware store. Jack could see that Cooper had something in the bag and was looking at the merchandise. Jack started walking back in the same direction; staying on that side of the street. Jack noticed that Cooper was no longer looking into the bag but, was looking straight ahead and stepping anxiously back toward the parked car. Jack finally caught up and was even with Cooper exactly across the street from him as both men were stepping lively. Finally, they turned the corner at Surf Street and they each hopped into the car with the bag of merchandise and sped away. They drove north along Clark Street and Cooper made a left turn onto Belmont Avenue and a moment later, a right turn onto Sheffield.

Cooper immediately parked a few doors north of Belmont across from the "1000 Liquors Bar and Carryout. "What's goin' on, Coop?" Jack asked. "Let's go in and sit at the bar…get off the streets for a while Cooper said. "Cool" Jack replied. The two men went in and saw patrons scattered along the bar and at a few tables. There was the usual meager crowd that one would expect on a Monday night. Cooper and Jack sat together at a table where they had a view of the streets. They ordered beers. Cooper brought the bag with him and began to rummage through it. Warily looking around and occasionally laying a piece of the design and costume jewelry in front of Jack on the table for him to look at; mumbling "check that one out…"" each time he pulled out a piece that looked interesting. "Damn, Coop…you know what, man…this shit looks real sweet and most of it has some silver in it with these fancy fake jewels…I know they ain't worth all that much but, they sho' as hell look good!" Jack estimated. "Yea…you're right….you're the salesman, Jack…what do you think you can do with this here stuff?" Cooper inquired. "Hey, bro'…do the best I can, that's what….when I try to sell it to people, I would downplay that they are fake jewels…instead, I would build on the fact that it is sterling silver, which most folks know has some value, and when you add that with the fact that the fake jewels look good…then, the price is wild…you might be able to get a real decent price that is based more on the pieces' good looks than what they're actually worth" Jack said. Cooper was impressed with Jack's analysis of the merchandise. "Damn, Jack…you sound like a sho''nough salesman….if you make your sales pitch like that then, we might be able to sell some o' this shit" Cooper said. "Coop…it all come from hustlin' in these streets, man…if you was as broke as I have been out here tryin' to sell shit then, you know…you either sink or swim…you get good or you give up…and you know me…I don't give up" Jack said, sounding confident and even cocky about his sales abilities.

"Alright, then…shit…let's go at 'em" Coop said spiritedly. With that, Cooper took some of the jewelry in one hand and folded the rest of the merchandise up in the bag and held it in the other hand. Jack scooped up the several pieces that Cooper laid on the table and they started toward the customers to make their pitches. The two went in opposite directions. Cooper went to one side of the room and Jack went to the other. The first couple of customers spent a few short moments listening to each man's pitch, glancing at the design jewelry and shaking their heads to say "no" Finally, Jack came upon a couple---a young female who was fairly attractive and looked to be about mid-twenties. She was dressed nicely, but casual. The man looked to be close to ten years older and he had on a mechanics uniform and looked as though he may have gotten off work not too long ago. Each was having a beer and a seemingly relaxed conversation.

"Hello good people" Jack greeted them cheerfully with a smile. The man looked up at Jack with a cordial smile and the woman beamed a lady-like, pleasant smile, as well. "How ya' doin', my man?....what can I do for you?" the man asked. "Excuse me, sir…and miss…I don't mean to interrupt the good time you all are having but, I have some design jewelry that is mostly sterling silver….some really nice pieces that I would like to show you…do you mind?" Jack said very persuasively and politely. "Well, you can show my lady-friend if she is interested…you care to see what he's got, honey?" the man turned to the woman and asked. "Yea…it's cool…what you got?" the lady asked very perky with a smile. Jack placed the several jewelry pieces on the table in front of them and sat down at their table. "Listen…my friend over there…this is part of his aunt's collection that she had for a number of years…very unique stuff…his aunt willed her estate to him…it was part of a lot of stuff she left behind….she passed about two months ago…anyway, he happen to have it in his car today and said he just wanted to get rid of it…he ain't in need of no money….she left him a little somethin'…. you know…he just wants to get rid of it and get a halfway decent price for the stuff" Jack explained. "Oh, my…these look pretty good…what are you asking for this piece right here" the young woman asked. "Oh…that piece…I know this….I was with him when he had the stuff appraised and each piece falls in the range of seventy-five to three-hundred dollars….make me your best offer and I'm sure if it's a half-way decent one he'll take it" Jack said with assurance, sounding very loose and casual about the matter. The woman shuffled around a few of the half-dozen pieces of jewelry that Jack had laid on the table. “Take your time…look ‘em over and see what you might like, miss…I’m just gonna step over and say somethin’ to my buddy for a minute” Jack said as the lady seemed interested and intently looked over the items, inspecting them and holding some of the necklaces up to her neck and fastening some of the bracelets on her wrist then, admiring them as she seemed to be negotiating with her companion.

Jack sat on one of the bar stools next to Cooper as he stood at the bar speaking to an older woman who was drinking at the bar. Jack could overhear Cooper’s pitch to the woman as he held a few of the necklaces in one hand and the bag of jewelry in the other. The older woman was fending off his sales pitch saying she had all kinds of such jewelry at home. Finally, Cooper relented and politely said to the woman. “Well…thanks for your time, anyway, miss” as he placed the pieces he held in his hand, back into the bag. “Hey, Coop…this lady with this guy over here might buy….I stepped away so, they could have a moment of privacy so she could sweet talk him into buyin’ some o’ that shit….watch…see…you can tell she is his mistress….he’s a married man….a sugar-daddy…he’s stuck…he cain’t say no to her…it’s gonna make him look bad, not to mention cheap…he’s startin’ to give in…see..see…told you” Jack said as he and Cooper stood back and observed the exchange between the man and woman sitting halfway across the room. Jack pulled Cooper by his arm several feet away from where he stood and, almost whispering, said “And you, Coop…man…I got to train you…you over there tryin’ to sell somethin’ to that *old* chick…you wastin’ your time, man…cain’t you see…see how she is dressed…she ain’t dressed like she wants to look attractive…she don’t look good no more…if she ever did and she just ain’t no good prospect for a sale…now…I went straight to those two because I could see there is some fire there…a little passion, and romance and all o’ that shit goin’ on and my man is payin’ for that koochie, sho’’nough!” He ain’t gonna pass up a chance to impress ‘cause he’s married and he wanna keep his little sweet thang on the side…check it out…see…she workin’ on him now…see…hehehahahahmm” Jack said as he attempted to muffle his laugh. Cooper just stood there next to Jack and fixed his eyes on the couple in a stunned, motionless stance.

"Watch the master go and collect his money, Coop" Jack said as he strolled back over to the couple. "Yea…my, man…she wants all three of these and we wanna' know what kind of a deal we can get for 'em" the mechanic said. "Well…I'll tell you, good people…my buddy is lettin' me take whatever price is fair and I know this piece here is one of the more expensive…for sure between one-fifty and two-hundred…this one about seventy or eight dollars and this other one, not that much…probably between forty to sixty dollars" Jack said with an air of confidence. "My price for all three…one hundred dollars!…that's my best offer…no negotiatin'…that's a damn good price, folks" Jack said in his persuasive salesman's tone. "The mechanic paused and rubbed his fingers thoughtfully over one of the bracelets that he had in his hand and seemed to be pondering Jack's offer. He looked at the young brunette sitting next to him and she grabbed his other arm lying on the table and caressed it as she looked into his eyes. "Aw, what the hell…take 'em, baby…they're yours" the mechanic said as he handed the young woman the hand full of jewelry and reached to his back pocket and pulled out his wallet. He pulled out two crisp fifty-dollar bills and handed them to Jack. "Thank you very much, sir…you all have a good night" Jack said very politely as he took the bills in his hand and stuffed them quickly into his pocket and a smile began to spread over his face. "You, too, my man…take it easy" the mechanic said as Jack began to walk away from them.

Jack walked back over to Cooper and by the time he was standing directly in front of Cooper, his wry smile burst out into laughter "Come on, Coop…hahahhehehha….let's ride, brotha'….hahahehe" Jack continued to laugh. He was laughing at the mystified, confounded expression that Cooper had on his face that told Jack all of what he was thinking and feeling at that moment. Cooper had seen Jack pull this off many times in the past. But, he was always dumbfounded as to how he made these sales and some of the other stunts that he had seen Jack perform, hustling in the streets. Cooper could not see how he did it----could not see anything special that Jack was doing to have so much success----how was he doing this? he thought. Cooper was more than pleased that Jack was able to do what he had done---he was benefitting from all of it. But, it made him feel a little envious of the way Jack ran his game with such ease while he was having no success at all. "I know…I know, Coop…it ain't no thang, man….I just get a little lucky sometimes, that's all" Jack said, trying to temper the effect that his seemingly effortless success was having on Cooper. Jack knew that Cooper did not take all of this seriously. He just wanted to have a little success of his own. Still, it did not mean that much to Cooper nor Jack.

The two men walked across Sheffield Avenue back to the car and got in and sped off. They drove around, making little hustles here and there---selling more of the jewelry and trading some of it for weed, and in turn, selling the weed. They stopped at bars and drank; flirting with some of the women at one bar that was somewhere further north up Clark Street. At one point, they stopped and bought a drink then, sat in the car for almost an hour drinking, laughing and joking and having the high-spirited time that they always had whenever they got together in this way. Neither one having any commitments of their time and just flowing free and easy with whatever came their way; enjoying their friendship and their good times to the fullest.

Finally, Cooper made up his mind that he wanted to steal some meat from a particular food store that he had stolen meat from in the recent past. Their security seemed pretty lax and he was pleasantly surprised at how easy his first couple of "stings" went at that store, he told Jack. "Jack…let's head for that store….cool?" Cooper asked. "You ain't said nothin' but a word, Coop….let's ride!" Jack said enthusiastically. Cooper drove back south on Clark Street and made a right turn at Irving Park Road. He continued west on Irving Park, sipping on the pint bottle of gin that they had been drinking from earlier. He arrived at the food store at Irving Park and Cicero Avenue with it's familiar black iron fences surrounding the parking lot. He swung the big '71 Pontiac up into the lot and parked.

Immediately, Cooper began coaching Jack on how the store was arranged inside and giving him the game plan. He asked Jack to go into the store first and buy something inexpensive; just so that he could get a store bag to work with while he stole the meat. After Jack returned to the car with the store bag, Cooper wanted him to go back in right behind him and they would act separately. He wanted Jack to behave a little suspiciously; acting as a decoy while Cooper made his sting. Jack went in and bought a bag of oranges so that he could get a big enough bag. He came back to the car and took the oranges out and gave the empty bag to Cooper. Cooper got out of the car first and walked deliberately across the parking lot to the store entrance; having folded the paper bag and sticking it in his back pocket where it could not be seen. After he was almost there, Jack got out of the car and walked behind him, entering the store about a minute later. Jack wandered around, picking up stuff and putting it back, occasionally looking around to create an air of suspicion about himself. He walked up and down the aisle along the check-out counters to make sure he was being seen and to draw attention to himself in a subtle way. This went on for about ten minutes as he walked up one aisle and then down another; occasionally catching a glimpse of Cooper moving here and there. Finally, he saw Cooper with a shopping cart with several items in it and the large bag that he had given him, apparently filled with the meat that Cooper had placed inside of it. Jack continued his act for about five more minutes and walked out of the store with no purchase after about fifteen minutes, just as Cooper had coached him. He walked back to the car that was unlocked and sat and waited for Cooper to show up.

He waited ten minutes, which became twenty. Now, Jack was beginning to worry. Cooper had told him that he expected to be out of the store not much more than five minutes after Jack came out. Jack could sense that something had gone wrong. Now, twenty-five minutes had passed and no Cooper. He decided to go back in and look for him. Jack had not drank anything for a couple of hours, now but, he was still high and feeling adventurous. He walked into the store and walked around and around, looking for Cooper. He knew that Cooper did not come out of the entrance, because he had watched it the whole time that he sat in the car waiting for him.

As he walked around in the store, Jack suddenly got a hunch and walked inside the double swinging doors that led to the back of the store that had "EMPLOYEES ONLY" stenciled on them. As soon as he entered, he saw Cooper lying on a big wooden table with his hands cuffed behind his back and a medium-built white man in a dark blue jacket standing over him and pulling on the cuffs that Cooper had on. His friend looked anguished by the position of his body on the table and whatever the man was doing to the cuffs on his wrist. Jack grabbed the man by his jacket and began shoving him and yelling at him, "What the-fuck you doin' to him, man!…huh?…huh?…fuck you think you're doin!…huh?" as he shoved the man violently around the back room where no other employees were. Jack was taller and maybe twenty pounds heavier. The security man was no match for his out-of-control energy. "I'm a Chicago policeman!….I'm a Chicago policeman!" the man finally yelled out defensively with fear and desperation in his voice. After the man spoke those words, Jack raised his open palms up on either side to say, "hands off" He did not want to make a bad thing worse by being charged for assaulting a Chicago Police officer. "Alright, man…but, you cain't be handlin' my boy like that…you alright, Coop?" Jack asked without looking at Cooper but, holding an angry glare at the stranger. "Damn, man…I wanted to sit up on this table but, he was pullin' me up kinda rough…damn….loosen these damn cuffs, man…shit..you got 'em too damn tight!" Cooper complained. "I'll loosen 'em" the man said as he stepped over to Cooper still sprawled on the table. The strange man, whom Jack could see was apparently working as security at the store, stepped over to Cooper and helped him sit up as he kept a wary eye on Jack who was standing on the opposite side of Cooper.

Finally, the store manager and one of the other male employees, burst through the swinging doors to the back room. "What's all the commotion about?" The manager asked. "I caught this one here stealing this meat over here" the security guard started, pointing to Cooper and then the bag of meat. "Then…this one here comes bustin' in here and started grabbin' on me…his buddy, I guess" the security guard explained. "Was he caught with him?" the store manager asked. "No…he came outa' nowhere" the security man said. "Well, call the cops to come and pick 'em up, Joe" the store manager said to the produce man standing next to him who, then walked back out to make the phone call. "Is everything OK here?" the store manager asked his security man. "Hey, man…I thought he was tryin' to hurt my friend here…that's all" Jack said. "I ain't gonna give you no problems…we'll just wait for the po' lice to come. "Okay…wait right here and don't pull any funny stuff, 'cause if you do…you're just gonna make it harder on yourself…you understand?" the silver-haired store manager said in an authoritative tone. "It's alright, man…I said we ain't gonna do nothin' but wait…alright?" Jack said in a defiant, annoyed tone. With that, the store manager left and the security guard left out behind him. "Damn, Jack…I'm sorry I got you caught up, man" Cooper apologized to Jack. "Hey, Coop…when a hustler agrees to go hustlin', he knows what the hell he is gettin' into…man, I'm three times seven and then some…I know what-the-fuck I'm gettin' into….I can handle it, man…it ain't your fault, Coop…I agreed, man…don't worry about it" Jack assured. "Well, I know the routine…we goin' to Foster Street station…stay overnight…we'll have a bond hearin' in the mornin'….they'll probably cut you loose in the mornin' and if I cain't get no "I" bond then, I'll be ridin' to twenty-sixth street to do thirty days around one or two o' clock tomorrow" Cooper surmised. "Yea…I guess you're right…we'll just lay back until the cops show" Jack said with resignation.

Fifteen more minutes passed before two burly, uniformed Chicago policemen walked through the swinging backroom double doors with the static of a police radio blaring. They were accompanied by the security guard. "Okay…who is the caught stealing" the first policeman to walk in asked as he turned back to the security guard. "The cuffed guy" he responded while pointing to Cooper sitting quietly on the wooden table. Both cops walked over to Cooper. "Who is this one here?" the same policeman asked, looking at Jack. "Oh…he wasn't stealin' but, he shows up later, busts in the back room here yellin' and bullshit" the security guard explained. "Hey…I stopped as soon as he said that he was a Chicago policeman" Jack said defensively. As soon as Jack made the statement, the cop who was doing all the talking, turned to the security guard and smiled broadly. "You slick-ass bullshitter, you…it's okay…we won't take you in for impersonatin'" the cop said, slapping the shoulder of security guard good-naturedly, who cut an embarrassed look at Jack. That statement made Jack realize that the man was not a Chicago police officer. He regretted that he let himself get bullshitted. But, it probably did not make much difference. He would still be going to jail with Cooper because he had associated himself with him by attacking the security guard. He was just glad that the man was not really a Chicago police officer. Otherwise, he would be facing more serious charges and would not get out of jail after an overnight stay as he expected would happen. The security guard did not press charges on Jack because he was too embarrassed to let the police know that he had allowed himself to be attacked.

The policeman took the security guard's cuffs off of Cooper and replaced them with their own. They cuffed Jack and he felt that sinking feeling that hustlers always felt whenever they were busted. Hustlers like Jack who had become accustomed to the rough-and-tumble life on the streets, took these situations in stride---it came with the territory and every hustler knew the code---you "rolled with the punches" That was the way it was. After they were both cuffed, Jack and Cooper were led out through the store's backroom where a police paddy wagon was waiting for them in the alley. They were led inside and the heavy doors were slammed shut. They sat in the dimly lit back of the wagon as a Hispanic man sat with his hands cuffed behind his back with his head down with long hair hanging into his face; seemingly half-asleep and sitting further up into the wagon. Jack and Cooper could feel the rumble of the wagon over the city streets as they sat; rocking back and forth; getting jostled around in the rough riding paddy wagon. "Hey…Jack…I got some squares" Cooper announced and he told Jack to go in his shirt pocket and take them out and they each lit a cigarette and smoked as the paddy wagon rumbled toward the Foster Street police station.

They went through the one-hour processing of getting pictures taken and being finger-printed along with a dozen other prisoners. It was 9:48pm, Jack had observed on one of the clocks inside the police station. They had a long wait before court in the morning. Jack could do nothing now but, allow his mind to wander. He began to think about his decision to attend college. The idea of attending was now reinforced by this experience which had served to remind him of what was in store for him if he did not make a change in his life. This "rough hustling" was a hard way to live, he thought. He needed some kind of hope to cling to because he was just drifting aimlessly and could sense some impending danger creeping ever closer to him. He could not describe it---see, taste, or feel it but, it was there and it was real. He wondered if he could really pull this off---attending college and living up to the challenge of being as disciplined as he could see Tina had to be; especially since his life was so utterly undisciplined. It all seemed very demanding. But, he felt that he could achieve something; that if he just put his mind to it---just get started---he could carry it through and be on his way to rise out of the craziness that was his life was right now. He knew that he would have to break all ties to his old habits and associations in the streets. He felt as though he could do it but, the temptation to gravitate to the on-going madness that he had become accustomed to would be a test for him.

He remembered announcing to his father one day, back when he was finishing high school, that he wanted to go to college. He had felt the desire to go to college since he was eighteen. He remembered his father's reply ringing like an echo in his mind whenever he recalled it. "You'd better get yourself a job and help your mother out with some o' these bills around this house" his father had responded firmly. The way his father talked to him always seemed so impersonal, Jack recalled; as though he was not really talking to Jack but, making some kind of pronouncement to a group of people and Jack was just there incidentally.

Jack and Cooper were placed in the familiar bullpen that prisoners were always placed in; a holding cell big enough for about three dozen people standing. But, right now, there was barely a dozen other haggard-looking prisoners along with Jack and Cooper; quietly spread about the cell. Some sitting, some standing and others sprawled on the benches and floor, trying to sleep; having the despaired expressions and postures that prisoners usually had while they seemed to be inwardly contemplating their situations. Jack sat up on the end of one of the metal benches inside the cell and Cooper spread out his jacket with the inside facing the cement floor. He laid on it in a fetal position to attempt to get some sleep.

As the time passed in the dimly lit cell, Jack was still awake and his mind wandered as he reflected on his life. His encounter with Tina had given him some kind of hope. It had let him know that he was a person that a normal, decent, attractive woman might want to be with. This was a surprising development and it had turned his thinking toward his being a more decent person---making something of his life. He could visualize a life with Tina where he would eventually finish college and they got married and were living a normal, happy life---and if not with her, with some other woman who was just as nice as Tina. Jack seemed to always be at odds with himself. His thoughts, hopes and dreams were of one kind; the exact opposite of how he was actually living his life---it was all a tangled, perplexing struggle for him.

Jack had been out of jail two days since his wild hustling spree with his friend Cooper. He had gotten a disorderly conduct charge and time served with his overnight stay in jail. Cooper was lucky enough to get an "I" bond and he got out of jail later on the same day another prisoner later told Jack on the streets.

It was Wednesday and Jack had talked to Tina on the phone earlier that morning when he called her from the public telephone booth inside of Frances' Tavern as soon as it opened that morning. He knew that it would be quiet enough for him to have a peaceful conversation with her on the phone. He was very happy with the way the conversation had gone. Her voice sounded soothing to his senses. It was refreshing to have her sweetness in his hard and brutal world. He told her about his hustling escapade with Cooper and getting locked up over night. The bit of embarrassment he felt when he told her felt odd but, he was honest with her, nonetheless. He knew that she had accepted him completely from the beginning with his beguiling street persona and all. She had said over the phone how she really wanted to be with him; but, that she had to prepare for her last semester at school; filing for graduation; buying her books for the next term and doing all kinds of running around; not to mention her part-time intern job teaching fourth-graders that would start soon after the semester had begun this week. She told Jack to keep calling her and perhaps, they could get together in a week or so. Tina told Jack, when they were together, how busy she would be once they had parted company. So, Jack was not surprised because she had warned him of the situation. He was just happy that she still wanted to be with him and had not had any second thoughts. He was full of yearning for her. But, it was difficult for him to express any tender feelings to her. So, he just said "I'm missing you" real quick and continued on with the conversation because of how odd it felt to hear those words coming out of his own mouth. Of course, whenever he would relate any of his interactions with her to his street buddies, it was always couched in macho terms that they understood.

He had to make his appointment with the recruiter at the Northeastern Illinois University Uptown Center so that he could sign up for the spring term that started in January. He had gathered up his social security card and his general assistance picture ID to take to the Uptown Center. He usually did not carry around these pieces of ID because he drank so much and was afraid to lose them. So, he kept them at his little studio apartment in the dresser drawer. His appointment was for 2:30pm this afternoon and Jack had already dressed the best that he could for his appointment after he had showered this morning. It was still only 11:15am. So, he decided to go back home and lounge around because he knew that if he hung around in the streets waiting for his appointment time, that he was likely to end up drinking before the appointment. He did not want to do that. He did not trust himself to not drink.

Jack had come home and laid down fully dressed on his Murphy bed and fallen asleep. Now, he was awake. As soon as his head cleared, it came to him that his appointment was at 2:30 today. He immediately looked at his clock-radio sitting on the dresser to see "1:42" ---he breathed a sigh of relief. He had plenty of time to walk over to the Center to fill out his papers for college. This was a big step for Jack and he hoped that he could carry it through. He went into the bathroom and brushed his teeth again. He was out of the door in five minutes and walked the several blocks to the Center.

At the Center, he met a young lady named Linda Chavez. Jack learned that she was a student herself and was also one of the Uptown recruitment coordinators who held their positions as work-study jobs. He sat across from her at her nicely organized desk in one of the offices in the Center. She had him to fill out all kinds of enrollment papers and he sat at a table out in the lounge area for almost an hour filling them out. He sat another half-hour with her going over his filled-out papers that included financial aid papers, as well. Finally, after she had to have him correct some of the papers and fill out another over again, she announced "looks like we have all of your papers filled out and ready to go….it takes about three to six weeks for all of your papers to be completely processed and if you are eligible for financial aid, you can start enrolling in classes in early November, okay, Mr. Rollins?" as she smiled pleasantly. "Uh…yea…yes…so what do I do next?" Jack asked. "Well…you should get some papers from the state and some from the federal Board of Education in a few weeks….just bring them in and we will submit them to the school to get you enrolled and have you set up for financial aid…alright?" the recruiter explained. "OK…so basically, I don't have to do anything but wait for that mail before I come back here, right?" Jack asked. "That's right!" the lady said with the same perkiness that she had been showing all along. "Alright, Ms. Chavez…thanks for all your help" Jack said as he shook her hand and started out of the door.

That was done and before he knew it, Jack was standing back on the corner of Lawrence and Winthrop. He had already talked to Tina. He had successfully completed his appointment at The Center to enroll in college and he was feeling pretty good about himself. But, now, he was alone again with nothing to do and nowhere to go. He was standing on the corner, just looking around---up the street one way then, down the street the other way. No one that he knew was around. It was the middle of the week. It was usually dead like this during the middle of the day. It was lonely and quiet for the most part and he was doing what he normally did during this time of day when there was nothing going on---he just stood around doing nothing.

CHAPTER 2
SWEET SURVIVOR

Jack awakened to the sound of his blaring radio that he left on last night when he came in drunk again from his wild night in the streets. His mind was still foggy and he did not feel so well. He could also hear the water running in the bathroom face bowl. It was one week into October and January, 1976 would soon be here when he would be starting school---if he survived himself and these crazy nights of drinking. Any day he would be getting that mail for college financial aid and enrollment----this had to stop, he thought. He was always full of repentance when that swirling, dizzy feeling was in his head and he was feeling hungover in the morning. He was a resilient young man and usually, he would recover and feel fine a few hours later, even without a drink. But, this was not one of those times---he needed to get out and get something to drink to smooth out his jangling nerves. Whenever he felt this way, he always mulled around his place; alternately lying down and sitting up in the bed; trying to will away the messy feeling inside while his mind was in a state of chaos; he could not keep a straight thought in his head; this usually went on for a while because he felt too nervous to get up and go out to the store---until the feeling had become too annoying and he dashed out to get something to drink; as long as he had money when he woke up—he was not so annoyed by it because he knew he could go out and get a drink right away; it was the times that he awoke without enough money in his pockets to buy even the cheapest drink that struck fear in him the most---to have to suffer and endure this crazy feeling for a long period of time was maddening. The clock-radio on his dresser read 11:03am when he woke up and turned the radio off and cut off the running water in the bathroom face bowl. He looked into his pants pockets and found $2.43. He had enough for a drink and he began to feel at ease right away---all he had to do was go out and get the drink. He decided that he would forego his usual shower and just wash his face and hands and go out of the door. He did this whenever he was not feeling so well in the mornings after drinking the night before. He was passing through the lobby of the Malden Arms on his way out to get his drink. Jack knew he should be checking with the desk clerk for his mail but, he was feeling too jittery to bother. He stepped at a hurried pace through the lobby and outside, turned left, heading south on Malden toward the Wilson Avenue Liquor store. When Jack arrived, he rushed in and bought a pint of vodka and when he came back out he could see the usual group of drinkers milling around the alley just east of the liquor store entrance. He ignored them and walked with the same hurried pace back north on Malden. He had decided to go back to his apartment and drink by himself. He did not like drinking alone. But, he needed a drink for maintenance -----just to feel normal again. So, he could not afford to share right now because he was broke. Jack was feeling relieved to arrive back at his apartment with the bottle of vodka. He took off his light jacket and sat on the edge of the bed. He took the bottle and immediately twisted off the top and began to drink---his entire body began to relax after that first drink. He paused to let the warm liquid drain down. Jack walked over to the radio and punched the button on the top to turn it on to hear his favorite radio station blaring out a favorite tune. His mind began to clear and he began to feel right again.

Jack's thoughts turned to Tina. He dwelled on her for a while. They had talked three times in the last week. It had been a little over one week since they were together for that first time. It was Tuesday and he had talked to her on Sunday night. They were supposed to get together Wednesday night for dinner and either on Saturday or Sunday, too. But, the weekend date depended on how things went with her getting some studying in and finishing grading papers for her fourth-grade intern class before the end of the week. He was supposed to call her tomorrow around 4:30pm before their date at about 8pm. So, for him, today was an open day and since he would not be speaking to her, he did not have to be sober. His rule for himself was---he would not be drunk when he called to talk to her. So, he would be sober tomorrow night; just as he had done on Sunday night. It was all part of his inspired effort to be a better person.

There was nothing to look ahead for today and Jack had nothing else to do---just a vast stretch of empty time. He sat on the edge of his bed; taking an occasional sip from the bottle and listening to the music and singing along in a low volume to his more favorite tunes while bobbing his head to the rhythm. He was beginning to feel better and better and his mood had turned happy and free from the anxiety he felt earlier before he began drinking. He lay down and dozed off. When he awoke again, his clock-radio read 2:17pm. He felt refreshed. He began to wonder what he was going to do now. He could not drink much today because he needed to be sober and feeling okay tomorrow evening. That was a long time away and he did not know what he would be doing aside from drinking or getting high on drugs. There had been many a day when he was broke---like he was now; and just passed the time feeling half-alive when he was not high. He decided to lie around for as long as he could before he went outside. He eventually would go to The Corner and just pass time hanging around, he thought. He would not get high. He had made up his mind; being straight when he called, then got together with Tina tomorrow evening was important enough to him that he could do it. He lay around listening to the radio for another two hours; occasionally turning the volume all the way down and lying down on the bed and closing his eyes for short stretches of time to make the time pass easier. Finally, he could not stay inside anymore. He needed to get out. He took his time showering to enjoy and appreciate it. It had not been all that long since he had begun taking regular showers. Only since he had began to get a steady assistance check and moved into the Arms had he been able to enjoy this simple necessity of his life. Afterwards, he dressed and went outside, heading straight for The Corner almost without even thinking about it, as he had done almost every day.

He finally arrived at the poolroom and there were a few tables being played, which was par for the middle of the week around 5pm. Inside, there were different-colored plastic seats built on top of long benches that neatly lined the inside of the poolroom in front of the big picture window that faced Lawrence Avenue. They also lined the window facing Winthrop on the east side of the poolroom. Jack went to the front seats in the far corner and sat in his favorite spot at the window facing Lawrence Avenue. Of the few tables being played, only one had anyone that Jack knew---Big Dune, a close friend of Fuzzy and Woody. Dune was a big, good-natured, easy-going fellow. Jack was on speaking terms with Dune but, did not get too personal with him because of his association with Woody, whom Jack had a falling-out with almost two years ago. Woody and Jack did not exactly despise one another, but the differences that they had back then had caused a rift in their acquaintance and Jack had fed Woody with a "long handle spoon" ever since then.

As Jack was sitting, the poolroom entrance door swung open and in walked Ray Foster, who was not so well liked by most people around the neighborhood; mostly because of his constant bragging and tendency to show off. He was a big and tall man; a couple of inches taller that Jack's 6'2" height with a slightly heavier than medium build. He was also about ten years older than Jack. He spoke with a southern drawl and people made jokes about how country he was. It was, perhaps a complex that Ray had that made him feel he needed to prove himself. He was always bragging and trying to present an image of himself as an exceptional person. He wanted to be accepted by the regulars around the neighborhood. But, it seemed to have the opposite effect. Many of the people around the neighborhood were either born in Chicago or were born in the South but, raised in the city. Calling someone country was a favorite put-down among those in the streets. These were the usual kind of mind games that street people played; trying to promote themselves in order to gain a respected street reputation. It permeated most every social gathering amongst Street Gypsies and the people they associated with. It seemed to be a way of life.

Ray strutted into the poolroom with his usual swaggering gait; walking straight for the group of pool players that included Big Dune. "I got next" he spoke out loud and boldly. The three players looked over at Ray as he approached and none of them spoke except Big Dune, who was standing at the front of the table studying his next shot. He acknowledged Ray by nodding his head. Jack watched the goings-on with Ray and the other pool players. Ray was not someone he knew very well and he felt a sense of fear and loathing for him. Jack got very negative vibes from Ray and felt that he was someone he needed to be wary of. Jack already knew that Ray was always trying to prove himself to be some kind of big-shot in these streets and that he did not have much regard for small-time hustlers like himself. So, Jack steered clear of him by keeping his distance. "Y'all don't mind if I get next, do ya?" Ray asked as he stood at the opposite end of the table from Big Dune and in front of some of the nearby plastic seats that lined the windows all around the poolroom. Finally, the game that Big Dune was playing ended and Ray began to play in the next one. Right away, he began his boisterous ways; saying little good luck phrases for himself and talking to the balls. After a while, he began to solicit the other three players for wagers; wanting to bet five dollars a game. They all declined perhaps, because of being aware of Ray's dubious reputation when it came to matters of gambling. They were also aware that he regarded this as a hustle and they were not going to let him hustle them. The game continued and Ray kept up his boisterous talk. Ray was loud enough that Jack could hear him clear across the poolroom from where he sat.

A woman entered the poolroom. It was Evelyn, the younger sister of Earline who lived next door to Jack more than a year ago when Jack lived in the 4848 Winthrop apartment high-rise building just north of the poolroom. She was also the older sister of Roxy, the youngest of the three sisters. Jack had dated Roxy back then, a little over a year ago. Roxy was ninteen years-old at the time and Jack was twenty-two. They all met during one of the wild parties that Earline had thrown back then. Jack became acquainted with them as well as some of their friends at that party as it spilled over into the hallway in front of Jack's door. He was leaving out of his apartment when Earline invited him to the party. Jack had found out almost a year after he broke up with her that Roxy had been the girlfriend of Ray Foster at one time. Roxy had mentioned a former, much older boyfriend. But, he would never have guessed that it was *this* Ray until Coley told him about it a while back. The affair Jack had with Roxy was short-lived, lasting only a matter of weeks. She was nice but, she was not mature enough for Jack and he politely ended the affair. Her hurt feelings had Roxy battering his chest with her fists as they talked inside of his apartment. The oldest sister, Earline had two small kids and their father, Tommy was somewhat of a weed-head who partied a lot. He and Earline had a sometimes stormy relationship. They did not live together, perhaps because of the welfare rules that said no unmarried father could live with the family; and he did not contribute much to the care of the kids; which was usual for most of the young men of his type. Evelyn's boyfriend, Michael was of a similar character. It was common knowledge amongst the regulars in the neighborhood that he was, sometimes extremely abusive to her. Michael fancied himself as a "player" and would boast out in the streets that he was an "eye-a-week" man. Evelyn walked into the poolroom; casually scanning the place by looking around to all corners of it as though she was looking for someone. She finally saw Jack in the far corner at the front. She stepped over to him with her characteristically slow walk and greeted him.

"Hey, Jack…how you doin'? "I'm cool, girl…what's goin' on with you?" he replied. "You seen Michael around here today at all?" she asked just as Jack had expected she would. "Naw…ain't seen him" Jack replied. "Shooot…I ain't lookin' for him that hard…believe me" she replied in a somewhat defensive manner. "He said to meet him up here…but, he always do that…don't show up…so…I don't care if he don't" she said in the same manner. Jack was like most men around the neighborhood. They saw Evelyn as a sexy woman because she was; and just like Jack, most of them probably had some sexual attraction to her, which was understandable. She had a nice figure and she kept herself looking well. But, she was in love with her boyfriend, Michael. She was also a little "dizzy" as some men liked to call it. So, most men did not approach her for those reasons. She was tempting but, her attachment to Michael, deterred them. He was always abusing her in one way or another---physically, verbally and in other cruel ways. She had too much baggage and everyone knew these things about her. Still, she was a physically attractive woman as were her other two sisters. She was a fixture around the neighborhood and all the men who knew her treated her like a friend. She was easy-going and pleasant for the most part. But, most people saw her as her own worst enemy because of how she allowed Michael to treat her so poorly.

"Oooh…look over there" Evelyn said as she looked toward the group around the pool table where Ray and Big Dune were playing "….there go that crazy-ass Ray Foster….always talkin' 'bout he got so much money" she commented. "Yea…he always tryin' to be "Flash Gordon"…look at him…talkin' all loud and stuff…for the life of me, I don't know what my baby sister saw in that nigga….I swear" she went on. "He even tried to offer me some money" she added in a confidential tone. "No shit?" Jack said, not surprised to hear her admission. "You know why he was offerin' me money….you know why" Evelyn went on. Jack paused with an air of indifference when she added that last statement. "With a body like that…I could see why he was offerin' money…"" he thought. "What you gonna' do now, Evelyn?" Jack asked. "Play it cool, brotha'…play it cool" she said as she patted Jack on his nearest shoulder and giggled at the same time and acted as though she had decided to throw all her cares away just at that moment.

Finally, Jack's friend, Coley walked into the poolroom. He looked to his left to see Jack and Evelyn sitting in the far corner. He walked over very slowly and sat near them. "What's goin' on people?" he greeted. "Hey, Coley" Evelyn said. "Big time Coley…my main man…what's happ'nin' brotha'!" Jack greeted energetically as he stood up and they did a soul handshake. "Ooooh, man…you just don't know, Jack…whooweeee!…man…I was hangin' out with these two freaky chicks…one white…one black….they wanted to take off…they didn't have nowhere to go…I met them in the restaurant over there on Sheridan and Lawrence…anyway…chick ask me…you got a place?….I said, hell yea…I got a place…she say…well can we go there to get high?…I said…maybe…what's in it for me?…dig what she said, Jack…dig this…she say…you can't have none of our dope, but we'll freak you off!…I say whaaaaaa!…"" "they looked pretty good, too…I already had keys to Skip's place…he gone off for about two days out of town…we went up there and, maaaannn…I'm tellin' you..them chicks was some stone freaks, man…didn't give me none of their dope…but, I didn't give a shit after they got naked….we freaked all afternoon after they got high…lawd have mercy…they done drained me, brotha'…I ain't never been so relaxed in my life…most dudes hope and pray they can get two good lookin' women at one time…without payin' nothin', of course…ya' dig…stone freaks, brotha'…stone freaks" Coley went on with a satisfied grin on his face and chuckling at the same time. "Ooooh…Coley…you cheatin' on your old lady like that?" Evelyn said, feigning disapproval as she facetiously chided him. “Buy me some weed and I won’t tell Shirley” Evelyn joked with Coley. “Alright, now…don’t try to blackmail me, now…I’ll make up some shit and tell Michael…watch it, now..”” Coley joked back with Evelyn as he smiled broadly and let out another light chuckle. “Shooo….I don’t care…he don’t care what I do…and if he did…he ain’t gon’ do nothin’ no way…he try somethin’ I’ll put his ass on punishment…hahaha…haha” Evelyn joked and laughed out loud “…whoooweeee!” she said at the end of her laugh as she shook her head from side-to-side playfully like a young kid that shown the light-hearted mood she was in and that she was getting a kick out of the verbal jostling with Coley. This was the usual kind of talk that went on between Street Gypsies and their friends; lots of joking and care-free banter. “Okay…alright Miss Evelyn…whatever you say…”” Coley said, still smiling but, seemingly ready to end that exchange.

“Check out ya’ boy, Ray over there, Coley…tryin’ to hustle Big Dune and them other studs…see him over there…”” Jack said to Coley, trying to solicit a comment from him that would tell him more about this man. Not only because he was wary of him but, also because he wanted to know what his ex-girlfriend could possibly have seen in a character like Ray. “Aw, shit…what is he doin?….tryin to get people to bet on games?….I don’t mess with him…they ain’t gonna’ mess with him, either…they not gonna’ bet his cheatin’ ass..…the only pool-shooters that will bet him are the ones that don’t know him…don’t nobody trust him…dig what I’m sayin’?” Coley said in a more serious tone. “You know what else about Ray?…he is a bluff…his bark is way worse than his bite…remember…if you ever get into it with him…he is a bullshitter….challenge his ass…if he says to you…I’m gonna kick your ass!…you tell him…well, do it then, nigga!…okay?…dig what I’m sayin’?” Coley said seemingly in his mentoring mode with Jack. “Yea…I hear ya’ Coley…I hear ya’” Jack responded as he listened intently to Coley whose advice he trusted more than anyone else around the streets of Uptown. Those were the exact notions that Jack had about Ray. He knew that he was someone not to be trusted and Coley only confirmed that. The talk between Jack, Evelyn and Coley became more toned down as the three of them just sat and occasionally exchanged short comments back-and-forth to one another. The pool game that Ray and Big Dune were playing carried on with Ray continuing to be heard throughout the poolroom with his loud talk. A few more players entered the poolroom and several moments passed before Woody came into the poolroom and walked over to the table where his friend, Big Dune was playing and announced

"Hey, y'all....they havin' a hell uva' fight out in the playground...Rick Floyd and Anthony...they battlin' like sho' 'nough gladiators!" Coley overheard what Woody had said and walked over to confirm it. Jack and Evelyn walked over to where Woody was standing. "Who did you say is fightin', Woody?" Evelyn asked. "Anthony and Rick in the playground" Woody replied seemingly trying to temper the excitement in his voice; and with that, they all rushed out of the poolroom to see the fight. Rick Floyd and Anthony were two of the biggest, strongest and toughest men in the neighborhood. Rick Floyd's father was known as "Sarge" around the neighborhood because he was a retired U.S. Army veteran who had spent twenty years in the service. He was a tough man and his son, Rick was even tougher some people said. Rick was now in the Army himself having signed up for two years but, contemplating a career in it as his father had done. Anthony was the oldest of three brothers and they had plenty of cousins and were known to "go for bad" as a lot of people liked to say. If you went up against any of the Blevins brothers, you had to go against all three of them and their cousins, too. But, because of his reputation, none of them ever even thought about messing with Rick Floyd. Anthony and his girlfriend, Peggy had been living together for four years in their apartment in 4848. Rick still occasionally stayed with his father and mother and one brother whenever he would come from the Fort Sheridan army base further up the North Shore where he was stationed. His folks lived a little further north of the poolroom on Balmoral Street where the residences were a little nicer. Rick was twenty-one years old. He would be twenty-two in a few months. Coley, Evelyn, Jack and Woody all rushed out of the poolroom door and turned the corner to go north on Winthrop where the kids playground was. It was between the rear of the Aragon and the south end of the 4848 building. There was already a crowd of about two dozen people standing on the outside of the playground fence at it's entrance; gazing intently at the action in the middle of the playground several yards away. When Jack finally could get an angle to see what the commotion was about, he could see two men who were entangled; locked in each other's grip; wrestling on the ground inside the playground. No one else was inside the playground and because of that, the spectacle seemed almost to be in an arena. "WOOooo!" The crowd gasped in sync as Rick broke out of Anthony's mighty grip, rose up and made what looked like a football tackle, slamming Anthony backwards to the ground. Anthony lay on his back for another few seconds before he raised his upper body up and smashed his right forearm into Rick's left temple. "Aw, shit…Whooo!…Damn!" were the gasps from the crowd. "They been fightin' for about five minutes, now!" one spectator said. …"Them some strong-ass niggas' there, man…I wouldn't wanna' fuck with neither one o' them" another commented. The mighty struggle carried on with each man gaining a little momentum at some point before it shifted to the other. Finally, it seemed, Rick Floyd had gained an extra surge of strength and grabbed Anthony with the grip of one of his powerful arms around one thigh and hip area on one end and the other arm gripped around his shoulder and neck on the opposite end and turned him upside down and rammed his head into the concrete ground. "Ooohh!...Oooww…Damn!…..Shiiit!…Oh Nooo!.." came the gasps from the crowd. After that, there was an eerie silence as the crowd, stunned by the last development, quietly stared and gazed at Anthony's body as it suddenly went limp on the ground. Rick gasped for air as he stood over Anthony's motionless form crumpled in front of him. He heaved momentarily as he tried to catch his breath. He stooped over and stuck his hand in one of Anthony's pockets and pulled out some crumpled bills; took a ten dollar bill out and put it in his pocket. He stuffed the remaining bills back into Anthony's pocket. "I told his ass not to fuck around with my shit!…I told him…now…that's what his fool-ass gets…don't fuck with me, nigga!" Rick yelled at Anthony's motionless body on the ground. "Somebody wake that fool up!…he just knocked out..that's all…tell him and any other chump-ass nigga' he wanna' get, to come on if they wanna' get down…y'all here me?…tell his ass!" Rick said with bitterly angry emotion as though he was talking more to himself than to the crowd. He walked slowly out of the playground area as Anthony lay unconscious on the ground behind him.

The crowd quietly spread out and back from him as he approached them at the open part of the playground fence. “Hey…what’s happ’nin’, Coley?….what’s goin’ on, baby?” Rick said in a tone that seemed to be seeking support; and as though he wanted to comfort himself with camaraderie. He reached out and did a soul handshake with Coley. Rick and Coley were not real tight. But, they had mutual respect and had always gotten along. “Yea...damn right...I wouldn’t let nobody take my money, either..yea..damn right…I wish a som’ bitch would try to take my money…I’ll do just like Rick did..yea…I ain’t bullshittin” Ray could be heard to say as he pranced around, talking out loud as some of the dispersing crowd glanced at him with smirks and other dismissive expressions. “Ray…Ray” Rick finally said after hearing the way Ray was carrying on; “Ray…Ray” he said once again before Ray finally heard him. “Huh…what?...what, Rick? he replied as he turned around to see Rick standing behind him. “Shut-the-fuck up!…okay?” Rick said sternly as he stared Ray down. After Ray saw the expression on Rick’s face, he just turned and quietly walked away. “Always runnin’ his fuckin’ mouth” Rick mumbled disgustedly. After Ray walked into the distance, Rick’s mood changed to a more subdued one.

“Come on… walk with me, Coley…let’s go get us a brew, alright…cool?” Rick urged. “Alright…yea…that’s cool with me” Coley replied, almost stammering with surprise at Rick suddenly picking him out of the crowd to hang out with. “Jack is with me..”” Coley quickly added, sticking to the principles of loyalty and fairness that he lived by in the streets. “That’s cool…come on ride with us, slim” Rick said, turning his head slightly and momentarily back to Jack who was a few feet behind he and Coley as all three of them stepped at a lively pace. They walked south on Winthrop, apparently heading to Saxony liquors to buy the beer. They arrived at Saxony Liquors and inside, Rick pulled out a wad of bills and selected one of them and held it in his hand. “Can y’all drink some Heineken with me?” he asked rhetorically, as they all stood in front of the take-out counter. “Yea…cool” Coley and Jack answered almost at once. Rick ordered a six-pack of Heineken, paid for it and they all left out of the store. As they stood outside of the store entrance, Rick said “Hey, y’all let’s walk away from around here…let’s go over to Wilson and Dover and hang” They walked together and as they did, Rick went into explaining what went on between him and Anthony to cause them to fight.

"Naw, Coley…you know…that nigga' deserved that whoopin' I put on his ass…dig this here…I'm over there on the Ainslie side of 4848 hangin' with some studs from the buildin'…James, Luther and Buddy…dig…we drinkin' a little brew out around the parkin' lot, right?…I wanna' get some weed…I see L'il Murphy…I decide to ask him to cop some weed for me…I pick him 'cause he know where all the good weed at…beside that…he copped for me once before.. before he came back…this dude who is in the army with me…I go to drop him off at his crib…I get caught up with him and these chicks he knows…I come back real late…you know Murphy held that weed for me a whole day-and-a-half?…no shit…now, how many of these studs around here can you trust with your weed for a whole day without them pinchin' off of it..huh? dig me…none, right?…none..I call him over…. I say "Murph…cop some weed for me, alright?...he know I'm always holdin' some paper…he know I ain't one of these fake-ass niggas' out here…but, dig this…the main weed man…he at the other end of the buildin' over by the play ground hangin' out there with Anthony and them….Murph said…"give me a dime bag" to the stud with the weed, dig…Anthony see him coppin'…he say "Nigga…don't you owe me some money?"...Murph say "naw…for what? Tony say…"nigga…you know you owe me" and took my money from Murph…*maann*…what he do that for….he showin' off in front of these studs he with…you know how he always talkin' big shit…dig…Murph come back and tell me…"Anthony took your money"…I cain't *believe* this here shit, man…I say…"Murph"…did you tell the nigga' that was my money?…he say "yea…I told him two or three times it was your money" "Man…I say fuck this" I walk on over there….I see the nigga' walkin' away…I know what he is tryin' to do….he gonna' slip away and disappear 'til the next day…then, lie about the whole thing that next day…dig…but, I catch up to his ass right in front of the playground…I say "Tony"…Murph say you took my money from him…what's goin' on?…he start this shit talkin' 'bout he didn't know it was my money and L'il Murph owe him and all this…I say "Well didn't he tell you it was *my* money..not his?…then he say…"yea…he said it but, I didn't believe him…I told him any nigga' that owe me and I catch him with some money…I'm takin' it if he ain't gonna' pay me…simple as that"…I say…"So…you sayin' you takin' *my* money…is that what you sayin?" he started talkin' all foxy and shit…finally, I say…"Hey, man…fuck all that…just hand me my money….he started to feelin' embarrassed in front of these two niggas he was gettin' high with…they walkin' along with him while we talkin'…I said…"I ain't gonna say it but one more time, Tony…hand me my money"…he start, to say "But I…" "I fired on his ass…knocked the cowboy-shit out of him…he hit the wall…them other two partners of his scattered like bitches…I say "hand me my money or I'm whoopin' yo' ass and takin' it" …we start to battlin'…nigga put up a good fight but, I knew I was gonna get him…knocked his punk-ass straight out!…end of story"…You know me, Coley…I might talk a lot of shit but, you don't never see me fuckin' with nobody….am I right or am I wrong?…tell me" Rick solicited. "Naw, brotha' Floyd…you are right…you don't mess with none of these people around here…I see you mostly keep to yourself…I don't see you around that much…and you know…he went out like a jap, fuckin' with your money like that" Coley offered.

"That's why I stay on the move…I don't stay around long enough for people to draw a bead on me and get me all caught up in some mess…'cause the more they know about you, the easier it is for them to set you up for some bullshit" Jack added with conviction. After a short silence, Rick spoke out "You know what, slim?…you're right…if I stay away from all these people out here who always gettin' into my business…I'd be better off…you said a mouth full right there…that's the truth" Rick said after he had taken a moment to reflect on Jack's comment. "Jack…you right, brotha'… I've been knowin' that for a long time…that is right" Coley added. …and I'm stayin' away from these niggas, from now on…watch me…I ain't bullshittin" Rick added in a dead serious tone.

Rick, Coley and Jack sat on the stoop at the southwest corner of Wilson and Dover for about an hour talking, laughing and drinking the Heineken beer. In that time, a few people passed that each man knew; a couple of them stopped and one stood for a while and spoke to Rick and the other, an old friend of Coley's that he had not seen in a few years, stopped for several minutes catching up and reminiscing old times. Jack knew many of the street characters and those that he knew, he greeted as they passed. This was the usual routine with Street Gypsies; sitting around the streets, drinking and generally having a good time. Jack had decided that he would only drink the one beer he had and stop drinking altogether after that.

As the conversation had turned more serious and philosophical, it prompted Jack to reflect on his own situation. He thought about his immediate future. Getting locked up with Cooper had made him realize that he could not afford to keep the kind of company and routine that he had been keeping for two reasons---school and Tina----or was it Tina then, school. He just knew that they were both important for what he hoped his future would hold. He wanted both to happen; to intimately be a part of his life. But, he was so much a part of these streets when he never really wanted to be. It occurred to him that he needed to move out of the midst of the madness that he had allowed himself to become accustomed to. He wondered what had been on his mind these last few years as he had been hanging around and prowling the streets and living this transient existence. How had he come to live this way? Now, suddenly, he had a change of heart and renewed ambition that he had not felt in so long. He had come to have aspirations to make his life better. As soon as the faintest element of hope had appeared with the idea of going to college and meeting Tina, those rays of hope had altered his thinking. He was hoping now that he might survive himself and this crazy street life. The thought of moving from the Arms so that he could attend school and be able to study in peace had come to mind. It was a simple solution to his situation; move to the YMCA where his friend, Willie-the-Weep lived. It was out of the area where he always hung out—just a mile west of Broadway at Wilson and Hermitage where the YMCA building stood. Jack had stayed there a few nights this past summer when he was "carrying a stick" and doing bad. The Weep sneaked Jack into the building and let him sleep in his room a few times. Jack remembered that the room was nice, clean and cozy--perfect for what he needed. He did not care that the rooms were small---he just needed the peace and privacy that they offered.

"Hey, y'all…there goes my brother, Charles in his car….let me catch him so he can give me a lift back to my ride over at 4848…let me get another brew…I'm gone, y'all" Rick said after he grabbed an extra beer from the six-pack and ran to catch up to the blue 1972 Chevy Impala his brother was driving after it stopped for the stop sign at the intersection of Dover and Wilson. "Charles! …Charles!" he could be heard as he faded into the distance and caught up to the car after it had pulled over to the curbside. "You see that, Jack?" Coley asked. "What?" Jack replied.

"Rick is a real good brotha'…he's in the army, workin' and gettin' all kinda' trainin'…he ain't fuckin' up like us…comes from a good family…I know his daddy real good…Sarge..he don't take no mess…Sarge likes to get high every now and then…when he does…he'll buy you drinks all day long…but, he ain't gonna' come outside…he knows himself…he knows he will spend all his money if he hangs outside with us broke-ass niggas'…Rick is a little like his daddy…if he likes you…he'll spend…if he don't like you…he plays broke…hahahaha…hahaha…I don't blame him though…it's a million broke-ass niggas' out here lookin' for somethin' free or somethin' that ain't tied down…..hahahaha" Coley said as he chuckled in-between his comments. "Yea…he used to come up to my crib almost two years ago to get high on that "hair-on"….he used to give me enough to snort. He would come to my place because all of them other dope-fiends, like Melvin and Andrew was too greedy and there was too many people goin' in and out of their cribs…while their wives was at work, they would be gettin' high at their apartments and they would have all kinda' niggas in their cribs…crowds 'uv 'em goin' in-and-out all day…Rick knew he couldn't get high at their cribs…he knew he couldn't do it in peace…so…he came to my crib because wasn't nobody there and all he had to do was take care of one person…me…so he could get high…every time he came, he would give me some to snort…I would snort it in the living room, then he would go into the bedroom and get high…he used to tell me all the time…"you wastin' good dope by snortin' it"…he kept on sayin' that…'til one day…I let him talk me into shootin' up..just like him…I remember that day…I shot that shit up and…I swear, man…I was so high…I couldn't even cross the damn street…no shit! ….but, I will tell you…he *is* a tough dude but, he was cool with me…he always looked out for me and gave me *somethin'* so he could get high at my spot…them other stingy, greedy-ass niggas…I wouldn't let none of 'em even come into my crib…especially that damned Woody!" "Yea…Jack..that low-down nigga' couldn't stay with his best buddy, Fuzz…so, he stayed with you for free…lyin' about he gonna' pay you and all along gettin' a check comin' to Fuzzy's house…that *is* low-down…sho' 'nough…I remember when you told me about that…me…I don't fuck with Woody…no way…but, I would like to tap his ol' lady…she sho' 'nough hooked up..''" Coley went on with a sly grin beginning to spread across his face.

"Yea…she *does* have a nice shape but, she is a little older than I like 'em" Jack responded. "She ain't too old for *me*…now, Jack…you know damned well, if she got naked in your crib…nobody but you and her…you would turn it down?…don't try to bullshit me…you would get it, now wouldn't you?" Coley chided Jack. "You don't know that, Coley…I'm in my twenties…she is in her forties…and I.." Jack started "Come on, now…hahahaha…stop it, Jack..stop, stop…hahahaha…whoooohahaha…stop it, fool!'…you know damn well you would get it…" Coley laughed and teased Jack. "Naw, naw" Jack tried to argue as Coley became more animated and loud, laughing and smiling. "I got to go home, Coley" Jack said calmly and with a straight face as he rose from the stoop they had been sitting on for more than an hour. He began walking east on Wilson from Dover. "You would turn it down, Jack?…stop lyin'" Coley went on as the two began to walk down Wilson side-by-side. Coley continued making animated gestures as Jack walked along calmly, smiling at Coley's chiding. They were good friends and this was how they always carried on. They arrived at Malden and Wilson and turned left onto Malden to go north. By that time, Coley's chiding had stopped and the conversation had changed and became more toned down. "You goin' in for the night, sho' 'nough, Jack?" Coley asked seriously. "Yea, man..''" Jack bristled with an annoyed inflection in his tone. "Damn, Jack….that ain't like you, brotha'…what's goin' on?.. you goin' in so early…you sick or somethin'?...it ain't even eight o' clock, yet" Coley asked. "Naw, man…I got business at the college tomorrow mornin'….I don't wanna' go there with alcohol on my breath so…I'm goin' in so I can be straight tomorrow…dig?" Jack said. "Okay, bro'…just wonderin' was you okay" Coley responded. They reached the Malden Arms and were standing in front of it. They did a soul handshake before Jack turned into the walkway to walk into the entrance. "I'll catch you, bro'.." Coley said. "Later" Jack said as he walked away.

Jack did not have any appointment with the college tomorrow. He did not want anyone, especially friends such as Coley to know that he was trying to stay sober for a woman he had just met. It sort of went against the Street Gypsy code of manly behavior; a code he knew instinctively. He was not really sleepy and he knew it would be a long, boring night. But, he was going to go in anyway. Jack fell asleep for a short while and he awoke to see that his nap had been short. He remembered that he had fallen asleep at about 8:15pm and it was now 9:39pm. He felt pretty good but, he wished that he could have slept through the night. He was stuck with all of this time on his hands and, now he was not even sleepy. It was going to be a very long night and this is what seemed to drive him crazy---just sitting around sober with nothing to do. He could feel a little anxiety begin to build up inside. Although he felt okay physically, he felt the mental pressure that he had put on himself of trying to live up to the foolish notion of not drinking for as long as he had planned—the better part of a day. He remembered that Tina had told him over the phone that she usually got into her off-campus apartment at around 2:15pm on Wednesdays. But, that she needed about another hour or so to settle in and feel ready to talk on the phone. Jack had decided that he would play it cool because he did not want to appear overly anxious by calling her at the very earliest time that he could; no, he did not think of himself as a player. But, he did not want to look like a chump, either. So, he had told a little white lie to Tina in that last conversation; telling her that he had "business" to attend to early tomorrow afternoon and he would probably not be calling until sometime after 4:30pm.

He finally decided "aw…to hell with all of that!..''" he wasn't going to worry about it. He was going outside to mess around for a while. He still intended not to drink. But, he was getting crazy from staying inside and he couldn't stand it any longer. He was broke, too so, he looked into his dresser drawer to look for any of the leftover "hashish" he would occasionally make. He usually threw whatever he had left over into his drawer. It came in handy when he needed something to make a hustle. He never knew when he might run into a mark out on the streets that he could sell it to. It had happened many times before and was a lifesaver when he was broke. He found one nice-sized chunk and another medium-sized one. Both still wrapped in aluminum foil. He stuffed them both into his pocket, washed his face and hands and locked his door and headed down the stairwell. When he arrived at the entrance door and stepped across it's threshold, he was immediately met by three men who were hanging around and talking near the building. Jack recognized them as residents of the Arms that he had seen numerous times around the building in his comings and goings. They were the usual hardened, rough-hustling street types, who were very much like himself and with whom he identified best. "Hey, y'all what's goin' down" Jack greeted them. "Hey, now"...."Hey" they all responded. "Got that weed, bro'" one said. "Cain't hang right now, brotha-man" Jack responded as he continued on. He could feel that the weather had changed somewhat from when he came home earlier. It was now a little warmer and windy. It had that balmy, Indian-summer feel to it that sometimes came about in the early Fall. He turned right to walk north on Malden to head toward the Lawrence Avenue strip where he spent most of his waking hours. The mild weather seemed to give the atmosphere an easy, mellowing effect with a tinge of excitement. Jack could feel the excitement welling up within himself and he could sense it in the air from the way people moved in the streets about him. As he passed people sitting outside on stoops and walking along the streets, he could hear a certain happier lilt in their talk and see an extra liveliness in their walk. The feeling continued to rise within him and he was glad that he had not stayed inside. He relished excitement and enjoyed life to the fullest. He certainly could not stay inside on a night like this when it was so clear and nice. Jack continued on, crossing Lawrence Avenue from the south side of it at Malden to the north side and walking east.

When he arrived at the northwest corner of Lawrence and Broadway, he paused and from where he stood, looked around slow and easy as he always did when he came to the strip. He had a view straight east down Lawrence. He peered into the distance to see if there were any body shapes that he could recognize hanging around Lawrence and Winthrop near the poolroom or anywhere around that intersection. He saw figures standing and moving on the streets but, no one he knew. He looked up and down Broadway to measure the mood of the streets and the level of activity. As he did so, he could hear the live music coming from inside the Green Mill. It was Live Jazz Night when the Mill usually booked a live jazz band to attract more customers. Jack strode slowly toward the front entrance and stopped directly in front of it but, a few yards away and very near the bus-stop bench near the curb. He paused and gazed; trying to see what he could of the action inside. A short moment passed before a man came strolling out from the entrance door that was set open. He strode out very casually and stood to one side of the door and scanned the streets in each direction. Jack recognized him as one of the part-time bartenders for the Green Mill whom he had seen before collecting admissions at the entrance door on Jazz Nights.

All of the bartenders at the Green Mill seemed to possess an attitude of indifference toward Jack. They were used to seeing him around the streets near the Green Mill. They knew, too that he was a small-time neighborhood hustler; so, they did not regard his presence inside the Green Mill as necessarily good because they knew Jack was always looking to make a hustle. Jack usually pretended to behave in a civilized manner in front of them because he wanted to be able to come in to try to make money whenever he might need to. On rare occasions, after he had made a good hustle, Jack would hang around the Green Mill until late; sitting at the bar, as opposed to sitting in a booth when he did not have money. He would be drinking and talking spiritedly while cracking jokes and spending money like a high-roller. This was how the bartenders became more acquainted with him. But, many times after that night of big-spending, Jack would be broke the very next day and would appear around the Green Mill looking to make money rather than spending it---he would be a big-shot one night and *persona non-grata* the next. When he came in and the bartenders could see that he was broke again, they would have disgusted expressions at the way he would try to hustle their customers. Sometimes they had to temper themselves from calling him off of the paying patrons. But, Jack's saving grace was the owner, Stanley who was in his sixties. Stanley's son, Barry, who managed the place on the weekends, and the other bartenders could not understand why his father treated a street person like Jack so well. Many times, Barry was on the verge of putting Jack out of the bar when he would have merchandise, trying to sell it to the customers; or was trying to pull some kind of scam. But,

Stanley would intervene and prevent it and occasionally do small favors for Jack; like give him free drinks. He even let Jack get up on stage one night to sing "My kind of Town" with the band. Barry never knew why that was but, he must have been told by his father to go easy on Jack, because he usually did.

Jack could see from where he stood, a number of patrons sitting inside; listening to the jazz band tuning up for their first show at 10pm. There was usually a one hour break after that one hour set then, another one hour set at midnight. The crowd was starting to grow with several more people walking up to the entrance door where the bartender took their admission fees. Jack felt subdued because this was not his usual mode; being sober when there was excitement going on. He did not mind that so much, because he was only killing time. He didn't have money to get in so, he just walked over and sat on the bench near the bus stop. He sat and took in the mild, late-evening activity about the streets.

Barely ten minutes had passed before he suddenly saw his old buddy Willie-the-Weep standing on the northeast corner directly across the streets in front of him. He stood up and yelled "Heeeyy Weep!"….heeyyy Weep!" The Weep looked around and spotted Jack across the streets from him. Jack made a quick, beckoning motion with his arm in the air. The Weep started across the street toward Jack after he had gotten the green light. "Big-time Jack…what you doin', bro'?" The Weep said as he stepped up onto the curb near the bench. "Hey, man… take a load off and sit down….I ain't doin' nothin'….just out here messin' around" Jack said in a subdued manner. "You tryin' to get up on one?" The Weep asked. "Naw, man….I ain't drinkin' tonight" Jack replied matter-of-factly. "What?....you ain't drinkin'?... Jack…oh 'lizabeth…I think this is the big one…I'm comin' to see ya', 'lizabeth…hahahaha…hahaha" The Weep said, mimicking a certain TV character while laughing at his own joke as he chided Jack. "Why you got to have the "big one" just 'cause *I* ain't drinkin'?" Jack replied with an expression and inflection that was good-natured, engaging and light-hearted. "Jack….'cause I know you…you ain't drinkin' is like a fish without water….like a duck that don't quack….a elephant without a trunk…a…"'" "Aw I get it!…that's enough…you got ya' point across..""" Jack cut in snickering to himself as The Weep joined in and they snickered and laughed together. “Hey…too bad you ain’t drinkin’” The Weep said as he pulled out a pint bottle of Richard’s Wild Irish Rose wine from his back pocket and whacked the bottom of it and began to twist the cap off. He looked up Broadway one way, then down it the other way before turning the bottle up to his lips and guzzling down some of the dark-colored liquid. “Ahhhh…”” he gasped afterward. “You know you wanna’ hit it….go ‘head, Jack…don’t torture ya’ ‘self like that….go on!” The Weep offered as he handed the bottle to Jack and tried to keep a straight face. “Jack cut his eyes at The Weep sitting next to him on the bus stop bench. “You must think I’m bullshittin’, huh?” Jack said in a half-serious tone that hid a hint of playfullness. “Go ‘head help yourself….”” The Weep continued. “hahahaha….hahaha…hahaha” Jack responded “…you cain’t break me, Weep…don’t even try it” Jack said, becoming amused with The Weep’s animated gestures and facial expressions. He turned his head away from The Weep and the bottle he was offering. “Okay, Jack….I see you serious…but, I been knowin’ you for a while…we drinkin’ buddies…and we done spent many-a-day hustlin’ up on a taste and only one other time, over a year ago…is when I last seen you turn down a taste…’cause you was followin’ that chick, tryin’ to get in her draws” The Weep said with a faint smile. “Oh, yea…good old Marilyn….she was a good ‘un, too, man…you know that, Weep?” Jack said with a reminiscing glimmer in his eyes as a smile spread across his face. “So, you *did* tap that, huh?” The Weep surmised. “Hell, yea, Weep…she was good to go, baby…sho’ ‘nough!” Jack said emphatically. The two men continued to sit on the bench and talk as The Weep took an occasional sip from his bottle. They continued to entertain themselves by cracking jokes, laughing and telling funny little stories.

Finally, a man who appeared to be a patron came out of the Green Mill. He was a white fellow of a fair height; close to six feet with a medium build. He appeared to be in his late thirties to near forty years old. He was dressed very nicely in a rust-colored blazer and an open-collared, pin-stripped dress shirt; dark-grey, well-tailored slacks and very nicely shined black, high-quality shoes. He walked out a few yards from the entrance and paused before looking around somewhat anxiously. His body language seemed to say that he was looking for something. He looked momentarily in the direction of Jack and The Weep sitting on the bus stop bench. He went into his pocket and pulled out a pack of smokes. They were the long, slender ones that were a cross between cigars and cigarettes that were the latest fad that so many people were smoking nowadays. They were supposed to make a person seem more sophisticated. The well-dressed stranger stepped out further from the entrance and lit his slender cigarette and began to puff as he stood in one place; occasionally gazing around the streets. He seemed to be trying to relax as he puffed away. He continued to occasionally glance over at Jack and The Weep in a manner that hinted that something was on his mind. Finally, after finishing his cigarette, he strolled over toward Jack and Weep sitting on the bench and his darting eyes seemed to belie the casual veneer that he attempted to present. "Look…look, Weep, be cool…ya' boy comin' this way…he wants somethin'" Jack half-whispered as he leaned out slightly and around The Weep to take a momentary glance in the approaching stranger's direction. He nudged Weep gently in his side with an elbow.

"Hey, fellas...nice night, huh?" the stranger greeted. "Hey, there…what's happ'nin'….." Hey…yea, beautiful" Jack and Weep replied almost in unison. The stranger stopped a few feet from the bench and paused and took a deep breath. "Ahhhh…I love nights like this in the Fall…warm nights when it's nice…where you can get out and have a good time...there ain't nothin' like it, huh, fellas?" the stranger said with an upbeat tone. "Yes, indeed" The Weep replied. The Weep, then looked the stranger up-and-down; taking note of his nice shoes and the nice manner in which he was dressed. "You lookin' like you ready for some action, my man" The Weep said like the seasoned old-timer he was. "Huh?…oh, yea…yessir…I'm always ready for some action…that's for sure" the stranger replied after being caught off-guard gazing in the opposite direction at a couple of unescorted, attractive women who had approached the Green Mill entrance and who could be seen pausing in front of the entrance. They were digging inside their purses to pay their admission fees.

"Hey….speaking of action, you fellas…uhhh, let me ask you.." the stranger started as he looked around the streets warily and moved a little closer; propping a foot up on the edge of the bench, a respectable distance from where The Weep sat. He leaned forward with a forearm resting across his knee and spoke in a more subdued tone "…hey, where is the good weed at?…you guys know where some good stuff is?" he asked. "Yea, man" Jack spoke up almost immediately after the stranger had finished speaking. "You know where to cop some good stuff at, buddy?" the stranger asked again, turning his attention to Jack and trying to suppress his anxiousness. "Yea" Jack said more calmly and casually; tempering his response after he realized that his earlier reply sounded a bit anxious.

"You ain't the po'lice are you?" Jack asked with a serious, straight face. "Aw, man…come on, now….do I look like the police?" the stranger responded with a reasoning gesture with his hands spread, palms-open on either side and a broad grin. "Yea, you look like the po'lice" The Weep responded with a straight face. "Sho' do…" Jack chorused in. "Hahaha…hahaha..ha..hahaha" the stranger laughed. Jack and The Weep, were playing their game of "setup" Putting the strange mark on the defensive so they could have more leverage to play him for whatever they could. All good hustlers knew this angle. "Hey, guys…I swear I am *not* the police…I'll swear on a stack of bibles…hey, you guys know Trent, the bartender in the Green Mill, right?" the stranger asked. "Yea…I know him" Jack responded. "Okay, then..if you know him…you know he is a sure enough pot-head, right?…am I right?…tell me" the stranger asked. "Yea….so" Jack responded with a bit of smug indifference. "Well…he and I have smoked a ton of pot after the shows over the last couple years since I've been coming here to Jazz Night at the Mill" the stranger assured. "Hey, my man…anybody can say they smoked weed with somebody…dig?…that don't tell me nothin'" Jack reasoned forcefully to show that he was not easily swayed and to reinforce the defensive posture of the stranger. "I'll tell you what, fellas…I will pay your way in the Mill to prove that I am not a cop" the stranger offered. "Hahahaha…aw…hahaha…hey, look here, we ain't that kinda' people…we ain't tryin' to make you spend up ya' money, for nothin' brotha'-man...we ain't like that…right, Weep?" Jack laughed. "Naw, man…we ain't like that" The Weep replied facetiously.

"Uhh…what's ya' name, my man?…my name is Jack" Jack said as he broke out into a broad smile and raised his open palm to shake hands. The stranger delayed for a second but, finally stuck his hand straight out for the conventional handshake. "My name is Steve" he replied. Jack slapped his hand with the man's and proceeded to do a soul handshake that the stranger was unfamiliar with and he just let Jack guide his hand to finish the shake. "My name is Willie" The Weep offered and lazily stuck his hand out to shake the stranger's hand, as well. "Good to meet ya' Willie" the stranger replied. "So…how about that weed you're talkin' about, Jack?" the stranger asked again much more cool and calm than before. "Oh…uh, Steve…yea…I can cop some weed for you…no problem…don't have to go too far, either…it ain't no more than five minutes away…it's good, too…that ain't no lie, either…everybody cops from these people 'cause they got the most fire weed around this way…dig?" Jack said convincingly. "How much you want?" Jack prompted. The stranger paused for a while before speaking; he seemed to be pondering the situation to see what his best option might be. "Okay…look…I'll tell you what" he began after a long moment had passed. "Since you say the spot is not too far away then, how about if I just cop a few joints and if the stuff is good, then I'll buy more…fair enough?" the stranger proposed. Jack paused after digesting what the stranger had said and a mild look of annoyed frustration began to tell on his face as he seemed to be pondering the stranger's proposal. "Ahhh…that's cool…but…the stuff is good and if you spend four-fifty for three joints…'cause they *are* a buck-and-a-half a piece, then, you wastin' ya' money…you could spend another five-fifty and get three times as much in a dime bag…besides…they really don't hardly sell joints most of the time…sometimes they feel like sellin' 'em…sometimes they don't" Jack said with an air of assurance. The stranger paused momentarily, looking up to the sky for a moment as he seemed to be giving the matter deeper thought. "Yea…that's a good point, my man and it's well taken…makes a lot of sense…but, what if the stuff's not good, then what?…if I buy a dime bag,…then I would have spent my money for nothin'…see…you might know it's good, but I don't…know what I mean?" the stranger reasoned. "Yea…okay…check this here, Steve…check this…tell ya' what…do this…they don't sell no nickels….I'm tellin' you…they don't sell 'em…but…these studs know me pretty well and I believe they will break up a dime bag for me and make a nickel…they won't mind doin' that long as you spendin' money…I'll just tell 'em that I got a customer for them…they ain't gonna know who, and they don't care, either…I'll say I got somebody who ain't never had none of their weed and they wanna' try it…then…if it's good…I'll be back to cop a dime…cool?…how does that sound, Steve?" Jack offered, breaking the offer down into fine pieces of logic and covering every angle like the consummate hustler; just as he had always done when negotiating deals and hustling in the streets. The stranger paused only a very short moment and his eyes seemed to light up as if it had dawned on him how much sense Jack's idea made. "That's cool, Jack…that's sure enough cool…that will work…you know what? …yea…two joints is three dollars…three is four-fifty…a nickel bag is five…good…now, you say it's good…well, we will see 'cause I'm gonna give you some money to cop…then, when you come back…I'm gonna give you a joint and a few dollars…how's that?" the stranger offered as he began to seem much more relaxed. A broad smile began to spread across his face. "Yea, Steve…that's square business, my man…sho' 'nough…yea…that's cool with me…a joint and a few dollars for coppin'…I'll go for that….yea…come on with it and I'll make that move" Jack said as the stranger reached into his back pocket for his wallet.

"Hey..hey, Steve…do me a favor, bro'…sit down on the bench before you hand me the money" Jack said as he began to speak in a wary tone and cutting his eyes up and down Broadway. "Why..wha…what's wrong?" Steve answered with the voice and facial expression of confusion. "Just sit down, man…'cause I don't wanna let any of these Slick Boys see you handin' me no money…if they happen to pass by and see you handin' me some cash…'specially with the way you dressed…they gonna be spottin' us all night and circle the block and try to ride down on us later..I don't wanna be bothered with them stoppin' and searchin' us..see what I'm sayin?" Jack reasoned. "You're talkin' about the police, right?" Steve asked. "Yea, man…the po'lice!" Jack said emphatically. "I don't understand...why you worried about them…you don't have anything on you do you?" Steve asked. "Nope" Jack replied. "You got warrants or something?" Steve added. "Nope" Jack replied again. "Then, what you worried about?" Steve reasoned. "'Cause I know them motherfuckas!….I know these streets…I have been busted by them before…one time, over a year ago…I was doin' the same damned thing I'm doin' now…talkin' to a white stud right out on the streets…he handed me some money in full public view to go cop for him…I takes the money…go cop, and I'll be damned if about ten minutes later them 'som-bitches didn't ride down on us…took the studs weed and locked both of us up…see, I saw 'em go by the first time just as this guy was handin' me the money…they saw that…then they laid in the bushes, then re-rounded on our ass…spent the night in jail…that's how I know and that's why I say sit down…now, you want the weed or not?" Jack said forcefully. "Yea, I want the weed" Steve assured. "Then sit down..take a seat…relax" Jack said as he segued into a lower, softer tone at the end. "Hahah..hahaha" Jack suddenly began laughing out loud, which took the stranger aback as his eyes grew wider while he stared at Jack and wondered why he was laughing. "huhuhaha..uhhh" the stranger stammered; trying to laugh along but, he was too confused by Jack's laughing to get into the spirit of it. Finally, he sat and began to look around somewhat warily himself after Jack had put the idea of police watching them in his head. "Here's five and when you come back I'll give you yours for coppin'…that OK?" Steve said.

"Okay, my man…I'm on my way right now…hey Weep, hang out with our man 'til I get back…I ain't gonna be long…okay?" Jack said as he got up and left the stranger and The Weep sitting side-by-side on the bench. "Yea…go 'head on, Jack…we'll just shoot the breeze 'til ya' get back, man" The Weep replied, and with that, Jack headed back around the corner towards the Arms to cop. Jack arrived in front of the Arms and all of the same few men he had seen earlier were still hanging around at the entrance. "My, man…you still holdin' that weed?" Jack asked the man who had given him the sales pitch for weed when he was leaving the building earlier. "Yea…I still got it, bro'…what you wanna cop?" the weed man asked, sounding more than ready to deal. "Yea…dig this…let me holla' at you" Jack said as he began to step away from the group and out of the building's walkway entrance and back out onto the streets a few yards. All hustlers spoke the same language in the streets and the Weed Man understood that Jack wanted to speak to him privately; and so, he followed Jack back out onto the sidewalk and they walked back several yards or so, far enough to be out of ear-shot of the other men still standing in front of the building "Hey, guy…dig this here" Jack started "You sellin' any nickels?" Jack asked hopefully. "Hmmm…..ah…uh…not really, man…we been just sellin' dimes…we don't usually break up no dime to make a nickel….we just do that for our best customers…people that's been spendin' with us on a regular basis…see…that's how we do…don't none of the weed people nowadays sell no nickels…very few…and if they got fire weed like we got….they sho' 'nough ain't sellin' no nickels…you know how it go, player…you know…"" the Weed Man explained in the street hustler language that Jack lived, breathed and understood so well. Jack paused after the Weed Man had spoken and seemed to be thinking about what to say next for a come-back. "Okay…okay, brotha', I can dig what you just said…understand me?….I dig what you sayin'…but, do me this one favor….'cause I'm hustlin', bro'…sho' 'nough hustlin'…I'm coppin' for somebody else and I need to show 'em that you got good weed 'cause they say if it's good, they gonna cop more…dig?....just this one time, player…I'll be back…see…I don't really know how your weed is…see…I don't know how good it is but, I'm tellin' the person that I'm coppin' for that it's fire…see…come on…break that nickel down for me…cool?" Jack pleaded. The Weed Man paused and pondered for a moment. The furrowing of his brow and the concentration on his face told Jack that he did not really care for his compromise but, he did not seem especially indifferent, either. As the silent moment passed, Jack could see a more relieved, comfortable expression come over the Weed Man's face as though, somehow, the idea had lost the bad taste to his palate that it had at the beginning. After he thought it through during that silent moment, his sour expression had suddenly turned sunny and at the end of his thinking he had found a rainbow in the proposition. "Hey, bro'…like I said before, we don't do that…break down dime bags to make nickels….normally, we don't…hey..I'll tell you what…you say ya' people gonna cop if they like our weed…that's what you said, right?' the Weed man asked. "Yea" Jack replied with an anticipating focus into the Weed Man's face as he spoke. "Okay, player…I'm gonna take you at ya' word this time…I'll do it just this once…if you don't come back to cop anytime tonight…if you don't stick to ya' word then, I'll have to cut you short…no more favors…dig me?…I'm serious, understand me, player?" the Weed Man said with conviction. "Yea…yea..I'll stick to my word…straight up…no lie" Jack replied. "Okay, then…you wait for me out here…I got to go to my spot in the buildin' and break the bag down…it won't take long…alright, brotha'?" the Weed Man assured. "Okay…but, my man…dig this" Jack started as he walked up close to the Weed Man and began talking in his low conning voice. "Treat me right..okay, man..'cause these people lookin' for a decent bag….look out for me, alright?" he implored. "I got ya' bro'…just be cool…you covered…be back in a few…" the Weed Man said as he walked back up the walkway and through the building entrance and disappeared inside after Jack handed him the five dollar bill. Jack just stood out on the sidewalk, casually looking around and after nearly ten minutes had passed, the Weed Man came strolling back outside from the entrance of the Arms and walked over to Jack. He glanced around the immediate vicinity and looked warily back in the direction he had come from before he shook Jack's hand and said in a staged tone of voice "It was good seein' you again, cous'….I'll see you around…be cool, now" Jack felt the small enveloped package transfer from the Weed Man's palm to his own and he immediately cuffed the package and stuck his hand in his pocket and turned and began to step casually away from the area toward Wilson Avenue.

Jack walked a half-block south of the Arms and turned left on the next side street, Leland. He passed one two-flat building and entered the next. He was familiar with the inside of the building and knew there was a stairwell leading to the basement that was usually quiet. He had gone there several times in the past to take a drink, duck the police or hide for a short while after making a sting. He walked down toward the basement to the bottom of the stairwell. Jack liked this spot because it allowed him to hear the creaky entrance door open and warn him of anyone entering the building. There was also an apartment door just left of the bottom of the stairs and there was a long hallway to the right of the apartment door that led to an exit door at the rear of the basement. He pulled out the reefer papers that he kept with him most of the time. He sat on the next to last step and began to roll joints. After he rolled all the weed into nine joints, he wrapped six of them into a cellophane cigarette package wrapper that he had picked up off the ground and tucked it safely into his pants pocket. He put the other three back into the small manila envelope that the weed came in. He had done it all in about five minutes. As soon as he was done, he got up from the steps and walked back up the stairs from the basement and after he was outside, used a different route by continuing east a half-block to Magnolia and turning left. He strolled up Magnolia back to Lawrence Avenue.

Jack turned the corner where the Green Mill was and he saw Steve sitting on the bench where he had left him. He and The Weep were still sitting on the bench near the bus stop. As he walked toward them, he could see them in the near distance turning to look in his direction. He strolled over and stopped. "Hey, Jack…finally made it back, huh?…I was hoping you didn't get busted or something" Steve said with sense of relief. "Yea…." Jack said very casually and did not say anything for several seconds as he sat down on the bench alongside The Weep. "Well, how did you come out?....did you get it?" Steve asked rather anxiously. "Hell, yea…" Jack replied, seemingly a little winded. "The stud didn't have no nickel bags…I almost begged him to make a nickel for me…I told him that if he broke down a dime to make me a nickel, that I would be back to buy a dime…maybe more, dependin' on how good his weed was" Jack explained. "But, he said he didn't have but a couple of dimes that were about to be sold in just a few minutes…he had to go and make up some more dime bags…said he would have a bunch of dimes made up in about an hour…all he had left was a half dozen joints from his personal stash..all I could do was buy these three joints from him for four-fifty…dig?...that's the best I could do…It took me so long 'cause I was tryin' to talk him into makin' a nickel bag…he just wouldn't go for it…said his money comes too slow sellin' nickels and joints…he didn't even wanna sell me the joints…I had to keep askin' him until he finally gave in" Jack added, making it sound as though the experience was so trying. "Hey, where can we go to check the weed out, then?…I'm ready to get myself a buzz going…I need to get high, man…where can we go?" Steve asked, acting squirmy and anxious like someone who needed to use the restroom. "Hey, Steve…slow ya' role, baby…slow ya' role…everything's gonna be cool…dig this…let's walk around the corner here and go to my special little spot…it's sweet…cain't nobody hardly see you from the streets…it's closed in, too so the wind won't be blowin' up in there, either…come on, Steve…it's that little gangway between the liquor store and the parking garage…let's go" Jack said as he began to step toward the curb to lead them across Broadway to the east side of it. "Hey, and by-the-way, my man, the fifty-cents you had left over, I bought some papers…is that cool? Jack asked. "Oh…uh…yea, that's cool…I just hope this weed is as good as you say it is…when we get there…I'll give you those bucks that I said I would give you….alright?" Steve promised. "Cool, my man…no hurry…I just want you to check this weed out…I believe you gonna like it…the Weed Man said it was fire…so we'll see in a minute" Jack went on.

The three of them crossed the streets and walked the short distance to the narrow spot between Saxony Liquor Store and the North Shore parking garage. Jack led them up into the dark gangway that had light at the back end where it was open and they could walk all the way out to the alley. There was an open space that had the garbage dumpsters that were at the back of each business surrounding it, and where they could walk around the back of the Goodyear Tire business that faced Broadway. This spot was good for whenever Jack would have to duck the police or make a quick getaway after a hustle. This was the reason that Jack liked to do his business here. Jack stopped in halfway into the gangway and leaned back against one of the metal rails that was on either side of the narrow space. He reached inside his pants pocket and pulled out the small manila envelope with the three joints in it. "Here ya' go, Steve…fire up, baby…get that buzz goin'" Jack urged. With that, he handed the manila package to Steve and watched him as he anxiously pulled one of the joints out of the envelope, then lit it with his fancy cigarette lighter that had a flashy silver hue to it and that caught Jack's eye right away. He had an urge to comment on the beauty of the cigarette lighter but, did not because his mind was already working on designs that he had made on it. He could tell that it had value above and beyond most any of the other fancy lighters he had seen in the past. After Steve lit the joint, he made the usual sucking noise as Jack and The Weep looked on. Steve grimaced and blew smoke out after holding it in. "Humph" he groaned after the first toke and then paused with the joint dangling low at his side as he pinched it between his thumb and forefinger. He toked again with the same inhaling and exhaling routine. He paused again afterward. Jack and Weep just stood quietly looking at the man kind of indifferently because they were drinkers and not weed smokers.

So, they were detached from the get-high ritual that Steve was going through. “Whooowee…damn….this weed is pretty good, fellas…wanna toke?” Steve said as he handed the joint to Jack. Jack didn’t smoke weed but, he did not want to seem like he was a square, either. So, he took the joint and pinched it in just the same manner that Steve had and took a drag off of it; not really inhaling that much of it. He exaggerated the sucking sound. He dared not let Steve know that he was not a smoker. “Pretty damn good, man just like you said, Jack…pretty good” Steve said, breaking out into a broad smile that told Jack that he had won the trust of this stranger. It was a smile that seemed to say that Steve was no longer wary of Jack and The Weep. That he did not have to worry and he could trust them. “Hey, Jack…tell ya’ what, my good man…”” Before he could finish Jack broke in and started chuckling out loud “ Aw…damn…did you hear that Weep?…it’s my *good* man, now…check him out…my *good* man…hahahah…hahahah…hahaha…first, it was my man…now, it’s my *good* man…look at him, Weep…he buzzin’ already…see…Steve…I told you, baby…it’s fire…just like I said..hahaha…hahaha…”” Jack went on laughing and smiling. This was all a part of his act. “Okay, Jack…you were right…here you go…just like I said…but…can I change one part of what I said….can I give you four dollars for goin’ for me instead of throwin’ in a joint…how’s that?” Steve proposed. “Aw…baby boy…no sweat…that’s cool with me…joint woulda’ been nice…but, I’ll take the cash…I like weed but, you go ahead and get high, man….it ain’t no thang…dig?” Jack assured the happy stranger. Steve pulled out his wallet and gave Jack a five dollar bill. “Here you go, Jack…you owe me a buck” he said as he handed Jack the five dollar bill. “Hey, Steve…check this, man…you gonna be around most of the night for the show, right?” Jack asked “Yes” Steve replied “Then let me get change a little later on so I can give you that dollar…cool?” Jack asked with an inflection that was soliciting favor. “Sure, man…don’t worry about it…I’ll probably be here all night…catch me later” he went on with a relieved, happy spirit that seemed to be climbing with his high. “Okay, you got your buzz goin’…now…what about the other dimes you said you was gonna get?...you still wanna cop, right?” Jack asked. “Oh, yea…you damned right…I got to have some more of this stuff to last me…all I’m gonna do is go back in and have another beer…that weed made me thirsty….after I have a beer and relax for a spell, then, I'll get you to cop a couple of dime bags...how's that?" Steve said with assurance. "Okay…okay…alright, then...you go ahead and enjoy ya' self…relax…me and Weep ain't goin' nowhere....we'll be out here most all night" Jack said. "Alright, then" Steve replied.

"Hey…but answer me one question" Steve said with a slightly furrowed brow. "Yea...what is it?" Jack asked. "Well…he said his name was Willie but, you call him Weep…what *is* his name?….why do you call him Weep?" Steve asked inquisitively. "Hey...I know but, let him tell you…you might get a kick outa' this..""" Jack said, seemingly leaving a curiosity hanging in the air. "Yea, Steve…let me tell you all about it" Weep started …my real name *is* Willie but, my nick name is Willie-the-Weep…I got that nick name when I was a boy…I was born in the south and we used to play in the creek near our place where I was born in Tupelo, Mississippi…I had three older brothers…we would play games around this muddy creek after school almost every day…grade school, ya' know…yea...after we got through playin' at the creek, we would race all the way home to our mother's good home cookin'..now I'm talkin' 'bout some sho' 'nough' down home southern cookin' and my mother, like a lot of our mothers, was a damned good cook…us Moss boys would be thinkin' about her cookin' all day long at school….anyway, we'd walk home from school about three miles….then, when we got to the creek..it was too early for dinner so, we played around…I was the youngest of us four brothers …the oldest brother, Jesse, was out of school so, he wasn't with us…anyway, when dinner time came…we could hear this old hand bell that our mother used to have…at dinner time she would step out on the porch and ring that bell about ten times…we would hear that bell from miles away…it would be faint…but, you could hear it 'cause it was pretty quiet in the south…anyway…we would hear that bell…then, we would all get to runnin' like bats outa' hell…we would race back home…well…my other two brothers was way faster than me and they would just wear my ass out tryin' to keep up with them…by the time I got home, papa would be done eatin' and be sittin' on the porch…my two brothers would be at the table and started eatin' already…and my mother always made somethin' good for desert 'long with dinner…I'm talkin' 'bout cakes…peach cobbler or bread puddin', blueberry pie…delicious home cookin..anyway…they would both be at the table before me…nobody else at the table but them…they be done stole all the dessert…I would come in way behind them and go straight to the table tryin' to make sure they left me some o' that dessert…but, them greedy bastards would hide and keep it all...whole cakes or pies and hide it from me…while I'm at the table tryin' to do this…I'd be askin' "what did mama cook for dessert?" and they wouldn't answer me…just keep on eatin'…then, when they got tired of me askin'…they would call mama to the table and say "mama…Willie standin' 'round the table with his nasty self…mud all over him botherin' us while we eatin…make him get away from us…then my mama would come to the table and see me all dirty and she would shoo me away…"get yourself 'way from my kitchen table, boy with all that mud on you…go wash yourself up before you sit down and eat…now mind me…you hear?...wash up good, too…" she would say…well, I used to wonder why they was so clean when they left the creek…they would wash up at the creek before we ran home for dinner…after I saw how they was doin' I tried to stay clean…but, I would get too much caught up in the fun we would have around the creek and still get dirty…anyway…when my mother told me to clean up, I would start cryin' boo-hoo..boo-hoo 'cause I know, I ain't gonna get much dessert and they would get two or three helpin's apiece, then steal the rest and hide it…mama would make plenty...but, they would eat plenty and steal plenty, too, then tell her it was all gone just to be mean…ya' see…in the South, you ate all you wanted…it was just our way…you never denied nobody somethin' to eat…you let 'em eat all they wanted and that's the way our mother was…if us boys ate everything on the damned table---it was okay…she would just cook more the next day…mothers cooked every day in the South…anyway…my brothers started callin' me "Willie-the-Weep because of that….it stuck" The Weep explained. Steve had sat and listened as he stayed quietly fixated on The Weep telling his little story.

"I'll be damned…and you're still Willie-The Weep after all this time!" haha..aaa…hahahahaha…Okay, Willie-the Weep…I enjoyed your story…hahahaha..'''' Steve chuckled out loud, seeming to be more loose, happy and care-free than at any time in the brief moments that he had come to know Jack and The Weep.

“Alright, guys…like I said…I’m goin’ in and relax until this buzz wears off…I’ll be back out later on to have you go get some more weed…you said you weren’t going anywhere…right, Jack?” Steve asked and waited for assurance. “We’ll still be out here…don’t worry about it…go ‘head on and enjoy the show” Jack said as he waved Steve away. With that, Steve entered the Green Mill.

Okay, Jack…what did you get him for?.....It ain’t like you to not get nothin’ out of the deal…what’d you rip him off for?” The Weep asked, as he held a knowingly mischievous smile. “Shiiit…you know me, Weep…I gots to get mine…got some joints” Jack responded with a cool and casual air. “And I ain’t done, yet…you know he gettin’ ready to get tore down before the night’s over…I’m gonna get that lighter, too before it’s over…watch me” Jack said with confidence. “Yea…he tryin’ to play like he ain’t got that much money…but, you can tell he got some kinda’ money ‘cause he sharper than a broke-dick-dog” The Weep said. “Sho-ya-right, Weep ‘cause I *have* seen him all pissy-faced before on Jazz Nights at the Mill…yea, high as hell…I just ain’t never had a chance to play him for nothin’ until now” Jack went on. The night wore on and Jack and Weep continued to hang around the front of the Green Mill, passing the time cracking jokes and laughing as they usually did whenever they were hanging out together.

Finally, they saw Steve come back outside accompanied by the two attractive ladies that he had been gazing at when the women entered the Green Mill earlier that night. “Look-a-there, Weep…ain’t that them two slick-ass ‘hoes Verna and Connie?” Jack asked rhetorically. “Hell, yea…that’s them bitches…them ‘hoes a’ steal the sweet’nin’ outa sugar” The Weep said. “Aw, shit…they got our boy, too…they gettin’ ready to fuck up our money, man…shit!” Jack said with frustration. “When them ‘hoes get through with his ass, won’t be nothin’ left to get” The Weep said. “I didn’t pay them ‘hoes no attention when they went in” Jack said. “Me neither…they dressed up so good tonight…better than I ever seen ‘em dressed…that’s why I couldn’t recognize ‘em from a distance.” The Weep said. “Me neither” Jack added. Steve and the two women made a left turn from the Green Mill entrance and began to walk north on Broadway and had only walked a short distance before they passed Jack and the Weep sitting on the bench.

"Hey, Jack" Steve spoke out as he passed the bench with one of the women on each arm as he was smiling and looking to be in a festive mood. "Jack…I'll be talking to you when I come back, buddy…alright…business, Okay?" Steve added. "Yea, bro'…cool" Jack said casually as he peered over his shoulder while he sat, watching Steve and the women pass by. The women and Jack cast a wary eye toward one another without acknowledging their familiarity with each other. They all knew the code of the game---to not give one another away. "Look at that shit" Jack said as he watched the two attractive black women walk arm-in-arm with their white male acquaintance; wishing and hoping at the same time that they did not spoil his plans to play the stranger for what he could. They walked further up the street, then stopped as Steve opened the doors to his parked car; a very nice Buick Park Avenue. "Damn…why them 'hoes have to show up now!" Jack said with the same frustrated tone. Jack was thinking about the street hustlers' code of never messing up another hustler's hustle---no matter who the hustler was, prostitutes, pimps, rough-hustlers---it didn't matter. You never tried to get in on somebody else's hustle---at least not knowingly. Sometimes, it was fair game to hustle a mark like Steve as the two women were doing now. It was a tricky situation. Jack had to adhere to the street code. The women did not know that he was trying to hustle Steve and he could not warn Steve against the two women because he could not prove that they were hustling him and not just having a good time with him. If he did warn Steve about the women, they could, in turn, warn Steve about Jack, and no one would make a hustle and he and the women would become enemies. Jack knew that this was not good for him if he wanted to continue to hustle in the streets and not have the women turn against him and have their friends go against him, as well. Their friends might be people he copped weed or "Ts and Blues from. He didn't know; they might be a relative or someone he already knew. Jack was very savvy and had to play it cool and not say a word and let things develop as they would. The women knew the code, too and had to adhere to it like any other hustler. If they did not, their reputations in the streets would suffer.

"Hey, Jack…he comin' back to send you to cop that weed…just get him for all you can then" The Weep suggested. "How the hell I'm gonna' do that, Weep…he wanna buy a coupla' dimes…he gonna give me even money, then give me a few dollars for coppin' when I come back…I cain't make much outa' that…"" Jack said with mild irritation. "Hey…I know…almost forgot, I got this hash with me…that's what I'll do, when he comes back…I'm gonna talk up this hash on his ass…only thing is, I'm gonna make him think that somebody else is sellin' it….yea…I'll say that The Weed Man got some fire hash…I'll sell him that script…yea…talk him into coppin' some hash..hell yea, baby...Weep..look like we might come out pretty good after all..hahaha!" Jack said as he chuckled with glee at how the idea seemed to magically come altogether in his mind. Jack and The Weep sat on the bus stop bench and talked about how they were going to play Steve when he came back to send Jack to cop the weed. They peered up the street several cars away between the other parked cars to where Steve's sleek automobile was parked. They could see the heads of Steve and the women sitting inside the car toking on the joints. They had sat almost half an hour before Jack and Weep could finally see the car doors swinging open and the three of them getting out. "Be cool, Weep…here they come" Jack warned as he gently nudged Weep with an elbow. Steve and the girls walked back in their direction much more slowly and subdued than when they had passed earlier. Their postures and gait told Jack and Weep that the weed they had smoked was now in full effect. As they drew closer, Jack could see that they were all smiling, but moving almost in slow-motion toward them.

"Hey, girls…go ahead on in…I got to take care of some business with my man here…okay?…I'll be there in a little bit" Steve said, as the women walked ahead. He walked over to Jack and The Weep sitting on the bench. "You ready to cop those dimes for me now, Jack?" he asked. "It ain't no thang, Steve…I'm ready when you're ready" Jack replied. "Now, don't reach in your pocket and hand me no money right now…you know how I feel about that…remember what I told you…I don't wanna' get busted…sit down…sit down before you hand it to me…and before I take it from you, I'm lookin' around…be cool, baby..dig me?" Jack said in his rhythmic, street savvy tone. Steve complied and sat on the bench on the end near Jack as he looked around the streets before going into his pocket to pull out his wallet; discretely holding it down low and turning his torso to the opposite side from Jack and The Weep as he picked some bills from his wallet. "How about getting me three dime bags?" Steve said as he turned back around after putting his wallet away and handing Jack a crisp twenty and ten dollar bill. "I know your fee has got to be more, the more I buy, so I'm giving you ten when you get back…is that good?" Steve said. "That's cool bro', Steve…that's cool…"" Jack said non-chalantly, not giving Steve the satisfaction of seeing him act excited because he was giving him more money to cop. This was the way hustlers behaved with marks. Jack looked around the streets again as he had come to do instinctively before taking the money from Steve. "Hey, Steve…look here, man…when I was coppin' them joints from the Weed Man the first time, I saw some dudes buyin' some hash from him…they had already bought some earlier today.. …man..they was ravin' to me about how good it was…they said it was fire, baby…I could tell it musta' been 'cause I know these studs from around the streets…they are some "get-high" connoisseurs, baby…sho' 'nough…and anytime you see them chumps goin' wild over somebody's dope…you can bet it's fire…my advice…pick up a chunk of it…he is sellin' fifteen dollar pieces…I'm tellin' you, boy…don't pass it up…hahaha…I ain't lyin'…you don't wanna' miss out, baby!" Jack raved on, giving one of his more stellar conning performances, gesturing with his body movements and facial expressions. This was the kind of act he would put on to persuade marks to listen to what he had to say---this was about money; how he made his hustle. He had to be good if he wanted to eat, sleep and get high. His survival hinged on these kinds of encounters. He maintained a care-free, casual facade. But, inside he was hoping that it would all pay off. "Aw, man…I don't wanna' mess with nothin' else when I know the marijuana is cool…"" Steve said looking a lot higher now than he had at first. When Jack finally sensed in that moment how high Steve really was, an inward feeling of elation and joy seemed to leap up within him; his mark was now high and less rational. This was a lot easier, now…he just had to get busy and go to work on him. Jack stepped up closer to Steve and began to talk low in his conning voice.

"Steve…Steve….Steve…look…listen to me, man…hold on, now…I'm ya' boy…I'm lookin' out for you…have I let you down, yet?…did I look out for you real good, so far?…huh?..huh?" Jack said in his most persuasive tone of voice as he forced the issue by getting up almost face-to-face with Steve. "Yea….yea..uh-uh..yea you looked out for me" Steve said meekly as he had begun to stammer slightly and have that ever-so-slight sway in his body that people who were high often had. "Okay, then…trust me…if I tell you it's good…then goddamnit!...it's good, okay…now, stop bullshittin' and give me fifteen more dollars so I can go on and get all this shit…you'll be gettin' high into next week offa' this hash, baby…no shit…I ain't lyin" Jack went on and then held his hand out firmly. "Uhh…" Steve started "Uh..uh…uh…my ass!...give me the damn money, man!" Jack shot back, his hand still held out. "Okay...you say it's good…it must be good…okay…hold on, alright?" Steve said as he walked over to the closed audio storefront next to the Green Mill to go into his wallet. He turned his back and began to rummage through his wallet for the money. He seemed to be fumbling. All night, Steve had been keeping his cool, but, Jack's aggressive, albeit benign style of talking to him was slightly unnerving; even though Steve seemed insulated from everything else because he was feeling good from his high. Finally, Steve walked back over and past Jack standing behind the bench and sat down on it and turned back around to ask Jack "You ready to go?...here it is…"" "Now, that's what I'm talkin' about…yea…see that Weep….the man listened to me…he remembered…yea…I can work with somebody who listens…he remembered not to hand me the money standin' up in the middle of the streets so everybody and their damned grandmomma could see what was goin' on….man sat down on the bench just like I asked him…I value my freedom…see…he understands that.."" Jack rambled on sounding kind of "preachy" Jack walked over after his little diatribe and sat down on the bench beside Steve. He did his usual scan of the streets before telling Steve "okay…give it to me" He took the money and walked back to the audio store entranceway and turned his back and counted the money before he turned back around and announced "I'm goin' to cop, y'all…don't go nowhere, Weep...Steve, I'll be right back, my man…just be cool…." He stepped away at a hurried pace. Twenty minutes had passed before Jack reappeared on the corner in front of the Green Mill. He saw the Weep standing near the bus bench. “Hey, Weep…our boy ain’t came back out yet?” Jack asked. “Naw, man…he been in there ever since you left” The Weep replied. “Okay…he can stay his monkey-ass in there for all I care…if he don’t never come out…I got me forty-five dollars…dig” Jack said rather sprightly. Jack felt good about the way things were going and he began to feel a little hope that things might get even get better as the night went on. All of a sudden, they heard a voice speak out.

“Damn right!...I get the most…I spent money in the club!” Jack and Weep turned their heads around to look behind them and they could see two rough-hustler types crossing Broadway at the light, coming from the east side of Broadway to the west side of it to where they were. The two were having a mild difference of opinion. “Aw, shit!...I’ll be damned…look who’s comin’, Weep…them fool-ass brothers!…daaammn!” Jack said with utter disgust. “Yea…here they come…that damned Tyrone and his brother, Calvin…them boys crazy ‘na betzy bug..and always tryin’ to play on somebody…let’s go” The Weep chimed in with the same measure of disgust. “What’s goin’ down, y’all!” Tyrone yelled out as he stopped several yards short of where The Weep and Jack stood near the bus stop bench. He began to do a little dance move to the Jazz beat emanating from the Green Mill doorway. It was the kind of jazz music that was strictly for listening pleasure. But, Tyrone’s mind was not in the best of health and so, he was oblivious to such nuances. “Hey…check this shit out, y’all…see that shit?…dig this” Tyrone said as he continued dancing while his brother, Calvin stepped back a few feet to check out Tyrone’s dance moves. He began to bob his head to the music and then broke into a little jig of his own. “Yea…get down…hahahaha…what the fuck you doin’, nigga?…the cha-cha..huh?…you cain’t fuck with my moves…watch this” Tyrone said to his brother who was doing his own out-of-control dance several feet away. Tyrone and his brother Calvin were fixtures around the neighborhood. They were pure alcoholics who, some years back, had fancied themselves as players. But, the game caught up with them just as it had so many others who thought they could survive their street lifestyles. Tyrone had been a good-looking man several years back. He was tall and dressed well and was very much favored by the ladies at that time; now, drugs and alcohol, over the years, had made him a shadow of his former self; he lived transiently; sleeping in abandoned buildings at night and roaming the streets during the day; he had accumulated numerous scars on his face; no doubt, some from various violent encounters and others from drunken injuries in the unforgiving streets of Uptown. The two brothers continued to dance wildly; swirling about with intermittent comments and outbursts of laughter as they danced maniacally around the small area of sidewalk in front of the Green Mill; it lasted about thirty seconds before they stopped and one placed his arm across the shoulder of the other and they shuffled wildly together to the bus stop bench and fell, sprawling upon it, laughing to themselves at the crazy fun they were having. Jack and Weep just stood back a few yards away looking at them. Jack gazed at them silently and it all seemed kind of pitiful to him because he knew their history. He knew that they were the street types that no one favored and that no one really wanted to be around; although he had wound up unintentionally in their company at various times in the past. Several years back, before the two brothers had become so pitiful, they were scandalous; not to be trusted and not very well liked because they were so underhanded and dirty out in the streets; occasionally, in the past, each brother had sustained some injury through the violence of someone they had double-crossed. When they were younger, they had been ruthless and they sold a lot of "wolf tickets" They had two other brothers, Pete and Smokey. When they stuck together in the past and before they were full-fledged drug addicts and alcoholics, they were respected and feared. Now, they were only despised by those who knew them and their history or those who had some kind of negative experience with them. Jack had been seeing these two brothers on a regular basis roaming the streets because they usually had no place to stay. Their other two brothers were heavy drinkers but, did not use drugs; they had places to stay and both of them lived with their girlfriends; they were not down-and-out like Calvin and Tyrone. Jack understood why they were acting so crazy. He knew that the life they were leading must be pure hell; and most times when he saw them on the streets, they were scuffling to survive; and if they were sober, they seemed miserable. So, he understood why they stayed high. Tyrone had been without a place to stay most of the last three years. He did nothing besides drink. He barely even hustled anymore. He did not try to dress decently at all. He seemed to have become void of all self-respect; beaten-down by the harsh existence on the Uptown streets. His brother, Calvin had served three years in prison and had gotten out about two years ago. He had been badly stabbed in '74 by a drug dealer. He had a couple of operations a year ago and was in the hospital for about two months back in the late winter.

"Ahahaha…aaahahaha..hahahaha..''" they laughed together, still sprawled out on the bench. "Hey, Tyrone…let me hit that bug juice, man…hand it here" Calvin asked as Tyrone sat up on the bench with a big, goofy smile and looking wild-eyed. "Here, Calvin" he said as he reached in his back pocket to pull out a half-pint bottle of gin. Calvin grabbed the bottle and turned it up in the air as he laid down halfway on the bench, partly propping himself up with his elbow. A police car passed by going north on Broadway and as it did, the policeman driving glanced over to see Calvin turning the bottle up. Jack and Weep were standing a few yards in back of the bench where the brothers were and Jack commented.

"See there….that's just the type of shit they do to make me not wanna be around their crazy asses…they drawin' heat on us doin' all this crazy shit…you see how he wasn't even lookin' or nothin'…just turned the damned bottle up and drank…now, I just hope that squad car don't come back around because of them" Jack said with a tone of disgust. "Hey..y'all…the fuck's goin' on around here…huh?" Calvin yelled out, looking lost and disoriented as he gazed over in Jack and Weep's direction from where he sat. He was high and seemed to be spaced-out as he gazed around wild-eyed. He turned to his brother next to him and started talking. He mumbled incoherently. "Fuck you talkin' 'bout Calvin?…speak up, nigga'…I cain't hear what you sayin'" Tyrone said in an irritated tone and sounding high, as well. "I said…is you still got the money?" Calvin said out loud, raising his voice and slightly slurring his speech. "Don't worry about it…hell, yea…I still got it!" Tyrone responded forcefully. "Give me five dollars" Calvin asked. Tyrone heard him but, ignored him. Several moments of silence passed. Tyrone did not respond, probably knowing that his brother was too high to really know what he was saying; or even to know what he wanted to do with five dollars. "Ty…Ty…hey, Ty..""" Calvin said. "Ty…Ty..""" he said again. "What-the-fuck-do-you-want!" Tyrone yelled out angrily with a stuttering pause between each word. "I need some money" Calvin replied meekly. "Man, you don't need no fuckin' money!…money for what?…you just had a good meal about an hour ago…you had plenty of drinks tonight…you don't smoke weed…what the fuck you want it for!" Tyrone argued. "I wanna' get a six pack" Calvin said mildly. "You already too high…six pack'll put you on your ass!...you know that, right?…right?" Tyrone said staring his brother in the face. Calvin paused and bucked his eyes with a wild looking stare at the way his brother was looking at him. His upper body swayed slightly with intoxication. Finally, Calvin sat up straight on the bench. "That's alright" he said wearily and drifted into silence before slumping back down on the bench.

Not quite an hour had passed when Steve came stepping out of the Green Mill. He looked over to see Jack and The Weep standing almost in the exact spots that he had left them near the bus stop bench. He stood in front of the entrance momentarily. Then, a broad smile began to spread across his face. He walked over to Jack and The Weep. "You got it right? He asked Jack. "Damn skippy…I went to get it didn't I?" Jack replied in a somewhat cocky manner.

"Hey…tell ya' what...forget about going back to that spot we went last time…I'm gonna' have Trent to let you guys in…I'll tell him you are guests of mine…then, we can go into the restroom inside…how does that sound?" Steve offered with a big smile. Jack looked back over at the bench where the two brothers were now sleeping side-by-side. "Hell, yea…that sounds real cool to me, man…we can get away from this crazy shit out here…you game, Weep?" Jack said. "You doggone right…I ain't been in that club for quite a while…I could dig some Jazz music right about now" the Weep responded. The three men walked inside the Green Mill and Steve walked over to Trent the bartender and said something to him and raised his arm to make a motion toward Jack and the Weep. Trent leaned over the bar counter to listen to him and Jack could see him afterward shaking his head in the affirmative. Steve walked back over to them. "Everything is cool, fellas…let's go to the back where me and the ladies have a booth" he said. Jack and Weep followed Steve as he strode energetically through the crowd past the row of occupied booths along the wall and stopped at the booth where the two women, Verna and Connie sat smiling and looking relaxed and seeming to be enjoying themselves. "Verna…Connie…these are my friends…Jack and Willie" Steve said.

"Hey..how y'all doin'?", Jack greeted. "Hello" each of the girls greeted, pretending not to know Jack. They were well acquainted with Jack from talking to him on rare occasions in the past out on the streets. They knew Weep too but, they did not know his name and called him "pops" perhaps, because of the very noticeable gray in his hair and beard. The comfortable look on their faces seemed to disappear as Jack and The Weep sat in the booth across from them. Before they were completely seated, one of the girls gave a look to the other that was telling and knowing and they turned back to The Weep and Jack sitting across from them and they each flashed a phony smile. The women had been quite comfortable playing their parlor games with Steve up until that point; knowing what they had planned for him. But, now they were in the company of Jack and The Weep. They did not feel threatened by The Weep but, they were very wary of Jack because they knew that he was a relentless hustler and that their plans for Steve had become compromised by his presence. They knew, too that Jack was playing Steve just as they were and they would have to play everything by ear from this point on. "Ladies, ladies…y'all lookin' mighty fly this evenin'…what's poppin'?" Jack asked with a broad smile. "Ain't nothin' goin on…we just havin' a good time with this handsome gentleman right here" Verna said, as she reached over to Steve standing next to her as she sat in the aisle seat of the booth and grabbed his hand to hold and caress it to emphasis her point and conjuring up all the charm she could. She knew how crafty Jack was and how he played the game. She knew his smile and friendly demeanor was well played and phony as a three-dollar bill. He was good when he wanted to be charming and it was hard for anyone to tell how sincere he really was. If you were not perceptive and street-wise he could easily suck you in---especially a woman like herself who had begun to like his looks some time ago as they had become acquainted while crossing paths in the streets.

The atmosphere inside the Green Mill on Jazz Nights always held the sophisticated liveliness that true Jazz fans loved for an evening of fun and relaxation. There were the nattily dressed hardcore Jazz fans---the cool cats, who were more than just casual listeners; a number of those types sprinkled the bar and booths of about seventy or so patrons on these nights. There were a number of attractive, nicely dressed ladies; some were escorted and others were with friends. There was the usual sprinkling of ordinary, more casually dressed patrons; some with groups and others there alone who looked to enjoy the music and perhaps, meet someone interesting while having a good time. The dim but, strategically lit lounge created the kind of sultry mood that the Jazz crowd loved. The long, curving bar of finely crafted maple added to the elegant décor. There was always the low-key murmur of conversation between the Jazz sessions and those spirited hoots of approval and polite clapping during the sessions that uplifted and roused the crowd.

"So what brings you gentlemen to the Green Mill tonight?" Connie asked with more curiosity underneath than she revealed outwardly. "Aw, baby…you know …we like to party, too…we was invited by my man, Steve…he's a cool stud…we like hangin' out with him" Jack responded, maintaining the same benign smile that he had been flashing since he sat down. The ladies knew that there was much more to it than that but, they smiled politely.

"Hey, Jack…let's go back there and take care of our business…okay?" Steve said. "Yea…right on, Steve…let's step it off" Jack said, stirring himself from the comfortable booth seat and rising up from it. "The bartender, Trent is sending somebody over to take everybody's order…just order what you want…it's on me…ladies…I'll be back in a little bit…okay?" Steve said. "Okay, baby" Verna said in her sexiest voice.

Verna and Connie were young black women who were in their mid-twenties. They were very good-looking women when they were doing well, took care of themselves and had their lives in order. But, they liked to get high and that made their lives full of ups-and-downs. They would have their place to stay. They were good at finding nice little apartments off the beaten path and out of the immediate area of where all the Uptown hustlers traveled. They were smart enough to know that if they stayed where no one knew they lived, their lives had some order and stability; even though they still got high and traipsed in some of the same circles as all the other fiends and hustlers in the various Uptown hot-spots. They had nice figures and looked especially good when they wore make-up and dressed well. When they did, they looked as respectable as any non-street type of woman. They knew that their ability to hustle well and survive in the streets depended on how appealing their appearances were---and they worked on that when they were not working over some chump who was full of lust for them. But, when they were having their down times, they did not look quite so stunning. They would go on drug binges for weeks at-a-time and their appearances would tell it. During those times, they could look as bad as any trampy street 'hoe that was around. But, they were slick enough that they stayed mostly to themselves; trusting only one another and not letting many of the street types they were acquainted with in their drug circles get too familiar with them. They were always trying to take the high road of seeking out respectable marks with money or catching one of the neighborhood chumps who had just gotten his check; and God help him if he had any attraction to them. They would play him for all he was worth by their masterful seductions.

Steve and Jack went into the back to the men's restroom. They entered a stall and closed it. "Here you go, Steve…check it out, baby!" Jack said with a broad smile as he handed Steve three small, puffy manilla envelopes and a small chunk of something wrapped in aluminum foil. Steve took the items and gazed at the rock-like object wrapped in aluminum foil. "What's this?…the hash?" he asked. "Sho-'nough, baby…that's that fire hashish I was tellin' you to get…don't take but a little bit to get you wrecked…no shit" Jack touted. Steve hurriedly stuffed the chunk and two of the manilla envelopes in the inside pocket of his sport jacket then opened one of the envelopes. "You still have those papers?"" he asked Jack in a whisper. "Oh, yea…"" Jack replied as he reached into his pocket and pulled them out. Steve rolled a joint and lit it and took a toke. "Yea…aw, yea…oh, yea…umhumm" he murmured after taking the toke and holding it in momentarily. "Just like the joints…gooooddd, man…really good" he commented again. "take it easy, slim…you don't wanna' get too toasted now do you?" Jack said just to sound as though he was concerned for his new acquaintance. In fact, if Steve was too high, that would be just what Jack wanted. It appeared that Steve was well on his way to being just that. “Hey, my friend…I’ve been doin’ this a long time…I can handle it…understand me?…it’s no problem” Steve said boldly and sounding a little cocky. “Alright then, bro’…knock ya’ self out” Jack responded, sounding as though he was backing away from his suggestion. ”Here you go, Jack” Steve said as he handed Jack a ten-dollar bill. “My man…solid, baby” Jack said, caught off guard but, sounding pleased as he took the bill and quickly pocketed it. Steve handed him the joint and Jack opened the stall door and paced around a small area of the restroom, out of Steve’s sight and pretending to be toking on the joint, making exaggerated sucking noises. After Jack took a couple more pretend tokes, Steve stepped out of the stall and said “Are you cool for now?…time to party, Jack…let’s get out of here” Jack pinched the “duck” of a joint and followed Steve out of the restroom. They arrived back at the booth.

The ladies and The Weep who had their drinks and seemed to be engaged in a lively conversation with laughs and giggles. “Hahahaha..whoooo…you a mess, Pops” Verna said as she laughed along with Connie as The Weep seemed to be keeping them entertained with his folksy humor. After the first Jazz session by the Norman Dupre Band ended at eleven o’clock, the four of them sat at the booth and had lively conversations with lots of joking and laughter throughout the night. Jack and the girls knew how to have a good time without letting their plans get in the way. Still, they were working on Steve; jockying for position to have favor with him. They knew that they would not be able to score on their mark until the end of the night, anyway, so----they continued to have a good time. Jack continued to sip lightly on a single beer and no one seemed to notice that he was not really drinking.

Jack could not understand why he seemed to be so much under control. He felt relaxed----even without a drink. It was eerie. He had been noticing this little feeling for the last week. It seemed to be an uncanny sensation of relaxation with a vague sense of calmness that was ever-so subtle. Jack knew that there was nothing physical that was affecting him in this way; at short introspective moments he had tried to detect the source of this pleasant but, unusual sensation. It was affecting him in a mental and emotional way. It was a curious sense of suppressed happiness. It must have something to do with Tina, he decided. He was suppressing the feeling because he had never really been truly happy except maybe during the most innocent times of his youth. He had not been so happy with the way he had come to this very difficult way of life that he had fallen into. Meeting a woman who lived a normal life and who seemed to be interested in him was affecting his mind and emotions in the most positive way. But, he was not allowing the joy to come fully to the surface because deep down inside, he wanted to live in it without acknowledging it; to enjoy those real moments of joy in being in Tina's company without identifying it; to not allow himself to be so submerged in it until he would drown; to not dwell on it. Now, these thoughts had begun to have him looking forward to his get-together with Tina tomorrow night. He thought about how he needed to have some money for the occasion. His next thought was just to play his game tonight like he knew he could and money would not be a problem when he meets up with his sweetie tomorrow evening.

The night went on with the group seated comfortably at the booth, continuing their care-free banter and laughter. Soon, the second show would start at midnight and the ladies had begun hinting around to Steve as they noticed he was gradually coming into the state of being less aware, just as they had hoped. Jack picked up on their little hints to Steve and he knew that he had to make some moves to counter the women's bid to spirit him off. He knew he would have to play his sharpest game tonight to outwit these women who, by their looks seemed to have the upper hand.

"Hey, girls…think both of you can handle me?…they call me "Steady Steve" you know.."" Steve said, feeling loose and free and smiling happily. "Hahahaha…hahhaha" the two women laughed out loud. "Steady Steve, huh?" Verna responded with an amused smile on her face. "Man…you must ain't never had no black girl before…have you? ….you cain't handle *one* of us let alone two…but, I'll tell you what…we'll give you a chance to show us what you workin' with…okay?" Verna challenged. "Cause when we get through puttin' some o' this black stuff on you…you ain't gonna know ya' name no more…" she added with sassiness. "Yea, Steve…besides, we heard that white boys ain't got enough to satisfy women like us…we like 'em long, strong and all night long…first time is a try-out..you got to prove yourself to come back a second time…understand that?" Connie chimed in with a sultry sassiness of her own. Steve was so tickled, and pleased by the two women's salacious comments, until he laughed out loud with a delight that was fueled by the mellow high he was feeling just then. "Yes, indeed…I'm havin' myself a good time!" Steve declared out loud.

Jack looked at the clock behind the counter and it read "11: 34". He knew he would have to start making his moves because the midnight show would be starting soon and once it did, any play he needed to make would be put on hold until after the show. Besides, the girls were moving in for the kill. "Steve…man…my shit done wore off…I need another hit…let's step to the back so we can get right…how about it?" Jack proposed "Aaahh..''" Steve started, sounding as if he wanted to say "no" "Ah..ah..ah, Steve" Jack began to cut Steve's negative tone short, then leaned over and whispered in Steve's ear "Them girls wanna' get with you tonight…you know you need to be feelin' right…come on" Jack said in a persuasive tone. "Okay….ladies…I will be right back…we need to check something out". As they rose from the booth, Jack grabbed a book of matches off of the table and they headed to the Men's restroom. "Alright, Steve..come on with it" Jack said. Steve responded by going into his pocket and pulling out the manilla envelope and fishing a joint out of it. "Okay…fire up!...you take the first hit" Jack urged. Steve pulled out his fancy lighter and Jack looked at it. He began to plot his chance to slyly gain possession of it. Steve lit up the joint with the lighter and put it back in his pocket as he began to toke. "Hummph…yea..yes, indeed" he commented after holding the smoke in momentarily. Jack said "Okay Mr. I'm gonna' smoke all the weed…can a brotha' get in on that…damn!" Jack commented sarcastically as Steve stood inside the stall, near the commode. Steve handed him the joint without a word and Jack took it and stepped out of Steve's view. He made a sucking noise, pretending to inhale and after a few seconds, exhaled and stepped back where Steve could see him. "Damn, man…this shit is better than I realized…this is some sho' 'nough fire…yea" Jack commented and handed the joint back to Steve. Steve began to toke again. "Man…you ain't tokin'….hit that mug like you mean it!" Jack urged him on. "Jack…I've been smokin' weed probably since you were knee-high to a grasshopper…you can't tell me how to smoke weed…if there's anything I know how to do well…it's smoke some weed"

Steve insisted in a light-hearted manner. “I cain’t tell, my man…cain’t hardly tell…you tokin’ like you scared of it or somethin’…smoke like a man…don’t let the girls see you tokin’ that way…I know women like them…they like a man who ain’t scared to get high” Jack went on. “Haha…you’re looking at the tokin’ champion, Mr. Jack…hahaha” Steve shot back, then began to toke the joint a few times in quick succession, perhaps unconsciously moved by Jack’s urging comments. “Take it easy, baby…take it easy…woa, woa…woa…save me some o’ that” Jack said feigning a desire to smoke on the joint before it was gone. He reached his hand at the joint while it was still in Steve’s mouth. Steve finally relented. “Can I knock this out” Jack asked. “Yea…go ahead” Steve replied. “Hey…you better get back and keep the girls occupied while I finish this off” Jack said as he slyly pinched the fire out of the joint as he held it extended down near his knee. Steve started out of the rest room on Jack’s urging; “Aw, shit…it done went out…light..light” Jack said. Steve went into his pocket and handed Jack the lighter. “Go ‘head..don’t keep ‘em waitin’…I’ll be out in a minute” Jack said as he held the piece of joint in one hand and the lighter poised to light it in the other. Steve went out of the door and Jack smiled to himself----he had the lighter. He hung around in the bathroom for a few minutes and then went out to the bar and walked over to Steve.

“Man…Steve…can I order me another brew?…weed got me thirsty” Jack asked as he stepped over to the booth where Steve was sitting on the aisle seat. “Yea, man…hey…order another round for all of us while you’re at it” Steve said. “Cool..be right back” Jack said. He meandered through the crowd of people standing around the barroom floor talking and drinking. He stepped up to the counter.

The low-key buzz of conversation inside the bar was suddenly pierced by a loud voice that seemed out of place; “Hey, Calvin…be cool…we goin’ in” a voice near the door spoke out. Everyone kind of noticed the louder voice and some turned to look toward the entrance to see if there was some kind of commotion. Jack looked over as he walked to the bar counter and was shocked to see Calvin and Tyrone entering the club. He was shocked and could not believe it because he had never seen them inside the Green Mill or any other bar except the very seedy Sheridan Liquors over on Sheridan Road. They walked in looking like zombies. Tyrone with all those scars on his face, not dressed so well and Calvin appearing very much the same with a face that was far less scarred than his brothers. Calvin's face looked somewhat comical, like a caricature---almost buffoonish. They walked in gazing around at the crowd inside the bar. Their scruffy appearances seemed out of place and the stench of vagrancy wafted in the air about them. Just as they were nearing where Jack stood at the bar, Calvin was walking in front of Tyrone when he stumbled into a customer seated on a bar stool and near where Jack was standing. "Oh..Oh..oh..man…damn…" Calvin mumbled with surprise after falling into the middle-aged man. "Hey…get off of me, will you!" the annoyed patron roared as he sat at the bar with the side of Calvin's head pressing into his back. Calvin was off-balance, almost on one knee after his stumble and was very slow in recovering himself. Tyrone stepped in and assisted him in getting upright and apologized profusely to the stranger that Calvin had stumbled into. "I'm sorry, mister...I really am sorry…believe me…this is my brother, he's tired and he should be at home in bed…I'm sho' 'nough sorry about that" Tyrone went on. The stranger did not say a word but, the annoyed expression on his face said all that he wanted to say. Calvin finally righted himself and stumbled again and stepped on Jack's foot. "Oh..uh..oh" he murmured as Jack caught his left arm to keep him from falling again. As Jack held Calvin's arm, Tyrone spoke.

"Cool Breeze…hey what's happenin', bro'?…you partyin' up in here, huh?" he said to Jack with a smile and a sense of relief that he had found someone he knew inside the strange surroundings. "Yea…what's goin' on?…what brings y'all up in here tonight?" Jack asked kind of indifferently and feeling a bit embarrassed that he was acquainted with the likes of Tyrone and Calvin in such a sophisticated atmosphere. "Aw, man…you seen us earlier when we was out there…the po'lice come up on us and told us to throw the bottle away or else we was goin' to jail…then, he said he oughta' take us to jail…anyway…after Calvin started clownin'….I had to cool him down and I told the po'lice that we was inside the lounge here and we just stepped out for some air and we was goin' back in…then, one of the po'lice said "you better get your asses back in there before you end up lookin' at some bars…we paid our way in to keep from goin' to jail…we gonna stay for a while 'til we know they gone…know what else?...we made us a sweet sting at the Boozery earlier tonight…caught a chump in the bathroom..drunk… money hangin' all out of his pockets…I couldn't pass it up…I clipped his ass for a nice little piece of change…that's how we was able to get up in here tonight" Tyrone rambled. "Yea…cool…I got to order for these people over here…y'all be cool, alright?" Jack added so that he could cut the conversation short and order the drinks.

"Another round of the same for us over there" Jack said to the bartender, Donnie as he pointed over to the booth with Steve, Weep and the girls. Jack had consciously made an effort to avoid talking to the bartender, Trent who was Steve's weed-smoking buddy. He did not want him to catch on that Steve was getting played. "What did you all have over there" Donnie asked. Two Heinekens, two Champales and one double shot of Courvosier" Jack replied. "One of the servers will bring it over" Donnie said and Jack moved away from that spot at the counter to another spot just a few feet away from the bar and just lingered there. He knew that the longer he stayed away, the less likely that Steve would remember that he had something that belonged to him; and once the show started, he would be even less likely to remember. Jack knew how people were forgetful once they were good and high. Jack stood at the counter a bit longer until he saw a server going over to the booth. He immediately stepped over to the booth as soon as the server was done. "I was chattin' with some people over there…I see we're ready for another round here…cool!" Jack said, as he attempted to get back into the flow of conversation at the booth.

The Norman Dupre Band had been back on the stage for about 20 minutes tuning up and they were soon to be starting the midnight show. Jack knew that, now, he had to play his best hand. "Steve…what color are your eyes, baby…come closer so I can see" Verna said as she sat next to Steve on the inside seat of the booth. "Why are you asking me that?…hahaha" Steve chuckled lightly with a blushing kind of giddiness. "Baby, 'cause you have some really nice eyes" Verna responded. "Well…I believe I took after my mother in that department…she was always getting compliments on her eyes…you know…hahaha" Steve commented with another light chuckle. "I think we're gonna have to get together tonight…I think I want you all to myself" Verna said in a seductive tone. "Oh, no, Miss Verna…you cain't have all the nice lookin' men for yourself" Connie cut in "You cain't be cuttin' me out of the picture, baby….no..no..no" Connie said in remarkable character.

Jack could see that the ladies were giving it their best shot and putting things into Steve's head at just the right time to assure that he would be leaving with them at the end of the night. Jack did not care about that at all as long as he had gotten something significant out of him before they left. In his head, Jack had begun to tally what he had hustled so far. Six joints and four dollars from his first run for weed; he pinched one joint from each dime bag on the second run and got fifteen dollars for the hash and ten dollars for buying the weed for Steve. He made twenty-nine dollars, so far and still had the lighter and nine joints---not bad but, he was not finished. He would eventually sell the joints and the lighter if he could get away with it, and anything else he could get out of him before the night was through. "Steve…look like you got somethin' goin' for yourself…you holdin' the best hand, my man…go 'head on with yo' bad self" Willie-the-Weep chimed in to flatter and placate Steve. Norman Dupre, the leader of the jazz band, began to prep the audience with a few words about the first tune they would play for the midnight show. After his introduction, the band began to play. Steve pulled out a cigarette and Jack immediately lit it for him with a match. They were all quiet at the booth and Verna grabbed Steve's arm and wrapped her arm around it. Steve turned to her and gave her a hazy smile. The midnight show proved to be especially entertaining and the crowd responded with vigorous applause at points when the players performed lively impromptu segments. Steve nodded off a couple of times during the show; perhaps, because he had to be still and quiet. Jack and the girls tried not to give away their predatory glances at Steve at the moments when he nodded out. The band finally finished the midnight show well past 1am; ending with the usually rousing rendition of a crowd favorite tune. They departed thanking the crowd and urging safety in their trips home.

"Damn…now, that was sweet…I need to get over here and see these shows on Wednesday nights…hahahaha….I really enjoyed that" Weep commented as a few of the lights that were darkened for the show were turned back on inside the bar. Steve was now more alert, although somewhat groggy as the group continued to sit at the booth and sip their drinks with Jack still pretending to drink. He continued to take little sips from his bottle of Heineken. "Steve, baby…you alright, sugar?…you feelin' okay?" Verna asked, continuing to make her play to have Steve's complete confidence before the night was done. "Oh…humm…ah…I'm okay…I was out for a little bit…but, I'm good…I'm good" Steve replied, still coming out of his haze with a yawn.

"Hey…Cool Breeze…you got a light on you?" Tyrone asked Jack as he was suddenly standing next to the booth. The ladies looked up to see Tyrone's face and Connie jumped with a startled gasp. "Uhh……oh, my..whooo!" after seeing Tyrone's heavily scarred face. "Whoooaa!" Verna gasped very quickly with the same frightful response. Each of the women gazed at Tyrone's face momentarily then, turned their eyes away, trying to compose themselves after the sudden fright. Jack cut a shameful glance around the table and immediately jumped up from his aisle seat at the booth and dug into his pocket to pull out a book of matches and took a couple of steps from the table. "Here you go" he said to Tyrone and struck a match and held it for Tyrone to light his cigarette. "Thanks, Cool Breeze…hey, man…this a fly joint…damn…you come here all the time?…some cool shit up in here…live music and everythang…huh? Tyrone went on. "Hey, Ty..Ty" Calvin said stepping up behind Tyrone seemingly from nowhere. "What you want l'il brotha'?" Tyrone responded, tempering himself to be kinder to his younger brother in the more civil atmosphere. "There's a booth right over there…let's get some drinks and sit down…come on" Calvin said. "Just be cool, man…ain't you had enough to drink?…just slow down….alright?.....damn" Tyrone responded. "Okay…tell you what...let's go over there and sit down..you *do* need to sit down…that'll keep you from trippin' over people and shit…let's go" Tyrone added with a sudden change of mind "Hey..ain't that ya' boy right there?…got some fine ladies…hey y'all…what's goin' on…y'all partyin' down…huh?" Calvin said with a big, silly grin and a little more alertness than he had earlier. None of the people in the booth spoke. They just gazed at the two brothers with curious stares as they stood only a few feet from the booth. "Hey, Cool Breeze…we gonna' be down here at the front" Tyrone said, picking up on the curious stares and silence that he and Calvin received from the group. He stepped away with his brother following as they headed to the just vacated booth near the front of the bar. "Goodness, gracious…what happened to that dude?…I been seein' him around the neighborhood for a while…how did his face get so messed up?…he scared the livin' hell outa' me..and that other dude with him lookin' all wild and crazy…I'm glad they went on about their business…whooweee..jesus!" Verna declared. "You ain't lyin, girl…I know they kinda' crazy…I been seein' them around, too…I ain't never had nothin' to say to them…I don't see them botherin' nobody, but, they just look too messed up to me…that's a shame he let himself get all messed up in the face like that" Connie added. "Who are those guys?" Steve asked curiously. "Hey, y'all….they cool…I know they look bad and everything…I been knowin' them for a coupla' years…they used to be trouble some years back…but, they're harmless, now…they just went all the way down, that's all" Jack said smoothing the situation over and adding his own bit of humane sentiment. "Oooohh, Steve…I am so glad you don't look nothin' like that... you're a good-lookin' man…baby, don't never let yourself get messed up like that..okay?..you hear me?" Verna said to Steve as she turned her attention back to her game of seduction. "You ain't got to worry about me, doll…there's no way I'll let myself go like that…that's too bad he's all cut up like that" Steve added with a mildly disturbed tone of sympathy.

"Why don't we get going Steve so we can have some real fun?…get away from here…you wanna see can we handle you….right, baby?" Verna continued, luring Steve further into her lair. "Verna, you ain't said nothin' but a word…good as you ladies look..what man is gonna' say "no" to you two…not me…that's for damned sure!…hahahaha…hahahaha" Steve laughed with absolute delight. alright…you're still sittin'…you ready, baby?" Verna said standing up part-way from where she sat to get Steve to begin moving and to motivate him with a glimpse of her curvaceous frame.

"Hey, Steve…take it easy and finish ya' beer, my man…why you in such a hurry?" Jack said trying to stall for time to make one more play on his "mark". "Let's go to the back and get right one more time…cool?…remember…you need to be ready to handle ya' business…right?" Jack urged. "That *would* be good because, like you said earlier….my shit done wore off! ..hahahaha!" Steve agreed, laughing at his play on Jack's words. Jack was pleased that he could get Steve away for a little while so that he could work on him. They entered the men's rest room and Jack immediately said "Let me fire it up this time, Steve…bust out one o' them joints" Jack said. Steve smiled as he went into his pocket to pull out one of the little manilla envelopes and plucked a joint from it. "There that baby is…go ahead…light her up" he said, still smiling as he handed it to Jack. Jack performed the same act as before; lighting the joint, with matches but, this time turning his back to Steve who stood partially outside the stall. He toked on the joint, letting most of the smoke escape. He did it again and pinched a small piece off the end of it to make it appear that he had smoked it. "Damn..this weed is fresh and a little damp…it keeps goin' out…gota' light it again" he said. He relit it and after another toke, passed it to Steve. Steve took several strong tokes, apparently determined to be good and high for his rendezvous with the girls. "I'm ready for them honeys….I'm feeling mighty fine…I don't know if they can handle this white boy here, Jack...I feel like a young bull…yes, indeed!" Steve exclaimed. "Come on…let's get out of here, man...I want to see what these girls are all about!" he said excitedly. Steve led the way out of the rest room and they arrived back at the booth.

"Steve, you keep foolin' around and you're gonna miss out on somethin' good…you know that?" Verna warned with the same seductive tone she had used all night. "Miss Verna…I just want you to show me what's good so I will know…I'm from Missouri, baby…you know what I mean..hahaha..hahaha…can you dig where I'm coming from, Jack?..ahahaha" Steve laughed and joked good-naturedly. "You're laughin' *now* but, we're gonna have your ass beggin' before the night is over…take a look, baby…can you handle it…can you handle it…can you…" Connie sang soft and seductively as she raised up from her seat and danced up close to Steve, boldly brushing her body lightly up against the front of his, swaying her hips from side-to-side and putting her fine figure on display. She stared deep into Steve's eyes with a lusciously enticing expression. "Whooo…damn! …it's getting hot in here!" Steve declared as he smiled broadly and looked back into her eyes. Jack looked on and he had to admit that he did not stand much of a chance after Connie's come-on. Still, he had to make a final play. "Jack…my man…you did me good…you took care of me, but now…I need something else that I can't get from you…hahahaha" Steve laughed heartily. "You damned right you cain't get it from me…I know what's on your mind, partna'…cain't say I blame you, though…you got to make ya' move while you can…dig where I'm comin'? from…hahahaha…for real" Jack laughed and joked.

"Let's go, baby" Connie said as she grabbed Steve's arm on one side and Verna immediately wrapped her arm around his other and they began to walk Steve toward the front to the exit. "Y'all be cool, now" Connie said as she turned around to Jack and The Weep with the expression of a vixen who had trumped them. "Hey…hey…Steve...""" Jack said as he stepped up quickly behind the three to catch up to them. "Steve…let me holla' at you one more time before you take off..listen, bro'…listen…hey, ladies…check this…I ain't gonna hold him but a minute…I swear…cool?...one minute" Jack pleaded. "Okay, brotha'-man…but, it's gettin' late, now…go on..…go 'head on and get it over with" Verna said with a cautioning sternness. "What, Jack?…I'm getting ready to go, man" Steve said with an annoyed tone. "Listen…step over here for a minute" Jack said as he wanted to get Steve out of ear-shot of the women. "Check this out…you know what this is right here?" Jack asked as he slyly held a small glass vial containing a grayish, powdery substance in his open palm. "You know what this is, right?" Jack quizzed. "Hell, no….what is it?" Steve asked with a tone of curiosity. "Spanish Fly..my man…Spanish Fly…look..this will get them hotter than they ever been in their life…they will freak your ass all night long after you slip this shit on 'em…put it in their drinks…""" Jack whispered. "Spanish Fly, huh?…I heard of that shit but, I never seen it or used it before" Steve responded. "Well…tonight is your lucky night, my man…you-are-in-luck…cheap…twenty dollars…" Jack continued to whisper. "Twenty dollars!" Steve said a little too loud. "Shhh!..you don't want them to hear you, man…be cool…I was gonna use it with my girl tomorrow night…but, I changed my mind…she already too damned freaky…she will wear my ass out if I use this shit on her…go on, take it off my hands…stud inside wanted to give me twenty for it, but, I wanted to let you get it off of me…here you go…hurry up..come on before they come over here to see what's goin' on!" Jack urged, still whispering. "Okay…alright" Steve said as he began to stick a hand in his front pants pocket. "Don't let them see you…okay…give it here, they got their backs turned to us…hurry up!" Jack urged as he kept his eyes on the women in the near distance. Steve went into his wallet and slipped a twenty dollar bill to Jack. "Cool, baby…later, Steve" Jack said feeling a smug sense of accomplishment after having sold some concoction that he created from an empty glass vial he found in the Men's room that he filled with cigarette ashes while taking a lone trip to the restroom earlier in the night. He quickly stuffed the twenty into his pocket while keeping an eye on the girls. At the same time, he felt as though he had hustled all he could from Steve. Jack figured that Steve had much more money than he was able to play him for. But, his time had run out and he should just be satisfied with what he already had. He watched Steve join up with the girls once again, knowing that they would get the better of him because they had him under their spell. He watched them walk to Steve's car and he could see the anxious body language in Steve's movement that told him how the women had him setup for an interesting night.

"So that's it, huh?" The Weep said after casually walking up behind Jack as he gazed in the distance at Steve and the girls entering the car. It was very close to 2 in the morning and the streets were near-silent with vehicle traffic almost non-existent and only a few people could be seen walking the streets in the vicinity. Jack felt another accomplishment, too. He had survived the night without drinking. He was glad that he had sipped only a few drops of the beer that he had earlier in the night; that he had left practically full on the booth table. This was significant for someone who could hardly resist drinking under any circumstances. But, he was on a mission that he had not been on before. He was not drinking tonight for reasons he that felt more motivated than ever. He wanted to continue this thing he had with Tina and his efforts tonight were a means of preserving the magic that he was feeling from it all. "Hey, Weep…they about to ride up outa' here…let's squat on this bench for a while…cool?" Jack said. "Yea" The Weep replied and before they began the first step toward the bus stop bench, they could hear commotion coming from just inside the Green Mill.

"Damn…what's goin' on up in there?" The Weep said. "You hear that?… that's Tyrone…let's check it out" Jack said and they hustled back into the Green Mill entrance. Immediately after entering, the bartender, Donnie could be seen standing over Tyrone and Calvin seated at the second booth just inside the door. "You can't come in here doing this kind of stuff!....I'm gonna have to ask you two to leave!" the bartender argued. "Come on, man...he didn't mean nothin' by it...let us finish our drinks...alright?...come on!" Tyrone pleaded. "No...no you insulted this lady here and that is unacceptable...you gota' go!" the bartender continued. An ample-chested, well dressed, tall woman in heels stood near the bartender, glaring toward the booth where Tyrone and Calvin were seated. "He don't know me to be talkin' to me that way....he's rude and ignorant!" the lady shot back angrily as she stood next to the booth that she was sharing with three other female friends. "Come on...he didn't mean no harm, man...let it slide...it won't happen no more" Tyrone continued to plead. "No...your buddy cannot walk up to a perfectly strange customer and say "You got some nice titties...that is uncivilized...where is he from, anyway?... talking like that to strangers in public...he's lucky that a man wasn't with her to knock his damned block off!....now, I'm giving you one minute to get the hell outa' here!" the angry bartender continued. "Hey, man...you wrong...you cain't talk like that to us, either" Tyrone said, standing up from his booth seat and seeming to have gone into a neurotic kind of anger himself. "Yea...back up offa' me, man!...I ain't done nothin' to you...leave me alone!" Calvin added, raising up from his seat, as well. After the two stood up from their seats and the confrontation began to appear close to getting physical, the bartender turned to the other bartender, Trent, who was keeping his eye on the situation as he stood behind the bar. The crowd inside had become sparse with most leaving after the midnight jazz session had ended. "Give me that club and call the police" he shouted to him. Jack immediately stepped in after he and Weep had stood for a moment watching the incident unfold.

"Hey, bartender...let me handle this...I'll talk to them, okay?...come on....let me talk...we'll talk outside" Jack whispered as he stepped between the bartender and Tyrone and Calvin. "Player..this ain't you, Ty...come on, man...forget about this...they gettin' ready to call the po'lice on y'all....you don't wanna go to jail, do you?...don't do it...hahaha...come on, now....let me holla' at you outside" Jack said, placating the two and placing his arm around Tyrone's shoulder and giving him an affectionate squeeze that also served to give the bartender and the two separation and pause in the heated moment. Jack didn't really like Tyrone and Calvin much at all. But, he intervened, nonetheless. He felt compelled by his association to them and to the Green Mill to broker the situation. He did not want the matter to escalate; acting out of his own sense of common decency. Still, his actions were self-serving. At this level of existence, everything was for barter. Jack knew that he could parlay his gesture into a measure of goodwill for himself later down the road. He was exaggerating his act of diplomacy to instill a sense of indebtedness in the Green Mill bartenders who were observing him tonight; and the act could be traded for a favor from them at a later time. These were the kind of mind games that Jack and all the street hustlers played. "Naw, Cool Breeze…that dude..come fuckin' with us for nothin'....Calvin ain't said nothin' out o' line to that chick….she just didn't like Calvin….if some other man in there hada' said the same thing Calvin said to her…she wouldna' said shit…now, tell me if that ain't the truth?...tell me, Cool Breeze" Tyrone went on. "Ty…Ty…listen to me, man…that ain't the point… it don't matter about all that…once she started to complain'…you shoulda' stepped it off…dig what I'm sayin', player?....it's easier to just step it off…'steada' doin' that…y'all standin' up in the man's face arguin' with him…'bout to go to jail…now you tell *me*.....is it worth it?….come on now…is it?" Jack insisted. "Okay…okay…alright…we outa' there now…forget about it…but, if he hada' tried to grab him…I'da' stole on his ass…I ain't playin'….know what I'm sayin', Cool Breeze?" Tyrone continued on excitedly.

The three walked outside near the bus stop bench standing close; still debating back and forth about the incident. The charged wrangling gradually subsided and before long, Jack and Tyrone were having a much more subdued talk. Meanwhile, Calvin had strolled to the bus stop bench, laid down and fallen asleep. The Weep had been standing back quietly onto himself several yards away to one side of the Green Mill entrance door as Jack and Tyrone continued to debate. The night had come into the mellow lull that always came during the night when most all of the bars were closed and the streets were bare of any activity and a light breeze whipped pieces of paper debris about the streets. This was that narrow space of time where a night reveler's exhilaration had calmed into a mellow mood of contentment.

Suddenly, in the middle of his conversation, Jack thought about Steve and the girls. He looked up the street in the near distance to see Steve's car still parked. About half-an-hour had passed since he, Tyrone and Calvin had walked out of the Green Mill. He began to wonder what was going on with the girls and Steve. He had expected them to have driven off and gone to wherever it was they were going. He thought it odd that almost an hour after the three had left the Green Mill, that the car was still parked. He could see movement inside the car. The girls seemed to be moving about inside. Jack could not make out much from where he stood. But, he could not see Steve's head at all. "Hey, Weep" he called out as he turned to look at Weep standing the few yards behind him, still standing near the Green Mill entrance door. There were more people leaving the bar than earlier; exiting in spurts of small groups and couples as they passed by The Weep The bar crowd was dwindling down as the closing hour of 3am neared. "Hey, Weep!" Jack yelled out again and motioned to The Weep whose mind seemed to be drifting as he casually watched the nicely dressed groups of people pass around him. He finally heard Jack call and noticed him make a wave of his hand in the air. The Weep walked over to him. "Weep…look down there where ya' boy's car is…I see them chicks movin' around in the car…where the hell is he, I wonder?" Jack said, puzzled. "They in there blowin' him or either jackin' him off…one or the other….hahahaha" The Weep responded with a light, casual chuckle. "You know what….you probably right…but, it seems mighty strange that they messin' around in the car and ain't drivin' off somewhere….you know…privacy…dig what I'm sayin'?" Jack reasoned. "Yea…but, think about it, Jack…they just after money…they don't wanna drive off with him to his crib or anywhere else…they just wanna' rip him off without havin' to put up with his ass too long…understand what I'm sayin'?" the Weep surmised "Besides….they don't wanna take the chance that he might be Jack the ripper, either.." he added. "Hey watch how you use that name….people with my same name are already in deep trouble around this area…people lookin' for 'em and they don't even know why…hahaheheha" Jack laughed at his little joke. "You got that right...scandalous as you is…if my name was Jack livin' around here…I'd either change my damned name or move…one of the two…hahahahaha" The Weep laughed at his own little barb. They traded a few more quips on the same topic and laughed heartily. As they did, Tyrone walked quietly and unnoticed over to the bus stop bench where his brother, Calvin was already slumped over on part of it. He was completely knocked out and was snoring mildly. The two tended to pass out together; sometimes, out in the open streets; or they would end up sleeping somewhere in an abandoned building. This was how they lived. Jack and Weep chatted a short while longer.

Suddenly, they could hear the two women's voices a short distance up the street. Car doors were slamming and as Jack and Weep turned to look, they could see the two women walking hurriedly away from Steve's parked car. They were talking to each other loudly. "That fool ain't got no damned money!...why you pick his broke ass to fool with?" Connie could be heard speaking to Verna. "Hey…hey…he was flashin', baby...how the hell was I to know he wasn't gonna have but twenty-two dollars left…shit!" Verna shot back and their voices seemed to reverberate in the quiet night air. They were walking toward Jack and Weep. But, before they got very close, began to cross over to the opposite side of the street, taking a slanted angle instead of crossing straight over; walking out in the middle of the streets where no cars were passing at this hour and still talking to each other. "Did you notice that he never did pay for them drinks he was buyin' for us at the booth…his boy, that bartender was hookin' him up with free drinks for us" Connie said as they walked. "Yea...and that fool is a car rental agent--that car is rented…lied his ass off talkin' about he is a buildin' owner and he sells insurance…he was bullshittin' us real good" Verna said in a tone of disgust and frustration. "Say, y'all…be cool, now…we are gone!" Verna shouted out to Jack and The Weep as they passed them before disappearing around the northeast corner of Lawrence and Broadway. "You heard that, didn't you Weep?" Jack asked seconds after the women had disappeared from sight. "What?" Weep replied immediately with a hint of challenge in his voice. "Them chicks was sayin' that our boy was broke…didn't have but a little bit of scratch on him" "Jaaaaccckk…come on, now…" The Weep replied wryly. "What?…what you mean?" Jack asked in a puzzled manner. "Jack…of all people…I thought you would be the last to fall for that bullshit" The Weep said with the same dry tone. "What?" Jack asked again, still puzzled. "Them 'hoes prob'ly ripped him off for everything…he mighta' had a bunch o' money…they walk by us talkin' loud 'cause they *want* us to hear what they sayin'" Jack paused after what The Weep had said and pondered for a moment, appearing to be thinking more deeply on the matter. Only a short moment passed then, he spoke "That is a damned good point you makin', Weep…but, somehow, I don't think that's the way it is" Jack said.

"Hey…let's walk over and look into his car…he's probably passed out…come on" Jack said as his words descended into a whisper. "Whoa, Jack" The Weep said quickly as Jack began to step in the direction of Steve's parked car while The Weep stood pat. Jack halted his steps immediately. "Why?" he said to Weep as he turned quickly back around to face him with a bewildered and pleading expression. "Think about it…you gonna go over there fuckin' around with a white man's car while he is inside sleep in the middle of the night…how that look?…think about it…then. when the cops see you out here doin' that…then what?....they gonna' lock your ass up…that's what….and if the dude wakes up and finds out you tippin' around his car…what is he gonna think?…huh?...he'll let the po'lice go 'head and lock your ass up, 'cause he thinks you *are* tryin' to rob him" The Weep reasoned with calm conviction. "Now, Weep…you know how I feel about robbin' people…that ain't even none o' my thing…I ain't for that…I'll play 'em…I just wanna see is he in there sleepin'….if his doors ain't locked…I'll lock 'em…that's all…I made my little hustle offa' him already…I'm goin' over there to his car…come on" Jack urged. "Naw, man…I'm gonna turn it in, brotha'…I'll check you tomorrow" Weep said wearily. "Okay, Weep" Jack responded with a sigh. With that, The Weep turned and began to cross Lawrence Avenue, heading south to Wilson to go west to the YMCA where he lived. Jack stood for a few moments contemplating what The Weep had said to him and decided that he agreed with him. Still, he was curious and just wanted to look inside the car. He looked up and down the streets as he began to walk the short distance up the street to where Steve's car was parked. He came near it and paused. He looked up and down the streets before he walked closer to it. He looked inside to see Steve lying across the front seat breathing lightly; fast asleep. He could see a back pants pocket turned inside out; and his pants unzipped. He tried the passenger-side door latch and it was locked. That was the end of it. When the door did not open, Jack decided immediately to not bother with the other car doors.

He walked away, heading back toward the Green Mill. He could see the entrance door closed as he came upon it. He stopped even with the bus stop bench where Tyrone and Calvin were passed out. Jack stepped over closer to them and shook his head at the pitiful sight of the two. Suddenly, he noticed something hanging out of Tyrone's shirt pocket. He couldn't believe it! A flash of excitement passed through his body when he noticed it was a wad of green bills----money! The excitement continued to build within him and he stepped over and reached into Tyrone's shirt pocket and frantically grabbed the bills. He could see right away as he clutched the wad in his hand that it was a fifty and several twenties---about a half dozen of them! As he began to put the money in his pocket, he thought to take two of the twenties, place them back into Tyrone's shirt pocket and close the flap. He stood back for just a moment to make sure that the bills he had stuffed back in Tyrone's shirt pocket could not be seen and they couldn't. Tyrone lay still, soundly asleep with Calvin next to him. Jack was satisfied and immediately began to step hurriedly away from the area. He remembered what Tyrone had said about clipping a drunk in the bathroom of the Boozery bar. But, Jack had dismissed it; not really knowing where the two might have gotten money to pay admission to come inside the Green Mill on Jazz Night. He thought when Tyrone told him the tale earlier that night, that it was just one of his fabrications. Because it was a strange thing about people like Tyrone who were once revered in the streets and had a reputation to uphold but, had fallen to the depths that he had. They were always trying to regain some of the notoriety they once had; trying to bask in even a few seconds of glory by telling tales that made them look good. Jack could not have fathomed that Tyrone had made such a big sting----that much money! Jack stepped lively, heading back to his apartment with a feeling of joy and pure exhilaration. Whenever he stepped out into the streets to hustle, he knew that the chance of making a good sting could happen anytime, anywhere and in any manner. He chuckled gleefully to himself out loud at his good fortune. This was how it was played out in the streets; as hard as it was to make money in the streets, you never passed up any money. He knew that one day in the near future, when he might be broke, that he would regret giving back the two twenty dollar bills by stuffing them back into Tyrone's shirt pocket. But, this was part of his finesse in the street game. He knew it was best to leave Tyrone with *some* money rather than *no* money because if he awoke with no money, he would remember being with Jack and knowing that Jack had something to do with the disappearance of *all* of his money. If he and Calvin still had money to drink with after they woke up, they would just dismiss the other money, probably not remembering what they had done with it and perhaps, not remembering exactly how much it was; maybe even thinking that they *did* spend most of it. As long as they had the two twenty dollar bills, the first thing they would do was go and buy a drink and get drunk again and remember even less of what happened and the entire incident would just fade into the past underneath all of the drunkenness and loss of memory. Jack knew this; besides, Jack knew what it was like to awaken with no money at all and needing a drink.

He continued to walk west on Lawrence Avenue in the dark night that was lit only by the tall street lights. He crossed over to the south side of Lawrence where it met Malden. He continued to walk and felt relief when he crossed over the threshold of the Malden Arms entrance door and was inside. He did not bother to take the elevator. He galloped up the stairs, two steps at-a-time. He nervously unlocked his apartment door and rushed inside, slamming the door closed and locking the dead-bolt. He felt even more relaxed, now. He sat on the edge of his bed and paused to think; letting the good feeling sink in and turning his thoughts to how he was going to prepare for his wonderful evening tomorrow. His racing mind began to calm down and he suddenly reached into his pocket to pull out all the jumbled bills. He had mingled the money he hustled with what he had gotten from Tyrone. He counted it----one-hundred and fifty-nine dollars! These were the glorious moments that kept him out on the streets. Most times, he hustled a lot harder to make this much money. He put the money under his mattress and lay down, fully clothed and fell asleep.

Jack woke up to hear birds chirping outside with streams of faint daylight piercing through his window. He rose up from sleeping on his back across the bed. He sat up and paused, letting his head clear from the grogginess. His mind instinctively turned to drinking as it did most every morning. But, he remembered that he would be meeting Tina tonight for dinner and whatever else they wanted to do----and so, he remembered that he still was not drinking again today. He began to have perplexed feelings about it all. He decided not to drink for his date with Tina to show her that he was not just a hustler in the streets; that he could behave like a civilized person and did not have to drink. He felt the warmth of anticipating her company and the mild annoyance at the thought of not drinking at the same time. His thoughts about being with Tina played a melody in his mind. It was as though most of the more pleasurable moments he had ever experienced had come together into these harmonious feelings and thoughts he was having right now. He looked over to his clock-radio on the dresser and it shouted "10:19am" He continued to sit on the edge of the bed contemplating and mapping out today's activities in his head. He wanted to take a good shower right now and he knew he would be taking another shortly before his date.

He ruminated for a while when suddenly, the thought of having the fancy lighter he had swindled from Steve came to mind. He felt his front pockets and could feel the hard, square, metal object through his pants. He reached in and pulled it out to look at it. It sure *looks* like gold, he thought as he looked at the gold-colored strips that criss-crossed the silver base on one side of the lighter. He looked closer to see what looked like a red gem imbedded exactly in the center where the gold strips crossed on the lighter. "Ruby?-----"couldn't be" he thought. The object looked sleek and classy and Jack was thinking that this may be worth more than he imagined. But, he did not want to build false hopes by speculating on it's value. He would just ask for it to be appraised at a pawn shop when he was out-and-about today----and once he did, he would perhaps, try to sell it to Jose, the owner of the Aragon.

As the haziness faded from his head, he began to feel a tinge of excitement at what lie ahead. He visualized himself dressed nicely but, casual when he met with Tina tonight. He was thinking of how he was going to go about gathering his attire. He could not afford new clothes. He would buy a new pair of shoes---not too expensive, some new underwear and he knew that he could go to his favorite spot at the Salvation Army store where Ida worked and get a shirt and perhaps a pair of slacks that were stylish and new or almost new. That was where he got most all of his clothes. He hardly ever paid for them. On numerous occasions, when he was high or drunk, he had sweet-talked and begged Ida, the store clerk to let him have what he wanted and she did most of the time when Josephine, the store manager was not present. Josephine alternated between managing two Salvation Army thrift stores and so, she was not at the Broadway store every day. But, when she was, Jack could not get anything free from Ida unless his timing was right and he brought his items up to the counter while Josephine was out to lunch or busy in the back room of the store. Ida was a woman who was probably in her mid-forties. She was fairly attractive and her looks appealed to many of the street urchins like Jack who came into the thrift store with the same idea in mind----to get a change of clothes; and some, like Jack, had the notion of taking items away from the store for free to sell on the streets. The items were usually not clothing, unless it was something worth selling, like a leather jacket in excellent condition or some other item of value. But, those items were rare to find because Jack knew that all of the items were donated to the Salvation Army from the public---sometimes entire estates were donated, and he also knew that the best items were taken when they first came into the Salvation Army by the people who worked there. Jack understood that the merchandise he saw in the stores were just the remnants of a far more valuable cache. So, he had no qualms about taking things out of the store without paying. But, that was neither here-nor-there. He just used the place to keep up his appearance and perhaps, make a few dollars. It was a happy day except for the fact that he would not drink.

Jack could feel a sense of freedom when he had money. It took a world of pressure off of him from having to wake up and be creative every single day to find a way to make a hustle. It was different each day. He had to navigate between putting money in his pocket and avoiding getting locked up and playing past all of the people in the streets who knew him and were looking for a hustle or a hand-out themselves. The grind of the streets was sometimes brutal. But, Jack had made survival an art form and seemed to thrive from the challenge. Finally, he rose up, walked over and pushed the on button of his clock-radio and an upbeat

R&B tune immediately blared out, adding to the special mood that he was in.

He undressed and showered. He decided that he would go over to the DelMar restaurant at Lawrence and Broadway to have a good breakfast. This was rare for Jack because, most days, breakfast came late-morning in a bottle. After he had showered, Jack put on his "kick-around" clothes---just his usual kind of dress for an ordinary day. But, he fancied himself a good dresser and looked forward to how he would put together his attire for tonight. He was still mapping out his day. He took the lighter with him so that he could try to sell it to Jose because he knew there was an element of trust and goodwill that he had forged with Jose who had always given him a decent dollar for his merchandise. He had decided just then to have it appraised only if Jose did not buy it, because he needed to know just how valuable the lighter was before he sold it to anyone else. He did not want to practically give it away. He also remembered the several joints that he had and neatly folded them up in an empty Newport cigarette pack that he had laying around. He put it in his pocket.

It was a partly cloudy day that seemed to be trying to get brighter as the sun shown full intermittently. Jack could hear the R&B tune playing in his head and he felt free and easy as he strolled down Lawrence Avenue the short distance to the DelMar. He went in and ordered a cheese omelet breakfast. He noticed that the unusual, relaxed feeling that he had been having for the last week or so was now even more pronounced today. He was not in his usual vigilant survival mode. He would just relax today and be the free spirit that he was because he understood that days like this came few-and-far-in-between. Jack finished his breakfast and tipped the waitress. When he stepped outside, he could see the Uptown National Bank clock reading "11:14am" He knew that Jose usually did not arrive at the Aragon early. If he arrived at all, it would be past noon most times. Jack knew that during mid-week, with the Foreigner show coming to the Aragon this weekend, sometime during the middle of the week was when Jose would be there to oversee some contractual and financial issues related to the upcoming show. Jack knew that this was the routine Jose had when these big rock band shows came to the Aragon. He had learned this from the many times he had come into the huge showplace trying to find Jose to sell him something.

Jack turned east after walking out of the DelMar and began to stride energetically down Lawrence Avenue toward the corner of Winthrop and Lawrence where he always hung out and where the Aragon, the poolroom, A&W restaurant and Frances' Tavern were. He could see in the short distance, standing in front of the closed poolroom, some of his friends; there was Jabo, Skip and Larry----all older men than Jack. They were a few of the many friends and acquaintances that Jack seemed to have accumulated around the neighborhood and throughout Uptown. They were three of the more pleasant people that Jack associated with. Jack had spent many hours with them hanging around this corner, drinking, laughing ,joking and always having spirited conversations. Jabo was the oldest. He was somewhere around his mid-fifties. He was an old dope fiend who was now too worn from the hustling life to chase dope the way he used to. He mostly drank and had a shot of heroin once-in-a-blue moon. He lived with "Puddin" his wife of 25 years. Larry was probably around his late thirties; a single man who lived with his girlfriend. He was not a hustler in the sense that Jack was. He mostly worked temporary jobs and occasionally had a job that would last more than six months. He was a regular around The Corner and mainly hung around with Skip and Jabo because all three were old dope fiends who did not do the hard hustling to get dope, nor did they engage in it as often as most fiends did; only getting high in that manner on rare occasions and mostly sticking to drinking.

They stood around The Corner sharing a drink and a laugh with the other Corner regulars and occasionally imparted their street wisdom to young men like Jack. They liked Jack because of his hustling ability and often witnessed his exploits on the streets. They admired his clever, relentless hustling and saw him in much the same light as themselves when they were younger and more active. Whenever Jack approached The Corner and saw them or any of his other friends, he would begin to have a certain feeling of joy and fellowship. It was subtle but, Jack recognized it and he seemed to thrive on these friendships. He knew that he needed them and their friendships; their support; their wisdom and their advice. He valued them because they were like family to him. Jack had seen the seasons change several times over, standing out on The Corner passing the day with these men. They had built a special camaraderie and over time, had discussed every topic imaginable, it seemed and each man added his own personality to the mix. It was the kind of association that made some of the rougher days for Jack out on the streets a littler easier to bear. Sometimes, on days when he was broke and the hustling had not been so good, someone would offer him a drink and their companionship because that was all any of them had; and it was more than enough for Jack to make it through the day.

"Fellas....fellas...what's goin' on?" Jack greeted as he approached and stopped right in the midst of where the men stood. Hey, Jack" How ya' doin', Jack" "Hey there, Jack" they all responded. Jack gave an abbreviated soul handshake to each of the three men. This was the kind of handshake that was given when there were too many handshakes to be had at once and it served to shorten the ritual to a reasonable length. "Brotha', Jabo...I ain't surprised to see you out at this time...I *know* you and Puddin' get up early...but, Larry and Skippa-Dippa'...I don't usually see y'all out here this early...what's happenin'?....old lady kick y'all out?...I mean...what's goin' on?" Jack chided good-naturedly to kick-off the lively banter that the four of them had become accustomed to. "Hey, brotha', Jack...I'll tell you what...the way Rita runs through my li'l scratch...she bet' not kick me out, 'cause, she know she cain't live high-on-the-hog no more....dig what I'm sayin'? ....she cain't buy all o' them fancy li'l do-dads and all of that other stuff she be blowin' my money on...ya' know?" Skip said, tongue-in-cheek...taking the bait that Jack had offered and engaging the group to respond in-kind. "Okay...okay...that's a damned good one, Skip...I'll go for that one...at least you're creative with your excuse...you in there...now what's up with you, brotha' Larry?...what's the scoop on you, baby?...tell it like it is" Jack chided as he turned to Larry while staying in the spirit of the moment. "Okay...I confess, my old lady *did* kick me out...she say get up...get out and get somethin'...I ain't gonna lie...our funds is short...I'm out here tryin' to get a hustle goin'...that's all...that's what's goin' on with me..hahaha..."" Larry replied as he joined in the banter. It was all smiles and lively conversation during these encounters that seemed more like a family reunion to Jack. He relished these exchanges and they filled him with exuberance. "Hey, Jack...I don't know why they sayin' all that about they old lady is spendin' all they money and runnin' 'em out the crib, but, I'm out here early 'cause I'm in the worst shape…my old lady kicks me out early, then she turns over in the bed and keeps on sleepin'…and she just as broke as I am…she want me to catch hold of somethin' and bring it back…dig *that*..how about *them* apples..hahahaha..""" Jabo chimed in with his part that served to be like the punch line in a joke. They all laughed heartily after his quip. "So, Jack…where you been?…I didn't see you all day yesterday…you alright?" Jabo asked in a more serious tone. "Aw..I'm cool…I had to lay low 'cause I had some business to take care of…I'm tryin' to get into college and I laid in the crib most all day so I could make it to my appointment at the college center on Sheridan" Jack said. "No shit?…what you takin' up?" Jabo asked. "I don't know yet, man…still tryin' to see if I can get in…I filled my papers out and everything…got to wait and see…" Jack explained.

"We tryin' to get up on one, Jack…what you holdin'? Larry asked. "Aw…I got a little somethin' on it…what y'all tryin' to get?" Jack asked. "I don't know…Smirnoff if we can get it..""" Larry responded. "Tell you what…""" Larry began as he opened his palm that he had been clutching the change in all along and began to count. 40..60..80…one-twenty-five…yep…that's what we got…" Larry continued after the count. "Yea, Jack…that's it between all three of us…can you handle the rest?" Jabo asked. "Give me the change…I got 'ya' faded..""" Jack said as he extended an open hand to Larry to drop the change in his palm. Larry did not hesitate and dropped it. "I'll be right back" Jack said as he turned and walked back in the direction he had come from toward Saxony Liquors just up the street. Jack bought a pint instead of the half-pint the group expected to see. When he arrived back among them, they responded cheerfully. "Damn, Jack…you got a pint, huh?...I'm glad you was able to do that" Larry said with a tone of gratitude. "Yea…me, too…this oughta' take the "haints"offa' everybody…hahahaha" Skip said in the rhythmic bee-bop tone that he always spoke in. Jack knew that it was not a good idea to let the others who knew him on the streets know that he had very much money. Everyone on the streets understood that and knew how to play the game. You could be generous but, only up to a certain point. You did not allow yourself to be a "soft touch" because some would abuse such generosity. So, Jack played it cool. The three men stepped away from the front of the poolroom and turned the corner to walk north on Winthrop to the playground to do their drinking. Jack did not drink and gave the excuse that he had to go to the college center today. He spent about a half-hour with the men, and had some laughs as they continued to crack jokes and share philosophies amongst themselves.

Finally, Jack decided to go on with his day and his plans. He said goodbye to the men and after he had stepped several yards away, he turned back to Jabo and casually and matter-of-factly called him to walk over to the short distance where he had stopped. "Oh…hey, Jabo…I forgot I wanted to ask you somethin' man…let me holla' at you" Jack said. After Jabo walked over to Jack and stood in front of him and asked "What's happ'nin, Jack?" Jack slipped a folded-up bill to Jabo and said "This is yours…just between you and me…you know" he said in confidence. "Aw, hey…thanks, Jack…good lookin' out…'preciate it" Jabo replied. "Keep that under ya' hat…cool?" Jack added. "Solid" Jabo replied and they parted. Jabo knew how to play it off. He slipped the folded bill into his pocket and when he would get back to the group, he would just say "He just wanted to ask me where that pawn shop down past Irving was" This was sufficient to placate them. Jabo and Puddin' had always been very friendly and kind to Jack and had shared their drinks at times when Jack had nothing. Jack felt closer to them and treated them like family; and so, whenever he had done well enough to give them money, he did.

Jack turned the corner where the poolroom had just opened and walked past it to go into the Aragon where some of the custodial workers were cleaning floors and the glass front entrance doors. He saw Rodrigo down the hall several yards away and called to him. "Rodrigo!..""" Rodrigo turned around and paused briefly to see who Jack was before beginning to walk toward him. "Yes, mi amigo…what is it?" He replied. "Hey…is Jose here yet?" Jack asked. "He is upstairs but, he just got here…you may want to give him another hour or so…Okay?" Rodrigo said. "Okay?…he's probably not settled in yet…pro'bly got a lot of business to take care of, huh?" Jack asked. "Yes…I think so…an hour or two later he will be ready to go to lunch…that is the best time" Rodrigo said. Okay, amigo…thanks" Jack said and walked out of the Aragon.

Jack headed for Broadway and Wilson where a number of men's clothing stores were to buy the underwear and shoes that he had planned to get. He went into the Woolworth's store because he knew that their underwear were just as good as the other fancier men's stores nearby, and he could get Fruit-of-the-Loom underwear for a better price. When he entered the store and came to the men's underwear section, he could not help but think about stealing them and his mind went through the usual calculations of how he would steal one or two three-in-a-pack underwear in the plastic packaging and walk out of the store. He had been successful in stealing from there several times in the past and the urge was overwhelming-----until he thought about Tina and of how the possibility of getting caught would spoil the wonderful evening he was looking forward to. Besides, buying and not stealing would help his credibility for any future times that he would come into the store. He grabbed two packs of his size of the three-in-a-pack Fruit-of-the-Looms and walked to the check-out line. It didn't feel right to him, but, he paid. Now, the shoes. He found a men's store along the Broadway strip between Wilson and Leland where many of the apparel stores were. There was a nice selection in the style of shoes he liked. Jack spent almost half an hour selecting a stylish pair of shoes that fit comfortably. He finally found a pair of black leather dress shoes that felt good. He paid and left the store, heading for the Wilson Avenue Pawn Shop just up the street and around the corner.

"Hey Bob…how ya' doin'?" he greeted the proprietor that he had come to know through the several times in the last couple of years when he had come into the shop and either sold or tried to sell something. "Whaddya' say there, young fella?" Bob greeted in his characteristic country-western drawl. Bob was an older man, somewhere in his fifties. He was an astute business man who had been in business at the pawn shop located underneath the Wilson Avenue "L" stop for most of the dozen years he had lived in Chicago after moving from Texas. He was well known by all the hustlers around the area and Jack had come to know him through J.T. Silk, his longtime friend. Bob bought a lot of items from the street hustlers in the area. But, he did not buy certain, risky items that could be traced by the police. He did not buy other items that he suspected were stolen from people too nearby his shop. He had very good instincts for such things and he had a good rapport with all the hustlers who did business with him. He was as fair as anyone. But, he did not buy or take into pawn anything that was not profitable. He was very knowledgeable in appraising merchandise; especially jewelry and he had done a lot of business with J.T and others. He had only become fully acquainted with Jack in the past year. “I’m cool, Bob…hey…I got somethin’ here I want you to look at…I need to know what you think as far as a price…okay?” Jack said. “Alright..let me see it” Bob responded in the calm manner he always spoke. Jack pulled out the lighter and handed it to Bob. Bob took it into his hand and immediately began to look at it intently. He walked over a few feet behind the counter and grabbed one of the magnifying glasses that he used to inspect jewelry. He was silent for about a half-minute before he spoke. “Okay…you got here some ten-karat on top of sterling….it’s nice…it’s worth somethin’ but, not a whole lot…the gem is not real..just a stone…what are you tryin’ to get for it?” Bob asked in his usual straightforward manner. He was a business man who understood “caveat emptor” and he knew that Jack understood it, as well. He knew that street hustlers like Jack did not take it personal that he was trying to make a buck off of them. Because whatever deal was made always benefitted both parties and Bob usually came to an agreement with most all the hustlers on whatever it was he decided to buy from them. “Okay, then…what can I get for it, Bob?” Jack asked. “Well…I’d say between forty-to-seventy dollars brand new…you might be able to get thirty-five dollars for it on the streets” Bob estimated. “Okay…what would *you* give me for it?” Jack asked. “One question…where’d you get it from?” Bob asked in a whispering tone. Jack began to talk low as some other customers walked in and had not approached the counter but, were milling around looking at merchandise in the shop. Jack leaned over the counter and spoke in a low tone. “I pocketed it off of a guy in the Green Mill last night…he don’t live around here….he lives way up on Milwaukee Avenue somewhere…he don’t hang in the neighborhood around here…he just shows up on Jazz nights at the Green Mill and that’s it…”” Jack confided. This was the way that Bob did business---he just wanted honesty about the source of the merchandise that hustlers were bringing to him so that he would know how to operate and handle the merchandise. It made the difference between displaying the merchandise in his shop and selling it by other means. He had plenty of fences and connections of his own from all of his years in the business. "Okay…as long as you're telling me the truth…I'll take it off your hands" Bob said. "Okay…how much?" Jack responded immediately; he was thinking that he did not want to waste any more time going back to the Aragon to find Jose and negotiate a deal for the lighter when he could possibly sell it to Bob right now. "Twenty five dollars…that's my best offer.." Bob answered. "Aw…come on, now, Bob…what..wha…thirty-five, man…alright?" Jack pleaded. "That's my best offer….take it or leave it…" Bob answered firmly. "Now, Bob…Bob…you know damned well, if you buy it, I'll come in here next week and see this piece in the case for three times that much…come on…tell the truth..''" Jack argued. "I got to make some money…you know how it is…we've had good deals before just like this one…last offer…okay?" Bob said with a tone of finality. Jack paused for a moment with a furrowed brow and finally said "Okay.." with a sigh of resignation. Jack really didn't care that much that he was getting the price that Bob had offered. He just argued because it was all part of his hustling technique----using the situation to hone his negotiating skills to see just how far he could go and how much he could get. He had picked this technique up from his hustling buddy, Melvin because he had seen the surprising success that Melvin had when he forced the issue. Jack had witnessed people give in to Melvin's persistence. He had seen how Melvin sometimes had gotten twice as much as he should have just from running his mouth. "Walk down here to the end of the counter and I'll take care of you.." Bob said in a whispering tone. Jack walked down to the end and signed a receipt Bob had prepared for him and after Bob gave him the twenty-five dollars, Jack left.

"Hey, Ida…you still lookin' good, girl...you gettin' hard to resist…you know that?" Jack said in his usual flirtatious manner to her. "Man..you always talkin' that mess…you scared of me and you know it…" Ida said in a calm, level manner. "Hahahaha…hahaha" Jack laughed. "Woman…you know I wanna' get next to you…don't fight it, baby" Jack said in one of his pseudo-sexy voices as he moved up close to her face. "Okay…what do you want, Jack?...go ahead and get what you want and stop talkin' all of that smack" Ida chided dismissively while fighting back a smile. She played along with the familiar routine that they both seemed to enjoy. Ida was an easy-going woman with a good heart and although Jack knew that he was taking advantage of her good nature, he really did like her and he thought she looked nice. He was sexually attracted to her too but, he only hinted at such possibilites in his light-hearted exchanges with her. He knew that she was a mature woman who did not play games. That she would not want to be involved with someone as unstable as him; although, she seemed to respond positively to Jack's hints about sex. Jack looked around the store that seemed to have just been restocked. He found a new shirt that was very nice but, it took much longer before he found a pair of slacks that he found acceptable. They were a pair of medium bluish-gray colored slacks that were semi-flaired Dockers with cuffs. They were new and flawless and still had one of the original manufacturer tags on it. They were his exact size, too. Jack decided that they only needed a little bit of pressing and that was it; he was delighted, too to find a new black leather belt with a stylish silver buckle that he thought would impress Tina. That was the last item he needed except for some new cologne that he wanted to get. Jack walked up to the counter and Ida checked-out a customer before she gave Jack a bag and a big smile and said "Here you go, man…now…go on about your business" Jack took the bag and said "You're beautiful, Ida…with your sexy self…I oughta…" "Go on and get outa' here, man before you get me all messed up around here!" Ida cut in before Jack could finish. "Hahahaha…hahaha…I love you, Ida…I'll see you later, baby" Jack said, still chuckling to himself as he looked back at her while crossing the threshold of the door on his way out.

He continued north on Broadway with his bags. He came near Montrose where "Pigeon Square" was----an almost triangular concrete island where the southbound Sheridan bus stopped on the east side of it and the northbound Broadway bus stopped on the west side of it. It was not called Pigeon Square because of pigeons; but, more for the manner in which the various street characters seemed to perch upon it; coming and going as pigeons do. The island had three large concrete planters evenly spaced in the center of it. The planters, with their small trees stemming from the middle of each and the concrete area surrounding it, was where many of the drinkers and drifters hung out; usually making a showy public display of themselves as they gathered up together; gabbing and chattering and causing little upheavals of insanity and skittish commotion from time-to-time. They languished on this island, panhandling for change from whomever they could to buy drinks; making little runs back-and-forth to the nearby take-out liquor store across the street on the southwest corner of Broadway and Montrose; passing great spans of the day during the warmer seasons drinking, drunk; cursing; lounging; laughing and forever seeking to maintain, to sustain, to forget, to fend-off and to find---something----what---they did not know. Some would stop there to keep company with the others who were already there or to just rest before going on their way. The sight of them on Pigeon Square and how they carried on epitomized their vagrant existence. This was how it was all over the streets of Uptown to varying degrees. Jack continued on and as he did, he could see that Pigeon Square was occupied with several familiar regulars. He could see from a short distance the desperation upon their faces; their darting eyes looking around for something; needing something, wanting something; their postures slumping from the weariness of the many long, empty hours spent traipsing up and down the streets. Jack did what every street hustler knew to do. He avoided them by continuing on his way on the east side of Sheridan Road. He knew that any time the "pigeons" saw someone they knew passing by with shopping bags who appeared in any way to be prospering, they would call out from Pigeon Square for them to come over or they would walk over to that person to see what they could get from them. None of the people he saw in Pigeon Square were his friends; there were a few of the usual characters that he was used to seeing every day. He walked past on the opposite side of the street and they did not notice him.

He walked on until he came to Wilson Avenue and turned left to go west to the Walgreens store two blocks away on the northeast corner of Wilson and Broadway. This was where he would find a nice cologne to wear tonight, he thought. That was all he needed now for his big night and his little bit of shopping would be done. He turned at the northeast corner at Broadway and Wilson and walked into the Walgreens store. He carried his bag in and as he was walking into the aisles, he could see from the corner of his eye, an undercover security person dressed in street clothes. He could also see from the corner of his eye that person, after spotting him with his shopping bags, walk forward in the next aisle over to cut Jack off and probably keep an eye on him by getting a better vantage point. Jack could smell security people and policemen. He had the keen instinct of being able to sniff them out. Jack knew what the man was doing and he could sense his presence. But Jack was not about to steal anything; even though the wheels were turning in his head right at that moment as to how he would steal something if he was not being watched. Jack walked around until he found the aisle where the men's cologne was. He looked at and smelled one brand of cologne and finally decided to buy the 4oz. bottle of a Ralph Lauren brand that had the scent he liked best. Jack could feel the plain-clothes security person looking at him and he stole a quick glance out of the corner of his eye to see the medium height man furtively peering around the corner at the end of the aisle. "Fool" Jack thought to himself. He hated these rent-a-cops and the way they thought they knew who was going to steal just by their appearance. He did not care what the security thought of him and it just made him delight just that much more whenever he got away with stealing from stores. Jack walked calmly up to the counter and got into the check-out line with his selection with two other customers ahead of him. The security man stood behind the line of people in the check-out line and it placed him facing Jack's back where Jack could not see him. He was also near the door. Jack turned his head casually to look behind him and caught the security person staring at his shopping bags with his shoes, slacks and shirt inside. He stared intently as though he was trying to see right through Jack's bags. His face held the usual suspecting expression that Jack would have expected. Jack already knew the attitude of these security types. There was never anytime that they did not hawk Jack or any other young black man like himself whenever they entered a store. Jack could remember this happening since he was very young----long before he became a street person and began to steal. He could only resign himself to the status of the perennial suspect because he *was* a thief. But, somehow, there was still something that stuck in his gut about the whole thing. As Jack walked out of the Walgreens store, he could feel his spirit soaring.

He felt a joy in his soul. It was as though all the stars and planets had aligned to make a bright rainbow around him. It felt like those days when he was just a boy; staring through the kitchen back window watching the rain as it poured down into the back yard and feeling melancholy because the rain had spoiled his day of fun out in that yard where he loved to play. Then, having the rain stop and the sun come out and that joyous feeling return of knowing he could go out and play again. Jack continued on. He did not own a watch, and what time it was had not mattered so much in his everyday life until now, when he needed to know because of his date with Tina tonight. He was good at guessing the time and he remembered that the clock behind Ida at the Thrift Store counter read about "1:17" About a half-hour had passed since then and he guessed the time to be about 1:45. He walked along the street with a bouncing stride that was full of energy and reflected the fabulous mood he was in. Jack had always been full of imagination and his mind was always full of the exciting possibilities for the future. He had always been full of hope about how good life could be. But, he could not figure out how he had come to be such a misfit when his thoughts and intentions had been so different from his actions. He had always been puzzled that for all the hopes and desires that he held for his young life, he had not come even close to fulfilling any such aspirations. How did he end up on the streets when his aim was to live the serene life of a sophisticated gentleman?----how had he, instead, come to this condition of subsisting----barely surviving, He did not know and right now, did not care. The thought was a fleeting one that passed like an exhaled breath. He would just continue on to be carefree and live life for the moment because it seemed so burdensome to think about problems and to worry. He did not like worrying at all----it was the one thing that he detested most. It seemed to be a human condition that was least like living or being alive; and so, he loved to live with a bit of recklessness. It seemed right and it felt good---to hell with worry!----that was what drinking was for---to forget; to be joyous; to live; and that is what he would do until something stopped him. Jack continued north on Broadway and began to cross from the east side of Broadway to the west side of it near the traffic light at Leland Avenue. He was stepping at the same lively pace when a voice called out to him

"Jaaaccckk….Jaaacckk!" he turned to his right to see Chump Boy and Cozell standing near the alley east of Broadway between the Majestic men's clothing store and the west end of the Leland building. They appeared to be socializing in the way that drinkers did when they drank together. They had probably just finished a drink, Jack thought. He knew the routine because he had done it so many times with each of them and many of the other neighborhood drinkers---you anted up all your change and bought a drink and then another and another until you ran out of drinks. Jack could see immediately that this was the purpose in them calling out to him. They had noticed the shopping bags that he was carrying and how he looked a little better kept than usual. Cozell was the neighborhood drunk; a man in his late thirties. He lived alone in a little kitchenette apartment in the three-story building across from the Tower building on Winthrop near Leland. He was a former westsider who once had a tough-guy reputation on that side of town. He had been to prison several times in the past. But, now, his hard drinking over the years had reduced him to a harmless drunk who slurred his speech even when he was not drinking; a true alcoholic whose life involved no activities other than drinking and hanging out on the streets. He did not care much about anything except drinking and his usual unkept appearance reflected as much. He was a fixture around the neighborhood. Chump Boy was a fifty-something year-old man from the south who was as country as could be; a good-natured fellow who had not been around all that long in Chicago or the neighborhood; just three years since coming from Mississippi. He was a hard working man who lived in a small apartment on Lawrence Avenue in the next block east of the poolroom. He was nick-named "Chump Boy" because of his unassuming, easy-going manner. But, mostly for how people took advantage of his good nature when he first came around. During that first year around the neighborhood, he was cheated, tricked, bullshitted, played and ripped-off. He was made a fool at every turn. But, after almost a year of this, he wised up and began to protect himself by just saying "no" to all the conning propositions that came his way from those who would beat him out of whatever they could. He went a step further, too by keeping more to himself. "Hey, Jaaaccckk!" Cozell called out again loud and strong. Jack knew that there was no choice but for him to go over to see what they wanted even though he was in a hurry to go home and get dressed for tonight. After looking in their direction and pausing momentarily, Jack started in their direction. "Wha 'ya say there, Mr. Jack…what's goin' on?" Chump Boy greeted with his southern drawl and the usual good-natured, broad grin he would have after a few drinks. Cozell just stood there next to Chump Boy, his head slightly wobbling from side-to-side in the same manner that the worst alcoholics' did. "Hey, Jack….how ya' doin' man?…what you got in them bags, man?" Cozell asked, never using any tact whatsoever, because he just didn't care. "Cozy Cozell…my main man…what's poppin' baby?" Jack greeted as he grabbed Cozell's right hand and started playfully giving a soul handshake. "Aw…these some clothes for me to go to school…they gave me a voucher from the school to buy this shit" Jack lied. "That's cool, man…hey…you got any chump?" Cozell asked. "Aw, man…I'm popped, straight up, man…I got to hold my little change for carfare so I can go up to the school tomorrow….it's way west around Kimball" Jack explained. "Aw, Jack…help us out a little bit…we need a little change to get us one" Chump Boy pleaded. When he first came around, Chump Boy would never have spoken that way to anyone by trying to persuade them to give him anything. But, his three years in the city had taught him to stop being so nice. He had began to pick up the behavior of the others after realizing how ruthless the game in the streets of Chicago was and how he just had to look out for himself and play the game the way that everyone else did. "Chump Boy…didn't I just say I didn't have no money?…what's up, baby?..you didn't hear me?" Jack asked sarcastically with the facial expression to go with it that soon gave way to a smile slowly spreading across his face. "Hahahaha…ahahahaha" Chump Boy laughed out loud at Jack's kidding around. Over time, he had come to recognize Jack's way of joking and having fun. "Hey, Jack-boy…you alright with me, man…you know that, right?….hahahaha" Chump Boy went on as he stuck his hand out and he and Jack shook hands as they all laughed together. "Hey Chump Boy…you don't look like you need no drink, man…look like you already been tastin' pretty tough…why you wanna' play on me for my little change…huh?" Jack continued to tease. "Naw..we just had a l'il ol' pint of that MD 2020, man…all that stuff do is make you mad…you know that…that ain't nothin' but a teaser for us, Jack…come on…help us out, sho''nough…we ain't near 'bout high" Chump Boy explained as his voice drifted into a more serious tone. "You need another one..sho' 'nough, huh?" Jack asked more seriously as well. "Hey…hey…hey,

Jack…no shit, man…that ain't no lie…I just came out about an hour ago…I still got the shakes, man…we need a taste…I ain't bullshittin' this ya' boy Cozell askin' you to help us out" Cozell pleaded. "Tell y'all what…y'all have helped me out before, so….here you go…get ya' self a brick" Jack said as he handed Cozell three one dollar bills. Cozell crumpled the bills in his grasp before he looked down to see how many there were. "Aw…damn, Jack…right on…you alright…you my guy, man…I ain't jivin' either…hahaha..hahaha" Cozell chuckled a lazy, slurring, happy, alcoholic laugh. The three of them slapped hands, giving each other "five" and laughed a little more before Jack said he had to go. The two men got what they were looking for, and although he tried to avoid them, Jack felt a little better at seeing the smiles on their faces after helping them out. He really didn't mind because they were his friends and they helped each other from time-to-time.

Jack continued on west on Leland to his place at the Arms and he allowed the joy to flow as the special rendezvous that he was anticipating drew nearer. He guessed that the time might be about 2:15 in the afternoon and with that in mind, he would go home and lounge for a while before calling Tina. He arrived at the entrance of the Arms and he rushed past several of the familiar residents loitering in the lobby and shot up the stairwell two-steps-at-a-time as he did when he was feeling especially good or was in a hurry; and right now----he was both. He arrived at his place and turned on his clock-radio to keep himself company as he rambled around his little place, taking the items he had bought out of the bags; measuring pant lengths and trying on the shirt, then the shoes, and so on. After he had done all of that, he decided that everything was fine and he bounced around to the beat of the several soulful tunes that played on his favorite radio station. Jack looked at his clock-radio again to see that it was now 3:32pm and he remembered that he did not want to seem anxious when he last talked to Tina about what time he would call her today before their date. He said that he had "business" to attend to in the early afternoon and that he would call her shortly after 4:30pm. Of course, this was all part of the little lover's games that new lovers played with each other to keep the passion flowing and the interest piqued.

He decided that he had time to go for a good haircut at Hank Jackson's apartment over on Leland over the Time Out bar near Clifton Street. He kept what he had on and rushed out of the door to head to Hank's place, which was only a few minutes walk away. When he arrived on the third floor of the old hotel building where Hank lived, he knocked on the door several times----there was no answer and he felt disappointed because Hank was almost always home because he had a bad leg and walked with a cane and had diabetes and didn't get out much and rarely drank for health reasons. Jack was going down the stairwell and, as luck would have it on one of his better days in quite sometime, he ran into Hank coming up the stairs. "Hey, Hank… I need one, baby…hook me up!" Jack said, smiling broadly as he looked down the stairwell at Hank who was at the bottom of the stairs, pausing to catch his breath. "I'll be glad when they fix that damned elevator" he said with a sigh after taking another deep breath. Hank started again from the bottom of the stairs with his cane to walk up toward Jack. "You need one…one what?…shit…I need me some damn ice water, that's what *I* need" Hank said with a little gasp between words. "Hank….a haircut…what else did you think I was talkin' about?…a hair cut, man…you gonna do that for me, huh?" Jack asked hopefully. "Man…I got to rest for a minute before I come up there" Hank said, continuing to gasp. "Okay…okay…go ahead and rest…you gonna do that?" Jack asked again. "Yea, man…damn…why you keep askin' me?…take it easy…I ain't goin' nowhere" Hank said again with a bit of annoyance. "You didn't say nothin' when I asked you the first time, Hank so, I asked you again, man…damn" Jack said with a little annoyance of his own. "Alright…come on" Hank said as he arrived at the top of the stairs and walked past Jack toward his apartment door halfway down the hallway. Jack followed him and after Hank unlocked his door, they walked in and Jack started walking around anxiously in the one-and-a-half room apartment. Hank plopped down on the old sofa almost in the middle of the room. "Sit down, Jack…you ain't gonna grow no taller" Hank said in the manner that he always did of speaking in one-line dialogue. "Okay" Jack said compliantly. "What you need a haircut for, Jack?…so you can look good when they lock you up and take ya' picture for stealin' everything that ain't tied down?" Hank said wryly with a light chuckle. "Now, Hank…that's cold…is that any way to treat a payin' customer, huh?" Jack answered with a note of sarcasm. "Payin?…Payin?…you gonna pay me?.....I'll be damned…I think you owe me for about two haircuts already, don't you?" Hank said with a tone of surprise and sarcasm of his own. "Hank…don't forget… I got you high twice…you remember you wanted me to get you high about three months ago and I did it twice and you said forget about what I owed you for the haircuts…you remember that?" Jack explained. Hank paused with silence and furrowed his forehead while he tried to recall what Jack was talking about. "I said that?….I don't remember that" Hank replied innocently. """That's 'cause you got good and high and you forgot everything after that…I helped you get home 'cause we was hangin' out by the lot next to the buildin' right here…I had to help your heavy ass up them stairs 'cause the elevator was broke…you was drunk…remember?" Jack went on. "Naw, naw, naw…I don't remember that" Hank said with assurance. "Aw, come on, Hank!" Jack said with exasperation. "Hey…well…just forget about the two haircuts, then and just pay me now…you gonna' pay me, right?" Hank asked to be reassured. "Yea…I'm gonna' pay you" Jack said with annoyance. "Come on, then, Hank…let's get started….I got a hot date in about two hours" Jack said in a lighter tone. Hank didn't say anything but, walked over to the old dresser near his closet and started rambling in one of the drawers and pulled out his electric hair clippers and a few attachments and started to clean the blades. He took a couple of minutes and he soon had begun cutting Jack's hair.

Jack rarely got his hair cut because he rarely spared the money to have it done. Most of his money went to buying drinks or occasionally T's and Blues. This was the new synthetic drug that was two prescription pills crushed in water, mixed and shot up like heroin with a similar high. Jack rarely got high in this manner and had started about a year ago to engage in this new fad. It proved to be dangerous because early-on, he had observed some of the people he was getting high with have seizures. The seizures he had seen were violent and whoever was around that person having the seizure would usually try to help them by making sure that they did not choke by swallowing their tongue. They held the tongue down by sticking a comb in their mouths. Jack had engaged in this way of getting high perhaps, a half-dozen times in that time without having a seizure. He had decided that the ones who were having the seizures were being greedy like fiends often were; abusing the drugs by taking too much at one time. That was the reason, he surmised, that they were having those seizures. He was careful not to use too much of the mixture to avoid having a seizure himself. As Hank was cutting Jack's hair, they engaged in their usual good-natured exchange of debates, arguments and put-downs.

Finally, Hank was done and Jack looked in the dresser mirror at his new haircut and he liked the way it looked and he thanked Hank. Before he could dig into his pocket to pay him, Hank said "Thank me by payin' me…that's the kinda' thanks I want…know what I mean, jelly bean…hahahaha" he chuckled. Jack paid him and gave him a two-dollar tip. "You did a good job, brotha' Hank…there you go" Jack said as he handed him several dollar bills. "Damn, Jack…you tippin' and everything…right on…this chick must be hot, man…to make you spend your drinkin' money on a haircut…hahahaha" Hank teased. "Hey, man…I don't just drink…a little mackin' ain't never hurt either…dig it" Jack answered spiritedly. Jack bounced down the stairwell of the hotel building on his way back to his place.

He knew that the time was very near for him to call Tina and he was trying to tell himself that it was all no big deal. But, the gradual rise of excitement inside was telling him different. He was trying to behave naturally, and he was on the outside but, inside he could sense a curious kind of merriment in his soul; a strange kind of good feeling. He did not want to let it overtake him. These kinds of feelings were so foreign to him and he felt awkward to even acknowledge their existence. Yet, he needed to feel them so badly. It was like a drink of water to one who had thirsted for an eternity; like peace in the middle of hell; like everything good he had never known. There was something spiritual about this woman and their connection. He felt it. And although he could not commit any notion of certainty to it, there was a sense of righteousness about it all. Jack arrived back at his place and as he pushed the unlocked door forward, he was anxious about the time as he focused on his clock-radio sitting on his dresser. 4:18pm, it said and he felt relieved that it was not later. He lie down across the bed and let his mind drift. He closed his eyes and he could feel the tenderness of Tina surrounding him. He could remember what her kiss tasted like. He could hear the sweet sound of her distinct feminine voice in his head. He could see her pretty face, so natural, pure and fresh; the sweet smell of her; her silky hair brushing across his face; her warm body underneath him; her loose and care-free sense of humor; the warmth of her spirit; it had all captivated his senses. He suddenly awoke from his semi-sleep, semi-daydream that seemed to last much longer than the few minutes it did. He looked over at the clock-radio to see 4:25pm.He turned the radio on. He got up from the bed and went into the bathroom and had a long and relaxing shower. He carefully cleaned his nails and took extra care to brush his teeth and rinse with mouthwash. He used lotion on his skin and dabbed on a little cologne. He groomed himself better than he had in as long as he could remember. The happy beat of the soul tunes that played on his radio kept his spirits high. He was surprised at how feeling good mentally could make him feel so good physically----it all seemed so strange to him. He had not felt good mentally, it seemed, ever. Not since he was young enough to be blissfully ignorant of the pitfalls in life. Jack finished his grooming and spread his clothes out on the bed. He dressed and looked at himself in the mirror, primping as he did when he thought he had a reason to. He was satisfied with his appearance. He had gone through extra care to select his outfit for tonight. He noticed that the haircut had made a big difference by making him look much more neat and respectable. He was glad that he had gotten it done. He looked at the clock-radio again. It was a few minutes past 5pm. Finally, he put his money in his pocket and walked out, locked his door and went down stairs to the lobby to a pay phone.

He called Tina. The phone rang several times before Tina picked up "Hello" her familiar voice spoke out, pleasantly piercing Jack's senses. "Hey, baby….it's me" Jack said with uncharacteristic gentleness. "Hey, Jack…I've been waiting for your call, honey…how are you?" Tina replied in a soft, sultry tone. "I'm cool…you gettin' ready?" Jack asked. "Baby, I've been ready" Tina purred with a scintillating sexiness in her voice. "I hope so, baby…I hope so…I'm almost ready….I want you to meet me on the platform as close to 7:30 as possible, okay?….just step off and we can talk while we wait for the next train…we're goin' downtown for dinner, then for a stroll around downtown….how's that?" Jack said. "Sounds good to me but, when I get off at the platform….all we're gonna' do is talk?" Tina said, playfully hinting at the obvious. “Baby…you know how we talk…we talk in different ways to each other….right?” Jack said in his own sexy tone. “Yes we do…and I’d say we’ve been having some very good talks lately…don’t you think?” Tina replied. “You’d better stop talkin’ that way or you might get more than you expect on that platform tonight” Jack hinted just as playfully. “You think I care…it wouldn’t matter to me where it was” Tina responded. “Okay…that’s it…stop…you’re gonna have me standin’ at attention out here and I might have to go back home and change…hahahaha” Jack laughed out loud. He could hear Tina laughing on the phone along with him. “I could just see you now with a big old wet spot in the front of your pants, trying to get back home to change…just picturing that cracks me up, Jack…hahahaha” Tina laughed. The laughing subsided, and when it did, Jack could feel a kind of release from it. It felt as though some kind of therapy had taken place and he barely noticed it. His mood was serene and he wanted to savor this very moment because it seemed so pure and innocent. “Ok, baby…get a move on…I’ll be waitin’” Jack almost whispered. “See you around 7:30 on the platform, honey…byyyyeee” Tina said very sweetly.

Jack was aware that he had about two hours to kill before he would be meeting Tina. He did not want to sit in his apartment because he knew the anxiousness would drive him crazy. He decided to go to his usual hang-out spot at the poolroom where he seemed to end up on most days. It was uncanny the way that seemed to happen, no matter what was happening on any given day for Jack, he seemed to always end up there at around 5 or 6pm. He walked out of the front door of the Arms and walked at an easy pace toward the poolroom. He decided, too that he would not think about Tina and their date so much. But, would just hang out for a while with any of his friends who happened to be around the poolroom. His interaction with them would keep him occupied and it would help him to relax before he met with Tina. He was kind of annoyed with himself that he was thinking about using diversions in this way. Why couldn’t he just act natural and not be so full of anticipation?----he didn’t know. But, he needed to compose himself, he thought. It was funny that he was thinking in this way, because he knew that as soon as he met with Tina and saw her, and began talking with her, he would feel relaxed right away. It was not her that was making him think and feel the way that he was right now because she accepted him completely and he knew that. It was something in his mind. Something about how he had been conditioned to reject others before they rejected him. It was about how his father never seemed to embrace him or treat him like a human being. It was about how he had landed on these streets all on his own with this way of life and not knowing how it all came to be. These thoughts vaguely ruminated deep in his mind; always blurred and in pieces; never in whole or complete thoughts. But, they manifested themselves in these feelings he was having that he knew were unnatural. But they felt natural to him-----feelings of guilt and shame that he could not understand where they were coming from.

Jack walked past the Aragon entrance, then the A&W restaurant. As he walked along Lawrence Avenue in front of the long stretch of the poolroom window, he peered inside momentarily to try to see if he saw any of his friends. He came to the entrance and swung open the door and walked in. He didn't see any of them and he immediately walked over to his favorite spot at the front in the corner where he could see everything without being so easily seen himself. There were several pool games going on with a few tables of the local regulars playing and a couple of tables of those from outside the area who visited the poolroom occasionally. Jack just sat quietly, trying to relax and momentarily checking his dress, picking off any little lint he saw and making sure his attire was flawless.

He thought about how he would try to make the night a pleasant one for Tina and which restaurant they would go to. He was familiar with where everything was downtown and although he had not decided which restaurant exactly, it was no big deal, he thought. He would just be spontaneous and pick the one that was most appealing at that time as they walked around downtown.

The audio system in the poolroom was playing a mix of soul tunes, rock and Mexican music. His mind drifted along with the music as a few romantic R&B tunes played in-between that seemed to be speaking to Jack suggestively; seemingly merging into his thoughts and setting a pleasant mood. Jack realized just then what he knew subconsciously---why he came into the poolroom all the time and just sat; why he sometimes used it like a sanctuary; because the music coming over the audio system seemed to sooth and rejuvenate his spirit. At other times, the poolroom served other purposes; to socialize with his friends; a base from which to hustle and to get high and to carry on the madness that seemed a part of his everyday life. He came there to not feel alone, at first. He remembered when he first moved into the 4848 Winthrop building and he lost his job and did not know anyone. That was when he came to the poolroom and gradually became acquainted with the local regulars.

Almost half-an-hour had passed while Jack sat in the front corner of the poolroom, trying not to let himself get too excited about tonight. For the most part, he was succeeding. He seemed to feel more serene as the time passed. He could see 6:12pm on the wall clock behind the service counter across the room where the service counter guys stood while they talked, laughed and joked while serving the pool-playing customers. Just then, the poolroom door swung open and in walked his friend, Coley. He stood in one place just to one side of the door for a moment. He did the same thing that Jack always did, gaze around the entire poolroom to see who was there; this seemed to be the mindset of certain hustlers to make themselves aware of their surroundings. Jack saw him do this and he understood this mentality of being aware and taking a mental snapshot of the scene. Jack and Coley both understood how dangerous these streets were and how such awareness was paramount to their survival. Finally, Coley saw Jack in the corner and walked over to him.

"What the hell's goin' on, Jack…you gonna' do some preachin' tonight or what?....you sharp this evenin', bro'..what's the occasion?" Coley inquired of Jack. "Nothin, man…just s'posed to step out with my little lady tonight" Jack replied, as he tried to project as much of an unconcerned, casual air as he could to hide the happy feeling he had inside. "Okay…cool…damn, you goin' out on a *real* date...this ain't just a wham-bam-thank-you-m'am kinda' girl, huh?" Coley asked pryingly. Jack paused and let a silent moment pass before he said "Aw…she cool…I like her…she ain't from around here" cutting his comment about the subject short because he did not want to let friends like Coley see his softer side. "She ain't from around here?…where she from, then?" Coley inquired. Jack paused again, then answered. "She's from Evanston, man" "Evanston, huh?…no shit?...go 'head on with ya' bad self, then, brotha'" Coley replied with the smile of a big brother that said he was happy for Jack and that he was pleased that he was doing things that were more sociable. “Let’s get a taste, then” Coley offered. “I ain’t drinkin’ tonight, man” Jack replied bluntly. “Aw, shit….aw shit…you ain’t just shuckin’ and jivin’ about this girl…she must be *about* somethin’…that’s cool, Jack…you need to go out with the ladies insteada’ hangin’ out with these hardlegs all the time…what time you meetin’ up?” Coley inquired. I’m s’posed to meet her on the “L” platform up there at about seven-thirty” Jack said. “Okay…then I can see her from a distance to see what she looks like, huh?” Coley asked. “Yea, man…you can check her out when you see me go up there…she gonna step off the train so we can talk…just look up there…you’ll see us” Jack said with assurance. “If she is pretty nice lookin’ then, I might have to come up there and meet her” Coley said with a wry grin. “She is fine, man…and you better stay your monkey-ass down there on the ground ‘cause me and her got some business to take care of on that platform…you dig!” Jack said jokingly but, shifting into the hardcore street dialogue that was so much a part of him and how he, Coley and all of the other street regulars talked. “Damn, Jack…she must look alright ‘cause you wanna’ feel her up when she step off that train, huh?…wanna’ get some o’ that sugar before you get back on the train…I can dig it, man….more power to ya’ brotha’…do yo’ thang, brotha’…do yo’ thang” Coley added in a rhythmic tone. “Yea…I’m gonna hang for a little while, man…then, I got to book” Jack said. Coley sat down next to Jack and they engaged in small talk for a while, laughing and joking in-between like they always did. Finally, Jack looked up at the poolroom wall clock behind the counter again and it read “7:10”.

“I got to go, Coley ‘cause I ain’t sure exactly which one o’ these trains she’s gonna be on…so, I better go now so I can catch her…later!” Jack said as he and Coley engaged in a quick soul handshake. “Hit it for me won’t ya’ Jack?” Coley added with his characteristically mischievious grin. “Go ‘head on, nigga’…I’m gone” Jack replied as he stepped away to go to the Lawrence Avenue “L” platform a short distance up the street. Jack stepped out onto the sidewalk from the poolroom door and the refreshing waft of a mid-October breeze blew about him and the clear sky held the dark-blue hue of night. The temperature was comfortable; perhaps, low-sixties and the atmosphere on the calm streets seemed to match the serenity he was feeling just then. He was sober and he was absorbing the beauty of the evening in a way that he never had before on the many nights that intoxication had muted his senses. He crossed Lawrence Avenue from the northside of it where the poolroom was to the southside to go to the train station entrance. He paid his fare and walked up the stairs. He knew that it could not be later than 7:15pm. He stood on the platform with a couple of other riders who were waiting for trains in each direction. He looked north in the distance to see if any train was coming----there was none. He paced just a little about the platform. After just a few more minutes, he could see the glimmer of the train lights on the track in the distance and he could begin to feel a mild anticipation. The train stopped in the far distance at the next station down the track. Finally, the train arrived at the Lawrence Avenue station and when it stopped, Jack stood back to allow the passengers to get on and off. He looked hopefully up and down the platform as people darted on and off the train. He looked for Tina to appear. The train sat for another moment---no Tina. The doors closed and Jack felt a mild disappointment. But, he knew that it was not quite 7:30pm; and so, he would wait for the next train. He knew that it would be perhaps, another ten minutes at least before the next one arrived. He waited. Finally a train appeared in the distance again. He could feel a little anxiousness begin to rise within him. The train pulled closer and closer and stopped at the platform. Jack did the same thing again. He stepped back to get a better view along the train doors while people were entering and exiting. Coming out of the middle of several exiting riders near where Jack stood, Tina stepped out, broadly smiling her vivacious smile and walking toward Jack with a joyful stride as though she was sneaking up on him. He was still looking past her along the car doors toward the end of the train. She was upon him before he knew it. She grabbed him by his arm and playfully said “Gotcha!” and when Jack finally saw her, he smiled broadly and spread his arms wide and wrapped them around her and held her, rocking her from side-to-side within a warm embrace, lifting her feet off the ground. She giggled while he did.

“You didn’t see me…if I was a snake, I would have bitten you!” she playfully. teased.They embraced and Jack continued the rocking back-and-forth for another moment before he spoke. “It’s good to see you, baby…missed you” he said softly. The train had pulled away from the station about twenty seconds earlier when they began a deep and passionate kiss while no one else was on the platform. Finally, they separated from their embrace and Jack placed his arm across Tina's shoulders as she placed an arm around his waist. They stood snuggling together on the platform facing north and looking up the track for the next train. "So, what have you been doing since the last time I saw you, Jack?" Tina asked as she gazed up sweetly at Jack who stood so much taller than her. "Stayin' outa' trouble….hangin' with my friends and thinkin' about you" he replied tactfully but, heartfelt. "Have you been stayin' out of trouble because of me?" Tina asked with a sparkle in her eyes and a broad smile. "Now that you mention it…I think so…I wanted to see you again and if I got locked up or somethin' then…I guess I couldn't" Jack replied with uncharacteristic openness. He was astonished at how open and honest he was being with Tina. He didn't trust many people in general and he was especially cautious with women. But, he had never known any woman like Tina. She seemed to be able to see right through him to his core; past the street character that he was and see something good in him--a woman who was in college; who lived a mainstream life and who would never engage in the things that he did. She was morally straight. In those terms, they were worlds apart. But, this feeling they were sharing right now made them seem inseparable. "That's very sweet, Jack…that's what I knew about you the moment I met you…the way you were looking at me…that hungry look in your eyes…the way you approached me…I could tell by your smile just what kind of man you were…you're not nearly as bad as you seem…I know" Tina explained with poised assurance. "Aw…you know, huh?…hey…and what do you mean hungry look?…hungry how?...what do you mean by that?" Jack inquired with a slightly puzzled expression. Tina paused and looked at Jack with that womanly expression of pursed lips, a stare and squinting eyes. Jack knew exactly what the expression meant. "What?…why you lookin' at me like that?" Jack asked with a smile. "Jack…yooouuu knoowww" Tina said as she smiled broadly and gave his waist a quick little squeeze. Jack suddenly came out of his quizzical mode to compose himself and said "You know what, baby…you are right…when I first saw you I *was* hungry…hungry for some roast beef and potatoes…steak and eggs…corned beef and cabb…""

"You know what I'm talking about, Jack!" Tina interrupted as she separated from Jack, stepped back and playfully gave him a slap to his chest and a sweet smile at the same time. "What?..wha..what's goin' on, baby?..what you talkin' about?..""' Jack said, continuing his ruse and trying to hold back the laughter that wanted to burst forward. Finally, Jack could not hold back any longer and he burst out with hearty laughter. They laughed together as Tina playfully smacked him on his butt a couple of quick times. The laughter subsided and Tina spoke "Jack, honey…I was talking about you were hungry for…me…can you dig that?" Tina said imitating Jack's favorite phrase. Jack paused for a long time. "Uh..Uh…uh.." He tried to talk but, the words seemed stuck as he was trying to be serious but, his expression was ambiguous. "You know what, baby…you looked real sweet and when you looked at me with those eyes when I passed by you in Frances' Tavern…I could see that it was different from any look that I got from any other woman…it was friendly and nice…uh…you know what I mean…you know" Jack said looking somewhat uncomfortable at expressing his true feelings to Tina. "I know, honey…I know what you mean" Tina replied with a sincere tone of understanding as she hugged up to Jack and put her cheek against his chest and they held a warm embrace. They were oblivious to the other few people who had gathered on the platform as they held each other in silence.

Finally, after almost ten minutes, the train could be seen in the distance coming toward them. It stopped and they got on. They sat silently side-by-side as the train roared down the tracks. The train was not so crowded, which was usual for the weekday evenings. As Jack sat, he could feel and see people cutting their eyes in their direction; stealing momentary glances at them. He understood---people were not so used to seeing black-and-white couples and they seemed compelled to sneak a look. It was no big deal, he thought. They could look all they wanted as far as he was concerned. He was comfortable. Tina sat beside him on the inside seat next to the window as the train moved along the tracks in the darkness. She grabbed Jack's hand as it lay in his lap and held it. He glanced over to her after she did. She flashed a happy, sweet smile to him. He was pleased with her touch and smile. It gave him that good feeling that this woman was really with him---connected to him in a sincere way. He smiled back at her and he could feel the change that she was causing in him. He even began to have a sense of trust with her. She was teaching him trust through the manner in which she was showing unconditional trust in him. After a while, they began small talk, making little comments to one another that seemed innocent and child-like in their simplicity. There was a sweetness that carried with their spoken words to one another and each of them could hear and feel it come across.

"State and Randolph…State and Randolph will be the next stop" the train conductor blurted out over the intercom. Jack and Tina stood to get off. They came up from the subway and walked to the northeast corner of State and Randolph past the Walgreens store on the corner. They crossed to the west side of State Street at the light and began walking south. There was the usual smattering of people that could be seen walking the downtown streets on a weekday evening. Jack and Tina walked at a casual pace holding hands. They came upon "Ceasar's" restaurant on State between Washington and Madison.

They entered and there was a quiet and pleasant ambiance. They sat and talked. "You been downtown much, Tina?" Jack asked. "Oh, yea…I've been down here many times with my parents…and lots of times by myself…I've been to Marshall Field's on State Street many times…the other big stores on State, the Shedd Aquarium, Adler Planetarium, Field Museum, Grant Park…everywhere..I love downtown Chicago…I wish downtown Evanston was like this…it's so boring compared to Chicago's" Tina said with a glowing smile and a tone of excitement. "How about you, honey…you come down this way much?" she asked. "Oh…uh…every now-and-then…yea…once-in-a-while…you know" Jack stammered as the question seemed to stir something uncomfortable within him. Jack recalled that as a kid, he didn't go many places. His parents worked hard and struggled and didn't have much time or money to take him anywhere. He remembered the many days he spent as a boy playing "strike-out" baseball with a rubber ball from sun-up to sun-down in the summers at the Cabrini-Green housing projects where he once stayed with his parents, sister and baby brother. He remembered how his father bought him a used red wagon when he was twelve years old and told him to go out and make himself some money like the other boys pulling groceries for the customers at the local grocery store.

He remembered, too back then how he had to fight off the bullies who tried to rob him of the money he was making with his wagon. The conversation with Tina had triggered a momentary flash-back of those memories. He snapped out of it.

"We was kinda' poor when I was a kid…didn't go too many places…I just played outside a lot…played baseball and all of that…I don't remember comin' downtown by myself until I was about seventeen to go to the show…me and my friend, Matt used to go to Jew-town to buy our clothes with the money we made…he worked inside the neighborhood store while I was still outside pulling groceries…finally, they gave me a job inside the store, too…we never went downtown to shop because we couldn't afford it…everything was cheaper at Jew-town… so, that's where we always went…I kept that job all the way through high school" Jack explained. "Wow…that sounds so different from how I grew up…sounds like it was kinda' hard…was it, Jack?" Tina asked with an expression that seemed a mix of sympathy and amazement. "Well, baby…I didn't know I was poor…didn't really think about it…when you're poor…I guess you're too busy survivin' to notice how hard it is…hahahaha…"" Jack laughed. "I guess it all made me stronger than I woulda' been if things was easy" he added. "I'm really glad you told me all of that…It's kind of exciting to learn all of these things about you, Jack that are so different from what I'm used to" Tina said with wide-eyed sincerity. "You are a survivor…my sweet survivor.." she added as she reached a hand across to Jack's laying on the table and held it while she gave a nurturing look deep into his eyes. Jack turned his palm up and held her's palm-to-palm as he smiled back.

"You know what, baby?…right now…I feel like I've known you for years, but since it's been just a little while, I'd like to know more…talk to me, sugar" Jack asked with genuine interest. "Oh…Okay…" Tina responded after a pause. "I already told you about my parents and how I began dating black men…humm…well, where can I begin…" Tina started. "I'll tell you what, Jack…you just ask me what you want to know and I'll try to answer…how's that?" Tina proposed. "Okay, baby…good idea…you're on…"" Jack answered. "What do you plan to do in the future as far as relationships, marriage and all of that?" Jack asked. "Tina turned her eyes upward and paused to think for a moment. "Jack, I don't really know but, I can tell you that I am just like any other woman…I want to marry one day, have kids, that whole thing but, I don't like to try to predict the future….I don't like making plans about those things because it's disappointing when things don't turn out your way" Tina responded. "Alright, …that's cool, baby…okay…how do you get along with your parents and what would they think about you being with me?" Jack asked. "Well, honey…like I told you that night we met, my parents really love me and my little sister and they would do anything for us…but, they have certain rules that they live by…" Tina offered. "Okay…like what?" Jack interjected. "Well, like with me going to college…I told my parents that I absolutely did not want to live on-campus…I was real strong about letting them know that because I didn't want to be around all of that little sorority stuff…I wanted to live off-campus and do my own thing…besides…I am much too mature for those geeky little sorority groups…so…since off-campus costs more, my parents said I couldn't have a car…that was their rule, and so, I had to give up a good used car that I could have gotten from them if I had stayed on-campus…and as far as what would they think about me being with you…I already told them that I am going out with a black guy…to be honest, Jack…like I said…my folks are quite liberal…they wouldn't mind that you are black…but, I know they wouldn't approve of how you are living which is really what interests me…you're different from other guys I've dated" Tina explained. "Okay, baby…I hear ya'….that's cool…okay…now…dig this…where are you at right now with respect to dating black men and dating white men?…what I'm tryin' to say is…where is you interest at right now? Jack asked, as he seemed to be asking more precise and to-the-point questions. "Wow, Jack..hahaha…you're good, man…now, how do I answer that?…whooo!...ahh…let me see…right now I have this thing for black men…I can't say for sure if it's a phase, but…I really am not interested in dating white guys right now…not that I wouldn't ever…I'm just having a good time dating black men…and I don't date just any black guy…I have to like him and trust him…and right now it seems to be more than just a curiosity thing…I still have white guy friends that I will always have…they are my friends and that won't change" Tina explained. "So you knew you could trust me so soon, Tina?" Jack asked. "Yes…I knew" Tina responded firmly. Jack paused and just looked across the table at

Tina with a faint smile and a glimmer in his eyes without saying a word. Tina smiled back with a shy kind of expression. She raised her eyebrows as if she was wondering exactly what Jack was thinking just then. She was silent for a long moment waiting for Jack to speak. "Okay…here is the big question, baby…this here is the sixty-four-thousand-dollar question…ready?" Jack teased. "Yes…I'm ready" Tina responded with a broad smile as she seemed engaged in the little game Jack was making of the question-and-answer session. "Uhh..okay..what do you think about me?" Jack asked kind of tentatively. "Ohhhh…Jaaacck" Tina said with a big smile. "Jack…I…I adore you…I know we've just met, but…I am having a blast…I love your company…It's exciting for me to be with you…we're so different but, we get along so great…I don't want this to ever end..''" Tina said with all the sincerity in her heart showing in her eyes and all over her face. They had dinner and talked; laughed and joked for another hour or so. Having such a good time until they had lost all track of time.

"Hey…it's ten o'clock already" Tina said after glancing at her watch. "Let's go for that walk around downtown you said we were going for, Jack" "Okay, baby…let's do it!" Jack responded with renewed energy. They strolled around downtown arm-in-arm, walking slowly while stopping and commenting on various places of interest. The meal and the long conversation in the restaurant seemed to have an unwinding effect on the two that made them feel extremely relaxed. This was the kind of good time that Jack had hoped he would have with Tina. It all seemed so surreal, given the lifestyle that he was living. Jack had not done anything quite so normal in quite some time. He seemed to crave this sense of normalcy. Right now, the madness that prevailed in his everyday life seemed light years away while he had Tina beside him. For the moment, he felt content and life seemed full of hope.

Jack rode the "L" to Evanston with Tina all the way to the Davis Street stop. He walked her out onto the street so she could catch a cab. They talked and made plans to go out on Sunday afternoon. Tina decided she would not wait to see how much studying she got done. She said she would get it done by Saturday afternoon so that they could have their date on Sunday afternoon. They shared another passionate kiss before she caught a cab from the Davis Street station to take her home. Jack jumped back on the "L" and rode back to Lawrence and went home.

Jack and Tina met at the Lawrence L Station on Sunday. It was a brilliantly sunny day that was crisp and cooler than recent ones. They took the Broadway bus south to Webster Street to go to the Lincoln Park Zoo. They strolled about arm-in-arm; hand-in-hand and sometimes hugged together. They had soda and popcorn and went into the Gorilla House. They marveled at the majesty of the lions and tigers and were mesmerized by the beauty of the exotic birds. They laughed at the antics of the chimpanzees and dolphins. They spent a good part of the afternoon immersed in each others company; seemingly in their own world; oblivious to the people around them who perhaps, had never seen two people from their two worlds engaged in such frivolity that so perfectly purged that human divide; interaction that was pure and void of the preconceived notions that society would foist upon them. As time went on, Jack and Tina fell into a routine of expecting to go out at least once a week. Jack found himself having to be sober more and more often. He had started to save his hustling money for these occasions. It placed a modicum of structure in his life and he looked forward to each outing. He was becoming astute at preparing himself each time; perfecting his dress and grooming; trying in little ways to improve his speech without losing who he was and how he expressed himself. He had even thought about meeting Tina with roses once but, he decided against it. It was too much of a leap for a character like himself and it was too square for him to contemplate further. But, he could find other ways to please Tina. Tina, for her part, seemed lost in all of the fun. She was really into Jack. She seemed to regard him as the man underneath the persona that glared out toward everyone else who casually observed Jack; but, did not know him or look beyond what they saw as she had done; using her feminine instincts to delve into the soul of a man as women are often able to do. It had come to a point when neither one wanted to look into the future as Jack had done way back on that second date when he attempted to gauge the affair by asking pointed questions of Tina. Since then, everything was spontaneous and focused on the moment. They were enjoying themselves very much. It was a time of glowing enchantment for each of them. Jack tried to negotiate a more masculine concept of the affair in his mind; even though his feelings for Tina were becoming as delicate as a flower.

CHAPTER 3
RING STING

It was the middle of November and Jack had been talking to Tina on the phone regularly. It was now as many as four times a week. Tina seemed very happy and she was excited to get Jack's calls. Jack was the same; not allowing anything to prevent him from calling his honey. Tina had been very busy with her demanding class schedule and her part-time intern job teaching those lively fourth-graders who seemed to energize her and wear her down at the same time with different challenges each day. She had expressed her passion for her work to Jack and how much she enjoyed it and looked forward to her career in teaching. These were the kind of conversations and topics that Jack was not used to. But, he found them inspiring. Tina's lifestyle seemed to be rubbing-off on him. Jack craved this kind of interaction with Tina. Not just because he had feelings for her and admired her secure sense of herself and how much of an independent thinker she was; but, also because he needed this connection with the normal world; some contact with mainstream society.

He could sometimes feel himself suffocating from this underground, anti-social, sometimes depraved existence that he lived. He felt cut-off. He could survive in the streets. But, his soul needed to survive, as well. Tina was helping him save his soul and Jack could feel an aura of salvation. While his street life could be full of excitement and fun at times, it was a tenuous one that was fraught with danger, as well. In the few years he had lived this way, Jack had seen plenty of violence and had been involved in several fights himself with various street characters. He had arguments and exchanged threats with others. It was all part of the tumultuous Street Gypsy life. Jack knew that he could not continue this way and survive. Drinking was a part of his survival and seemed to insulate him from all of the madness. But when he was with Tina, they went away from Uptown where he was calmer and his mind seemed to relax and everything was pleasant and civilized when they went downtown or to the park or a restaurant; doing what people living normal lives would do. Somehow, he felt more sane, even serene when he was with her in these places and doing these things. Tina was not afraid to be in Jack's environment. But, hanging on the streets was not something she cared to do. She would visit a bar like Saxony's or Frances' and she did visit with Mike at his apartment that once after she could see that he was a nice guy. But, that encounter may have been born of her loneliness; not having a boyfriend at the time and enduring the boredom of studying all the time.

Jack had been awake for a little while; trying to decide what he would do today. His money was low----eight dollars and some change when he counted it after waking up. It was Thursday and his clock-radio read 10:47am. He talked to Tina last night. But, on Thursdays she always had to do some extra things at the school for her internship; like grading the class' weekly test papers and attending the once-a-week teacher's meeting that sometimes went late before she could go home. So, they never talked on Thursday nights. It was the only night during the weekdays that they did not talk. But, they were together every Saturday and Sunday. Sometimes Jack did not have money on their get-togethers because he had stopped doing a lot of the rough-hustling he had been doing in the past; all because of Tina, of course. Tina did not mind his being broke. Sometimes she would just visit him at his place in the Arms. Jack insisted on her not coming there alone. So, he always met her at the Lawrence Street L station. They would talk in his apartment and Jack had bought a little TV that they sometimes watched when they were not talking or making love. Other times, Jack would visit her by taking the Evanston L to her off-campus apartment. Sometimes, staying the whole weekend. Tina still had to study. So, she would go to the campus library for a few hours during the day on those weekends while Jack stayed at her place or just went out for a walk until she came back. When they went out, they went to bars and restaurants in Evanston and at other times in Chicago. When Jack did have money, he was happy to pay because he wanted their outings to not be a strain on Tina. He didn't like for her to pay. But, when she did, he insisted on just having coffee in a restaurant or going for a walk around downtown.

Jack had cut way down on his drinking because of being with Tina. He had begun to just drink beer and not very much of it at that. He also had abandoned all ideas of getting high on the T's and Blues or heroin that he occasionally did. Because he did not speak to Tina on Thursdays, those days always seemed so much lonelier for Jack than they used to. Before, he never knew what day of the week it was because it didn't matter and he didn't care. But, his life seemed to have changed dramatically in just a month and somehow, it seemed as though it had always been this way with the routine he had with Tina. Now, he not only kept up with the days of the week but, he found himself keeping up with the time of day, as well. He finally turned on his radio and took a shower. He dressed and went out of his apartment.

He was walking past the front desk in the lobby of the Arms when the desk clerk called out "Rollins!.....you got some mail here….you want to get it now or later?" Jack stopped in his tracks just before going out of the door and swerved around. "Whoa….yea….let me get it" Jack said as he walked back to the desk and the clerk handed him two pieces of mail. "Thanks" Jack said as he walked back to the elevator reading the face of the two letters intently. After a few seconds, his heart skipped a beat as a wave of excitement passed over him.

"It's those school papers" he thought as he noted the sender addresses. The elevator arrived and Jack got on and went back up to his apartment. He excitedly opened one of the letters that was from the U.S. Board of Education. It said that he had qualified for student aid at the federal level and after he filled out the enclosed forms, he was to give one to the school he would attend and the other to be mailed back to the U.S. Education office. The other letter were forms from the State of Illinois Department of Education that said that he must submit the enclosed forms to the school after filling them out and the school would return the forms to the State Department of Education with all of the requested information. A feeling of joy spread over Jack. He was very happy to read those words "You are qualified" on the two letters. He was relieved. The first thing he thought about was to tell Tina all about the good news-----but, they were not talking tonight and he felt excitement and frustration all at once. He sprang up from the edge of his bed and started pacing. "Should I call Tina anyway and just speak a few minutes to tell her?.....yes?....no?....wait....let me think...." "calm down...look at how you are acting" he told himself----this was not like Jack to get overly excited. But, this matter meant the world to him. It was almost a matter of life and death; and at least a matter of survival. His mind raced with all of the possibilities. He thought about moving from the Malden Arms where he was now living to accommodate his soon-to-be student lifestyle. He had to start planning this right away. Spring classes would be starting the second week of January 1976. So he had about seven weeks to make that move. As his mind raced, a groundswell of hope began to fill Jack. He began to think that some spiritual force was at work on his behalf; and although he was not religious and did not attend church, he had his own vague sense of reverence for a higher being. Jack sat at the edge of his bed for several more minutes, thinking and allowing the good feelings and excitement to resonate. It took almost an hour before Jack could calm down enough to think about what he would do with his day. He decided to play it cool about calling Tina tonight to tell her. He would just relax and try to contain himself enough to wait and tell her tomorrow night when they had their usual talk when they seemed to talk longer because it was the end of the week.

He decided that he would go out and hang around at the poolroom as he usually did. Even though he was now happily and hopelessly connected to Tina and he now had hope for his future, he still had to live the life he had. He had become extremely well versed in the art of survival. He had already begun to dial his profile down; keeping his visibility around the neighborhood low-key in anticipation of the changes he was planning in the very near future. It had been almost a month since he could say that he had really been high.

The time he was spending with Tina was changing him little-by-little. She had seen Jack high when they first met and they had gone to the Machine disco. Still, he was very sweet to her then, she had told him. But, she liked him even better when he was completely sober. She could see the real Jack at those times, she had said. She told him that he seemed out-of-place living in these streets the way he did. She could not understand how he had come to live this way and neither could Jack. She had commented on his intelligence and how, although he was a little “rough-around-the-edges” he had a sense of common decency that she did not see in many of the other street types she had observed around his neighborhood. Jack put the letters away in his dresser drawer and started back out of the door, headed for the poolroom.

He arrived and walked inside and immediately went to his favorite spot in the front corner to sit and watch the activity inside and occasionally look out of the window facing Lawrence Avenue. Thursdays seemed to be one of the more quiet days of the week; perhaps because it was the last day before the weekend and the day before many people’s payday. Jack sat for quite a while listening to the music over the audio system and casually observing the sparse pool playing activity inside. None of his friends were around. So, he went outside to stretch his legs and to be out in the air. He stood at the corner of the poolroom facing south straight down Winthrop Street where he could see all the way down the street a block away to the corner of Leland and Winthrop. He slowly paced and looked around and soon he could see a male figure in the distance round the northwest corner of Leland and Winthrop, walking at an energetic pace. He recognized the figure with the cool stride right away----it was Suge; another one of his hustling buddies whom he had not seen in weeks. Suge continued to pace hurriedly in Jack’s direction and Jack could see that Suge had a large shopping bag in his hand as he drew nearer.

“Brotha’, Jack!.....what’s to you, baby?…what’s goin’ on!” Suge greeted spiritedly. “Ain’t nothin’, man….ain’t nothin’…what’s poppin’ with you, baby boy!” Jack greeted with matching energy. They each smiled broadly as they engaged in the customary soul brother handshake. “What you holdin’ there, brotha’ Suge?” Jack asked as he turned his attention to the large shopping bag that Suge sat on the ground near them. “Man…let’s get inside and I’ll spit it to you” Suge responded in his usual flamboyant manner. They walked inside and Suge seemed to be moving in that excited manner when he had been hustling good and making money.

“Yea, brotha’ Jack….man, I made me a nice little sting….I met this chick named Honey, right…bumped her about two weeks ago….met her at a little house party I just stumbled up on one night…you know me….I didn't know a damned soul up in that party…but, I just started usin' my gift-o-gab and started talkin' shit…charmin' the ladies and what-not…everybody up in there was cool with me…after about one hour of conversation….I had 'em eatin' outa' my hand…anyway…I run up on this Honey chick…she kinda' cute….I start layin' my mack down…chick tell me she works at Carson Pirie Scott downtown….I say "yea…no shit?…I stopped down there to see her one day….man, I see she's workin' on the first floor in a blind little corner…I seen this big ol' display of men's cologne not far from the cashier counter where she works…so I set it all up….I start to workin' on her…talkin' sweet, man…sho' 'nough…I was treatin' her like a queen…after about two days of that, I tell her…hey, baby….I just start havin' a streak of bad luck…my uncle is sick and I have to go over to his place and help him out…he got back problems…his insurance done ran out…I got to try to take him to the County Hospital all the time and my funds is runnin' short…she say she wish she could help me out but, she ain't exactly rollin' in dough from her workin' there as a cashier…I finally get to the point I'm tryin' to get at….I say…hey…I wanna' knock off that little cologne section over there around the corner in that blind spot near her counter…it was in her line of sight but, out of sight from anywhere else on that floor" "Can I go ahead and do it? I ask her….at first she was scared about losin' her job, but, I put this thang on her that night and she said go ahead…but, make sure you don't implicate me if you get busted…said she'll just say she was busy with a customer and never saw anything…I say "baby…I would never get you caught up…believe me….I'm just gonna make this a one-time thing…cool?" She told me when that old sore-foot security guard goes to dinner…that's when I made my move…I cleaned up brotha' Jack…cleaned up….I musta' had about sixty bottles of all kinds of nice men's cologne in this bag…I done sold about twenty bottles of it and I still got about forty bottles left…if you want to, you can help me knock off what I got left…cool?" Suge offered.

Jack paused and fixed his eyes on the large shopping bag as he peeked inside to see it full of fancy new cologne cases stacked on top of one another. He ruminated for a moment before responding. "Hell, yea, man…hey…I might be able to off it all at the Aragon next door…you know they're my best connect…" Jack offered. "…they love this kinda' shit, Suge…they buy this kinda' stuff all the time…they sho' 'nough dig fancy colognes like these….if I sell it all, can I get a few bottles off the top?" Jack asked. "Jack…you my boy…I was gonna give you a couple off the top, anyway….but, if you can sell it all or most of it in one shot…I' ll let you get four bottles…alright?" Suge proposed. "Cool!....tell you what…get your four bottles now…then, take the bag on over there…okay? Suge added. "You ain't said nothin', bro'" Jack said as he sat down next to the shopping bag in the front corner and started to pull out the fancy shapes and different sizes of colognes to see which he wanted to keep. He was looking them over and in a short time had set aside the four he wanted.

Suddenly, just as Jack had finished, he heard a voice speak out---- "Hey…what y'all got there?…that's for sale?" Jack looked up to see that it was Ray Foster standing nearby. Jack immediately shifted seamlessly into a defensive mode that he shielded from Ray. "Hey, man….aw…this already sold, I'm gettin' ready to take it on over to the guy who bought it" Jack responded. A bewildered look spread over Ray's face. "They bought it but, you ain't gave it to 'em yet?.....I don't understand that" Ray puzzled. "Stud works in the Aragon…I showed it to him earlier…he said he would buy the whole thing…just come back a little later for the money….time to go back now and get the money" Jack explained. "Man…I can tell that's some damn good cologne…y'all cain't sell me some of 'em before you take it over there?" Ray asked. "'Fraid not, my man…I already told him how many is in the bag…that's how many he's expectin'" Jack continued to explain with an air of indifference. Jack had already come to know enough about Ray that he did not want to have any dealings with him what-so-ever. He knew that Ray did not respect the kind of hustling that he and Suge did. So, why should he benefit from it by buying from them, he thought. He understood, too that he would have to continue to handle this exchange tactfully. "Tell you what, bro'…after I come back, I'll sell you one of mine….cool?" Jack offered. "Hey, man…look here….I got the money to buy a whole bunch-o' that shit…dig what I'm sayin'?.....you cain't sell me ten or fifteen of 'em?…look…I got the money right here….think I'm bullshittin'….see here…look …cash goddamn money….you can sell some of it right here…I ain't bullshittin'" Ray went on in his characteristic style of being more concerned with impressing than listening to anyone's reasoning. "You ain't listenin' man…. did you hear what I said?…this whole bag is already sold….I'll sell you one of mine…dig?...hold on 'til I come back…okay?" Jack said, trying to control his exasperation. "See there…I don't know what kinda' hustlers y'all is…passin' up cash money right here to run and give your shit away to the white man…see…ya' hustlin' backwards…yea…I ain't never seen no hustlin' like this…"" Ray went on. After Ray made that statement, Jack tried to control himself. He grudgingly digested the insult. He felt anger and fear at the same time. He felt fear that he would respond angrily to Ray. He paused to temper himself to respond with tact if not grace. "What you want, man?….the stuff already sold…I got to go take care of my business…later" Jack responded, brimming from the exchange as he stepped past Ray toward the poolroom exit. As he did so, Suge, recognized immediately that he needed to be tactful as well so as not to be left in the company of Ray for any more antagonistic exchanges. "I'm goin' that way, Jack…I'm goin' to Saxony to get me a taste" he said to excuse his leaving. Jack and Suge had come to know of Ray Foster from a distance; never really talking to him but, becoming familiar with his loud, boisterous and annoying ways from being around the poolroom. They maintained a nodding acquaintance with him and kept him at a distance. They could see that his personality was somewhat volatile. But, just like everyone else, they could also see that he was not all that he tried to present himself to be.

"That's a silly-ass nigga'…. ain't he?" Suge said to Jack after he had caught up to him in front of the Aragon entrance. "Sho' 'nough, man….that fool' pissed me off….always talkin' 'bout he got this and he can do that….try to put studs like us down on the sly….criticize our style of hustlin' then he wanna' buy from us…I don't wanna do no business with him….I know how studs like him is….you sell him somethin'….even somethin' like cologne…he'll be cool when you sell it to him…but, later on, he'll be complainin' about it…he'll find somethin' wrong with the deal…dig what I'm sayin' Suge?" Jack responded. "Yea…I hear you…he definitely is that kinda' nigga' with his Huckleberry Hound Dog ass" Suge said with cutting sarcasm. "Hey…while you tryin' to sell that to ya' boy in the Aragon, I'll be buyin' a taste down at Saxony…vodka cool with you?" Suge asked Jack. "I'm gonna pass on the vodka…get me a beer…alright?" Jack asked. "I got you" Suge responded as he strode up the street towards Saxony Liquor store.

Meanwhile, Jack swung open one of the several tinted glass entrance doors to the Aragon and hauled the large shopping bag inside. Suge was strolling back with the packaged vodka and beer in hand. After he stepped in front of the entrance doors of the Aragon, he could see Jack inside walking out toward the second set of doors before he burst through one of the outside doors. "You got a deal…right?" Suge asked, as he noted Jack's excited movement. "Sho' 'nough…check this, Suge….one-ninety for the whole thing…is that cool?" Jack asked as his breathing seemed slightly accelerated with excitement. "Hell, yea…let me think…what is the price I'm gettin' a bottle?…let me see" Suge said while he mumbled under his breath, counting to divide the number of bottles by the price. "That's somewhere around five dollars a bottle, ain't it?" Suge asked. "It's a little bit more than five dollars a bottle….you had thirty-seven bottles after I took four out of the bag" Jack responded. "Humph….let's see….the prices I'm seein' on these bottles is from about eight to fifteen dollars….most of 'em somewhere in-between….that's cool….probably about good as I'm gonna get out here…Jack….you done did it again, baby….you handlin' your business, sho' 'nough!....hahahaha….my mothafuckin' guy!...go on back in there and tell him he got a deal….shit…you got the right connects, baby….I ain't lyin'!" Suge raved, smiling broadly and moving excitedly. The two slapped "five" so hard until their hands were stinging. With that, Jack shot back inside through the Aragon entrance doors and in a few minutes came back out beaming. "Let's step back into the bathroom and count this scratch" Jack said. They both took a step toward the poolroom in the short distance.

But, Suge stopped immediately after taking one step. "Aw, hell naw!" Suge said. "Ya' boy still up in there…I don't wanna be bothered with his crazy ass…let's step into your office over by Saxony….cool?" Suge suggested. "Fa' sho' Jack agreed. They walked back in the opposite direction toward Saxony Liquor store to go into the secluded breezeway next to it that Jack called his "office"----where he made many of his clandestine transactions.

Jack could have easily handed Suge the wad of cash from the cologne sale in plain view out on the sidewalk. But, they both had come to know from experience to make money exchanges of this type somewhere out-of-sight because they did not want to be beseeched by the local regulars for drinks and small loans or to draw suspicion from passing police or detectives in unmarked cars who would stop them out of curiosity. They could never know when either one would pop up unexpectedly. They entered the breezeway and Jack pulled the wad of cash out and handed it to Suge. Suge counted it. "On the money…one-ninety" Suge said as he peeled off thirty dollars and handed it to Jack. "Good lookin' out, Jack…them connects you got is payin' off…you handled that real smooth, brotha'….is that cool right there?" Suge asked. "Yea…this is cool, Suge…I needed some paper" Jack said with gratitude. After the money exchange, they continued to stand in the breezeway to talk and drink.

"So, Suge how come I ain't seen you for a while, man?....been over a month, ain't it since I seen you around this way?" Jack asked as the conversation had become social and more relaxed. "Shit, man….I just did thirty days in the County for theft….I was boostin' over there in New Town and the store owner busted my ass and run out into the streets and flagged down the po'lice…got that little time behind that…store owner had a little sugar in his shorts so, before they put me in the paddy wagon, I tried to cop a plea with him to make him think he might get hold to somethin' but, it didn't do no good…they took me on over to Foster" Suge explained. "Damn, man…that's rare for you…you hardly ever get busted 'cause I know you pick your hustles real careful" Jack said. "Yea…that's true but, sometimes you take a chance on a new spot to hustle and it don't turn out like you thought….you know how that go…all part of the game…ya' know?" Suge philosophized. "Yea…you got that right…all you can do is roll with the punches….just be glad you didn't get no more than them thirty days" Jack said. "Other than that…how you been doin' Suge?" Jack asked. "Aw…just gettin' high…I was stayin' with Al and Brenda for about two weeks before I got busted….they had a nice little crib over on Drake near Irving Park…they let me stay because I was hustlin' good and I was gettin' T's and Blues cheap as hell from my boy Tank…you know Tank, the stud with the silver Brougham…yea, Al and Brenda was diggin'' that 'cause they was gettin' high as hell offa' me…then, I got busted and when I got out and went back to their crib, come to find out the apartment was vacant and locked 'cause they had got busted two weeks before I got out and now they're in jail…I rented me a room for two weeks at that little Grace Hotel on Sheffield…you know…just south of Irving…it's cool for now…I'll keep it for long as I can" Suge explained. "That's the way the game go don't it?....up and down…yea, buddy…only the strong survive, huh, Suge?" Jack said spiritedly with a chuckle. "You know that's my motherfuckin' motto, baby…I keep remindin' myself to take whatever the game is dishin' out 'cause that's just the way it goes" Suge said with conviction. Jack and Suge remained in the breezeway for a while longer catching up on how things had been going for each other as they exchanged stories. Jack talked about how he met Tina. He bragged on all of her good qualities but, used the macho street terms that he and all the other hustlers used. The code was to never expose any tender feelings to the other street hustlers. You never wanted to seem weak in any way out on the streets.

Finally, the two walked out of the breezeway after they had finished their drink. Hustlers always looked around to make themselves aware and Suge was doing just that as he and Jack were nearing the underpass of the Lawrence Avenue L station as they walked on the north side of Lawrence, heading back toward the poolroom. "Aw, shit…don't look….behind us…it's Kato….he done spotted us and I just *know* he gonna jump out on us…be cool" Suge almost whispered. A moment later, a blueish-gray unmarked detective car made a u-turn from going east on Lawrence to swerve alongside Jack and Suge and facing west as they strolled along. Jack and Suge could hear the beep from the siren that only lasted a split-second. They heard the screech of the tires near them. A medium-built, wiry Asian man in blue jeans jumped out of the car from the driver's side and another detective jumped out from the passenger side and stood on the opposite side of the car.

Kato was a detective who was well known and recognized by the street hustlers in the area. Many of them had stories about how he had outwitted them or sneaked up on them to bust them. Jack had never been busted by Kato but, had seen him in action and heard several stories of his exploits to become aware of his reputation. The name was one given to him by the street hustlers for his tenacious style. “Hello, gentlemen” Kato greeted in a cool and relaxed manner with the underlying cockiness that hustlers had come to know of detectives. “Hold it right there…okay?” Kato added. “Where are you guys coming from?” he asked. A long pause ensued. It was the usual fear that gripped hustlers when they were stopped for a search. “We just walked from the liquor store back there” Suge finally said with a hint of measured caution. Kato was slow to respond. “Liquor store?…I don’t see any bags” Kato said. “We drank it already” Jack responded. “Put your hands on top of the car and spread” Kato said. “Anybody carrying any weapons or illegal drugs?” Kato also asked before patting them down. “Not, me” Suge responded. “No” Jack answered. “Anybody got any warrants?….I know you don’t have any….I saw you at Foster about a month ago, right?....you just get out?” Kato asked Suge. “Yea…I just got out three days ago” Suge responded. “What about you?….what’s your name?” Kato asked Jack. “Jack Rollins” Jack answered. “Let me see some ID” Kato added. Jack pulled out his general assistance picture ID and handed it to Kato who, in turn, handed it to the other detective who quietly got into the detective car. Jack had only began to carry his ID in the last several weeks at Tina’s urging. “Relax for a few minutes…he is going to run your name…okay?” Kato said to Jack. Jack did not have any warrants and only had two other warrants in the past----one traffic that was cleared up when he got busted last year and a theft warrant that he served a month’s time for earlier this year. Jack and Suge stood silently for several minutes before the detective got out of the car and handed the ID back to Kato and said “He’s clean” “Okay, gentlemen…have a nice day” Kato said as he handed Jack’s ID back to him and the two detectives got back into the car and sped away.

“Dammnn, boooyyy….just think if they had rode up on us while we still had that bag of cologne…luck was on our side that time, Jack!” Suge said with a sigh of relief. “Yea, buddy….I sho’ ‘nough didn’t wanna get locked up!” Jack said with the same tone of relief. Jack seemed to have been more sensitive to the entire incident of coming close to going to jail; perhaps, because his head was clearer now than when he was getting high everyday. Also, because he had begun to have purpose in his life. “Hey, Jack….that was my cue to call it a day, man…I’m goin’ on back to the crib…I'll see you later, bro" Suge said as he and Jack engaged in a soul handshake before Suge walked away. Jack decided that he would do the same. As he walked back west on Lawrence toward the Arms, he thought about how he was going to achieve his goal of cleaning his life up and going to college. He was hopeful. But, the incident with Kato had reminded him of what a stretch it would be to shift from his street life, such as it was, to the life of a college student. He was thinking about how he would survive financially.

After arriving at his place in the Arms, he continued to think about it and he remembered what the recruiter, Linda Chavez had said about financial aid; that he could get grants, loans *and* he could get a work-study job at the college to supplement his income. He did not know how all of that worked. But, he had to go forward and trust that it would all work out. If he could live the rough-and-tumble life in the streets of Uptown that he had been living for the last few years; then, any other challenge paled in comparison, he thought. Somehow, he felt that his street life had prepared him for what he was about to embark upon ---another episode of survival.

"That's so neat, Jack…I am so happy for you, honey…congratulations!" Tina said excitedly after Jack told her the news over the phone about the financial aid letters he had received. It was about 6:30pm, Friday evening and they were having their usual long session on the phone. Jack had gone home Thursday evening and stayed in the whole night. He went to the local library late this morning and spent a couple of hours reading various materials to pass the time. He had not done much reading before that. It also served the purpose of preparing him for all the reading he anticipated he would be doing as a student. "Thanks, baby…I'm feelin' pretty good about it…I'm gonna' have to start gettin' ready to move from where I'm at right now…I know you'll be glad to hear that, huh?" Jack said. "Yes, Jack…you know I don't mind coming to see you there but, I do wish you could go to a little nicer place somewhere else so you won't be around all of those really wild people that I see there" Tina said. "Well…I think I'll start lookin' for another place right away and then see if I can move at the end of this month after I get my check…I was thinkin' about goin' to the YMCA on Wilson Avenue just west of Ashland…it's cheap…don't need a security deposit…it's a good area....quiet residential neighborhood...the rooms are small, but, nice and clean...plenty of heat...only thing is, I won't be able to have you in my room...guests have to stay out in the guest area in the lobby" Jack explained. "Oooohhh....I don't think I like that part of it...but, if that's where you want to go, Jack...it's alright with me...you can always visit me at my place" Tina responded. "Well, baby...first...I'm gonna look around to see if I can find some other cheap place in a quiet area where they don't ask for a security deposit, because I don't think I'm gonna be able to pay it...but, we'll see" Jack said.

"Jack...you are doing so well...you know you are very special to me...did you know that?" Tina said, as her voice changed to a sweeter tone. "No...I guess I never thought about it...but, I'm glad to hear that, baby....you mean a lot to me, too...I feel like I've known you forever and it's only been a short while...I care for you very much" Jack confessed. "You know, Jack...when I'm with you, I feel so much like a lady...I feel protected and cared for and respected...I not only feel it...I can see it in your eyes...that's why I enjoy being with you so much" Tina said. A long pause ensued before Jack spoke. "You still there, honey?" Tina asked, breaking the long silence. "Oh...yea..yea..I'm here, baby..." Jack stammered. "So what do you think about what I said?" Tina asked. "... I feel...uh...uh....very happy about what you said....no one ever said that to me before" Jack said with a rare tone of humility that he had never revealed to Tina before. He tried to restrain the emotion inside that seemed to rise up suddenly. He was surprised at the power of the feeling that seemed to envelop him.

He could not remember anyone ever saying those words to him before. It seemed that as far back as he could remember, there was some kind of hostile human interaction in his life. His parents may have loved him but, they had never said the words and he could not tell by their actions; his sister and brother may have but, they didn't know how to say it; and he could not utter the words himself to them or anyone else. He had heard the words used throughout his life----care, need, want, love. But, they were never addressed to him. Everything had been a battle from the very beginning. He didn't understand the interaction between people that was called love. He had only a couple of short-lived affairs with women in the past where they satisfied each other's needs for a little while and then, things changed and each moved on. It was fun and exhilarating at times but, never approached this feeling that he had heard described so often. He only knew that he had to be strong and resourceful in order to survive and very little had meaning beyond that. The early years of his life seemed to have prepared him more for savagery than the civilized notion of love. But, perhaps, now he was experiencing it. The trust and care that Tina was showing him had broken down all of his defenses and he was happily engaged in her positive world of civility, nurturing and caring.

"Okay…alright…good!..now…you're staying with me after we go out tomorrow night...that's what you said…right?" Tina asked as she shifted to a more upbeat tone. "Yea, baby…sho' 'nough!" Jack replied enthusiastically. "Good…I'm glad you're in the mood because I wanna have a good time at my place…you know…like we always do…" Tina hinted. "You mean you want to play some of our little games that we always play?" Jack asked with a note of mischief. "Oh…yes, my dear…you know which games I like to play…right?" Tina asked with a salacious tone. "Oh..yea….tease-n-please…right?" Jack said. "Right…and if I don't get pleased….I'm gonna have to spank you on your naked butt…can I do that?" Tina asked. "Hahaha…girl….you are wild..hahaha… "okay…okay…" Jack said as he attempted to let his laughter subside. "Where do you want to go to eat, this weekend, baby?…you wanna go to that restaurant that you said your folks took you to that you liked so well but, you haven't been back for a long time?" Jack asked. "Oh..oh…uh..uh…RJ Grunts!...you wanna go, honey?…can we go this weekend?" Tina asked excitedly. "Sho' 'nough, baby…I ran into a little money the other day…yea, I can handle it!" Jack assured. "Oh…that's teriffic, honey!...I'll be ready for it tomorrow night!" Tina added with excitement.

The routine of meeting every weekend was something that both Jack and Tina had come to look forward to and enjoy so much. It was about not being alone so much anymore and dispelling the on-going boredom of student life for Tina. She had become so bored with studying constantly and traveling in the same circles as other students in Evanston; studying all week at the campus library; hanging out on Saturday nights at the same local pubs and seeing the same people at those places; other students whose lives were as predictably unexciting as hers was at the time. That was why she had begun, almost a year ago, to occasionally go out of the familiar area in Evanston, at the cheap cost of a train fare, to go into Chicago and visit some unfamiliar places for excitement; going to bars to meet men---and if the man could be a nice, good-looking black man then, it was just that much more exciting. She was very happy to have met Jack and she cherished their relationship.

Jack had not really been looking for a woman or a relationship. He had been too consumed with surviving for it to matter that much. But, when he met Tina, he had not expected that he would meet someone like her who would accept him so unconditionally and who seemed so pure and normal. He had not expected, too, that a relationship with a woman could be what it had become between them. It had added so much to his life and magically brightened his existence. It was all so pleasantly strange and he felt curiously elevated by it all.

Almost every Saturday and Sunday for more than a month, Jack and Tina had met by him going to her place in Evanston; or, if they were going out in Chicago, Tina met Jack at the Lawrence L station and they went on from there. Since they were going to RJ Grunts this weekend, the hippie-inspired restaurant that became popular just a few years ago located near Lincoln Park Zoo, Tina was meeting Jack at the Lawrence L station this Saturday. When he woke up this morning and looked outside to see the rain and had heard the forecast over the radio, Jack prepared for his date with Tina by going out and buying an umbrella at the Woolworths store on the corner of Broadway and Wilson.

It was Saturday evening at a little past 7 pm. Jack stood on the platform at the Lawrence L with his umbrella in hand while waiting for the next southbound train to arrive. It was especially dark. The lightning flashed across the sky with the echo of the thunder as the heavy rain pounded the structure of the station that had a wooden canopy that protected most of the platform. He expected that Tina would be on the next train. When it finally arrived, Tina stepped out from one of the cars and yelled out "Jack!.....over here!" and Jack saw her immediately. He walked over to her and they hugged and shared a short, warm kiss as the train pulled away. They hugged up together as they walked down the platform stairs. They walked the half-block through the pouring rain out on the street, huddled under the wide umbrella that Jack held as they crossed Broadway to catch the southbound number 36 Broadway bus. They had the routine of going to the back of the bus and sitting in the corner of the long rear seat. They sat in back of all the people seated on the bus where they could not be seen. It also allowed them to steal an occasional kiss without drawing the curious stares of onlookers. Their conversations on the trains and buses had become much livelier than their earlier dates. Their affair was still very new and fresh and the excitement seemed to come naturally. They were playful with one another and they teased, joked, engaged in horseplay and laughed quite often. At other times, they had more serious conversations; answering each other's questions and exchanging ideas and opinions----being introspective and giving little bits of their inner-selves to each other. Those exchanges seemed timeless because they went on for hours without their noticing the passing of the time.

They talked low but, freely in blissful oblivion from the people around them. Jack and Tina arrived at RJGrunts and after a short wait, were comfortably seated. The waitress placed them at a corner table, just as they had asked, so they could feel a little more privacy and they asked for time to order. The place was crowded and buzzed with lively conversation, as was usual on a Saturday night. The rain had slowed to a drizzle in the pitch darkness outside that was windy and a few faint flickers of lightning occasionally flashed across the dark sky. All of this made the inside of the restaurant with its clientele of mostly hippie-folk-types seem all the more cozy as the two warmed themselves from the chilly rain they had endured. There was a joyous ambiance inside the restaurant and the two seemed lifted by the atmosphere as they occasionally scanned the room with broad smiles and a feeling of excitement. They looked at the pictures on the walls of all the waitresses who had worked there for at least one year in the four years the restaurant had been in existence. A man with a Polaroid camera was roaming about in the restaurant taking customer's pictures. Jack and Tina took two pictures, one for each of them to keep. Jack loved these moments that seemed so far away from his street life. It was so pleasurable to him. He was not used to this dining out at nice restaurants and he did feel a little out of place and his actions were a bit crude from time-to-time. But, he enjoyed it and hoped to continue doing these things. They ordered and ate; sitting for about two hours talking and enjoying themselves. Finally, they left and took the same bus route back to the Lawrence L train and rode the train to Tina's place in Evanston.

"Honey….why did you decide to be with a white girl like me instead of a black girl?" Tina asked Jack as they lay in her bed with their night clothes on. Jack paused to give the matter a moment of thought before answering "Well, baby…it's kinda' like what you said about curiosity but, it goes a little deeper than that….check this out…what if you went into a store to buy some cookies and you always bought the same kind of cookies because they were the only kind your parents ever bought you…but, there were other kinds of cookies on the shelf….now….you remember your mother always sayin' the other cookies were no good…that the family always bought those same kind of cookies…okay?…listen to me…you followin' me?" Jack asked. "Yea…go ahead" Tina replied. "Okay…now…you are grown now and the same variety of cookies is still on the grocery store shelf…you keep buyin' the same ol' cookies your mother used to buy and you keep seein' the other cookies on the shelf…you finally say to yourself…hey…I ain't never tried them other cookies…how do I know they ain't no good?…why was mama sayin' they ain't no good?...then, finally you buy some of the other cookies that you wanted to try…you find out that they are delicious….you like them…you also find out that your mother probably was tellin' you they was no good 'cause they were more expensive….see?…can you dig that?....see where I'm comin' from?" Jack explained and waited for Tina's response. "…Uh…I guess….are you sayin' that you are with me because you wanted to try a white girl out?" Tina asked, with a quizzical tone. "Not exactly…more because you are a good person and you are attractive and I don't like the idea that I can't choose a woman because of her race or mine and dig this….a lota' black people feel that a black man should only be with black women…but, this is a free country…right?....that's only a belief of theirs….those are *their* beliefs…not mine….besides…I'm a grown man….I make my own decisions…nobody can tell me who to be with….how would those same people like it if I said somethin' to them like…Hey, John…you shouldn't be with Mary,…she's too light-skinned…you should stick to darker women?"….see what I mean?…they wouldn't like it, now, would they?…wouldn't like me tryin' to tell them who to be with...see...get my point?...so…they can't tell me who I should be with just because I'm black….who do they think they are?...they can tell me who to be with…but, I can't tell them…huh?...I can be with a white girl if I want…it's not against the law…I'm not hurtin' nobody…it's my right and it's my business...I'm not scared to do what I want…nobody runs my life but me…and the man upstairs….see…and the same goes for white people who don't like me bein' with a white woman…I'm not scared of them…they don't intimidate me….somebody's got to have the courage to do what they want and not give a damn about what people think…they can all kiss my ass…see…mind their own damned business!" Jack said with conviction. "Wow…you have a really strong opinion about all of that...don't you?…I like that about you…"Tina said. "Hey, baby…in the streets I learned you can't be no punk…tryin' to please people all the time….you gota be yourself no matter who doesn't like it" These were the kind of conversations that Jack and Tina had all the time. Each of them feeling completely free to be themselves. They had become each other's confidant. They would always talk a little before they made love and quite a bit afterward with the talk going late into the night before they fell asleep.

It was a Tuesday in late November and Jack was back at his place. He enjoyed his weekend stay with Tina and he had called her Monday evening and they had a short talk. He had continued to stay low-key in the neighborhood. Now, he had begun to hang around the poolroom for shorter periods of time. He was there in the early afternoons for a couple of hours. But, he would leave before the evening came when all of the patrons and other street hustlers began to hang around in the area. Jack did not want to be tempted to engage himself in anything risky while he was waiting to get into school. He had also begun to stay in his room more. He still made small hustles here and there that were low-risk; selling little items like toasters and radios that he had gotten from the Salvation Army store for free by his usual charming pleas to Ida. This kept a few dollars in his pocket. He had begun the habit of going out to buy a newspaper to look at apartment ads. This morning, after he had his morning shower, he headed out at a little past 9am to buy one.

He walked out of the Arms and was walking south on Malden heading for Wilson Avenue. As he was walking and nearing the intersection of Wilson and Malden, he could hear loud voices in the area. Some of the voices sounded angry and violent and he could hear one of the voices pleading. He came to the intersection and sensed the voices coming from a little bit west of where he stood at the corner of Wilson and Malden. He looked across the street to see two men beating another. They were punching and kicking him at the edge of the alley next to the Norman Hotel. He recognized the two men doing the beating. They were dope dealers that he knew from Sheridan Road. The man they were beating was one of the fiends that he had only seen around a few times; a man that he knew was new to the Uptown area and had gotten out of jail a few months ago. They called him "Low-down" "Where's my damn money at, nigga!" Jack could hear one of the dope dealers yell at the man as he and his partner were beating him. Jack paused for a moment and watched as the punching, kicking and scuffling continued while the man kept pleading "I ain't got it…I'll get your money…come on…I'll get it for you…Aaaahhh!" Jack continued on and went into the Wilson Avenue Liquor store to buy his paper. Jack was used to seeing these kinds of things and he had become fairly insensitive to them; having been involved in fights, arguments and the like himself on occasion. But, he seemed to be a bit more sensitive to what he had just witnessed; perhaps, because he had not really been drinking for a while and because he was trying, as best he could, to change his mindset and how he was living. He had sank much deeper into this depraved existence than he had expected; and now, he was reminded more than ever by the violent scene that he did not want to live this way.

Jack walked back to the Arms with his newspaper. As he passed through the lobby, he thought to stop to see if he had any mail. "Here you go" the desk clerk said as he handed Jack a piece of mail. Jack looked it over and could see the "Northeastern Illinois University" name on the corner of the letter. When he got inside of his apartment, he opened it up and read it. The letter said that he had a date set on Wednesday, December tenth to take a math and an English placement test. It went on to explain that this was usual for new students in order to gauge their math and language abilities to place them in the appropriate classes. After Jack read the letter, he did not think much about it, except that he was getting a sense of how much a person had to do to get into college. It was not as simple as he had thought. But, he was committed and he was going to take the placement test and whatever else they wanted him to do so that he could get in. Nothing he had to do could possibly compare to the challenge of living in the streets, he thought. He continued to hang on the streets for short periods of time; being careful not to get himself caught-up in risky hustling schemes that might get him locked up. He was careful to avoid Melvin and his other hustling buddies that he ran with and did all of the risky hustling in the past. But, he still needed to make money, so he hung around the poolroom, occasionally selling other hustlers' merchandise up-and-down Lawrence Avenue to the various fences that he knew. This was all a part of his plan to pass the time until he was in school and had begun the routine of college life.

Jack had been looking everyday for an apartment where he didn't have to pay that security deposit. He began waking up earlier than he had in the past and walked out of the area to look; usually walking several blocks west of where the Arms was. All of the studios and one-room places he inquired about required a security deposit. It was nearing the end of the third week of November and he was hoping to find a place before the month was over. Each evening that he spoke to Tina, he would give her accounts of his search for a new apartment. He could express his frustrations to her and she gave him her usual unwaivering support. While he hung around the poolroom, Jack would occasionally sip on a beer and sometimes when the beer was having it's affects upon him, he could feel those old urges rising up within him where he wanted more; maybe some hard liquor or wine or even some drugs were the kinds of cravings he would have for fleeting moments; but, they were mild enough that he could mentally fight them off and resist the temptation.

Jack and Tina went out on the weekend and everything was more low-key because neither of them had much money this weekend. They did what they usually did when their money was low; they spent long periods of time in coffee shops and went for long walks and having timeless dialogue as they always did.

It was Saturday, November twenty-ninth. Another week was passing and Jack was running out of time to meet his goal of finding a new place to stay by the end of the month. He had spent most every day looking for the last few weeks. He had this final Saturday morning to look. But, he decided that if he did not find a place this morning, he would have to make his last resort choice of getting a room at the YMCA this afternoon. He knew his monthly Aid check would likely be at the Arms today. Jack got up early this Saturday morning. He had his usual long talk with Tina Friday night and had told her that he would try one last time to find an apartment this morning before he went to the "Y" this afternoon to rent a room. It was 8:20am when Jack went out. He went out to get his newspaper and came back to his place to look through the rental ads. He saw a couple of ads that he could afford the rent and he wrote down the phone numbers. He went downstairs to the lobby to call them. But, one was already rented and the other insisted on a security deposit. His hope to get a place somewhere other than the "Y" had faded. He had hoped to get a nice, clean little place; either a single room or studio out of the area where he now lived. Somewhere that he would not see any of his fellow hustlers or any of the street people he was used to seeing; where there was peace and quiet. He had visualized a nice little place in a good neighborhood where he could invite Tina. He wanted to be able to have her at his place where she could feel comfortable in coming and going.

From the first time he met her, he was impressed and mystified at how she would patronize the bars along Lawrence Avenue and visit him at the notorious Malden Arms and not show any fear and behave as if she belonged. Jack was more concerned about her safety than she seemed to be. The Y was in an ideal location. But, he could not invite Tina to his room. Whenever she visited him there, they would have to sit out in the lobby area where the community TV was and where there was no privacy. They would be surrounded by the mostly single male residents who would be watching the TV. He did not care for that scenario and that was the reason he had looked so long and hard for an alternative. But, it appeared now that he was not going to be able to avoid it. After he had spoken to the last renter on the phone, he decided that time had run out. He was going to go forward and rent the room at the Y this afternoon. He was fairly certain that he could get a room there. He had come to know from his experience of visiting with Willie-the-Weep, that the room occupancy was transient, with renters coming and going often. Many of the residents were much like Jack; only a step away from being out on the streets.

Jack had not seen The Weep to tell him that he was moving into the Y where he lived. But, Jack thought he would surprise him if he could get a room there today. It was now almost 10am. Jack had to wait until about eleven-thirty for the mailman to arrive before he could get his check from the desk clerk. Meanwhile, he mulled around his place, looking all around at his few belongings and thinking about how he was going to transport them to the YMCA several blocks away. He decided that he would just take a cab because he would have to make two trips to carry everything on foot. He felt joy from the prospect of moving to make a new start in his life. But, he felt a bit wistful, as well at leaving the craziness that had become so familiar to him. There was something about this insane lifestyle that was addictive and maddeningly exhilarating and that was the part that made him reflective. It was the struggles and looming danger that he would not miss. Jack nodded off for a short while and when he awoke, he went downstairs to the lobby and picked up his check from the desk clerk. He continued on to the currency exchange at Lawrence and Ashland where he always cashed his check. He cashed his check there because it was out of the area where other Street Gypsies could see him. He wasted no time and walked the several blocks to the YMCA at Wilson and Hermitage. It was a very sunny and cool day and he walked anxiously because, although he felt he could get a room today, there was no absolute certainty. He hoped that it would go okay and he would get the room. He arrived on the block where the Y stood with homes surrounding it on a quiet street. There was a small grocery store across the street that many of the Y residents frequented. Jack had been there before on one of his visits with The Weep and he found it very convenient.

Jack walked into the YMCA lobby and up to the desk. "I want to rent a room" he announced. "Okay" the clerk responded cheerfully. "Give me a minute to check what we have available" he added. He began to look and Jack grew a bit anxious as the man kept looking. As he did so, Jack noted that the man seemed very relaxed and easy-going. So unlike the people he was used to dealing with in the area he had come from. Everyone there seemed more tense, on-guard----wary. "How's the second floor?" the clerk finally said. Jack breathed a sigh of relief when he heard the man say those words. "Oh…uh….yea…that's good" Jack responded. Are you going to rent by the week or month?" the man asked. "Monthly" Jack replied. The desk clerk completed the transaction after Jack paid him the months rent. I want to leave a note for Willie Moss on the third floor" Jack said. The clerk gave Jack a blank slip of paper and he wrote a message with his room number on it "I'm in room 212, Weep. Check me out" The clerk took the note and put it in The Weep's mail slot. Jack accepted his receipt and key after the clerk explained the house rules to him and gave him the handout. Jack walked out feeling an enormous sense of relief. It felt like the relief he used to feel in the past when he would pay his rent at the Arms before going out to blow the rest of his money getting high. That had been his routine month-after-month before now. Jack walked back to the Arms and before he went upstairs to his room, he told the desk clerk that he was moving today and that he would give him the key after he came downstairs with all of his stuff to put into a cab. Jack went to his room and began to gather his things. He needed to find something to carry his clothes in. He had a large canvas laundry bag that he had been using to carry his clothes to the laundromat. He began to pack his clothes in it. He packed away his hygiene stuff and a few other items in one shopping bag. He wrapped his few pairs of shoes in newspaper and stuffed them in another grocery bag that he had lying around. He could carry his small thirteen-inch TV by the handle. He folded the few towels and one blanket and bound all of it with a bedsheet. He had gathered all of his worldly possessions in about half-an-hour. Finally, he plopped down on the edge of the bed and looked around the room. He was somewhat disappointed that he would be moving to the Y. But, he knew he could continue to look for another apartment while he was living there.

As he sat, Jack looked all around the little place that he had called home for the last six months. He was happy that somehow, he was able to make this change of residence. He knew that none of this could have happened on it's own without his meeting Tina and having a desire to change because of her influence upon him.

He rose up from the bare mattress and walked downstairs to the lobby to call a cab. The dispatcher said the wait would be ten to twenty minutes. When the cab came, Jack had all of his things stacked near the lobby door. When he heard a car honking outside, he knew it was the cab and he began to take his things out to load into it. He gave the desk clerk the room key. "You might have to still come back for your mail a few times after you file your address change, you know" Roger, the desk clerk advised. "Yea…I'm goin' over to the Post office on Broadway and file my address change on Monday morning" Jack replied. With that, the desk clerk said "Take it easy, Rollins….I'll see you around" "Not too often, I hope" Jack replied. The desk clerk understood exactly what Jack meant----any move from the Malden Arms could be nothing but a good one. After he had gotten settled in his room at the Y, Jack called Tina later that afternoon and told her that he had gotten the room. She was happy that he was out of the Malden Arms and indifferent to the idea that he was now staying at the Y. They talked a little while and hung up to prepare for their get-together tonight.

It was Wednesday, December tenth and Jack was showering; preparing for his appointment to take his placement test at Northeastern. He was feeling a bit apprehensive because he had not been in school for several years. Except for Algebra, he had been a good student in high school. But, he had not taken any kind of academic test since high school. He had been to the local library a few times in recent weeks, trying to familiarize himself with basic math by reading old text books. He was hoping that it went okay and that he didn't score so low on the tests that they would change their minds about letting him enroll. He did not know how all of this worked nor how well he would do; but, the one thing he did know was that he was going to give it his best try. All of these thoughts ruminated in his mind as he showered in the community bathroom on the second floor of the Y. Jack had begun to settle in and get used to his new surroundings. He had been there just a week-and-a-half now, and he found it interesting. The rooms were always warm with the radiator heat sometimes making his room too warm. But, this was okay with Jack because he could always open the window. There was a housekeeping crew that brought fresh towels and bed linen twice-a-week to each resident. The entire Y was kept very clean and it was usually quiet.

Many of the residents were older men with a smaller number of twenty-somethings like Jack mixed in. Many of them seemed a bit odd---not so normal. But, Jack hadn't quite figured out what the oddity was. He had begun to feel much more comfortable than he did at the Arms. He noticed subtle changes in his mind and body. He was sleeping better and his appetite was a bit sharper. His thoughts seemed clearer. A short introspective moment told him that this was all because he was no longer in the tense, edgy atmosphere of the Malden Arms and the area surrounding it where he had been hanging out. He enjoyed his new-found peace of mind.

Lately, his thoughts were focused on his near-future and he envisioned how happy his experience in college would be. He could also see his relationship with Tina progressing into a permanent bond--- at least, that was what he hoped. But, with the knowledge and experience that he had from his past and all of the beliefs about women that he had picked up in the streets from the "player" mentality that prevailed, he kept some reservations. He had been warned not to put all of his faith in a woman. He had been indoctrinated with this philosophy in bits-and-pieces over time from various encounters with his brethren in the streets. He had been warned not to get played by a woman; because to do so would be the worst kind of strike against his manhood. He wondered, though, had any of these men met a woman like Tina who seemed to be so unconditional in her regard for him; someone he felt that he did not quite deserve. But, he had seen for himself and had heard the stories of men who had lost in the game of love and how they had to live down the rejection and humiliation that they had not foreseen; forever reciting their tales of loss and analyzing it from every angle; he felt that he had been sufficiently cautious; but, how should one proceed with an affair such as the one he had with Tina? he could exercise only so much caution; be reserved only to a point; but, as long as the affair was meaningful and rewarding, he had to jump in with both feet and let things be as they may; he could not calculate love.

Finally, Jack got dressed and started toward the Northeastern Illinois University Uptown Center at Sheridan and Montrose to take his placement tests. Since he was now living at the Y, his walk was several blocks longer. But, with all of the walking Jack did on a regular basis, it did not make much difference. He arrived and went up the long stairwell to the Center. He went to Linda Chavez' office. "Jack Rollins…how are you?" she greeted in her usual cheerful manner as Jack peeked his head into her office. "Hello" Jack responded politely. "Yes…please sign in on this list here on the clipboard….and we can get started" Linda Chavez said as she led Jack to a room while she carried a handful of official looking papers. She sat him down in the empty classroom and gave him a couple of number two pencils. She also gave him one set of those papers she was carrying. It was a folded test paper with numbered answer spaces. She then gave him a thin booklet with several pages of test questions and a couple of sheets of scratch paper. "This is the English Placement Test…to test your language skills level" Linda explained. "Also, you can take your Math placement test today or schedule it for another day if you're not quite ready" she added. "Can I let you know after I take this test?…I need to see how I feel after this…can I do that?" Jack asked. "Sure….you will have one hour to take this test…if you finish sooner…just come back to my office and let me know that you are done…okay?" Linda said. "Alright" Jack replied. As Jack took the test, he found himself concentrating and he was doing better than he expected. He skipped a few questions and came back to answer them. He took almost the whole hour but, he finished in reasonable time. When he went back to Linda Chavez' office, he told her that he wanted to take the Math placement test in about a week. "That's okay…how about Wednesday, next week?" Linda asked as she looked at her testing schedule. "That's good….perfect…I wanna get ready, but, not take too long…you know what I mean?" Jack said. "Sure…I know what you mean…a little time to prepare is always good…I'll see you on that day at 1pm…okay?" Linda said. ""Yea…I'll be here...goodbye" Jack said before he left.

It was nearing Christmas time and for the first time in a along time, Jack had to think about preparing for this holiday. He had not given or received any Christmas gifts in a couple of years now; not since the short-lived affair that he had with Earline's sister Red that lasted most of December two years ago. He remembered that she bought him a nice knitted sport shirt and he gave her a brand new watch that was part of some things he boosted from a retail store on Broadway during the busy Christmas shopping season a couple of years ago. Back then, Jack loved the crowded stores with throngs of shoppers. This was what he and many other hustlers who engaged in boosting wanted----a store so full of shoppers, that it was almost impossible for the security to watch everyone, or even for the security people who watched hidden camera monitors in a backroom somewhere to identify a theft when it occurred. But, this Christmas was very different from then. He was no longer the gregarious, freewheeling, down-and-dirty hustler that he had been just last Christmas. Back then, he was high most of the time when he was hustling. Nothing mattered and he didn't give a damn. He took all kinds of risks back then. But, now, he had good reason to not take such risks anymore. He had changed and sometimes surviving required one to change. He had learned this over the last few years from his life in the streets. There were times he had to be a chameleon when he was hustling; sometimes changing his entire persona to con or get over on a mark.

It was Tuesday, December sixteenth and Jack had begun to think seriously about what he was going to do for Christmas regarding Tina. He had not contemplated these matters in quite some time. For the last few years, it had been just another day and last year he was so high that he didn't realize when the day came. Now, he wanted to do something nice for Tina because he cared for her. He suspected that he loved her but, he did not want to acknowledge it in his mind; even though his heart was telling him all that his mind would not. He could not deny that he was being guided by those very feelings. He had no choice. He had avoided being involved this way with a woman in the past because they had always given him an excuse----a way out; a reason to not go any further; usually, they were demanding; asking for commitments and such, and making other demands that he was not ready for. He had learned from his experiences and he had become prepared for those demanding types. But, Tina had done none of that. She seemed a bit mysterious in that regard. She was entirely different. She had become his friend and lover all at once and he was baffled at how this all came to be; he had no defenses and he was not ready for the manner in which she had gained his trust so immediately.

Today, Jack went through the routine that he had begun in the last month or so of getting up by 9:30am, showering, going to the Bezazian Library and reading math books and other materials. He had to take his math placement test tomorrow, so he laid low today and went in early.

Hello, Ms. Chavez" Jack greeted as he peeked his head in Linda Chavez' office. Hello, there, Jack…how are you?....come on in" she responded pleasantly. She sat Jack in the same room and gave him another test. She recited the same thing she did for the last test about having an hour to finish and she gave Jack the test materials. "Okay…you can start now" she said as she closed the door to the room leaving Jack alone inside. Jack began with the math test and after confidently doing several problems, he got stuck and he felt confident on only a few of the next several problems as they seemed to become more difficult as he went along. The last several problems seemed especially hard and he answered them as best he could. He took the entire hour and he did not feel that he had done so well. He remembered struggling with math in high school and it was his most difficult class back then. He barely made a passing grade, he remembered. Jack finished the test and walked back to Linda's office a few minutes after the hour was up. "Ms Chavez….I'm done…I don't think I did all that good" he said with a somewhat worried expression. "Well…we will see how well you did in about a week when the tests are scored on campus for all of the applicants who took the test this week…don't worry…you finished high school math, right"? Linda asked. "Yes…but I barely passed…and have been out of school about six years" Jack replied. "How did you do in the rest of your classes?" Linda asked. "Oh…I did good…really good in some, like English, History, and Science…that Math was pretty hard, though" Jack explained. "Well, you still shouldn't worry….if you didn't score well enough on the math test, you probably will have to take one, maybe two below college level math classes when you start classes…but, I doubt if you will be taking two…probably just one…and when you complete that class successfully, then, you will have achieved college level Math and you can go on from there" Linda explained. "You mean even if I failed the placement test, I can still get enrolled?" Jack asked with a hopeful tone. "Yes…and it's not exactly looked at as failing so much as it is seen as a way to measure what class level to place you in…you understand?" Linda asked. "Yea…I understand…that makes sense…the test is not a pass or fail…it's for placement...right?" Jack said. "Exactly" Linda responded. "Okay…I feel better already....Miss Chavez" Jack started. "Linda" she responded "Linda…so, I can still enroll…no problem?" Jack asked. "Oh, yes…definitely….and I've got your English placement test right here, if I am not mistaken…let me check your score…you'll get a letter soon with that score…but, I can give it to you now….let's see here" Linda said as she looked over a document that was lying on her desk. "Rollins…Rollins….Rollins…oh, here we are….Jack…you did excellent...and it looks like one of the higher scores…very good!" Linda exclaimed after she found Jack's score. "You got a twenty-eight and our highest score was thirty out of a possible thirty-two!" She went on. "So…I wouldn't worry very much if I were you….you're in good shape" she assured. "Right on!...hahaha…I don't feel so bad about the math test, now…since I can still get enrolled…so I'm good to go!...hahaha…Thanks, Linda!" Jack said excitedly. "Sure…don't forget, enrollment starts in the first week of January…make sure you come in on Tuesday, the sixth of January, just like the letter you got says…okay?" Linda reminded Jack. "Yes…for sure…I'll be here, thanks again" Jack said as he shook Linda's hand before he walked away down the hall and bounced energetically down the long stairwell before he burst outside onto the sidewalk.

Jack turned and began walking briskly north on Sheridan Road. He was feeling very good about things, in spite of how the math test had gone for him. He was gliding along Sheridan Road, heading north to Wilson Avenue and thinking about the day he would be enrolling in classes. He was in his own world, when suddenly, he heard a voice speak out to him "Hey, Big Slim…Slim…check it out..""" It was the character that Jack knew as "Slick" an older hustler whom Jack had become acquainted with over the last couple of years. He had walked up on Jack before he knew it. Jack found him to be interesting and entertaining because He was odd, a little crazy and amusing all at once. In spite of all of that, Jack would talk to him and hear him out because, between the neurotic chatter, he occasionally imparted to Jack some game that was worth hearing, and Jack would listen closely to pick it up. Slick was always moving hurriedly about the streets; sometimes talking out loud to no one in particular about this and that; complaining and sounding irritated about whatever the issue was; he was an old-time dope-fiend and hustler from forty-seventh street who occasionally traveled to the northside to hustle because, as he was always saying, hustling was harder on the southside and besides…."them Southside niggas' crazy!" he would declare. "Slim..looka' here…look…check this shit out, man…I got a whole bag o' shit I just boosted, man…eye drops, brand new scarves, foot medicine…a whole buncha' shit…can you use any o' this…?" he asked as he raised the shopping bag that he was carrying with an offering gesture toward Jack. "Hahaha…naw, naw…I ain't in the market for none o' that…I'm cool, Slick.." Jack replied calmly with a light chuckle. "Man…you know what…that's alright, Slim…I got to get outa' here, anyway…I think the po'lice might be trailin' me…I got to throw them motherfuckers off!...I got to go…be cool!" Slick said as he craned his neck around, looking in the distance behind him and moving with a jerky, hurried motion before he turned the corner just as they arrived at the corner of Sunnyside and Sheridan. He cut in front of Jack heading east on Sunnyside while walking with the same wild, hurried gait and looking all around as he faded into the distance.

As Jack continued north on Sheridan Road. His encounter with Slick made him suddenly realize that he was on the main drag where many of the hardcore fiends and hustlers congregated. He could see some of them milling around in the distance at the corner of Sheridan and Wilson. He decided that he would avoid them and he backtracked just a few yards and crossed from the east to the west side of Sheridan and cut westward on Sunnyside. As he approached the corner of Sunnyside and Broadway, he could see the dispersing crowd of people from the Salvation Army soup line that formed every day around eleven-thirty in the afternoon. People came and went for a couple of hours to get a free meal. It was part of the Salvation Army Center building that stood on the corner. It was a place that provided a variety of social services, such as a food and clothing pantry, transportation vouchers and drug and alcohol recovery programs; and of course, church services; Jack weaved through the group of people lingering around the sidewalk who had just finished their lunch at the Center. They were the usual down-trodden, bedraggled assortment he would see traipsing the streets of Uptown daily. They were not hustlers or dope-fiends but, more docile types and some were derelict. Most of them were drinkers like the majority of street people in the area. Jack had not been able to bring himself to go to the soup line when he was broke and hungry. He had too many ways to make money and feed himself. He found a way to get enough money for his basic needs most every day. It was probably the bit of pride that he had left that made him hustle so hard to keep from becoming someone who had to stand in the soup line. But, he understood the necessity of all the social services that the Salvation Army provided. Uptown was a place that certainly needed them, he thought. Jack continued on home to the Y, taking short cuts all the way to avoid seeing any of the regulars he usually saw on the streets.

It was Wednesday, December seventeenth and Jack and Tina had made very little mention of the upcoming Christmas holidays but, the issue was now pressing on Jack's mind more than ever. Tina had told him that she would be off the whole day on Tuesday, December twenty-fourth and on Christmas day. She had asked Jack did he want to do anything special and he responded by saying "of course" But, Jack didn't have any money to speak of right now and the holidays were fast approaching. So, he told Tina that he would let her know on the weekend what he wanted to do. Tina never put pressure on Jack for anything; although she had a way of challenging him when he had any doubts about what he could or could not do. Whenever Jack had a dilemma that he had not quite figured out, Tina would make suggestions to him that would set off a train of thought for Jack and he eventually figured things out for himself from there. But, right now, he felt that this was something he would take care of himself. It was not the kind of issue that he could bounce off of her because she was the subject of the issue. Quite simply, he needed some money to celebrate the holidays with Tina in the way he hoped. He began to think about it after the first week in December passed. He thought about what safe hustle he could make that would make him enough money to buy Tina a nice gift and for them to have a good time around Christmas. But, the safe little hustles that Jack had been doing for about the last two months were not what he had in mind. The money he had been making was just enough to get by. He needed a good "sting" He began to think that these kind of thoughts and the actions behind them must surely mean that he loved Tina. He had to admit it to himself and let go of that last bit of manly pride that kept him from acknowledging it. Lately, Jack had been almost pensive about his Christmas dilemma and he made up his mind to talk to his friend, Coley about it. Coley was the type who didn't bother with a hustle if the payoff was not significant. He did not engage in the small-time hustling that Jack did. He had connections of his own and he knew the hustling game as well as anyone because he was experienced in all phases of it.

Jack remembered that Coley had offered him to work in a hustling scheme that Coley had done before. But, it was somewhat involved and he needed a partner who was smart enough to help him pull it off; someone who was a good actor and con like Jack. But, Jack had turned him down a couple of times in the past when Coley had excitedly made the proposition to him. Jack felt that the scheme was too drawn-out and the payoff took too long to materialize; and that was why he did not want to get involved. Jack's style had always been quicker, smaller hustles. But, now Jack needed some real money. The twos and fews he had been hustling lately were not going to get it. He needed to go for something bigger to get him over the hump. His time was running out and he felt he needed to make his move soon. He had wracked his brain for the last two weeks trying to figure out what he was going to do. Now, he was more than ready to get busy.

It was Thursday, December seventeenth. Jack made a phone call to Coley to ask him to come down to the poolroom this evening to discuss the scam. Jack would not be talking to Tina on the phone tonight, as usual, so, he had the entire evening to hang out with Coley and get something going on the hustling side. Coley agreed to meet Jack at the poolroom at 7:30pm. "Hey, Jack….what's to ya' brotha'?….talk to me" Coley greeted. "Hey, Coley…how ya' doin' man?…yea…I just wanted to know was you still up on that sting you always tellin' me about?" Jack asked. "What sting?....oh…oh…yea….that one…you talkin' about the gay doctor sting…you wanna get down?….we could make a nice little piece of change, ya' know" Coley said.

"Yea…you know what I said before when you asked me…I didn't wanna have to deal with no gay marks 'cause I don't know how to deal with them… I ain't never played no gay mark before"

Jack explained. “Hey…quiet-as-kept…him being gay is good far as gettin’ over….they’re more willing to fall for some bullshit than straight marks is…’cause they’re lonely and they’re eager to make friends” Coley explained. Jack paused a moment before he responded as he seemingly pondered the logic of what his friend had just said. “I guess you’re right…you been around and you know all types of people…I seen you dealin’ with them at Saxony and the other bars around here….but, I never did meet them ‘cause I rarely drink inside a bar….I only do it when I’m tryin’ to play a mark or when I got money, I’ll hang at the Green Mill for a little while…other than that, you know I drink on the streets” Jack explained. “Jack…you know, man….anytime you see me hangin’ around with some square motherfuckers…it’s all about the paper….dig what I’m sayin’?” Coley asserted. “Yea….but, you be playin’ it off so tough ‘til I don’t know if they’re your friends or just marks that you’re playin’…and you know me…I be knowin’ you up to somethin’ so, I steer clear so you can do your thang…I don’t wanna walk up and say the wrong thing and blow it for you…dig?” Jack explained. “Yea…that’s cool, Jack and I appreciate that ‘cause you’re one of the few young brothas out here who understands that and what I’m tryin’ to do…actually…you see…a lota’ times they are both…a mark and my friend..mostly square white dudes and sometimes they’re gay….they’re lonely and they have money…that’s the main thing…when you see me with them, it’s ‘cause they got money…people with money are sittin’ there at the bar gettin’ high…I get acquainted and party with them…get their trust…after a while, they get to know me and they’ll say…James…you’re a really nice fella…that’s ‘cause I play it off so well…I buy ‘em drinks and everything…after I get their trust…I play ‘em…I get paid…dig what I’m sayin’?” Coley said with the seasoned confidence of someone well-versed in the game. After a silent moment to allow what Coley had said to sink in, Jack finally said “Okay…cool…so run that game by me again that you always tellin’ me about” “Okay…this is how it goes…this one mark you have seen me with before….I have been knowin’ him almost a year…he’s the gay doctor…he’s single, of course, and he got all kinds of money stacked away….he’s been a gynecologist for almost twenty years….he’s got one weakness…he’ll buy anything once he gets high…I have sold this fool all kinda’ shit after he got high on different nights we were drinkin' at Saxony...he have bought old watches…and he would pay me once….and it's always way more than the shit is worth…and then forget that he paid me and pay me again…ain't that some hellified shit?….I ain't bullshittin' then he buyin' me all kinda drinks at the same time…so I'm sho' 'nough gettin' paid" Coley explained. "Okay…so this is the one you wanna' run this game on…right?" Jack asked. "Yea…this is how we gonna do it…he'll come to the bar and drink if I call him up…I'll have him come to the Saxony bar Friday or Saturday night…I need two people to play this off…one to come in and sit at the bar and act like he don't know us and another to come in with a piece of jewelry tryin' to sell it…now, both people got to be dressed nice and act as if they don't know us or each other…the jewelry is gonna be fake…you know that shit they sell in Jew-town?…anyway…the person will come in with the jewelry…it'll be a man's ring the size this mark wears…he'll sit at the bar…start drinkin' then, pull out the ring and tell some kinda' sob story about why he's gota' sell it…but, the catch is…Kevin…that's the mark's name…got to be good and high before this person comes to the bar to show the ring…I want our man to ask about twelve hundred for the ring and claim he paid over three grand for it…he'll show it to the other person who's in on it who will be sittin' at the bar…this person will start ravin' about the ring and make an offer for it… and carry on about how nice it is and how much it's worth, then pull out a wad of money and count it…then find out he only got about half the money…he makes a phone call to somebody at the phone booth in Saxony to get the rest of the money…but, he don't have no luck…then, he sits at the bar actin' all dejected and stuff..talkin' about what a bargain price it is and on-and-on…dig…then I don't make it no better…I talk to the guy…and console him after he misses out on the bargain of the century…dig?…I know this mark, Kevin is gonna' try to buy the ring after that…I know him and I know that is what he is gonna do…" Coley explained.

"So…who you gonna get for the two people?" Jack asked. "Well…I already got Whiteboy Freddy B to agree to do it …'cause he don't drink that much…I need somebody who won't get drunk on me and blow the whole thing….he will be the person sellin' the ring" Coley explained. "Alright…sounds good, so far…who is the second person?" Jack quizzed. "I need somebody smooth who is believable …somebody who looks trustworthy but, of course they're really not, to play the part of the assistant…they cain't be stupid…got to have some wits about they damned self…dig what I'm sayin'?" Coley said with conviction. "Okay…so who is it gonna be?" Jack asked again. "I got to think on this one…I don't want no pillheads 'cause they will want too much pay so they can buy some pills…don't need no big drinkers…already said that…cain't use no silly motherfuckers…. damn.…I'm runnin' outa' people.….who the hell am I gonna' get?…damn……let me think…anyway…I'll have somebody by tomorrow" Coley said.

"Hey…Coley…I think you forgot one important thing…what the hell is my role in all of this?" Jack asked with a puzzled expression. Oh..yea…hahahaha…you…my brotha'…will sit with us and drink a little and talk and bullshit…that's all I want you to do…just sit…talk and bullshit…but, don't get drunk…cool?…you ain't hardly drinkin' nowadays anyway…alright?" Coley said. "Just sit with you and the gay stud and just keep y'all company?...I don't understand what good I'm doin'" Jack said with the same puzzled look. "Hahahaha…ahhhh…young Jack….even though your role don't seem like much…it's the key to the whole thing" Coley chuckled. "How?…why?" Jack asked again. "Well, ya' see….he *is* gay…he gonna be conversatin' with a young buck like ya' self…gettin' all happy and stirred up…he really let's himself go when he is in the company of strangers…especially young dudes…just be cool…you ain't got to do nothin' else…just be cool and friendly…that's all…he gonna try to buy the ring to show off in front of you to show that he is a big-time dude and he got money…you bein' there is the hook, brotha'…you the hook, bro- man…dig?" Coley said with supreme confidence and a broad grin.

It was Friday, December eighteenth. Before Jack and Coley parted company last night, Coley vowed to have his second person by 6pm that Friday evening and he would meet Jack at the poolroom with that person to discuss the sting amongst themselves. Jack had made it to the poolroom at 5:52pm. He sat at the same place in the front corner looking out of the long picture window that faced Lawrence Avenue. He peered vigilantly eastward down Lawrence waiting to see Coley's familiar frame appear in all of the Friday night pedestrian traffic. But, he knew that it was still a bit early, yet and he should relax. He was thinking about the scheme and was feeling some apprehension about how it might turn out. He had no choice now but to place all of his hopes in it going okay. He was reminded, as well, by all of this preparation, why he did not like this kind of hustle that hinged on too many things having to go right. At a few minutes past 6pm, Coley burst through the poolroom entrance. He was alone. "Hey, man…" He greeted Jack.

"Hey, Coley…where's ya' boy at?" Jack asked with a hint of worry in his voice. "Be, cool, man…don't worry….I talked to him….it's Skip" Coley assured. "Yea…smooth-ass Skip…right on!" Jack said cheerfully. "That's right….ran into him in the Goldblatts store today…he was with his wife, Rita …they was shoppin'" Coley said. "He might work out good" Jack speculated. "I think so….anyway, he's supposed to be here sometime before seven o' clock…said he had to make a run around five and he know he won't make it down here until between six-thirty and seven" Coley said. "What made you pick Freddy B?" Jack quizzed. "Hey, man….I think he was the best choice…he's white…nobody would suspect he was in cahoots with us on this thang…besides.. I asked a couple other people….pool shootin' Ernie and Tommy Jackson …but, they talkin' like they want half the damn money for the role of sellin' the ring…I say naw, man…this is *my* sting….I ain't givin' you half…and they tried to negotiate their cut and I said…that's alright…forget about it…good thing I didn't tell neither one of 'em when or where it was gonna jump off…you never do that…you tell a nigga' where and when a sting is jumpin' off and they'll be there to try to get a cut even if they ain't in on it…you know how that goes" Coley explained. "You know I know" Jack confirmed. "Yea…I picked Whiteboy Freddy B 'cause he *is* convincin' you know" Coley said. "Sho' 'nough…he does have that way about him…he is persuasive and you can trust him, too…if I was a stranger…I would believe what he was sayin' Jack commented. "Besides that…he ain't tryin' to be greedy like them other cats…he thought about it for a minute…then, he agreed to do it for the money I quoted him…it will make everything even more believable with him in the picture…dig?" Coley said. "Hahaha…we ready to go, then…huh?" Jack chuckled as he raised his hand to slap five with Coley. "Yea..if everybody shows up and they play their part right…we cool” Coley said with assurance. “Right on!….when you wanna do this?” Jack asked. “Well…after Skip agreed to do his part…I called the doctor up and he’s gonna be at Saxony at seven-thirty tomorrow night” Coley said. “Damn, Coley…I’m s’posed to meet my girl around that time” Jack said with a bit of concern. “You wanna get paid, don’t you?” Coley asked. “”That’s alright…I’ll just call her and make some other arrangements” Jack responded quickly, not hesitating to acknowledge the gravity of the situation.

Finally, at around 6:50pm, Skip walked into the poolroom. “Hey, fellas…” he greeted as he approached Jack and Coley sitting in the front corner. “My, man, Skippa’…have a seat and let’s iron this thang out….I already told you scandalous Jack is in on this…right?” Coley said as he motioned toward Jack. “Hey…yea…how ya’ doin’ Jack?…yea…Jack is my man…he helped me out of a coupla’ tight spots a while back” Skip said in his usual rhythmic manner as he extended his hand for a handshake with Jack. “Hey…what’s happ’nin…my man, Skip!” Jack greeted as the two shook hands.

“Okay…Skip…check it out…the mark is this gay doctor….you mighta’ seen me hangin’ with him before at the Saxony bar, drinkin’ and shit…he got money…I’m talkin’ ‘bout some sho’ ‘nough money…dig me?…he been a women’s doctor for almost twenty years…he’s lonely…he comes down to the Saxony bar a couple of nights a week….takes a cab there, then, takes one back home…I ran into him almost a year ago…now…you know me…I ain’t prejudiced….I’ll play on any som’ bitch…understand me?...anyway….when he gets high…he gets real happy…that gay happy….maybe that’s why they call ‘em gay…I don’t know…he will start to buyin’ people drinks…then, he starts buyin’ shit offa’ people…sometimes he wanna’ buy shit offa’ people even when they don’t wanna sell it…he gets silly…I noticed this about him way back when I first met him….like I said…almost a year ago…I’m in the bar drinkin’…he introduces himself and starts buyin’ me drinks…I guess he took a likin’ to me….kept buggin’ me to sell my watch to him…I kept sayin’ “no”…my daughter bought this for my birthday…it was a good, solid watch…but, not very expensive…my daughter was seventeen at the time…she didn’t have much money…anyway…he kept buggin’ me so much ‘til I finally sold it offa' my arm for a ridiculous price….I said to myself…I'm gonna' fix this fool from botherin' me about this damn watch…my daughter probably didn't pay more than thirty dollars for the watch…I sold it to his ass for seventy-five…then he got even higher later that night and forgot he paid me and paid me again…dig me?…yeah…I know…soon as he paid me the second time…I got the hell out of the bar…went home…the next day, went out and found the same damn watch on sale…I bought it and my daughter will never know the difference….ever since then…when I see him around the Saxony bar…I stick to his ass like glue…hahahaha…damn right…" Coley cackled as he told his story. "Anyway….to make a long story short…I'm givin' you background on him so you can know how to play this thang…you gonna come in the bar real non-chalant and sit at the bar sippin' on a drink…try not to drink much at all..just sit there and when Freddy B' comes in with the ring…it's gonna be exactly the marks ring size…dig?…I already coached him on how to play it…you look at the ring and say…damn…you sellin' this for what?...and act like it's such a bargain and act like you gonna buy it…but, you say you're short…you make a phone call to get the rest of the money…but, you don't have no luck…dig it?...you know how to play it…I guarantee you…our boy is gonna jump up and start actin' like he's a super high-class motherfucka' and start tryin' to buy it…he wanna be the center of attention…wanna show off…I know him…watch…that's what's gonna happen…you game?" Coley asked. "Am I game?…am I game?…hahaha…do a hog love slop?…damn right I'm game…shit..when a mark is that easy…there for the pickin'…I got to have him…sign me up, baby..it's all over but the shoutin'…dig" Skip said spiritedly in his characteristic bee-bop style. "Alright then, goddammit…that's what I wanna hear…somebody game to make a hustle…we got to stick together like a band of gypsies to make this work…and one more thing…whenever we pass the ring around amongst us and the mark…don't let none of them other people in the bar get a good look at it…in fact, we wanna keep any of them from holdin' it too long in their hand…now…the ring does look good…these dealers in Jew-town sellin' that fake jewelry, got some stuff that looks like the real thing…dependin' on how much you wanna' spend…the more you spend…the more real the ring looks…I spent a little change on this ring…it looks damn good…you would have to look very close to tell it ain't the real thing…some of them studs you see in Jew-town makin' a livin' offa the real good lookin' stuff…anyway…one of us oughta' cut in and hold it and look at it and bullshit around so none of them can get a chance to see that the ring ain't real expensive…okay? Coley said. They all chimed in with agreement.

"Yea, baby…I cain't meet you tomorrow night" Jack said to Tina from a phone at the bank of phones down the hall from his room. "Why, Jack?…what's going on?" Tina asked with a tone of disappointment. "Oh, baby…I found some work…I talked to a guy who lives here at the Y…he said he could use a little help with his plumbin' work late this afternoon….he needs an assistant…I don't have to know nothin'…he will just show me what he wants me to do…I cain't pass this up" Jack lied. "Well….I guess you're right…you *do* need the money…besides….I could just go over to my folks and spend the evening after I do my laundry and my studying at the library" Tina said resignedly. "Don't worry, baby…we're still goin' out on Sunday…we'll do somethin' special and we'll still get together on Tuesday or Wednesday, Christmas eve, too…cool?" Jack said. "Okay…that's cool" Tina sighed. They talked a little while longer before they hung up.

It was eleven-thirty in the morning and Jack began to sense the mild feeling of anxiety arising within him about the scam that was going to jump off at the Saxony bar this evening. A myriad of scenarios ran through his mind about what could go wrong. Usually, Jack had been carefree and unconcerned about the many scams he had run on marks in the past. But, now he was anxious because of how much he found himself depending on the outcome. It all sounded good but, if Freddy B or Skip did not pull this off, or the mark just decided not to buy the ring because a grand was a lot of money to spend with a stranger in a bar, then, his plans to have a good Christmas with Tina would be dashed and he really wanted in the worst way to have spending money for the holidays; for them to have a good time and for him to be able to give her a really nice gift. But, he realized, too that if it did not work out, it would not be the end of the world and that she would still care for him just as he cared very much for her. They would enjoy being together, anyway.

Jack had stayed at the Y all day to kill time. He read some magazines; went out to the Village restaurant on Montrose to eat lunch and came back and watched television in the community area of the lobby. He did not want to start drinking before the sting was supposed to jump off. He thought it was best that he only drink a couple of beers at the table while he sat with Coley and the doctor. Besides, he was supposed to call Coley at 5pm to make sure everything was okay before he walked toward the Saxony bar.

"Hey, brotha' Jack…yea…everything is still a go, my man…you're on tonight…what do them show business people say?…break-a-leg..hahahaha…you got to perform like you goin' for the academy award, baby…dig…yea…you ready ain't you?" Coley said, seemingly in very good spirits. "Hell, yea…I'm ready…ready to get paid!" Jack responded as he fed off of Coley's spirited mood. "Alright, then….show up about eight o' clock and come on in and sit down with us…I'll introduce you to the doctor…just be polite and like I said…friendly…we'll start drinkin' and bullshittin' and then Skip s'posta' show up about eight-thirty and just sit by himself…at the bar if he can…or whereever…dig…then Freddy B should be along closer to nine…now, I coached the hell outa' him to not be too heavy on the actin'…dig…just act natural…this will jump off just like I said…now just look real neat …tell him you got a regular job…act like you're a regular upstandin' guy…dig me?" Coley went on. "Yea, man….I got this…you know me, Coley…I'm like Laurence Olivier when some goddamn money is involved..hahahaha….I'm ready, man" Jack chuckled. Alright, then…see ya' there!" Coley said before he hung up. Jack took a nap around four-thirty then, he just sat in his room watching TV. He was trying to psyche himself to accept that things might not turn out as planned. He was trying to cushion himself for any disappointment. At the same time, he had to have some kind of faith, too---for whatever good it was worth.

Jack had taken a good shower and put on some decent clothes that didn't look too flashy. He needed to create a more conservative persona about himself. He was good at these subtle shifts of personality and mind-set because he had put it into action so many times before for exactly the reasons he would tonight. He checked his drag once more before he was out of the door. He walked the distance through the dark, cool, clear evening from the Y to the Saxony bar in his old stomping ground. Jack arrived at the bar. As he strolled in, he glanced at the wall clock at the far end of the bar to see that it was a few minutes past eight. The warm air in the room wafted into his face. The occasional clinking of drinking glasses along with the aroma of liquor all seemed more heightened to his senses than at any time before. The upbeat conversational buzz was livelier than usual; perhaps, because of a festive holiday mood in the air. There were little bits of holiday décor here-and-there and Smitty, the bartender was serving the customers in a Santa hat. Jack walked halfway in along the narrow path between tables against the wall and the bar on the opposite side before he saw Coley and the doctor at the last table along the wall in the back. They looked jovial as they were both smiling and seeming to be having a good time. "Jack!...Jack…over here!" Coley yelled out just as Jack spotted them. Jack walked over and he constrained himself from responding to Coley in his usual manner.

"Hey, how are you all doing?" he greeted politely as he had set his mind to be in perfect character. "Sit on down, Jack….meet doctor Kevin….Kevin…this is my good friend, Jack" Coley said with a broad smile as he stood up from the table and gestured toward the doctor seated next to him. The doctor looked at Jack and smiled broadly. He stood up and extended his hand to shake. "It is really my pleasure, young man….Jack, huh?....that's a strong name for a tall fellow like you…be seated by all means" the doctor said as Jack could see that he was a bit tipsy. The three sat closely with Coley sitting between the doctor wedged in the corner seat and Jack sitting on the aisle side of the table. The doctor ordered a round of drinks. He ordered a shot of cognac for himself and a pitcher of beer for Coley and Jack. They began to chatter spontaneously about whatever came to mind and in-between the laughter and quips, the doctor would ask questions of Jack "where do you work?…where are you from?…where do you live?" and Jack responded with answers that were not entirely truthful but, that cast himself in the best possible light. In the meantime, Coley was playing his game, using hints to urge the doctor on to get as high as Coley wanted him to get; occasionally shooting a covertly sly glance at Jack to emphasis something about the doctor that he wanted Jack to take note. It was not long before Skip walked in and sat anonymously at the bar and ordered a drink. He hardly even looked in the direction of the table where the three were gathered.

At about ten past nine, Freddy B strolled in. He was already in character with a facial expression that shown a subtle hint of distress. He sat at the bar and before long, he was making small talk with some of the patrons sitting at the bar around him. Skip sat two bar seats away from Freddy B near the entrance end of the bar. Things were going pleasantly at the table with Coley, the doctor and Jack. The doctor was not the flaming type of gay, Jack came to notice. His personality and mannerisms were more androgynous than anything and Jack was relieved about that. He sensed that he would not feel so comfortable playing his role with a more aggressive type of gay person.

Finally, after almost an hour of sitting, drinking and chatting, Freddy B struck up a conversation with Skip after the people between them had departed. Skip moved to the seat next to Freddy B and they began to make small talk. Freddy B pulled out the ring and shown it to Skip. "My goodness…you're kidding, man…that is a beautiful ring!…you sellin' it for what?...well, I'll be!…hold it…let me see….very nice….I think I might be interested" Skip could be heard to say just over most of the buzz of conversation in the room. Skip and Freddy B began to engage for several minutes in some low-key price haggling before Skip went toward the phone booth that was just around the corner, in the back, across from the Men's restroom. He stopped near the table where Jack and the others sat and turned back toward Freddy B to speak. "Hey…my, man…hold onto that ring…don't do nothin' until I make this phone call…alright?…do that for me, will ya'?" he said in a perfectly pitched tone that could be easily overheard. Skip made the gestures and motions of a man who had suddenly become anxious. He dashed into the phone booth and stayed for a few minutes. He dashed back out and stopped near the group's table. "Hey, gents…anybody got change for a dollar?…I got these people on the line and this damn operator is hollerin' about puttin' in some more money…anybody got it?.....yessir…I'm tryin' to take care of some important business…I sure would appreciate it" Skip rattled off quickly as he took anxious breaths for effect. "Oh… I probably have it" the doctor said as he went into his pocket to fish some change out" "Let me see what I have" Coley added. Coley and the doctor reached into their pockets and fished out change. “Here ya’ go, partner…I got you…” Coley said as he handed Skip the change and Skip gave him the dollar bill. “Hey…I’ll give you a dollar bill for that change you got there, too, my man...” Skip said to the doctor as he pulled out a wad of bills and fished out a dollar bill. “Thanks a lot” he said as he exchanged the bill with the doctor. Skip turned back to the phone booth and shut the door again. “Looked kind of nervous…didn’t he?” the doctor said after Skip left. “Yea…tryin’ to take care of business…I guess” Coley said non-chalantly.

“Jack…I expect a young fellow like yourself is looking to get married one day…got anybody special?” the doctor asked with a bit of a drunken lisp and becoming bolder in his questions. “Oh…well…I have a girlfriend…she’s real nice…we haven’t been together too long…she’s special to me…but, I don’t know about marriage…I’ll wait and see how things go” Jack replied with straightforward humility. “Is she good-looking?” the doctor asked, obviously using small talk to advance the acquaintance and making his interest in Jack more apparent. “Pretty good-looking I would say” Jack replied. “Good…what’s she doing with her life?” the doctor asked “Oh…she’s about to finish college…she’s going to be a school teacher” Jack responded with a hint of pride. “That’s terrific, Jack…don’t you cheat on her…you hear?…don’t run around giving her stuff away” the doctor said with a grin that seemed to be holding a bit of mischief. “Aw, shit…Kevin..I know what that means when you start talkin’ like that…look out, Jack…the doctor is on the prowl…watch ya’ self..hahahaha..” Coley said before laughing out loud. A guilty smile spread over the doctor’s face. “Jack and I are friends…right, Jack?” the doctor said as he reached across the table and gently patted the back of Jack’s hand as it lay on the table. “Sure…we can be friends” Jack said. “Well!...I am feeling quite extraordinary right now!…I’m going to order us another round, gents…I want to keep this party going!” the doctor said as his spirits seemed suddenly lifted.

Several more minutes passed before Skip came out of the phone booth. He stepped with a slower pace while he held a mildly frustrated expression on his face. “You come out alright, my man?” Coley asked just as Skip was passing in front of the table. “Naw, man…not at all…shot down, baby…I was just about to make a helluva’ deal with my man over there” Skip said in a dejected tone as he shot a glance in the direction of Freddy B sitting at the bar. “Oh, yea…how’s that?” Coley asked. “Well..” Skip started as he stooped down a little and leaned forward to speak in a hushed tone. “My man over there’s got a helluva’ ring for sell…he kinda’ knows how much it’s worth…but, then again, he don’t…I worked in a jewelry establishment once and after I saw it…I can tell you…that ring is worth way more than he’s askin’…I was tryin’ to get it offa’ him…I got part of what he’s askin’ right now…I got on the phone and tried to get the rest from my uncle…I forgot he’s outa’ town for another week…just my damned luck!” Skip whispered. “So…what is the ring worth?” Coley asked as Jack and the doctor were slightly leaned forward and listening intently. “It’s an eighteen karat, white-gold, two-and-a-half karat-weight man’s diamond ring…worth around three grand easy” Skip whispered. “So…what is he askin’?” Coley asked. “Twelve hundred…can you believe that?…twelve hundred, man…I couldna’ done much better if I’da’ robbed him…but..don’t have to…he’s practically givin’ it away” Skip said convincingly. “Hey, Doc…you hear that?…twelve hundred for a three-thousand-dollar ring” Coley said in a hushed tone. “The doctor looked at Coley for a long moment that seemed eternally suspended as far as Coley was concerned.

This was the moment of truth and the doctor seemed to be trying to force himself to think. Intoxication swayed his upper body ever-so-slightly and he paused as he looked into Coley’s face. There was a long moment of silence and Coley and Jack seemed to hang on the doctor’s answer. “Well, hell…let me see the damned thing!” he finally burst out loud. “Okay…y’all be cool…just take it easy while I try to get it from him to show to you…I think he’ll trust me” Skip said with a low, cautioning tone. He walked back over to Freddy B and seemed to be negotiating. “Man…that sounds like a deal…I wish I had the money…I love nice jewelry...really touches up your appearance, I think” Jack said matter-of-factly. “I think so, too…I have a few pieces of jewelry at home…not much…I mostly wear my graduation ring that I got from medical school…but, I do appreciate nice jewelry” the doctor chimed. Several moments passed before Skip came back to the table. “I got it y’all…look…he said go ahead…see if somebody wants to buy it” Skip said before he handed it to Coley. Coley took it into his hand and held it closely. “Nice diamonds…looks damned good…man….it's a nice size…this is sho 'nough nice…damn…I cain't afford nothin' like this…wish I could, though…that *is* a deal…" Coley gushed before he handed it to the doctor. "Let me see here.." the doctor mumbled as he slipped the ring on the ring finger of his right hand. "How about that…well I'll be damned!...it fits perfect!...just my size!" the doctor said with surprise. "Let me see…wow…yea, it fits you beautifully, Kevin…man.. and it looks good on you…what do you think, Jack?" Coley asked as Jack looked on. "Yea...looks good on you…no doubt" Jack added in a low-key, spontaneous manner as he looked at the glimmering ring on the doctor's hand. "I'm jealous, my man…I sure wish I coulda' got that ring…it looks good on you just like they said" Skip said with a broad grin as he stood in front of the table where the three sat. The doctor held his hand out and admired the ring for a moment and smiled a gushing, happy smile. "It does look fabulous on my hand…truly does…the more I look at it…the more I want it...hell…I'm gonna buy it!..." he finally said. "But..you know…I don't have that kind of cash on me, of course….my good man…can you ask him if he'll take a check?" the doctor asked Skip.

Immediately, an expression of doubt spread over Skip's face. "I really doubt it….I know he don't want no check…but…I can ask him, anyway…here goes nothin'.." Skip said as he wasted no time walking back over to where Freddy B sat quietly alone at the bar. The three sat at the table and watched from the distance halfway across the room as Skip and Freddy B engaged in a conversation. They could see a brief exchange of words and finally, Skip walked back to the table where the three sat. "Naw…he says he needs the cash…he don't wanna' deal with no checks" Skip said. "Oh, well…how can I do this…" the doctor began to contemplate. "Kevin…it's easy, man…think about it…just go over and ask Smitty…he's been knowin' you umpteen years…he knows you're a doctor…you've been a regular here forever, it seems…you must have spent enough money in here over the years to buy the damned place…cash the damn check with him…then give the cash to your man to pay for the ring…simple" Coley advised. "You want the ring…right?…go on over there and ask him" Coley added.

"Well…I will…except for one thing.." the doctor said as he continued to sit. "What's that?" Coley said with a puzzled expression that seemed a bit worried, as well. “I need to get the receipt that he got when he bought it…if I can get that…and I can get the cash…we have a deal” the doctor said in a slightly sluggish tone. “Well…my man…did he have a receipt for the ring?” Coley asked Skip as he seemed to take on the role of an arbitrator. “Uh…yea…when I first spoke to him about the ring…I think he did mention a receipt…let me ask him..” Skip said as he took off again in Freddy B’s direction. There was another session of close-up negotiating between the two and Freddy B could be seen digging into his pocket and pulling out his wallet. He began fishing something out of it. Skip accepted the item that Freddy B handed him and he walked back to the table. “Here we go…got it right here” Skip said as he handed the folded piece of paper to the doctor. “Hey, gents…I don’t mean no harm but…could somebody take care of me for all this negotiatin’ I’m doin’…can you look out for me?” Skip asked as he stood before the three seated at the table. “Hey, brotha-man…we got you faded…don’t worry about a thing…we’ll look out for you” Coley assured. The doctor pulled his glasses out of his sport jacket and put them on and perused the document after he unfolded it. “What‘s those first two numbers say right there, Jack…can you read that for me?” the doctor said as he held the paper over closer to Jack and pointed on the paper. “Hmmmm….let me see…“three…coma-two…three-thousand-two hundred” Jack responded. Oh…so…he paid thirty-two-hundred-something…I see the jewelers name at the top…yep…the description fits…okay…looks fine…now, let me go over here and talk with Smitty and see what I can do…you guys want another round?...what are you drinking, sir?” the doctor asked as he turned to Skip. “Shot o’ Hennessy will do me…thanks” Skip repiled. “Alright…you’ve got it…be right back” the doctor said. “Okay…I’ll let him know that you’re tryin’ to cash a check with the bar…alright?” Skip offered. “Sure…that’s fine…go ahead” the doctor said as he continued to step away.

“Hey, Kevin…let me hold the ring so we can admire it while you’re gone” Coley said. “Oh…uh…sure…hold onto it, okay?” the doctor said as handed the ring to Coley before he continued on strolling toward the bar. The doctor stopped at the end of the bar near the little swing door where the bartender could enter and exit. He began talking to Smitty and he leaned on the bar as Smitty continued to serve customers. Between servings, Smitty would walk back over to the end of the bar where the doctor stood and the exchange continued. Meanwhile, Coley and Jack sat at the table. "I hope he can get it, Jack…come-on….come-on…Smitty…don't blow it…don't let us down…" Coley chanted to himself in a low tone and speaking to Jack all at once. "Jack…we're halfway there…this is it, baby-boy" he murmured as he fixed a stare on the doctor standing at the bar across the room. The doctor stayed for quite a while and the exchange seemed to go on-and-on. Coley and Jack focused on the proceedings, trying to glean anything they could from the gestures and expressions of the doctor and the bartender as they talked. They could not hear what was being said over the music playing and the buzz of crowd noise in the room. Meanwhile, Skip was standing near Freddy B, still seated at the bar as the two continued to talk.

"Slick-ass Jack" a voice suddenly spoke out, piercing the noise. Jack and Coley were startled to see Dinky, one of the neighborhood regulars and Jack's nemesis standing nearby with a beer in his hand. The two had differences on several occasions over a year ago and wound up fighting one night in front of the Boozery bar around that time. Dinky was about the same age as Jack. He was a little heavier by about twenty pounds with slightly shorter height. But, he was much slower than Jack when it came to fighting. The fight ended with Jack fracturing Dinky's finger and him with a very sore knee. The regulars who witnessed the fight that night, raved about Jack's rapid-fire punches that neutralized Dinky's heavier frame. They had not fought or argued since but, whenever they ran into one another, did not hesitate to let the other know that the dislike was still at the surface.

"Hey, Dink…what brings your jive-ass up in here" Jack replied. "I might be checkin' up on *your* ass…see what kinda' hustle you got goin' up in here…I know you don't come in this bar…so you must be hustlin" Dinky said with a silly grin and his usual sarcasm toward Jack. "Don't worry 'bout it, fool…get you some business….then, maybe you can stay the hell outa' mine" Jack said with cutting indifference. "Hahaha…you still talkin' shit.. that don't faze me" Dinky said with the same smirky grin as he stood several feet away from the table. "Makin' any money, Jack?…I know you up to somethin'" Dinky went on. Finally,

Coley, who had kept his eyes on the doctor nudged Jack with his elbow. "Jack…get rid of that sucker before he blows our thing…get him away from here before the doctor comes back. .I think he is about to walk back over here…go ahead" Coley whispered. "Hey, Dink…let me holla' at you outside" Jack said as he raised up from the table and walked over to Dinky and placed his hand on his elbow as if to guide him outside. "Hey, man…I don't appreciate you grabbin' on me…watch yourself" Dinky said defiantly, snatching his arm back. "Watch myself?....watch myself…'the hell you talkin' to, chump?" Jack challenged.

"Meet me outside, fool…alright!" Jack said sternly with a piercing stare. "Ain't no thang!" Dinky responded with the same defiance as he followed Jack outside. Coley could see the two through the large front window of the adjoining liquor store, arguing outside on the sidewalk. He took his eyes off of them and turned his attention back to the doctor who was still talking to Smitty. Coley looked outside again and saw that Jack and Dinky were fighting. But, he sat watching the doctor closely as he continued to talk to the bartender. Coley looked outside again and he could see the two throwing punches and moving out of view. Coley was feeling anxiousness between waiting for the doctor to return and wondering how things would turn out with Jack outside. Several minutes passed as Coley watched the doctor continue talking and laughing with Smitty.

Finally, Jack came back looking a bit disheveled and walking hurriedly. He walked past Coley and said quickly "gota go to the restroom…be right back!" Coley wondered what had happened outside. He peered outside into the night that the street lights partially lit. He was looking for Dinky but, did not see him. Finally, Jack burst back out of the men's restroom and sat down quickly. "I was tryin' to get back before he came back to the table" Jack said as he seemed to be holding his right hand with his left and nursing it. "You made it just in time 'cause here he comes back" Coley said as he watched the doctor turn and begin to walk back toward them. "What happened outside?…I saw y'all fightin'" Coley asked. "I think he went home…I don't think he's feelin' too good…" Jack said as he held back a grin. Suddenly, Jack and Coley burst out in unison with laughter.

The doctor returned to the table and stood near his seat. "Well, James…looks good, so far…Smitty can do it…he just has to tally up some receipts in the back in about ten minutes…Joe is gonna come over from takeout and help bartend while he counts the money…he's got to make sure of how much he has on hand before he cashes my check…he's sure he's got it, plus plenty of cash left to make change at the bar" the doctor explained. Coley and Jack shot quick, veiled glances at one another with muted grins that held a mirthful glee. "I've got our drinks coming over in a few minutes" the doctor added. "So, Jack…you like my ring, huh?" the doctor asked with a broad smile and a playfulness in his voice. "That is a sharp ring you got, doctor Kevin…you are gonna be stylin' with that nice piece of jewelry…yes, indeed…I like it a lot!" Jack assured emphatically, as he seemed to still be trying to shift out of the mode of recovering from his fisticuffs with Dinky. "You know, guys…I love to make a good deal….nothin' like it….you see…when deals like this come along…it's great to be able to take advantage of them…hey…I'd like to talk to this guy selling the ring…he's sat over there the whole time…I wanted to let him know that I really appreciate this deal… I guess if that other fellow talking to him over there would have had the money…I wouldn't have been able to buy it…" the doctor said with a tone of satisfaction. "Just be glad he didn't have the money and you got a shot at it, doc….you're a good business man…that's all" Coley patronized before shooting another quick, sly glance to Jack.

"I'm gonna go over and chat with him for a little bit…you guys hold onto my seat, will you?" the doctor said before walking over to where Freddy B and Skip sat on bar stools next to one another. He stayed for ten minutes or so, happily chatting away and Jack and Coley could hear the occasional laughter from the doctor punctuating the conversation as they sat at the table. Finally, the doctor came back to the table and sat down. Their drinks came and the three sat together drinking and admiring the ring after the doctor put it back on his finger while he laughed and talked away. A short time later, the doctor said "Oh…I see Smitty waving at me…I'll be right back" before he raised from the table and walked over to the bar. Jack and Coley could see Smitty and the doctor closely negotiating. They could see the doctor hand him the personal check he had written earlier and Smitty hand the doctor an envelope.

“Jack…you see that, man?…hahahaha…we did it, brotha’!....hehehe…I told you…didn’t I!”” Coley whispered with glee as he tried to keep a straight face. “Yea, baby…this turned out just like you said, Coley…sweet, man…sho’ ‘nough sweet!” Jack whispered in the same manner, trying to contain his joy. As the doctor walked back toward them, he turned and walked over to Freddy B at the bar. He said something to him and Freddy B raised up from the bar stool and they walked together to the back of the bar around the corner from the table where he sat with Jack and Coley. They continued toward the end of the little hall past where both the men and women bathrooms were. Coley and Jack watched silently as the two passed their table and went into the back. They knew that the wall in the back was where patrons could go to speak privately. They knew that even though he was a little tipsy, doctor Kevin knew to be discrete and make an exchange of this type in as much privacy as he could; lest any observers saw the exchange and came to believe that he carried large sums of money around all the time. The doctor was careful to a point. This was the reason that he did not roam around to the other local bars. Everyone knew him at Saxony and the bartenders and some of the other patrons, in the past, had made sure that he got a cab home safely. After several years of patronizing the place, he had come to feel confident and safe there. It was like home for a person like himself who spent long hours at his practice and who lived alone. “Jack…check it out…I told Freddy B to leave as soon as he got the money....to wait for us at Frances’ until we got there….we‘ll hang for a few minutes….then, I’m gonna tell doc’ I’m sleepy and that I’m goin’ home….you make up whatever excuse you want…dig me?…then we both will get some hat…alright?” Coley explained. “Hell yea…I got you…we gonna get outa’ here as soon as we can and go get our funds…” Jack responded.

The two sat quietly with perhaps, more that a little anxiety knowing that the money had changed hands. When Freddy B and the doctor came back into view, the doctor was talking and he was thanking Freddy B for giving him such a great deal. As Freddy B passed the table, he gave a little purse of his lips and a faint nod to Coley that was veiled enough to go unnoticed. Freddy B stopped and shook hands with the doctor and they exchanged parting pleasantries before Freddy B walked out of the bar with a casual, relaxed stride. “You know…he really is a good man that Quincy guy is…yes, indeed…a pretty bright fellow, too…too bad he has to sell his valuable things…tells me he’s going through a divorce and having a bit of a time…shame” the doctor sympathized. “Hey…you guys want another round?....I’m gonna order myself another double-shot of cognac…what-do-you-say, fellas?” the doctor said cheerfully. “Hey, doc…we already got this pitcher…this is cool…this is plenty…save ya’ money, man…don’t spend so much..besides…I’m gonna have one more glass of beer…then I’m goin’ home” Coley said.

“Aw come on, James!...I’m just getting started here!....why are you going home!” the doctor said emphatically with a note of disappointment. “Gettin’ sleepy, Kevin…I been tryin’ to fight it off for a while, now…just cain’t hang no more” Coley responded. “Yea…me, too…it’s getting late and I’ve got to work tomorrow” Jack chimed in. “Okay…well…I have had a good time tonight…it was a pleasure meeting you, Jack…let’s do this again soon…how about it, guys?” the doctor said. “Oh, yea, Kevin…no problem…we enjoyed your company…right, Jack?” Coley said. “Yea…it was nice meeting you doctor Kevin” Jack said very politely as he shook hands with him before he and Coley began to rise from the table to prepare to leave. “Say, doc…you’re gonna make it home okay tonight….right?” Coley asked with concern. “Oh…yes…I’ll finish my cognac, then call a cab…I won’t be back until after Christmas…I’ll probably be in here on the Tuesday after Christmas…stop by and check to see if you see me…okay?” the doctor said. “Sure, doc…I’ll look for you then…take it easy” Coley responded.

“So long, doctor” Jack chimed in before the two walked out of the bar. The two began to walk east on Lawrence away from Saxony bar and waited until they were several yards away before they began slapping five and acting like kids; smiling and grabbing each other, and behaving triumphantly over the success of their sting. ‘Aw, shit…hahahaha…we did it, Jack!…I told you, man…am I the man?…huh…am I the man?…hahaha…that was a hell of a sting…wasn’t it?…damn right…I know my shit, man…I know my people…told ya’ how it was gonna jump off…didn’t I?…hahaha..” Coley went on-and-on excitedly. “Hell, yea…I can have a good Christmas, now…thanks to you, man…I swear…I didn’t think we could pull it off…but, we did…that was a smooth hustle, baby…I ain't lyin!" Jack said with the same excitement as they walked hurriedly toward Frances' tavern.

"Let's hurry up and catch up to our money, man…no time to waste!" Coley said as the two continued to step at a lively pace. They burst through the entrance door at Frances' tavern and looked around anxiously for Freddy B. There were just a few patrons there seated at the bar---they did not see Freddy B-----panick set in for both men. "Damn!"Coley…that sucker done made off with our money, man!" Jack said in a frustrated tone. "Be cool…be cool…"Coley cautioned Jack before he raised his voice to Frances behind the bar and made a beckoning motion to her. "Hey, Frances!" Frances was not busy and she strolled over slowly to the front of the bar where Coley and Jack stood. "Hey…you seen a kinda' slender white guy come in here with a beige jacket on?" Coley asked. Frances looked around the bar momentarily then, said "He went into the men's room" Jack and Coley breathed a sigh of relief and immediately began walking toward the men's restroom in the back. Just as they began, the men's room door burst open and Freddy B calmly strolled out.

"Hey…you made it" he said with an innocent grin. "Hey...let's go back in the restroom to take care of business" Coley said. Just as he spoke, Skip came through the front door and they all looked back to see him enter. Coley made a waving motion of his arm to Skip and he walked through the bar to join them. They all entered the restroom. The four men gathered around one of the stalls with Freddy B inside of it. "Okay…let me get that…I'm gonna give you your's right off the top, Freddy" Coley urged as he held his hand out. Freddy B went into his pants pocket and pulled the envelope out that the doctor had given him. Coley took it and opened it. He counted out some bills and gave them to Freddy B. "You get that extra 'cause you played your part so sweet…that was sho' 'nough smooth, the way you did it" Coley complimented. He then pulled out a few more bills and folded them twice-over before handing them to Skip in a manner where no one could see how much it was. "Like I told him…you did damned good" Coley said to Skip after he took the folded bills. "Now…. here you go, Mr. Laurence Olivier…hahahaha….here's your damned academy award!" Coley teased Jack as he turned his back to the other men to shield the transaction of handing a wad of money to Jack. "….and I get the most…anybody got any objections to that?" Coley asked rhetorically. "Alright, then….didn't think so!" he said after a short moment of silence passed. He folded the now thinner envelope and stuffed it in the front pocket of his jeans. "You dirty, rotten band of gypsies…you did good…everybody happy!" he said out loud. After Coley spoke those words, the men chorused a hearty "yea!" and began to chatter excitedly all at once. "You know, Coley…we *are* livin' like gypsies…street gypsies!" Jack declared with a triumphant, happy smile. "I got to get goin' Freddy B said. "You know me, Coley…got to take care of my beeswax, brotha'" Skip added. "Yea…I hear ya'" Coley replied. He knew exactly what Skip was about to do with some of his money. Jack felt happy and relieved after Coley gave him his cut. The men stayed another several minutes in the restroom, happily chattering away about their good fortune. They took turns making comments on what they would do with their money.

They all shook hands and gave brotherly hugs and each gave Coley a compliment on his improbable caper and how it came off so well. Freddy B thanked him because he said it gave him credibility with his new woman that he could hustle a little money in the streets aside from his modest salary at his job. Skip commented that he needed to give some money to his wife, Rita because she had been the main provider far too often. He also added that he needed a "bump" Finally, the men left out of the restroom to leave the bar one-at-a-time until Jack and Coley were left standing in the restroom.

"Let's get away from around here, Jack…let's go somewhere else and hang out" Coley suggested. "Where you wanna go?" Jack asked. "Let's go to the Mystic Lounge up on Sheridan Road and just relax and have a few drinks before we turn in…kick it for a while…alright?" Coley said. "Cool…but, I ain't stayin' too long…maybe an hour or so…okay?" Jack responded. "Let's catch a cab up there, then" Coley said.

They caught a cab the mile or so further north on Sheridan Road and went into the quiet lounge that featured late-night amateur jazz shows. It was a popular venue for Jazz fans and upcoming local Jazz artists who were striving to make a name for themselves. The performing musicians were well screened by the owner who always sought out the most talented amateur and sometimes professional artists to play at his lounge. He served as somewhat of a mentor to most of them.

Cuda Watson had played a number of years as a professional tenor sax player. But, his career was cut short by a car accident that severed tendons in his arm and shoulders. The incident cut his rising career short and he received a large settlement because of the effects the accident had on his career. He had resigned himself to be a fan and he used his sizeable settlement to establish the Mystic Lounge; named after the most successful of two jazz albums that he made early in his career before it was cut short.

The Mystic Lounge was small compared to most lounges. But, there was a special coziness to it's atmosphere; perhaps, because the clientele was more sophisticated, laid-back and classier that any other place in the immediate area. Along with a clientele of discrete tastes, it was a place that the biggest pimps and hustlers frequented because the usual assortment of ordinary street hustlers did not. Most could not afford the prices and the sophisticated clientele could make them feel out-of-place. It was a more peaceful venue that was off the beaten hustling path where Jack and the other hustlers hung out. It was a retreat for the upper echelon hustlers who enjoyed it's low-key atmosphere; a good place to go after making a good hustle. Coley would visit the place now-and-then and he seemed to fit right in. He had even made friends with Cuda a year or so ago; occasionally being invited to the party rooms, tucked away upstairs that were reserved for special guests. "My man, Coley…how ya' doin' brotha'?" Cuda Watson greeted as he stood behind the bar as Coley and Jack strolled in. "Cuda…what's goin on, man" Coley responded as he reached over the counter to shake Cuda's hand. "Hey, Cuda…I got my main protégé with me…this is Jack…a good young brotha' in the game" Coley said as he introduced Jack to Cuda. "Nice to meet you, my man…Cuda" Cuda Watson said as he reached across the bar and shook Jack's hand. "What you fellas drinkin?...I got your first round" Cuda said. "A coupla' champales, Cuda…thanks" Coley replied as he began to walk to an empty table in the corner and near the bar. Jack followed and they sat comfortably. A sultry waitress brought their drinks. Jack looked all around at the smattering of well-dressed clientele spread around the bar. As he settled back, he could sense the mellow atmosphere and the feeling of comfort that enveloped him. "Nice place" he commented.

"Yea, Cuda got him a nice place here…it seems to get little better every year…he works hard to build it up..but, he's a freak…loves the ladies….would you believe he's single…actually divorced" Coley said. "Almost every night, after closin' he goes upstairs with a different woman" Coley said quietly. "Freaky-deek, huh?" Jack responded. "Yea, buddy…sho' 'nough….he has invited me up a coupla' times when the lady had a friend….he got two rooms up there with beds in 'em…he would go in one room with a chick…I go in the other one with the other chick…he's cool…not too many studs would do that….he will only do that if he really likes you…I think he does it because he likes to brag the next day about how freaky he got the night before….I think that's what makes him keep this place up so good…so he can meet new chicks to freak-off with" Coley explained. "Cool…he's alright, then" Jack surmised. "Yea…me and him are real tight" Coley said.

"Hey, Coley…about them studs we did the sting with…ain't you worried about them knowin' how to play that mark-ass doctor?" Jack asked with genuine concern. "No…not at all…why do you ask?" Coley asked. "Because they might go back to Saxony to try to play him again while you ain't around…maybe blow your good thang" Jack surmised. "Jack…think about it….can any of them dudes go back and show their faces after the doctor finds out he paid all that money for a fake ring?...huh?" Coley asked before pausing. "Hahahaha…hahaha…yea…I guess you're right" Jack laughed with a certain gleefulness after the logic struck him. "And…besides…you and me are in the clear…we don't know them dudes…remember?…we didn't know the ring was fake, either…it looked so good…it fooled us, too…dig where I'm comin' from?" Coley added. "Yea…right on…you're right, brotha' Coley" Jack agreed.

"Hey…that was real thorough the way you had that receipt thang setup, too…real clever, my brotha'…sho' 'nough clever" Jack complimented. "I had that setup because I know him…and because I know him…I knew he was not gonna' unass that money until he had a receipt…that's the way he is…I know that" Coley explained. The two sat and chatted for about twenty minutes before Coley spotted Cuda waving his arm, beckoning to him from behind the counter.

"Hold on, Jack…Cuda wanna' holla' at me…be right back" Coley said before he raised from the table to walk over to the bar. Coley leaned over the counter closely as Cuda seemed to be almost whispering to him. Several minutes passed before Coley returned to the table with Jack. "What'd I tell ya'…he wants me to hang with him later on…says he got two chicks over there in the corner who wanna get down with him tonight…looks like I might have to cut you loose tonight, my brotha'" Coley said with a gleeful tone. "That's cool with me…remember I told you I wasn't stayin' long" Jack replied. The two sat and sipped on their drinks and talked casually about their Christmas plans. It had, indeed been a wonderful night for them to succeed in their scam. This was the way things went in the streets of Uptown for those who lived the Street Gypsy life. It was predatory and there were no taboos----everything went; except, you lived by the codes that street hustlers understood. Jack finally finished his drink and he felt the easy relaxation and sense of peace that came now-and-then when he had this kind of money in his pocket. He was relieved and happy that he was now able to do the things he wanted to do to have a happy Christmas with Tina.

He said his goodbyes to Coley and Cuda and he flagged a cab outside. Cab drivers were familiar with the club and it's clientele, so Jack was able to get a cab right away. He lay back in the cab as it sped through the streets of Uptown toward the Y. He was thinking happy thoughts about his get-together with Tina on Sunday afternoon.

When he arrived at the Y, he went to the third floor and knocked on The Weep's door. Jack knew that Weep might be up because he knew his routine of staying out in the streets drinking, then coming in late. "Who is it?" The Weep's voice spoke out from inside the room. It's me, Jack, Weep" Jack spoke out. A moment passed before The Weep opened the door. "Hey, Jack…I guess we been missin' each other because when you in school…I'm out on the streets…then, when you come in and go to bed…I'm still out…what's hap'nin' man?" Weep said. "Nothin' much, partna'…just thought I'd catch up to you…check this out, brotha'…got somethin' for you" Jack said before he reached in his pocket and peeled off a few bills from a wad. "Here you go…that's you" Jack said as he handed Weep the money. "Damn, Jack…what you done did…robbed a bank?" Weep said with astonishment after he took the bills and looked at the denominations. Jack knew that Weep could use the money because he received a disability check once-a-month that was not very much; barely enough to get by. "Not exactly, Weep…lucked up on a little hustle" Jack said. Jack knew how the game went and he was especially forward thinking and cautious when it came to running game out on the streets. Even though The Weep was his good friend, Jack knew not to tell him anything about the sting with the doctor because Weep was a drinker and when drinkers get drunk, they tell everything. So, Jack knew not to breathe a word, lest it got back to the people that they had stung. "You sho' you can stand this, Jack?" The Weep asked. "Weep…you know me…I wouldn't give it to you if I couldn't…dig what I mean?" Jack said with a broad smile. "I guess you right…I sho' 'nough 'preciate it, too, Jack…you know that" Weep said with a sincere tone of gratitude. "I know, Weep…I know" Jack said. The two sat in Weep's room and talked for about twenty minutes, catching up to what each other had been doing before Jack left for his room to go to bed.

"Hey, baby….it's me…how ya' doin'?" Jack said to Tina from one of the phones on the second floor down from his room at the Y. "Hey, Jack…I'm glad you called me early…I was gonna go out in a few minutes…what are you doing?" Tina asked. "I just finished showering a little while ago…you ready for today?" Jack replied. "Yesss!…what are we gonna do, honey?" Tina said with the gleeful excitement of a child. "Whatever you wanna do, baby!" Jack replied spiritedly. "So…everything went okay with the work you did for the plumbing guy, huh?" Tina asked. "Oh..uh…yea…real good, baby…sho' 'nough…I worked and he paid me good…he gave me regular plumbers pay…you know they make pretty good" Jack lied. "How long did you have to work?" Tina asked. "About seven hours, I think" Jack replied. "That's really good, honey…so what time do you wanna get together?" Tina asked. "Tell you what…it's about nine-thirty right now…I need to make a couple of runs…how about two o' clock?" Jack asked. "That's fine with me, honey…I can't wait to see you since we had to skip our regular Saturday…I missed you…I went to my folks like I said…did my laundry…studied….I'm ready to have some fun, now" Tina said with the same excitement. "Okay, then…meet me at the Lawrence stop…we'll figure out what we wanna do then…okay, baby?" Jack said. "Okay, honey…I'll see you, then…bye" Tina said.

Jack went back to his room and finished dressing. He decided that he needed a newer, heavier coat because the weather was steadily getting colder. He decided to go to his usual spot at the Salvation Army store where Ida worked. He would look around there to find a decent used coat that he could get for very cheap. He left the Y and walked all the way back to the Del Mar restaurant to have a good breakfast. He took his time eating. Jack was aware that he did not eat right most of the time. So, whenever he was able to have a decent meal, he would have one. Of course, it all relied upon how much money he had at the time. In the recent past, he was always high and getting high seemed to come before eating during those times. He was happy and felt better about himself that he had stopped getting so high. He had minimized his drinking considerably last night when he sat with Coley and the doctor and he took almost an hour to drink the bottle of Champale that he had at the Mystic Lounge. It all amounted to a very light buzz that he barely felt. For him, it was almost like not drinking at all. He was feeling no effects from it this morning. Jack left the DelMar restaurant and went to the Salvation Army store.

"Hey, Ida, baby…how you doin' today?" Jack greeted as he strolled into the store and could see Ida standing idly behind the counter. "Uh-oh….here comes trouble…what are you up to now, man?…and what do you want?" Ida responded stern and sassy. "Nothin' Ida…can a brotha' be nice and friendly sometime?…*my goodness*" Jack replied with exaggerated annoyance. "Usually, nice and friendly comin' from you is gonna cost somebody somethin'" Ida said with her usual tone of sassiness and sarcasm. "So…what is it?" Ida reiterated. "You know somethin' Ida…that's what I like about you…you challenge a brotha'…keep him on the up-and-up….the straight and narrow…always…" "Enough of that, man!..don't try to jive me!…go on and do what you always do and stop tryin' to be so slick" Ida interrupted. "Okay…Ida….I still love you" Jack said with feigned innocence. Jack looked around in the store after his little exchange with Ida. He found a heavier coat that was used but, in very good condition and it had the bit of style that appealed to his taste. He stopped at the counter and paid the full price that was on the tag. "What!...I am gonna have a *heart attack*!....wait a minute…hold on….let me mark this down on the calendar…Jack-paid-for-something-in-the-store" Ida teased as she pretended to be writing on a piece of paper before she burst into laughter. "Man…you mean you got money and you spendin' it in *here*?" she said, with a tone of amazement. "Yea..you know…I'm just a poor sharecropper out here on these streets, but, even a sharecropper can get hold to a few dollars, Ida...give me a little credit" Jack joked as he continued the spirited verbal jostling. "And another thing…man, you mean to tell me…you ain't high, either, are you?…what done came over you…you tryin' to be a saint or somethin'?" Ida said with a broad smile and a chuckle. "Hush-up, woman and give me some sugar!" Jack replied in his usual playful manner as he puckered his lips. "Get outa here, man and quit that mess!" Ida said, feigning indignation. This was the way Jack and Ida communicated all the time. Each knew that the other enjoyed these exchanges that had come to define their relationship. They joked around often but, occasionally had more subdued, serious conversations, as well.

Ida was in her early forties and Jack was a young man nearing his mid-twenties but, there was an underlying attraction between the two that seemed to give these encounters a warm friendliness. Jack knew that whenever he had the kind of money that he had in his pocket right now, he should pay at the store where Ida worked. He needed to give himself some kind of credibility with her to show that he was not coming to take all the time; that he would pay if he could and to show her that he was not trying to take advantage of her. Ida knew that Jack was like many of the other street people in the area; someone who was caught up in the street life and who were mismanaging their lives because of alcohol and drugs among other reasons. She knew that they were not bad people but, were needy and desperate in the streets of Uptown. Jack paid for the coat. Ida wrapped it up and he said goodbye to her. "Jack…" Ida said before he began out of the door. "What?" Jack replied. "You're a whole lot better when you ain't high…you know that?" Ida said with a tone of sincerity. Jack paused, turned around and chuckled before he continued on.

He walked back to the Y and in his room, he tried on different combinations of clothes to see what he would wear today on his outing with Tina. He put the clothes away neatly and wore his old sweat outfit while he lounged around his room. He read the newspaper that he picked up on his way back to the Y and watched a little TV. At 1pm, he began to get ready and after he dressed and put on the coat that he bought, he was out of the door.

He walked the mile or so back to the Lawrence L and waited on the platform for Tina. Finally, she arrived and she stepped off of the train near where Jack stood on the platform. "Hey, honey" She said as soon she saw him. She walked toward him with open arms and he gave her a bear hug. "Hey, sugar…good to see you" he said with a broad smile. She beamed a glowing smile up at him and gently caressed his cheek before she kissed him. They stood on the platform alone, talking for several minutes before a few other people arrived to catch the train. "I got off because I didn't know if you wanted to stay on the train or catch the Broadway bus, Jack" she said. "Well, I want to go and have some lunch downtown, then go to the movies after that…how's that?" Jack offered "That's fine, honey…then we can go back to my place and hang out all night 'cause…guess what?" She said before pausing. "What?" Jack responded. "I am out of school for good!…hurrraaayyy!" she said with glee. "Oh…yea…that's right, Tina…hey…let's celebrate, then…what do you wanna do, baby?…it's on me!" Jack replied. "That's alright, Jack….you don't have to do anything special…I appreciate what you're doing already…besides….we're gonna do something special for the holidays…that's what you said…right?" Tina said. "That's right…and we are gonna talk about it over lunch downtown today…okay?" Jack said. "Yes! that's really cool!" Tina replied as she jumped into Jack's arms and hugged him as he lifted her off her feet and swirled her around. These were the blissful moments that Jack and Tina had come to expect; they were spontaneous, pure and magical; their romance had come to be more meaningful than either could have imagined and they enjoyed the fun and frolic that came with each outing. They took the next train downtown to find a restaurant for lunch.

They got off of the Jackson Park-Howard train at Randolph and walked briskly in the overcast, cool afternoon. There was a festive mood in the air and the streets were teeming with the usual crowd of Christmas shoppers. They walked past the Marshall Fields store with adults and children huddled closely to the store windows as they marveled at the fancy Christmas displays. There were symbols of Christmas everywhere. They weaved through the crowds and turned east onto Washington street and walked to Michigan Avenue as a light snow flurry began. Just a couple of blocks south of Randolph, they found a nice restaurant. They went in and were seated.

"Jack….my folks want to meet you and I want you to meet them…is that okay?…I've been kind of hesitating because I didn't know how you would feel about it…so…what do you think?" Tina said. "They wanna meet me?....they know I'm black?…huh?...hahahaha…guess who's comin' to dinner, baby!…hahahaha!…cool…it's okay…I don't mind meetin' them…when you talkin' about doin' this?" Jack asked. "Oh…yes…they know you are black…remember those pictures we took at RJ Grunts…I let them see it…they said you seemed nice…mom said you were nice-looking…how about Christmas day for Christmas dinner…my sister and grandparents will all be there…they are already expecting you…so…you'd better say yes, boy…can you dig where I'm comin' from?" Tina said in an animated, playful tone to tease Jack in her favorite way by imitating his style of talk. "Christmas dinner is cool…I'll be there with bells on…and you cain't sound cool as me…forget about it …okay?" Jack teased back. "What you talkin' ' bout, man…I can sound more like you than you do…yea…right-on…dig…what's happ'nin', my brotha'…yea..hahaha" Tina said before they both burst out laughing. "But…Jack…you are gonna have to tone down the coolness when you meet my folks…okay?" Tina said in a more serious tone. "No doubt, baby…I will…don't worry" Jack replied more seriously. "They are very nice, but, they *are* parents…you understand, right?" Tina added. "I got ya' baby" Jack replied. The two ordered lunch and sat for almost two hours talking, the usual length of time they seemed to spend when eating out. "Jack….I have a suggestion for Christmas eve…you can come home with me tonight and stay 'til Christmas day….I want you to help me finish decorating my place while you are with me…okay?" Tina said. "Decoratin?…what can I do?" Jack asked. "Just little stuff, Jack…hanging up things…decorations on my little Christmas tree…stuff like that…it's easy…I just like us doing things together…alright?" Tina asked. "Okay, baby….I'll do it" Jack agreed. "Goody…then, on Christmas Day we'll just walk over to my folks for dinner" Tina added.

The two finished their lunch. They went on to the Woods theatre to see a movie. They enjoyed it with popcorn and soda as they snuggled together in the dark theatre quietly transfixed on the film. After the movie, they spent the next hour or so strolling about downtown. They seemed relaxed and carefree as they walked around enjoying the excitement and Christmas cheer in the air; stopping to look at displays and to admire the bright Christmas décor all about them.

As the evening arrived, they took the L train to Evanston and back to her place where they had their usual long and intimate bedroom talks in-between passionate sessions of lovemaking. "Baby…tomorrow, I have to take care of some business…I have a few things I need to do…so, I have to go back to my place in the morning" Jack said as the two faced each other while lying on their sides in Tina's bed late in the night.

Jack realized that he needed to take some time to do Christmas shopping for Tina while he was alone. As soon as she said she wanted for him to stay at her place until Christmas, he knew he couldn't do it. But, he agreed to keep from spoiling the mood at that moment. He also knew that he did not want to wear the same clothes through Christmas day. He knew that Tina did not think about that. Jack had never experienced any of this before. He had never had a girlfriend who treated him so special and who regarded him with such respect and who challenged him in a nurturing kind of way. The whole idea of him meeting her parents and him staying several days in a row at her place seemed to give him a sense of family with Tina. She had this way about her that made him feel that he belonged with her. He could see that her upbringing was an entire world apart from his own. Tina seemed to live with the idea of preserving the dignity of everyone around her while she could be herself in every aspect of her being; these were subtle characteristics that one could not pick up immediately; one had to be around her for a while to see these wonderful things about her as Jack had.

Jack's world had been so full of cruelty and indifference from the outset. His orientation to life was one of suspicion and distrust. In his world, he had come to expect the worst from human beings;

that was the premise of his survival mode. He had come to understand that whether people treated him well or treated him poorly, that he still needed to survive. This was why being with Tina had come to be so joyful for him. He could relax, not be on-guard; be completely free with another person as he had never been before; he didn't have to worry about protecting himself against her; and he had learned from being with Tina the value of having someone who cared.

"What do you have to do, Jack?....why can't you stay?" Tina asked softly. "Because I need to get a change of clothes for one….and I have some runnin' around to do…I'll do it tomorrow and come right back here tomorrow evenin'…..alright?" Jack said. "Okay…" Tina replied. "You understand…right?" Jack added. "Yea…it's cool…I can finish cleaning this place up real good while you're gone…I didn't have much time while classes were going on...now I can" Tina said. They said their good nights and went to sleep.

Jack woke up the next morning and showered, dressed and kissed Tina before he went out to take the L train back to the Wilson stop. He walked home and took a nap because he still felt a little sleepy. He and Tina usually kept each other up during parts of the night and this would have them sleeping late in the morning until around 10am whenever they went to bed together. But, Jack had gotten up a little earlier so that he could take care of his business and get back to Tina's place before very late. He awoke from his nap feeling refreshed and he could see his clock-radio on the night stand reading 1:10pm. Right away, he began to think of what he wanted to buy Tina for Christmas. His thoughts seemed so magnanimous when it came to her; and because he was feeling so much love for her, he was thinking of getting her something very nice that she would really like. He had a decent chunk of money for his holiday spending. He dressed and walked over to the Wilson L stop and took it downtown. He got off at Lake Street and strolled southward on State Street. A feeling of joy began to rise within him. It seemed to have sprung up suddenly. It was curious and strange. But, it seemed to have him moving effortlessly. He felt light in his body and his mind seemed carefree. There was a warm feeling in his chest as he strolled along the street. He could visualize the warm, sweet smile on

Tina's face when he would present her with Christmas gifts. He knew he was being guided by what was in his heart.

He rode the L downtown. He went into a few of the nicer stores and bought some fancy perfume and a saleslady helped him pick out a couple of sexy lingerie outfits for Tina. This was all new and exciting for Jack. He remembered last year when he was hustling on the streets and trying to survive around Christmas time. He was in an alley, sharing a bottle of Richards Wild Irish Rose wine when someone reminded him that the next day was Christmas Eve. That caustic revelation alerted him to how far his life had degenerated. After he was done buying gifts for Tina, he took the L back north and went to his room at the Y.

Jack moved about his place gathering up a few changes of clothes to take back to Tina's place. It was nearing 6pm and he packed all that he would take with him in his large duffle bag. He went out the door and walked up to Lawrence Avenue and Ashland to take the bus to the Lawrence L stop near Broadway. When he got off of the bus and was walking toward the L, he saw Coley in the distance standing near the Lawrence L station in front of Sharon's bar.

"Hey, Jack…where you headed with all that stuff, man?" Coley asked as Jack came within a few feet. "Goin' to my girl's place…gonna spend a few days.." Jack replied. "Jack…man…you done changed a hell 'uva' lot since you met this girl…I got to meet any woman that can turn your scandalous ass around…I ain't lyin'…before you met her…you was on a see-saw with the devil…you know I ain't lyin…you know that…right?" Coley chuckled. "Aw, man…I wasn't that bad" Jack said with a broad grin. "Come on, Jack…you was knockin' off one sting after another for a good while…remember?" "Yea…I kinda remember…but I was high all the time back then…I cain't remember what-all I did" Jack relented. "Damn right…I seen you, Jack…I'm ya' boy…I watched you go through all your changes…am I right?" Coley asserted and paused for a response. "Am I right?" he reiterated. "You're right" Jack finally responded. "Alright, then…I know what I'm talkin' about…so…what's your girl's name?" Coley asked. "Her name is Tina" Jack responded. "I'll tell ya' Jack…that one time I seen her…Tina was lookin' sharp, brotha'…I don't know how you got her, but…*that* girl looks like somebody…no shit" Coley grinned as he spoke. "She *is* nice…I meet her over at Frances Tavern one night a few months ago" Jack said. "And y'all been together ever since?" Coley asked. "Yea…pretty much" Jack responded matter-of-factly. "That's good bro…don't blow it...treat her right and don't fuck up…you'll be straight…dig" Coley advised. "I'm cool…everything is cool between us…I'm tryin' to keep it that way" Jack said.

"Hey, Jack….dig this…me and Freddy B chippin' in to throw a little get-together party at his crib for the holidays…him and his old lady stay over on Foster about a block west of Broadway…the set gonna be tomorrow evenin' about seven o 'clock…bring your old lady…me and Shirley gonna be there…you gonna' come?" Coley asked "Oh, yea?…that's a nice little spot over there on Foster…let me talk it over with my girl and I'll get back with you before late tomorrow…cool?" Jack said. "That's cool, brotha'…call me at home tomorrow…alright?" Coley asked. "Dig this here…I didn't tell my girl about the sting with the doctor…I don't want her to know about it…okay?….tell Freddy B for me, too…alright?" Jack said with a serious tone. "Okay, botha' Jack…I can dig where you comin' from…she don't need to know about that, anyway…I'll make sure nobody brings it up at the set…alright?...you my boy…I'm lookin' out for you" Coley replied with assurance. "Cool" Jack said before he turned and dashed into the L station.

Tina heard a knock on the door and she knew it was Jack. She opened the door and Jack stepped in and dropped his bags on the floor. "Hi, honey…you made it back!" she said with an excited smile as she jumped into his arms before they embraced. "Let me help you with those bags" Tina said as she fussed with the bags, grabbing them and putting them into her closet. "You eat anything yet, baby?" Jack asked. "No…I got to cleaning everything in here and I forgot all about it….but, I am starving right now" she replied.

"Okay, then…we're goin' out to dinner….where is a good place to eat around here?" Jack asked. "Oh, Jack…thanks…the Prairie Moon on Sherman Avenue is really good" she replied. "What you waitin' for, girl… lets go!" Jack said as he gave Tina a playful spank on her rear. "I'll get my coat" she said with a giggle. They walked in the dark evening on the quiet streets for several minutes to the restaurant. They sat, ordered and had dinner along with their usual long session of talking.

"Hey, baby…what do you think about going to a house party where some of my friends will be?… these are some of the best people I know, like Coley….you saw him one time about a month ago…remember?....and a few other good friends…it's gonna be at Whiteboy Freddy B and his old lady's house…they live in a nice spot…they don't live around the Aragon…what do you think?" Jack asked. "Honey…I would be glad to go and meet some of your friends...but, why do you call your friend Whiteboy Freddy B? and why do you call his wife-girlfriend his old lady?...is she old?" Tina challenged Jack in her usual way. "Aw, baby…that's just the way we talk….it don't mean nothin'….Freddy B is my boy…we just call him Whiteboy Freddy B 'cause….I don't know…'cause he's white…he don't care…he knows he's just one of the fellas far as everybody is concerned…and old lady…that's just a figure of speech...we say that if she's old…young…it don't matter….just come to the party and you'll see how we are…everybody is cool…you'll see" Jack explained. "Okay…whitegirl Tina *will* be at the party with blackboy Jack" Tina said with tongue-in-check sarcasm. A short pause ensued before they both burst out laughing. "Okay…I get your point" Jack said as his laughter subsided. After dinner, they returned to Tina's place. Jack called Coley and told him that he and Tina would be at the party. They had a pleasant, quiet evening, curled up together on the sofa watching television until late. It was Tuesday morning, December twenty-third. Jack and Tina lie lazily in bed, both drifting in and out of a dreamy, half-asleep state; occasionally tossing and turning to flop over on one another in a warm snuggle. They finally rose from bed and could see from the window a dusting of snow outside.

"Look, honey…a little snow" Tina said with excitement as she pushed the curtains back to look out of the window facing the street. "That's cool" Jack replied as he came up behind her and hugged her from the back and gave her a little peck on her neck before he nestled his chin in the crook of it. "Finally, we can be together without school or anything else to get in the way…don't you just love the holidays, Jack?" Tina said. "Well…this is the first chance I've had to celebrate in a few years" Jack replied. "So…what kept you from celebrating before now?" Tina asked.

"You never got to see me at my worst but…I was pretty wild and crazy the last few years…I guess I didn't have any reason to celebrate" Jack said matter-of-factly. "And now you do?" Tina quizzed. "Uh…yes…yes I do" Jack responded with slight hesitancy. "And…" Tina urged. "And what?" Jack responded. "You don't wanna say it…do you?" Tina went on probing with a slowly spreading smile. "Say what, baby?" Jack answered with a little discomfort. "That you are crazy about moi!" Tina said with a light chuckle. "Who the hell is mo-i!" Jack puzzled. "Me, silly….me!" Tina said with a gleeful smile. "You love me don't you, Jack?" Tina pushed on. "Come on…let it out you silly goose!" Tina teased as she began to tickle Jack in the vulnerable spots she had come to know. "Hey watch it, now!....this is interrogation…this ain't fair….leave me alone…hahaha…" Jack said as he began a weak protest while he tried to fend off Tina's tickling and trying to suppress his laughter at the same time.

The tickling turned to smooching and then torrid passion as they undressed from their few night clothes and had their session on the carpet near the window. It was more intense than ever before and they became lost in the ecstasy----and then silence---- "I love you, Jack" Tina finally said in a soft whisper as they lie side-by-side on the carpeted floor. "I love you too, Tina" Jack replied softly with all the sincerity that was in his heart. They showered, got dressed and went out to a nearby restaurant for breakfast. It seemed that a newer, stronger bond had somehow formed between them.

They had crossed over into a new dimension of their romance. There was a renewal of their spirits; warmer affection between them; more patience listening to what the other had to say; more caring----it had all culminated from those three words they had spoken to one another; being together had become all that mattered.

"Today is the day for the party…you ready, baby?" Jack asked Tina with a tone of excitement. "Yea…I'm ready…I'm looking forward to meeting your friends" Tina said in the usual unconcerned, carefree manner that Jack had come to know of her. He marveled at her inner strength. She didn't seem nervous or afraid at all. She was certainly different from what he expected of her. He had been pleasantly surprised. "Jack…while we are at the party….do me a favor?" Tina asked. "Yea….what?" Jack asked with wide-eyed inquiry. “Let’s not drink very much at the party…let’s just sip on our drinks…and if there’s too much drinking and people are getting drunk…let’s leave…okay?” Tina asked. “Sure, baby…don’t worry…everybody is cool…you’ll see” Jack responded. “I’m not really worried, honey…I just want us to have a good time…I don’t want for things to be like they were with your friend, Mike…I mean…he really liked to drink and he got drunk pretty fast…he was nice…but, drunk…I just don’t want that type of situation” Tina said with a smile. “Listen, baby…it’s not gonna be that kind of party…this is gonna be very private…we’re not gonna have people stumblin’ in off the streets…this is gonna be certain people that Freddy B, Coley and me know are cool people…dig…it’s gonna be peaceful…wait….you’ll see” Jack said with assurance.

Tina and Jack went back to her place and spent the afternoon by finishing Tina’s place with Christmas decorations. They worked together with Jack placing the star-shaped, flashing light at the top of the Christmas tree and framing the inside of the apartment windows with Christmas lights. After they finished, they sipped on eggnog and watched a couple of TV shows through the afternoon. Finally, it was 5:30pm. “We should start getting ready for the party, honey” Tina reminded Jack. Tina urged him to shower first while she went to her closet to pull out what she wanted to wear. It was shortly past 6:30pm when they were ready to leave and they took their usual route on the Evanston L. They got off at Berwyn, the stop before Lawrence because it was closer to Freddy B’s house on Foster and just a short walk away.

“Hey, people…come on in!” Freddy B greeted Jack and Tina at the first floor apartment door in the nice two-story, brick apartment building. “This is my lady, Carmen…Carmen, Jack…and….” “Tina” Tina said quickly. “They stepped inside and there was music playing. The apartment was very clean, nice and neat. A large, well decorated Christmas tree stood in the living room near the draped windows. The furnishings were modest but, very well kept. Hi, Tina, Jack…welcome to our little place…let me take your coats….have a seat” Carmen greeted, undertaking her role as host with enthusiasm. “Y’all got a nice place here in a nice neighborhood” Jack commented, looking around as he took his coat off. It’s alright…we like it” Freddy B said with a broad smile. “Coley didn’t make it yet…huh?” Jack asked. “He called about half-an-hour ago… said he was on his way…we thought you were him” Freddy B responded. “He’ll be here soon, then” Jack said. “We have plenty of food… ham, potatoe salad, chicken, lasagna, sweet potatoe pie, …all kinds of stuff…we got plenty of drinks, too…what you folks wanna’ start off with?….food?…drinks?…help yourself” Freddy B said with sincere hospitality. “Let me have a beer, Freddy….what you want baby?…you hungry?” Jack asked Tina. “Give me a beer, too…I’ll eat later” Tina said.

“Hey…want you to meet my friends sitting in the kitchen…come on…I’ll introduce you” Freddy B said as he waved Jack and Tina to follow him into the kitchen. There were two couples, a Spanish couple and a black male and white female couple sitting around the kitchen table that had several covered food dishes sitting on it. They were talking, laughing and drinking. They all stopped and looked up as Freddy B entered. “Hey Juan and Teresita, Joe, Monica…these are our friends Jack and Tina” Freddy B said with perfect host etiquette. They all exchanged greetings with big smiles and handshakes. Meanwhile, Freddy B went into one of the couple of coolers sitting next to the refrigerator; “Hey…Schlitz, Budweiser, Heineken, Miller…name your poison, Tina” Freddy B asked from across the kitchen. “Budweiser is cool” Tina responded. Give me a Bud, too, Freddy” Jack yelled back. Soon the modest apartment was filled with cheerful conversation and laughter before the door bell rang. Two more couples and a lone male came in together. Minutes later, Coley appeared at the door dressed to the nines with his main squeeze, Shirley who was dressed rather fashionably, as well. Several more people arrived; then Skip and his wife, Rita appeared. Coley was usually the life of the party because he was the most out-going of anyone there. He was always full of jokes and interesting conversation. Jack usually fed off of Coley’s lead. They began a rousing round of spirited jokes and quips between them with Skip joining in; entertaining the hosts and guests. It loosened everyone up and soon, the place was rocking with party cheer. There was party music and some danced. Everyone mingled well, with most everyone becoming acquainted with the others. Everyone ate and complimented the hosts on the delicious food and how enjoyable the party was. Tina was having a glorious time with Jack’s friends. She seemed to have made friends with

Coley's woman, Shirley and Freddy B's mate, Carmen. She talked with Coley, Skip and Freddy B and most all of the guests at one point or another. She was enjoying the party and Jack was completely engaged in whatever conversation he was having during the festive evening. Coley stood in the middle of the festive group and proposed a toast. "To a great band of gypsies who make good things happen…everybody toast!" he spoke out heartily, and everyone toasted and cheered. Finally, it had gotten late and people began to leave. When Jack asked Tina, she said she had a great time but, was ready to go. Jack announced to Freddy B and Carmen that they were about to leave. Soon after, Coley came over to Jack to speak privately. "Jack…dig this…we chipped in on the food and everything that Freddy B bought for the party…but, that's all…we need to give them somethin' for the big cleanup after the party…they will be doin' all of the cleanup themselves…let's put in and give them somethin' for that…okay?" Coley whispered under the noise to Jack as they stood in a corner of the room. "Yea…that's cool…what should I chip in?" Jack asked in a low tone. "Give me fifteen and I'll put in fifteen…okay?" Coley proposed. "That's cool" Jack said before he went into his pocket and slipped Coley fifteen dollars. "I'm not gonna ask Skip for no money because his cut wasn't that much" Coley added. Coley walked over to Freddy B and spoke to him very privately just inside their bedroom doorway. They came back out and Freddy B said "You didn't have to do that, Coley" "Me and Jack wanted you and your lady to have somethin' for the cleanup and for goin' outa' your way throwin' such a nice party" Coley responded with a tipsy hiccup. "Well…we appreciate it…that's real cool of you guys" Freddy B said with heartfelt sincerity. Coley and Shirley, Jack and Tina were the last to leave and they departed with smiles at the door saying over and over what a great party it was and what a good time they had. Because it was late, Jack decided they would take a cab and they rode it all the way back to Tina's place in Evanston. "Jack…what did Coley mean by band of gypsies?" Tina asked in the cab as it sped homeward. "Nothin' baby…it's just one of our little names we gave ourselves..that's all" Jack replied.

"Jack…Jack…wake up…time to get up…let's start getting ready to go to my folks" Tina said as she was raised up in the bed shaking Jack who was still asleep, trying to rouse him out of bed.

"Hummm....what!" Jack mumbled, still half asleep. "Get up, Jack!" Tina urged a little more forcefully. Finally, Jack sat up and stared, blurry-eyed at Tina momentarily until he became fully awake and aware. "What time is it?" he asked hazily. "It's ten-fifteen…you don't have a hangover do you, Jack?" Tina asked with concern. "Uh..humm…naw…I feel fine…I only had three beers all night…I'm cool" Jack said lazily. "So you'll be in a good mood when we go to my folks today…right?" Tina quizzed. "Sure, baby…I'm alright…I'm ready" Jack replied. "Smack!...then get that butt going!" Tina said as she smacked Jack on his butt as he lay on his stomach. Jack grabbed her and they wrestled giddily for a brief moment as she playfully tickled him to fend him off. "Okay…you wanna shower first?" Jack asked. "No…you first…so it can wake you up" Tina advised. Jack grabbed his bag of hygiene things and went straight to the bathroom. "They are expecting us around noon and we will have dinner around one o'clock" Tina informed Jack after he was showered and dressed and she was making her last touch-up of the very light makeup she sometimes wore. She also gathered gifts she had planned to give her parents and grandparents.

They walked about ten minutes through the breezy, overcast weather to Tina's parents home on Maple Avenue. "Hi..come on in" Tina's dad greeted at the door. "This is Jack, dad" Tina said, introducing them. "How are you doing, sir" Jack said more nervously than he expected as he shook the father's hand. "Mom…we're here" Tina yelled out before her mother came walking out of the kitchen. "Hello, dear…and this is Jack, I presume" she said cheerfully, turning to Jack with a smile before she gave him a hug. "Hello, Mrs Newberry" Jack said as politely as he could. "Let me take your coats and you two go on into the living room and, Tina…introduce him to everyone" the mother urged. Jack and Tina went into the living room and Jack could see an elderly couple sitting together on the sofa and Tina's sister, whom he had never meet, sitting in a sofa chair.

"Jack, this is my grandma Celeste and my grandpa Oscar…grandma…grandpa…this is Jack" The grandparents seemed a little surprised at the sight of Jack but, they smiled politely. "Hello" they said. "Hi" Jack said a little stiffly. "And that is my sister Jessica" Tina said as she made a slight gesture toward her sister seated in the sofa chair across from the grandparents.

"Hi, Jack…didn't know you were so tall…Tina's told me all about you" Jessica volunteered with the spunkiness of a younger sister. "Jessica!" Tina admonished in a slightly embarrassed tone. Tina and Jack sat down on the far and opposite end of the sofa from the grandparents. There was an awkward silence. "grandma….grandpa…can I get you more drinks?" Tina asked as they were already drinking beverages. "I'm fine, honey" the grandmother said. "I could use more cranberry juice" the grandfather said as he handed an empty glass to Tina. There was another awkward silence as Jack sat alone in the presence of the grandparents. He felt a slight discomfort. He tried to relax. He could imagine what they must be thinking of a young black man like himself keeping company with their granddaughter. But, the thought was fleeting and he would not let it make him uncomfortable, he thought. "You go to school with Tina, Jack?" the grandfather asked. "No, sir…I don't" Jack replied. "Oh…humm….well…you'll be glad she invited you…we're going to have a fantastic dinner today…Tina's mother is a great cook" the grandfather said. "Yes…I taught her a lot about cooking when she was a young lady growing up…we come here every Christmas for dinner and they come to our place every thanksgiving" the grandmother added cheerfully.

The conversation they were making seemed to melt Jack's defenses away and he was suddenly feeling more relaxed. He was glad that his preconceived notions about Tina's grandparents had not panned out. They chatted more, making small talk in the few minutes that Tina was gone. "Here you are, gramps" Tina said as she handed him a fresh glass of cranberry juice to the grandfather. "I see everybody is getting acquainted" Tina said with a big smile that said she was pleased with the flow of conversation she heard just as she stepped in the room. "Okay, everyone…dinner time" the mother said as she suddenly appeared in the doorway of the living room. They all meandered to the dining room that was on the opposite side of the hallway. Tina's father said grace and they began dinner.

"So, Jack…were you raised in Chicago?" the father asked. "Yes, sir" Jack responded. "Which high school did you attend?" the father asked "Waller, sir" Jack replied. "Yes…I'm familiar with that school…I worked there as an English teacher about four years after I started teaching…it has become a very good school…very well integrated, I understand" the father added. "Yes, sir…it is…I liked it very much" Jack said. "What year did you graduate, Jack?" "Nineteen-seventy, sir" Jack responded. "Tina tells us you're enrolling in college…is that right?" the father asked. "Yes, sir…I'm enrolled already…I'll be starting in January" Jack said with a note of pride. "That's terrific....from what Tina tells us…you've had a few challenges in your life…you lived in the projects at one time is it?" the father inquired. "Yes, sir…we lived in them for three years before we moved" Jack explained. "Well, son…I'll tell you…Catherine and I have participated in a lot of causes for equal education because we believe in it and we have been using our position as teachers to help our students understand that…when you start, Jack…do your best to stay until you finish…an education is so important" the father said. "Yes, sir..I'll take your advice" Jack said politely.

The dinner conversation went well after that and Jack was relieved that no one else asked him any more personal questions as the talk turned more to family matters. It seemed as though Tina's family had accepted him and he felt as though he had conquered a mountain. It gave him a certain glow inside. After everyone left the table, the conversation continued in the living room where they gathered to exchange gifts with the parents giving Tina money among other gifts. The mood became festive with the opening of the gifts and there was joyful conversation and delightful quips here and there that made everyone laugh. Jack seemed to continue making a favorable impression, cleaning up his speech as much as possible. Jack was certainly feeling a sense of family at this time and that haunting feeling of disconnect that he would constantly have during his waking hours seemed to have diminished for now. It all felt uplifting. Finally, it was near 5pm and the grandparents prepared to leave. Tina saw it as an opportunity for her and Jack to leave, as well. "We'd better get going, ma…we have a few things planned" Tina said. "Okay, dear" the mother replied and then, she began to prepare plates with mounds of food for Tina and Jack wrapping them in aluminum foil and packing it all in bags for them to take away. "Here, you kids…take this…you can eat a good meal for a few days…okay?" the mother said in a nurturing way. Thanks, Mrs. Newberry" Jack said. "Thanks, ma" Tina said; and the two were off back to Tina's place.

They spent time together at her place for several days and on New Years Eve, they went to a popular disco club in Evanston; meeting up with a few of Tina's friends to party the night away. They let all of their inhibitions go as the group of four women and three men joined in with the club crowd in the raucous celebration; standing on top of chairs and tables; hoisting their drinks high in the air as the revelry rose to a deafening cheer as the midnight hour was approaching. Amid all of the cheering, Jack took a private moment that became caught in space and time where he could hear nothing but his own thoughts; see nothing but his own visions. He was reflecting on this wild past year that had brought so much turbulence to his life. But, that ended with the sweet harmony of a blissful union that quieted the anxiety and discord in his soul. For him, it was a divine transformation of mind and spirit that was delivering him from the hell he had known for the last few years. It was time for a new beginning---he had found sweet redemption.

CHAPTER 4
COLLEGE FRESHMAN

It was Wednesday, January 7th and Jack felt a nervous excitement welling up inside as he stepped back into his room at the Y after coming from the community shower. It was his first day of school at the Northeastern Illinois University Uptown Center where he would start his freshman classes. He could barely sleep early last night. But, the tossing and turning finally subsided into a restful sleep later in the night. He awoke feeling refreshed and full of excited energy. This was the first step toward his new life, he thought. He certainly wanted to get off to a good start. He had gone over to the Salvation Army store where Ida worked during the first few days after New Years to select some choice pieces of clothing such as a nice thick winter jacket and some sweaters and knitted jerseys. Dress slacks and jeans were hard to come by in good condition. But, he managed to dredge up a couple of pairs of each to accentuate his college wardrobe. Jack had his clothes for his first school day picked and laid out last night after he tried on different combinations of clothes and checked how everything coordinated. He had been cautious not to spend much more of his money after the splurging he had done during the holidays. He still had a fair part of his money left from the sting. He wanted to make sure that he did not have any money problems during the first weeks of school. The financial aid letters he had gotten recently and Linda Chavez had both informed him that he would receive a financial aid check in about four weeks. He would get a voucher for books in the first week. He would also see a counselor who would help him find an on-campus work-study job. His mindset was that this was all very exciting because it was his dream coming true.

He still remembered what his father said to him five years ago when he graduated from high school and Jack told him that he wanted to go to college. His father's response was disappointing but, realistic. There was no way he could afford a college education for Jack, or even take care of him while his tuition was free. It was something that was not even considered by most black people. An education seemed a far-fetched notion that was only realistic for some white folk. But, times had changed and over the last decade, or so, the socially conscious government had begun to implement programs so that poor people like Jack could have an opportunity to get an education without the tremendous financial strain.

It was a cold but, sunny day outside and there was still a fair amount of frozen snow on the ground that came mostly during the first two days after New Years. Jack was finally dressed and he checked his drag completely from back-to-front and from head-to-toe. He felt good and he looked good, he thought. He grabbed his note tablet and his pen for taking notes that Linda Chavez had advised him to bring on his first day. He put on his nice winter jacket and he was out of the door. He walked the distance to the Center through the cold that had become more winter-like in the last week.

"Hello, Jack…how are you?" Linda Chavez greeted after Jack arrived at her office in The Center. "I'm fine…and you?" Jack responded. "I'm good, thanks…there is coffee and donuts in the lounge for all of the new students who will be starting today…we are going to wait for everyone to arrive before we start orientation… it starts at ten-thirty and it's ten-ten now so, you can go in there and wait…hang your coat up…help yourself to the coffee and donuts and relax until orientation starts…okay?" Linda said cheerfully. "Alright…thanks" Jack replied. Jack did just as Linda said and he was there only a minute before another student arrived.

"Hi…I'm Marvin…you here for the orientation?" the neat-looking, fresh-faced Hispanic man greeted. "Yea…I'm startin' school for the first time…you, too?" Jack asked. "Yea…trying to have a future…you know" the upbeat young man said. The two made small talk about their college aspirations. Other new students arrived every few minutes until there were almost two dozen of them in the lounge. Linda Chavez came into the student lounge "Okay, people…I am going to call off names and I want you to acknowledge by saying "here" She began to call off the names and everyone answered except for a couple of called names.

Jack took a moment to look around at the other new students. He observed how they moved with such innocence, naivete and eagerness to conform. None of this seemed to match the underlying hostility, suspicion and defiance that he could feel just below the surface. Jack knew that he needed to tame these savage urges even more so than he had done recently for the sake of his relationship with Tina. He needed to fit into this college environment. Jack kind of envied the other new students for seeming so decent and innocent. It made him wonder how he seemed to be at such odds with them in his experiences and social conditioning. Why did they not seem defensive and wary as he was? These people were nothing like the hardened street characters that he had become used to interacting with. They appeared carefree and relaxed as if they were right at home. He felt a bit ashamed about his street life. He knew that he was not willing to disclose his seedy past to any of these people. So, he would just act as though he was a normal person with a normal past; only kind of poor. Aside from those outings with Tina, he had not been in such a civilized setting in quite some time.

The orientation started with the recruiter, Linda Chavez explaining the itinerary and giving instructions. A financial aid person and a counselor followed to give students their orientation on financial aid, classes and other school matters that were important to the new students. Jack sat and listened closely and took notes. He was glad that he brought his pen and note tablet because he realized that it had been a long time since he had to remember details in this manner. Although he was able to keep up with the instructions, he could still feel the haziness in his thinking from the many days and nights of drinking. He had been near-sober for a while, even though he had a few drinks over the holidays. He was feeling a huge sense of accomplishment about not getting drunk and cutting so far down on drinking for the last couple of months. He could not understand how he was able to do so without falling back into his old habit of drinking constantly.

He found himself hardly even thinking about it. The session lasted an hour-and-a-half and afterwards, each of the students received a formal schedule of their classes. After the orientation was over, the group of students began to disperse and little low-key conversations were going on between a few remaining students. "Take it easy" Jack said to Marvin as he departed.

"Good-googly-moogly" a voice spoke out. Jack looked up from studying his schedule as he sat in one of the student lounge chairs. When last he remembered, there were no other black male students in the room as the voice seemed to indicate. Jack looked up and he could see a student who was about his age who was on the short side with a stout build, standing in the middle of the room, not far from where he was seated. He was white but, his voice sounded black. "Man!...they done messed me around" he mumbled to himself as he stood there closely examining his schedule. Jack looked up at the short, stout-looking man and when he noticed Jack looking at him in a mildly amused manner with a hint of a smile on his face, he looked back and said in a tone of fellowship "They got me twisted, man…damn…I'm gonna' have to work with this" as he held the paper schedule in one hand examining it. "What?…they messed up your schedule, man?" Jack asked in a friendly manner. "Well…looka' here, bro'…on Tuesday-Thursdays, I got this Biology class that ends at 2:15 in the afternoon here at the Center…then, I got to go back to campus for my Lab for this Biology class at 5:15pm…that's three hours between classes…ain't that some stuff?….messed up ain't it?...see…I tried to get a lab right after the Biology class…I signed up for the three-thirty lab but, it was full and they bumped me to this five-fifteen lab" the spry stranger said.

"I don't know, my man…I'm a freshman…my first time in college" Jack said. "Uh-uh…a newbie…look out…I thought I smelled milk on your breath…my name's Billy….who you be?" the stranger asked very loose and carefree as he held his hand out in the fashion of a soul handshake. Jack was somewhat taken aback at the white stranger offering a soul handshake and speaking in the hip street language that he was so familiar with. But, he engaged himself, nonetheless. "My name is Jack…Jack Rollins" Jack responded with a light chuckle as he seemed tickled by his new acquaintance's personality and lively wit. "Yea, bro'…this is the start of my second year…I take most of my classes on-campus but, I got this Biology class here at the Center…that's why I was kinda' disappointed at the schedule because I have to go back to the campus for the Lab on the same day…but, you know what….it's all gravy, baby…I'm rollin' with the punches" the spirited character said a little more subdued and with a hint of bravado.

"You stay around here?" Jack asked out of curiosity, wondering if he was a local person. "Yea…up on Montrose and Ashland…got me a little studio up there" Billy replied. "Hey..I'm not too far from you…I'm at the Y over there on Wilson!" Jack said with a tone of excitement. "Yea…that's cool…here…take my number…I know what it's like startin' off…if you have any problems or questions…give me a janga-lang…okay?....now don't be callin' up for no loans…I cain't help you with no money…but, holla' at me if you need some direction…alright?" Billy said with a notable tone of sincerity. "Okay, my man…I'll do that…'preciate it" Jack responded. "Okay, then…later…I got to get to campus" Billy said before he left. Jack was a bit mystified at the street-savvy stranger. But, he felt a kinship right away. He was curious as to how this white dude had come to be so black in his expressions and mannerisms.

Jack's first class, Man & His Physical Environment was coming up at 1:50pm today. All of his classes were at The Center. He decided to kill time by reading some of the college material lying in the lounge area. He read for a while then, he went outside to buy a newspaper at the nearby newsstand on Broadway before deciding to have some lunch at Jakes burger and hot dog restaurant at the corner of Sheridan Road and Montrose next to the Center.

Jack decided to give Tina a call because she was almost always on his mind. She had been going out looking for a job every day and visiting her college campus to attend to school related issues for graduating students, including preparations for her graduation ceremony. Most days, she was back home before 3pm. Jack made the call at a pay phone inside of Jakes restaurant before ordering. The phone just rang and rang so, he hung up. He figured that she just had not made it home yet and shrugged it off.

After lunch, he went back to The Center and found the room for his Humanities class. When he entered the room, a few students were already seated. Jack nodded to them before he sat down; eventually, several more students arrived until there were slightly more than a dozen seated in the room. Jack sat silently, occasionally looking around the room and feeling somewhat out-of-place. But, he felt good at the same time because this was what he wanted. When the instructor came, he was a middle-aged man who seemed of some European descent; perhaps, Greek or French, Jack guessed. He seemed to be fairly fit and well-taken care of; perhaps, late-thirties, early-forties in age. He appeared alert and focused just as Jack had expected a college instructor would be "Good afternoon, everyone" he greeted pleasantly and firmly. "This is Man and His Physical Environment" he started. "…and my name is Dr. Brian Gouston" he continued. The teacher talked for about twenty minutes before he engaged the class in a session of going in order around the room and having each student tell a little something about themselves. When Jack's turn came, he said he was a plumber's assistant and eventually wanted to get a college degree but, was not sure in what field. The professor handed out the class syllabus. The session was lively with the instructor engaging the students in a question-and-answer exchange on geography related issues that the students seemed to enjoy. Jack found himself consumed with interest. The instructor dismissed the class early and urged them to be prepared for a full session on Monday.

Jack's second Monday and Wednesday class was called Intro to Uptown Center. It was a class that orientated the new freshman students on how the Uptown Center operates and was designed to teach civic and community values. It gave them hands-on experience interacting with the community by performing various voluntary services for the surrounding neighborhood. He attended and there was no book to buy, just a syllabus with handouts describing the various voluntary services a student could get involved with. The class was instructed by one of the Uptown Center teachers and counselors, Barbara Chaffee. She was a pleasant, enthusiastic woman in her late thirties that Jack felt he liked right away. Jack's first full day at school had been a positive experience. It had been as good as he could have expected and he enjoyed it. It felt good and he decided "I can do this" It all left him with a heightened sense of hope that he could change his life.

After that last class, Jack began to sense a mild feeling of melancholy. Usually, when these puzzling feelings arose, he would become introspective; trying to figure out what had caused them to occur. It came to him that it might be a couple of things. First, that he may have been a little more disappointed at not getting Tina on the phone than he let himself believe. Another thing was that he was no longer living the carefree street life that he had for what seemed an eternity but, was actually only little more than two years. It had filled his life with uncertainty; but, finally, he was no longer relying on his friend, the bottle that had been so much a part of that life. The near-sober state he was in had it's pleasant side and gave him a certain stability. But, this was the first time he was really alone with it without having something to look forward to that would occupy him and fill him with anticipation as the recent holiday activity had done. His life was changing just as he had hoped. But, he did not expect this surprising lull in his spirit where he seemed more alone than he had been in some time. The thought of drinking popped into his head. But, it was fleeting as soon as the thought of Tina came to mind. He understood that he missed getting her on the phone and that was all---no big deal; and his mood immediately shifted into a brighter space with that encouraging thought.

It was almost 3:30pm when Jack left the Center and that lonely feeling that began earlier continued to linger. He decided to head for the poolroom to hang out for just a short while. He had no intentions of drinking. But, he was not sure what would happen and what he would do. He walked north along Sheridan Road and deep inside, he was hoping that he would see someone he could talk to from the usual street crowd. But, as he walked, the streets were sparse of people because of the cold temperature. He walked past Sheridan Liquors near the corner of Wilson and Sheridan Road which was usually a hub of activity no matter the day or time and particularly late on any evening. But, there were only a couple of people hanging outside that Jack did not know and they appeared to be going inside the bar. He continued on past the Peanut Barrel at the corner of Leland and Sheridan Road. No one was hanging around outside there, either. He noted the temperature on the Bank of Chicago sign across Leland that read °21 before he turned left onto Leland heading westward. He walked the two blocks to Winthrop and turned north to go the one block to the poolroom. As he approached the corner of Lawrence and Winthrop, he could sense that he had missed being there.

There was almost a feeling of having been away from home. The familiarity gave him a feeling of ease that he really did not want to embrace---but, it was comforting, nonetheless. From across the street, he paused at the corner and could see into the poolroom through the glass window that fronted Lawrence Avenue. He was surprised to see so many familiar faces all at once. There was Mo'tic and Obie, Coley, Jabo and Larry all congregating inside near the front row of plastic chairs along the window facing Lawrence Avenue. Jack began to have ambiguous feelings as he started forward to cross Lawrence Avenue

"Fellas..fellas…fellas" he said as he strolled into the poolroom, greeting the gathering. "Hey, Jack…brotha', Jack…whaddya' say, Jack" they all responded almost in unison, each of them, in turn, engaging Jack with an abbreviated soul handshake. "Where you been young fella?…I ain't been seein' you around" the old-timer, Jabo inquired. "He been held hostage up in Evanston by his girlfriend" Coley interrupted with a broad smile. "No shit…huh, Jack?" Jabo responded with a wide grin. "Yep" Jack replied. "Yea, man…he got him a good-lookin' snow girl…college girl, too" Coley added to bolster his friend's street credentials. "No wonder I ain't been seein' you…got ya' self a li'l honey, huh?" Jabo teased. "Yea…she's cool" Jack responded modestly trying not to make a big deal of it.

"I don't blame ya' partna…stay the fuck 'way from these hardlegs, man…they ain't got nothin' for you…dig what I'm sayin', player?" Mo'tic chimed in. "Hey…what you tryin' to say, Mo…he shouldn't be hangin' around us?" Larry asked with a tone of feigned indignation. "Damn right…If I had some money right now…y'all wouldn't see me" Mo'tic said with a straight face in his usual antagonistic manner. "Aw, you just hang with us when ya' money short, huh?" Larry jumped in with the same tongue-in-cheek manner. "What?…you'll do the same damn thang, Larry…don't try to bullshit me…all of us do it…we only get together like this when our money is short…tell me I'm lyin'….if you had a grand…naw…just a hun'ud dollars right now…couldn't nobody hit you in the ass with a red apple…am I right or wrong?…you tell me…yes or no, Larry?" Mo' tic challenged, knowing he was stirring up the kind of banter that he loved to create. "Yea…you right, Mo…I'd be somewhere layin' up with one o' these chicks…high as a kite" Larry relented.

"Mo'tic began to giggle after Larry's admission. "Hahahahehe….you know damned well I'd do the same damn thang….If I had some real money right now…I'd be runnin' so fast 'way from 'round y'all…the street lights would look like a picket fence when I run past 'em…dig what I mean?…hahahahehehe" Mo'tic said as he cackled a hysterical laugh while he and Larry gave each other "five" "Hey, Mo…don't get too high and mighty 'round me…I'm ya' home-boy…don't be tryin' to run 'way from me when you got money…I was raised with ya' in Memphis…I remember you when ya' nose was runnin' and you was beggin' for cookies" Obie said, fueling the fun-filled exchange. "Whoooaaa!" the others whooped in sync, laughing at the cutting remark.

"I'll tell ya' what…my nose mighta' been runnin' but, I ain't never begged for *nothin'* let alone some damned cookies…one thang you knew about me, Obie…down in Memphis…I didn't beg…I *took!*…just like I do right now…ya' understand?…tell the truth…that's what the hell I did…yea…I won the Golden Gloves the year I made eighteen…remember?" Motic went on in the same blustery manner. "Yea…that's right..you could sho' 'nough throw some hands…best I ever seen" Obie admitted. "Matta' fact…I'll tell y'all how I learnt' to fight…when I was 'bout thirteen..down in Memphis ol' boy we call Shoetop used to whoop my ass almost every day when I got outa' school…I used to battle his big ass fightin'…but, he used to get the best o' me every time…didn't matter what I did…then…school was out for the summer then, September come back around…I had gained about twenty pounds and I got strong 'cause that was the summer I was workin' with my daddy at the lumber mill…anyway…when school started, I said to myself…I'm tired o' these ass-whoopins…I'm gonna' fight hell outa' that damn Shoetop…first fight that semester…I got him down and went to wailin' on his ass…they had to get the gym teacher to pull me offa' him…yessiree…felt so good to whoop his ass…look like I just lost my mind…I went to whoopin' asses every where I went…I used to start shit *just so* I could whoop some ass…I went to whoopin' asses comin' then…I went to whoopin' asses goin'….then, somebody went and signed me up for this boxin' shit…I went on and had a bunch o' fights…next thang I know, I'm the goddamn champ!...I'm tellin' ya' man…that ain't no lie…is it, Obie?....hahahahehe…I ain't lyin'!" Mo'tic said as he burst out into another fit of hearty laughter.

"Hey, Mo…how come he was called Shoetop?" Jabo asked. "Hehehehaha…huuuhh…'cause that big som' bitch would wear hell out of a pair o' shoes…look like every time you turn around, he done wore the bottom out of his shoes…pair o' shoes wouldn't last no time…he would have a new pair in April…May…he need a new pair…his daddy got so tired o' buyin' shoes all the time for his ass …told him…you better make them shoes last a few months 'cause you ain't gettin' no more until such-and-such-a-time…then, when he wore that hole in the sole…he'd be too scared to tell his daddy…he either had to save his li'l money and buy 'em hisself or fix the shoes up…he spent all his li'l money on candy..so, he wasn't gonna' buy *nothin'*…anyway…he start puttin' paste-board in the bottom of his shoes…the soles got so wore out 'til he didn't hardly have no bottom to his shoes…just the top…that's why we start callin' him Shoetop…hahahaha.." Mo'tic explained with a chuckle.

"Hey, Jack…we tastin' pretty good right now…I got a pint of vodka and Larry got some Schnapps….come on…lets go in the back so you can get a good swig.." Jabo offered. Ambiguous feelings began to pull at Jack. He paused and it seemed to last an eternity. He wanted to take the drink and share in the banter and camaraderie. But, he began to think of the consequences and what was at stake. He could not afford to go on a drinking spree at this crucial time, he though. Besides, it would be disappointing not only for himself but, for Tina, as well. He knew that a little too much to drink would set off a craving for drugs and no telling what after that. He fought the urge off. "Naw…that's alright, Jabo…I'm sleepy, man….I need to go home and lay down…" Jack said as the excuse seemed to roll right off of his tongue. "You're welcomed, now…I'm tryin' to look out for you" Jabo urged. "I know you lookin' out for me, Jabo….you always do and I 'preciate it…but, I got to pass this time…thanks, anyway" Jack responded.

"What you got there, Jack…ya' school notebook?" Coley asked. "Yea, man…classes started today" Jack replied matter-of-factly, trying to de-emphasize the issue. "You ain't just shuckin' and jivin' about that school thang, huh?" Coley commented. "Well…I'm gonna try my best to go through with it, Coley…I really wanna do this, man" Jack said with more sincerity than he ever had shown before on the subject. Jack didn't say much to his friends about school. He knew that they were wise enough to know the value of it. But, it was not something that held any particular value in their own lives such as they were. Jack understood this so, he did not make much mention of it.

"Got to ride out, y'all…I'll holla' at y'all later" Jack finally said after about an hour or so of mingling. He took off for home. As he walked through the cold in the winter twilight to the Y, he was thinking that he was glad that it was not summer time because going to school would have been harder for him during the warmer seasons. During the winter time, it was much easier. He could at least get into the routine of going to school before the warm weather hit. He was not as tempted to engage in his old habits during the cold weather. It was going on 6pm when Jack arrived at the Y. He had stopped at a restaurant and bought himself a carry-out dinner to take home. He went to his room and ate his meal. He relaxed for a while before he went out into the hallway to call Tina on a pay phone.

"Hey, honey…how are you?" Tina replied after Jack spoke. "I'm cool…what ya' up to, baby?" Jack asked. "Nothing much…I stopped over at my friend Vicky's place today after I came back from Northbrook applying for a job…mom let me use her car to go job-hunting…Vicky lives in Skokie so, since I had the car, I figured I would stop by…I called her from Northbrook and she said come on over, so I did…how was your first day at school?" Tina asked with a hint of excitement. "Oh…baby…it was real cool…no problems…everything went smooth and I met a few people…my next class is Monday…I have two afternoon classes on Mondays and Wednesdays and two morning classes on Tuesdays and Thursdays" Jack said with a happy lilt in his tone. "Jack…I'm really happy you liked it…it's a lot of work…just take it a little at a time…you'll get through it" Tina advised. They talked another half-hour. They made plans to get together on the weekend before hanging up. Jack felt so much better after the long talk with Tina. He felt a little melancholy and disconnected earlier but, now he seemed centered again and he was reminded again how much Tina had come to mean to him. Jack went to the poolroom and mingled for a couple of hours with his friends on Saturday afternoon without drinking.

Then, he and Tina went out late that afternoon to the movies in downtown Chicago. After the movie, they went into a downtown restaurant and had hamburgers and their usual lively conversation. Jack spent the night with Tina at her place in Evanston and they had another fulfilling weekend together; with no holidays to celebrate and Tina out of school and not working yet and Jack not having class work just yet, it was a peaceful time where the two were blissfully bound the entire weekend.

It was Monday morning and Jack and Tina exchanged their usual passionate affections as they said goodbye before Jack went out of her apartment door to head for the L train home. His first class was not until 1:50pm today so, he had time to go home for a nap. He was still a little sleepy because, whenever he and Tina slept together, there wasn't so much sleeping. It was 8:30 am when Jack arrived at his room in the YMCA. He always felt completely unwound whenever he arrived at his place after spending time at Tina's place. He was a little tired and sleepy but, completely relaxed. He also seemed to have this enormous peace of mind, as well. He undressed and laid down and napped. When he awoke, it was almost noon. He showered and came back to his room and dressed.

He went out and walked the couple of blocks to the Village Restaurant on Montrose. He had an egg breakfast and came back to his room and bumped around for a while before taking his notebook, pens and class syllabuses and heading out of the Y for the long walk to the Uptown Center for his first afternoon class. Jack was on time for his 1:50pm Man and His Physical Environment class. There were a few more students than before. Dr. Gouston gave a lecture for about half an hour. He advised everyone to take notes. He gave a short quiz of five questions afterward. This was all new to Jack and he was reasonably happy with getting three of the five questions correct. The instructor referred to the class text that Jack noticed most of the students already had. He had taken notes at the orientation session and he referred to them to remind him that his voucher for books would be ready tomorrow at Linda Chavez' office. Aside from being the in-house recruiter for the Center, she coordinated Financial Aid matters between The Center and the campus that was several miles away on the Northwest side of the city. It was time for his second class, Intro to Uptown Center and it seemed to be a full class with a couple more students that he had not seen at the first class session. It turned out to be a lively session with a fun-filled exchange of comments and good-natured barbs between the students and the teacher. Barbara, the instructor seemed to have this way of inspiring a lively debate of ideas among the students; and as she beamed the same happy smile that she had at the very first class, Jack thought to himself that these were the kind of people he should be around; not the street urchins like himself who lived in that predatory world of no rules; no principles; no conscience and no remorse. The realization that he had wasted so much time in the streets passing away many empty hours achieving nothing was being illuminated by the contrast of what he was doing now. His life had been drifting perilously out of control and he seemed not to have cared where it ended because drinking had insulated him. It occurred to him that somewhere along the way, he had chosen hope over despair; action over apathy. He had somehow been transformed into the person now sitting in this college classroom. But, curiously, he did not feel responsible for this dramatic change. He did not feel that much effort on his part had caused this to occur. Intervention of some sort was at work here, he thought. Jack could not figure it out right now but, he decided in this moment of reflection that he did not want to return to that life he had been living so recently but, seemed as though it had been so long ago. This classroom setting and the interaction between the others and himself had given him a sense of grounding, normalcy and calm. There was nothing to fear here; no desperation; no anger; no madness; none of the neurosis that raked his nerves daily when he was in his survival mode out on the streets.

After his last class, Jack went into the student lounge and spent some time reading the college materials lying around. He wanted to immerse himself in the Uptown Center atmosphere. Already, it was beginning to feel like a kind of sanctuary. Hanging around helped him to kill time and would help him to be in the streets that much less, he thought. Finally, he left and that odd feeling of aloneness arose very mildly. But, he was beginning to understand that he had made changes in his life and now, he needed to learn how to adjust. Idleness and carefree carousing were no longer a part of his daily activities. He had to teach himself to adhere to this new lifestyle; he was beginning to see that the transition was not so easy. There were little emotional and mental upheavals that he needed to overcome. But, these feelings were not so much of a challenge when he compared them to his days of desperate survival over the last couple of years; that experience had expanded him; stretched every fiber of his being; tested him to his limits; he had been twisted, bent and mutilated by the raw experience. It gave him a wealth of savvy and wisdom for which there was no other price except the brutal experience itself. He was grateful that he had survived to see this day when his life had changed.

Jack walked back toward the YMCA in the blustery winter wind as it whipped thin streams of snow flurries through the air. He took Wilson Avenue. He was coming upon the Wilson Avenue Liquor store when he suddenly noticed through the wind and snow blowing in his face, a couple of people he recognized standing in front of the store. It was Po' Boy and Lowside. They were regulars who mainly hung around Sheridan Liquors. He did not know them so well. He had become barely acquainted with them over time during the many nights out on the sidewalk in front of Sheridan Liquors where the usual gathering of dope dealers, fiends and other shadowy characters would congregate. Jack could feel a mild surge of fear rise within. These were two characters whom he knew to be gang affiliated. They were members of the Demons; the notorious street gang that had terrorized Chicago neighborhoods for decades. There were various loosely organized factions all over the city. Jack had come to be aware of most of those who identified themselves as members within the group of regulars out on the streets. Like most others who were not members, Jack avoided having much contact with them. He had come to know how they operated out on the streets and how they regarded those who were not members. Mostly, if one avoided them, there were no problems. But, Jack had learned that being a member held more danger than being a non-member. Out on the streets, he had witnessed the punishment that higher ranked gang members meted out to the soldiers; the back-alley beatings; the maimings and injuries issued out to members who had violated some gang code had forewarned him. The mere knowledge of these things had guided him in how to tread the streets and what to avoid when it came to their element.

"What's goin' on homey" Lowside, the heavier one greeted

Jack. “Hey…what’s goin’ on, y’all” Jack responded very casually, masking the bit of fear he was feeling. “Where ya’ headed, my man?” Po’ Boy asked rhetorically, making conversation. “Just up the way…to my partna’s crib” Jack lied. “Yea..hey, man…we got this car cassette player here…you know anybody that might be interested?” the tall, wiry Po’ Boy asked as he pulled the bulky item out from under his long wool coat and displayed it to Jack. Jack could sense the toxic vibes emanating from their presence. He knew, too to be careful not to engage himself too much because these types of characters would take advantage of anything he said to use him. “Hey…that looks sweet, man…but, I don’t know nobody who even got a car” Jack said. “Help us sell it and we’ll split with you, slim” Lowside offered. “Cain’t hang, brotha’…I’m already late tryin’ to get up to my boy’s place” Jack lied again. “Okay, then…alright” Po’ Boy responded very casually as though the issue was not really as important as he had first made it seem. “Hey…you smokin’ anything?” Po’ Boy remembered to ask just as Jack had taken several steps away. “I’m popped, baby” Jack turned to respond. “Okay…later, Slim” Po’ Boy said. Just as Jack turned to continue on his way, a police car was passing and had slowed as it pulled in front of the Wilson Liquor store. The car stopped in front and the police peered at Po’ Boy and Lowside momentarily before they pulled off. Jack was walking away when he noticed the squad car pulling up. He breathed a sigh of relief as he stepped up his pace toward home. Jack was grateful that he did not linger and that he was spared from being caught up in a bad situation. These were the usual kind of encounters Jack had on the streets. He had to know how to play his hand to navigate around the kind of nefarious games that people on the streets were plotting around every corner.

Jack continued on home to the Y. After he settled into his room and put on his relaxing clothes, he ate some leftover food he had in his room. He turned on his little TV. He watched it for a while but, this mundane activity of just sitting and watching television seemed trite and unfulfilling. But, Jack was wise enough to disregard that notion. He had decided to regiment himself to these kinds of ordinary activities that did not seem to affect other people in the ways that they were affecting him. He needed to be calmer and to accept that this was just the manner in which ordinary people lived. Life could no longer be the full-throttle, reckless folly it had been if he wanted to achieve his goals. He looked at his clock-radio and it was barely 5pm. He wanted to wait until later to call Tina. At 6:30pm, he called. The phone just rang and rang. He called again at 7:30pm---no answer.

It was Tuesday morning and Jack needed to leave home earlier for his morning classes at the Northeastern Illinois University Uptown Center. He awoke feeling the weight of disappointment that he had last night when he could not get hold of Tina. He wondered what was going on. He was feeling somewhat disoriented as the thought of not getting Tina on the phone occupied him the whole time he was preparing to leave out. He showered and dressed and decided to leave a little early so that he could have breakfast at Jakes next door to The Center.

After breakfast, he was standing in Linda Chavez' office. There were several students standing in line for their book vouchers. Jack got in line and things were quiet except for when Linda spoke to the next person in line to ask their name, check them off the list and give them their book voucher. "Hi, Linda" Jack said when his turn came. "Hello, Jack" here you are" she said as she checked his name off the list and handed him a book voucher with his name on it. "Everything okay so far?" she asked. "Yea…so far, so good" Jack responded pleasantly, still feeling a little odd hearing himself sound so civilized as he was still adjusting to this lifestyle change. "Where is the book store to get the books?" Jack asked. "Just up the street on Broadway on the west side of the street a few doors south of Wilson…it's Beck's Book Store" she responded. "Okay…thanks" Jack said as he took off to go for his books. When he arrived, the store was full of students. It was 8:50am and his first class was at 9:30am. He was hoping to get his books before his first class started.

He arrived at the book store and the process of finding the books he needed as he referred to his syllabus was difficult. He had trouble following the number and title sequences and had to be careful that he was getting the right book because some of the books resembled others. Jack began to feel a bit of anxiety. But, he kept at it until he had the four books for his classes; one for each class except Intro to Uptown Center, which required no books and an extra one for his Expository Writing class, his first class on Tuesdays and Thursdays.

He made it back to his Writing class for the first session at The Center with a few minutes to spare. The instructor, a man of medium height was already standing near his desk at the front of the classroom. He had written his name "Thomas Walker" below the title of the class on the blackboard. Most of the students were already there and a few more streamed in as Jack took a seat. The new student, Marvin was one of the students who came in after him. "Hey" he acknowledged as he smiled and made a small waving gesture of his hand to Jack before he took a seat in the back. The instructor looked up at the wall clock over the blackboard and began when he saw that it reached 9:30am. "Good morning students…is there anyone who is not here for Expository Writing?" he asked, then paused momentarily. "Good" he continued on after none responded. "This is Expository Writing" he started and lectured for almost twenty minutes. Then, he did what the teachers in Jack's other classes had done; start around the room to have each student tell a little bit about themselves and what they hoped to get from the class.

The rest of the class was interesting but, Jack could not get his mind off of Tina. He was hoping that everything was okay with her and between them. Deep down inside, he did feel a little worried for the very first time ever about his relationship with Tina. But, the feeling was very mild because, in his heart, he knew she loved him and there had to be a good reason why he could not get hold of her last night. Besides, he thought, she was probably enjoying her newfound freedom because he knew how tired she was of those four years of school she had endured and how boring it all had been. He knew her spirit----that she was an adventurous kind of woman who would explore all of the possibilities to enjoy her life. He knew she was responsible and she was loyal to her commitments. After Jack had reminded himself of all of these things that he knew of Tina, he was a little calmer. He concluded that he was not so worried ----just a little bit disappointed because he missed her.

The writing class ended at 10:50am and Jack's second class began at the next period at 11:00am. It was his Community Organization class taught by a slightly built, grey-haired woman who seemed a bit high-strung and who spoke fast and moved at a quick pace. Jack found the class topics interesting because it centered on the science of people and societies with an emphasis on American society. With thoughts of Tina still ruminating in the back of his mind, he was not so focused as he might have been. Otherwise, he was feeling fine; even a bit grand at sitting in these classrooms as a college student. He seemed to be feeling much better about himself these days because his world was clearly on a much more civilized plain. Each day his mind seemed a little more relaxed, his nerves more calmed and the fogginess from daily drinking seemed to be lifting. His outlook on his future seemed to have brightened enormously. He was developing the feeling that he did not want to give all this up; certainly, not for the madness he had already experienced. He just had to somehow endure the monotony that this more peaceful existence seemed to bring. As Jack was sitting in class thumbing through his notebook, he saw that one of the notes he took at the orientation session said that he should see his counselor in the first week of school and to see the person who recruited him to find out who his counselor would be.

When the class was over, he headed for Linda Chavez' office. She was busy with one student and a couple of others were sitting in the reception area of her office waiting. When he entered, she looked up and said "Hi, Jack…you need to see me?" "Yes…to find out who my counselor is" Jack responded. "I am probably going to be tied up with students for a little while….you can wait in here or wait in the student lounge….what do you want to do?" she asked. "I'll wait in the student lounge" Jack said. "Okay…when I am done with these students, I will step over to get you…okay?" Linda said. "Yea…okay" Jack responded. He went into the student lounge and began reading the college materials, magazines and pamphlets. There were other students seated at one of the several dining tables in the back of the lounge having their lunches and talking.

Jack was sitting in the lounge area near the entrance when a heavy Hispanic woman who was well-dressed and wearing lots of makeup entered the lounge area. As she plopped down in a seat near Jack, she began talking right away. "I woke up late for my first class today….I rushed getting over here…didn't make it…hey…you must be new, huh?" she said. "Yes…how did you know?" Jack asked. "Cause I practically live here at The Center….how are you?…my name is Guadalupe…everybody calls me Lupe" she said, extending her hand to Jack to shake.

"Jack" Jack responded as he reached over to shake. "They finally got some cute guys in here…it's about time…hahaha" Lupe chuckled. "Oh…don't mind me…just talking to myself" she added. "How long you been goin' to school here?" Jack asked. "Almost a year-and-a-half…I'm supposed to be taking my classes on-campus but, I just hate to go to the campus because I live two blocks away from The Center…this is the first semester I should be on-campus but, I got a schedule with all my classes here…I got lucky" She went on with a smile. "Say…how do you go about gettin' a job on campus?" Jack asked. "Just see your counselor…I got my job that way….I run the Community Day Care here at The Center" Lupe said. "How much do these campus jobs pay?" Jack asked. "Not much, Jack…three dollars-and something an hour….but…I'll tell you…it's a big help" Lupe advised. "You married?" Lupe asked. "No…I'm…"

"Jack Rollins…you can come in now" Linda Chavez unknowingly interrupted as she stepped just inside the lounge doorway. "I gota see my counselor…nice talkin' to you, Lupe" Jack said to Lupe as he raised from his seat and walked over to Linda's office. "Have a seat, Jack…let me see who your counselor is….then, once I find that out…I'll look at their schedule and see where we can schedule an appointment with them for you…okay?" Linda said after Jack had come in. "Okay…looks like your counselor is Barbara Chaffee…you meet her yet?" Linda asked. "Yes…she is my Intro to Uptown Center teacher" Jack said. "Okay…excellent….she really is a very beautiful person…great teacher and counselor…you'll love her" Linda said. "Yea…I enjoyed her class…she *is* good…I like her" Jack responded. "And she can help me get a campus job?" Jack added. "Perhaps…depends on what is available and what kind of work you are willing to do…but…yes…that is part of her job here as well as mine" Linda said. "Okay…now…I see an opening here for Barbara on Thursday at one-thirty….you have class then?" Linda asked Jack. "No…my last class ends at twelve-twenty on Tuesdays and Thursdays" Jack said. "Okay, then…I will put you in for one-thirty for this Thursday to meet with Barbara…okay?" Linda said. "Good…I'll be there" Jack replied. Jack began to leave when Linda said "Do you have a locker yet, Jack?" she asked. "No…I don't" Jack responded. "Well there are lockers in the lounge along the south wall as you may have seen…pick one…get yourself a lock to put on it…and give us the number you are in….okay…try to do that as soon as possible…alright?" Linda said. "Yea…okay…I will…I won't have to carry all of these books everywhere" Jack said.

"Oh…one other thing, Jack…we want all of the students to meet the staff…we will have a little social get-together for all new students and the staff next month on the twentieth of February…we do this every Winter term to help everyone get to know one another and to help keep new students connected and staying in school…but, I would like for you to come back to my office after you meet with Barbara on Thursday to meet the Center director, Sam Martinez and the assistant director, Glen Lafleur…they are not here everyday…they are at the campus some days…but, they will be here on that day…okay?…I'll make a note for Barbara to remind you when you meet with her…alright?" Linda said. "Yes…that's good…I'll be here after I see her…thanks" Jack said before he left The Center.

Jack headed for home after meeting with Linda Chavez and he decided to take Montrose. It was the nearest street to The Center that was ran east and west that he could use to walk westward home to the Y without seeing very many of the usual characters he knew in the streets. It was cold and there were fewer people on the streets as would be expected. But, many of the street people had nowhere to go or anything to do. Even if they had a place to stay, most came outdoors to get hold of something; perhaps, to make some kind of hustle to buy food and drinks; or to ante-up with any of the other drinkers to buy cheap drinks to at least diminish the misery of being broke and cold. Jack could see a few of them mingling around the Broadway-Montrose intersection.

As he started westward on Montrose, Jack could see a police paddy wagon in front of the Tipaway bar just across Broadway where he had bought take-out liquor many times. He was passing in front of it on the opposite side of the street and he could see Robert Williams, a tall fellow that he grew up with in his old neighborhood in Cabrini-Green. Robert was being led out of the bar in handcuffs by the police and Jack could see a splattering of blood on his shirt through the open winter coat he was wearing. A few of the street regulars were standing several yards away, watching the incident unfold. Robert looked disheveled; appearing as though he had just been in some altercation. Jack was not surprised to see Robert involved in some incident. Jack was well acquainted with Robert from seeing him in the last few years around Uptown. Robert was a little crazy. He seemed sane when he was sober. But, whenever he began drinking, he would really get crazy and there was no predicting what he would get involved in. Occasionally, he would get locked up. Robert had already been to prison a couple of times. Jack never remembered him being odd in any way when they were youngsters growing up. But, in the time he had seen Robert around Uptown, he was always getting into trouble. Robert dressed nicely most of the time. Jack remembered him always being dressed neatly when he was younger in the old neighborhood. Robert was sometimes seen with Michael Carlton, who was a friend of both Jack and Robert. But, Mike felt the same way about Robert that Jack did---he could not tolerate him when he was high and whenever he began to behave obnoxiously in his company, Mike would sneak away from Robert. Jack found Robert annoying to be around, as well because he was always wanting to box with Jack. Jack used to engage when it first started. But, he learned quickly that after he gave Robert a few good body shots during their impromptu matches, Robert would begin to get serious and hit a little too hard. Jack would try to tell Robert he wanted to quit. But, Robert would continue until Jack knocked the wind out of him before he stopped. Jack watched as the police loaded Robert into the Paddy wagon. "He'll be out in a month or two" Jack thought to himself.

Jack continued on walking westward on Montrose. He had begun to think about Tina. He planned to call her around 4 or 5pm. He was hoping that she would be home. He picked up some carry-out dinner again at the restaurant on Montrose. Jack stopped at the lobby desk to see if he had any mail. He had one piece of mail from school and one of those pink message slips that he had seen the clerks use to take messages for the residents. He read the message and the thing that jumped out at him was "From: Tina" The message said "call me when you get home" He was very happy to get the message. He went to his room and ate his dinner. It was 3:15pm when he laid down for a nap.

He awoke at 4:50pm and went out to the phones in the second floor hallway to call Tina. "Hello" Tina answered. "Hey, Jack…I called you a couple of times today…I wanted to let you know I was out with some friends last night…I should have called you and left a message while I was out. But, I was with my friends Vickie and Maryann while they were out shopping and we were just having a blast…Maryann's older brother is getting married and that's why she was out shopping...how are you, honey?" Tina rattled off in her usual upbeat manner. "I'm cool, baby…I tried to call you last night but, I couldn't get hold of you…I thought you skipped town on me" Jack said. "Hahaha…I'm sorry, honey…I should have called you earlier…I don't have enough money to skip town, anyway…hahaha" Tina apologized with a laugh. "Well…as long as you're okay…that's all I care about" Jack said. "Thanks, honey…that's sweet…I'm okay…what's been happening with, Mr. College?…that's what I'm gonna start calling you from now on" she giggled. "Nothin'…Mr. College is really gettin' into this school thing…so far it's been pretty good…I'm still meetin' people and the teachers and everybody are real cool" Jack responded. "So…are we still on for the weekend or do you have a lot of homework yet?…cause I know how that goes…believe me" Tina commented. "Well…I think we should be able to have our usual get-together 'cause I really didn't get much homework, yet…just a chapter to read from one of my classes…that's all…we'll get together" Jack promised. "Oh…good…I miss you already" Tina added. "I miss you, too, baby" Jack said. They continued to talk for another half-hour and the conversation was upbeat as it always had been. But, Jack could tell that the freedom of being out of school seemed to make Tina a little less reliant upon their get-togethers. But, he was happy that their talk had the usual cheeriness.

Jack went back to school the next day and things went just as well as before. He chose a locker and bought a combination lock to put on it. He bought a book bag from the Woolworths store on Broadway. He was settling in to his student life and it all seemed bright, new and exciting to Jack. The structure of his everyday student life felt meaningful. He was enjoying meeting new people at The Center. After his last class, Jack went toward home, buying dinner, as usual, on the way. He studied by reading a chapter for one of his classes. He began to realize that seeing people everyday at The Center and talking to them was replacing the socializing he once did on the streets. But, he still had a sense of longing for the streets and his friends out there. They were bonds that he could not easily break after a few years of developing them. He knew, too that associating with those friends in the streets was detrimental to his goal of going to college and finishing. He knew that he would still be going to The Corner and the poolroom and mingling with the street crowd there because he enjoyed it. He decided his plan would be that he would go around them only occasionally; not staying very long and certainly, he would not be drinking. For the last two months, he had done well at drinking very little and being practically sober.

It was Thursday and today, Jack would be seeing his counselor to see about getting a campus job. He remembered too, that he would return to Linda Chavez' office after classes to meet the Center director and assistant director. He attended classes and after having lunch, went to see his counselor, Barbara Chaffee. "Well, hello there, Jack Rollins" Barbara greeted Jack after he announced himself in her office. "Have a seat, Jack" she offered. "So…how is everything going for you, so far?" she asked. ""Pretty good, so far, Ms. Chaffee" Jack replied. "Just call me Barbara…okay?" she said. "So, classes are going okay and you're not having any problems adjusting…you've never been to college before…is that right?" Barbara inquired. "No…my first time…although I have wanted to go ever since I finished high school…but, it's really hard when you don't have money" Jack said. "That is quite true, Jack and that is why the staff here at the Northeastern Uptown Center works hard to get and keep disadvantaged people in college…we support all kinds of grass-roots organizations that fight for federal dollars so that more people who can't really afford it can get an education…it's very important work and I am proud to be a part of it all" Barbara said. The counselor's words seemed to give Jack a profound sense of importance about what he was doing and he could feel the sincerity of what she said. He could see what Linda Chavez meant in her earlier praise of Barbara.

"Anyway…let's get down to the nuts and bolts…you will need a part-time job…most every student we have has one…either an on-campus job that they get through our office or an off-campus job that they get either through the campus employment office or ones that they find on their own…it's tough to make it without one for most students" Barbara said. "Here, Jack…here is a list of on-campus jobs that may or may not be available…we will have to check on a case-by-case basis…take it with you…take some time to look it over and pick a few of those occupations that you think you would want to work in" Barbara said as she gave Jack a two-page handout. "Okay….I'll look it over" Jack replied. He and the counselor talked casually for about fifteen minutes more. She was full of information about school that Jack found helpful. He felt good about the meeting because he realized that these staff members at The Center were sincere people who cared about their work and the students they were helping. Jack left Barbara's office after she set another appointment for him to return on Friday next week.

He went to Linda Chavez' office to meet the Center director and the assistant director just as she had advised. "Oh…hello, Jack…have a seat and let me go to Sam and Glen's offices to see if they are ready to meet you" Linda said as she rose from her desk and walked out of her office to go to the office next door. After about a minute, she returned and said "They're ready to meet you, Jack…follow me" Jack followed Linda into the office next door. There, he saw a neatly groomed, well-dressed Hispanic man who was not very tall and another man who appeared to be Caucasian standing in front of the large desk in one of the two offices. The offices were side-by-side with a wall partitioning them. Jack was impressed at the pristine, well arranged office setting that seemed fitting for a director. "Hello, Mr. Jack Rollins…how are you?" the Hispanic man greeted. "Hello" the other man greeted and they took turns shaking hands with Jack as they smiled pleasantly. "Have a seat, Jack…we just want to meet you and welcome you to The Center….we'll be doing this for each of the new students we have this semester….I am Sam Martinez and this is the flying Frenchman, Glen Lafleur, the assistant director" The two men sat in seats in the reception area near where Jack was seated. "Jack, this Center has been here for six years and I have been the director for the last two…Glen has been the assistant director in that same time…our mission here is to recruit new students from Uptown and the other surrounding neighborhoods and let them know about the educational opportunities they may not be aware of here at Northeastern…we want to enroll as many as we can and keep them in school until they finish…so, we know you just started a week ago and we want to know how things are going for you and how you like it, so far" Sam said. "I'm going back to my office" Linda said softly before leaving and before Jack spoke. “Well…I like it…it’s been good…everybody has been very helpful” Jack said. Jack was a little uptight at first but, the friendliness of the two men seemed to loosen him up and toward the end of the ten minutes or so of talking with them, he was feeling very comfortable. “Jack…if you have any problems or questions or if there is anything we can do for you…let us know” Sam said before the two men shook Jack’s hand again and Jack left. Afterward, Jack decided to spend some time in the student lounge. He put most of his books away in his locker and kept one out to study.

“Newbie…what’s up, baby!” a voice spoke out as Jack was comfortably seated in one of the cushiony sofa-chairs in the lounge reading his text book. He looked up to see that it was his gregarious new acquaintance, Billy. “Hey, what’s goin’ on, my man?” Jack greeted with a smile. “Hittin’ them books, huh?....that’s the way to do it, man…get on down with ya’ bad self” Billy said. “I’m just takin’ a little break right now…been runnin’ all day” Billy said as he plopped down in a nearby seat. “Everything cool, so far?” Billy asked. “Yea…so far” Jack replied. “Now, don’t forget…you got my number…you can holla’ at me like I said…don’t be shy” Billy urged Jack. “Yea…I won’t forget…I’m cool right now” Jack replied.

“Hey…what’s your story, Billy…what brought you up in here to school?” Jack inquired. “How much time you got?..hahaha…it’s a long story, bro’….a looonnng story” Billy said with an amused tone. “Hey…I been strugglin’ with this school thang…I did a bit not too long ago and now…I’m back in school” Billy said. “You was in jail?” Jack responded. “Jail…huh!…I was in the joint, baby....Menard…prison” Billy confessed. Jack was a bit shocked at the admission and he wondered just how Billy was managing to be in school after doing prison time. “They let you in school after you did prison time?” Jack asked with surprise. “Yea, man…these people at The Center been pullin’ all kinda’ strings for me ever since I been goin’ here” Billy added. “Like what?” Jack asked. “Well…I did time for a robbery after my second semester….wasn’t no reason in hell I shoulda’ been gettin’ myself caught up like that…but, I got high one night celebratin’ my good grades at the end of that semester….got a little too crazy…spur of the moment thing….don’t know what got into me…my money was low…but, it wasn't that low to be doin' what I did…was drunk…robbed a liquor store way over on Marshfield on a dare from my cousin, Monty…gun was empty…I was a damned fool!" Billy said with a sincere tone of self-admonishment. "So....that was not that long ago?" Jack asked. "Almost a year now" Billy responded. "So what happened?" Jack asked. "Well…I did about thirteen months and got three years parole…Center got me a free lawyer from the Legal Aid service…them lawyers…The Center staff was dedicated to helpin' me, man…they're like family to me right now…had it rough growin' up, man…I won't get into that…but…right now…by the grace of God…I'm back in school…these people at The Center really seem to like me…I keep 'em laughin'…they're real good people" Billy said. "Cool….that's good, man…yea they do seem like really good people…all of 'em" Jack said. "Yessir…and you know….all they did for me helped me make up my mind about what my major is….Sociology…social work….that's my callin' baby…my family…myself…we needed a lot of help when I was growin' up…we was a messed up family…it wasn't good, man….when I get my degree, I plan to help a lot of people….dedicate myself, man" Billy said with a hint of a quiver in his voice. "That's a hell 'uva' story you got there, Billy…that's cold-blooded!" Jack said with a bit of amazement. He was surprised that anyone who was already enrolled in school would have a background more depraved than his own. But, he was beginning to feel even more of a kinship with Billy; not just because of his upbeat personality but, also because of his relevation of his trials and tribulations. He found him to be not much different from himself; especially when Billy spoke of his family issues.

"Well….you know what…I came straight off the streets and enrolled here…I ain't got nothin' but my little room at the Y…I'm tryin' to get myself together" Jack admitted. Jack knew that he only shed light on his background because Billy had been so forthcoming about his. But, he knew he would not make any such admissions to any of the others at The Center. "You was buck-wild out in them street…wasn't ya'?….doin' some o' everythang, Huh?" Billy said. "Yea…gettin' high everyday…stealin'…everything, man…you know how it goes…don't say nothin'" Jack said in a somewhat hushed tone. The two talked confidentially for a while, revealing things about themselves that neither would to the other students.

They were brethren of the same background and experience in spite of their differences of color and race.

"What kinda' name is your last name, Billy?" Jack asked. "Eneas…it's Greek…William Eneas…that's my name….I'm Greek-Italian" Billy said proudly. "That's real cool…dig that" Jack said. "Yea…daddy is Greek, mother is Italian" Billy said. "Well…how come you soundin' like a brotha' when you talk?" Jack asked. "'Cause I grew up in a mixed neighborhood with brothas' around Taylor Street on the Westside…played plenty of basketball on the school-yard courts over there and I have spent enough time in jail with brothas 'til I guess I just became one…know what I mean?…without a doubt…from the streets of the ghetto, baby" Billy said with an animated tone and expression. Jack chuckled at the comic inflection. As they were talking, another of Jack's new acquaintances, Lupe came into the student lounge.

"Hi, Jack..." she said very spirited and then "Hey, Billy" with a dour tone. "What's happ'nin' Miss Guadalupe?…how you doin' baby?" Billy said with a tone of familiarity. "I'm alright…Jack look out for this guy…he has problems" Lupe said to Jack. "Hey…what's that all about…I got problems?…everybody got problems…why you frontin' me off like that, Lupe?…that's kinda' cold, baby" Billy said with a facetiously pleading tone. "Jack is a nice guy and I don't want to see you playin' your little games with him that you played with me" Lupe said with a bit of sternness. "Come on…come on now, Lupe…let by-gones be by-gones, baby…you ain't gonna' never leave me alone about that little incident, are you?…my goodness!" Billy lamented. "Hahaha…sounds like you two got some old issues to settle…what's the deal?" Jack said. "Aw, man…almost a year ago she got all salty at me, man…" Billy started. "It was barely six months ago" Lupe interrupted. "He invited me out and then, stood me up" Lupe said. "Aw come on, Lupe…see…that's the whole problem between us right there…you have a whole different interpretation of what happened…we was supposed to get together to study and you callin' it a date…I'm sorry…I fell asleep and that's why I never showed up" Billy pleaded. "It was a date because you said it was…you were going to take me out to pay me back for helping you out by filling in for your time watching the kids at the daycare when you worked with me" Lupe said. “Aw…here we go, again” Billy said, a bit peeved before he rose from his seat. “Lupe…have a nice day, baby…later, Jack” Billy said as he left the student lounge.

“Hahaha…he’s alright…I just like to needle him every now-and-then” Lupe chuckled. “What are you doing right now, Jack?...would you mind keeping me company for a little while in the daycare in about twenty minutes?” Lupe asked. “Well…I was tryin’ to get a little studyin’ done right here in the lounge” Jack said. “Okay” Lupe replied. Jack could tell by her recent comments to him, that perhaps, Lupe was a little lonely and was looking for a boyfriend. She had a nice-looking face but, she was approaching morbid obesity. Her beautiful personality however, was sparkling and friendly. She seemed as decent as any woman could be. “Lupe…I can study here for the twenty minutes then, I’ll meet you in the daycare…where is it at?” Jack said. “It’s down at the end of the hall on the left before the next hallway” Lupe said. “Okay” Jack said. Jack wasn’t doing anything else and he had planned to do some studying at home tonight, anyway. So, he could spend some time in the daycare with Lupe.

After twenty minutes, or so, he went down the hallway to where Lupe was and walked in. It was a large room with tiny desks and chairs and a wide open play area with a few scattered toys. There were child-type murals on a couple of the walls and a fair-sized desk at one side of the doorway where Jack found Lupe sitting as she was opening and closing drawers. “Hey…this is pretty nice for the kids…huh” Jack said with a good-natured smile as he gazed around the room. There was another female student who apparently was there before Lupe and was turning over the daycare duties. “Okay…I’ll see you tomorrow, Lupe” she said before leaving. There were several pre-kindergarten kids playing in the open space as Lupe stopped her rummaging at the desk and looked up at Jack then, beamed a warm smile at the children playing. “They’re really something, aren’t they?” Lupe said to Jack. “Yea…they’re so full of energy…look at ‘em” Jack said as he smiled an amused smile at the kids playing. “Have a seat, Jack…over here next to my desk” Lupe offered before Jack walked to the opposite side of her desk and sat in a stout wooden chair. “So, Lupe…how long you been runnin’ the daycare?” Jack asked. “A solid year…since the start of my second semester here in ‘75” she said. “So, this is your on-campus gig, right?” Jack asked. “Yea” she replied. “I can tell…you really enjoy these kids…you have any?” Jack asked. “No, unfortunately…I would like to have some, though” Lupe said. “I’m gonna’ really miss these kids whenever I leave school and I get a real job” she added. “You got any kids, Jack?” Lupe asked. “Nope…not yet” Jack answered. “I was trying to ask were you married the other day when you went to see your counselor” Lupe said. “No…not married” Jack answered.

“You got a girlfriend?” Lupe asked. “Yea…I got a girlfriend” Jack answered. “Oh…that’s good…where does she live?” Lupe asked. “She lives in Evanston” Jack answered. “There’s not that many African-Americans in Evanston…are there?” Lupe asked. “I’m not sure…but, she ain’t black…she’s white” Jack answered. “Really?…I never would have thought that…you don’t seem like the type who would be with a white girl” Lupe said with surprise. “And what type of black man is it that *would* be with a white girl?” Jack asked with a challenging inflection. “I don’t know…a softer type…I guess” Lupe said. “You sayin’ I’m too rough to be with a white girl?” Jack asked. “No…don’t get me wrong…I’m just sayin’ that I’m surprised and you just didn’t seem the type…I don’t know why I have that impression about you…I just do” Lupe explained. “That’s alright, Lupe…I surprise a lot of people ‘cause I don’t think like other people…I think for myself…I don’t go along with everybody else’s program…dig what I’m sayin’?” Jack said. “I’m just kind of stubborn…I got my own way…that’s all” Jack added. “I understand…I know what you mean” Lupe answered. The two went on talking about different things and telling each other about their ways, likes and dislikes for another half-hour, or so. They seemed to have struck a friendly chord. “It’s about time for me to get goin’ Lupe…I’ll see you around…you here tomorrow?” Jack asked. “I’m here for an afternoon class then, the daycare” Lupe replied. “Okay…cool…I’ll check you later” Jack said before he left The Center.

Jack was taking his usual route walking west on Montrose toward the Y. He was on the north side of the street and was crossing Clifton Street where his friend, Annie Mae lives when he heard someone call out his name. “Jack!...Jack!” He looked around and he could tell that the voice was coming off of Clifton Street. But, he did not see anyone. He stopped walking and stood still; trying to gauge the direction the voice was coming from. "Over here, Jack!" the voice called out again. Finally, Jack could see that the voice was coming from a car parked on Clifton Street. It was a street that was cut short because it was behind the Truman college property and it ran north and south. It was a little enclave of four courtway buildings; two on either side of the shortened street. The car was a yellow Chrysler Lebaron that was familiar to him. It was usually parked on that street. Jack turned and began walking north toward the parked car. As he approached it, he could see a head leaned out of the back driver's side window. He could not see right away who it was because the cold vapor from his breath momentarily blocked his view. Then, he could see that it was his friend, Suge. "Jack…come on...get in, man" Suge spoke out as he popped his head back in the car. Jack leaned over to look inside and he could see that the owner of the car, an old-timer that everyone called "Poppa Jones" was sitting in the driver's seat comfortably nursing a pint bottle of Old Crow. "Hey, now" he greeted Jack. "how ya' doin' Poppa" Jack greeted before he slid inside after Suge opened the door and slid to the opposite side of the rear seat and Jack slid in to sit where Suge had sat. As Jack settled into his seat, he looked over at Suge and noticed that he was dressed magnificently; better than Jack had seen him or most anyone on the streets before.

"Damn, Suge…you sharper than a broke-dick-dog, man...what you been doin'?" Jack asked in amazement. "Lucked up, baby…Jack…I made a sting you won't believe, man…couldn't believe it myself" Suge said. "No shit…what happened?" Jack said with amazement as he scrutinized Suge from head to toe. Suge was wearing a brand new, very stylishly cut overcoat of some high-quality wool blend; dress slacks of the same quality and brand new shoes. He even had a ring on his left hand that appeared to be genuine. He looked resplendent. "Go on and take a hit o' this Hennessy" Suge said as he handed the bottle to Jack. Jack took the bottle but, did not drink and just held it. He was still sitting, with an amazed look at how Suge was so well dressed.

"Man…I lost my connect with my boy, Tank…remember, I told you about him before?…anyway…I couldn't get no more Ts and Blues from Tank 'cause he caught a case and he's out on bond…he say he knows the cops is watchin' him real close right now and he don't wanna' catch another case before he beats this one out…anyway, my funds ran out…I had to start doin' some rough-hustlin'….one night I'm breakin' into cars….now, Jack…you know that ain't even none o' my hustle…anyway…I'm breakin' into this one car to steal the tape-deck…I gets the tape-deck out…I see some buttons inside the car…didn't know what the buttons was for…I start pushin' buttons…it was one o' them fancy Mercurys…one of the buttons popped the trunk…I figure I might as well check the trunk out…I find two little canvas bags, man…cash goddamn money…it was a nice chunk…for real…set me straight…I paid my rent at the Grace Hotel for four months…still okay money-wise…I ain't gonna say how much, Jack…'cause you know how the game go…but, I'm straight for a little while" Suge said confidently. "Yea…I was tellin' him it sounds like somebody who has a business and they was prob'ly gonna take that money to the bank in the mornin'" Poppa interjected. "Damn…you lucky bastard!" Jack said a bit enviously. "I just copped me a nice package of weed from my man, Poppa here…I bought him out and, now…we just sittin' here waitin' for his cop man to deliver the rest of my package" Suge said. "That's cool, Suge…all the way cool!" Jack said. Suge went on talking excitedly about how he was going to lay low and invest his money in weed and sell it. Jack sat in the car for a half-hour talking with Suge and Poppa. The conversation consumed all of his attention.

"I got to get goin' man…I'm still in school and I got classes tomorrow" Jack finally said as he prepared to get out of the car. "Let me stretch my legs while I'm waitin' Poppa…I'm gonna get out and walk my boy down to the corner…I'll be right back" Suge said before he got out of the car with Jack. They walked together and Suge was still talking excitedly. Before they parted, Suge said "Here, Jack…I know you could use a little boost…that's not a loan, either…just from one brotha' to another 'cause you my mellow" Suge said after he handed Jack two fifty dollar bills. "Damn, Suge!…what you doin' man?…I cain't make this up no kinda' way!" Jack said. "Naw, naw…that's you…no strings attached…'cause you musta' put me up on a hundred stings where I made money by myself or we made it together…you add all that money I made because of what you did when you was hustlin' like a mad-man back then…that ain't nothin'…and don't worry…I got it like that" Suge said with heartfelt sincerity. "The reason I got out of the car is I didn't want Poppa to see me hand you that package…I already gave him a little extra for gettin' his cop-man to fill my order…I don't want him to get carried away…dig where I'm comin' from?" Suge explained. "Yea…I can dig it…well…thanks, man…you know you my guy..I 'preciate it…you know that" Jack said with the same sincerity before he and Suge parted with a soul handshake.

Jack continued walking homeward, stunned by Suge's revelation of his good fortune and how he decided to share a little with him. Jack loved his friends out in the streets. He never thought about how he may have helped someone else survive because it was the spontaneous manner in which he lived. Survival was a twenty-four-hour-a-day job as far as he was concerned and sometimes friends surrounding him while he was deep into his hustling would benefit just from being there. Jack treated them like family and when he was hustling good, would share some of his bounty. They were the only family he had out on the streets. Suge was no different. He was the same as Jack, experiencing the same voluntary disconnect from his family; not staying in touch with them and immersing himself in the street life. Jack stopped at the same restaurant on Montrose and bought a carry-out dinner as he did most evenings. He spent a little more and bought some dessert, as well. He had not been doing that lately because his money was getting low. He was trying to stretch it and if he spent his money reasonably, he could make it until he received his big financial aid check in a couple of weeks. The money that Suge had just given him was a big help. They had developed a true friendship over the few years they had known one another. Jack met Suge when he was meeting all those people that Fuzzy introduced him to back when Jack first moved into the 4848 high-rise building. They had been good friends ever since.

Jack arrived at the Y and when he checked for his mail at the lobby desk, he had a message from Tina. "I will be home later tonight. Call me after 10pm" the note read. Jack decided that Tina was still enjoying the free time she had while she was still looking for a full-time job and he shrugged it off. He would call her after 10pm. He fell asleep early in the evening a little past 8pm and he called Tina after he woke up shortly before 11pm.

"How's my honey?" Tina asked after Jack greeted her on the phone. "I'm cool, baby…ain't nothin' goin' on….everything is the same" Jack answered. "What's new with you, baby?" Jack asked. "I went to a bar and met up with Vickie and Roger and his girlfriend for a few drinks at the pub on Sherman…that's where I was tonight. "Cool…you had a good time?" Jack responded. "Jack…you know me…of course I did, honey…you thought about what we are going to do this weekend?" Tina said. "Well…you know….dinner, as usual…then we can go to a disco club on Rush Street for some dancing…you in the mood for that?" Jack said. "Actually, honey.. I've done so much running around this week looking for a job until I'm a little pooped…I'm feeling a little more laid-back….how about jazz this weekend?…I've only been to a jazz club a couple of times before but, I enjoyed it….I feel like just laying back and being entertained instead of working up a sweat entertaining myself…how about it, honey?" Tina said. "Whatever you want, baby…you're my baby and you can get what you want" Jack replied with a salacious tone. "Well then, sir…I will have the usual…a large side of beef…how about that?" Tina said with the same tone and an amused chuckle. "Will that be the six ounce or the eight ounce, m'am?" Jack teased back. "Uhhmmm…how about a nine-inch or a ten inch…do you have any of that?" Tina joked. "Uh…why, certainly ma'm…will you be having steak sauce with that?" Jack said, bursting out into laughter before he could finish saying the last words. "Yessir…I want all of the sauce you have…hahahaha" Tina burst out into a hearty laugh along with Jack. The two talked for about another fifteen minutes or so. They planned to have their usual talk on Friday evening and they would plan their weekend then.

Jack awoke and it was Friday, the only day that he did not have classes. It was the second Friday since he started school. He had not gotten into any routine of what he would do on Fridays. But, he began thinking about it this Friday morning. He had an appointment with Barbara Chaffee at 1:30pm today but, he did not have anything else to do. After taking a shower and mulling around his room, he decided that he would use Fridays to get most of his studying done. Tina was out every day looking for a job and he had not even suggested their getting together on the weekdays unless it was a holiday. He realized that too much togetherness could get in the way of what each of them was trying to do; that sufficient space and time from one another was good. He had learned that lesson over time from his previous affairs.

After dressing, Jack went out to the Village Restaurant on Montrose where he went for most of his meals, He had his usual egg breakfast and stayed for a while reading his newspaper. He went back to the Y and gathered up his book bag and headed for The Center at almost 11am. He decided to look over the handout that Barbara Chaffee gave him to figure out what campus jobs he may want to work. He would do it when he got to The Center before he did some studying and before his appointment.

When he arrived at The Center, he immediately ran into Lupe in the hallway. "Hey, Jack…how are you?" she greeted. "I'm cool…how you doin'?" Jack responded. "Hey…I'm seein' my counselor today to find out about a part-time job…you got any suggestions 'cause…you know…I'm new to all this" Jack said. "Well…all I can say is that you might have trouble finding anything here at The Center…most everything is taken…all of the daycare slots under me are taken, too…you might do better going on campus to the student employment office and finding an off-campus job…those jobs usually pay more than the work-study, on-campus jobs" Lupe advised. "Okay, Lupe…that's right on…I'll ask my counselor about it" Jack said. "You got classes today?…if you don't, come on by the daycare" Lupe said. "I'm not for sure if I will…I got some studyin' to do today" Jack replied. "Okay, then…I'll see you when I see you…I have my class a little later and then the daycare…bye" Lupe said before she headed in the opposite direction down the hall and Jack went to the student lounge. After taking some time to go over the handout and checking off the work-study jobs he was interested in, he studied in the student lounge for about an hour as a few students came and went. Others studied, lounged or had their lunches at the tables in the back.

"Hey, man…you tryin' to become Einstein overnight, huh?'" a voice near Jack spoke out. Jack knew immediately that it was his new friend, Billy. "You ain't playin' around…are you?" Billy continued in his characteristically upbeat manner as he took a seat near Jack. "Hey, Billy …how ya' doin' my man?" Jack greeted with a smile. "I'm straight, bro…what's new?" Billy said. "Nothin…just tryin' to keep up with my classes and I have to see my counselor this afternoon about gettin' a part-time gig somewhere" Jack said. "Yea…that's cool" Billy replied. "Hey, Billy …you got a part-time job…don't you?" Jack asked. "Yea, man…as a matter-of-fact, I got myself an off-campus job through the Student Employment office…I got lucky and got a job at this supermarket on Addison about nine months ago…at first, I was just cleanin' up and helpin' out…they liked the way I was workin' and the jokes I was crackin' so well until they wanna' give me an apprenticeship so I can get into the butcher's union one day…I started learnin' how to cut meat and they gave me a raise a few months ago…helped me out a lot" Billy said. "Go to the student employment office on-campus, Jack…you might luck up and find somethin' that might pay a little somethin' Billy added. "Thanks, Billy…I think I will do that…that's pretty much what Lupe told me" Jack said.

"Oh..you been talkin' to *her*, Huh?…she say anything to you about me?" Billy asked. "Naw…why?" Jack asked. "Hey…don't say nothin' to her but, dig this, man…she was mad at me about that little incident because she's all frustrated 'cause she cain't find no boyfriend…she was hopin' I was makin' a move on her that time when we was supposed to get together…and no…it was not a date…Jack…you see she's real big and everything…she all pent up with emotion 'cause she ain't got nobody and she took her frustrations out on me…she knows she cain't hardly get nobody because she's so big…if she would just start doin' somethin' to lose some of that weight…I'm sure she would have guys checkin' her out 'cause she has a pretty face, she's real neat and dresses real good…she's nice…very feminine…just overweight…that's all…still…she's cool with me…so just be careful dealin' with her, man…she tends to be a little sensitive…stay off the subject of weight when you talk to her…dig" Billy explained. "Yea…I know where you're comin' from…you know damned well I ain't gonna' say nothin' about weight…I wouldn't front her off like that, anyway" Jack said. "Just look out, man…she might try to make a move on you" Billy warned. "Oh, no….I already told her I got a girlfriend" Jack responded. "Shiiittt…that don't mean nothin' my man…cain't you see she's havin' a drought…she needs it no matter who it's comin' from…hooked-up…not hooked up, married, not married…dig what I'm sayin'?" Billy said with a broad grin. "I know…I can deal with that…she will always know that we are just friends…I ain't lookin' for nothin'" Jack said. "Just watch ya' self is all I'm sayin'…you'll be spendin' time with her one day and next thing you know…she done tore you off for your stuff..dig..hahahaha" Billy laughed and joked. "Then..when I see you hangin' out with her a little too tough…I'll know what's goin' on….Billy said with a chuckle. "Go 'head on with that bullshit…I ain't even that type o' stud…cain't nobody hook me up that easy" Jack said with a broad smile as he took Billy's barbs good-naturedly. This conversation with the teasing, laughing and joking seemed to advance the friendship between Jack and Billy; making them more familiar and comfortable with one another. Their similarities seemed to have made them instant friends. They talked a while longer before Jack went to see his counselor, Barbara Chaffee.

They had a good session where she helped him outline a strategy to get a part-time job. She went over the choices he made on the handout she had given him and she said she would take time to review all of the work-study jobs he checked off to see if any of them were available. She set another appointment for him to return a week from today so that she could give him the results of her efforts to place him into an on-campus work-study job. Jack was feeling enthusiastic about the prospect of finding some part-time work that he could do; the idea of having something to do; somewhere to go each day was appealing to him. He could sense a healing was taking place. For too long he had experienced the monotonous hum-drum of day-to-day idleness; the aimless drifting; the stifling of an empty existence. It was almost 2:30pm and Jack went back to the student lounge to study more. He remained another hour-and-a-half reading his text books.

Finally, he left. It was almost 4pm and that meant that there was a vast amount of time, at least four hours before he would be calling Tina tonight. That curious void rose within him again; that vague feeling of aloneness. There seemed to be a tinge of a dark feeling that accompanied it. It seemed to guide him to the poolroom where he had unconsciously decided to go at this time. There was no where else he knew to go; nothing else he could think to do. He was at The Center for as long as he felt like being there. He began to yearn for some human interaction. After leaving The Center, he walked over to Broadway and turned right and began walking north. He walked past the Salvation Army Center at the corner of Sunnyside and Broadway; then, the Harris Bank on the same side of the street. He arrived at the main intersection of Broadway and Wilson that was a pulsating hub of pedestrian and vehicle traffic where the elevated Wilson train stop was. He walked on past the Walgreens store on the corner. As he walked along, he saw various street characters that he would see every day traipsing and mingling here and there; spread about up and down the strip of Broadway stores. He passed the Woolworth store and across the street, he saw some street people lingering in front of the L station entrance; perhaps, panhandling for a drink; he saw a band of Indian street people that he usually saw; three men who always drank together. They were drunk and raising some sort of ruckus amongst themselves on the other side of the street in front of the big picture window of the restaurant that was next to the L station entrance. He continued on past the Brothers clothing store; a couple of shoe stores; the pizza shop; the Military Supply store and then the Jupiter store that sold underwear, school supplies, towels, household and other useful items. This was where Jack had done quite a bit of stealing. Whenever he came upon the store, his mind would compulsively go into a calculation of how he would plan to steal something and this moment was no different. Jack knew that it would take a while before he could break his old habits and he walked on past it. This was the setting in which Jack would normally be a player from day-to-day; just another wretched soul engaging in the same aimless folly that these characters were. But, he had made a monumental change in his life in just a short time. He wanted to keep things the way they were because he had not felt such validity in quite some time. He now had direction and he wanted to stay the course.

As he walked along, Jack could feel those same old urges gnawing at his insides; why couldn't he just go and get a drink and forget it all?---go crazy like the feeling inside of him wanted to do. But, the bit of sanity he was trying to cling to was helping him to fight the feeling; trying to forge a partition in his mind between the constant madness that had become so much a part of him and the new, civilized, sane person he was discovering. He walked on to the corner of Leland and Broadway and he looked across the street at the Boozery bar where he had bought many a drink and where he had his fight with Dinky. As he crossed Leland and passed the Majestic men's clothing store on the corner, he looked across the street at the huge Goldblatts store that stretched the entire block on Broadway between Leland and North Clifton Street where quite a bit of his stealing took place, as well.

He continued on past the Uptown National Bank and crossed Lawrence Avenue from the south to the north side of it where the Delmar restaurant stood on the corner. He turned right and headed east to pass the Saxony Liquor store; his favorite store where he bought most of his drinks. He walked on and passed the Aragon Ballroom with it's gigantic marquee looming overhead with the latest posting of an upcoming rock concert.

As he walked along the long picture window of the poolroom, he peered in to see what activity there was and to catch a glimpse of who was inside. He saw Melvin and Andrew. He also saw his friends Skip and Coley. When Jack saw Melvin and Andrew, he began to feel a little apprehension because he knew they were always trying to get high. In the recent past, when he was still drinking and carousing, he had thought nothing of taking part in the risky schemes they would plot together. But, now he was still battling his demons and he knew in a short time that he would have to fend off their overtures to engage him. Jack swung the entrance door open and stepped inside the poolroom, "Jack…what's goin' on?" Coley greeted. "Hey…Coley" Jack replied. "The smooth operator himself…what's poppin' brotha'?" Skip said in his usual colorful manner. "Hey Skip…how you doin' man?" Jack greeted with a broad smile. Jack was genuinely happy to see his friends. Whenever he was around them, there was a lifting of his spirit that seemed to occur and whatever problems that were on his mind seemed to magically vanish.

"Brotha', Jack…my ace-boon-coon…hey, man" Melvin said with a broad grin as he and Jack shared a soul handshake. "Hey, Jack" Andrew greeted. Andrew was more an acquaintance to Jack and they were not as close as he and Melvin and certainly not as close as he was to Coley or Skip. Andrew was a tall, wiry man; not quite as tall as Jack; perhaps, barely six-feet. He was a family man with a wife and two kids. He was also as much of a fiend as Melvin. Their Vietnam experience had made them brethren of the same sort. They seemed to share the same mentality when it came to the pursuit of getting high. In his acquaintance with them over the years, Jack had become much closer to Melvin than Andrew. Andrew was a bit more standoffish and private than Melvin. Andrew had a reputation for being brazen in the kind of hustling he would do. He liked to rob people and he worked alone. Jack did not like robbing people; it was not his kind of hustle; and it was perhaps, part of the reason he was not so close with Andrew. Melvin was put off by Andrew's hustling style but, he did not mind doing the kind of rough-hustling that Jack liked to do; and so, they began to hustle together a couple of years ago. It had come to be expected that whenever they met up, they would venture off into one hustling escapade or another. Time-after-time in the past, they had joined up to make something out of nothing; creating a hustle almost out of thin air. They would sometimes amaze themselves at how resourceful their dope-fiend instincts had made them. Melvin seemed to always find Jack hanging around The Corner. Melvin had a wife and two kids; five and six year-olds. He held jobs for short stints of time. His long periods of unemployment and his meager contributions to the household were an on-going point of contention for he and his wife, Diane. Her good job at the phone company that she had held steadily since graduating high school and her determination were what held the family together. "What's to ya', Road Dog….hey 'Drew" Jack greeted the two. Jack knew what to expect from these two and he braced himself for the conversation that was about to ensue.

"What you been up to, Jack?" Melvin asked. "I ain't raisin no hell, man…same old thang goin' on" Jack replied. "What's been goin' on with you?" Jack asked. "I'm workin' a temp job right now…makin' a little money…ain't much but, it will pay some bills" Melvin said in a dispirited tone. "Hey, check this out, Jack" Melvin said as he stepped away from the others while they were talking amongst themselves. Jack followed Melvin as he continued to step away. "Yea…what's happ'nin?" Jack asked. "Hey…I got a little money…you wanna go in on a bump?" Melvin almost whispered. "I'm popped, Road Dog…I ain't holdin' nothin'…besides…I got to get up early tomorrow to see if I can get this job in Lincolnwood…all I have is a couple of bus tokens at my place at the Y" to get there tomorrow" Jack lied. "You wanna' try to make a hustle somewhere so we can get high?" Melvin asked with a hint of pleading in his voice. "Look, Melvin…I got to be cool tonight…if I start gettin' high…I ain't gonna' make my appointment tomorrow…I'm tryin' to keep my little spot at the Y" Jack explained. "Come on, Jack…a little bump ain't gonna hurt you" Melvin said with the pleading becoming a little more pronounced. "I know if I get a bump…I'm gonna start drinkin' after that..I don't wanna wake up with no hangover 'cause I know I ain't gonna make it to that job appointment…so, I got to be cool for tonight" Jack said with more conviction. "Damn, Jack…I'm gonna have to get high by myself, huh?" Melvin said, finally relenting.

After that, Melvin went over to Andrew and began to say something to him. They stepped several yards away and it appeared to be a private conversation of the same kind that he just had with Jack. Jack began talking with Coley and Skip and they carried on their usual kind of banter. After about twenty minutes, Skip said "Anybody wanna get up on a taste?…I got some chump" "I ain't holdin' nothin' Skip…I got to get goin' anyway…got a job interview tomorrow" Jack lied, staying consistant with what he had said to Melvin earlier. "Jack ain't drinkin'?….you ain't tryin' to be one o' them…what they call it…teetotalers are you?…hahaha" Skip quipped. "Naw, Skip…just got some business to handle tomorrow…Coley…I'll holla' at you, man" Jack said to Coley standing a few yards away, puffing on a cigarette. "Okay, Jack…see you later, brotha'" Coley replied. Jack walked out of the pool room.

As he walked toward home, Jack could not help but have the ambiguous feelings of wanting to keep company with the only friends he knew. But, not being able to hang around them because he was trying to change his life. He was realizing that it was difficult trying to fend them off from engaging him in the same useless routine that he had in the past; trying to break those destructive habits. It was fortunate that he had Tina and she was nothing like his friends. She had become his anchor. He seemed to have increased strength, endurance and faith because of her. He seemed to be able to persevere as long as he had her encouraging devotion. Otherwise, Jack did not know how long he could resist his friends urging him to partake in the same craziness that had stagnated his life. But, as he walked home, he was devising his strategy. He would make his visits to The Corner and the poolroom fewer and further in-between. He would begin to immerse himself in his student life. He would make more friends in school with those more civilized people. He realized that his friends did not quite understand what was in his mind and what was in his heart. What Jack was trying to do was a rebuke to everything his friends were about. It seemed to Jack that those friends had already accepted their lives as they were. They seemed to have no other aspirations; no hope; no intentions of changing their existence. But, Jack knew that he was different. He was passionate and determined about changing. He had a vision for himself of a more wholesome, sane and happy life. He knew that he did not want to live the street life; even though the life had almost saturated his soul; he did not want to go on; he did not want to continue into that wretched darkness of despair and hopelessness that he could see had drained the spirits of so many around him.

In the past, he had worked at jobs and he was striving toward that ideal life that he had envisioned. But, several times along the way, unwise choices had sabotaged him; and each time he had picked himself up to start again. Jack understood that this was one of those times he was once again picking himself up. He was also beginning to see that the peaks were getting higher to reach but, the valleys were getting dangerously deeper, as well; and so, now was the time to redouble his efforts to save himself.

As Jack strolled through the dark, chilly winter evening, his thoughts turned to Tina. There seemed to always be a feeling of comfort that came with thinking of her. Jack arrived at home and he felt grateful for the cozy warmth of his one-room place at the Y. He tinkered around his room for a while before he went down stairs and watched the community TV with a smattering of residents. He could watch TV in his room. But, sometimes he just felt like sitting around the community area and observing the other residents and how they behaved as he watched TV; even though he did not converse with any of them, it seemed to alleviate some of the aloneness he was feeling at times. He sat there for about half-an-hour before he saw the clock in the community area reading 6:30pm. It was his usual routine to have eaten dinner by the time he spoke to Tina. So, he went back upstairs to his room to get his coat and take his usual trip to the Village restaurant to get his dinner. He had his dinner at the restaurant that closed at 8pm each night. It was shortly after 7pm when he finished and returned to his room.

He took off his coat and went back out to the bank of phones in the second floor hall to call Tina. "Hey, Jack, honey…how are you?" Tina's cheerful voice spoke after Jack greeted her on the phone. "Ready for the weekend?" Jack asked. "I was ready on

Monday" Tina quipped. "Yea…I know you said you've been kind of tired…I'll see if we can just relax when we go out this weekend…how does that sound, baby?" Jack said. "I appreciate that, Jack…you're sweet" Tina said. "You decide on which Jazz club we will be going to?" she added. "Well…you know for sure it won't be the Green Mill….there's a Jazz club called the Happy Medium on Rush Street…it's supposed to be pretty nice from what I've heard…I haven't checked out the show schedule yet but, I will check on it and find out about some other clubs around town, too…alright?" "Yea, honey…cool" Tina replied. The two talked a while longer and planned to meet at 7:30pm on Saturday at the Lawrence L stop, as they usually did. Jack and Tina had decided to dress nice-casual for their weekend Jazz show. Jack called the Happy Medium to find out about the show schedule. He decided they would go to see the Marvin Harris Quintet jazz group there at the 8:30pm show. Jack had begun to think about the immediate future and how things between he and Tina might change.

Because his head had become clearer recently with his not drinking, he was beginning to have some forward thinking. He tried to imagine what changes might occur in the near future when Tina would get a full-time job and when he would be more involved with school, homework and a part-time job. But, he cut that thinking short because it was leading into thoughts that he did not want to entertain. Jack had begun to notice that being sober had it's little drawbacks; like having little worries and fears; his excessive drinking over the last couple of years had spared him from such annoyances. But, now he found a little bit of worry creeping into his conscience. He hated worry; despised it; it was perhaps, a big part of why he drank; "this is what happens when you start givin' a damn" he thought. Still, he was barely noticing these subtle changes. He was far too hardened for them to have much effect.

It was a chilly, overcast Saturday afternoon. The steam heat made a light whistling noise from the radiator. It was nice and warm inside as Jack rummaged around his room, preparing the clothes he would wear for his outing with Tina tonight. Jack was feeling the usual excitement as he sang the Temptations song "My Girl" to himself as he moved about. It was 6:15pm and he had just finished his shower. He had never been to any places on Rush

Street; at least not as a patron. In the past, any such adventures into that part of town had been for hustling only. But, now he felt a certain esteem from going there as a patron for a good time. This was true for all of his outings of this kind with Tina. Somehow, these experiences were helping Jack to regard himself as less of the street person he had been and more as someone who was civilized and respectable. This was part of why he liked these ventures so much. He could escape from that wretched sense of worthlessness that he carried around with him on the streets when he was living so recklessly. He could relax and forget about his cares. He felt very happy being out with Tina. He finished dressing and he admired himself in the mirror. He dabbed on some very nice cologne and put on his good overcoat.

He walked out of the Y very close to 7pm and walked through the dark, chilly evening all the way to the Lawrence L station. He arrived a little early. He went up to the platform and stood waiting in the cold. He peered north along the train tracks into the distance to see if a train was coming---nothing. Several more minutes passed and he began to see train lights in the distance. When the train finally reached the station, Jack stood back to allow riders to exit and to get a better view as he looked for Tina. She did not appear. He looked at his watch. It was just a couple of minutes past 7:30pm. He expected that she would be on the next one and he waited. Another train appeared and when it stopped, he did not see Tina right away but, she grabbed him after hiding behind another rider exiting the train. “Hey, handsome” she said sweetly. “You just love to catch me off-guard, don’t you?” Jack said with a broad smile as he grabbed her and gathered her in for a big hug. “I just like to play…my favorite game when I was a kid was hide-and-go- seek” Tina chuckled. “You’re still a big ol’ kid…now, you’re just playin’ hide the weenie” Jack said as he laughed out loud at the quip. Tina giggled and they began to walk slowly together arm-in-arm, meandering around the platform; talking for several minutes before the next train arrived.

They boarded. They rode to Chicago Avenue and got off. They walked east one block to Rush Street and turned north to walk a few blocks to the Happy Medium club. When they arrived, Jack was impressed. It was different from any other place he had been. There was a regal atmosphere about the place and a small crowd of people were lining up to go in. They walked up to the entrance and entered along with the modest crowd. They arrived at the admissions area and Jack paid. As they walked in, Jack saw mostly older people. They appeared to range in age from thirties to sixties. There was a fragrance of sophistication in the air that seemed intoxicating to Jack. It reminded him of the Mystic Lounge that he had visited with Coley; except that this was a larger venue in one of the city's best entertainment districts. The crowd of patrons surrounding Jack and Tina seemed calm and congenial as they walked in near the main staging area where seating tables were spread all around.

"Jack…this is perfect…just what I had in mind, honey" Tina said with a tone of both relief and excitement after they were seated. "Yea…pretty nice, huh?" Jack responded with a broad smile as they both gazed all around at the accoutrements of the main room. There was a kitchen entrance and bar area on the opposite side of the room from where they entered. They sat for twenty minutes or so as more people filed into the large room and were seated. A waitress came and asked if they wanted to order from the menu. "Jack…I am going to have a drink…is that okay?…I know you haven't been drinking…but, I would like to have one" Tina said. "Baby….don't worry about it…it don't bother me…drink if you want to…I want you to have a good time…if I decide to drink anything…it probably won't be anything but a beer…I'm cool…don't worry about me" Jack said with conviction. "Okay, honey…I'm just concerned about you…that's all" Tina said with sincerity. "I know, baby…it's cool" Jack assured. With that, Tina ordered herself a gin and tonic and they ordered food.

It was about half-an-hour before the Marvin Harris Quintet appeared on the stage and began their warm-ups. There was a polite, low-key murmur of conversation in the room from the patrons. Jack and Tina were seated only a few feet from the next table where an older black-and- white couple sat; perhaps, in their fifties, Jack surmised. The man was black and the woman was white. They were impeccably well-dressed and groomed. The man turned and looked at Jack and spoke. "This Marvin Harris Quintet is one of my favorites…I have followed them for a long time…I have most of their albums…you and your wife are in for a real treat, young man" he said with the knowing smile of a seasoned fan. "They're pretty good…huh?" Jack responded. "Oooh..yeeesss" the older gentleman responded with an accompanying facial expression for emphasis. “This is our first time here at this place and our first time seeing them…but, we’re not married…not yet, anyway” Jack said in the tone of polite civility that he could muster on demand. The older man leaned over and spoke softer. “Listen…she seems like someone who could make you very happy…hang onto her” and he sat back upright in his chair and smiled that knowing smile and gave Jack a little wink. Jack just kind of stared at the older gentleman momentarily and he felt as though he had been touched by something mystical. Jack had a look of awe fixed on his face and a faint smile that wanted to burst forth into laughter. The entire exchange seemed to lift him in a way that he could not quite understand. Tina was quietly gazing around and did not see when Jack spoke to the older gentleman. She turned her head back around to find Jack with an amused smile on his face. “What, honey?…what’s going on?” she asked. “That old-time player over there…he was tellin’ me that you seemed like a good woman…you know…in so many words” Jack said with a little mirthful giggle. “So what’s so funny about *that*?” Tina asked with a note of wonderment. “Hahahaha….I don’t know..hahaha…he was just a funny dude…aaaahhh…I’m just feelin’ goofy right now…don’t mind me…hahaha” Jack went on with his private little amusement. Jack did not know what it was about the older gentleman or what he said that set him off into such a giddy mood----but, it was a good omen, of sorts because it seemed to set his mood for the night. “You’re not cracking up are you, Loverboy?” Tina asked teasingly. “No, that’s not it…I cracked up a long time ago…can’t crack no more” Jack said playfully, even though the statement may have had a bit of truth to it.

Their food came a little later and they were just finishing their meals when the Master of Ceremonies appeared on the stage to introduce the show. Afterward, the lights dimmed and the show began. The audience was very quiet as the band played several numbers. The show went on for about an hour before the band stopped and left the stage. The lights came back on. The MC returned and announced a half-hour intermission.

“Jack…you know, I’ve been thinking about how much we are going to be able to see each other from now on” Tina said, only a moment after the lights came back on. “Yea, baby…what about it?" Jack replied non-chalantly. "Well…I just want us to be together as much as possible…I don't know how much time we are going to have for each other after I find a full-time job and you find part-time work along with your classes" Tina said with a hint of worry in her voice. "Aw…don't worry about it, baby…let's just take things as they come…I don't like to look into the future and get worried or afraid about it…I like to stay loose and deal with things when they come up" Jack responded. "Well…things are going to change in some ways between us…I just want to be ready…that's all" Tina said. "Look, baby…I love you…right?" Jack said. "Yes" Tina replied. "And you love me…right?" Jack said. "Yes" Tina answered, again. "Then…as long as we care about each other…we will get through this…right?" "Yes, honey…you are right" Tina replied with a sorrowful expression before she leaned over to Jack and pressed her cheek up to his and they had a sitting-down hug. "Now…let's not worry about anything right now except havin' a good time…alright?" Jack said with a note of encouragement to Tina as he put his arm around her shoulder and gave her an affectionate squeeze.

"So...this is what you said you wanted, right, baby?…laid-back---is it laid-back enough for you?" Jack asked with a bit of the playful rhythm in his voice that urged Tina to come back in tune with the playfulness they always shared. "It's laid back like I wanted…thanks for everything, honey?" Tina replied with a bit more enthusiasm and a warm smile. The show started again and lasted another hour before it was over. Jack and Tina were strolling back to the subway station on Chicago Avenue. "You have a good time, baby?" Jack asked Tina. "I sure did…it was very relaxing" Tina replied as they strolled slowly arm-in-arm.

As they were walking south on Rush Street and were about a block away from Chicago Avenue, a group of revelers, a couple of young men and a couple of women walked past Jack and Tina strolling. The men were holding open bottles of beer. They were talking loud and whooping it up. As they passed Tina and Jack, one of the men stumbled and brushed hard up against Tina's right side while Jack was on her left. "Whooaaa!" Tina let out as the swipe pushed her over into Jack. Jack immediately became angry. "Wait right here, baby" he said and he took off after the drunken revelers. "Jack..Jack…don't bother about it!" Tina yelled as Jack rushed ahead into a trot to catch up to the group.

"Hey, man..my man" Jack said as he approached the group and they stopped and turned to face him. "Yea, dude…can I help you?" the one who had brushed up against Tina asked. "Ahh..yea..my, man…you can do somethin' for me..you know…you know what that is?" Jack said as he paused and bit his lower lip with anger. "So…what's the problem, man?" the reveler asked, slurring his speech. "Watch where the fuck you're goin'!!!" Jack yelled before he leaped forward and pushed the man so hard, he fell backward violently to the ground and the beer bottle flew from his hand and rolled wildly along the sidewalk. "You understand that mothefuckin' shit, punk!..you understand!!" Jack yelled as the anger grew like a rising tide inside. "Hey, man…what are you doing?" the other man in the group asked in a tone of alarm. "Shut-the-fuck-up!...you want some o' this!" Jack said angrily as he pressed his chest and face into the man's. "Hey, dude..…we're not looking for trouble" the man said meekly as the two women stood by silently watching the development "Well, then…tell your drunk-ass buddy to watch where the fuck he is walkin'…other people are on the streets, too…he almost knocked my girl down a minute ago and didn't say a damned word…just kept goin' with his stupid ass…I'll beat his fuckin' ass!…you understand?" Jack said very angrily. "You understand!!" Jack yelled out louder when the man did not respond. "Okay…we're sorry…he's sorry…he didn't mean to do it…it was an accident…sorry" the man pleaded while his friend still laid on his back on the sidewalk. "Alright, then…watch ya' fuckin' self!" Jack said before he walked away from the group and back the several yards to where Tina stood.

"Sorry about that, baby…I couldn't help it…I just hate stupid, rude motherfuckers…sorry" Jack said apologetically. "Jack…it was no big deal…really…I wasn't hurt or anything…he just brushed up against me" Tina said. "He brushed up against you mighty hard and didn't say "excuse me…that's what got to me" Jack said. "Maybe I overreacted but…it's just how I am …and besides…I guess I just always expect the worse from people and I react that way" Jack said with a hint of remorse. "I shouldn't be behavin' that way, either…it might put you in danger…I wasn't thinkin'" Jack said. "I agree, Jack…you started acting like a mad man over a very small thing…that's what I was going to say to you but…you beat me to it…you promise not to go berserk next time?" Tina admonished Jack in her usual manner. "Yea…I promise" Jack replied contritely. "But…you have to understand…my life is not easy like theirs…they probably got money…a nice place to stay…all of that…they can afford to be easy-goin'…my life is all the way different…I cain't come home to a nice house and pet the dog and ask what's for dinner and kick my heels up…life is a constant battle…you cain't expect for me to go around grinnin' all day…that ain't me" Jack said with a bit of angst. "Don't worry about it, Loverboy…when we get back to my place…I'm gonna see if I can do something to calm down that beast in you" Tina hinted with a warm smile.

"Yes, indeed, baby…you know just what to do, too…don't you?" Jack said as he smiled back at Tina and they continued walking to the subway arm-in-arm. It was around 11:15pm when they boarded the L train at Chicago Avenue to head to the end of the line for the Evanston train. It was shortly past midnight when they entered Tina's apartment. They prepared for bed. They stayed up talking for about half-an-hour before they both fell asleep. They awoke around dawn and had their usual lovemaking session before falling asleep again.

It was Sunday morning and Tina awakened first, as usual. She spread open the bedroom curtains as she always did to see a partly sunny day outside. "Wake up, sleepy-head" she spoke out while Jack still laid in the bed fast asleep. When Jack did not respond, Tina went over and started playing with him. She played with his nose and he stirred and moaned. She squeezed his cheeks to make his lips poke out. He stirred again and rolled away from her. Finally, she smacked him very hard on his butt and his upper body popped up and his eyes sprang open with a look of grogginess. "Hey…over here, Mr. Sleepy-head…yoo-hoo…hahaha" Tina chuckled, laughing at the disoriented expression on Jack's face. Jack was still groggy and looking all around to get his bearings and allowing his head to clear. Tina sat on the edge of the bed, still giggling at him. "Hey…what's happ'nin'?…what time is it?" he asked. "You always ask what time it is when you wake up…it's about 9:40, honey" Tina replied. They both showered and got dressed. "I'm gonna make breakfast this morning, Jack…I went out grocery shopping Thursday…got some good stuff" Tina said. "That's cool, baby…what you got?" Jack asked. "I have eggs, of course; Jelly; I know you like wheat toast so, I have wheat bread…I have orange juice, milk, oatmeal and pancakes if you want that…what do you want, honey?" Tina asked. "Uhhhh…three eggs…scrambled soft and the wheat toast" Jack replied. "Okay…I'll get started" Tina said. Tina finished preparing and they started breakfast and Jack gave Tina a kiss on the cheek and said "Thanks, baby…'preciate it" as they sat at her kitchen table eating.

"Jack…so how does it look for you getting a part-time job at school?" Tina asked. "I don't know…I have an appointment with my counselor this comin' Thursday…I'll know more about it then" Jack replied. "What about you?…how's your search comin' along?" Jack asked. "Nothing, yet…I've given out my resume to quite a few places…filled out a ton of applications, it seems, at schools…I have been on about a half-dozen interviews…nothing, so far…it's hard to get started when you are a new teacher…my mom and dad are looking out for me…they know a lot of people in the education field but, all the people they know are in Evanston and I told them that I didn't want to work in Evanston…I'm sick of being around this town…I need a change…I want to work somewhere else" Tina said. "So where do you want to work?" Jack asked. "I don't mind working near Evanston…somewhere like the north suburbs, like Northbrook, Skokie, Schaumburg…and I would love to work in Chicago, too" Tina said. "Anyway…my folks will be glad when I get something because they are paying my rent here and when I get a job, I will start paying it myself" Tina said. "Damn…your folks got money, huh?" Jack said. "They're not rich, of course but, they have been working about twenty-five years as teachers…you've got to be able to put a little something away in all that time" Tina explained. "Yea..I guess you're right?" Jack said.

After breakfast, the two went out for a long walk that lasted about half an hour. Tina was showing Jack around downtown Evanston where they had never gone and other places of interest. They stopped at a coffee shop to get out of the cold and warm up. They had coffee and stayed a little while before they left and came back home. The two spent the rest of this lazy Sunday relaxing and watching television.

Morning came and it was Jack's routine to get up early and leave to go home on Monday mornings after a weekend at Tina's place. The two never had breakfast on these Monday mornings when they had a busy day ahead. Tina got up early, as well because, since she had finished school, she would get the Sunday newspaper and peruse it for job opportunities on the weekends; making a list of the ones she would contact on Monday morning. She would call them at the earliest business hour she could so that she could, hopefully, get an interview. "I'm gonna get goin' baby…I'm gonna take a little nap soon as I get home then, get ready for my afternoon classes" Jack said as he stood in the doorway of Tina's apartment with her standing just inside. "Okay, honey…have a good day at school…call me, alright?" Tina said. "Okay…see ya'" Jack replied before they kissed and he took off.

As Jack walked toward the Evanston L train station, he could not help but think about the matter Tina brought up about things changing for their get-togethers in the near future. He did not like looking into the future just as he had told her. But, he could not help but let thoughts of it linger in the back of his mind. He did not want to dwell on it or examine it and consider the possibilities of how things would change. When he began to sense that same feeling of worry creeping into his conscience, he dismissed all thoughts of the matter from his mind. Nonetheless, he still had to prepare for how he would handle attending his classes, studying and working a part-time job. He knew that he would have to manage all of this and still have time for his sweetheart. But, he had to take his own advice that he had given to Tina at the Jazz club --- "take things as they come…don't worry about them ahead of time" Jack arrived at the Wilson L station. He got off and walked through the cold, overcast weather to get home. When he got home, he undressed and laid in his bed and napped. He arose at shortly past noon.

He began to get ready for school. He left early so that he could have lunch at Jake's restaurant next door to The Center. He left the Y and walked briskly through the freezing temperature. He crossed Broadway and turned south and passed the Harris Bank with it's sign that read "°19 at 1:07pm" In just a few more minutes, he was at Jake's where there already was fast-paced serving of the customers. The warmth inside began to thaw him and the smell of lunch food was stimulating. Jack ordered food and took his time eating. Afterward, he arrived at the student lounge with plenty of time left before his Man and His Physical Environment class that began at 1:50pm. "Hello, Jack" Marvin greeted as Jack stepped inside the student lounge that was buzzing with several groups of congregating students spread around the room. “Marvin…how ya’ doin’ my man?…what’s goin’ on?” Jack greeted. “Nothing…getting ready to go to my afternoon classes” Marvin replied. “Yea…me, too…what do you think of the classes and this Center, so far?” Jack asked. “Uh…pretty good…I like the counselors…that Linda…she’s smoking…too bad she’s engaged…and the directors, Sam and Glen…they are real cool…I like it here” Marvin replied. “Yea…I’m gettin’ the same impression…I think it’s gonna be alright, my friend…yes, indeed…alright” Jack said. They continued to engage in small-talk until it was time for their classes.

There was a long lecture given by the professor in Jack’s first class, Man & His Physical Environment. There was a good amount of homework given out, as well. After the first class, Jack went to his second class, Intro to Uptown. It was a very involved and detailed session and Jack had to take lots of notes. The day was busier than last week but, it went well and Jack decided not to stop at the poolroom after school. He headed straight home; sticking to his plan to make his visits there fewer and further in-between. Besides, he had plenty of homework to keep him busy. Jack seemed to hit it off well with his fellow students Willie, Lupe and Marvin, too. This was all starting off very well, he thought. He felt better about having them as his friends in this college environment. It seemed more natural and safer; although, he felt that his relationships with his friends in the streets were genuine.

But, there was a sense foreboding that seemed to surround that street life. There was nothing that Jack could look forward to in that existence; no hope for anything better. He was fully experienced in all of it’s trepidations; completely indoctrinated with all of it’s nuances. The few years he had lived that way had seemed an eternity. Now, he was trying to cleanse himself of the habits, tendencies and neurosis’ that had infected him. He wished that he could have a new past. But, he could not. Before, he had no avenue to climb out of an existence that he seemed to have fallen into precipitously. Now that he had found a way out, he was going to hold on.

Jack went home with all of his books in his book bag. He kept his usual routine of stopping at the Village restaurant to pick up dinner to take home. He liked taking his dinner home to take his time eating it while watching television, rather that eating it at the restaurant. He seemed to enjoy it better that way. When he arrived at his room and changed into his lounging clothes. He turned on the TV and ate his dinner slowly, savoring it until the last bite. He watched TV another half-hour before he opened his book bag and pulled out the textbooks for homework that was due at the next Man & His Physical Environment class and his Intro to Uptown class. He paused and looked at the new books. The scent of their newness wafting faintly to his smell. Here he was engaging in something that would have been completely out of his realm as early as six months ago. He was studying college material. It was all new and for some reason, Jack's mind began to wander. He began to think of his days on the streets; thinking of all the times that he wondered where he was going to get money from; how he was going to get his next meal; where was he going to lay his head down at night; who was looking to harm him; what could he steal and sell to make money; how could he get another drink; when was he going to get busted for stealing; who would he have to fight today. These were a constant stream of thought that played havoc on his psyche and nerves when he was living that way out on the streets. But, drinking had helped him to survive. Jack was grateful that he was now doing something as simple and straightforward as studying. A strange urge suddenly emerged within him that made him want to take the books and press them to his face and inhale the new smell. It was odd, and crazy but, that was the wild urge that flashed through him and was suddenly gone. The strange feeling must have symbolized something, Jack thought but, it was too complex for him to even begin to understand. This was perhaps, a lingering remnant of his madness. Jack studied by reading the required chapters in his Man & His Physical Environment book and studying his notes for his Intro to Uptown class. He studied for an hour-and-a-half before he stopped. That was all he could do for his first real study session. But, he felt real good about it. Afterward, he gave Tina a call and they always seemed to talk a shorter time on Monday evenings because they had just left each other early that morning. The conversation was very low-key and they said their usual affectionate goodnights before hanging up.

It was Tuesday and Jack had to get up earlier today for his morning classes at The Center. He went through his same routine to get prepared then, he was off; arriving at The Center about fifteen minutes before his Expository Writing class. He headed straight for the student lounge, as he usually did. There was the usual smattering of students spread around the lounge area and Jack scanned the room as he always did and he noticed Billy sitting in one of the large sofa chairs that faced away from the entrance.

Immediately, a feeling of cheer spread over him and he walked over to surprise his new friend. "Big-time Billy…what's goin' on, man?" Jack greeted with a broad smile. "Hey…how ya' doin', Einstein?…what's to ya' baby?" Billy greeted in his characteristically gregarious manner. "Everythang cool?" he asked. "Aw…I'm straight…goin' right along, you dig" Jack replied. "Have any luck findin' a part-time gig?" Billy asked. "Nothin' yet…I'm supposed to meet my counselor Thursday…she is lookin' into somethin' on-campus for me" Jack responded. "Good luck, man…things kinda' tight on them campus jobs but, somethin' might jump off for you…you never know…I hope you can get somethin'…I know how tough it is when you just startin' off…I'll look out for you if anything opens up at the supermarket where I'm at…alright?" Billy said. "Yea…thanks, Billy…I 'preciate that, man" Jack said. "Hey…ya' girl ain't tore you off, yet?" Billy asked with a wry grin. "Who?…oohh…Lupe?…you still messin' with me about that?....go 'head on, man" Jack responded with a wide smile. "I done told you, boy…you might have to strap it down…'cause she might get close to you one day and just snatch her some…hahaha…I'm tellin' you…you keep hangin' around her…it's like puttin' food in front of a hungry woman…hahaha" Billy said, trying to suppress his laughter. "Shut up, man…leave me alone…just 'cause I'm a nice fella, tryin' to be cool with everybody don't mean I have to get freaky" Jack said as he playfully punched Billy in the shoulder. The humorous banter seemed to advance their friendship.

Each went his separate way to start the school day after a few more laughs. Jack attended his morning writing class and then his Community Organization class that came immediately at the next period. The day went well and he got more homework from each class. Jack was now beginning to feel the challenge of the college student life. After his last class, he was leaving The Center to go straight home and get a start on his homework when he ran into Lupe in the hall.

"Hello, Jack…how are you?" she greeted pleasantly. "Hey, Lupe" Jack responded. "What are you doing right now?...if you're not doing anything, come on down to the daycare" Lupe offered. "Cain't hang this time, Lupe…too much homework…I'm goin' home to get some studyin' done" Jack said. "Oh..yea?…I can certainly understand that..okay…stop by when you can" Lupe said. "Okay…take it easy" Jack said before he bounded down the long Center stairs leading out to the street. Jack headed home, grabbing some take-out lunch on the way at the Village restaurant.

He arrived at home to begin studying. After eating lunch in his room, he started. He had to read a chapter for his writing class then, read a chapter and do a quiz of multiple questions for his Community Organization class. He could feel the lingering fogginess in his mind that made the studying a bit difficult. He had not done this much concentrating since he had taken evaluation tests for jobs several years ago. But, little-by-little, he could feel himself getting used to it. He finished his homework at almost 5pm and he felt much better about it at the end than he did at the beginning when he seemed to struggle.

He decided to skip dinner and he called Tina at 7pm. But, he did not get an answer. He called her again at about 8:30pm and she answered. She told him that she was out with friends again; that she had a couple of job interviews today and she was feeling excited because she felt encouraged and thought that she might get a job offer from one of the interviews. "Yes, Jack…I really, really hope I can get this job at Andrew Middle school in Skokie….keep your fingers crossed for me, honey…okay?" she went on excitedly. "Yea, baby…that's good news…I'll keep my fingers crossed for you…I hope you can get it" Jack responded with the same excitement in his voice. Jack was happy that Tina was excited and he was feeling the same hope for her that he could hear in her voice. In the time they had been together, sharing all of their hopes and dreams and everything about themselves with one another, Jack had become perfectly in tune with Tina. He could almost see into her soul and he was sure that she could see into his. They had become inseparable over the last several months. He could see that this was the point at which things would begin to change. He was beginning to be immersed in his student life and she was perhaps, about to become employed. But, none of that seemed to matter to him as long as her feelings for him remained the same. She had come to mean everything to him in the short time they had been together. He never dreamed that he could love anyone the way he had come to love her and he had never had anyone to make him feel as significant; as cared for as she did. It had all come about by happenstance; and now that it was here, he had come to cherish it. He could feel her presence with every beat of his heart; she was on his mind much of the time. His connection to her had vanquished his anxieties. He had never felt so at ease as he had been in their time together. He noticed the changes within himself where he wanted to improve; to be a better person. He had never felt such sweet inspiration before. "I'm gonna be out late tomorrow night, too, honey…I'll be with Vickie and Roger and his girlfriend at that same bar again…we're gonna' hang out…I don't know what time I'll be in…you can still call me…okay?" Tina advised. "Well….that's okay, baby…if you are gonna be out late…I'll just wait and call you on Thursday night…how about that?" Jack responded, putting on a brave front, even though he felt a mild twinge of disappointment when she said those words. "Okay…you sure?....it's not a problem, honey?…I could come in earlier…like around eleven if you want to call" Tina offered. ""Naw, baby…go ahead and have a good time…it's alright…I'll talk to you on Thursday" Jack insisted more earnestly this time after he had accepted the situation in his mind. "Okay, honey…love you…goodnight" Tina said.

Jack continued his routine on Wednesday. He had breakfast in the morning at Jake's restaurant. He attended his afternoon classes and got a little more homework to do. He came back home to do more studying and to do more homework for his Tuesday-Thursday classes. Jack's classes were completely underway now, and he was realizing how he had to regiment himself to manage his time for classes, studying and homework. It was all a bit challenging. Linda Chavez had explained to him that in order to maintain his financial aid, the rule was that he had to pass seventy-five percent of his classes each term. Jack understood that this meant passing three of the four classes he would take each term. It was all still a matter of survival and it always seemed to bring out the best in him when things were on those terms.

It was Thursday and Jack was up early for morning classes again. After his usual preparations, he was off to school. Today was the day he needed to meet with Barbara Chaffee to see about an on-campus job, he remembered. He would have lunch at Jake's after class and see his counselor afterwards. At 1:30pm sharp, he was standing in the doorway of Barbara Chaffee's office. "Come on in, Jack…how are you?" Barbara greeted. "Hello, Ms. Chaffee" Jack greeted as he walked up to her desk. "Have a seat…I just need to take a moment here to finish up something I'm working on…then, I can pull your file and see what we have" she said. A couple of minutes passed before she finished with the papers she was working on. She raised from her desk and went into a file in her desk drawer. "Okay, Jack…let's see…" she said as she thumbed through the folder files. "Rollins…okay" she said as she pulled out a lone file folder. Okay, Jack….I see that I called each supervisor and department head where you checked off a job in their departments…hardly anything is available as I suspected…however, there is a reception job at the library where a student will be leaving because of class scheduling conflicts…the student got the job at the start of the semester then, she had to change her class schedule and can't continue in the job…do you think you might be interested?" Barbara asked. "I don't know…what's the duties of the job?…reception…is that like secretary work?" Jack asked. "Yes..pretty much" Barbara answered. "Hmmm…I might…can I think about it?...is it like just sittin' all day in one spot?" Jack asked. "Yes..it is...but, with one stipulation…once you start the job…you will have to keep it for the whole semester…they want you to be sure you can go the whole semester because the job will count toward your financial aid award and it may cause you to lose some money if you stop the job after starting it" Barbara explained. "Well..in that case…I think I'll pass on it so that I can try to get something else…besides…I don't know if I can stand sittin' in one spot that long, anyway" Jack said. "Okay, Jack…that is just fine…now…the next thing that I am going to suggest for you is to go to the Student Employment Office on campus…you can look for off-campus jobs there when you have time…I am going to give you a carfare and a lunch voucher…you should be receiving a financial aid check next week along with all of the other new students…I'll give you enough money on the voucher for several carfares and lunches…that should tide you over until then…okay?" Barbara explained. "Alright, Ms. Chaffee…that's good…thanks" Jack replied. "Here you are, Jack…you can just cash it at Ms. Chavez office….she keeps carfare tokens and lunch credit slips in her office" Barbara said as she handed Jack a slip of paper she had filled out. "Alright…thanks-a-lot" Jack said. "Can you also stop in my office every week at this time, Jack…we can have a short session to discuss your job situation each week until you get something…can you do that?" Barbara asked. "Sure…no problem, Ms. Chaffee" Jack replied before he left. He went to Linda Chavez' office and received a bunch of CTA tokens and several slips of paper that said "Northeastern voucher for" and in a blank space was written "Lunch to $5" Jack took them. "Have you been to the campus yet, Jack?" Linda asked. "No, I haven't" Jack answered. "Well, then…let me give you directions" she started and directed Jack in a couple of ways to get there by CTA bus and train and she explained where to enter the school and how to get to the Student Employment office. "Thanks, Linda…that was a big help…I think I can get there, now" Jack said before he left. Afterward, he decided to have lunch at Jake's and head for home after that. He had enough homework to keep him occupied the entire evening. He stayed in and studied for most of the afternoon. He stopped around 5:30pm to go out and get dinner.

After dinner, he relaxed for a while by watching a little television before he called Tina at almost 8pm. "Hi, Honey…how are you?" her pleasant voice greeted Jack over the phone. "Hey, baby…what's new?" Jack greeted. "Well…I'm gonna tell you…I got the job!!" she said with a high-pitched tone of excitement. "No, kiddin'?….that's great, baby!…I'm glad you got it!…is it that one in Skokie that you wanted?" Jack asked. "Yes it is…we can celebrate this weekend…what do you say, honey?" Tina said. "Hell, yea…we can celebrate…no doubt about it!" Jack said with a smile in his voice. They laughed and giggled over the phone at the momentous occasion. Her first full-time, permanent job out of college. Tina continued to rattle on with excitement about how she planned to work hard and learn as much as she could and how much fun the two of them would have together. Jack felt a sense of relief for her and he was happy that she had found a job and did not have to look anymore. The conversation ended on a very cheery note. Jack had come to know Tina as a generally cheerful person and it seemed to give him a good feeling inside to hear her sound especially happy about her circumstances. Her personality always seemed to glow with a certain kind of warmth. Her happiness was contagious. After he hung up with Tina that night, Jack decided that he would get up early on Friday morning and take the Montrose Street bus to the campus. He had no classes on Fridays so, he planned to go to the Student Employment office to see about a part-time job.

He woke up at 7:30am and showered. He went to the Village on Montrose for breakfast and took the Montrose bus from there west to Kimball. He caught the number 34 Kimball bus from there going north to the campus. He got off at Catalpa just as Linda Chavez had directed him. He went into the main entrance. Inside, he walked around wide-eyed. He had never been on a college campus before. It appeared to be a clean and well-organized place. There was a rush of people walking through the hallways. They appeared to be a mix of students, staff, teachers and other employees of the school. They were a variety of ethnicities and nationalities. Jack could see the intelligence and sense of purpose in their strides. He passed by offices, art work and bulletin boards full of flyers and other information. He asked a passerby about directions to the Student Employment office. The person was very friendly and gave him clear and concise directions. He was liking the campus already. It was all making a positive impression upon him. He made it to the Admissions office that was near the Student Employment office. A worker there directed him to some stairs that went to the basement. Jack walked down the stairs and was greeted at the receptionist desk. “Hello…how can I help you?” the very young woman said. “Hi…I’m a new student from the Uptown Center…I want to apply for off- campus jobs” Jack answered. “Okay…this is your first time here….so, you have to fill out a form for us to keep on file” the young lady said before she handed Jack a clipboard with the form on it. “You can go over there to fill it out” she added, pointing to an area inside the office that was behind her. Jack went on to fill the form out. He gave it back to the receptionist and after he sat waiting for a few minutes, another attractive young woman came out and called his name. “Jack Rollins” she said. “Yes” Jack answered. “You can come with me…how are you?…my name is Deidra Perez” she greeted him pleasantly with a smile. “Hi…nice to meet you” Jack responded. Jack followed her to a cubicle. He sat down. "Okay, Mr. Rollins…do you have your student ID with you?" she asked. "Yes…right here" Jack responded as he went into his wallet and fished it out. "I'll be right back…I'll need to make a photocopy of it" she said before she disappeared in a back room. Jack looked around the office area that had other little offices spread around and a more open area in the middle with booths and a large table in the middle. There were several other people in the office performing various tasks with a couple other students being interviewed. Everything seemed so organized. Jack was getting a feel for the college atmosphere on-campus and he looked around with the same wide-eyed gaze. The young woman returned and she interviewed Jack, asking him what kind of work he was interested in doing. After the short interview, she directed him to the Job Board that was back upstairs and out in the hallway just outside of the Admissions office where he first came in. The interviewer explained to him that the jobs were posted on the board for all students to see and that each job was categorized by type and each had a corresponding number. She also explained that the contact information for those listed jobs were not posted; that this information was kept confidentially in the Student Employment office for the use of enrolled students. She advised him to write down up to three of the posted job numbers on paper and return to see her so that she may contact the employers for each job. Jack did that, perusing the board carefully for fifteen minutes or so before he had three job choices. He returned to the Student Employment office. "Okay, Mr. Rollins…let me know which job you would like for me to call first" Deidra asked. Jack asked her to call one for a part-time transportation assistant at a hospital. She called and they said the job was filled. Jack had her to call for the next job; another part-time job in a warehouse as an order picker; the contact person said that they filled the position a couple of days ago with another person at their company. Finally, she called the last job for a gas station attendant. Deidra spoke with the manager and he said he still needed someone to fill the position; working a couple weekdays part-time in the evenings and Saturdays full-time during the day. Jack had her to arrange for an interview set for Tuesday afternoon at 3pm. Jack felt encouraged that he was going to a job interview on his first visit to the Student Employment office. This was nothing like the State

Employment office. This whole school thing was much more accommodating, he thought.

Afterward, Jack hung around the campus, walking all about to see everything he could. He walked up and down the stairs in the classroom building. He walked over to the campus library that was a separate building about a hundred yards away. He finally went to the lunchroom in the lower section of the main building and used his voucher slip to get lunch. The food was very fresh and good and he enjoyed it. He sensed the relaxed, congenial atmosphere; something he was not used to. It was all that he hoped it would be and he wished that things would continue to go well in the future to allow him to stay in school so that he could one day start classes at this beautiful campus. Since he was very young, he had hoped he could go to college. He felt very fortunate to have it actually happening. Being around the campus gave him a certain pride in being a student. He felt that his life had finally begun to mean something. He didn't want to leave but, he finally went home.

He arrived at his room at the Y close to 2pm. He decided to try to get most of his homework done so that he could have plenty of time on the weekend to be with his sweetheart. He got comfortable in his room and he studied until almost 6pm. Afterward, he went to the Village restaurant for dinner. He came back home and relaxed before calling Tina. "Hey, baby" Jack said when Tina answered the phone. "Hey, Mr. Good-n-Plenty" she answered in a sultry tone. "Hahaha…how you doin' girl?" Jack chuckled, knowing exactly what her reference was. "I'm okay, honey" she responded. "Have a good time last night?" Jack asked. "As usual, my dear…Roger got a little drunk and started debating with me and Vickie over some nonsense last night and Sandra, his girlfriend hustled him out of the bar to get him home 'cause he was getting totally wrecked" Tina explained. "Couldn't hold his liquor, huh?" Jack commented. "Most of the time he does, but, for some reason he got a little goofy last night...Vickie and I hung around for a while after they left…then, we went home" Tina said. "Hey…I have an idea for us to celebrate my new job" she offered. "Yea, baby…come on with it" Jack said. "Well…I was thinking you and I could go on a horse and carriage ride early Saturday evening…they seem so romantic, Jack and I've never been on one…then, we can have dinner after that…I'll spring for the ride…how's that?" Tina offered. "Aw, baby…I don't want you to spend your money before you make any" Jack replied with a bit of concern. "It's okay…I can do it…I have some savings…it's cool" Tina said. "Yea...but, I don't want you spendin' your money like that on me…dig what I mean, baby?…I mean…if we do somethin' like that….let me pay…you want me to pay?…I can.." "No..no, Jack..I will pay….this is what I want to do….I don't want it to cost you…please…just let me do this because I just want to mark the occasion with something I can remember…it's important to me and I know you don't have extra money right now…so, let me do this…okay, honey?" Tina interrupted. "Uhhh…alright…I guess…but, you understand where I'm comin' from, don't you?...I just feel a little odd about it" Jack said with a mild tone of frustration. "Jack…just relax…don't worry about it…do this for me…okay, sweetie?" Tina said as she coaxed Jack with a little purring tone in her voice. ""Okay, baby…I'll do it for you…this is what you want…so..yea...okay" Jack relented. "Goody…we can get a carriage on Pearson street right at Michigan Avenue and I want to start the ride around 8pm…we can go on a half-an-hour ride…so, we will have a late dinner around 9pm…let's meet at the L stop at seven… okay?" Tina suggested. "Yea, baby…that's cool" Jack replied. The two chattered on for quite a while and Tina seemed especially talkative and upbeat. Jack was fully engaged as he usually was; listening to all of the happy talk that was pouring out from her. He realized then just how much happiness was inside of Tina and it seemed to come to her so naturally. She did not seem to have any of the emotional, angry, pent-up feelings that used to be more at the surface for him. He realized, too that she had shown him that he did not have to be that way; that he could be happy if he allowed himself to be. He was learning these little lessons from her almost unconsciously. She had taught him to relax; to smile more and not be so defensive and suspicious. It was one of the many reasons that he adored her.

Saturday was here and soon after Jack awoke, he could sense that feeling of excitement welling up inside. He knew that Tina would be brimming with happiness today when they went on their carriage ride and then dinner to celebrate her new job. Jack also knew that his check would be in the mail today. This would make it extra special because it meant that he did not have to pinch pennies while they were on their outing. He was up at around 9am and he went into his closet to see what he would be wearing to the outing. He mused around; pulling out several garments to decide what combination of them he would wear. He finally decided and hung them together back in the closet. He went into the community shower and showered before he put on some of his every day clothes. Their get-together was not until this evening and he had all day to do other things. Jack had already decided that he needed to get as much studying done as he could this afternoon. After he put his clothes on, he left his room. He went downstairs to the desk clerk and asked for his mail. His check was there just as he expected. He immediately walked over to the currency exchange at Lawrence Avenue and Ashland Avenue. He cashed his check and went to the Village restaurant to eat breakfast. He came back to his room and studied until he couldn't anymore. He finished at shortly past 2pm. He tried to watch television but, he felt too antsy and excited to sit still for very long; and since there was so much time left before his outing, he decided that he would go to the poolroom because he had nothing else to do and nowhere else to go. It was not very difficult to keep himself occupied on the weekdays when he had classes; when he had structure in his day; when he could talk to his new friends and others at the NEIU Uptown Center. But, on the weekends when he had leisure time, he found it difficult to spend so many waking hours alone and not having anyone to talk to. So, he was off. It was a cold but, sunny day and he made sure to put on his long underwear before he took the long walk to the poolroom.

When he arrived, he came upon several of the regulars; Jabo, Larry, Skip and his best friend, Coley. They were all congregating inside the poolroom. When Jack could see them inside as he passed along the outside of the Lawrence avenue poolroom window, he felt the usual sense of relief and uplifting that being around them seemed to bring. He walked in full of cheer; greeting everyone with an extra energy. "Brotha', Jack…you done dropped off the scene for a while…huh?" Jabo asked. "Kind of" Jack responded. "I'm in school,…been goin' for a few weeks now" Jack admitted proudly. "That's cool…that oughta' keep you outa' trouble" Jabo replied. "I hope so, Jabo…you kinda' noticed I been layin' low…huh?" Jack asked. "Yea…I miss you when you ain't around for a while…I miss you comin' to the rescue when I'm out here and I'm either broke or I'm short on a drink…you know yourself that you have come through for me a thousand times and got the shakes off of me…I really appreciate that…ain't but a few will look out for me like that" Jabo said with a tone of gratitude. "Well, Jabo…I don't even think about it…you know if you're cool with me…it's alright…I will look out for you if I got it…especially if we're tight as you and me" Jack explained. "That's sho' 'nough the truth, too" Jabo said before he nudged Jack gently with an elbow and whispered "step on outside…I got somethin'" Jack followed because he knew what Jabo had. Often times, the regulars hid their bottles from the others while they shared with those they preferred. This was usual behavior and everyone did it at one time or another as a measure of survival. When they got outside and stood at the outside wall of the poolroom where there was no window and they could not be seen by the others, Jabo pulled out a pint bottle of vodka. "Go 'head on and hit it real good" he said as he handed the bottle to Jack. Jack took the bottle and halfway turned his back to Jabo before he turned the bottle up to his lips and drank as though he was drinking a fair amount of it. But, he only pretended to. He gulped a couple of short swallows before he grimaced and handed the bottle back. Jack did not really want to drink. But, did not want to disappoint Jabo by turning his offer down when he was trying to show his gratitude. Jabo being a much older man who hardly ever had much extra money and who collected a monthly disability check; and because he was a bit up in age, he did not engage in the energetic kind of hustling that Jack and the other young hustlers did. He only came across extra money once in a great while; and so, he relied on Jack and some of the other younger friends he had to look out for him on the streets; and most all of them did because they had a certain reverence for his age and his wisdom and how he occasionally imparted to them some street game that they found useful.

Jack and Jabo continued to chat out in the cold for a few minutes when Andrew appeared in the near distance, walking toward them from the 4848 building where he lived. He was all bundled up with a big, heavy winter coat. "Hey Drewski….what's goin' on, man?" Jabo greeted. "Hey…what y'all up to?" Andrew replied. "I'm sellin' some good dope, y'all…got some fire" Andrew offered. Jabo and Jack paused and did not answer for a short moment. They were a bit taken aback. But, they were probably taking a moment to let the pronouncement sink in and to formulate a response. They had not ever known Andrew to sell any heroin as he was referring to. They also knew that he was a fiend for it himself; and they both probably digested his advertisement with skepticism and a grain of salt. "Man…I sho' 'nough would like to, Drew…but, I am tapped, brotha'" Jabo said with the standard street response for such a dubious claim. "Me, too, man" Jack responded, knowing that something was amiss with Andrew, as well. "Okay, y'all…but, if y'all run into anybody lookin'…send 'em my way" Andrew said before he stepped past them toward the corner.

Just as he did, a plain detective car was passing, going in the same direction. Two detectives leaped out of the car while the driver stayed. "Hold it right there, fellas!" one of them said as they stepped anxiously toward the three men. Then, both of them veered toward Andrew. "Put your hands up against the wall and spread" one of them said to Andrew. While one patted Andrew down, the other stepped over to Jack and Jabo "Turn around, put your hands on the wall" the officer said. "Officer…we just out here havin' a friendly talk" Jabo said. "Yea?…that's alright…you got anything on you?…either of you?" "I got a little taste on me…that's all…it's open" Jabo offered. The officer did not respond to Jabo's admission. He patted them both down. "Let's see some ID, fellas" he said afterward. Jack and Jabo both fumbled through their pockets to pull out their identification. "This is a college ID here…you in college?" the officer asked Jack after he examined his picture identification from school. "Yes, officer" Jack replied. "You guys know that man?" the officer asked as the other detective was patting Andrew down several feet away. "Yea, we know him" Jabo said. "What's his name?" the officer asked. "I don't know his real name…we call him Drew" Jabo said. "You were talking to him…but, nobody knows his real name…come on…somebody talk or everybody is going down to the station for some questions" the officer barked. As soon as he heard those words, Jack became anxious. He immediately visualized his entire evening with Tina being spoiled. "Officer…we call almost everybody by a first name or a nick-name….we just know people from them comin' to the corner here…don't hardly none of us know the others real name…we all call him Drew....we don't have no reason to know his name…that's the honest truth" Jack pleaded, hoping to avoid any trip to the police station. "Alright…I believe you…but…this guy is a suspect in some recent criminal activity in this area…we're taking him down…you guys know anything about that?" the officer asked forcefully. "No, officer…I just come around once-in-a-while…I don't know what's goin' on around here lately" Jack offered with the same placating tone. "I ain't heard nothin' either, officer" Jabo added. "Okay…I'm going to let you guys off this time…just don't lie to me or I will come back and lock yous up…okay?" the officer said as he turned to step away. "Yessir…yes" Jack and Jabo said almost at once. The detective stepped over to the other officer who had handcuffed Andrew and each held an arm as they led him to the back of the detective car with his hands cuffed behind his back.

After the detective car sped away, Jabo spoke. "You know, Jack…people been sayin' for about two weeks that they was lookin' for somebody around here for a couple of strong-arm robberies…Drew probably got a case on him if they can make it stick…you see how they went straight to him…they goin' by a description that they prob'ly have" Jabo said in a confidential tone. "Well…I don't know nothin'….I ain't tellin' nothin'….if he catches a case…he catches a case" Jack said philosophically. "He does act kinda' mysterious, though…wouldn't you say?" Jabo added. Yea…that's right…he does…lets go back in the poolroom…that was close…and I got a hot date tonight, man…I didn't wanna' mess it up" Jack admitted.

"Oh, yea?…same little honey?" Jabo asked with a broad grin. "Yes, indeed, Brotha' Jabo…she's sweet, too, boy!" Jack said spiritedly. "I don't blame you, man…don't let nothin' stop you from havin' a good time" Jabo encouraged as the two walked back toward the poolroom entrance. "Yea…another thing…you believe he had any good dope to sell?" Jabo asked Jack with a knowing grin. "Hell, naw…if he had any to sell, he prob'ly used it all up gettin' high…I wasn't fallin' for that for one minute…who does he think we are?…Joe Sausage-Head?" Jack said dismissively. "Hahaha…for sho!" Jabo responded before swinging the poolroom entrance door open as they both stepped inside.

"Where y'all go, man?...I was lookin' for you, Jack….I had somethin' to tell you" Coley said as soon as they walked into the poolroom. He walked over to Jack and put his arm across his shoulders and walked him over to a corner of the poolroom for privacy. "Hey…dig this, Jack...we all gettin' together at the Mystic tonight…Freddy B and his old lady and me and Shirley…bring your lady, man…we gonna have a good time" Coley said with a tone of excitement. "Sounds good…what time y'all gonna be there?" Jack asked. "Me and Shirley are gonna be there about nine-thirty…Freddy B said him and Carmen are gonna be there around the same time…not much later…you comin'?" Coley asked. "Well…let me talk to my lady…we're goin' downtown on a little carriage ride tonight and then, we're havin' dinner after that…we should be done around ten-thirty…I have to get her to agree first…but, I think she will....she met all of y'all and she likes everybody…we should be there" Jack finally assured. "You sho?'" Coley asked again. "I'm pretty sure, Coley…mark it down, brotha'" "Okay…cool..that's all set…damn brotha', Jack…you livin' it up with your girl…huh?" Coley said with a big smile, glad to know that his friend was enjoying himself. "Yea…Coley…thangs been real cool with us" Jack said. "You slick rascal…keep handlin' your business, man…and invite me to your wedding…okay?" Coley said. "Yea…I don't know about that, Coley…maybe…maybe not….you know" Jack responded. "Anyway…just enjoy it…that's all" Coley said. "You know…me and Jabo had the Slick Boys roll up on us a little while ago…they grabbed Andrew, cuffed him and took him to the lockup" Jack said. "No, shit?" Coley said with surprise. "Yea…ask Jabo" Jack said as he motioned toward Jabo who was describing the police stop to Larry and Skip near one of the pool tables half-way across the poolroom. Jack mingled around the poolroom for almost another hour without drinking anything else. He decided it was time to go home to prepare for his special evening. "Okay…I'm gonna get goin' y'all" he announced to the group. "Okay…see you later" Coley said and all the others said their goodbyes before Jack took off. The incident with Andrew and the idea of almost going to the police station seemed to unnerve Jack somewhat. He was reminded of how much his life had changed in a short time. In the past, he would have thought nothing of such an encounter where he might have been taken to the police station for questioning; nor would he have been fazed by seeing Andrew getting locked up. But, a taste of freedom from that street life and the peace and civility of his new life had changed his perspective and his sensitivity. He would still make his occasional visits to The Corner. But, he realized that he needed to be even more cautious when he did.

Jack arrived back at his room in the Y at around 5:30pm. He usually called Tina an hour or two before their outings. So, before he began to shower and dress, he called her. They spoke briefly. Jack finished showering and dressing and was on his way. The walk to the Lawrence L station was not as cold as recent days. But, it was still cold enough for Jack's best and heaviest coat. He felt good and he stepped briskly. He arrived at the L station at ten-to-seven and a train came right away. Tina poked her head out from a car not far from where Jack stood on the platform. Very few people were getting off so, he noticed her right away. "Jack…come on!" she beckoned, leaning out from the train car. Jack hustled over to the car and darted in. They laughed and giggled and hugged each other as the other riders looked on. "I didn't want to wait out in the cold for another train" Tina said after they found a seat. "Me, either, baby…it seems like they take extra long when it's cold" Jack replied. "Listen, baby..check it out…Freddy B and Carmen, Coley and Shirley…they are gonna' be partyin' at this really nice lounge tonight…it's about fifty-four-hundred north on Sheridan Road…it's real nice…a small Jazz club..I told Coley we would be there" Jack said. "Oh…you did, huh?" Tina asked with a faint smile and a bit of challenge in her voice. "Yea…you wanna go don't you?…you met everybody…you like them, right?" Jack asked. "Yes, I did and yes I do…but, you just said yes before you asked me?" Tina said with the same inflection in her tone. "Uhh..yea, baby…we ain't doin nothin' else after we have dinner tonight" Jack argued. "Hahahaha" Tina began to chuckle. "I'm just playing with you, Jack…I just like to see that little boy look come over your face when you feel a little guilty…of course, I'm going with you…wouldn't miss it" Tina said. "You had me goin' for a minute" Jack admitted with a smile.

"You ready for your first carriage ride?" Tina asked excitedly. "Yea…I guess so" Jack said with a kind of muted response. "You don't seem excited, Jack…what's wrong?" Tina asked. "I'm excited…it's just that…I never did this before…romantic stuff like this" Jack replied. "But…as long as I'm doin' it with you…it's cool" Jack added. "Jack…you're very romantic…I know that….you will love this ride…wait and see" Tina said with a big smile as they rode the L train that jerked and screeched along the tracks through the dark Chicago winter evening. They got off at Chicago Avenue and walked east to Michigan Avenue. They walked the short distance through the small Water Tower area before arriving at the corner of Pearson and Michigan. They waited about five minutes before a horse-drawn carriage was ready. After paying, they got on and started the ride. The air was cold and clear and there was a light wind as the horse began to draw the carriage through the brightly lit Michigan Avenue. The driver followed the route that Tina requested; going south on Michigan Avenue one block with the horse's hooves clopping on the pavement; then, turning west onto Chicago Avenue to go one block to Rush street; turning there to go north on Rush street. Jack noticed the faces of some of the Rush street crowd; mostly men who seemed to cast a noticing eye at the interracial couple riding prominently through the bustling hot-spot of night life. But, Jack was having a good time as he was engaged in a barrage of happy chatter with Tina as they huddled inside the carriage and talked excitedly; making comments on what they saw as they enjoyed the scenic route. When the ride was over, they were all smiles. "That was a sweet little ride we had…I really liked it" Jack said with a broad smile as they stood on the sidewalk after climbing off of the carriage. Tina paused for a moment, beaming into Jack's face with a warm smile before she gave him a passionate kiss. "That was really special" she said afterward.

They had decided earlier to go to the Carlton restaurant on Rush Street when they passed it at the beginning of their carriage ride. It looked interesting because the restaurant had big picture windows that the patrons could look out to see the Rush street activity and passersby could look into the restaurant to see the people dining comfortably. They walked back westward on Pearson and turned north to go the one block to the restaurant at the corner of Chestnut and Rush. Jack had gotten used to the telling expression on some people's faces when they glanced at him and Tina as they entered the restaurant together. He expected it and it did not seem to faze him. "Let's just relax and just take our time eating…what do you say, honey?" Tina said. "No doubt, baby…this is your day…we're celebrating!" Jack said encouragingly. "Tell me about the job…I know you're a teacher….but, what grade?…what do they expect you to do, baby?" Jack asked after they were led to a nice booth with a window facing Chestnut Street and were seated. "Well…I will be teaching mostly third and fourth-graders…I'm new so, I will be expected to do substitute duties, too…but, I don't care…I'm just happy to be hired!" Tina said with the same excitement she had been showing all along. Jack just looked at Tina and smiled. He was just enjoying her being so happy. It gave him a certain glow inside. In a suspended moment, he looked deep into her happy face; seeing her magical smile and her wavy brunette hair; it all meant "Tina" to him and that was all; he did not see her in any other way except that she was the burning bright light in his life and that she was special in so many ways.

They ate and laughed and the happy chatter continued. "You know…I'm goin' for an interview for a part-time job at a gas station on the northwest side on Tuesday…I hope I can get lucky like you did, baby…I need that job to help me out" Jack said. "I'm keeping my fingers crossed for you, honey…call me about seven-thirty that night and let me know…you will have to start calling me around that time from now on, anyway because of my job…okay?" Tina said. They sat for a long time relaxing and talking about their future plans. But, they still never talked beyond the immediate future just as they each had agreed long ago. Jack had told Tina several times before that he never liked looking too far ahead and spoiling the moment. She agreed, saying that they were both still very young and they would just enjoy what they had today.

Finally, after about two hours, they left the restaurant and headed back to the L train. After a forty-minute ride on the L, they got off at the Lawrence stop. They walked to the corner of Broadway and Lawrence because it was easier to catch a cab there. They arrived at the Mystic Lounge at shortly before 11pm. Jack and Tina walked into the dimly lit lounge with it's relaxed and sophisticated atmosphere. Jack noticed that, just as before, the patrons were the usual mix of blacks and whites of good taste; the same kind of low-key crowd as before. Jack liked it better than other places he and Tina had been because the people here seemed too enlightened to gawk at a mixed couple. There were a few mixed couples there tonight. The place was buzzing with warm vibes. It had a charm that was captivating. After they stepped just inside the entrance door, Jack stood in one spot, holding Tina's hand and gazing around, looking for Coley and the others. Finally, he saw them on the other side of the room. They were all seated at a big table near the bar except for Coley who was leaning on the bar nearby talking to his friend and the owner, Cuda Watson. Jack started toward them, still holding Tina's hand. Just as he was approaching them, Coley turned around as he was talking to Cuda and saw Jack. "Aw…hey, Cuda…this my young protégé and his lady…you already met Jack…and this is Tina…Tina…meet Cudda, the owner of this place" Coley said. "Hey, brotha' Jack…hey there, Miss…Tina…glad to meet you…Jack…let me compliment you, my brotha'…you have very fine taste in ladies…that ain't no lie!" Cuda commented as he gazed admiringly at Tina and took her extended hand and held it momentarily. "Hi…thank you" Tina said, smiling. "What you say Cuda?…he got good taste?...damn right he got good taste…that's my main man right there…everybody I run with got good taste" Coley boasted and laughed. Jack could see that his friend was already feeling good and after their greetings with Cuda, they walked over to the table.

"Hi, Jack, Hi, Tina…good to see you, girl" Carmen greeted cheerfully. Shirley, who was also seated at the table greeted them, as well. "How are you doin, baby" Shirley greeted Tina. "I'm okay…good to see you, Shirley" Tina replied. "Jack…you hangin' on tight to that girl, ain't you?…you better, boy…terrible as you are…you got lucky…and you know you got lucky, too…don't you?" Shirley teased good-naturedly. Jack had spent many an evening at Coley and Shirley's place drinking, talking and watching television. Shirley knew Jack well and treated him like family. "Look at James…he loves to come here and get with Cuda, tell lies and laugh all night…he is a mess...I'm tellin' you" Shirley said as she cast a knowing expression in Coley's direction.

"So what have you two been doing since we saw you at the party?" Carmen asked Jack and Tina. "Well…I finished school in December and I just got a new job this week…and Jack is in school!" Tina said eagerly. "That's great, girl!" Carmen said as she and Tina seemed to have formed a bond from their first meeting. "That's real good, Tina…I'm happy for you, girl…but, you must have put a spell on that one right there…I never would have dreamed he would straighten up and go to school…I am in shock!…you must have his nose wide open…'cause he is a stubborn one…wouldn't change for nobody….not since I have known him" Shirley said. "Well, I get to see the really good side of him that he doesn't like to show everybody else" Tina said, sticking up for Jack in her own little way. "Hey, y'all…I ain't so bad…am I?" Jack said with a smile and feigning defensiveness. "No, Jack…you are my favorite one of James' friends…he's told me about how you have done favors for him that he couldn't get from anybody else" Shirley confided. The lively conversation continued on through the night with everyone appearing to be enjoying themselves. Jack had two beers that he sipped on throughout the night. Tina was feeling proud, not only for herself for having finished college and finding a job but, for Jack, as well. She knew that Jack had led a seedy kind of life. But, as she listened to his friends talk with each of them saying something good about his character and seeing how much affection they had for Jack, she had confirmation that the gut feeling she had about deciding to be with him was not a mistake. She sensed something about him early-on that transcended his street persona and his circumstances at the time. There was something much more; there was a mysteriousness about him that intrigued her. She wanted to delve further as if digging for gold or diamonds and becoming elated at finding something beautiful and valuable in the dust. The night ended with Shirley taking Coley home early because he had gotten drunk. The others began to disperse shortly afterward. Their departures were full of promises to get together again and there seemed to have been a greater bond formed between the newly acquainted members of the group.

Jack and Tina took a cab all the way to Tina's place because it was so late. They arrived at around 2am. Lying in bed, they had their usual heart-to-heart, probing talks about anything and everything that night; and their usual love session, as well.

They awoke very late Sunday morning. It was going on noontime. It was a much colder day that was ominously overcast with blustery winds and snow from what they could see through the apartment window. The TV news blared on-and-on about the stormy weather. The two decided to nestle inside all day. Tina prepared a very late breakfast and it was past noon when they sat down to eat. They finished and Tina had Jack to help her clean up her place. They engaged in a bit of horseplay and joked around as they tidied up her apartment. The phone rang. "Can you get that Jack?" Tina yelled while she was in the bathroom. Jack answered the phone. "Hello" he said. "Hello…is Tina there?" a man's voice asked. "She's in the bathroom right now…who is this?" Jack asked. "This is Jason from school…I'll call back" the man said before hanging up. "Who is it, Jack?" Tina asked as she was coming out of the bathroom. "It was some dude named Jason…said he would call back….who is he?" Jack asked. "Oh…he's a friend of mine from school…he graduated with me" Tina said non-chalantly. "Oh…okay" Jack replied, trying to hide the mild bit of concern he had about a man calling his girlfriend. Jack did not want to seem jealous so, he left it at that.

Monday morning came and they arose early together at around 6am because it was Tina's first day at work and she wanted to have plenty of time to get there on time. To save time, Jack just freshened up because he did not have classes until the afternoon on Mondays. He would go home and get his customary extra bit of sleep before preparing for school. Jack and Tina kissed outside her apartment door after she locked it and they parted outside of the apartment building with Jack giving Tina encouragement for her new job before they went in opposite directions out on the sidewalk. Jack took the L train home and got off at Wilson Avenue and walked to the Y. He undressed and went to bed. He woke up at 10:30am after a couple hours of sleep. He showered and dressed before taking off for his walk to school. The weather was much more settled today and it was sunny but, cold as he trudged eastward through the snow toward The NEIU Uptown Center on Sheridan Road. He arrived at the student lounge almost half-an-hour before his Man & His Physical Environment class. His friend, Marvin was there. "Hey, Jack…how are you?" he greeted. "My man, Marvin…what's goin' on" Jack said. "I'm okay…how are classes going for you?" Marvin asked. "I'm doin' okay…startin' to get a lot of homework, though" Jack said. "Yea…me too…it's not real easy, either" Marvin said. "College classes…just have to concentrate, right?" Jack said. "Yea…but, as long as I have time and I can study in a quiet place…I do okay…I stay caught up…but, I have to study at the library…I have younger brothers and sisters at home…they're kinda' noisy" Marvin said. "Yea…I can dig it" Jack said. Marvin's comment about the noise at his home made Jack realize how easy he had it; living in the Y where it was fairly quiet and he was undisturbed. He did not have to go to the library to study. He could see the good character in Marvin; seeing how much he wanted to go to college just as he did; seeing that he was going to certain lengths to get his studying done with very few resources just as he was. These were the kind of people that Jack was glad to meet and he wanted to embrace them because they were so unlike himself; unassuming; honest; untainted by the kind of depravity that he had exposed himself to in the streets. Deep inside, Jack longed to be just that kind of person. He was hoping that abstinence from his former street life and his gaining an education would transform him into a better person. He was baffled at how his dreams had been so at odds with his reality. Jack's life had been rife with contradictions.

After his afternoon classes were done, Jack picked up dinner on his way home and studied for a couple of hours after he got there. He called Tina and they spoke briefly, as they usually did on Monday nights. She talked about her new job and Jack was glad to hear her say she liked it. She wished him luck for his interview tomorrow afternoon before they hung up.

Jack made it to Sheridan Road early the next morning; and after having a hearty breakfast at Jake's, he got to his first morning class minutes before the starting time. Both classes went well and he went back to Jake's for lunch afterward. He was in the mood for socializing so, he decided to go to the student lounge. His mind was on his interview at the gas station this afternoon. He was trying to unwind before he took a bus to go there. He was just relaxing when Billy walked up.

"If it ain't the Dalai Lama himself…check you out…all laid-back and what-not" Billy said. "Hey, fool…what's goin' on?" Jack responded as he lay lazily reclined in one of the cushy sofa chairs in the lounge. "What you up to, man?" Billy asked. "Aw…nothin'…just relaxin' for a little while" Jack responded. "Ain't too many folks around here right now, huh?" Billy commented as he looked around the lounge to see no one else there. "Yea…I think a lot of people have the same mornin' classes and they just wanna get back home in the afternoon" Jack commented. "What's been goin on with you, Billy?" Jack asked. "Man…the big boss at the supermarket called me into his office"

Billy said with a tone of seriousness. “Yea….what happened?” Jack asked curiously. “He was talkin’ about my application and my criminal record” Billy said. “Damn…no shit!....you been there almost a year….what did he say?” Jack asked. “Oh…I didn’t get fired or nothin’….he just said that they have periodic reviews of their employee file information and he wanted to know the nature of my criminal background…he said that they are goin’ out of their way, bendin’ the rules a little bit to get me into the butcher’s union…he wanted some assurances that I wasn’t gonna embarrass them further up the road…dig what I’m sayin’?” Billy said. “Yea…I get the picture” Jack replied. “Damn, man…I’m goin’ for my interview a little later this afternoon…I don’t know what I’m gonna put on that application where it says have you ever been convicted” Jack said. “You got any felonies?” Billy asked. “No…all I got is two thefts and a disorderly” Jack replied. “You cool then, man….the application will say felonies….those are misdemeanors” Billy said. “Where is your interview?…what kinda job is it?” Billy asked. “Gas station attendant at a Clark station on Western near Irving Park Road” Jack replied. “Another thing is…I ain’t worked in two years…I don’t know what to put on the application for job references” Jack added. “Man…just say you been a student for the last two years…that’s all…then, they won’t have to call up nobody…just verify that you’re a student…show ‘em your student ID…dig” Billy advised. Jack paused after Billy’s advice. He thought about it in a moment of silence. “Yea…that might be the best way to go, Billy …I think you’re right, man…that’s just what I’m gonna do” Jack said with a smile as he extended his open palm to Billy for the usual soul handshake. “Hey, Billy…got to ride…time for me to hop on this bus and get to that interview…wish me luck, man” Jack said as he rose to depart. “No doubt, Jack…good luck, man” Billy said as they finished their departing soul handshake.

After leaving The Center, Jack walked south on Broadway to Irving Park Road. He took the Irving Park Road bus west to Western. He arrived at the corner of Western and Irving Park Road. He looked around to see where the gas station might be. He looked at the referral slip that he got from the Student Employment office. The address on the slip indicated that the Clark station was on Western Avenue about a half-block north of Irving Park Road. Jack peered into the distance where he could see the familiar red, white and blue Clark sign. He walked toward it and he could see from his watch that he had arrived about twenty minutes early. He arrived there and walked inside the station. A young white male employee with a blue Clark shirt with his name on it standing behind the cashier counter spoke to Jack "Can I help you?"

"I'm here for an interview…looking for the manager, Gus" Jack replied. "Yea…that's him over there talking to a customer…he'll be here after he's done" the young attendant said. After a few minutes of waiting, the pot-bellied, middle-aged man began to walk from several yards out on the lot toward the station. "Excuse me, sir…you're the manager?" Jack asked after the man was near him. "Yes…what can I do for you?" the manager asked before he stopped in front of Jack. "I'm Jack Rollins…here for a job interview" Jack said. "Oh…yea…that's right…come on in so I can give you an application" Gus said. He took Jack into his office behind the door that said "Employees Only" and was on the right side of the cashier counter. "Here…fill this application out and after you're done…we'll talk…okay?" Gus said. "Yes…okay" Jack replied before he proceeded to fill out the application on a clipboard with an ink pen attached. "I'll be back when you're done" Gus said before he walked out of the office. Jack was finished in about ten minutes and the manager returned a few minutes after he was done. "Okay…all done?" the manager asked. "Yes, sir"

Jack replied as he handed the clipboard with the completed application to him. Gus was silent as he perused the application for about a minute. "Okay…you're a college student right now?" Gus asked. "Yes" Jack replied. What kinda work did you do before that?" I worked in a warehouse five years ago, then I worked at Michelin tires after that for two-and-a half years" Jack said. "Why'd you quit there" Gus asked. Jack could feel a little nervousness begin to grip him. "I wanted to go to college and get my education" Jack replied. "You done any part-time work since you've been in school?" Gus asked. Jack began to feel the nervousness grip him again. "Well...I worked at the school daycare in my first year of school for about six months and I had a job in a Salvation Army thrift store for a while after that…now, I am out of work and looking for something steady part-time" Jack said. "Okay…you have real good handwriting and good spelling, I see…you don't have any health problems…do you?" Gus asked. "No…none…I'm in good health..I almost never get sick" Jack replied. "Okay…you seem alert…you have good manners…healthy…I have a few other applicants…I'll give you a call in the next couple of days and let you know what I decided…okay?...take it easy" Gus said as he shook Jack's hand. "Thanks" Jack said before he departed.

As he headed back home, Jack realized he had to cover the lies that he told about the daycare and Salvation Army jobs he said he once had. He would see Lupe tomorrow at school and tell her what he said at his job interview and ask her to go along with it. He also would call Ida at the thrift store and ask her to cover for him, as well. Jack arrived back home at about 4:30pm. He checked for his mail at the lobby desk and dropped off his book bag full of books in his room. He was hungry so, he went to the Village Restaurant to pick up dinner and bring it back to his room. He went through his usual routine of watching television while he ate. When he was done, he turned the television off and studied for about an hour. He was thinking about the gas station job the whole time; hoping that he would be hired over the other applicants. He did not know how this would go. He had not applied for a job in months and he felt a little odd when he went for the interview today. Gus, the manager was friendly enough. But, Jack could not glean much from his interaction with him. He did notice Jack's good handwriting and spelling and the other things he mentioned about Jack did seem encouraging. Jack would know in a couple of days. He was gradually becoming acclimated to this normal lifestyle. He was realizing how much he had been insulated from it all with being high every day in the past. It took effort that he had not exerted in quite some time. It took being forthright. He realized that he could not deviate from this course. He could not drink much, lie, cheat or steal and still do the things he was doing right now. He had to maintain some basic decency and not lapse back into his wanton ways.

It was not quite 7pm when Jack decided that he would call Tina. "Hello, honey…how did you do?" Tina asked when Jack greeted her on the phone. "Right now…I don't know, baby…I went to the gas station…filled out the application and talked to the manager…he asked me some questions about my work history…I had to lie a little…said he'd call me in a couple of days to let me know whether I got the job or not….he said he had some other applicants…so, I don't know what my chances are….that's it" Jack said. "Okay, honey…I still have my fingers crossed for you" Tina said with her usual cheeriness. "But, he did say I had good spellin' and handwritin'…you think that might count for somethin'?" Jack asked. "I don't know, honey…but, I'd say it was a positive sign that he noticed" Tina offered. "You know…I think we'll have to put our plans for the weekend on hold until I find out if I got hired" Jack said. "Yea…okay, Jack…we'll wait and see" Tina agreed. "How was your day?" Jack asked. "Oh…it went okay…I did have a little rougher day with the kids today…one kid had to be sent home because he had a bathroom accident…another kid kept falling asleep in class…and I'm still learning the rules about what to do with the kids in certain situations…sometimes they're a handful….but, I really love this kind of work" Tina said. The two talked a little while longer before hanging up.

It was Wednesday and Jack had afternoon classes today. He had a quiz and an exam in today's classes so, he woke up and studied for a couple of hours before showering and going out to the Village restaurant to have breakfast. He read his favorite newspaper and then went back to the Y where he lounged around in his room before dressing for school. He realized it was the end of January already and at the end of next week he would be getting that big financial aid check from school. The check was supposed to be almost fifteen hundred dollars and Jack had already been thinking that he needed to get a bank account. He hadn't had one in over two years; since he had his last steady, full-time job at Michelin Tire Company. He took off for school a little early. Jack arrived at school almost an hour before classes. He was walking down the hallway when he ran into Lupe who was going in the opposite direction toward the Daycare room and was accompanied by another female student.

Hi, Jack…how are you?" she greeted cheerfully. "Hey, Lupe…what's goin on?" Jack replied. Jack…this is my new person in the daycare…meet Sheri" Lupe said, introducing Jack to an attractive African-American young lady who was shapely and slender with a pretty face. "Hello, Jaaaacck" the woman said drawing Jack's name out with a soft, sultry tone as she smiled pleasantly. "Hello, Sheri…nice to meet you" Jack said as he extended his hand to feel the softness of her's in his palm as they shook. "She just started…I'm showing her the ropes" Lupe said. "That's real cool…welcome to The Center, Sheri" Jack said pleasantly. "Thank you" Sheri replied. "Can you come down to the daycare after classes if you have time, Jack?…I need a little help moving some things around?" Lupe said with a smile. "I'll drop by after classes…alright?" Jack said. "Thanks, Jack" Lupe said as both women smiled before Jack continued down the hallway.

"Get up off ya' ass and make somethin' happen, man" Jack teased Billy after he entered the student lounge and observed him scooted down in a sofa chair. "Be cool, now…don't make me break these size tens off in that behind o' yours" Billy teased back. "Go ahead…they gonna call you hop-along-Billy after that, too" Jack quipped. They both laughed before engaging in a soul handshake. "What's hap'nin' Jack?" Billy asked more seriously. "I'm cool…what you been up to?" Jack asked. "studyin' my ass off….that's all…this school thang don't never seem to end…you know how it goes…work….school …pinchin' pennies…the usual routine" Billy said. "I wish that was the usual routine for me…I'm still lookin' to get hired somewhere…you know I went on that interview yesterday" Jack reminded Billy. "Oh, yea….how did that go?" Billy asked. "Well…good as could be expected…filled out the application…talked with the manager…I took your advice and said I've been a student for the last three years…he still asked me if I worked while I was in school" Jack explained. "He probably knows you wasn't goin' to school offa' your well-to-do parents…..that's for sure….he's probably had lots of students work for him part-time…he knows how it goes….he knows students need a part-time job" Billy surmised.

Jack and Billy were talking when Glen Lefleur, the assistant director of The Center came into the lounge. "Gentlemen…I need to ask a favor of you two…we just had our soda vending machine delivered a little while ago but, the delivery men say that there is no way for them to get it up here because it's so big…they refuse to take it up that long stairwell here at the entrance…we need some help from a couple of strong guys like you two…would you please help out?" Glen asked with a tone of urgency. "Sure" "No problem" Billy and Jack answered. "Where is it?…we'll bring it up" Billy offered. "It's downstairs….outside on the sidewalk near the door" Glen said. "Okay..we need to put our book bags up" Jack said. "Here…I'll take them and put them in my office….okay?" Glen said. Glen took both book bags and took them to his office. He came back. "Guys…it's pretty big….go down and look at it….then, tell me if you can handle it or not….please don't say you can if it's too big…because if it is….we'll find another way to get it up" Glen said. "Okay…let's go, Billy" Jack said. The two bounded down the long stairwell leading outside. When they got to the sidewalk, they looked at a huge Coke machine that was taller than Jack. "Damn, Billy….this sucker *is* pretty big" Jack said as he gazed at the brightly colored machine. "Yea…you're right…but…if we could get the right size dolly….one of us could pull while the other pushes it up the stairs" Billy said. Jack paused and walked all around the machine looking at it's circumference. "Well…I think we can handle it if the dolly is big enough" Jack said. "I'll go back up and ask Glen does The Center have a big dolly anywhere" Billy said. "Okay…I'll wait out here" Jack said before Billy bounded back up The Center stairs. He was back in about a minute. "No luck…we don't have one….sure would be nice to have a Coke machine in the student lounge…what do you say?" Billy commented. "Yea..sure would" Jack replied. "Hey…got an idea…the Spanish store here next door…we could ask them can we borrow a dolly….you *know* they got one…probably got a big one, too…I'll go ask 'em" Billy said before he walked over to the Spanish-owned grocery store next door and entered. He was gone for about five minutes before he re-appeared with a very large dolly in tow. "Got it, man…check this bad boy out…big enough ain't it?" Billy said beaming as he stood to one side to let Jack have a good look at it. "Yea…it's big enough, alright…you pull…I'll push…alright?" Jack offered. "Cool..let's get started so you can get to class" Billy said. Jack tilted the big machine so that Billy could get the plate of the dolly underneath. After that was done, Billy leaned it back and started backwards up the stairs as he pulled it and Jack pushed. They had to pause a couple of times on the way up while they grunted and groaned as they made incremental progress. Finally, they were near the top of the stairwell with the machine and a few steps to go when the huge machine suddenly shifted slightly to the right side. "It's slipping, Billy!" Jack yelled out franticly. Jack looked at the huge machine and he was aware that there was not much leeway on either side of it between the walls. He was also aware that the stairwell was very long going down and if the Coke machine slipped back toward him, it could be disasterous. He could almost see his life flashing before his eyes "Billy!…you got this damn thing!...I'm gonna put my shoulder up against the right side …can you pull it up the rest of the way real quick!…I'm a goner if this thing slips again…okay!" Jack spoke frantically. I got you man!…I'm gonna give it a big pull and you push on the count of three…ready!" Billy said real quickly. "Yea!" Jack shouted out. "One…two..three!" and they both grunted, pushed and pulled mightily. The machine rolled the last three steps very quickly up the stairs and Billy took it's momentum to swerve it up against the nearest wall in the second-floor hallway and sat it up quickly in one motion. Neither of them said a word as they heaved, and breathed heavily for a moment

"That was a close one, Billy" Jack said. "If you wasn't strong enough to jerk that thing up those last few steps…I woulda' been through!" Jack said with a sigh of relief. "I wasn't worried, man…long as you had some weight up against that side that was shiftin'…I had you" Billy said confidently. "You a strong-ass, short white boy, ain't you?….you been eatin them greens and grits that's what it is" Jack said. "Somewhat…a lot of it is that Greek food, baby…lots of vitamins in a Greek diet…you oughta start eatin' Greek food and get like Hercules, my man…you know Hercules was Greek don't you?...yea…you eat that Greek food…you'll be able to carry this damn machine on your back all the way up them stairs…dig what I'm sayin'?" Billy said with a tongue-in-cheek diatribe. "Hahaha...get the hell out o' here, Billy…fool…I almost died tryin' to help take this one up the stairs...you talkin' 'bout me carryin' it up them stairs by myself...ain't no kinda food in the world gonna help me do that" Jack chuckled. The two had a good laugh before Billy checked his watch. "You got ten minutes before your class, man" Billy said. "Damn…let's find out where Glen wants us to put this machine and after we do that…we can get our bags…okay?" Jack suggested. "Cool" Billy replied before he went into Glen's office. In a few seconds, they both came back out with Glen carrying their book bags. Jack and Billy wheeled the machine into the student lounge with Glen showing them where to place it. He thanked them profusely. “Billy …I’m thankful that you got that strength, man” Jack said. “That’s alright, bro’…I wasn’t gonna let nothin’ go wrong....you know that now…don’t you?” Billy said before they shook hands again more meaningfully than ever before. Jack went to class and Billy returned the dolly to the store.

Jack attended his classes and after he was done, he headed for the daycare just as he had promised Lupe. When he walked in, it was shortly before 5pm. “Hi, Jack” Lupe greeted him as soon as she saw him enter the daycare room, There were a couple of kids left romping around on the floor of the wide play area. “Hey, Lupe…I’m ready…what you got for me to move?” Jack asked cheerfully. “Oh..thanks-a-lot for showing up…I asked a couple of people before you and they said they would help move stuff for me then, cancelled out” Lupe said. “See this bookcase?…can you move it over there?…then, I need this table moved to that corner over there…then slide my desk up this way to right here…can you do that for me?” she asked. “Sure…no problem” Jack said as he slung his book bag off of his back and sat it down to start. Not much more than five minutes passed before Jack was done. “How’s that…is that how you want it?” Jack asked. Lupe looked up from some crayon drawings by the kids that she was shuffling and looking at. “Oh…yea…just like I wanted…you’re a sweetheart, Jack….thank you very much” Lupe said.

“You got time to hang around until these kids’ parents pick them up?…they should be here in ten or fifteen minutes…then you can walk me to my place…I cooked some chicken breast and rice, Mexican style…it’s really good…you can have that for dinner as my thanks for helping me out…how’s that?” Lupe offered. Jack paused and thought about it for a quick moment. “You live in one of those courtways a couple blocks up Montrose, right?” Jack asked. “Yes” Lupe responded. “Okay…that’s cool…it’s on my way home, anyway” Jack said. “Good” Lupe responded. The two sat around making small talk and watching the kids play. “How did your new person do today?” Jack asked Lupe. “She did good…I was just explaining things to her and letting her see how everything is done…she went to her afternoon classes after you saw her earlier…she was supposed to work this late shift that I’m doing right now…but, she is new so, I will do it with her for this first week she is here…I sent her home early” Lupe said. “Ooohh” Jack said. Soon, the parents of the last two kids came and picked them up. Lupe locked up the daycare and she and Jack walked toward her place. “You have a real nice place here, Lupe…nice furniture…lots of space, too” Jack commented as he scanned her neatly arranged and well-decorated apartment after they had entered. “Yes…I like it…those school checks helped me get this furniture…I got this apartment real cheap…I couldn’t afford a place this nice anywhere else…but, you know this area is not all that safe…I got burglar bars on all my windows” Lupe said. “Yea…don’t blame you” Jack replied, feeling a twinge of guilt about his past transgressions. Jack relaxed on Lupe’s nice couch and she asked him if he wanted some refreshments before she began to warm up the dinner she had cooked. “I cooked up this food this afternoon between classes” Lupe said as she handed Jack a can of soda with a glass of ice. Finally, the food was heated and ready. They sat at Lupe’s table in her kitchen and it seemed very nice and homey in her apartment as they ate and talked.

“So…you and your girl…you plan to get married?” Lupe asked. “We haven’t been together that long…not quite six months so…I don’t know…we’ll see” Jack said. “You ever plan to ask her?” Lupe asked. “I really haven’t given it much thought…we have an agreement to wait and see how things turn out without tryin’ to force somethin’ to happen” Jack explained. “That makes sense…she taking good care of you?” Lupe asked. “Taking good care of me?…I’m takin’ care of myself” Jack replied. “No…I mean in other ways” Lupe continued. “Other ways how?” Jack asked. “She go down on you?” Lupe asked boldly. “Hahahaha..aaahhh…Lupe…gettin’ kinda’ personal ain’t you?” Jack said. “You like your dick sucked?” Lupe asked. Jack paused and his smile disappeared as he realized what Lupe was leading up to. “Well, Lupe…I cain’t answer that…I don’t know what to say about it” Jack said, politely side-stepping her leading question. “I didn’t think it was all that personal…most men like it…sorry…you don’t have to answer”

There was a short moment of silent discomfort before they changed the topic of conversation. “I really got to get goin’ home to get some studyin’ done, Lupe…I really appreciate the dinner…it was very good…you’re a good cook” Jack finally said. “Glad you enjoyed it…thanks again for helping me out today” Lupe said. Jack gave her a big hug before he departed. As he walked home on the dark streets, he was thinking about his day. He could have gotten killed by an oversized Coke machine and he almost got propositioned for a blowjob, it seemed. He was not really so offended by Lupe's remarks. But, he did feel kind of sorry for her. She is a nice person who is getting her education. She is bright and keeps a very clean and beautiful apartment; a good cook; she was just overweight, he thought. But, Jack's care for her as a friend seemed to increase with the realization of just how lonely she must be at times. He knew very well himself how it felt to be alone.

Jack made it home and it was almost seven-thirty. He would be calling Tina around 8pm. He got comfortable and turned on his little television and watched it for a while before he went out to the bank of phones down the hallway from his room. He called Tina. "Hello, honey" she greeted Jack after he spoke. "How was school?" she asked. "It was cool…me and Billy took a huge Coke machine from the sidewalk up the stairs to The Center…it almost fell back on me" Jack said. "Oh, my god!…you okay, honey?" Tina gasped. "Yea…I'm alright…I didn't get hurt or anything…I just didn't realize it was a dangerous job we were doin'….the manager of The Center asked us to do it after the people who delivered the machine refused to take it up the stairs….I see why, now" Jack said. "That's awful…they delivered it but, wouldn't take it up?....they sound like real jerks" Tina said. "Yea…but, we got it up the stairs and if Billy wasn't strong as he is….you might not be talkin' to me right now" Jack explained. "Oh, my…that was brave of you guys…but, be careful, honey…okay?" Tina said. "You heard anything from the gas station guy?" Tina asked. "Not yet, baby….he said he would call me in a couple of days…it's only been one day since I applied" Jack responded. "Yea…okay…just have to wait…huh?" Tina said. "He should call tomorrow….I'll let you know when I call you tomorrow night…okay?" Jack said. They talked a little while longer before hanging up.

It was a chilly Thursday morning and Jack arose early to get to his morning classes. Right away, he was thinking about that gas station job. He was already feeling a little anxiousness about his prospects. He showered and dressed. He was thinking, too about how things would play out for an outing with Tina this weekend. He lived for these weekends where he seemed to be living the surreal life of someone else; going out to nice places to dine and being entertained seemed more like a dream. He had not lived quite this well in the past even when he was working a full-time job and things were going very well for him. He expected that whatever the news was about the job, he and Tina would be going out. He left his room and walked to The Center. He stopped at Jake's and did not have much time before class. He ordered a three-egg breakfast and woofed it down. He was in his Expository Writing class a few minutes later. The day went well but, he was hoping all along that he would be fortunate enough to be hired. His reckless ways had never allowed him to care about these kinds of matters before. A bottle of Rose or a good shot of dope would have been remedy enough anytime worry would creep into his conscience. But, now that he had hope, he had allowed himself to have a bit of faith, as well. So, he said a little prayer in his mind. He could hardly wait to get back to the Y to see if he had any messages. He was uneasy in his Community Organization class and he was not paying as much attention as he should. Finally, the school day was done and he did not hang around The Center. He kept a couple of books in his book bag to study at home tonight.

He left as soon as his class was done and walked anxiously the several blocks home. He could feel a mild palpitation in his chest as he walked up to the YMCA clerk's desk where he got his mail and messages. "Any mail for 212?" he asked the clerk. "Here you go" the clerk said as he handed Jack a regular piece of mail and two of the pink message slips. Jack looked at the messages hopefully. He could see one was from Tina. "Good luck. Call me soon as you can" it read. The other was from the gas station manager. Jack's thoughts leaped with excitement and he could barely contain himself as he read it, "I haven't made a decision, yet. Call the station tomorrow around 11:30am" it read. He was puzzled. He did not know what this meant. He went to his room in a daze; wondering what the message could mean. He arrived at his room, still mystified. He kept thinking about it. But, he could not glean anything from the ambiguous message. Suddenly, he decided that he could not wait until tomorrow to call as the message suggested. He would call right now. "Clark Gas…how can I help you?" the voice said. "Hello…is Gus there?" Jack asked. "Gus leaves every day at five-thirty…he's gone" the voice said. It took almost half-an-hour after he returned to his room for

Jack to settle down and accept that he had to call Gus tomorrow to see how things had turned out.

Finally, he opened the letter he also received and it was from "Northeastern Illinois University Financial Aid" office. He read it and it gave him instructions on how to pick up his check at the campus on Friday next week. He found it somewhat consoling. He mulled around his room a while before calling Tina shortly before 8pm. "Hi Honey…any good news?" Tina greeted. "Hey, sugar…not yet…he left a message for me at the Y to call him tomorrow mornin' at eleven-thirty" Jack said. "Hmmm…wonder what he is going to say" Tina said. "Don't know, baby…I wish he coulda' just left a message tellin' me whether I got the job or not…why do I have to call him" Jack said with a hint of frustration. "Yea…I know what you mean...when I got hired, they did leave a message for me to call them back before they told me I got the job so, don't be disappointed…you still might get the job…think positive, honey" Tina encouraged. "Okay…yea…you're right…I'll try to keep an open mind" Jack said. They talked a bit longer and Jack promised that they would plan for the weekend if he was not hired to work.

It was Friday morning and Jack felt good that he could sleep a little longer and not have to rise early; but, as soon as his head cleared and he was fully conscious, the thought of his prospects to be hired at the gas station was on his mind. The thought of planning a weekend with Tina was on his mind, as well. He did remember that he needed to be at the Northeastern campus at 1pm today to pick up his financial aid check. Jack was showered and dressed by 10am and shortly after, was at the Village restaurant for breakfast; he came back to the Y and waited around in his room until it was 11:30am; he was a little nervous when he went out in the hallway to call the gas station. "Hello" the gas station worker greeted.

"Hello….yea…this is Jack Rollins…I was there on Tuesday and I applied for an attendant job…is Gus there?" Jack said. "Hold on a minute" the voice said. A long, anxious moment passed for Jack before a voice spoke out. "Yea…hello" the voice spoke. Jack could tell right away that it was the manager, Gus; he had not anticipated that he would feel so nervous over this situation but, he was feeling very anxious. "Hello…this is Jack Rollins….I was there on Friday…I applied for the attendant job and you left a message at my home to call you back today" Jack explained. "Oh....yea...Rollins...yea...you're hired" Gus said in the plain and straightforward manner that Jack had come to notice. A feeling of elation and relief came over Jack all at once. "Thank you" were the words he mouthed silently as he closed his eyes and looked upward for a short moment. His prayer was answered. "Thanks a lot, sir...I really appreciate that" Jack said trying to control his excitement. "Now...it was close....you beat out some good candidates...even some older fellas with lots of experience who are out of work...I need smart, young school guys....you guys seem to be my best workers" Gus elaborated. "What time can you come in on Monday to fill out some tax papers?" Gus asked. "Well...I have classes in the afternoon, sir...I can come in the morning around ten" Jack replied. "Perfect...we will work out a schedule for you, too..alright?" Gus said. "Okay...I'll be there at ten in the morning on Monday, sir" Jack said. "Good...I'm not here on the weekends so...I'll see you then" Gus replied before he hung up. A feeling of joy began to spread over Jack. He was feeling giddy. Everything was going well in school; he was going to get his school check and now, he had the part-time job that he was hoping for. He was glowing. All he could think of was how joyous the moment would be when he shared his good news with Tina.

Afterward, he left the Y and walked the couple of blocks east to Ashland Avenue to take the Ashland bus north to Foster Avenue and then the Foster bus west to Kimball Avenue; he walked the few blocks to the campus from there. He arrived at the Financial Aid office to see throngs of students standing in lines that led up to the counter where students could be waited on. He waited and waited; almost two hours had passed before he inched up in line to get to the counter and give his name. "Jack Rollins!" a lady behind the counter called out a little later. "Come this way" she said after Jack answered. He went back into an office and she asked him a number of questions about his enrollment. She asked for identification; his state and school IDs. Finally, she handed him a check from a pile of paperwork with checks paper-clipped to each batch. Jack left the school staring at the numbers on the check that was fourteen-hundred and forty-nine dollars. Jack couldn't believe he would receive this kind of money for enrolling in school. But, he did not regard the windfall in the way that he used to. He was serious about school and he planned to put it to it's best use. He had already begun to be a bit frugal ever since he had cut his drinking down to almost nothing. Still, he could feel those old, wild urges trying to rise up inside; the urge to just go out on the streets and begin drinking and spreading money around and being as loose and carefree as he had been in the past. Suddenly, there was that churning feeling again that had not been there for some time; that same old feeling twisting his gut into a knot; the feeling he used to get when he was hustling on the streets and getting high; he was surprised that it flared up so easily and so quickly. It had come out of nowhere. It reminded him of who he had been and who he still was; he could feel his intellect kicking in; trying to suppress the beastly feeling. Finally, he began to talk in his head to himself; trying to convince himself not to do anything foolish; that he would be remorseful if he did. It only took a moment of recalling the misery that he had been so familiar with. His thoughts changed immediately and the twisting in his gut began to go away. He began to calm down. He looked at his trusty watch to see that it was almost 4pm. He decided to try to make it to the Ravenswood Bank on Lawrence Avenue before it closed. It was the closest bank to where he lived. He went to the bus stop near the campus. The Kimball Avenue bus came right away and he rode it to Lawrence to take the Lawrence bus east to the bank. He opened a bank account and it was near closing time before the process was done. He had deposited the check. He felt relief when the banker told him that it would be several business days before the check cleared and he could make withdrawals.

After leaving the bank, Jack walked back toward the Y that was not very far away. He decided to go to the Village restaurant for dinner. It was shortly past 5pm when he finished dinner and went back to his room at the Y; he tried to sit and watch TV but, he was getting restless and bored. He had too much pent-up excitement to lounge around his room for long. He knew that his friend, The Weep was never home at his room in the Y at this time of day. He was always out in the streets drinking and carousing around this time. He usually came in well past 9pm most nights when Jack was fast asleep. On days when Jack went to school in the afternoon, The Weep was usually still in bed late into the morning, sleeping off his high from last night. So, Jack and The Weep rarely saw one another around the Y during the weekdays.

So, he couldn't visit with The Weep. The restless feeling had Jack walking toward the poolroom before he realized it. He just felt like being sociable; especially when he had so much to feel good about as he did right now

He walked through the dark streets. There was the usual teeming of activity out in the streets. There was an excitement in the atmosphere that characterized these Friday evenings; people glad to be off work and looking forward to the weekend; spending money and getting ready to unwind from the long week. Jack loved the feeling that Friday evenings seemed to bring. There was a lively bounce in his stride as he walked along. Before long, he had arrived at the poolroom. Just as always, there was the usual growing crowd inside; lots of noise and high-spirited chatter. He walked in and stood for a moment near the entrance, looking around for familiar faces. He saw Big Dune and an assortment of the other regulars shooting pool. Skip and Jabo were standing around. Others were milling around laughing and joking. Jack walked in to where Skip and Jabo were standing.

"Whooaa!" Jabo yelled out. "If it ain't the mack-man himself… brotha' Jack…how ya' doin' man?" Jabo greeted. "Jack could see that Jabo was certainly in a groove and enjoying his high. "Hey, y'all….what the hell is goin' on!" Jack replied just as spirited. He engaged in soul handshakes with both men and everyone was all smiles. "I thought we wasn't gonna hardly see you no more, Jack…thought maybe that l'il honey of yours had you on lockdown" Jabo teased. "Not quite, Jabo…she let's me come out once-in-a-while" Jack replied in the playful language that they all understood. "It's jumpin' in the house tonight…ain't it?" Jack said "Yea…this is as crowded as I have seen it in a while….look like all of these chumps in here tonight spendin' a little scratch….'bout three different people in here done offered me and Jabo drinks since we been in here…and you know old war horses like us don't turn down nothin' but our collars….dig what I mean?" Skip said. Jack could tell that Skip was high off of more than liquor by the occasional drooping of his eye lids. Jack always enjoyed the comaraderie with his friends on The Corner but, it was tricky for him to socialize with them without being solicited to get high. "You bubblin' ain't you Skippa'?" Jack said with a smile, tickled at Skip's actions when he was as high as he was now. "Listen, Jack…you know the deal, baby…yea…I'm bubblin' off' this horse…yes, indeed…whooweee!...I feel like a million bucks!…dig me…hahahaha!" Skip chuckled as his eyelids continued to alternately droop lazily then, pop back open. Jack mingled for a while with the group before his friend, Coley finally showed up. "Hey, Jack…how ya' doin', brotha'?" Coley greeted after he entered the poolroom and walked over to Jack. "My main man, Coley" Jack greeted. "Lota' folks in here tonight…what you been doin' since I saw you at the Mystic?" Coley asked. "I'm surprised you even remember I was there...you was wiped out when Shirley took your ass home" Jack said with a tone of amusement. "Yea…Cuda was feedin' me free shots of Martell…and before I knew it…I was out of it, man" Coley admitted. "Hey…I just got me a part-time job today, man" Jack said with a glowing smile. "No shit?…what kinda work you gonna be doin'?" Coley asked. "Gas station attendant…over on Western" Jack said. "Cool…now me and Shirley can drive over there and get us some free gas" Coley said tongue-in-cheek. "You a damned lie…you ain't gonna get me fired, fool" Jack said before they both burst out laughing. "You know I wouldn't front you off like that, Jack" Coley said as their laughter subsided. "How's Tina?" Coley asked. "She's cool…she got a full-time, permanent job last week…so, she's really happy about that" Jack said. "Yea…I know she must be…jobs pretty scarce these days" Coley commented.

Jack was having a good time laughing and joking when he happened to look outside to see his old nemesis, Dinky. He was standing just outside the poolroom entrance talking to a man who was bigger than he was. Jack noticed that they seemed friendly with one another. The evening had been going good for Jack. He was having a good time with his friends and he did not drink. But, now that Dinky was on the scene, he faced a dilemma. He did not feel like the hassle that a confrontation with Dinky would bring. It would certainly spoil the evening and the good mood he was in. But, just as he was always determined to do; he was not taking any bull off of anyone and if it came down to another fight with Dinky then, so be it, he thought. Jack continued to mingle with his friends inside the noisy poolroom. In the back of his mind, he was thinking about Dinky standing outside the poolroom. He was hoping that Dinky would just go away before he decided to leave. But, almost another half-hour had passed before Jack looked through the poolroom window again to see Dinky still outside on the corner talking with his friend. Finally, it was getting closer to 8pm, the time he wanted to call Tina. He had to go now and he decided that he would just leave. “I’m gonna make it home, y’all” he announced to his friends in the group, Coley, Skip and Jabo. “You walkin’ toward Saxony, Jack?” Coley called out to Jack as he started toward the exit. “Yea” Jack replied. “I’m goin that way…hold up” Coley said. They walked together out of the poolroom.

As they walked out onto the sidewalk, and were several yards away from the poolroom, Jack heard Dinky’s unmistakable voice call out to him. “Jack…hold up, fool…got somethin’ to say to you’” Dinky said as he walked up behind Jack. Coley and Jack both turned around to see Dinky and the larger man walking close behind them. Jack knew that this would be their usual confrontation so, he prepared himself for a fight. “Yea…thought you got away with that little fight we had…huh?....yea…you wanna get down now?…yea…you got ya’ boy with you…I got my potna’ with me…let’s do it!” Dinky said as he began to dance around in a boxing stance. “I got ya’ back Dink…go on and get down!” the larger man said as he began to start moving around shifting his feet and watching Jack and Coley very closely. “You a damned fool, Dinky…same thing gonna happen just like it did before…I’m gonna kick your stupid ass!” Jack challenged as he took a boxing stance and began to dance around himself. Jack had gotten very angry and he wanted to hurt Dinky more than ever. “My man…this ain’t your fight…okay…let them go at it!” Coley yelled out to Dinky’s friend. “Hey…I’m lookin’ out for my boy…anybody jump in it…that’s when I jump in!” the larger man replied. Jack stepped right up to Dinky and fired off several rapid punches to the head, landing the first shot squarely and missing the last two. Only a few more seconds passed before Jack started landing body shots and Dinky landed two good shots to his chest; they scrapped a while longer, trading punches and Dinky began to seem a little tired. Jack was using his strategy of wearing Dinky down by making him move around quite a bit by making threatening motions to throw a punch while conserving his own energy. This was always the strategy he used with Dinky. It had worked every time he fought him before. Jack started stalking Dinky and Dinky continued to dance around. But, he was beginning to look more weary and Jack took notice. Jack began to measure him before he moved in for another rapid-fire flurry of punches. He threw two quick shots to Dinky's left ribs and when Dinky dropped his elbow to protect them, Jack quickly went to the head and landed a major blow that stumbled Dinky backwards before he fell on his back to the ground dazed. This was when the larger man jumped between Jack and Dinky and made a wild swing at Jack and missed. Jack ducked. Immediately, Coley swung from the blind side and punched the large man on the side of his head, staggering him. As soon as Jack saw him stagger, he moved in to push him down to the ground and began kicking him in the head while Coley kicked him in the back. Jack turned around to see Dinky trying to recover and he stooped down and punched him in the face a couple of times very quickly. Dinky slumped back and laid on his back, stretched out on the sidewalk, bleeding from his mouth. He was done. Meanwhile, his friend raised his large frame from the ground, taking a flurry of kicks and punches from Jack and Coley before he got to his feet and began to run. Jack and Coley just stood in place watching him run before he disappeared around the southeast corner of Lawrence and Broadway where the Uptown Bank stood. "Look at his big, punk-ass run…I don't think we'll see him around this way no more" Coley said. "Yea…I'm tired of Dinky's bullshit…let me tell his ass somethin'" Jack said to Coley before he walked over to Dinky lying on the sidewalk. "Dinky…Dinky…you hear me?" Jack said as he stooped down to talk to him. "Listen, Dinky.." Jack started. "Whaa..what?" Dinky moaned as he lay on the sidewalk dazed. "Listen…this is the last time I'm gonna fight you, man…you hear?…next time I'm gonna hurt you real bad….next time I see you, don't start no shit…okay?....don't start no shit, won't be no shit….understand?" Jack said. "Yea" Dinky said wearily.

"Alright, then…get your ass up…here…let me help you up" Jack said as he began to help Dinky up from the ground; Coley helped. After assisting Dinky in getting to his feet, they walked him to Saxony Liquor and bought him the drink of his choice and Coley bought the drink he went for; all the while talking to him friendly and encouragingly. They used tissue and handkerchieves to wipe the blood off his face; they continued to make him promise not to start any fights with Jack in the future. After leaving Saxony, they walked him to the Delmar restaurant and Jack bought him a meal and paid for it in advance. They walked out of the restaurant and left Dinky inside dining.

"Man…Coley…thanks for keepin' that big stud off of me…that was a big help" Jack said. "You my ace-boon-coon…what else I'm supposed to do?...I know one damned thing…If I need your help like that…you better jump in" Coley said with conviction. "Aw, man…you know me…have I ever let you down?…you know I don't mind thumpin" Jack replied. "Yea…I know that…I know if don't nobody else stand up for me…you will, Jack…that's for sure" Coley said. "Alright…I got to get home and take care of some business, Coley" Jack said. "Awww…I know…you got to call Tina…don't make it sound like you got all kinda stuff to do" Coley teased with a smile. "Yea…you're right…let me get goin" Jack said. "Later" Coley said after they shook hands and Jack took off.

"Hey, baby" Jack said to Tina on the phone. "Hello, Jack…any good news, honey?" Tina asked excitedly. "Yes, indeed…got the job!" Jack said in a joyous tone. "Yeaaaaah!" Tina cheered. "Things are lookin' up for Mr. College….huh?" Jack added gleefully. "That is so great, Jack….we are going to celebrate just like we did for me…oh…do you have to work at all this weekend?" she said. "Nope…free for the weekend to party with my baby….got my school check, too….you ready for some fun, girl!" Jack said. "Yes!....where are we gonna go!" Tina asked, still brimming with excitement. "Well…tell you what…you think about it and I will think about it…we'll both sleep on it and tomorrow, I'll call you around one in the afternoon…we'll decide then…okay?" Jack suggested. "That's cool, honey" Tina replied. They talked on a little while longer with the same excitement. "I love you" each said before they hung up.

Jack's favorite time of the entire week was always Saturday mornings. He remembered how exciting Saturdays had come to be back when he had started working part-time as a teenager in high school; the excitement of cashing his paycheck on Saturday mornings; taking the bus to Jew-town at Halsted and Roosevelt Road with his best friend from the Cabrini-Green projects; shopping for dressy clothes; haggling with the merchandise sellers at their sales stands along the streets and in the stores on Halsted

Street; going back to his friend's house to listen to his Temptation albums; getting ready for those Saturday nights; going out drinking and chasing girls; showing off the new outfits they had bought. Those days were gone but, Jack still relished these Saturday mornings. They were especially exciting nowadays, since he met Tina. After he arose this Saturday morning, he felt that same joyous feeling he used to feel back in those days when he was younger. This was the kind of happiness that Jack had always hoped for and now, it was here. It was magical how his life had transformed in these last several months from the wretched depravity that had almost consumed him to the sunlight of a brilliant new day, glowing with possibilities. There were nothing but good thoughts in his mind and he felt the world was his to play with. He hummed some of his favorite tunes as he rummaged around his room, preparing to shower. He sang all while he showered. He went out to his favorite restaurant, The Village, and had a hearty breakfast. It was shortly past 10am when he finished his breakfast and returned to his room. Jack told Tina that he would call her at 1pm so that she and he both could have time to do their personal stuff; errands and such. He realized there was a void of time before he would be calling her. He felt too excited to try to do any studying. He knew that he would not try to kill time by going to the poolroom; especially after his run-in with Dinky yesterday. He would still be going to the poolroom from time-to-time but, he didn't feel like it today.

Jack decided that he would go and pay a visit to his buddy, Willie-the-Weep in his room on the third floor. "Weep…it's me…open the door" Jack called out as he knocked on The Weep's door. "Hey…who that is?" Jack could hear The Weep speak out faintly from inside. "It's me, Weep…open the damned door" Jack replied. Jack could hear The Weep bumping around inside the room as a moment passed before the door popped open. "Hey…scandalous Jack!…what's goin on, potna'?….come on in" The Weep greeted. "ain't seen you in a month o' Sundays" The Weep added. "Yea, Weep…just wanted to holla' at you 'cause I ain't seen you in a while…what you been up to, brotha'?" Jack asked. "Nothin'….I was out last night drinkin' with Bow-tie and them…Bow-tie got his check and soon as everybody found out…they was on his ass like flies on shit…he got high and started spendin' money…got me and a few of 'em drunk as hell, man…I wish I had one o' them dranks now" The Weep said looking a bit weary and washed out from last night. "Got the shakes…huh, Weep?" Jack surmised. "Not too bad…but, I got 'em…sit on down, man…tell me what you been doin'" The Weep said. "Aw, Weep…everything, man…I'm still in school…just got me a little part-time job and I'm still goin' out with the girl I met way back in September, man…remember?…I told you about her" Jack said. "Yea…I remember…I ain't never seen her…but, I run into Coley not too long ago…he said he met her and everything…he say y'all went to a party together…he says she's a college grad and lookin' pretty good, too…you still with her?" The Weep asked. "Yea, Weep" Jack replied. "Damn, Jack…that ain't like you…I been knowin' you a few years now…I ain't never knowd' you to stick with no chick that long…what's the matter?" The Weep asked. "What's the matter?…what do you mean what's the matter?" Jack asked. "You know what the hell I mean…I mean what's the matter…do she got your nose wide open!" The Weep said in the same loose, joking, tongue-in-cheek manner in which everyone spoke on the streets. "You want the truth or a damned lie?" Jack asked facetiously. "Let me see…I'll try the damned lie first to see if like it or not" The Weep chuckled. "Okay…she hangin' out with me for my money" Jack said. "Hahahaha…hahaha" they both began to laugh out loud. "Hahahaha…okay…now…let me hear the truth" The Weep continued, still grinning broadly. "Okay..I don't admit this to too many people, Weep…I'm just tellin' *you*, now…I am crazy about this girl, man" Jack admitted for the first time to anyone other than Tina herself. "No, shit?…well….I heard from Coley she was crazy 'bout you, too" The Weep replied. "I hope so, Weep…I hope so…'cause I done jumped in…ain't no turnin' back" Jack said as forthright as he could. "That's cool, Jack…you ain't frettin' about it are ya'?" The Weep asked. "Hell, naw" Jack answered. "Okay, then you oughta be happy…don't worry 'bout the destination…enjoy the ride" The Weep advised. "Hmmm…you're right, Weep" Jack said in a quick moment of musing. "That's it…that's what I'm tryin" to do" Jack said. "Alright, then…stop standin' around lookin' crazy and go out and get me a damn drink before I shake myself to death" The Weep said jokingly. They both chuckled. "What you want to drink?" Jack asked The Weep. "Get me a Smirnoff…okay?" The Weep said. Jack went out to the local grocery store a few blocks away and bought the drink for The Weep. He came back with it and they sat in Weep's room for over an hour as The Weep sipped on his drink and became more-and-more animated and loud; laughing and telling funny little, folksy stories to Jack about things that had happened to him in the past. Jack was used to hearing these kinds of spirited talks from The Weep that he enjoyed so much. Before long, The Weep's shakes were forgotten. "I got to get goin' Weep" Jack finally said after he looked at his watch to see that it was past noon. "Here…take this" Jack said as he reached in his pocket to peel off fifteen dollars and handed it to The Weep. "Aw, Jack…that's sho' 'nough good lookin' out…thanks, man….'preciate it" The Weep said with sincerity.

Jack went out to the cleaners down the street to retrieve his dry cleaning for his outing tonight. He went back to his room and called Tina. They talked about their plans on what they would do tonight. Jack wanted to have a simple evening of a movie and dinner in downtown Chicago;

Jack met Tina at the Lawrence L station as they always did and they arrived downtown at around 7:30pm to see the movie. They found a nice restaurant afterward and they dined comfortably. As they were together, Tina chattered away happily, smiling all the while. She told Jack how happy she was that things were going so well for him. She talked about things they could do together. She talked about her plans to get a bigger, nicer apartment outside of Evanston because she was so bored with the monotony of seeing the same things in the town that she grew up in. She talked about them possibly living together and she hinted at them sharing their lives. Jack was very happy to hear her words of devotion that were so comforting. As they talked, he began to feel her love enveloping him like a warm blanket. He had been experiencing a curious sense of inner healing in the time he had been with her. For as long as he could remember, his life seemed a bit fractured. He could never remember anyone being on his side. Growing up, his father's way of speaking to him had always seemed distant and impersonal. His mother seemed to love him. But, she was suffering her own emotional traumas and was unavailable for him as a child. All his life he had experienced haunting feelings of abandonment. His spirit seemed wounded when he reflected on his childhood in his mind's eye. Deep-seeded anger and sorrow seemed to be lurking somewhere underneath. He never realized how well other children were treated until he was older.

In the midst of their happy talk, it was dawning on Jack that Tina was giving to him what he never seemed to have before; something that was making him more whole than he had ever been. She was transferring to him what had been given so freely to her. It was a poignant moment of revelation and a tear fell from his eye. “Jack…are you alright?” Tina asked when the tear suddenly appeared and rolled down his cheek. “Yea…I’m cool…my eyes are stinging…must be that cigarette smoke from that table over there…let me go to the washroom and rinse ‘em with some cold water” Jack said before he rose quickly from the table and hurried to the restroom. He was in the restroom for a good while before he reappeared, standing at the table, a little more settled and composed. “Your eyes okay, honey?” Tina asked very concerned. “I’m cool…everything is cool…little cold water…you know…I’m alright…” Jack said as he sat back down in his seat. They finished their dinner and afterward, strolled around downtown in the cold, brisk air for a while talking about everything before they took the L train back to her place in Evanston.

They had their usual lovey-dovey weekend of togetherness and before they knew it, Monday morning was here. They both got up early and showered and dressed. They had their usual passionate kiss just inside Tina’s apartment door. They parted, going in opposite directions out on the sidewalk in front of the apartment building. Tina went to work. Jack went home on the L train as he always did. He felt the usual tranquility that he always felt when he was leaving Tina’s place. He had never experienced any other feeling quite like it. It was peaceful and soothing; it was nirvana.

He remembered that he needed to get to the gas station for his appointment with the manager, Gus at 10am so that he could fill out those employee tax papers and make out a work schedule. So, he was not going straight home but, would go directly there. He arrived at Western and Irving Park Road half-an-hour early so, he stopped at a little nearby restaurant and had breakfast. He was at the gas station shortly before 10am. “Hello, Gus” Jack said as he approached him in front of the station door. “Oh…hey,

Rollins…you're right on time…I got all the papers ready for you…come on in" Gus said. He led Jack into his office and when Jack sat down, the manager handed him several employee forms to fill out. Jack filled them out while Gus continued to serve customers. When Jack finished, Gus returned to the office shortly afterward. "Everything done?" he asked Jack before Jack handed him all of the filled out forms and said "Yes" Gus perused the forms for a moment and said. "Good…that's done…now let's work out a schedule for you" Gus said. "I need around sixteen hours a week out of you, Jack…that's what you put on your application…right?" Gus said. "Yessir…that's right" Jack responded. "Okay…I need a couple of weekdays from you for four hours a day…I don't care if it's daytime or evening…then, I will need a full eight hour shift from you on one of the weekend days…doesn't matter which day…okay?" Gus said. "Yessir" Jack said. They sat down and Jack filled out a work schedule for Tuesdays 2 to 6pm, Fridays 8am to noon and Saturdays 8am to 4:30pm. The gas station opened at 8am every morning and closed at midnight each weekday night and 11pm on Saturdays and 10pm Sundays. "We have company coveralls and shirts…I will have to order yours with your name patch on them…in the meantime, we have some new ones with no names on them in the back…go in the back room there and pick three shirts and two sets of coveralls…you keep those and wear em' to work…we have an employees bathroom in back of my office…alright?" Gus said. He led Jack into the back storage room where a pile of new and laundered Clark Gas Station work clothes were lying. "Pick through this and look for your size…the coveralls are only three sizes…small, medium and large" Gus explained. Jack took his time picking out the work clothes and Gus gave him a bag to carry it home. "One more thing…four dollars a week comes out of your paycheck for getting your uniforms cleaned…turn em' in on Fridays…get 'em back on Mondays…okay?" Gus said. "Welcome aboard" Gus said before he and Jack shook hands and Jack was on his way home. Jack was feeling especially good about himself. His life had begun to have order and make sense. He was now seeing that his plan to attend college was working out just as he had hoped. All those days of going to the State Employment office proved to be a waste of time. Being a college student had benefitted him immediately in finding a part-time job.

This was something that would not have happened otherwise, he thought. These last couple of weeks had been better than the entire last two years of his life. It all still felt surreal. But, he still could feel the occasional twinge of madness pulling at his gut like an addiction; reminding him of the savage instincts that guided him before. He was being very careful nowadays to not give in to them. Jack realized, too that this new life of his was much easier than his former one. It was still not so secure but, he no longer felt that maddening sense of free-falling desperation.

He took the bus home so that he could prepare for his afternoon classes. When he got to his room at the Y, he had time to take his customary Monday morning short nap. He awakened after an hour and freshened up before dressing, grabbing his book bag and heading to The Center. His day in school went well and he received exam and quiz papers back. He did fairly well, getting an eighty-seven percent on one and a ninety-one percent on another; Jack was happy and very encouraged by the grades; he ran into Lupe in the hallways in between classes where they talked briefly before she went to her daycare duties. He found Willie in the student lounge at the end of his last class and they had their usual lively, good-natured exchange; he came across Sam Martinez and Glen Lefluer, the director and assistant director of The Center a little later. He had an interesting, casual conversation with them just outside of their office where they gave Jack good, useful information and encouragement about how to navigate through the school environment and to succeed academically and financially. They were friendly and down-to-earth and Jack felt comfortable with them. Sam also handed Jack a yellow-colored flyer with a message about the NEIU Center Freshman Party coming up on the 20th of February. They had just posted it in the student lounge as well, he said. Jack was settling in and he had begun to fit in, as well. The people at The Center were beginning to feel like family to him. Jack headed straight home after his last class. He was thinking about his new job that he would be starting tomorrow. He was excited and happy. He followed his usual routine of picking up dinner on the way home and after dinner did a little over an hour of studying. He called Tina. They had their usual brief Monday night talk and she wished him luck on his first day of work tomorrow.

Tuesday morning had arrived and Jack planned to get a good

start by rising early. He showered and was out of the door shortly before 8am for his 9:20am class. He had begun taking Montrose Avenue to walk to school in the last few weeks because he was occasionally running into some of his friends and acquaintances along Wilson Avenue, which also ran east and west and was a straight route east to The Center. He had avoided them in that time when he was walking along and would see them in the distance milling around on the streets. He would change his route and take a side street to avoid them. He knew that they were doing the same old things that he used to do with them; staying out all night getting high and after sunrise, stand around the local liquor stores and hustle for drinks. Jack knew that his survival meant avoiding his old friends; leaving them alone. He could not afford to mingle with them and do what they were doing. As he walked along on this morning, he was approaching the Tipaway bar on Montrose that was a short distance west of The Center. He was passing the bar and was crossing the alley on the east side of it when he heard his name called out "Jack!" He looked to his left to see Robert Williams and two other men standing in the alley near the sidewalk, drinking.

"Aw, shit…we in good shape now, y'all…that's my home-boy right there!...Jack!…come here, man…let me holla' at you…hahaha…you dirty dog, you!" Robert began to jabber as he began to seem excited, moving about with a jerky motion; Jack could see that he was high and very near that stage of drunken insanity that Jack always dreaded. The other two men were local regulars that Jack always saw around the neighborhood. They were big drinkers. Jack had come to regard them as annoying from his past encounters with them. He tried to avoid them whenever he could, just as he often did Robert Williams. "Hey…Robert…what's happ'nin?…you outa jail…huh?….I got to run, man…I got to go…" Jack said, as he slowed down but, kept walking. "Come on, man…slow down, goddamit!...let me say somethin'…whoa..whoa…hold on!" Robert yelled out to Jack as he began to step away from the two men he was drinking with. "What's happ' 'nin, man?…come on now…make it quick….I got to be somewhere" Jack said as Robert stepped over to him. Robert was close up to Jack, wreaking of alcohol; looking wild-eyed and drunk. He bounced around in that insane manner that Jack had come to know of him. "Hey…hey…check this out…let me hold somethin'" Robert tried to whisper but, was probably speaking louder that he wanted because of being high. "Hold what, Robert?…I ain't got no scratch, man…I'm tryin' to make some money…if you let me get on my way" Jack said with the standard line that one used in the streets from one bullshitter to another. "Aw…come on…I know you holdin' somethin'…two dollars…that's all I need…two dollars" Robert begged. "Hey..hey…look..take this…that's all I got…I'm short…that's the best I can do" Jack said as he handed a lone dollar bill to Robert. "Come on you dirty dog..hahaha!" Robert said with a laugh as he took the dollar and began to throw little playful punches at Jack in the manner that he always did when he wanted to box. Jack knew what to do from all of the other encounters he had with Robert. So, he punched him very hard in the chest, making him stagger backward a couple of steps, looking disoriented. "See you later, Robert" Jack said as he continued on his way, walking very fast and chuckling to himself at Robert's reaction to the hard punch.

Jack attended his morning classes and mingled with Marvin and Billy in the student lounge between classes. After the last class, he hurried home and had enough time to grab something to eat. He changed into his work clothes before hopping on the bus and heading for his first day of work at the gas station.

Jack arrived at work a good twenty minutes early. Brad, the young white dude that he met the day he came to apply greeted him. "Gus went on a tow job…he left your time card right here…try to punch in close to your start time…like inside of five minutes…you start at two…right?" he said. "Yea" Jack responded. "Okay…here you go…you'll be workin' with me…I'll train you on what to do" Brad added. "Okay…cool" Jack said. Brad seemed friendly and easy-going enough. He seemed like someone Jack could get along with. They chatted for a few minutes while Brad stocked the soda coolers and snack shelves. Brad told about how he had moved out of his parents' house a year ago and was living with a roommate after dropping out of school. Brad told Jack that he worked at the gas station full-time. Brad's problems with his parents sounded very much like his own, Jack thought. At a few minutes before 2pm, Jack punched in and started his training; Brad taught Jack how to take the meter readings off of the gas pumps at the beginning of the shift. Brad served customers by ringing up sales on the cash register and pumping gas. In between time, he trained Jack. Jack pumped customer's gas and Brad taught him the cash register later in the shift and stood by as he rang up a few sales. He taught him other details of working at the gas station. "I'll be working with you until four-thirty…Roberto will come in at four and he'll work with you" Brad said. Jack was picking up things fairly easily. At 4pm, Roberto showed up and introduced himself to Jack. He was a young Hispanic man, around Jack's age. He was pleasant for the most part and more quiet than Brad was. Toward the end of his four-hour shift, Jack was beginning to feel that he was catching on to everything. He decided that he liked the job and the people he worked with were cool. His first day was done and he felt good about it.

Jack picked up a take-out dinner at the Village restaurant on the way home to the Y. He ate and relaxed in his room before he called Tina; he spoke excitedly to her about his first day at work; saying that his co-workers were young guys like himself. Tina told of how she was getting along well at her teacher's job and how she was saving up money to get an apartment somewhere outside of Evanston. She said she was hoping to move by the Fall of the year. Another week passed and school had gone well with Jack taking more exams and quizzes and passing them with increasingly better grades. He enjoyed laughing and joking and just having good conversations with his new friends and fellow students at the school. Meanwhile, at his gas station job, things were developing nicely.

It was Friday morning. "Yessir" Jack said to the customer who had pulled up to the pump for gas. "Five dollars regular" the man responded. Jack began to pump the gas; as he had learned to do as a routine of his work duties. He cleaned the windows with the water and squeegee near the gas pump. Jack liked to do a little extra cleaning of the customers cars so, he carried an extra cloth rag that he wiped little spots and dirt off of the customers cars. As the weeks went by, the customers seemed to like the extra little cleaning of their car where Jack cleaned their windows as a station courtesy but, he always took it further; being careful to not leave any streaks on the customers windows. As the weeks passed, some of the customers kept coming back and going out of their way to have Jack pump their gas because of the extra little care that he seemed to show their cars. Jack seemed to have a lot of energy for working on this job. He seemed to enjoy expending it. He liked staying on the move. It was just his nature. He played a lot of sports growing up and he was athletic. He had also spent many hours traipsing the streets of Uptown hustling. These things had conditioned him to have a relentless drive.

"Hey…my man…can you guys clean a car here?" the gas customer asked. "We don't do car washes here but, I can clean it for a price" Jack answered, letting his hustling instincts kick in. "Okay…can you wash my ride and clean out the inside too?…I got to get somewhere not long from now...after you finish pumping my gas…I'm headed over to that restaurant up the street…I should be back in about half-an-hour" the customer said. "Sure" Jack responded. "How much?" the man asked. "Six dollars" Jack said. The customer left the car and walked the couple of blocks up Western Avenue to the restaurant. It was almost 12 noon, Jack's quitting time. Gus was gone from the station for lunch. Jack's relief man, Roberto was already there at 11:30am; Jack drove the car to the back of the station and began to wash the customer's car with a bucket of detergent water and a wash rag. He moved fast. He ran back-and-forth between waiting on customers and cleaning the car. Finally, he was done with the car in about twenty minutes. He had cleaned the inside thoroughly and he used some gas station car cleaning stuff to put some finishing touches on the car after drying it off. The customer was back about thirty minutes later. "Goddamn!…that's a great job!...how'd you get it so clean?" the customer asked in awe after he returned to get his sparkling 1968 maroon Chevy Impala. "Just washed it" Jack responded coolly. "Well…I'll be damned…you're good, my man…here's your six and an extra tip…how's that?" the customer said. "Cool…'preciate it" Jack said as he accepted the nine dollars the man gave him.

The next day, on his Saturday shift, a customer drove up to the pump. "Say..my man…my buddy was here earlier this week…he says you do a bang-up job cleanin' a car…he recommended you to me…can you clean my car like you did his for the same price?" the customer asked. "sure…no problem…pull it to the side of the station over there" Jack said and after parking the car. The customer walked up the street, smoking a cigarette as Jack started on his car; washing it and cleaning it with the same care as he did before for the customer's friend. "Yes, indeed…that looks mighty fine…good job on the inside, too" the customer raved after he returned; showing a glowing satisfaction on his face. "Look here…can you do a wax job for me?…I'm goin' to my brother's wedding next Saturday…I want this baby lookin' sharp by then" the customer added. "Yessir.….can you bring it in the day before…Friday?" Jack asked. "Sure can…how about Friday morning?…then I can pick it up after I get off work at about four…how about that?" the stranger proposed; "Good…I'll have it ready for you by four, sir" Jack said. "So…how much?" the customer asked. "Wax is twenty-five and detail another ten" Jack offered. "That's a good price…you got it…give me the works and I'll see you on Friday" the customer said. "Listen…I do this on the side…I don't want my boss to know...next time you come in…bring your car in on Tuesday afternoon, Friday or Saturday mornings…that's when I can do it…that way I can keep givin' you a good price…okay?" Jack advised. "Deal!" the customer replied. The customer paid Jack and gave a couple of dollars tip, as well. He drove off happily. Another customer arrived shortly after that customer, pulling up to a gas pump just as Jack was standing near it. "Fill 'er up, will ya" the man said, driving a sparkling champagne-colored Cadillac. Jack pumped the gas and began cleaning the windows carefully with a squeegee, admiring the car as he did. "seven-sixty-five, sir" Jack said to the customer after he finished pumping the gas.

"You the car-wash guy?" the man asked as he handed Jack a twenty-dollar bill. "Uh…yea…how did you know?" Jack stammered with surprise. "I heard about you from one of my customers…guy bought a car from me and had you wash it…said it was the best job he'd ever seen…I decided to check you out…I don't normally come this far for gas" the strange customer said. "Think you could use some more business?….I'm Don Hardy, owner of Don Hardy Cadillac-Chevrolet over on Cicero and Belmont…I can bring you a few cars a week for washes and waxes…how about it?" the customer added as he held a business card in his hand, offering it to Jack. "A few a week?…yea…sure…yessir I could do that" Jack said, taking the card. "Okay…how much a car?" the man asked. "Six dollars for washes on a regular sized car…twenty-five for waxes…another ten for detail….for vans add ten for wash and ten for wax" Jack explained. "Yea...that sounds fair" the older man said.

"Listen…bring the cars in on Fridays after twelve noon or on Saturday mornin'…I cain't let my boss know…alright?" Jack said. "Yea…that's fine…I'll do that" the stranger said. "Listen…you ever wanna trade your car in, come on over to my dealership….I got some good deals…got some very nice new and used cars…okay?" the stranger added. "I'd take you up on that except….I ain't got no car" Jack said bluntly. "You don't have a car?....man…everybody needs a car…you got a job and a hustle on the side…..that qualifies you right there…whenever you're ready…come on over to my lot…I'll have my people to work out a deal for you…I see you're a hard workin' young man…that's good enough for me to finance you…okay?" Don Hardy said. "Okay…cool…I might take you up on that one day soon" Jack said, feeling a little uplifted by the encouraging compliment and offer. The hustling wheels in Jack's head began to turn. He was thinking that he could enterprise this a bit further like he did his street hustling. Besides, Valentine's Day was coming up next Saturday and he wanted to have enough money to do something really special for Tina.

He decided he would stop in the neighborhood and talk to some of the other hustlers sometime soon. It was a common practice for Jack and many of the other hustlers on the streets who were really good at boosting to take orders from customers; people who wanted to buy certain items but, did not want to pay the full retail price. They knew that some street hustlers would sell these boosted items for at least fifty-percent off. Jack had stopped stealing and doing any of the hustling he used to do. He did not want anything to interfere with his college life. He did not want to take any chances; and so, he had a couple of hustlers in mind that he wanted to boost car wax and other car cleaning items like sham rags, wheel and upholstery cleaner for him. He wanted to get a big supply to keep his new hustle going. He could get it from those hustlers real cheap. When Jack got home, he showered and went to the Village and had lunch there. Later on, he planned to walk over into his old stomping grounds in the neighborhood so that he could find those people he was looking for to make a deal to boost for him. One that he was thinking about was Patch-eye Slim because he was an old-timer and a master booster. Patch-eye got his name when he lost an eye in a dope house several years ago where his eye was accidentally put out when two dope-fiends began fighting. He had worn a patch over the eye ever since. Jack had gotten to know him when they both were living at the Malden Arms. During that time, he had heard of his reputation and had seen his handiwork. But, Jack would go to him only as a last resort. He knew that old-timers like Patch-eye, who was around forty years old, thought they were slick and could outsmart young hustlers like Jack. But, Jack was already ahead of the game. If he had to deal with Patch-eye, he knew that he had to negotiate shrewdly to get a fair deal. Jack knew that hardcore dope-fiends like Patch-eye would try to pull something if you weren't careful when you dealt with them.

Jack really favored Mezzi who had a reputation on the streets as the best boosting chick around. She would boost exactly what you ordered. She refused to do a lot of haggling over the price. She knew that the prices she asked were good. So, she set them and she would not budge. Mezzi was a mix of East Indian and black. Even though the hardened, dope-fiend life that she lived seemed to have worn away some of the soft side of her feminine appeal, she was still an attractive woman with jet-black, silky, wavy hair. She did not have the average black features. She looked more Mediterranean. So, she didn't draw the usual suspicion that other black hustlers did when they boosted. For that reason, she was much more successful. Also, because she went all around the city and suburbs to do her boosting instead of the local areas in and around Uptown where certain store owners were vigilant and prepared for thieves. The only problem with Mezzi was that she was not around that often. So, Jack would have to ask around to find out where she could be found. He knew that his best chance of locating her was to ask some of the fiends and dealers who hung around the Sheridan Liquors bar on Sheridan Road and Wilson Avenue; because Mezzi was a fiend herself and no matter where she was, or what she was doing, if she wasn't in jail, she would always come around the Sheridan Road strip and cop her dope from the dealers she knew.

It was not as cold this Friday afternoon as it had been in recent days. After he finished having lunch at The Village, Jack walked back home and studied for an hour in his room. It was still early in the afternoon so, he took a short nap. He awakened feeling refreshed at around 2:30pm. He dressed and put some extra cash in his pocket to buy Tina something nice for Valentine's Day tomorrow. He headed for the streets looking for either Mezzi or Patch-eye Slim. He walked eastward on Wilson Avenue. He had been avoiding people he knew along the way when he was going to and coming from school. But, now he was hoping to run into some of those street people he knew. He passed the Private Pie pizza restaurant and the Wilson Liquor store next to it at Wilson and Malden. All he saw were the usual assortment of drunks and drifters milling about. He continued on and purposely walked on the side of the street where the notorious Wooden Nickle bar was; a violence-prone, dingy bar patronized mostly by native Indians and many of the other local drunks and troublemakers. He walked along the sidewalk in front of it as a few of the regulars were hanging around the entrance; none of them were people Jack knew or who could serve his purpose. Jack looked across the street from it where Truman College stood. Students were coming in and out of the building. The surrounding grounds near the building were favorite spots for the local drunks to sit in the grass and on the concrete ledges of the college building and drink; even during the chilly winter days; and some of them were there doing just that.

Suddenly, Jack spotted Whiteboy Silver sitting on one of the ledges to one side of the entrance walkway of the college. He appeared to be just resting and trying to blend in. Jack knew Silver well. He had gotten high with him several times in the last couple of years and Silver taught him the recipe for the phony hashish concoction that had been so useful to Jack's hustling game. Jack suddenly felt hopeful because he knew Silver had some kind of misguided love for Mezzi. They were friends but, Silver regarded her as a love interest and on occasion, Jack would see them together. But, he was not sure of the nature of their relationship; because although Mezzi would find these occasions to run with Silver on the streets for short periods of time, she did not seem to regard Silver in the same way. He seemed to be more of a flunky for her when Jack saw them interact. But, Jack really needed him now because it was very likely that Silver knew her whereabouts. Jack hustled across the street and walked over to Silver.

"Hey, Hash Man…what you doin' around this way?" Jack greeted. "Nothin, man…takin' a break from all this runnin' around" Silver responded. "Doin any good out here?" Jack asked. "Not really…I sold a gold ring in the pawn shop right here earlier…I done shot all that up…I'm lookin' for somethin' else to make some money…ain't nothin' goin' on right now…what about you?" Silver said. "You ain't gonna believe it but…I done straightened up…I stopped drinkin' so much…got in school…workin' a part-time job, too" Jack explained. "Hahahaha…damn…that *is* hard to believe…what happened?…you got religion or somethin'?" Silver said with a broad grin. "Naw…you know damned well I ain't religious….I just got tired of that crazy stuff I was doin'….'specially goin' to jail…I ain't been to jail since I got straight" Jack explained without telling the full story. "I'll be damned….I know *you* didn't stop gettin' high….I know that" Silver said emphatically. "Just about" Jack replied. "You ain't drinkin' or nothin'?....you done went crazy…who are you, man?….I don't know you" Silver said facetiously with a bit of genuine astonishment. He was probably wondering how someone like Jack could go without getting high even one day, let alone for any extended time beyond that. He regarded Jack as one of his fellow misfits; brethren of the streets. They had gone on a few wild hustling escapades together in the past; they had been the same street creatures with the same instincts and motivations. Silver was confounded that Jack could make such a change. But, he took him at his word and he could tell that his admission was sincere and true. "Yea…you *are* lookin' kinda' cleaned up…buy me a drink…I know you got some money…since you're all straightened up" Silver said. "Okay…but, you got to do me a favor" Jack said. "Like what?" Silver inquired. "I need somebody to boost somethin' for me…Mezzi…that's who I need to do it…that's ya' girl…right?" Jack said. "Well…you know how that goes…we're tight…what you want me to do?" Silver asked. "Find out where she is so I can negotiate a price for the stuff I want her to boost" Jack said. "Hahaha…you know Mezzi could be anywhere…you know that" Silver chuckled. "Yea…I know…come on…let's walk back to the Wilson Liquor store…I'll buy you a drink" Jack offered. The two began walking together back in the direction that Jack had come from, going a couple of short blocks to the liquor store. Jack bought a pint of vodka for Silver. They walked a short distance to a nearby building where they went inside to stand in the hallway and get warm while Silver drank the vodka. "So…Silver….where do you think she might be?" Jack asked. "Hard to tell…I know sometimes, she stays at that Chateau Hotel back on Broadway at West Sheridan Road...or she might stay with Big Red at his place… especially if he's pitchin'" Silver said. "Okay…that's a start" Jack said as he seemed to be ruminating at the same time. "You don't wanna hit this vodka?" Silver asked, grimacing after swallowing then, handing the bottle to Jack. "Naw, man…go ahead" Jack replied. Jack and Silver stood in the hallway for a while longer, socializing and catching up on what was going on with other hustlers in the streets. "Silver…let's walk back to the drug store on the corner…I wanna give you my number where I live in case you run into Mezzi or find out where she is…if you do….give me a call…alright?" Jack said. "Alright..that's cool with me" Silver replied. The two walked back to the drug store on the southeast corner of Magnolia and Wilson Streets. Inside, Jack got a piece of paper and borrowed a pen from the cashier and wrote his number down and gave it to Silver. "I'll look out for you real good if you can find her and you call me" Jack said as he handed Silver the torn piece of paper with the phone number to the YMCA and his room number written on it. Silver understood exactly what Jack meant by "looking out" He knew that what Jack was offering him was just another hustle and nothing else needed to be said. Jack knew that although he had the money, he could not afford to pay full price for those car cleaning supplies. The wax alone would be expensive. He needed enough of those supplies to last for a long time and Mezzi was his best hope to save himself a lot of money.

Jack spent another half-hour walking around the streets, hoping to find some of the other people who knew Mezzi and could give him some information. But, it was getting late and he had not seen any of those people. Jack's thoughts turned to his plans to get Tina something nice for Valentine's Day. He stopped at the Goldblatt's store on Broadway that always stayed open until 9pm on Friday evenings. He went to the jewelry counter and took quite a while mulling over the women's jewelry display, contemplating on the perfect gift for his sweetheart. Finally, he settled on a magnificent gold chain with a heart-shaped pendant that had a couple of small diamonds and a ruby in it. Jack paid almost all the cash in his pocket, save a few dollars. He went back home feeling especially good about his purchase. In his room, Jack was thinking that he would also have to buy a small amount of those car cleaning supplies until he could get someone to boost a larger amount. He lounged around watching television and called Tina a little later. They had a warm, playful and happy talk. Tina told Jack that she had a surprise for him. He hinted that he had something special for her, as well. They both understood that the surprises were for Valentines Day. Jack spoke excitedly about making the extra money on his side hustle. Jack would bring his duffle bag with his overnight stuff in it; his hygiene stuff, a few pairs of underwear and a special change of clothes. He would go straight to her place from his gas station job.

Saturday morning came and Jack was up early. After his shower, he dressed and the bus dropped him off near the gas station at 7:45am. Roberto and Brad were already there. "Hey, Jack" Brad greeted. "How ya' doin' Brad….you opened up?" Jack asked. "Yea…I'm the weekend manager" Brad replied. "You can pump gas until things slow down, then you might as well operate the cash register for a while after that" Brad said. "Okay...that's cool" Jack replied. The tone that Brad spoke to Jack was more like an equal rather than that of a boss. Brad seemed to have an unassuming, easy disposition. Jack took note of that. He was calculating how he would maneuver around to do his side hustle of washing and waxing cars. A contentious weekend manager would not have served him well, he thought. He was grateful for the likes of Brad. Jack was thinking of employing a bit of the mind games that he played in the streets, albeit of a more benign nature. He would show slightly more reverence to Brad's authority than he normally would. He would be an especially conscientious worker. He would give Brad a sob story about needing more money. Jack decided to talk to Brad right away about his hustle; giving him a long drawn-out story about needing to pay off overdue rent and some other debts. Brad said it was okay as long as Jack did not neglect the customers. Jack had a couple of washes and a wax job that day. He was very pleased at making the extra money. He knew that he had to get along well with Brad if he wanted to continue his hustle. At the end of his shift, Jack slipped Brad a ten dollar bill and said "That's for helpin' me out…thanks" before he walked off with his duffle bag to take the bus, headed for Tina's place. On the way to the L station, he bought a dozen roses for Tina.

It was nearly 6pm when Jack arrived at Tina's place; she gave him a big hug and kiss after she swung the door open. "Hi, honey…give me your bag…Ohhh, sweety…ohhh…these are beautiful!....flowers!...and she hugged Jack and gave him a passionate kiss. "That's not all, baby" Jack said after their kiss. This is for you, too" Jack added, smiling broadly as he pulled out the little jewelry box. "Ohhhh, Jack…you did all of this!" Tina gushed, letting her happiness burst forward with giddy laughter. "Jack…every time I think I know you…you surprise me….thank you so much, honey!" Tina continued to gush. "Hey…come here…I have something special for you, too!" She said before she grabbed Jack's fingers, pulling him toward the closet. "Here!" she said as she reached on the closet shelf and handed Jack a small package that was gift-wrapped. "What is it?" Jack asked. "Open up and see" Tina said excitedly. Jack opened the package and it was a gold bracelet with "Jack" cursively written into it. "Damn, baby!...you musta paid a nice dollar for this!" Jack said with awe. "Don't worry about the price…okay?" Tina said with a wide smile. The two laughed and giggled, smooched and hugged; they played around affectionately. "Hey…I've got one more surprise" Tina said.

"I arranged for us to have dinner at Truffants….a really nice restaurant in downtown Evanston….we'll have a special Valentine's Day dinner…it's what I wanted us to do…so I made reservations" Tina said. "Aw, baby…promise me one thing though…I pay…okay?" Jack said. "No, Jack…that's alright….we can go dutch….okay?" Tina insisted. "Okay, baby" Jack relented before Tina jumped into his arms and gave him another passionate kiss. Tina said she had already showered; so, Jack was able to jump in the shower and take his time. Afterward, they lounged around for a while. Jack brought some of his nice things to wear for the occasion. He got dressed and Tina dressed in one of her best outfits. Their reservation was for 8pm sharp. They called a cab and rode to downtown Evanston to Truffants. It was a classy restaurant with an elegantly subdued ambiance. There were many other couples of all ages already seated; obviously celebrating the holiday and their romantic unions. Jack and Tina took their time ordering. They were just as immersed in each other's company as when they first met. The peaceful, romantic dining atmosphere was the perfect setting for a celebration of their love. They sat for over two hours before leaving for Tina's place.

They arrived back at her place near 11pm; they changed into their night clothes. They stayed up on the sofa watching television, drinking soda and tea. The TV played with the sound down low as they snuggled on the sofa. They talked their usual warm, snuggly talk in the living room with only the light from the television. Tina always liked to lie on Jack's chest while he held her. Whenever they lounged on the sofa, they touched each other tenderly. When they were together, time seemed to always stand still. Since being together, they had become intimately familiar with each other's little idiosyncrasies. She liked his animated facial expressions; his quirky sense of humor; his street cool and savvy street knowledge. Tina was first attracted to Jack's nice looks, his height and his noble, well-formed chin. But, it was his gentler side that surprised and captured her. From his seemingly rough exterior, she could never have guessed that a gentle side existed just from looking at him when she first met him. But, as she came to know him better, she could see that he was much more than he appeared. He was intelligent and clever. But, it went without saying that his sexual prowess was a key factor in their searing romance. Jack was first attracted to Tina's pretty face and shapely form; as were most men who gazed upon her. But, it was her gracious manner and a mysterious confidence that accompanied her attractiveness that was so mesmerizing. She seemed very bold at times and that was very exciting to Jack. He had come to learn that even though she was very decent and civil, she had a bit of that living-on-the-edge mentality that he had. She also did not possess the smugness that some attractive women seemed to display. She was humble and down-to-earth, which made her all the more appealing. When he first saw her at Frances' tavern, he noted that subtle, classic beauty about her. They lounged on the sofa until well past midnight before going to bed. A round of passionate lovemaking put them to sleep.

Sunday morning came and the weather outside still seemed cold and the air still from what Tina could see from her window after waking up. Jack was still snoozing in bed, as was his habit. It was about mid-morning; shortly past nine. Tina gently nudged Jack and he stirred. She rubbed his head dotingly as he slept. She moved about the bedroom before heading to the bathroom while Jack dozed. Jack finally rose from bed; sat up on the edge of the bed, waiting for Tina to finish her shower so he could take his.

Finally, she came out. "Let's go out for breakfast, honey…okay?" she said. "Sure…wanna go to the same place we always go?" Jack asked. "Yes" Tina said. After Jack showered they went out and had breakfast; afterward, they romped along the streets in the cold cracking jokes and engaging in horseplay by making snowballs and having a snowball fight on the way back to Tina's place. It was an especially peaceful and relaxing weekend.

It was Sunday evening; Jack and Tina had gone out for dinner and returned to her place. "We're havin' a Freshman Party this week on Friday, baby…you wanna go?" Jack asked Tina as they both lounged on the sofa. "Really?…yea…I remember you mentioned it once before…what are they going to do?" Tina asked. "Just a party with food, music, dancin' for the new students like me and the staff so everybody can get acquainted…just their way of helpin' students get familiar with everybody so they can stay in school…lota freshmen drop out before their second year…they're tryin' to prevent that trend" Jack explained. "What time on Friday?" Tina asked. "Six pm" Jack replied. "I think I can make it…I'm usually off work at four on Fridays…I can make it a little later than six…maybe six-thirty" Tina said. "Cool…you'll get to meet some of my friends…the staff…it'll be real cool…I'll meet you at the train station…I'll be there at Lawrence around six-thirty…we'll talk Thursday night…alright?" Jack said. "Yes, Dear" Tina replied playfully with a smile.

Monday morning came and Jack and Tina rose early and went through their usual routine when Jack stayed the weekend. They both showered early and after a passionate kiss just inside the apartment door, Tina went to work and Jack rode the L train home to get ready for his afternoon classes. After arriving at home, he took his morning nap for almost two hours. He awakened, dressed and headed for school. The school week went well and for the first few days he went straight home, except for Tuesday when he went to his gas station job.

It was Thursday and Jack had attended his morning classes. He did not have to work at the gas station today. So, he had lunch at Jakes and went home. He napped for a couple of hours and then studied for an hour-and-a-half. It occurred to him that he had time to go around Sheridan Liquors where he could possibly achieve two of his objectives; finding out where Mezzi might be and perhaps, running into Patch-eye Slim. Both frequented the notorious Sheridan Liquors because there was always dope being sold in and around it. It was a well-known hub of clandestine activity. Patch-eye Slim had longtime friends in the dope game like Big Red; another old-timer who mainly sold heroin but, also began selling T's and Blues because they were the popular new synthetic heroin, of sorts. Jack had not been to that spot to hang around it for months. In the past, he would go there to cop T's and Blues mostly, with his hustling buddy, Melvin. The crowd around Sheridan Liquors were the more hardcore dope crowd of buyers and sellers. Most of them played a more ruthless hustling game in the streets. They played for higher stakes. They were the crowd that carried guns and put hits out on their rivals or those who owed them an unpaid debt. They played for keeps. They were a more dangerous group that Jack knew to tread lightly around. But, Jack was wise enough not to engage himself with them in the wrong manner. He was careful not to owe any of them any money; he did not mix with them. They were much more private and guarded because many of them were dope dealers who were wary of stick-up artists. It was now dark outside at just past 4:30pm; Jack dressed and put on his heavy coat and went out, headed for Sheridan Liquors. Since his dramatic lifestyle change over the last several months, Jack had not cared to walk in the path of Sheridan Liquors. But, he was going there now because it made sense. He needed to get all of those car-cleaning and waxing supplies because to pay retail for the amount he needed would eat at any profit he made. So, being the calculating hustler that he was, he knew what he had to do.

He trudged through the dark streets down Wilson Avenue; taking that route rather than avoiding it as he had done recently; hoping to see some of the same element of street characters that he had been avoiding recently. He arrived at Sheridan Liquors. He realized it was early for the Sheridan Liquors crowd. But, most of the time, he could find someone who knew something that he needed to know. Jack arrived at the northwest corner of Sheridan Road and Wilson Avenue; he turned left and the front of Sheridan Liquors sprang into view in the near distance. He could see the dark figures of several people spread about in front of the Sheridan Liquor bar entrance with the street lights offering a modest bit of lighting on either side of the bar's front.

Immediately, Jack recognized Big Red standing in his familiar pose in front of Sheridan Liquors when he was pitching and waiting for customers. He was standing there alone. Big Red was a man in his mid-forties. But, the many years he had spent in the streets made him look older. Jack walked over to him and spoke. "Hey, Big Red…let me holla at you" Jack said as he approached him. "Yea…what's hap'nin' Slim?" Big Red replied. "Yea…I'm tryin' to catch up with ya' boy, Patch-eye…I need to talk to him" Jack said. "Aw, damn…I thought maybe you wanted some o' this fire horse I got…I got them T-shirts and Blue Jeans, too" Big Red said, staying true to his purpose as a hustler; always thinking of selling. "Naw…I ain't tryin' to cop…I got to talk to him about some business…you seen him lately?" Jack asked. "I was over to his crib earlier…he said he was gonna be down this way pretty soon…you might see him a little later on" Big Red advised. "Cool…hey…one more thing…you seen Mezzi around?" Jack added. "Naw…ain't seen Mezzi for a coupla' weeks" Big Red said. Julius, one of Mo'tic's friends came strutting out of the Sheridan Liquors door. "Red…old black-ass Bo in there buyin' chicks drinks….but, he gonna ask me for some damn credit….I say…nigga…what I look like….a bank?…you spendin' money tryin' to impress them 'hoes and you askin' me for credit?…he tell me….let me get a coupla' bags on credit….I say, fool…this ain't no damn charity…you better get the hell on…ain't that some shit…must think I'm a goddamn fool…talkin' 'bout he'll pay me tomorrow…he sound like that l'il hamburger eatin' stud that run with Popeye…what his name is?….Wimpy…yea…that's him…Wimpy…I'll gladly pay you Tuesday if you give me a bag o' dope today…I told him…what you think I'm sellin' fool?…this some fire-ass dope!" Julius said, chuckling and talking in the loud manner he always did. This was the usual kind of fun-filled, blustery bravado that entertained and passed the time for these characters who lived in the streets. Julius and Big Red continued to talk and Jack walked away. He walked across the street to the southeast corner where the Burger King restaurant stood He went in to stay warm. He bought a cup of coffee. He sat near a window where he could look out and see the front of the Sheridan Liquors bar; hoping to see Patch-eye Slim or Mezzi. A little more than half-an-hour had passed when Jack recognized Patch-eye's unmistakable form appear strolling along the sidewalk in front of the bar. He raised up immediately from his seat and rushed out. In a matter of seconds, he was approaching Patch-eye Slim out on the street several yards from the bar entrance. "Patch-eye…what's goin' on, my man" Jack greeted. "Oh…hey, Young-blood…what's to ya' baby" Patch-eye responded. "Got a deal for you, Patch-eye" Jack said. "Yea…what's poppin'?" Patch-eye said, angling his good eye toward Jack and wearing a black patch on his bad eye with a thin strap that went around his head. At the same time, he leaned his head over slightly to hear Jack better; his long frame being a few inches taller than Jack's. "Yea…I need to get hold of a bunch of car-cleanin' stuff…mainly car wax…I need other stuff, too like car wash, shams, wheel cleaner, upholstery cleaner…dig what I mean?…I need a bunch of it…like about thirty cans of car wax and as much of the other stuff as I can get" Jack proposed. "Okay…I dig what you sayin'….humph" Patch-eye said before pausing and ruminating for a long moment. "So…you need somebody to boost it for you…huh?" Patch-eye finally asked. "Yea…I'm offerin' half-price on whatever I can get…I got a little part-time gig…I started this car wash and wax hustle on the side at my job….I'm gettin' steady customers and I need a supply to keep my hustle goin'" Jack explained. "Young-blood…how come you don't do it ya' self?" Patch-eye asked. "I'm tryin to be cool…I'm on probation…don't wanna catch no case" Jack lied rather than going into a long explanation of the truth. "Okay…I'll do it…but, I need some front money" Patch-eye said. "Front money?…what you need front money for, Patch-eye?" Jack asked with a curious expression on his face. "You know…front money…so when I go to knock the stuff…I got money to buy somethin' to front like a payin' customer" Patch-eye explained. "Yea…I can dig what you sayin'…but….I don't do business that way, Patch-eye…matter o' fact…don't nobody hand out no front money when they put in an order for boostin'" Jack reasoned. Jack knew that this was Patch-eye's way of trying to make a hustle off of him by just talking; that Patch-eye was just seeing how much he could get away with. "Cain't do it then, Young-blood" Patch-eye said with a tone of finality. "Alright….that's cool, Patch-eye…I'll holla' at you…later" Jack said before starting to walk away. He turned around soon after and said "You seen Mezzi around lately, Patch-eye?" Jack suddenly remembered to ask. "Mezzi…Mezzi….Mezzi…you know what…she probably hangin' out at that Chateau Hotel down on Broadway…you know….right at West Sheridan Road" Patch-eye responded.

Jack was surprised to get any kind of positive information about Mezzi from Patch-eye Slim. But, he was grateful and decided to take the Broadway bus south to the Chateau Hotel. The Chateau Hotel was a couple of grades better that the other transient hotels in the area where fiends and other street characters tended to stay. These were the places Mezzi could usually be found; quieter, more peaceful venues where the usual rift-raft didn't go. It was worth a try Jack thought. It was the first lead he had gotten on Mezzi's whereabouts. He walked back west the couple of blocks to Broadway and Wilson and waited for a bus. He took it to West Sheridan Road. He got off the bus and walked into the Chateau Hotel that stood conspicuously on the southwest corner.

"Hey, my man…lookin' for a friend of mine…she might be stayin' here right now" Jack announced after he strolled up to the hotel registration desk. "Yea…what's the name?" the desk clerk asked. "First name is Mezzilina….last name…I'm not sure" Jack said. "Okay…let me check" the clerk said before he browsed his registration book, mumbling in a low voice. "Oh…hey…Mezzilina Fharquar…that sound like it?" the desk clerk asked. "Yea…yea…that's it!...she here?" Jack blurted out with raised excitement. "Yea…got her right here….she's checkin out today, too…what's your name….I'll call up" the desk clerk offered. "Cool!" Jack said in a hushed and excited tone before giving his name. Jack stood by as the clerk called up to Mezzi's room. "Hello…Ms. Fharquar….yes….you have a person down at the desk who wants to speak with you…yes…he's right here…okay…hear you go" the clerk said before he handed the phone to Jack. "Hello" Jack said. "Yea…who is this?" Mezzi's distinctive voice said over the phone. "Mezzi…it's me….Jack…the guy who hustles sometimes with ya' boy Silver…remember…tall…I'm always around the Aragon… yea…yea…that's me" Jack responded to Mezzi's inquiries to identify him from all of the other street characters she knew. "I'm comin' down" Mezzi said on the phone before she hung up. "Hey…my man…thanks…she's comin' down…thanks" Jack said to the desk clerk as he handed the phone back to him. "No problem" the clerk responded.

Jack waited about five minutes before he saw Mezzi's short, voluptuous frame walking toward him after getting off of the elevator. "Hey man…what's hap 'nin'?" Mezzi greeted in her characteristically easy tone. "Hey, baby…how you doin'?" Jack said as he opened his arms to give Mezzi a hug before they stepped over to the lounge area of the lobby that was nearby. They sat down on the lobby sofa. "What are you trackin' me down for?" Mezzi asked with the same challenge in her voice that she always used with all of the people who knew her in the streets. "Aw…check it out, Mezzi…I'll pay you to boost some stuff for me" Jack said. "Why are you payin' somebody…you know how to boost…right?" Mezzi said. "Yea…I could boost it myself…but, I started goin' to college about a month ago…I'm tryin' to stay straight…ain't hardly drinkin' either…I don't wanna get busted and have to drop out…you dig where I'm comin' from?" Jack said. "No shit?…wild as your ass is, man…you're tryin' to straighten up?…that's hard to believe….I have seen you do some way-out stuff…humph…alright…I believe you…I can dig it" Mezzi said after digesting what Jack said. "Well…?" Jack said prodingly after Mezzi fell silent and seemed to be thinking on the matter. "Well, what?" Mezzi asked with a hint of defiance. "Well, will you take the order?" Jack asked. "You got the money?" Mezzi asked. "Yea…I can prove it, too…see this deposit receipt….that's my account….that's what I got in it from my school check that I got about a week ago" Jack said after pulling out the thin little plastic bill folder that he used for a wallet and fishing out the bank deposit receipt. He unfolded it and showed it to Mezzi. "I'll be damned….you savin' up money, too…you really have changed…and I mean a lot, too" Mezzi said as she smiled broadly, probably more so after seeing Jack's deposit slip and knowing he had the money than anything else. "Okay…I'll do it…but…you got to do me a favor" Mezzi propositioned. "What's that?" Jack asked. "Help me move my stuff a little later on…about an hour from now…alright?" Mezzi replied. "How much stuff you got?" Jack asked. "Not that much….just my clothes…shoes…couple of boxes…a few bags…that's all" Mezzi said. "Well….let's go, then" Jack said enthusiastically. "First…I need to get somethin' to eat…I was gettin' ready to walk down to the restaurant on Addision....you wanna go?" Mezzi said. "Yea...let's go" Jack replied. "You're buyin'....part of my fee...dig?" Mezzi said real sassy-like. They walked the few blocks south and went into the restaurant. They sat and talked. They talked about how Mezzi would boost the car cleaning supplies for Jack and what day she expected to have the merchandise ready for him to pick up. Then, Mezzi began talking about how she had gotten locked up for theft about three weeks ago. She went on-and-on about the series of events that occurred with the theft arrest. She said she was moving tonight to her girlfriend's apartment to stay. Her friend lived a few miles west at Western Avenue and Montrose. Jack agreed to take a cab with her to help move her belongings after they finished eating and returned to her hotel room. Jack enjoyed Mezzi's company because she was so plain-spoken when she talked. She knew how to relate to the men on the streets and still maintain her feminine aura. She was extremely clever but, forthright when she found it necessary. She could be extremely devious, too if you made enemies with her. She had many powerful male allies on the streets; mostly the dope dealers that she had spent lots of money with on a regular basis. They had become like family to her over time. Others were men who desired her. They were her protection when she needed it. She did not allow other fiends to get close to her. She mostly kept her distance from them because she knew that they would cross her without a thought for a hit of dope. Despite her dope-fiend habits and lifestyle, she still maintained her appearance and men continued to be attracted to her.

"Let's go" Mezzi finally said after bending Jack's ear for almost an hour about all of her recent exploits and adventures. The two left the restaurant and walked back to her hotel. Jack went with her up to her room and helped her finish packing. There were not too many things to carry, just as she had said. But, she did need help with the couple of heavier boxes that she had. They hauled her stuff onto the hotel elevator and through the lobby. Mezzi stopped at the desk to collect her deposit and they towed her things out to the sidewalk and flagged a cab.

They were at her new residence in a short time. They hauled her things up to the second floor apartment in a nice courtway building. Mezzi pulled out a set of keys. "Angie is not here so I have to let myself in" Mezzi said as she fussed with one key trying to unlock the apartment door before trying another. In a moment, she had the door open and they dragged her things inside. “You cool, now…right?” Jack said in a tone that sounded like he was ready to leave. “Be cool, man…don’t you wanna relax for a while?” Mezzi said. “Well…I guess I could sit down for a minute” Jack relented. “Damn…you helped me move my things…catch your breath…what you in a hurry for?” Mezzi said kind of fussy-like. Jack sat down on the sofa in the living room and looked around the apartment. It was nice and well-kept. It was easy to tell that it was a woman’s apartment because it had that touch to it’s arrangement and décor. As he sat, Jack could hear Mezzi bumping around in the back rooms of the apartment, opening and closing closet doors and so on. Before long, she emerged from the back rooms and walked into the kitchen behind him. “You want a drink, Jack?…we got beer and some Chianti wine here” Mezzi called out from the kitchen as Jack could hear the refrigerator door opening and closing. “Naw…that’s alright….I’m cool” Jack replied. “You sure?…you’re welcomed to have a drink” Mezzi called out again. “Naw…I’m gonna pass, Mezzi” Jack reiterated. A moment passed before Mezzi stepped into the dimly lit living room. Jack was taken aback to see Mezzi’s shapely form appear in a very thin slip. She was carrying a bottle of beer and a glass of wine. “I need to relax and have myself a drink” she said before she sat in the matching sofa chair across from him. She crossed her legs and Jack could see the smooth flesh of her thighs up to her crotch. He was affected and he could feel an involuntary arousal stirring within him. Then, it occurred to him in times past, before he met Tina, that he was no different from the other men on the streets who talked and interacted with Mezzi over the years; that underneath her hardened, dope-fiend exterior was a voluptuous feminine form. Psychologically, notice of it was somewhat muted by the hardcore language she used on the streets. She related to the men on the streets in such a way that she became like a friend and fellow hustler to many of them. They respected her hustling ability; her savvy instincts and cleverness. They knew about her powerful allies on the streets, as well. While interacting with those men, she seemed to mask any hint of weakness that would make her vulnerable. She knew that fiends on the streets would exploit her if she showed any such weakness; because they were ruthless and didn't care. So, she always displayed her toughness. Like herself, they cherished a hit of dope above all else; even any opportunity to lay down with her. "Ooohh, man…it feels good to relax in this place….that hotel was alright…but, not as comfortable as Angie's place" Mezzi said with her legs still crossed high. Jack gawked at the flesh on the underside of her smooth, well-formed legs and thighs and he was reminded of how he had desired her before. Jack just sat looking at her and trying to negotiate in his head how to control his rising lust. "Let me turn on my favorite Jazz station" Mezzi said before setting her drinks down on a nearby end table and rising from the sofa chair. She took two steps over to the stereo and turned her back to Jack as she fiddled with the stereo knobs. Her shapely, well-defined buttocks jutted out at him through the thin, satiny slip. This was not helping any of the control he was trying to maintain over the affect she was having on him. Jack was now realizing that being sober had made him more sensitive in every aspect of his being; and this was the first test of this kind aside from his desire for Tina. He remembered that in the past, when he desired Mezzi, it was all kind of drowned-out by the priority of getting high. Now, his desire was in full force and there was no defense. The stereo music suddenly blasted on and Mezzi turned it down to a lower, softer level. "How's that?…is that too loud?" she asked sweetly before she plopped back down in the cushy sofa chair, looking very relaxed and crossing her legs high just as she had done before. Jack was thinking that, as clever and astute as Mezzi was, she must know the effect she was having on him---her entire persona had suddenly changed to ultra-feminine. Was she trying to seduce him?----was she running game because they had a business deal going?--was she trying to play him for his funds in the bank?--or was she just horny?----Jack didn't know. But, it didn't seem to matter to other parts of him. "Jack….you look a whole lot better than you used to….you're all cleaned up…talkin' and actin' all proper…you're doin' alright" Mezzi commented.

"Listen…do me a favor, Jack…can you massage my neck for me?…I got a crook in it or somethin'" Mezzi added before she walked over to Jack sitting on the sofa and laid an arm across his shoulder. "Would you please do that for me?" she asked coaxingly as she was so close up on Jack that he could feel the heat from her body and he could see through the thin garment she had on.

"Yea…okay" Jack stammered. Mezzi sat down right next to Jack on the sofa, allowing her thigh to brush up against his before she turned slightly away to let him massage her neck from that side he was sitting. "Ooohh…that feels good, Jack….real good…mmmph!" Mezzi purred after Jack began the massaging. "Oh, Jack….let me lie down in your lap so my neck won't be so stiff while you're doing that" Mezzi asked. "Okay" Jack mumbled. Mezzi stretched out horizontially on her stomach and laid across Jack's lap with mostly her chest in the middle of his lap. "Oohh, Jack!…I feel somethin'!….what do we have here!" Mezzi said with a playful giggle after she felt the protruding in his lap. "Hahahaha" Jack chuckled nervously with a little embarrassment. Mezzi raised up from her lying position and stared at Jack in a seductive manner; piercing his eyes with her sultry stare. A short moment passed before she straddled his lap. Jack was not quite sure where his mind was. For the moment, his mind seemed suspended in a neutral zone. He did not know how he was going to react. He was just frozen. He could feel the heat of her body as she lowered her crotch into his lap with the silky garment riding up her luscious thighs. There was silence. Mezzi placed each arm on Jack's shoulders. She began to lean forward when suddenly, a jingling of keys and a jostling of the front door could be heard. After hearing it, Mezzi hopped out of Jack's lap just before the door sprang open. "Hey, hey, girl…hahaha…you made it!…what's goin' on, Mezzi!" Angie, Mezzi's friend and the resident of the apartment greeted with a spirited cheeriness. She was carrying two bags of groceries; one in an arm and the other she slid into the living room; sliding it along the floor to just inside the door. She carried the bag in her arms into the kitchen without looking around; still talking as she did so. "Yea, girl…I got somethin' *good* to cook for dinner tonight…I hope you like it….whooo….I'm tired of runnin' around…girl…I cain't wait to tell you what's been goin' on" Angie went on from the kitchen as she still had not looked around to see Jack sitting on the sofa in the recesses of the living room where it was dim. Meanwhile, Mezzi had scurried into a back room. She returned to the kitchen with her jeans on underneath a robe. She had slipped them on in about half a minute while Angie was busy putting groceries away in the kitchen and chattering away excitedly. "Hey, Angie…let me help you with that stuff" Mezzi said, acting as natural as she could. The two continued to put groceries away. Mezzi went back into the living room to retrieve the other bag of groceries and finished helping Angie put the groceries away. "Hey…I want you to meet my homey, Jack" Mezzi announced after they were done putting the groceries away. "Oh" Angie said with a little surprise after Mezzi pointed toward the living room. Angie followed as Mezzi casually led her into the living room. "Jack…this is my ace-boon-coon…Angie" she said. "Hey, there, Jack…how you doin' baby?" Angie greeted, extending her hand to Jack to shake and flashing a broad smile. Angie was a thinner, taller and darker-skinned woman than Mezzi. She appeared to be around the same age as Mezzi and she was a fairly nice-looking woman. "Nice to meet you, Angie" Jack said as he shook her hand and greeted her very pleasantly. "Man…I didn't even see you sittin' there" Angie said with a light chuckle. "Yea…he helped me get my things over here…he's from Uptown" Mezzi added. "Yea?…that's cool…you wanna stay for dinner?" Angie offered. "Naw, thank you…I got to raise…got to get back to the crib…take care of some business" Jack said as he stood up to emphasis that he was on his way out. "You leavin' now, Jack?" Mezzi asked. "Yea…I got to get goin' Mezzi" Jack said. "Okay…let me holla' at you about our deal" Mezzi said before she led Jack out into the hallway. There, they confirmed that Mezzi would call Jack in a few days when she had the merchandise that Jack wanted her to boost and that he would come to where she was to get it and pay her what they agreed. "Okay…cool..I'll see you soon" Mezzi said before she opened her arms to give Jack a hug. "We can meet up and finish what we started in here, you know" Mezzi added with a seductive inflection in her voice as they were still embraced. "Yea" Jack said almost involuntarily. Mezzi surprised Jack with a quick kiss on his lips after they broke their hug. "Be cool" she said. "Later" Jack said before he bounded down the stairs on his way out of the building.

Jack made it back to the Y at about 8pm. He had picked up a carry-out dinner at the Village restaurant. He was glad to get back inside as the weather had gotten considerably colder. He also remembered that tomorrow was Friday, the day of the Freshman Party given by the NEIU Uptown Center. He was feeling excited about calling Tina tonight and talking about having a good time with her at the party. He changed into his lounging clothes and had his dinner in his room while watching television. After he was done eating, he went out to the hallway to call her. “Hi, honey…how are you?” Tina said after Jack spoke. “I’m good, baby…ready for the party tomorrow?” Jack asked excitedly. “Yea…I really would like to have a good time right about now” Tina replied somewhat subdued. “What’s the matter?…you don’t sound excited” Jack said. “Oh…I’m excited…it’s just that I’m a little sad today…one of my favorite little students is leaving us after this week….they’re moving out of state…I’ll miss little Ruthie…she is a funny, happy little girl” Tina sighed. “Well…I guess you *can* get attached when you’re the teacher to those little kids…huh?” Jack commented. “Yes…and you know me…I can get a little emotional sometimes” Tina said. “That’s alright, baby…I like that about you” Jack said. “Thanks, honey…you’re so good to me” Tina said. “Alright, now…time to perk up, baby!…party time tomorrow!…no long faces allowed…can you dig that?…you’ll be ready…right?” Jack said, attempting to change Tina’s mood back to the happy state he was so used to. “Oh…hell, yes…I will be ready to party, Jack…I’ll be at the Lawrence stop at around six-thirty tomorrow…okay, honey?” Tina said with a lot more spirit. “Be there or be square, girl…I’ll be there at that time…cool?” Jack said. After a few more minutes of talking, they hung up and Jack went to sleep.

Jack rose early Friday morning feeling especially chipper. Since he had stopped drinking, everything was going his way, he thought. He dared not look into the future. But, right now, he was going to enjoy all of his good fortune. He showered and dressed and hopped on the bus. He arrived at the gas station almost half-an-hour before opening time because he anticipated having car wax customers this morning. He started work at eight sharp and not more than ten minutes after he did, the customer he had spoken to last Friday about a wax job pulled up to the gas pump. “Hey, buddy…here we go…I’m gonna leave the keys with you for my wax job and I’m ridin’ to work with my-co-worker in the car in back of me…I know you’ll do a good job....I’ll see you at four” the customer said before he handed Jack the keys and got into his co-worker’s car and rode off. Jack took the car and immediately parked it out on the side street next to the gas station lest Gus ask about it were it to sit on the gas station lot too long. Roberto was the only other attendant working with Jack today besides Gus. Jack waited on customers, pumping gas for almost half-an-hour before a black Cadillac pulled up with a man about Jack's age driving it. "Hey, Bro'….Don Hardy sent me over here to get this Caddy washed and waxed….you the guy that does that?" the young brother asked. "Yea that's me…park it over there" Jack said, pointing to an open space on the gas station lot on the left side of the station building. After the man parked the Caddy, he walked over and spoke to Jack. "I got to wait for this other dude from the dealership to pick me up in about ten minutes…he had to stop up the street to drop somethin' off to a customer" the man said. "Okay…man…that's a cold ride there…they sellin' that one?" Jack asked as he looked over to admire the black Cadillac Coupe De Ville with Vogue tires that looked immaculate. "Yea...it's for sell….rides like a dream, too" the man said to Jack. "What year is that one?" Jack asked. "Seventy-two" the man replied. "What kinda deals your boss got over there?….I met him last week when he came in here…said he had some good deals…told me he could give me a good deal on a ride…but, I don't know about that…can he?" Jack asked. "Aw, man….let me tell you…I got a dark blue Coupe I got from him cheap…had a bad engine when it came in so, he was sellin' it dirt cheap….I bought it. "I got a good engine real cheap from one of his suppliers, too….got the mechanics at the dealership to install the engine….they did it in their spare time so, it took a while….altogether…didn't cost me that much…..it's paid for…..seventy Coupe…clean as a whistle drives real smooth" the young man said with a broad smile. "So…he wasn't lyin….I *can* get a good deal over there…huh?" Jack asked with a focused interest. "Yea…Don is cool…he's money-hungry but, he will give you a good deal…he don't pay us a hell 'uva' lot…but, he always doin' favors for his workers" the man said. "Cool…hey…I'm Jack" Jack said, extending his hand to shake. "Johnny" the young man said as the two shook hands. Shortly afterward, a pickup truck swerved onto the gas station lot. "Oh…here my boy is to pick me up…what time should I come back to pick the ride up?" Johnny said after handing Jack the keys. "About two…alright?" Jack said. "Cool…later" Johnny said before he trotted over to the pickup truck, hopped in and rode off. Jack immediately parked the black Cadillac on the street behind the first one. He worked his shift until noon. Then, he started on both cars after Gus left the station for his lunch hour. He washed both cars and applied wax to the first one. He returned them both to the same parking spots on the nearby side street. Jack had come to know how to time Gus's lunch hour to anticipate just when he would return; Jack had come to notice that he always returned back at the station between an hour-five and an hour-fifteen minutes after he left for lunch; these were the kinds of details that Jack had come to take note of during his survival in the streets. Over time, he had come to make a habit of such observations. When Gus returned, Jack was off work and applying wax to the second car. He thoroughly cleaned out the inside of both cars and then polished the wax off the first, then second car. As he did so, Jack was admiring the luxurious features on the inside of the Cadillac. As he continued to clean, he was thinking more-and-more about buying one of these cars. He imagined how proud he would be to have the regulars in the neighborhood see him in a magnificent ride like this Cadillac. He thought about what Don Hardy had told him about making him a good deal. He though about how his worker had confirmed that when he dropped the Cadillac off. He kept cleaning and daydreaming. After he was done, he hung around for the dealership worker, Johnny who arrived shortly after 2pm being driven in the same pickup truck. He paid Jack and raved about how the car was gleaming before he drove it off. Jack walked over to Roberto and gave him the keys to the other customer's car who was to pick it up at 4pm. Jack asked Roberto to collect the money for him, as well because Jack did not want to wait around until 4pm for the second customer to show up. He was excited about getting back home to get ready and to pick Tina up at the L station for the Freshman Party tonight. Jack caught the Western Avenue bus toward home.

Jack was in his room getting ready for the big night. He felt especially good that he and Tina would be together in the very civilized atmosphere of the NEIU Center. He could feel the excitement welling up inside. He wanted to show Tina a good time and introduce her to his new friends and the staff. It was shortly past 4pm and inside his little room at the Y, he began to prepare for the big night; picking out a suit of clothing that he wanted to wear; showering and putting on his best cologne. He could hardly contain himself as he sat in his room trying to watch television. He went downstairs and walked around in the lobby because he could not sit still. He went back upstairs to try to take a short nap but, just laid there with his eyes open. Finally, it was time to go to pick Tina up at the L station.

After walking the one mile distance in the cold, he arrived at the L station at shortly past 6pm. He stood in the mouth of the stairwell at the Lawrence Avenue CTA platform to stay off the cold and windy platform; he huddled there with a few others who were waiting for the Loop-bound Englewood-Howard train. It finally arrived and Tina was one of the first people off of the train. She smiled broadly as soon as she saw Jack. She was dressed very nicely in a long black coat and a stylish black hat that covered her ears; she was wearing a fashionable pair of winter boots, as well. She was always a vision of loveliness to Jack and he was feeling especially proud of her appearance tonight. They embraced and shared their customary passionate kiss on the platform.

"Let's get a cab…okay, baby?" Jack suggested. "You don't want to walk there?…it's not that far" Tina replied. "Naw…I wanna' get there quick because the party already started at six" Jack said. He also did not want to encounter any of the street people he knew on the way to The Center. He knew they would only be an annoying delay if he ran into any of them. "Okay, honey…I'll get the cab" Tina said. It went without saying that Tina always flagged down the cab whenever they took one. After they caught a Yellow cab in front of the train station, they arrived at The Center in not more than five minutes. They walked up the long stairs and at the top of it, music and the buzz of party conversation met them at the second-level hallway. There were people lined along the hallway chatting. There were bright-colored balloons hanging from the ceiling that read NEIU Freshman Party. As he and Tina walked along the hallway toward the student lounge where the activities were centered, Jack could see a few familiar faces he had come to know at The Center. "Hi, Glen…Sam…this is my lady, Tina" Jack greeted. Glen and Sam greeted Jack cheerfully and shook hands with Tina, welcoming her to the party. There was a festive atmosphere and lots of faces that Jack didn't recognize amongst those he had passed along the hallway.

He and Tina arrived at the student lounge doorway that had a stream of bright light emitting from the room into the dimmer hallway. When they entered, there were many of the other students that Jack always saw on school days. They were scattered all about the large room, chatting, laughing and most everyone seemed to be smiling. They were all dressed nicely. There were several tables of food lining the back wall and a DJ was setup in a far corner, playing music. Jack and Tina paused in the middle of the room. Jack scanned the room for any of his friends and in a few seconds, he saw Billy. A broad smile spread immediately over Jack's face. "Tina…let me introduce you to my friend, Billy …come on" Jack said as he took Tina's hand and they meandered through the crowd to get to where Billy was standing. Billy was talking to a young woman who appeared to be about the same age as the other freshman students. But, Jack had never seen her before.

"I told you we cain't go to my place tonight…I'll take you another time" Billy could be overheard saying to the young lady who was silently wearing an exasperated expression on her face. "Billy" Jack said as he and Tina stopped a few feet from where Billy stood. "Aw hey, Jack…how ya' doin' bro'?" Billy greeted with a broad smile and an affectionate slap of Jack's shoulder. "Man…they really went all out for this party didn't they?" Jack said with a bit of awe in his tone. "Yea…the first one that I went to last year wasn't as nice as this one…yea…they went all out" Billy replied. "Meet my lady, Tina" Jack said, stepping aside to allow their introduction. "Hi, Tina" Billy said gazing at Tina wide-eyed. "My goodness!…Jack…where did you find her?…she is fine!" Billy said emphatically. "Why, thank you" Tina gushed as Billy continued to hold the hand she had extended. "I'm sorry, miss…I didn't mean to sound rude" Billy added quickly, gently releasing Tina's hand. "That's alright…I appreciate the compliment" Tina replied. "His brains don't work that well but, his eye-sight is excellent!" Jack quipped, turning to Tina with a light chuckle. "That's cold" Billy said with a straight face that quickly burst into a broad smile. "You're right, mister…his brain is not working too good" the young lady accompanying Billy chimed in. "Oh..hey, y'all…this is my friend, Karen" Billy said.

"Friend?" Karen said with a stern glare at Billy. "Come on, now…why you doggin' me?…be nice" Billy leaned over and whispered, grabbing her nearest hand and abruptly pulling her closer to him all at once. "Karen….this is my Road Dog, Jack and his lady-friend Tina" Billy said to Karen. "Hi, you-all" Karen said. "Hey, Billy …who are all of these strange, older people I see in the hallway?" Jack asked. "Aw…those are mostly Northeastern staff and a few teachers from the campus….they come to help support the party and show support to the new students and encourage 'em to stay in school" Billy said. "Hey, Jack, Tina…y'all better go on over and get some of that buffet over there…I ate soon as I came in…they got some pretty good food over there" Billy advised pointing to the tables full of food lining the back wall. "Yea…you wanna get somethin' to eat now, baby?" Jack asked Tina. "I'm starving….let's go" Tina replied; and with that, they both got into the buffet line and prepared themselves plates of food. They walked over to one of several eating tables that were set up not far from the end of the buffet table on the perimeter of the room. They sat, ate and talked and seemed to enjoy the music being played. Billy and his friend, Karen joined them at the table to just sit. The DJ was playing mostly popular disco and funky R&B dance music. Some of the people were already dancing in the center of the floor. The Center Director, Sam Martinez walked over to the DJ spot and took a microphone into his hand.

"May I please have your attention, everyone…for those who don't know me…I am Sam Martinez…director of the NEIU Uptown Center…as many of you know, this is our annual party for Northeastern Illinois University freshman who came in the Fall semester of last year and the Spring semester this year that began last month…this is the University's effort to encourage the new students to stay in school by taking advantage of all of the resources that we have in place to make your transition into college life a smoother one…we have an excellent counseling staff…part of that staff consists of an outreach program for students having financial, social or personal problems during their first year at Northeastern…we have a tutoring program and we have an excellent partnership with the campus Student Employment office to help these newer students find part-time work….I encourage the new students to mingle, the staff and teachers here to introduce themselves to our new students...and most of all….have a great time at this party!…have fun, everyone!" Sam said smiling and waving as he walked away to a thundering applause.

The buzz of the party crowd returned. The DJ started the music again, as well. Jack, Tina, Billy and Karen sat for a while at the table chatting and having a good time. Before long, Lupe appeared at the room entrance; Jack and Billy turned around at the same time when they heard a familiar and odd laughter that pierced the buzz of party chatter in the air. "Hahahaha" they could hear Lupe laughing from where they sat. "Hey, Billy …there ya' girl is" Jack announced with a hint of sarcasm. "What you mean *my* girl…she ain't tryin' to get next to me" Billy said before he realized the implications of what he had said. Jack gave Billy a silent facial expression that said "watch what you're saying…my lady is here" and Billy picked it up right away. "Although she *is* tryin' to get next to ya' boy, Marvin" Billy said to clean up the earlier comment. Tina and Karen just sat with blank expressions as the curious moment during Billy's comments seem to hang in the air and then pass. The women seemed to be momentarily puzzled at the comment but, let it pass after Billy's last comment.

They both turned to look toward the front of the student lounge to see the overweight Lupe laughing loudly and becoming somewhat of a spectacle with her loudness. After a moment of observing her, Billy commented. "You know what, man?…she is toasted already…better hide because she is way-out when she gets high" Billy warned. Just as Billy had made the comment, Lupe stumbled into a table full of literature that was set out for the partygoers to take. A couple of men standing near her caught and held her up when she almost fell over. "Look at that man…I went through somethin' like this with Lupe last year…I talked to her and she told me that she is very self-conscious about comin' to these parties….she said she has so much anxiety about it…but, she wants to come to 'em and have a good time…so, she gets blasted before she comes…that way, she can have a good time without bein' so self-conscious" Billy explained. "Why are you trashing her, Billy?" Karen asked. "I'm not trashin' her…she gets a little crazy when she drinks…that's all…watch…you'll see what I mean" "She seems to be a nice-looking woman…just overweight" Tina commented. "And she is a very smart student and a nice person, too" Jack added. "How do you know, Jack?" Tina asked curiously. Jack looked at Tina with surprise. "I have talked to her on school days…I helped move some furniture around for her in the Daycare Center where she works" Jack replied casually. “Uh-oh…here she comes, y’all…better hope she don’t see us” Billy said with a tone of warning as he observed Lupe making her way through the crowd; steadily coming closer to where they sat. She was stopping momentarily here and there to make small talk along the way. Intermittently punctuating the talk with loud, intoxicated laughter. “Aw, man…she is almost here” Jack said. Billy and Jack turned back around to sit facing the table and hunching their shoulders in a posture of trying to hide or not be noticed. Jack was on the side of the table where he could look to his right and see the front of the room and Lupe advancing toward them. Billy had his back to that view. “She still comin?” Billy asked as he and Jack both held serious, anxious expressions. “Aw, man…uh-oh…here we go” Jack mumbled.

“Jaaaacckk!” how are you?...you came to the party!…good to see you!” Lupe said out loud enough to be heard by everyone in ear-shot; with that, she walked over to Jack and leaned over to pepper him with a few quick kisses on the cheek. “Thanks again for helpin’ me out….you are a good friend….come on…let’s dance!” Lupe said, still leaning over but, now smothering Jack with a hug that almost buried his head between her large breasts as he sat in his chair. In the meantime, Karen raised her eye-brows. Tina’s mouth went open with a look of surprise as they both stared at Lupe’s actions. Billy turned slightly away in his seat and propped his elbow on the table, attempting to hide his face with his hand. “Billy!...is that you?….still trying to be a player…huh?...hahahaha!” Lupe said with loud, happy and mocking laughter. Billy responded by removing his hand from his face to show a look of exasperation. “Hi…I’m Tina…Jack’s girlfriend” Tina injected at the end of Lupe’s laughing. A look of seriousness suddenly came over Lupe’s face. “Oh…oh..hi….how are you?…I’m Guadalupe…nice to meet you” Lupe said politely but, slightly slurring her words as she extended her hand across the table to Tina. They grasped hands for a quick moment to serve as a handshake. “I feel like dancing…anybody wanna dance?… Billy …you can’t dance, anyway…you Jack?” Lupe asked. “Uh…not right now, Lupe…we just got through eatin’…maybe later” Jack said. “Okay…alright…I’ll go out on the floor and dance by myself, then….see you” Lupe said before she returned to the dance floor to join those already moving to the driving beat of the DJ’s music. “See there…I wasn’t trashin’ her but, she didn’t waste no time trashin' me…see that Karen?...talkin' 'bout I cain't dance….I can get down" Billy complained. The two couples continued to sit at the table watching the dancers and listening to the music. They were chatting with one another when suddenly, they could hear chanting coming from the floor "Go!.go!...!go!" and they all turned toward the dance floor to see Lupe in the middle of the floor gyrating suggestively to the beat of the music as other dancers on the floor were dancing and clapping with broad smiles as they watched Lupe dance with a very tall black man who was moving in a similarly suggestive manner.

"Look at her…she can really dance!" Karen said in awe. "Wow!…I never would have thought she could dance like that!" Tina said. "Look at her cut loose…ol' boy dancin' with her looks like he is really gettin' heated up, too!" Billy added. The rousing spectacle lasted another half-minute before the dance song ended and Lupe trotted back toward the table to the cheers and applause of the other dancers; giggling and laughing and seeming to be having a glorious time. The tall man who had danced with her was behind her; following her to the table. He was a well dressed, slender man. "These your friends…these your friends?" the tall stranger asked Lupe after they both arrived at the table. "Lupe was still laughing. "Hey…yes…these are my friends" she said as she continued to giggle. "Hey, y'all…she can dance…cain't she?…she is really good….smokin'…hahahaha…huh?....she got down…didn't she?" the stranger went on. "Yea…yeaaaa, Luuuppeee!" Jack and Tina yelled together, raising their hands with exaggerated clapping. "Girl…how did you learn to dance like *that*?" Tina asked. "Hahaha…my aunt was a Spanish dance instructor for many years…she taught me since I was a little girl" Lupe said. "Spanish dance?....then how did you learn to dance to that kind of music?" Karen asked. "After you learn how to dance…comes natural" Lupe answered.

"Hey…mind if I sit with y'all?" the tall stranger asked. "Yea…go ahead….sit on down, man…just put ya' tongue back in ya' mouth…lucky the music stopped…otherwise, I thought you was gonna catch a case out there on the floor close as you was dancin" Billy commented in his usual sarcastic tone. "My name is Eddie…Eddie Sloan…..nice to meet you, Lupe" the strange man said very politely with a bit of a twinkle in his eyes. "Hello, Eddie…my pleasure" Lupe answered before the man surprisingly took her hand and kissed it. "Check out Mister Rico Suave" Billy commented. It became immediately obvious to everyone at the table that the stranger was feeling something amorous toward Lupe. Lupe let out a lady-like giggle as she was obviously flattered by the stranger's advances. They began to chat in a low-key, soft manner, exchanging warm, polite comments. After a few minutes passed, Tina spoke out. "Hey, Jack…let's get out on the floor and shake a tail-feather…let those two get acquainted" Lupe and her new friend were so immersed and attentive toward one another, until they were oblivious to what Tina had said. "Yea…good idea…I need to show off my moves, anyway" Billy commented spiritedly. And with that, Karen, Billy, Tina and Jack walked out to the dance floor that seemed to have gotten more crowded. The beat of the music fueled the festive atmosphere of dancing and fun that continued on. They danced to several songs in a row; finally breaking for a while and having soda refreshments. Then, joining back in again. It was a fun-filled night and everyone seemed to have a good time. Lupe had, apparently, found a new admirer.

Jack and Tina had already had a lot of fun at the NEIU Freshman Party on Friday night. The weather was very cold. So, before leaving the party, they decided to spend the weekend mostly indoors at her apartment in Evanston. Tina took a cab all the way home Friday night while Jack took one to the Y. Jack arose early on Saturday morning and made it to his gas station job. He had one wash and two wax customers that morning as he was working with Brad and Roberto. He did those himself. He got two more wax jobs early in the afternoon and gave one to Roberto because he didn't have time to do it. After his shift ended, Jack took his duffle bag full of his things for his weekend stay with Tina and went to her place that Saturday evening. They spent another glorious weekend together.

It was Monday morning and Jack was riding the CTA L train from Tina's place back to Uptown so he could go back home to the Y and have his usual morning nap before his afternoon classes. He arrived in the lobby at the Y and remembered to stop and check for his mail. There was no mail but, the desk clerk handed him one of those pink slips that they used for phone messages for the YMCA residents. "Got your stuff…call me" it said with a phone number scribbled on it; the Caller section had

"Mezzi" written in it. Jack was elated; but, he felt a curious sense of apprehension, as well. He was glad to know that Mezzi had boosted the merchandise he wanted. But, he also did not know what would happen when he came face-to-face with her. He knew he could not control his lust for her; and he knew she wanted to have him, as well. He didn't know what was going to happen. But, he wasn't really worried about it, either. Jack took the note and read it again as he walked up the stairs to his room; he stopped at the bank of phones on the way to his room and called the number.

"Hello" a voice said. "Hey…Mezzi?" Jack said. "Yes..this is her…Jack….is that you?" Mezzi asked. "Yea…it's me" Jack replied. "Got my message….huh?" Mezzi said with a smile in her voice. "Yea…I did…that's cool…you boosted the stuff…huh?" Jack said. "You know me…it was a piece of cake" Mezzi replied confidently. "No, shit?...good" Jack said. "So…when you comin' to get your stuff?" Mezzi said with a strong hint of sexiness in her voice. "Uhhh…where you at?…the same spot?" Jack asked. "Of course, Jack…same place you and I were before we were so rudely interrupted" Mezzi said with the sexual overtones becoming even more pronounced in her voice. "Do you remember how to get here?" Mezzi asked. Western and Wilson….right?" Jack asked. "Western and Montrose, Jack….twenty-four-seventeen West Montrose in the courtway….apartment 2B….okay?" Mezzi said. "Hold on a minute….I'll write it down" Jack said before he hustled to his room a couple of yards down the hall and hurriedly unlocked the door and rushed in to get a pen. He walked back out and picked the phone back up. "Give it to me again" Jack asked; Mezzi recited the address and Jack wrote it down. "I got it" Jack said afterward. "Okay, Jack…when are you coming?" Mezzi asked soft and sweetly. "Oh…uhh…tonight after school…about six" Jack replied. "Okay, Jack…I'll be waiting for you" Mezzi said in the same sexy tone. Jack hung the phone up and after hearing Mezzi's voice over the phone, his mind seemed to be in a state of suppressed excitement. Jack went into his room. He had already showered at Tina's and he was tired; so, he undressed, got into bed and took his Monday morning nap. He awoke around 12:30pm, dressed and was off to school, taking more than enough money with him to pay Mezzi. He arrived and attended his classes; all the while, having occasional erotic images flashing in his mind and the heated feelings that went with them.

He was trying to fend off those thoughts and feelings. His conscience was playing havoc with him as he struggled to negotiate between the natural lust that pre-existed and his commitment to Tina. At some point during the day, he decided he wasn't going to worry or fight it. After his last class, Jack went to Jake's and had a quick hamburger and fries dinner. He hopped on the Montrose bus to go to the address where Mezzi was. As he walked into the courtway building, a stream of ambiguous feelings coursed through his mind and body; excitement, dread; apprehension; he was trying to suppress them as he went forward on his mission. He walked up to the second floor apartment and knocked on the door that read 2B. He waited for a moment and there was no answer. He was beginning to feel a mild anxiety rising within.

He knocked again a little harder. "Who is it?" Mezzi's distinct voice spoke out through the door. "It's me…Jack, Mezzi" Jack said. Another short moment passed before the door slowly opened. Mezzi was standing behind it with a dress and house slippers on. "Hey, Jack….come on in" she said with that same soft, alluring tone that she had before. She stepped aside and drank him in with her gaze. "Hey, Mezzi" Jack greeted. "I got your stuff back here…come on" she said, beckoning him with a little flip of her wrist as she walked toward the back rooms of the apartment. "Where is your roommate" Jack asked. "She won't be home until about nine tonight" Mezzi said with a smile. Jack followed her into the open door of a bedroom. She walked over to a large canvas bag and untied the rope drawstrings and opened it. Jack looked inside to see several dozen cases of car wax, each containing multiple cans and numerous brand new sham rags and an assortment of other items he had requested for Mezzi to boost. He stooped down and went through the merchandise; sorting through it to see everything that was there. "Yea…this is good…exactly what I wanted…you did real good, Mezzi…what's my damage?" Jack said. "Retail…it's a little over three-hundred worth…I want what I asked…one-fifty" Mezzi said. "Okay….here you go" Jack said as he reached in his pocket and handed Mezzi a roll of bills. "Count it" he said after she took hold of the money. She counted it. "One-fifty…cool" she said after she finished. Then, she laid the money on the nearby dresser. She walked back over to the bed and sat on the edge of it. Jack was stooping down across from her, still looking through the bag before tying the drawstrings. Mezzi leaned back on her elbows on the bed and propped one of her feet up on the bed. Jack acknowledged the invitation.

Chapter 5
Abstinent Love

All of the workers at the gas station had become part of Jack's extended work force for his wash and wax hustle. They were all glad for the opportunities to make a little extra money whenever he gave them a wash or wax job. . They went about the jobs with enthusiasm; having fun and relishing each chance to make the extra money. The arrangement was, Jack let them have all of the money from the washes and kept fifteen dollars from each thirty-five dollar wax job they did because he was providing all of the wash and wax supplies. He would chide them if their wash or wax jobs were spotty; urging them to do a better job. Jack coordinated everything around when Gus was not at the station; mostly on the weekends. He made sure that each co-worker had an equal chance to make money. Sometimes, good-natured little spats broke out between the workers over the wash and wax jobs. But, Jack would jump in and smooth things out. There was a different atmosphere around the gas station. The workers seemed to be in higher spirits. Before, long, they were making as much money each week from this side hustle as their gas station pay. They had come to work as a team for the car wax and wash customers; all of them being especially courteous to those customers and treating the washes and waxes as though it was a regular part of the gas station business. But, being careful during the weekdays to not let Gus, the manager know what was going on. Jack always gave Brad, the weekend manager a little something whenever he had a good day with the washes and waxes. Jack knew that Brad was not the type to tell; but, he knew that the money insured his silence. Jack was getting more and more cars from Don Hardy's car dealership who was becoming his best customer; bringing in four or five cars every Saturday and Sunday for washes and waxes. Jack's hustle was growing and his understanding with his co-workers at the station was a good one. He was beginning to save up quite a bit of money from his venture. He began to have more cash stashed away in his room at the Y; being careful to lock it up where the cleaning people would not have to see it. He was accumulating enough money that he was making a trip to the bank at least once-a-week to make a deposit. He had begun to buy more clothes and nicer ones at that. Several weeks had passed. School and work were going well.

Finally, Jack looked at his bank book and decided that he had enough for a down payment on a car. It was time to pay Don Hardy a visit to see what kind of deal he could get on a car. But, before he did any of that, he had to get his driver's license back again. It was a simple matter of applying and taking both the written and driving test again. It took him a few weeks before he took both tests.

His college friend, Marvin, who had an old '65 Buick that he drove, took him to the State Drivers License facility to take the driving test after Jack had passed the written test the week before. Early Friday afternoon after Jack had finished his shift at the gas station, Marvin picked him up there and took him to the North Elston Avenue Drivers License facility. Jack used Marvin's car to take the driving test. He passed and got his license. Jack was elated and he chattered away excitedly as Marvin drove away from the facility and back to the Y. Jack thanked him profusely and talked about how he was going to go about picking out a nice used car to buy. Marvin was quiet, smiling all the while as he drove; pleased that his friend was so happy with the favor he had done for him.

It was late afternoon and Jack was sitting in his room at the Y. He was feeling too excited to sit around. He was hungry and went to have an early dinner at the Village Restaurant. He decided to walk from there to the poolroom where he had not visited in nearly a month. He was already feeling the pride he would have when he showed his friends on The Corner his new drivers license. He knew he would be bragging to them about his plans to buy a nice used car; even though his friends would calculate that Jack must have enough money to buy drinks. But, Jack knew how to play the game in the streets. He would intentionally carry only a few dollars with him so he would not be tempted to be too generous. He usually was, when buying drinks for his friends while not drinking himself.

The blue sky was clear and the sun shown brightly on this cold day. Jack took a different route; walking north to Lawrence Avenue before turning east to head toward The Corner. The sunny day seemed to add to the happy mood he was in. Finally, he arrived at Lawrence Avenue and the street was already bustling with the usual late Friday afternoon excitement. As he walked eastward, he could see the large, bright Aragon marquee with it's flashing lights. It advertised the big weekend rock show that was starting Saturday night. He could see the stir of activity inside as he passed the Aragon entrance. When he came to The Corner, he peered through the long picture window of the poolroom, as he always did, to see who was inside. He could see his friends Coley and Jabo seated side-by-side in the plastic chairs that lined the wall. There was sparse pool playing activity. Immediately, his spirit was lifted and he smiled to himself as he strolled inside. Jack knew that it was best that he didn't visit The Corner very often; but, he missed it, nonetheless.

"What's goin' on, y'aaalll!!" he spoke out loudly as he walked in amongst the group. Coley stood up and he and Jack engaged in a soul handshake. Jack and Jabo did the same. "Boy…you a sight for sore eyes, Jack" Jabo said. "You got that right" Coley echoed. Jack noticed that his two friends seemed a bit dispirited. "Why y'all lookin' all tired, man?" Jack asked. "Broke, man" Jabo said. "Me, too, Jack….and you know that I am hardly ever *flat* broke" Coley said a bit subdued. "We need a drink, man…can you handle that, Jack?" Coley asked. "Yea…what y'all want?" Jack asked. "You know what we drink, Jack….vodka" Coley replied. "Alright…let's go to Saxony" Jack said before they all walked out of the poolroom and began to walk together eastward toward the Saxony liquor store. Jack bought the drink for his friends and they went back to the poolroom. Inside the Men's restroom, Coley took a drink from the pint bottle of vodka and passed it to Jabo. Jabo took a drink and in turn, handed the bottle to Jack. "Naw….I still ain't drinkin', y'all" Jack said. "You still ain't drinkin, Jack?" Jabo asked. "Nope…still not drinkin'" Jack repeated. "That's alright…more for us" Coley said wryly before he reached and grabbed the bottle from Jabo and turned it up again. "Hey….check it out, y'all….got my drivers license back!" Jack announced proudly as he pulled out his drivers license ID and flashed it. "No shit?" Coley said as he took Jack's drivers license and looked it over. "Nice, man….now all you need is a ride" Coley said a bit wryly once again. "Yea…I think I'm gonna start lookin' for one pretty soon, too" Jack said with a broad smile on his face. "You are?…you must have some money, then" Coley quickly surmised. "Not really…I'm tryin' to scrape up a little money…my girl is gonna help me with the down payment" Jack lied in the spontaneous manner that everyone on the streets did. "You still with Tina, huh?" Coley asked. "Yea…we're still cool" Jack replied. "Okay…so ya' girl is gonna help you with the down-payment….how you gonna pay the car note?" Coley asked. "I got a little part-time job…plus…I get financial aid at school" Jack replied, purposely leaving out the information about his side hustle. "Yea…I know the school gives Shirley a nice chunk of money a coupla' times a year" Coley said. "Yea…I get the same thing" Jack added. The men walked back out to the poolroom, sat and lounged around.

Before long, Andrew came into the poolroom and walked up to them. "Hey, y'all" he greeted. ""'Whaddya' say, 'Drew…hey, 'Drew" they all greeted. "Where you been, 'Drew?….we ain't seen you in at least a month" Jabo asked. "Remember back when I was out here with y'all and the cops swooped down and took me to jail?" Andrew said. "Yea" Jabo replied. "I caught a case behind that…my wife just scrapped up the money to bail me out a few days ago" Andrew explained. "So, what's happ'nin' with your case?" Coley asked. "Man….I'm gonna beat it…'cause they got me on somebody else's strong-arm robbery….I just hope they don't find out about the ones I *did* do…if they don't…I'm cool" Andrew said with all the non-chalant expression of someone who was completely carefree. There was a spell of silence after that comment. "Yea…well, at least you can fight the case from the outside instead of from the inside of a jail cell" Jabo offered with a light chuckle. "Yea…believe me….I'm glad as hell to be out of that Cook County jail…they givin' out a lot of time over there right now….I seen a coupla' studs in my division get life" Andrew added. The men continued to chat as the regular Friday night pool shooting crowd began to trickle in; and with them, the usual buzz of excitement.

Finally, Ray Foster came in. Then, Woody and Fuzzy and their group of friends came and began shooting pool. Jack, Coley and Jabo were in their usual mode of sitting on the side watching the games and taking in the lively atmosphere of manly fun and leisure. They traded comments; laughed and cracked jokes; sneaking drinks from the pint bottle of vodka in-between. They mingled with the other regulars engaged in games and those who were loitering on the sides as they were.

Finally, three men who were well known around the area walked into the poolroom just as the evening hour began. They were revered in this part of town. There was a bit of a hush in the air as the three men strolled in looking very relaxed. They were Roger, T-Slick and Cassanova--all known to be big-time hustlers and pimps. Each of them made rare appearances in the poolroom. But, more rare was them appearing there together. They were well-acquainted with one another from traveling in the same circles and seemed to share a certain respect for one another. They regarded themselves as peers in the street hustling game. They were considered the top dogs in the game, as well. Their reputations were well-established far and wide across the city and even into other states and towns. They didn't mingle with ordinary folk nor allow lesser hustlers to associate with them. Everything was on a higher plain. Their reputations were shrouded in a certain mystique. Ordinary street hustlers aspired to be like them because of the respect they received. The mystique was as much about image as anything else. Maintaining an air of cool in the public eye was paramount. These three men were true to the game and the image by always dressing well; being flamboyant; driving big, fancy, expensive cars and flashing large rolls of cash. Whenever they spoke, it was always something very hip, clever or passionately philosophical with respect to the game. They were pacesetters. They were also known in the streets for being extremely ruthless; making money by a variety of means; all of it from the streets. Working ordinary jobs was for squares. They lived by an entirely different code. But, the thing that made them most respected is that they were dangerous characters. One would be served well to tread lightly around them and their affairs in the streets. You never wanted to make enemies with them. They had gained much of their respect by bringing harm to those who had crossed them, stolen from them or owed them an unpaid debt. They owned guns and associated with other dangerous characters. All of this was upon which their reputations were built. And so, these things were common knowledge amongst the ordinary folk in the streets. This was why there was a certain hush that came over the poolroom when they entered.

They strolled in; each with a regal bearing; with an air of supreme confidence and cool. They stopped at the counter to pay for a game. All eyes were on them when Roger pulled out a large roll of bills. "I got this" he said as he paid. All of the regulars in the poolroom seemed to suddenly be a little less talkative. They did not want to say or do anything in their presence that seemed especially square. There was a heightened consciousness. The three men strolled over to an unoccupied pool table. As they played their pool game, they talked spiritedly amongst themselves. As they did so, certain words that pimps were known to use could be overheard like "bankroll, trap, 'hoes. The others around the large poolroom who knew of them, were picking up on their language; no doubt, logging the inflection of the clever phrases into their memory. Some of the regulars were talking in hushed tones to others; giving out little tidbits of one or the other of the three big-time hustlers' storied episodes.

"Which one of 'em got the slickest ride?" Li'l Murphy, one of the youngest regulars, asked of Coley. "I think T-Slick…he got that Cadillac Seville…black with red leather interior…a customized silver-plated grill….vogue tires…and a lot of stuff on the inside, too" Coley said not too loudly. "Yea?...wonder where he parked it?" Li'l Murphy asked as he craned his neck, looking through the large picture window on the Winthrop-side of the poolroom. "Is that it there?" Li'l Murphy asked. Coley and Jack looked together. "Yep…that's it…cold ain't it, Jack?" Coley said. "Yea…sho' 'nough….I know I cain't even afford the tires on that bad boy" Jack commented as he gazed in admiration. "Look up the street…now, I know that's Roger's ride" Coley said, pointing as they all strained to peer further up the street through the window. "Is that it?…that Silver Brougham?" Jack asked. "Yea…cain't see it too good…but, it's sharp, too…ain't it?" Coley said. "Yes, indeed" "without a doubt…" Li'l Murphy and Jack commented. "Them studs is doin' it big!" Li'l Murphy said with excitement. "Now…Cassanova…he got a sweet ride, too…a maroon Cadillac Sedan Deville with a customized gold-colored grill….I don't see his…he musta' parked it further up the street…anyway…you don't wanna mess with none of them, y'all…you do…they might find you in a dumpster somewhere…dig?" Coley said with a tone of warning. With that, Jack and Li'l Murphy both gazed in awe across the room at the three men enjoying their lively pool game. They ogled the fine clothes they were wearing; mostly custom-tailored outfits and their flashy jewelry. Jack noted the hardened expressions ingrained into their faces. They looked determined and hardcore, he thought. The atmosphere continued to be lively inside the poolroom, albeit a bit more subdued than usual.

Jack, Coley and the others were carrying on their usual lively conversations when Bow-tie and Willie-the-Weep walked into the poolroom together. Bow-tie was carrying a large, black plastic bag over his shoulder. The two continued walking to the area where Jack, Coley and the others were seated. They stopped. Bow-tie leaned over and let the large plastic garbage bag slide off of his shoulder onto the poolroom floor. "Whaddya' say, gents?…Bow-tie on the hustle tonight…got somethin' y'all might be interested in" Bow-tie announced in his familiar southern accent. "Hey, Bow-tie…Weep" Jabo spoke first before all of the others who were sitting or standing nearby greeted them, as well.

Bow-tie was one of the neighborhood regulars who lived in the Tower apartment building on Winthrop in the forty-seven-hundred block south of The Corner. He was a man of short stature. He was likeable, charming and funny. He had a gentlemanly demeanor that seemed to carry from his southern roots. His tawdry style of dressing was how he got his nick-name. He loved to drink and have a good time with many of his other drinking neighbors who lived in the Tower apartment building. "What you got in the bag, Bow-tie?" Coley inquired, curiously cutting his eyes at the bloated black plastic bag sitting on the floor in front of them all. "Coley, my friend….I know yous' a player….you likes to style…right?" Bow-tie started. "Yea, man…you sellin' somethin'?....open the doggone bag and let's see what you got" Coley said anxiously; eager to view the bag's offerings.

"Well…I'm 'bout to do just that if you can hold on to ya' britches" Bow-tie said calmly before he untied the knot at the top of the plastic bag. Bow-tie opened the plastic bag and pulled out a couple of brand new men's leather coats; a jacket and a long leather with the tags still on them. "Ooowwwee!…Bow-tie…them is really nice!....where the hell did you get them?…I know you didn't knock for 'em yourself" Coley surmised. "Naw, naw, Coley…you know me….I ain't into hustlin' thata' way….man…I bought these one night from a boy out in front of the buildin'…he hustled 'em from somewhere…he needed him a hit real bad…sold it to me for a hell'uva price, too…couldn't turn it down…anyway…I had got my check that day….and you know me….I was high as a kite when I bought this stuff….it's been sittin' in my closet ever since…but, now my money done run shawt and I gots to put some scratch in my pocket" Bow-tie explained. "Man…I wish I could buy 'em…what size is they?" Coley asked. "This 'un here is a forty-six long and this long one is a forty-eight regular…I got another nice one in the bag but, I don't wanna be pullin' all of it out at once" Bow-tie explained. The others inched forward and looked the coats over and commented on how nice they were and how they wish they could buy them. But, most all of them didn't even have a decent amount of pocket change, let alone enough to buy the expensive leather coats. "Why don't you let me have this one here on credit, Bow-tie?….I guarantee I'll pay you in a coupla' days" Coley offered, touching the stylish leather jacket laying inside the plastic bag. "Naw, naw, my good buddy…I cain't work like that…sorry, Coley…C-O-D, baby…that's what I need…cash on the barrel-head" Bow-tie said with a serious expression. "Okay….I can dig it" Coley sighed with resignation. "Weep…why don't you watch over this stuff while I take this jacket right here and go 'round and try to sell it to one o' these fellas up in here?" Bow-tie said to Willie-the-Weep.

With that, Willie-the-Weep grabbed the plastic bag and pulled it closer to him as he sat in front of the long picture window with the others. Bow-tie walked around from table-to-table talking to the pool players with the leather jacket in hand. This went on for almost an hour before he returned to the area where The Weep and the others were sitting. "No luck, Weep….we done tramped all around tryin' to sell these coats in these bars and taverns up and down the streets before we hit this poolroom…I'm surprised we ain't got a sale on these nice coats....they beautiful...ain't they?" Bow-tie said.

"They sho' 'nough is....but, I'll tell you what...I see you didn't go over to them boys who really got the money...T-Slick and them over there...I didn't see you ask them did they wanna buy anything....there your sale is right there" Coley said, making a vague motion of his head in the direction of the three big-time players. "Coley...you right....Weep...yo' turn, man....I'm pooped out, brotha'...see if them pimp-boys might be interested in them leathers...know they got some money...if I had their money...I'd throw mine away...hahaha" Bow-tie quipped with a light chuckle. "Okay...let me try...I'll take the long leather....see if they like this one" The Weep said before he opened the plastic bag and pulled out the brand new long leather and walked toward the three men playing their pool game. Jack, Coley and many of the others turned their attention to the action as they watched

The Weep walked over and began speaking to the big-time players. They were too far away to hear the conversation over the noisy poolroom. But, Bow-tie, Coley and Jack could see the interaction with each of the men looking the leather coat over. Roger even tried it on. It seemed to fit. For a moment, there was a conversation between Roger and The Weep. Finally, Roger took the leather coat off and handed it back to The Weep. The Weep strolled back toward Bow-tie and the others with a look of disappointment on his face. "Man...he talkin' 'bout he'll give me thirty bucks for it" The Weep whispered. "That ain't even close" The Weep continued. "You damn skippy.....man...I'll keep 'em and wear 'em my damned self before I give 'em away like that" Bow-tie spoke in a hushed tone. "Damn, Weep....we ain't did nothin'...and I'm shakin' like a dog shittin' 'simmon seeds" Bow-tie said. "Me, too" The Weep said.

Jack was sitting just a few feet away as he overheard the exchange. He felt sorry for his two friends and drinking buddies. "Y'all need a drink, Weep?" Jack asked. "Yea, Jack...we sho' could use one...we been trampin' 'round for a while....can you help ya' pals out?" Bow-tie asked. "Yea...step it off with me, Bow-tie" Jack whispered as he raised up from his seat and walked toward the Men's room in the back with Bow-tie following. "Be right back, Weep" Bow-tie said. "Here ya' go" Jack said inside the Men's room as he handed Bow-tie a few dollar bills. "That's for both of y'all….look out for Weep, too" Jack said. "Thanks-a-bunch, Jack…you sho' is a lifesaver….I sho' 'nough 'preciate this….you know I'm gonna look out for our boy, Weep…this'll take the haints off of us" Bow-tie responded with gratitude.

"You know what else?....you know I'm pretty good at sellin' stuff…right?...you want me to try to sell them leathers for you?" Jack asked. "If you think you can do any good…by all means…do yo' thang, brotha…me and Weep trust ya" Bow-tie said with renewed enthusiasm. "Okay…I'll tell you what…I'll try at the Aragon next door…the owner is there tonight and I deal with him all the time sellin' him stuff…I'll go over there first…okay?" Jack said. "Right on, Jack…you know me and Weep know ya….we done seen you in action hustlin' like a mad Russian…we know what you can do…go get the bag and try ya' luck…me and Weep will wait in the poolroom" Bow-tie said. "What you want to try to get for all three leathers?" Jack asked. "Jack…try to get much as you can but, don't settle for less that two hundred for all three…okay?" Bow-tie said. "Okay, Bow-tie…I'm on my way right now" Jack said. With that, they walked back into the noisy poolroom and Jack grabbed the plastic bag that had all three leather coats and headed out of the poolroom to the Aragon next door. He was gone for about half-an-hour before he returned. When he walked back toward the poolroom without the plastic bag, he could see through the glass window of the poolroom as he passed in front of it. He could see Bow-tie and the Weep inside. He noticed the excitement on their faces when they saw that he didn't have the bag anymore. He saw the wide smiles on their faces as he walked toward where they were seated. "Let's walk to the back, fellas" Jack said in a low tone. The Weep and Bow-tie followed. Jack led them to a bathroom stall. On the streets, everyone operated in a highly private mode when it came to money. . Money was scarce amongst the street regulars. If they drew a bead on you, they would beg or play you for as much as they could. One had to be very discreet--even with friends. "Okay…this is what I got…two-thirty" Jack announced to both men in the cramped stall space. "The two men whooped and giggled gleefully like little kids. "Damn, Jack!…that is sweet, man!…that's real good!….I ain't lyin'!" The Weep said with a huge sigh of relief. "Jack…you my ace, baby-boy'…hahahahaha!…I know'd if anybody could pull it off…you could…hahaha..” Bow-tie cackled with joy. Jack handed him the roll of money. “Yea…the owner bought ‘em…you know he got big-time money…he knew it was a good deal….bought all three of ‘em” Jack explained. “Here ya’ go, Jack” Bow-tie said as he handed Jack a twenty dollar bill. “You did good” Bow-tie added. “Better than good….that’s my buddy…you can count on Jack to give it a good try if nothin’ else” The Weep commented. “Jack…you know we got to play it off…you know the vultures is out there lookin’ for somethin’…let’s go” Bow-tie said. With that, they walked back into the poolroom, pretending to still be negotiating; walking to the opposite side of the poolroom from the group they were with earlier. They were still sitting and standing around.

The Weep, Bow-tie and Jack walked closer to the front of the poolroom but, stayed on the far end of the vast room. Then, Bow-tie slipped out of the front door of the poolroom while The Weep and Jack stayed and continued to talk in a corner far from the others. Then, The Weep slipped out of the poolroom front door not very long after Bow-tie. Jack followed a little later. They all met up in front of the Tower building where Bow-tie lived. “Yea…look like we got away clean as a whistle….If we’d a’ stuck around that poolroom, it woulda’ been a beggin’ contest ‘twixt all o’ them chumps that was hangin’ around” Bow-tie said. “Sho’ ‘nough” The Weep chimed in. “Weep…here…you can go get the taste….get some Southern Comfort for me…then get what you want…I’ll look out for you when you get back….come on up, Jack….I’m goin’ in the crib for the night” Bow-tie said after he handed The Weep a crisp twenty dollar bill. “I’m goin to the Boozery…okay?” The Weep said before he took off. Bow-tie led Jack into the Tower building. It was understood that they would go up to Bow-tie’s third floor apartment and fellowship with drinks as they had done so many times in the past. “I’ll hang with y’all for a while Bow-tie but, I ain’t drinkin’” Jack said casually. “Not drinkin?” Bow-tie said with genuine surprise as he paused on a step while they were going up the stairwell. “What’s the matter?…you on medication or somethin’?” Bow-tie asked somewhat seriously. “Naw…just stoppin’ for a while” Jack said to mute the curiosity. “Okay…well…come on up, then” Bow-tie said as they continued on up to Bow-tie’s place. Willie-The-Weep returned and he and Bow-tie sat on the sofa and began to drink and tell old stories and crack jokes; kicking their heels high up in the air, they were laughing so hard. They seemed to be feeling better-and-better. All of their cares suddenly seemed far away. Jack enjoyed their crazy talk and wild sense of humor. He loved to hang out with them because they were so entertaining and he knew they were good people. Jack spent more than an hour enjoying their company in Bow-tie's apartment; never taking a drink the entire time but, having a good time, nonetheless. It made Jack feel good that he was able to help his friends out. He knew they appreciated it and thought well of him for it. They were his family and he cared about them.

He went home, still tickled from the two men's carryings on. Jack arrived back at his room at the Y. He could see that his clock-radio read 8:32pm. He took off his coat and went immediately back out into the hallway to the phones and called Tina. "Hi, Baby" Jack said after Tina answered. "Hi, Honey" she replied. "What you doin'?" Jack asked. "Nothin'….just finished my dinner…watching television" Tina replied. "What you wanna do this weekend?" Jack asked. "Oh, Jack…I need some time to get some things done…some projects I have for my classes…it's gonna take some time…I have to go to the library to do a little research on Saturday afternoon…plus, my mom wants me to come over on Sunday and help her with some cleaning and re-arranging she is going to do…is that okay, honey?…we get together almost every weekend…can we skip this weekend?" Tina seemed to be pleading. Suddenly a knot was forming in Jack's stomach and he did not know why. Tina's request was not unreasonable, he thought. They *had* been together almost every weekend for months. "Aw..yea…okay..yea…that's cool, baby…no problem" Jack said, trying to mask his surprise. "Ohhh…thanks, Jack…I do need some time to do stuff this weekend…we can talk on the phone…call me late Saturday or early Sunday…okay?" Tina advised. They talked a little longer before Jack hung up.

Jack knew that he should not be feeling the weighty disappointment he was feeling. It seemed out-of-line with the situation. Indeed, he had enjoyed all of those splendid weekends in the company of his sweetheart. Each weekend had been as delightful as he could have ever dreamed. Besides, he had been alone many-a-day before he met Tina. He had become used to being alone; used to being occupied full-time with survival. Now, he had to admit to himself that he had come to expect too much of the affair and Tina. He had to voluntarily turn his attention elsewhere this weekend. “A car!…go to Don Hardy’s car place to see about buying a car!... …yes…that would get him excited all over again!” he thought. Jack could go to Don Hardy’s car lot and look at some cars this weekend. Then, he could tell Tina all about it when they talked on the phone. He planned to go there after work this Saturday. He felt a new surge of excitement welling up; even though he missed Tina already with the thought of not being with her physically. He knew that they were still together in each other’s heart. That thought comforted him and diminished the bit of disappointment he felt.

“Hey, Jack…check out my new watch I bought…pretty cool…huh?” Brad said with a broad smile as Jack entered the gas station to start his shift. “Hey, Jack…I got the money for those last two wax jobs…I’ll give it to you in a minute…those two cars on the lot are both waxes” Roberto said as he passed Jack on his way out of the station to the lot to attend to a gas customer. Jack was a little subdued this morning as he paid scant attention to his co-workers. Things had really livened up around the station lately and the guys were all smiling a lot more these days. But, Jack was a bit pre-occupied with himself. He had been deeply introspective since he spoke to Tina last night. Even though they were not getting together this weekend, he still had plenty to be happy about. School was going well and he wasn’t broke anymore. He wasn’t drunk all the time, either. Life looked so much brighter and promising through his sober eyes. So, why was he so introspective? So pensive? There seemed to be a sense of foreboding deep inside that eluded him. All of this was leading into worry. Jack hated that. So, he decided that it was him worrying himself and nothing more. He needed to let go of his expectations regarding Tina. He realized he had taken their get-togethers for granted. He needed to back up and re-assess himself; let go of the silly notions he was entertaining.

Jack waited on a parade of gas customers before he could start on one of the wax jobs. He gave the other to Roberto before Johnny from Don Hardy’s came to drop off two more cars for wax jobs. “Brotha’, Jack…what’s goin on, player?” Johnny greeted in his usual lively manner as they engaged in a soul handshake.

"Nothin, man…comin' over there today…check out some rides" Jack announced. "No shit?…you comin' after you get off today?….cool!…got some smokin' rides over there right about now…better come on…you might find a deal like I got…got some caddys that need a little work…clean bodies, too" Johnny said with a sense of excitement.

"Yea…comin' right after work" Jack assured. "Hey…why don't I pick you up?....I'll come in my car…the caddy I bought from Don…cool?" Johnny said. "Yea…can you come at 4:30?" Jack asked. "Hell, yea…I'll pick you up, then…you can see my ride…see the deal I got…alright?" Johnny said with the same excitement. "Okay…I'll wait for you" Jack said. Johnny's co-worker, Oscar, took the other car to be waxed off of the tow truck bed and Johnny got into the truck with him after leaving the car that he drove. They rode back together to Don Hardy's just as they had done each time they dropped the cars off at the gas station. Jack finished the wax job and continued on to have a busy workday. Finally, it was 4:30pm and he had cleaned up and was waiting for Johnny to pick him up.

Finally, a dark blue Cadillac drove onto the lot and Jack could see Johnny behind the wheel as he swerved up to the gas station entrance. Jack hopped in and they rode toward the Don Hardy lot on Cicero Avenue. As they did, Johnny coached Jack on how to deal with the sales people; telling him which sales people to talk to and how to negotiate a deal and so on; treating Jack like a personal friend rather than an ordinary customer. "I 'preciate you pullin' my coat on what to do….that info sho' 'nough will come in handy" Jack said to Johnny as he drove. "Aw…Yea, man…. I just don't wanna see a good brotha' get played like they done played some of the customers….that salesman Rico….he's real greedy and cold-blooded….he'll sell you a piece of garbage for the highest price he can get…commission, you know….he's real cutthroat…avoid him at all costs…either deal with Jim Richmond or Don himself…they got authority to make you a good deal…they can drop the price like they want to…they are both the owners….but Don is the main owner…Jim is part owner and manager" Johnny explained. "Okay…cool…this ride of yours is real slick, man…this is the one you had the engine put in…huh?" Jack said. "Yea…see how smooth it rides?" Johnny asked. "Yea…rides real smooth…and it's clean, too" Jack said.

Soon, Johnny pulled off of Cicero Avenue and onto the Don Hardy lot. It was huge; spreading an entire city block with a sea of cars. Many customers were walking around on the lot looking at cars. “Come on…I’ll introduce you to Jim Richmond…you’ll see Don, too” Johnny said as they approached the office and showroom building at the center of the lot. Johnny led Jack into the bustling office and showroom. They walked around for a moment before Johnny spotted Jim Richmond engrossed with a customer. He could see Don Hardy from several yards through the glass partitions of his big office; he was also with a customer. “Just be cool for a while…Rico is an Italian stud…dresses real slick….if he comes by and asks can he help you…tell him you’re already bein’ helped…okay?” Johnny advised. “Yea….alright” Jack replied. “Come on…let’s go out on the lot…look at some rides….I’ll show you some nice ones and which ones to avoid” Johnny said. “Cool” Jack replied. They walked out onto the lot and they walked around and Jack began to feel the excitement welling up as he looked at the numerous cars on the lot. There was a black 1969 Chrysler New Yorker with silver trimming that he liked; a 1968 Mercury Monterey that was sharp looking. “This Monterey….I remember this one…leaks too much oil…might need some valve work, too….forget about that one” Johnny advised. Finally they came upon a gold-colored 1969 Cadillac Coupe Deville that looked immaculate. “Man….I like this one, Johnny…this is real nice….just what I had in mind…what do you think about that price?” Jack asked with a tone of excitement. “Thirty-four-hundred-five?.....they’ll come down off that a little, I believe” Johnny said. “I don’t know about this one, though….looks real clean…nice interior…go back inside and wait for Jim Richmond….let him know right off the top that you got a job but, you cain’t pay too high ‘uva’ note…let him know you’re interested in this Coupe…dig what I’m sayin’?” Johnny advised.

“Right on…let’s go talk to him” Jack said excitedly before the two headed back to the office building. “You know what?....I think I might stand a better chance with Don…I met him already…he knows about my hustle…he is my main car wash and wax customer…that’s what I wanna do…talk to him” Jack said, still bubbling with excitement. “Yea…that makes sense to me…Jim is cool but…go ahead…talk to Don…he can cut you a sweet deal if you talk to him right” Johnny advised. As the two re-entered the office building, they could see Don Hardy shaking hands with a customer and the customer left shortly after. “Come on, Jack…I’ll walk you up to his office door” Johnny said as he led the way for Jack. “Don…you got a customer here lookin’ to see you” Johnny announced as he leaned his head into Don Hardy’s office. “Oh, yea…who is it..ohh…ohh…yea…my wash and wax guy…come on in!” the blustery Don Hardy said, flashing a broad smile. “Good to see you, young fellow…everyone’s been pleased with the work you’ve done on our cars…real good work you’ve been doing” Don Hardy said as he extended his hand to shake Jack’s. “Hi ya doin’, Mr. Hardy” Jack said. “Sit on down…what can I do for you?’” Don Hardy said. “I’ll see you later, Jack” Johnny said as he turned and walked away. “Uhh….I think I’m ready to buy a car from you” Jack said. “Well…that’s great…have you had a chance to look over the lot to see which one you might be interested in?” Don asked. “Yessir…I saw a sixty-nine caddy coupe out there that I liked” Jack said. “Alright…here…I need you to do something, then…take this pad and pen and write down the make, model, color and the VIN number….okay?” Don said as he handed the items to Jack. Jack immediately went back out to the lot and wrote those things down, being careful to get the VIN number right. He returned to the office and Don was talking to another salesperson before Jack could talk to him. When he was done talking, he beckoned Jack back into his office. Don looked over the information that was written on the pad and looked over a wide printout he had amongst a lot of other papers and reports that were spread out on his desk. “Okay…let’s see here” he mumbled as he compared the information. “Okay…here we go…yes….that is a sixty-nine Cadillac Coupe….looks like we got it all squared away with our inspections…looks to be in good mechanical shape…everything else…alright….we’re asking thirty-four-hundred-fifty for that one…okay?” Don said. “Alright…uhh…Mr. Hardy…how much would my car note be?” Jack asked. “Well…depends…how much can you put down?” Don asked. “Ohh…about a grand” Jack replied. “Okay…now….we got to run a credit check on you…and then figure out how you’re gonna get financed…can you get a bank loan on your own?” Don asked. “I doubt it…I ain’t never got a loan before….never really had any credit” Jack said. “Oh, boy…well…I’ll tell you what…we’re doing business together…I know you're a hardworking young man…let me crunch some numbers here and see what I can do for you" Don said before he started punching the numbers on the calculator sitting on his desk. "Okay…now…can you pay about one-ten a month?" Don asked. "Yessir…I can pay that….long as I keep gettin' business from you" Jack said with enthusiasm and a big smile. "Oh don't worry about that…Don Hardy's business isn't going anywhere….you'll definitely keep getting cars to do from me…okay, young man…I think we've got a deal!" Don said. "Right on!....I mean…thank you, sir" Jack said excitedly. "Now…what I am going to do is….I'll finance you myself…now…I'm giving you a great rate…eight percent over twenty-four months…the most time I can finance a car that old…for a person with no credit history, I usually charge at least twice that rate…but, we're doing business…I like your hard work….and I trust you…I haven't had a single complaint about the work you've done for me…now when can you give your down payment?" Don asked. "I can bring it on Monday" Jack said with a smile and a gleam in his eyes. "Okay, then….I'll have the paper work drawn up…when you come in Monday…you'll sign some papers…give us the down payment and you'll be all set to drive away!" Don said.

They shook hands and Jack left the dealership feeling very excited about the car deal he just made. He couldn't believe that it was so easy. Things had turned out in his favor without him doing very much, it seemed. He realized that the business relationship with Don Hardy that he happened upon had paid big dividends. He was very happy. He found Johnny and talked excitedly about the deal he struck with the owner himself. "Damn, brotha'….he gave you a sweet deal!....I told ya….see there….my advice paid off….you gonna be ridin' slick pretty soon…that's real cool!…give me some dap" Johnny responded to Jack's excited talk as they did a little soul hand-slapping. "Look out for my ride for me until I get back on Monday, Johnny….alright!" Jack yelled out excitedly as he trotted away to catch the bus.

Finally, after he was sitting on the bus, heading back to the Y, Jack's mind drifted back to Tina. He couldn't wait to tell her about the car he was buying. Even though he was feeling excited to call her, somberness still lingered underneath the joyous feelings. It gave him an odd sense of ambiguity. He returned to the Y and remembered that he had mid-terms. The last week of

March was beginning and his mid-terms were next Thursday. He decided that he would stay inside and study before calling Tina. It was almost 8pm. He studied but, his mind did not seem as clear and focused as it had been before. But, the studying was useful nonetheless. Finally, he relaxed for a while by watching television until the news went off at 10:30pm.

It was almost 11pm when he decided to call Tina. "Hi, Honey…my mom called me to come over for dinner tonight….I went and she tried to get me to spend the night…but, I told her I had to get back to my place because I had something to do…how are you?" Tina said. "I'm okay…guess what?...I bought a car!…a real nice one, too…wait until you see it!…it's real cool!" Jack said, trying his best to contain his excitement. "Oh, yea?…that's great, Jack…really great" Tina said. She did not respond with the degree of enthusiasm that Jack expected. It was kind of lukewarm, he thought. "I'm pickin' it up on Monday…I could drive by there on Monday night!" Jack said excitedly. "Ohh…uh…I'll be trying to rest on Monday night, Jack…can we do that some other time?" Tina replied. Jack was a little surprised at her response. "Uh..wha…what's the matter, baby?…you don't want me to come by on Monday night?" Jack stammered. "No, Jack…it's not that at all…I just need to rest on Monday…take it easy…I've been really busy lately…okay, honey?" Tina pleaded with a tone of frustration. "Okay, baby….I understand…you still want to get together next weekend…right?" Jack asked. "We can get together…let's talk about it later in the week…I'm just tired right now…alright, honey?" Tina said. "Okay…we'll talk later" Jack said. The two talked a couple of minutes more before they hung up.

Jack was feeling a bit mystified about the exchange with Tina. He could sense a change in her. He couldn't quite understand what it was but, he was feeling it. Or was he just being overly sensitive? He wasn't quite sure. He needed to contemplate to sort it all out. He already recognized that he may be putting a little too much expectation on Tina; that she was human and she did get tired and maybe she had too much to do recently. Whatever it was, he was surprised to find himself being so sensitive about it. In the streets, he and his friends had always been so cavalier; always subscribing to the player mentality when it came to women. You could say you cared for a woman. But, it wasn't cool to show it. Jack had been through quite a bit in his life; especially in the last few years. He had put himself through the rough-and-tumble life of surviving on the streets. He had experienced the insanity of it all; the brutal, raw madness. Yet, he had been durable through it all. But, somehow, the disturbing twinge of emotion he was feeling right now seemed more pronounced; perhaps, because he was feeling it where he had never felt it before; in his heart. He also realized that he had not been sober long enough to feel this way about a woman before. Jack went to bed. But, it took a while longer than usual for him to fall asleep.

Jack woke up late on Sunday morning. He remembered having a crazy dream about he and Tina riding in his newly bought car. Something about them being chased by another car and a man yelling from the pursuing car calling out Tina's name. It was all very vague now. He sat up on the edge of the bed to let his head clear and to get his bearings; all the while, feeling a bit mystified by the curious dream. He could also feel a strong urge to want to hold Tina tight; to embrace her warmly. He didn't know why the urge had suddenly come about. But, it seemed like what he needed just at this moment. Somehow, having that feeling told him that Tina was now deep in his soul. She had become a part of him. Then, gradually his head cleared and the curious thoughts and feelings faded.

He looked at his clock-radio on the dresser and could see "10:33am" He hurried to throw on his robe and grabbed some change from his drawer before he rushed out into the hallway to the phones. He remembered that Tina had told him to call her early on Sunday morning. He called and there was no answer. He realized that she had gone out and she had not called him. He remembered that usually, she would have. It wasn't a big deal, he decided. He would talk to her later. His thoughts turned to the day ahead. There was nothing to do today; no plans; no get-together with Tina; no work; no school. He decided he would go out to the Village restaurant to have breakfast and come back to study for his mid-term exams for a couple of classes next week. He had his breakfast. After returning to his room, he studied for as long as he could. When he was done, he just kind of laid stretched across the bed for a long while; letting his mind drift into stagnation. Then suddenly, that creeping feeling of loneliness spread over him. It seemed to engulf him completely. It was that familiar old feeling that he used to have; that always seemed to linger and lurk inside; it never felt good; that feeling he would have just before the urge to drink would come about. Right now, just as always, the thought of drinking popped into his head. He could never intellectually identify these feelings. He just had them; then reacted to them; usually by drinking. What was he going to do next? He didn't know. He felt a strong urge to get out of his small room. It began to have a suffocating feeling. He sat up on the edge of the bed trying to think of something he could do or somewhere he could go that was not part of his usual routine. But, no ideas came to him; only the compelling urge to go to The Corner. The only other people he knew other than his friends on The Corner were his new friends at school. But, he only saw them at school. He needed to be around people right now.

So, he got up, showered, got dressed and he left out of the Y. He headed to the only place he could go where people knew and accepted him. The weather was much warmer today. Spring had just begun. Jack was beginning to feel much better as he strolled along the street underneath the partly-cloudy sky. The wind wafted about him warm and softly. The warmer weather seemed to awaken that familiar sense of excitement within him. His mood seemed to gradually brighten as he continued on. He saw more people gathering together outside along the streets than he had seen in recent Sunday afternoons. He marched on.

As he passed the entrance of the Aragon, he could see his friends Coley and Li'l Murphy across the street from the poolroom, sitting on a favorite concrete stoop. He smiled to himself as he walked toward them. He also heard Fuzzy's loud, animated voice echoing from across the street. Jack glanced over to see him gathered with his friends drinking at the rear of the E-Z-GO gas station lot. Cozell, the neighborhood drunk, was hanging around Frances Tavern with a couple of other notable drinkers. The warm weather had brought out the usual array of street characters. Jack was back in his element where he felt most at ease; where he felt a glorious sense of freedom and fellowship.

"Hey, Jack is back…Jack is back…Jack is back…hahaha" Coley called out playfully as Jack approached them. "Surprised to see you today, Jack…what's hap'nin' brotha'?" Coley greeted as they engaged in the usual soul handshake. "Nothin….just figured I would come and hang out on a nice day like this" Jack replied.

"What's goin' on L'il Murph?....what's to ya, baby!" Jack said as he greeted him spiritedly with a handshake. There seemed to always be this tone of merriment in these exchanges with his friends. Jack's mood was always lifted by it. "Still with Tina…huh?" Coley asked. "Yea…we still together" Jack replied, not wanting to expound on the subject. "How ya' school thang comin' along?" Coley asked with genuine concern. "Still in school….doin' alright….you know.." Jack answered. "what's been goin' on around this way?" Jack asked.

"Chucky died" Coley said flatly. "You mean dope-fiend Chucky that hangs with Skip and them sometimes?" Jack asked with a tone of surprise. "Yea…him…OD'd in the hallway where Jabo lives…died last Saturday" Coley said. "No shit?…they didn't set him outside after he got too high did they?" Jack asked. "Naw…he was gettin' high somewhere else…then, later on, he went and bought some more dope…tried to do it all by himself…it was too much…killed him" Coley explained. "It was good he wasn't at Jabo or Skip's place when he died…they woulda' caught a case" Jack surmised. "Yea…you're right…they investigated and found out he wasn't at either one of their places before he OD'd" Coley said. This was the kind of conversation that Street Gypsies would occasionally have when someone they knew from the streets met a tragic end. It was expected and accepted as part of the street life.

"Hey…check it out…gettin' me a ride, man!" Jack announced. "Yea?…your old lady dropped that down-payment money on you…huh?" Coley asked. It took Jack a few seconds to remember the lie he had told Coley about Tina helping with his car down-payment. "Yea..yea..uhh..yea she did a little somethin' for me….dig" Jack replied. "Let me get another brew over there, Coley" Li'l Murphy asked. Coley reached behind a nearby bush and into a brown paper bag to pull out a tall can of beer. Jack looked at the can of beer with the film of frost on it and it looked appetizing.

Before he knew it "Let me get one too, Coley" seemed to come out of his mouth involuntarily. "Naw?…you drinkin' again?....you really want a beer?…no bullshit?" Coley asked Jack after he handed Li'l Murphy a beer. "Yea, man…give me the damn beer…stop askin' questions" Jack said with a bit of annoyance. Jack took the can of beer Coley handed him. "Hey, y'all…pour a little out for Chucky" Coley said. "To Chucky" they all said in unison as each poured a little of their beer onto the ground. After that, Jack turned the beer up to guzzle some of it down. He felt the little alarm deep inside go off. But, he ignored it and took a few more swallows of the refreshing brew. He was tired of trying to walk the tightrope of civility; of trying to be righteous; trying to balance his life on a double-edged sword. For some reason, he had suddenly become uninspired. Jack hung around in the same spot for a good while, laughing and joking with Coley and Li'l Murphy. Later on, Skip and Larry came along and joined in. When the beer was gone, Jack sent Li'l Murphy to Saxony Liquors to buy another six-pack. The spirited banter continued. Jack had completely forgotten how he felt when he woke up this morning. His cares seemed to have vanished in all of the revelry. Street-corner bullshitting was the order of the day; especially when the weather had broken as it had recently.

Suddenly, Jack remembered that he needed to go to pick his car up at Don Hardy's before his afternoon classes tomorrow. He did not want to get drunk and not be able to get up in time to do that. Besides, he had to stop at the bank before he went there. He stood around for a little while longer with his friends. He was enjoying the fellowship. But, the thought of what he needed to do was gnawing at him. He certainly did not want to get drunk and spoil the joyous day he had anticipated tomorrow. "I got to cut out, y'all" Jack finally forced himself to speak out. "Why you leavin' Jack?" Larry asked. I got to finish studyin' for my exams comin' up at school in a few days….got to pick up my ride in the mornin' too" Jack explained. He departed with a soul handshake for each of his friends before he walked away. Jack did not like leaving in the middle of having a good time with his friends. But, he did not want the regrets that would come tomorrow had he stayed.

As he walked back to the Y, it felt a little odd to once again have alcohol in his system after a few months of not drinking at all. He felt just a hint of the wild, mischievous feeling he used to get. But, he had intentionally drank only beer. He knew that any hard liquor would have launched him into that same familiar madness that he knew so well; that drunken insanity that was so unpredictable. Jack made it back home and it was just approaching the evening hour. He thought about calling Tina. But, she had left out this morning without calling him. Before, she seemed to always look forward to being with him; talking to him on the phone. Now she didn't quite seem the same. Jack was feeling a little bit of the defiance that he used to feel when he got high. He began to think "Hey…forget about callin' her…let her call me" This would be his new attitude. He was not going to behave like a love-sick chump, he thought. He was trying to muster up his emotional strength. But, deep in his soul, he could feel that burning sensation of desire and yearning for Tina. He tried to mentally fend it off. He undressed and laid in the bed, wrestling with his thoughts and feelings for a little while before the effects of the beer allowed him to drift to sleep.

Jack woke up early Monday morning. He sat up on the edge of the bed. He paused there, trying to detect just how he was feeling; and he felt fine. He did not feel any ill effects what-so-ever from his little deviation yesterday. He was happy that his day could proceed without any problems. His clock-radio read "7:52am" and it was perfect timing for him to shower and be on his way. His thoughts turned to what lie ahead this morning. With the excitement of purchasing a car, his mood turned upbeat and happy as he moved about his small room. He finished his shower and dressed. He grabbed his bank book and walked out of the Y. He did not plan to have breakfast right now because he was too excited about buying the car. He walked the several blocks to the Ravenswood bank at Lawrence Avenue and Ravenswood. He went in and withdrew about eleven hundred dollars.

He caught the Lawrence bus to Cicero Avenue. Then, the Cicero Avenue bus to Don Hardy's dealership. When he got off the bus, he walked at a hurried pace through the car lot before he arrived at the offices. He walked over to Don Hardy's office and the door was locked. Jack could see through the glass walls that no one was inside. He turned around and was met by a man. "How ya' doin' there…can I help you?" the man asked. "Oh…I was lookin' for Don…I'm supposed to sign some papers and pick up my car today" Jack said. "Well…I'm Jeff Carter.....I'm a salesman….let me see if I can find out about your deal…okay?…just hold on while I check it out" the man said before he walked over to another office where another man was sitting behind a desk. Jack stood on the opposite side of the showroom as he watched and waited as the men engaged in a conversation. Before, long, the man walked back to where Jack stood. “Yea…that’s Jim Richmond over there…he’s probably got your papers all ready to sign…go see him” the salesman said. “Thanks…’preciate that” Jack replied before he walked over to Jim’s office.

“Yessir…come on in…have a seat….can I get your name?” Jim Richmond asked as he shuffled through a stack of papers on his desk. “Jack Rollins” Jack replied. “After a moment, Jim pulled some of the papers out of the stack. “Here we go…Jack Rollins…sixty-nine caddy coupe…yes…you’re supposed to give me a thousand-dollar down payment…right?” Jim said. “Yessir…got a cashier’s check right here” Jack said before he reached into his billfold and pulled the check out and handed it to Jim. “Good…alright…need you to sign here…here and here” Jim said as he handed Jack the papers and pointed to the signing places on them. Jack signed the papers and immediately his mood was lifted. “Okay…now take this paper here and give it to the guys over there in that garage…that’s where your car is…they will give you your car keys…look the car over inside and out before you drive off…if you notice anything wrong with the car right then…let them know…if you have any kind of problems after you drive away with the car…bring it back in as soon as you can and we’ll see about straightening it out…alright?” Jim said before he reached his hand out and he and Jack shook hands. Jack was so excited, he seemed to be walking on air as he strolled across the lot to the garage in the distance. When he arrived, he saw his friend, Johnny inside congregating and talking loud and spiritedly with a group of co-workers in coveralls. “Brotha’ Jack….come to pick up ya’ ride huh?....theses my co-workers….Chills and Jonesy” Johnny said. “Hey y’all” Jack greeted hey now, brotha’ Jack…Hey, Jack” the two co-workers said as they took turns shaking Jack’s hand. “You got that gold coupe…Huh?” Chills, a tall, light-skinned fellow with a bushy afro asked. “Yea…that looks like it over there” Jack said as he gazed at the gleaming gold Cadillac that was parked in the stall furthest away. “Oh…that’s it for sho’…I had our helper here to clean it up a little….it’s already been through the certification inspection…I made sure they looked at it good….not that spot check they do on a lot of cars” Johnny said with a boisterous tone and a wide grin. “You looked out for me…huh?” Jack said, looking at Johnny appreciatively and smiling broadly. “Yea…I got you, man” Johnny replied in the spirit of brotherhood. “I got to have you look the car over….go and start it up and let it run for a little bit before you sign these delivery papers” Jonesy said to Jack. “Aw…yea…cool” Jack said as he took the car keys Jonesy handed him.

“Let him drive it a few blocks…then come back and sign” Johnny suggested to Jonesy” “He can do that…go ‘head” Jonesy replied. “Jack…let me ride with you…see how you rollin’…alright?” Johnny asked. “Aint no thang…come on” Jack replied and they both jumped into the car and Jack pulled out of the garage, through the lot a short distance before taking the exit opening and driving out onto Cicero Avenue. “Drive south to Belmont, then turn around and come back” Johnny suggested. Jack felt proud and excited as he began to get the feel of the luxurious automobile. He enjoyed the smooth ride and the powerful acceleration . “Punch it, man…see what she can do!” Johnny said excitedly as Jack raised the speed. The car glided along the road and the sound of the engine was like music to Jack’s ears. The two laughed out loud at the feel of the car’s power. They returned from the short ride and Jack dropped Johnny off at the garage. Jack signed the papers for Jonesy. “You got that temporary paper number that we put in your back window….your tags oughta’ come in about a week…okay?” Jonesy said before Jack drove off. It all felt surreal to Jack as he drove toward the Y in his car. He could hardly believe he bought it. He felt immensely proud. But, right now, he needed to get back to the Y to prepare for his afternoon classes. He suddenly had an urge to drive to Tina’s place. But, right away, he decided against it. He loved her and respected her wishes too much to go against them. Still, he yearned and wanted to see her tonight and have her share in his joy.

Jack arrived back at the Y. He parked his car on the street where he could see it from the window of his room. He went to the lobby desk and registered his car with the clerk so that he could park in the YMCA parking lot. He rummaged around his room for a while before grabbing his book bag and going back out to his car. He decided to drive over to the Village restaurant to have an early lunch before driving to school.

After lunch, he drove to school feeling excited. He could already feel himself swelling with pride as he anticipated showing his car off to his friends at school. Billy, Marvin, Lupe and a few others. He arrived and was lucky enough to get a parking space across the street from The Center. It was shortly past 1pm. There was almost an hour before the start of his first class. Jack walked into the student lounge and looked around excitedly to see if any of his friends were there. He saw several students lounging. Finally, he spotted Marvin seated in a far corner. He walked over to him. "What's goin' on, Marvin?" Jack greeted. "Hey, Bro'….how are you?...what are you up to?" Marvin greeted in his usual easy-going manner. "I'm cool, man…got my ride!" Jack announced gleefully. "No shit?…you drove it here today?" Marvin asked. "Yea…it's parked right out front!" Jack said. "Let me check that bad boy out" Marvin said.

"Come on….let's go!" Jack said as he led Marvin out of The Center and across the street to where his car was parked. "Man…how did you get the money for this?...I'm struggling to get by and you're riding in a Cadillac!" Marvin said as he gazed in awe at the gleaming automobile. "Hustlin' man…pullin' strings….I got connections, baby!" Jack bragged. "So, really…how are you doing it?" Marvin asked with a broad smile. "Well…tips from my job…that's all" Jack responded. "At the gas station?" Marvin asked with a puzzled expression. "Yea" Jack replied calmly. Marvin walked all around the car gazing at it before Jack opened the door and said "Hop in, man" They sat in the car for a while talking and looking at the features on the dashboard. "If I had the money…I would have bought a Chevy…that Cadillac drinks a lot of gas" Marvin said. "Marvin…what do the girls like to ride in?....Cadillacs…right?" Jack said as he rolled his eyes with a smile" "Yea…I guess" Marvin said as they continued to talk while walking back to The Center. Jack and Marvin split and headed for their classes. Jack left his Man and His Physical Environment class to go directly to his Intro to Uptown class. The professor prepped the class for the exam coming up next week. Jack couldn't wait to get out of class to drive his car once again. He was very happy to have it.

But, the happiness seemed to be tinged with a bit of melancholy. He could not share it with his sweetheart. She had placed rest and convenience ahead of their getting together. They had been so close until they could read each other's mind; look into each other's soul. He knew her spirit; and even though Jack had conceded in his mind that she was entitled to skip a weekend now and again; and to rest; her spirit had not seemed the same; she seemed bothered; worried; her tone had been curiously uncharacteristic. That was what disturbed him the most. Jack had a protective nature and he never liked to see the people he loved suffer in any kind of way. He wondered if something was bothering her. But, it took a lot to bring that side of him out and let it show; because he had a hardened exterior that was almost impenetrable. He was stubborn and defiant; always prepared to fight.

Finally, the class was over and Jack was leaving out of The Center when he ran into his friend, Billy. "What's goin' on, Potatoe Head?" Billy teased. "Nothin' Twinkle Toes" Jack teased back. "What's poppin' baby?" Billy greeted more seriously, offering his opened palm for a soul handshake. "Aw, I'm cool, Billy ....what's to ya' man?" Jack said. "Just studyin' my ass off...tryin' to keep up with these exams comin' up...ain't got no time and no money, either" Billy said. "Yea...I can dig it...the student life ain't easy is it?" Jack commented. "You got that right...but...it's cool...you ready for your mid-terms?" Billy asked. "Aw...I'm straight....I been studyin' too...I got two exams comin' up Thursday" Jack said. "Hang in there, Jack...it *will* pay off, brotha'...tellin' you what I know" Billy said.

"Check it, man...got my ride parked outside!" Jack said with obvious pride. "No shit?...done knocked you a ride already...huh?" Billy said. "Come on...check me out" Jack said as he turned to walk and gave a beckoning motion of his hand. "Aw...okay...it actually starts and runs...right?" Billy said with a hint of sarcasm and a smile spreading over his face. "Haha...you'll see...come on" Jack retorted with a little sarcasm of his own. They went out onto the street and Billy did just as Marvin had done. He walked around the car to look it over and finally commented. "Lookin' sweet...you done knocked real good...you musta' made yourself a good little sting here lately" as he appeared sincerely impressed. "I'm doin' alright...doin' a little square hustlin'....dig?" Jack said. "Yea?...keep it square...you don't wanna catch no case...believe me...I know about catchin' cases...don't do like I did" Billy said seriously. "Man....right now…I won't even throw a piece of paper on the ground…that's how straight I've been" Jack said. "That's good…you doin' good, Jack…I like to see that...you my boy…keep it up" Billy said before they parted with another soul handshake.

Jack jumped into his car and began to drive away. As he drove, he began to think ahead to the evening. He knew he would go home and study for at least an hour or so. But, he knew that after he was done, the lonely feeling would return. He decided not to call Tina. She had already said that she wanted to rest tonight. So, it went without saying that calling her was discouraged.

He was driving westward along Montrose Avenue when he suddenly noticed through the remaining light of dusk, his friend Suge. He was standing on the corner of Clark and Montrose. Jack was shocked to see Suge on crutches. He also noticed that his face was a little bruised. He immediately pulled over to the right side of the street and parked. He walked back to where Suge stood. "Suge….man….what happened to you, brotha'?" Jack asked as he looked him up-and-down with a surprise-stricken gaze. He noticed Suge's left foot wrapped up in a cast. "Hey, Jack...my man….I'm glad to see you, bro" Suge said somewhat subdued. "What happened to you?" Jack repeated with sincere concern and shock. "Man…let's go somewhere so we can kick it….I'll tell you all about it" Suge said. "Come on…get in my ride….we'll talk" Jack said as he led Suge across the street while he hobbled along on the crutches. They got into Jack's car. "Damn, Jack…you ridin' slick, baby…how in the hell did you knock this?" Suge asked before he slid his crutches into the back seat and hopped into the passenger seat. After he was seated, Suge looked around the inside of the car with admiration. "This is a cold ride, Jack…what you been doin'?....musta made a big sting" Suge said. "Naw…just a little car wash and wax hustle I started on my little part-time job" Jack explained. "You bullshittin'…..how did you get the job?" Suge asked. "Through school, man…I stopped drinkin' for a while…got into college" Jack said. "Damn…you been doin' a lot o' shit since the last time I saw you" Suge said. "Yea…but, forget about that….what happened to you, brotha'?" Jack asked once again. "Long story, Jack…remember I made that big sting…right?" "Yea…a while back" Jack recalled. "Well…remember I told you I was gonna start sellin' weed and just live offa' that hustle?" Suge began. "Right" Jack said. "I was doin' real good for a while…got me a little studio way over west on Addison and Keeler…got it set up real sweet…bought me a little stereo…sounds is bumpin'….got my weed connect all set up…I been rollin'…been sellin' some good weed…but, I sell my weed back around Ashland and Montrose…built up a good clientele, too…dig…then, somebody pulled by coat…motherfuckers was gonna try to stick me up…I bought me a gun….then, I got me a henchman…big-ass Skull…used to be Tank's body guard…you know him…paid him in weed…you know how I play it…never did tell him he was a bodyguard…I would just let him follow me around and feed him joints…I just let whoever the stickup men was that was watchin' me see me with him all the time…then…sometimes I would hang around with these Puerto Rican studs, too…couple o' Latin Imperials…I would just give them a good deal on some weed and they would be hangin' around me pretty regular…you know my game, Jack…my shit is smooth" Suge said as he extended his hand and they slapped five. Then, he continued. "Anyway…them fools would see me with them Imperials…I know they didn't want no parts of them Imperials or big-ass Skull, either…so, my little plan worked for a while…some weeks went by…then…I *did* get stuck-up…just when I thought I was in the clear" Suge explained.

"You didn't know who was gonna try to stick you up?" Jack asked. "Well…I had a pretty good idea…some dudes from the westside was hangin' out around here…they would buy a little weed from me but, they was always beggin'…even tried to talk gangster to me…but, you know me…I started talkin' foxy back to 'em….real hardcore…you know…droppin' names of the people I run with…like Tank…Saheeve…they saw that little gangster talk they was tryin' to scare me with wasn't phasin' me…they backed up offa' that shit…they didn't cop for a while after that…then, they started coppin' again…but, then I started seein' them with some dirty niggas I knew from jail…I knew they was in jail for stickups…so, I was thinkin' it was them….when I got stuck up…it *was* them" Suge explained. "So how did they finally stick you up?" Jack asked.

"A bitch, man…a fine-ass bitch….the way I was sellin' was…I kept my stash at my crib way 'cross town on Addison…right?" Suge started. "Yea" Jack said. "I would bring out about eight or nine bags…a coupla' lids and a bunch of joints…then, I would go to my girl's crib…my little girlfriend lives on the first floor up the block here…I would leave the weed I brought with me at her crib…whenever I had a sale out on the street…she would toss it out the window where nobody could see her…she would toss it in the gangway where the police or anybody else couldn't roll up on you too easy…after they gave me the money, I would tell the customer…there your weed is…go on and pick it up…that way…I didn't carry nothin' on me" Suge explained. "That was sho' 'nough slick, Suge…so…what about the stickup?" Jack asked curiously. "One day I'm outside in my usual spot…playin' it off….waitin' for customers…sweet lookin' chick roll up on me and say…my friend told me I could get some good weed around here…I say….oh yea?…who is your friend?" "The chick say…her friend's name is Vanessa…and she starts describin' her….the description sounds like most any chick…so, I ask her….you ain't the po'lice are you?...you know 'cause she lookin' so good….well-kept….she say no…I'll prove it…she shows me some tracks on her leg where she been shootin' up…that was good enough for me…she say come on over to this empty apartment over on the next block…now, I admit…I was lookin' to get next to her…she so fine and everything…dig…so I did what I never did before…I got my girl to toss a bag out to me…we go into the empty apartment….them niggas broke in on us…she played it off like she was scared….they let her run out…they pulled a gun on me...I kept tellin' them I didn't have nothin' on me…I'm talkin' my ass off…they smacked me a couple of times in the face with the gun…took my money…then, I jumped out the window…lucky it was the first floor…broke my foot…I started yellin' in pain…hurt like a son 'uva bitch…they ran off…that was it" Suge explained.

"So how ya' funds holdin' up?" Jack asked. "Aw…I'm straight…I still got money…I put that money from the sting in the bank so I won't be tempted to splurge and play big-shot 'cause that's what I was doin' at first…I cut that shit short…I try not to touch that money….I just keep turnin' over my weed money…I mainly been livin' offa' that" Suge said. "So…what are you gonna do, now?" Jack asked. "Nothin'…gonna keep sellin' my weed in the same spot…just ain't gonna get caught up like that no more…I ain't scared o' these suckas out here" Suge said defiantly. The two sat in Jack's car talking for a good while longer; reminiscing and catching up on what each had been doing lately. Jack spoke positively about his affair with Tina. But, even though he knew he could open up and tell Suge anything, he did not want to mention his little disappointment in the midst of their heartfelt talk. His perspective on it seemed to have changed while he was talking with his friend. Somehow, his feelings did not seem so serious as they did when he was alone in his mind ruminating about them. "You wanna get a drink, Jack?" Suge asked. "Naw…I got classes tomorrow…I better be cool" Jack said even though the drink he had yesterday had stirred a hint of that old craving today. "Okay…well…drop me off at my crib…alright?" Suge asked. "Right on, brotha'" Jack replied before he cranked the car up and drove Suge home. It was shortly past 7pm when Jack arrived back at the Y. After being in his room for a few minutes, he noticed the lonely feeling that he anticipated did not materialize. He sensed that it was because his encounter with Suge had dispelled that lonely feeling for now. Still, he went to bed with Tina on his mind.

Jack remembered to rise early on Tuesday for his morning classes. He also would be going to work at the gas station today. As he began to stir in his room, preparing for his shower, thoughts of Tina immediately popped into his mind. He began to think of what their conversation would be on the telephone tonight. He was hoping that she would be her usual happy self; that she would have the same sweet, engaging disposition that he had become so accustomed to. He hoped that their talk could go back to the way it was. Perhaps, her getting some rest was all that was needed, he thought. Jack showered, dressed and was on his way. When he went out into the YMCA parking lot to get his car, it always lifted him to see it. Changing his ways and pursuing his ambitions was paying off so positively. Evidence of his improved life was encouraging. It buoyed him and seemed to deflect some of the disappointment he had with Tina skipping their usual rendezvous. He was also dressing so much better these days since he started his hustle at the gas station. All of this made him feel good about himself.

He parked on Sheridan Road in front of The Center and dashed up the stairs to get to his Expository Writing class. His Intro to Uptown class came immediately after. After his last class, Jack grabbed a sandwich at Jake's restaurant next door before he jumped into his car. He stopped off at his room at the Y for a short while before he drove on to his job at the gas station.

When he arrived, Roberto had just finished waiting on a gas customer as Jack walked past him. "Hey, Jack…Gus wants to see you in his office" Roberto said. "What for?" Jack asked, furrowing his brow. Gus had never asked to see him in his office before. "I don't know, man…right now, he's in there doing paper work" Roberto added. "Alright…cool" Jack responded. He was still puzzled and wondered what Gus could want. He walked into the station and opened the door that said "EMPLOYEES ONLY" "Yea, Gus…Roberto said you wanted to see me" Jack said as Gus sat behind the gray, scratched-up, metal desk. "Yes…sit down for a minute, Jack" Gus said casually.

"I found out about your little enterprise" Gus said. Immediately, a feeling of fear, shame and guilt began to grip Jack. He stared silently into Gus' face, waiting to hear what he would say next. "You're running a little car wash operation on this property…that's a no-no" Gus said authoritatively. "I'm sorry, sir" Jack said resignedly. "I can't have all of these cars out on the lot like that…plus, I can't have you guys doing that instead of waiting on the customers" Gus added. Jack knew he had to think of something fast; so, he just started talking. "Gus…I'm sorry…but, we took care of all of the customers…we wasn't sloppy or nothin'….I swear…Gus…I got a dealer givin' me cars to clean up on a regular basis…I really need the money 'cause I just bought that car out there and I need to pay the note on it…plus, I need the money because I got to catch up on some bills…I'm in school full-time and I ain't hardly got no other money comin' in except this job and you know we ain't makin' much money here…the other guys need the extra money, too…Brad got a baby on the way…please, Gus…can we work somethin' out…we really need that money…please" Jack pleaded. Gus paused for a long moment. Then, he placed his big rough palm across the back of his neck and rubbed it hard as an anguished grimace appeared on his face. He turned his back to Jack and walked a couple of steps, He was silent for another moment before he turned back around to face Jack and spoke. "Jack…you *have* been a good worker…I can count on you…tell you what…I'm gonna let you keep your little side job…just keep those cars parked on the street as much as possible....at least keep them on the edge of the lot out of the way of the customers…then…I want you to pay the water bill for the station…we have to pay a water bill every month that runs about thirty-two dollars…you pay that…take care of the customers…and do like I just said and you guys can keep your side job…I know money is scarce for you guys…trying to work and go to school, too...and one more thing…keep this under wraps just like you did with me…I don't want the corporate office finding out about this…okay?" Gus explained. Jack stood in the middle of the floor seemingly speechless. "Thanks, Gus…I really appreciate that…I really do…thanks-a-lot!" Jack gushed as he walked over and shook his boss's hand. Gus just smiled. "Now get to work!" he barked.

Jack put on his issue coveralls and started working. He felt that he had died for just a moment when Gus told him he had found out about his hustle. But, now he felt as though he had been reborn, He suddenly had a new appreciation for everything that was going so well for him. He worked his shift with renewed energy. He had two wash customers toward the end of the shift just as Gus was leaving for home at his usual time of 5pm. Jack felt especially relieved now, because he no longer had to hide his hustle from the boss. This made things even better than before. He stayed a little past his work time to finish the two car washes before he jumped into his car to leave.

As he drove home, his mind was on Tina. He intended to call her at the usual time. He would behave naturally, he thought, as though nothing had changed. He would not show any effects from the bit of emotional turbulence he had experienced over the weekend. It had been a bit glum and he did not realize he would miss her so much. Jack parked his car in the usual spot in the YMCA parking lot. The lot was never crowded because most of the residents did not own a car. As Jack entered the building to go up to his room, he began to feel a fluttering inside; and in his mind, there was a myriad of thoughts that accompanied the feeling. He did not know how their talk would go tonight. But, suddenly, he did not feel so natural and spontaneous. There was a mild sense of apprehension that put him in a different frame of mind than before. He didn't like the feeling because he had always felt completely free with Tina; and now, he was beginning to wonder what to expect. He tried to mentally fend those thoughts and feelings off; shut them out of his mind. Jack was feeling a nervous excitement, as well. He was feeling happy that he would be talking to his sweetheart tonight. He missed being with her and he yearned to hear her voice. All of these feelings and thoughts seemed to mix together in an ambivalent way. Jack did not feel hungry because of the way he was feeling right now; so, he would skip dinner. He decided to try to relax. He changed into his lounge wear. It was about an hour before the time Tina would expect his call. So, he tried to unwind by watching television. He began to feel a little more relaxed.

Finally, he went out into the hallway and called Tina. "Hello" She answered. "It's me, baby" Jack answered. "Hi, honey…how are you?" Tina greeted. That familiar greeting seemed to mean so much to Jack and it sounded good to his ears. He felt an immediate sense of relief and joy that perked him right up. "I'm good, baby…how are *you* doin'?…that's what I'm concerned about…you alright?" Jack asked with a tone of seriousness. "I'm okay…I know you didn't expect us to skip the weekend…then, I said I wanted to rest on Monday when you wanted to come by with your car…I'm sorry but, I've been way too busy lately…I had a little pressure…but…I'm alright" Tina explained. "Well…I'm glad…I thought maybe it was me…or you mighta' changed your mind" Jack said. "Well…I do have to change my mind about some things" Tina said. "Like what?" Jack replied. "I'm thinking that I won't be able to go out both days every weekend or have you over for both days every weekend" Tina said. Jack could feel that little tight feeling in his gut return. "Ohh…okay" Jack replied and paused to let her explain. "So what do you wanna do?" Jack asked after she did not fill the pause.

"Jack…remember when we talked about how things were gonna change between us?…when I brought it up at that Happy Medium jazz club?…remember when I said I was worried about that?" Tina said. "Yea, baby…I remember that" Jack replied. "Honey…when we first started going out…I was finishing school…I was kind of busy but…not like I am now….then, I was just looking for a job for a while…so, we could go out the entire weekend…but, now that has changed and I have to do a lot of preparing outside of my classroom teaching…and I feel tired from dealing with those kids…I knew things would change and I do need more rest than I used to" Tina explained. "Hey…you're not…uh…" "No…I am not if that's what you're thinking, Jack…you know I use the pill religiously" Tina said. "Okay…so…you wanna go out this weekend?" Jack asked hopefully. "Yea, honey…sure…we can go out" she replied. Jack was relieved once again; his spirit seemed to automatically be lifted in that moment. "But…just on Sunday…okay, honey?" Tina added. "Yea…sure…can I stay over?" Jack asked to force the issue and leave no ambivalence about where he stood with Tina. "Yea…that's fine, honey…I guess we'll both be winding down…getting ready for Monday like we always do on Sunday evening" Tina replied. "Okay…I wanna call you during the week like always…cool?" Jack asked to have some assurance. "Of course, honey…but, I won't be in 'til late on Thursday…you know…as usual" Tina said. "Okay" Jack replied. They talked a little longer and Jack told her about what happened at the gas station with the manager, Gus and how things were even better with him not having to sneak and hide his hustle from the boss. Finally, they hung up with their usual "I love you"

Afterward, Jack walked back to his room. He seemed to be sorting his feelings out about the conversation he just had with Tina. Overall, he felt happy about it. But, at the same time, he had a sense that things were still not quite right. He could not put his finger on it; except that Tina had altered their get-togethers by cutting out half the time they would be together. It meant that he would see her just once-a-week. His feelings for her seemed to require more than that. She seemed comfortable with it; but, he realized he loved her and he was not comfortable with seeing her so seldom; and there was the crux of the problem. "She seemed comfortable" he thought. Jack was happy. But, not like he was before. He could see that things had, indeed, changed somewhat with he and Tina just as she had predicted. But, what he really wanted to know was---has her heart changed. He would not care that he was only seeing her once-a-week as long as her heart was still with him and had not changed. But, he was sensing that perhaps, her feelings for him may have really changed. He pondered for most of the night; thinking about what she said in their phone conversation tonight; dissecting everything; trying to glean something that could tell him more. But, nothing came to him. He fell asleep.

It was Wednesday and after Jack woke up, showered and

dressed, he went out to have breakfast at the nearby Village restaurant. He noticed that his mood was much brighter than it was before talking to Tina last night. He still had a bit of that curious notion in the back of his mind that something was still not quite right. Everything she said about her responsibilities at her job and being busier and, therefore more tired made sense. Her requests to change things was not unreasonable. So, he just needed to adjust himself mentally and emotionally to the change. Negotiating all of this in his head allowed Jack to accept the change and be more comfortable with it. They were still together and that was all that mattered, he told himself. So, he decided to dismiss his qualms and to take things as they were. Jack finished his breakfast.

Now, his mind seemed more relaxed and less cluttered. So, he decided to go back to his room at the Y and study a little while for his exams tomorrow before he went to school for his afternoon classes. Finally, after the studying, he drove to school and parked. He entered the student lounge. There was a smattering of students sitting here and there. Some eating; some studying and others talking. Jack had almost half-an-hour before his first class at 2pm. He looked around the lounge and noticed Lupe seated at a table, gazing out of the window.

"Hey, Lupe…how ya' doin'?" Jack greeted after walking over. "Oh…hey, Jack…have a seat" Lupe said. "What have you been up too?" Lupe asked with her characteristically broad smile. "Oh…not much…what's goin' on with you?" Jack asked as he sat down across the table from her. "You know what?…I'm dating that guy I met at the party…remember?…that tall black guy that was dancing with me…Eddie?" Lupe said almost with a whisper and a hint of giddiness. "No, shit?....I noticed he was all over you…just like Billy said…his tongue was almost hangin' out when he was followin' you all around at the party" Jack commented with a light chuckle. "Ohhh, Jack…he is a very nice man…he treats me so good…we've been out a few times" Lupe said, still showing a little giddiness. "So…everything is goin' good with you and ol' boy…huh?" Jack said with a smile. Yea….real good" Lupe said with a happy, satisfied smile. "That's good, Lupe…good for you, girl….that's what you wanted…right?….a nice dude?" Jack said.

"Let me guess…y'all talkin' about Eddie" a voice interrupted. Jack and Lupe looked up from the table to see Billy standing in front of them, slinging his book bag off of his shoulder onto the table they were sitting at, then sitting down with them. "What's the word good people?...she tellin' you about Eddie, ain't she?" Billy said to Jack. "Well…" Jack began. "So what, Billy …we can talk about whatever we want…Jack is my friend" Lupe bristled. "Oh…here we go again…she done already bent my ear out o' whack praisin' Eddie….you'd think he was the second comin' of Jesus…let her tell it" Billy commented with a wide smile. "Why are you bothering me about Eddie…you don't want to see me with a boyfriend…do you?" Lupe said to Billy in her usual antagonistic tone. "I see you peeled him off of you long enough to come to school" Billy said, knowing that he was annoying Lupe. "Leave me alone….you hear me you little…" Lupe said as she leaped from her seat at Billy and grabbed his ear and began to playfully twist it; perhaps a bit roughly. "Hahaha…hey…what are you doin'….let go my ear!…Jack…help me, man!" Billy yelled out as he turned his head to alleviate the twisting of his ear. A few seconds passed before Lupe let go of Billy's ear and they all had a good laugh. "See there, Jack…you had a good demonstration right there…don't never say nothin' bad about Fast-Eddie…dig what I'm sayin'?" Billy said before Lupe raised her hand at him again and he dashed several feet away, laughing. "Yea…you gonna get tired of Eddie, the way I see him stickin' to you like glue…you'll be callin' the po'lice on him pretty soon…watch what I say" Billy teased as he stood a safe distance from Lupe, still chuckling. "You're just jealous…that's all" Lupe said as she sat back down, a bit more relaxed. The three talked for a few minutes before it was time to go to classes. Lupe had to go to her daycare job down the hall. After the fun-filled exchange, Jack walked to his class, smiling to himself at the antics of Billy and Lupe. He realized that he had formed a special bond of friendship with them and his other friends at school. He had connected with Sam and Glen and the other staff, as well. He enjoyed being around them and they had become like a family to him. He needed them. The wholesome school environment had become his safe haven; his sanctuary of hope.

Jack arrived at his Man and His Physical Environment class and the instructor went over the preparation for the exam coming up on Monday. He took notes and he felt prepared because he had been studying and keeping up. When that class was finished, he went to his Intro to Uptown class at the very next period. There was the same preparation for the exam on Monday. When that class was over at 5pm, Jack had not decided what he wanted to do. It was too early to go in for the night.

So, he decided to go to the corner and show off his car because none of his friends, except for Suge, had seen it. He could barely contain his pride as he drove the few blocks north on Sheridan Road and made a left turn at Lawrence Avenue to go west. He found a parking spot on Winthrop near Frances' Tavern where the regulars liked to congregate. Jack was wearing a nice leather sport jacket and dress slacks. His hair was well-groomed with just a touch of relaxer. He wore a pair of stylish shoes. He looked nothing like the street urchin he had been almost a year ago. Jack got out of his car and he could see many of the neighborhood regulars congregating here and there; up and down the streets. He noticed a group of the neighborhood girls across the street from him. They were gathered up together talking in front of the courtway building just south of Frances' Tavern. Jack could feel and he could see from the corner of his eye, their continuous gaze in his direction

He walked on to the corner where a few of his friends and other regulars were loitering on the corner of Lawrence and Winthrop near Frances' Tavern. There was Jabo, Skip, Larry, Obie and Motic. "Jack…what's hap'nin' bro'?" Jabo spoke out first. "Hey, Jack…Jack" the others greeted. "Where you goin' so sharp, brotha?" Skip asked. "No where, man…just got outa school" Jack replied kind of blasé. "What *have* you been doin, Jack?…lookin' mighty sporty there…nice leather jacket" Larry commented. "Yea, thanks" Jack replied. "That was you gettin' outa that coupe over there?" Jabo asked. "Yea…yea…that's me" Jack replied, beaming with pride as he looked into the near distance at his parked car. "Looka' here, will ya…Jack…you done made a hell 'uva turn-about…ya' sharp…drivin' a caddy…eyes done cleared up…what you doin' man?...last year you was lookin wild as all get-out…now, look like you ready to do some serious mackin…yessir!" Skip commented with a chuckle. "I stopped gettin' drunk…got into school" Jack replied.

"Damn all that!" Motic interrupted. "How much you got on this drink?…you sharp, brotha'…real sharp…but, you know what?....you'll like a prince to me if you could drop somethin' on this taste…yea…that's what the hell I wanna know…all that shit they talkin' 'bout don't mean nothin'…what you doin'…nice leather…blah-blah-blah..la-la-la…give me a coupla' nice dollars so I can go and get this pint of vodka…hahaha" Mo'tic cut in with his usual blunt and blustery style and a hearty laugh. He was clutching a couple of dollars and some change in the palm of his hand as he stepped closer to Jack. Jack began to laugh out loud and just reached into his pocket and gave Motic a few dollars. "See that shit, y'all?…you standin' around lolly-gaggin' when you know you wanna ask the man for some money…I just had the nerve to come right out and ask him…that's all…that's how you do it" Motic chided the others; glaring back at them as he marched ahead toward Saxony Liquors around the corner and up the street. None of them ever took Motic seriously because they knew this was a showy act; his shtick he put on just to keep things lively. They continued to stand out on the corner beside Frances Tavern, having their usual spirited fun while they waited for Motic to return with the drink.

As they were congregating, one of the girls that Jack had seen near the courtway was walking toward the group, heading toward Lawrence Avenue. "Hey, Jack" she spoke out as she passed them, flashing a brilliant smile and looking directly at Jack as she did. Jack was surprised to hear her speak to him alone. "Hey" he spoke back to her kind of off-guard. Billy Ruth was a very attractive neighborhood girl who was a few years younger than Jack. She was wearing a short jean skirt that revealed her sexy legs and that turned men's heads. She was a member of the Jackson family that lived in a house down the street on Winthrop across from the Tower building. Jack knew her and they had a nodding acquaintance. But, he knew her father and brothers much better from occasionally talking with them on the streets. "Hey, Jack…can I talk to you for a minute?" she asked after stopping several yards past where the group of men stood. Jack was again surprised that she had something she needed to speak to him about; because they never had very much to say to one another on the streets; although, she knew he occasionally associated with her brothers. Jack casually walked over to her as a hush fell over the group of men as they gawked at the meeting between Jack and the girl. “Yea…what is it?” Jack asked after he came face-to-face with her. “Yea…could you please do me a favor?” she asked. “What?” Jack asked. “I need to get up to my cousin’s house on Morse Avenue real soon…like in a half-hour…if you’re not doin’ anything…can you drive me?” she asked coyly. “Well….let me see….I guess so…give me about five minutes…okay?” Jack said casually; a bit puzzled and surprised at her request. “Okay…thanks…I have to go to the store around the corner....I won’t be too long…alright?” she said, flashing another seductive smile. “Okay…cool” Jack replied calmly. She took off stepping energetically. After she turned the corner, the other men started their banter. “Whooweee!....Jack!...you mackin’ now, baby!…that sweet little tender thang givin’ you some action!” Obie howled. “Yea…she makin’ a sho’ ‘nough play for you, Jack” Jabo chuckled. “Yea…what did she say to you, Jack?” Larry asked. “Oh…she wants me to drop her off up on Morse…said she had to get there real quick” Jack said casually. “Man....If I was your age, Jack….I’d be all over that!...dig what I’m sayin’?” Larry commented. “”Me, too” Obie said. “Yessir….without a doubt….you know it!” the others chimed in succession.

Before long, she reappeared around the corner and walked straight up to Jack. “I’m ready!” she said, standing rather closely in front of Jack. “Okay…hey ‘y’all…I’ll see y’all later” Jack said as he and Billy Ruth walked together toward his parked car. “I hope I’m not puttin’ you out too much by askin’ this favor…but, I really have to get up there quick…I’m supposed to go somewhere with my cousins on a short trip and they are about to leave soon…they are gonna leave me if I don’t get there in time…I was waitin’ for my dad to take me after he got home from work…but, he is runnin’ pretty late…I really appreciate this, Jack” Billy Ruth said, smiling sweetly. Jack opened the car door for her and she slid into the passenger seat with her jean skirt riding up high to the thick part of her thighs until Jack caught a glimpse of her pink panties. Many times in the past couple of years, Jack had seen this young woman around Winthrop Street near her home. She was, indeed, very attractive with a beautiful body and very smooth caramel-colored skin. She always dressed very nicely and was graceful, feminine and lady-like; keeping her appearance so immaculate. She was desired by most every man in the vicinity.

Jack was no different. In the past, he had fantasies of his own about her. But, right now, he didn't seem to be feeling that desire. He was preoccupied with thoughts of Tina ruminating in his mind. Billy Ruth gave Jack the address to drive to. As he drove along, he found her to be quite open and engaging; chatting with him the whole time; talking about the neighborhood and volunteering plenty of insight into her thoughts and feelings; talking as though she wanted to establish a rapport with Jack. Jack responded politely; being a perfect gentleman; occasionally glancing over at her as she sat so closely next to him; not helping but to notice her well-endowed physical attributes. "You got a real nice car here, Jack…where do you work?" she asked politely as they rode along. Jack explained that he was in college and he had a part-time job and the car-wash hustle. She mentioned that she had broken up with a boyfriend a couple of months ago after a short-lived affair. Jack found it curious that he was not feeling excited to be in the company of this young woman; that he did not seem motivated to take advantage of the opportunities she was presenting. Her subtle advances were met with polite indifference on Jack's part---his mind was elsewhere. After he stopped in front of the address, she hugged Jack warmly; pressing her chest into his and whispering softly "Thank you so much…I'll see you around the neighborhood…okay?" before she got out of the car. As Jack drove home toward the YMCA, he felt a strong undertow of melancholy; a sense of tragedy. He knew something was very wrong that he did not try his best to get next to Billy Ruth so that he could have his way with her.

Soon after he arrived at the Y, Jack called Tina. "Hi, Honey" she greeted after Jack spoke. "How are you doin' baby?" Jack asked. "I'm alright, Jack…you okay?" she asked. "Yea….I'm cool…what you wanna do this weekend?" he asked. "I don't know, honey…I've really been too tired to think about it…you think of something and let me know by Friday….but, remember…Sunday…okay?" Tina said. "Yea…that's cool…is everything okay with us, baby?…I feel like somethin' ain't right" Jack finally let out. He was a bit bothered that her communication with him did not seem quite the same. Somehow, it seemed a little off-kilter. He noticed that their conversations were not as light-hearted, free and easy as before. They hadn't really joked in their last few talks like they usually did. He could sense a bit of tension in her. Suddenly, Tina seemed subdued as she paused a little long before speaking. "I'm sorry, honey…it's like I said before…I've been tired…I'm doing a lot of stuff at work…why do you say that?" Tina said with a somewhat somber tone. "I know you said you've been tired…but, you don't seem happy like you used to…if somethin' is botherin' you….let me know…if it's me…I wanna know" Jack said with a tone of rising emotion. "I'm okay, honey…I didn't notice that I changed…you think I've changed?" Tina asked. "Yea, baby…you're not the same…is there somethin' you wanna tell me?" Jack asked. "No" Tina said. "You sure?" Jack insisted. "Yea" Tina replied. "Okay…alright" Jack relented his probing with a little exasperation in his voice. "So, I'll be callin' you tomorrow and probably Friday night, too…I know you said you'll be in late tomorrow night…I'll try to call late…is that okay, baby?" Jack said. "Yes…alright, honey" Tina replied. "And I'll think of somewhere nice we can go on Sunday…okay?" Jack added, dotingly softening his tone. "Okay" Tina replied. "I love you" Jack said, very much needing to hear those words back from her. "I love you, too" Tina replied before they hung up. Jack felt so much better afterward that he finally let out to Tina what was bothering him. He felt a weight and worry lift immediately from his mind. He also thought he would go all out; do his best to cheer Tina up on their planned outing this weekend. He missed her cheerful, happy mood so much. It always lifted him and made him feel that all was right with the world. She had filled him with so much hope and buoyed his spirit with her joyfulness. Yes, it would be a special outing this weekend. With his mind much clearer, Jack studied for a little while to brush up for his exams tomorrow morning. He slept a lot better this night, as well.

Jack scooted into his chair after arriving at his 9:30am Expository Writing class, just as professor Walker began to speak. He had lectured at the last class that he would make the mid-term exam an essay on a current event to test the students writing skills. Jack sat quietly focused in his seat as the professor prepared the class and gave instructions on how to take the exam. Jack felt confident as he had been getting good grades in this class and had inspired several lively debates in recent class sessions. It demonstrated his enthusiasm, curiosity and quirky, unconventional outlook on various subject matter. The instructor always engaged Jack and was obviously impressed with his intelligent input. The students were given an hour to finish the exam. Those who finished earlier were allowed to leave. Jack did just that, leaving after completing his exam in about forty minutes. Jack went into the student lounge for a while and there were hardly any students. He happened upon his counselor, Ms. Chaffee. He had a nice, polite conversation with her before taking off for his Community Organization class. There was a short exam there and the instructor lectured at length afterward. Jack was feeling anxious to get out of class. When the class was finally let out, he went out of The Center and next door to Jake's to have a cheeseburger lunch.

As he was eating and looking out of the large picture window of the restaurant, a few of the street wanderers that he knew from the tramp trails suddenly appeared in front of the window walking along the sidewalk. Jack knew the routine. They were probably broke and looking for a hustle, just as he had so often in the past. He knew that as soon as they spotted him, they would speak to him and ask for a handout. So, Jack turned his face away from the window, hoping they did not see him inside the restaurant. He could faintly hear their talk coming through the window. "Oh…hey…ain't that ya' boy…Jack?" one of them said to the other. He knew that next, they would be entering the restaurant. "Hey, brotha', Jack…how you doin' man?" Doogie said, smiling as he led the other two, Marcus and Hondo into the restaurant behind him. They looked weary and bore the usual scraggly, unkept appearances that many of the street types did. On rare occasions in the past, Jack had mingled with them during some of his wild drinking episodes. He knew what came after such a hearty greeting.

"Jack….ain't seen you in a while, baby-boy…what's hap'nin' with ya?" Marcus said, trying to muster up some cheerfulness and forcing a smile. "Hey, brotha' Jack" Hondo greeted, all of them smiling hopefully. "Man…we tryin' to get up on somethin'….I ain't lyin'" Doogie said with a bit of angst in his voice as he sat down at the table with Jack while the others stood. "Hey, y'all…what y'all up to?" Jack greeted, sounding lively and masking how he really felt. Doogie went into a little diatribe about his recent bad luck; pulling up his trouser leg to show Jack an injury to his leg from some unfortunate incident on the streets. He spoke of how the three of them had been roaming around the streets together since the morning, trying to make a hustle. Jack half-listened; knowing the listening was pointless; that it was leading up to one question. “Let me hold somethin’ Jack?” Doogie finally asked, drawing inference from Jack’s much improved appearance since last he had seen him. “Man…you caught me at the wrong time, Doogie…I’m short, baby…I spent my last on this food…hold on…I might have some change…here…here you go” Jack said as he stuck his hand in his pocket and rustled some change out and handed it to Doogie. “Aw…okay, brotha’…’preciate it” Doogie said as he continued to make small talk for a moment before the restaurant owner, Jake asked “Can I help you?” prompting the three men to leave out of the restaurant. Jack knew the game in the streets; you had certain allies and loyalties; and although he was generous with his friends; he knew to dismiss all others. The game of survival in the streets of Uptown was a hard, cold existence; but, it was fair.

It was early afternoon and Jack had just finished his cheeseburger lunch. He felt his mind begin to drift free and easy. He loved the sense of freedom and serenity he had when he felt this way; no worries; everything seemed okay; his talk with Tina had eased his mind and the happiness he once knew had returned. Now, it was early afternoon and he had confidently completed his exams; his last two mid-terms of the semester not coming until Monday. He had been studying and had plenty of time to study for them this weekend. He had a full day of work at the gas station on Saturday; but, no outing with Tina until Sunday. He thought about what Tina said about coming in late tonight. He had the rest of the day and the evening to do whatever he wanted; but, what would he do? That same old feeling of loneliness seemed to be lurking somewhere underneath. But, he was fending it off with his new-found peace-of-mind. He actually felt upbeat and decided to go where he always did-----to The Corner.

He left Jakes, got into his car and drove the short distance to Lawrence and Winthrop. The poolroom didn’t open until around 11:30am most days and the poolroom patrons rarely trickled in much sooner than 1pm. So, Jack knew that few people would be inside. He parked his car a half-block from the poolroom on Lawrence Avenue across from the E-Z GO gas station. In the near distance, Jack could see a few of the regulars mingling on The Corner as he locked his car doors. It was a mild and partly cloudy day. There was the promising balminess of spring in the air that had come on more days over the last couple of weeks. It was the first week of May. The atmosphere seemed to hold that same old excitement that Jack felt at the beginning of each spring for the last few years when he could hustle without the burden of winter weather threatening his existence; taking the sport out of the game of survival. It was intoxicating. This had always been the time of year when the madness on the streets ensued in earnest; when the crazy hustling accelerated and the wild, free-wheeling insanity of the Street Gypsy life was on full display. When the warm weather came, an array of streets characters would be out and about; scattered up and down the streets; their laughter and crazy talk echoing in the city streets; the euphoria of being high erasing all inhibitions and setting spirits free. As Jack strolled toward The Corner, he could see Coley and Jabo standing near the poolroom entrance as a few others were hanging around across the street near Frances' Tavern.

"Jack....what's goin' on, brotha'?...still sharp...huh?" Coley greeted him spiritedly as he approached. "My man, Jack...hey, bro" Jabo said. "Hey, 'y'all...what's the deal" Jack greeted, smiling broadly as he engaged each with an energetic soul handshake. "What's been goin' on around here?" Jack asked to initiate conversation. "Nothin' man...weather breakin'...these fools back out on the set....we just seen ya' boy Dinky arguin' out here a little while ago...gettin' ready to fight some stud we ain't never seen before" Jabo chuckled. "Yea?....I'm not surprised...that boy is crazy...I don't wanna see him myself....*tired* o' whoopin' his ass" Jack said flippantly as Coley and Jabo burst into laughter. "You say you tired of whoopin' that ass...huh?...hahaha" Jabo laughed heartily. "Yea...Jack been whoopin' his ass about twice a year for the last two years...hahaha" Coley added with animated laughter. Of course, Jabo and Coley had a bottle with them and offered Jack a drink. He declined. "Got to take mid-term exams on Monday, y'all" Jack explained with a sense of pride. He was also feeling more comfortable talking about his college life with his friends on the streets. "You takin' mid-terms?....you sho' 'nough serious about that school thang...huh?" Jabo commented. "Yea...I'm tryin' to straighten myself up....I don't wanna be on these streets for the rest of my life" Jack said, suddenly realizing how his comment reflected on his two friends. A short moment of silence came afterward. “Pass me that wine, Jabo” Coley said, breaking the silence. Jabo passed a pint bottle of Richard’s Wild Irish Rose to Coley who looked around the streets before turning it up to take a drink. The three continued to talk; standing on the Winthrop side of the poolroom.

Before long, they could hear laughter and loud talk coming from near the 4848 Winthrop building up the block. Jack peered into the near distance to see several men walking toward them; their animated talking, hoots and laughter reverberating around the street. As Jack looked up the street at them, he recognized Andrew, Melvin, LV and another man he had never seen before. They seemed to be having a rousing good time. They continued to walk toward him “Andrew and them…Jack…them your get-high buddies…they been gettin’ high at Andrews crib for the last few days….that dude with them…he’s been buyin’ dope for them…that’s Cocoa…..he’s from Sixty-Third Street….Sixty-Third Street Gangsters….he’s LV’s cousin….they tell me he robbed a currency exchange out in the far south suburbs a few days ago…he been hidin’ out in 4848 at LV’s place since then….Jack…don’t hang with them…police lookin’ for that dude…don’t say nothin’” Coley said to Jack a moment before the group of men approached them.

“LV….I’ll box yo’ ass all night, nigga…you cain’t get down…come on” Cocoa said as he went into a boxing stance and danced around for a moment and shot a couple of playful jabs at his cousin. “Sit your country-ass down somewhere, fool….you already fell out of the chair upstairs…chair whooped your ass…you don’t want none o’ me…hahaha” LV said as he chuckled and made a couple of quick play swings over his cousin’s head. Both men seemed to be off-balance from their high; moving jerkily about in their fake match. They were all in high spirits. Jack could tell that they all had that mellow, satisfied kind of high that fiends were always trying to achieve.

“Hey…Jack…what’s poppin’ baby?…my roaddog….hey, Cocoa…hey…hey…hey…check this out, Cocoa…come here” Melvin said with droopy eyes and trying to get the stranger’s attention. “What you want, man?” the stranger responded. “Hey, Cocoa…this my hustlin’ buddy I was tellin’ you about….Jack…me and him done made many-a-sting together….he's down, man….hustles his ass off….Jack…meet LV's cousin, Cocoa" Melvin said, seeming proud to introduce the two. "Hey, brotha' Cocoa…what's goin' on?" Jack responded tentatively; extending his hand for a soul shake. "Hey, bro'…Jack…how you doin'?" Cocoa responded. Jack felt a mild sense of apprehension from being in the stranger's company; knowing what he had just learned about him. At this moment, Jack reflected and realized he was at a crossroad. He looked at them and the delightful insanity dancing in their eyes was mesmerizing; enticing. It reminded him of how he felt when he got high with them in just that same manner on several occasions in the past; how devilishly exhilarating it all had been. Just then, he could feel a slight twisting in his gut; a craving to be in that same state of delirious madness himself; in that space where nothing mattered. But, he was viewing all of this from clear eyes and a sober state of mind. It was not as alluring as before. He had set himself on a new course; to save himself from this kind of incremental suicide. He had Tina and his college life. He had hope for a future. He realized in this reflective moment what he really wanted; to marry Tina and get a college degree; to eventually be normal; to somehow return to the life he once knew before he slipped into this crazy Street Gypsy existence. Right now, he had to seize his opportunity; to not let it slip away. It was the first time that his true desires had come to his conscience with such clarity. He knew he wanted this sober, sane, normal life that he was living right now. But, would he have the strength?---the will to maintain it? "Yea, brotha' Jack….they been tellin' me a lot about you…tell me you a top-flight hustler 'round this way….studs be bringin' their merch' to you to fence….that's cool, brotha'…real cool" the stranger commented as his eye-lids drooped lazily. "Yea…me and Melvin…we *have* hustled together quite a bit" Jack responded modestly, not wanting to elaborate and get too friendly with the stranger.

Hey, Jack…check this out, man….let me holla' at you" Melvin said, touching Jack's elbow to lead him a few paces away from the group and out of ear-shot. "Hey, man…this stud made a big sting….he's been gettin' us high every day….I stashed some of the dope we was doin'…want me to save you some?…you want a hit?....it's fire, too…you see I'm already bubblin'" Melvin whispered. Ambiguous feelings tugged at Jack. He could still feel the urge gnawing at him.

He remembered all of the changes and trouble he and Melvin had gone through together in the past; plotting; scheming; traipsing up and down the streets to make enough for a hit; committing bold, brazen acts during their small-time hustling escapades; maneuvering with fiendish guile. It would be a curious mental twist to bring himself to devalue what he had valued so highly before. But, for several months now, he had tasted the sweet serenity of peace and civility; love; and everything that seemed decent and right. He did not want to lose it all and fall back into the abyss.

"You know what, Melvin….I've had a touch of bronchitis for a couple of days…been takin' medication for it…I cain't mess it up gettin' high…I'll get sick again" Jack lied right off the top of his head. "Hey, Cocoa….better get your ass off o' these streets…know what I mean?" LV cautioned his cousin. "Yea….you right 'cous'…..I better move before the Slick Boys come rollin' through" Cocoa replied. "Yea, man…I'm out on bond…I don't need them to try to put another case on me" Andrew added. "Okay, then…we're goin' in the poolroom for a while…you wanna hang?" Melvin responded to Jack. "I'm gonna kick it with Coley and Jabo for a while" Jack replied. "Okay…cool…you change your mind about that hit…let me know…okay?" Melvin said. "Yea" Jack responded, not saying anything more to show Melvin that he was serious. Jack understood Melvin's offer; that he was showing his friendship and loyalty. Jack felt relief when the four men walked away, continuing on to the poolroom. He felt very good about himself that he was able to resist the temptation. "Yea, Jack…you did the right thing…let your get-high buddies go 'head on…I know you didn't wanna be hangin' with somebody the po'lice is lookin' for" Coley commented. "Right on…they bad news…that's' the stick-up crew right there" Jabo added. "Man…I ain't got time for them" Jack said with firm conviction.

So…Jack…how's everything with Tina?" Coley asked. "Everything's cool" Jack responded. "Been a while since we all got together at Freddy B and Carmen's around the holidays….get your girl and let's all hook up again at the Mystic Lounge like we did before…whaddaya' say?" Coley suggested. Jack paused and thought for a moment. “You know what?....that’s a good idea, Coley” Jack said. “We had a real nice time…all of us together…we really enjoyed that…Tina had a good time” Jack added. “How about this weekend?” Coley asked. “That’s cool…only thing is…it will have to be Sunday….Tina is tied up on Saturday” Jack said. “Sunday should be cool….early like about nine…how about that?” Coley said. “That’s cool…I’ll call Tina and ask her….we’re goin out Sunday afternoon anyway…we could stop at the Mystic that evenin’ Jack said. “Cool…I know Shirley will go with her partyin’ ass…she wanna go so she can gossip…hahaha” Coley said with a light chuckle. “I’ll call you Friday evenin’ after I get off from my part-time job…alright?” Jack said. “That’s a bet” Coley responded. Jack, Coley and Jabo congregated on the streets for a while, eventually going inside the poolroom when they saw Melvin and his group leave out. Jack hung around with them a good while longer; not drinking and enjoying the camaraderie and fellowship like old times.

Jack finally arrived back at his room in the Y around 8:30pm. It was always hard to leave his friends when he was having such a good time. But, he had real self-discipline nowadays that was inspired by all of the positivity in his life. It was still too early to call Tina. He planned to call her in a couple of hours. After making himself comfortable, he watched television for a while. Then, he laid down and took a short nap before snapping out of his restful snooze; allowing his head to clear before he looked at his clock-radio to see that it was going on 11pm. He grabbed some change from his dresser drawer and went out into the hallway to call Tina. The phone rang and rang. He decided to try again around 11:30pm. When he did, the phone rang and rang with no answer once again. The curiously disturbing feeling returned and he wondered what happened with Tina. It took him a good while to finally fall asleep.

Jack awakened and when he rolled over to see that the clock read 7:52am, he leaped out of bed. He was late for work. He felt a slight panic before he told himself that he had never been late before and he would just call the gas station and let them know. Right away, he grabbed enough change and went out into the hall to call. “Yea…I should be there before 9:30” Jack said to Brad who opened the station on a few weekday mornings before Gus arrived at 8:30am. Jack hurried to take a shower and got dressed.

Finally, while he was driving to the gas station, thoughts of his failed attempts at calling Tina popped into his mind; and immediately, the annoying thoughts of wondering why she was not home to pick up the phone began.

When he arrived at work, he was barely there mentally; feeling disturbed by the growing pattern of Tina being less-and-less available for him. He was pensive as he went about his duties at work. There was that usual sense of aloneness that accompanied this state of mind. He wished that he could call her right away to find out what happened last night to ease his mind. But, Tina was at work. He dreaded being preoccupied this way. It was robbing him of the little peace-of-mind that he had finally found in his tumultuous life. Jack had a few car-wash customers. He was grateful when Johnny came by to drop off a couple of wax jobs from Don Hardy's. He was able to laugh and joke with him for a short while and momentarily forget about those annoying thoughts. Before he realized, it was noontime; his quitting time. He stayed longer to finish his wax jobs; taking his time to forestall when he would be off work and alone once again with his thoughts. Finally, he was done and it was time to go. "Brad…collect that wax-job money for me will you?….I'll get it Monday…alright?...thanks" Jack asked before he got into his car and took off. Jack thought about going to The Center to kill some time. But, he knew that few of the students or even the staff lingered very late on a Friday afternoon at The Center. There were hardly any classes and most of them usually left early; anxious to get a head start on their weekends. The only person he knew would be there at this time was Lupe who would still be there at the daycare center with the kids. Jack didn't feel like spending time with her and have to listen to her raving about her new boyfriend. He could go home and study. But, he didn't feel like it. Besides, it was a beautiful, warm and sunny day and right now, he didn't want to spend it indoors. He needed to be around people. But, he didn't have anywhere to go. His last visit to The Corner had convinced him to make himself scarce there and that's what he would do today; find somewhere else to go.

Jack got into his car and decided to just drive around; not going anywhere in particular; but, he seemed to be instinctively driving back toward Uptown. As he did so, the incessant thoughts about Tina began. He didn't like this at all. It was an odd feeling that he had never experienced before---until lately. It was worry; the very thing he despised most; stealing his mind; his thoughts from him; even when he was on the streets with nothing; at least he was in possession of his mental functions; but, not now; he seemed to have lost that; to what? There was an unfamiliar sense of powerlessness that accompanied these rambling thoughts. He thought about how he and Tina had already planned to go out Sunday. But, they would not be together Saturday evening like before; about how he had spoken to her on Wednesday evening; but, he couldn't get hold of her Thursday night. But, she never made any guarantees about being available that night. When he spoke to her tonight---could he really complain about not getting her on the phone last night? He didn't know what to think about all of this. It was all a bit perplexing. It had come to the point that he had to just relax and dismiss all of these thoughts that seemed to be going in circles. Besides, he needed to be in a pleasant mood when they went out Sunday if he was going to cheer her up as he had planned.

As Jack drove toward Uptown, he decided to take a certain route to avoid the usual crowd of regulars on the streets that he expected to see. His mind seemed to guide him toward the lake. He drove on to the Wilson Avenue part of the lakefront. There was a smattering of people out; casually enjoying the warmth of the afternoon sun. He parked his car on the paved drive where cars passed through and others lounged in their parked cars here and there just as he was. It was also a popular spot as a sort of lover's lane. Jack leaned back in the driver's seat and rested with the windows down; mostly trying to rest his mind; to relieve himself, at least momentarily, of all his concerns. He looked out past the nearby trees and grass as he faced Lake Michigan in the distance. The waves gently rolling up-and-down; back-and-forth; his mind seemed to come in tune with the natural surroundings; drifting in sync with the lake's waves. He was beginning to feel peaceful. He nodded out. Jack's eyes opened little-by-little as he awakened. He stretched and yawned before he sat up in the driver's seat of his car and allowed the grogginess to clear from his head. He looked at the clock on his dashboard and the time told him he had napped for about an hour-and-a-half.

He got out of his car and rolled up the windows and locked the doors. He decided to walk along the lake. As he walked along, he was enjoying the warmth of the sun beaming down and the sound of the water sloshing back-and-forth; splashing up against the huge rocks that lined the shore; every twenty or thirty yards, he encountered a person or two lounging in the noon-day sunshine; a sub-bather here and there. It was a relaxing, peaceful atmosphere. As Jack strolled along, he observed couples; lovers who perhaps, had abandoned their afternoon obligations to steal a little happiness. He took note of how they interacted. He understood how they seemed oblivious to all observers like himself; how they seemed so lovingly focused and intertwined with one another; he certainly understood. He was walking north on the lake when he came to Foster Beach which was not very far from where he had parked. He saw mothers with small kids frolicking about on the sandy shore. It all kind of reminded him of the kind of peace and joy he was seeking in his life; the kind of blissful serenity that he had hoped he could find with Tina. This solitude was allowing Jack to come in tune with his thoughts without the noisy distractions of the inner city streets. He was enjoying the peaceful surroundings. But, he could feel the loneliness begin to weigh on his conscience. He realized that he was walking that fine line again; that high-wire act of striving for a better life by avoiding his friends on the streets; and this is what it had come to---aloneness. He couldn't be with Tina as much anymore. But, he felt he needed to be with her more than ever right now. He couldn't keep hanging around his friends as he had recently---but, they were all he had right now to keep him company. He was thinking those thoughts again and he wanted to shut them off. The thoughts did not come to him clearly. They were vague and indistinct. But, for Jack, at the bottom of it all was the instinct to survive. That was what it all amounted to. That much was crystal clear.

Finally, Jack had an idea. He would go to visit Sandra. She was one of his friends that he could just drop in on her at her apartment. He especially liked to play with her two little boys. He always had a good time with them; behaving like a kid himself and having fun playing games with them; that's what he could do! It was a perfect idea. He could be with her and the kids for a while without feeling the peer pressure and urge to get high like he always did with his friends on The Corner. The thought filled Jack with exuberance; and he was already anticipating the silly little games that he and the little boys liked to play. He baby-sat the boys on several occasions last year. He and Sandra had an understanding. Whenever Jack was worn and beat from his life on the streets, he would go to Sandra's place to dry out. She would leave the boys with him because she knew Jack would be sober while he was with them; that he loved them and would take good care of them; at times, spending all of his hustling money on the boys. She needed a break and would leave out and go on a drinking binge for a day or two; occasionally calling in to check on the boys. Then, she would return and Jack would be all dried out and rested so he could return to the streets. Jack casually strolled along the lake shore back to his car. He got in and drove toward Sandra's place. He stopped and called her on the phone. She was there and told Jack to "come on" He stopped at a grocery store. He bought food. He bought toys and candy, as well. He drove to Montrose and Malden to go to the apartment building Sandra lived in. She lived a block south of Wilson on Malden Avenue. But, Jack took Montrose to avoid people he knew on the streets. Finally, he arrived at Sandra's place.

"Who is it?" Sandra's distinct voice could be heard through the apartment door. "It's me, sista-in-law" Jack called out from the hallway. "Okay…hold on a minute" she said. The door sprang open shortly afterward. "Man…you don't know how glad I am to see you….what's all these bags you got" Sandra said with her characteristically wide smile. "Hey…check it out…I got food….I got some candy and some toys" Jack said as he wrestled with the bags, dragging them inside the apartment. "Man…you brought all this for us?" Sandra asked. "Sho' 'nough sista-in-law….we gonna party, now" Jack said with a gleeful chuckle as he sat the bags on the dinner table. "Where my boys at?....where my boys at?" Jack asked excitedly. He loved to stir up excitement with the boys and have a good time acting silly with them. "They in their room watchin' television" Sandra said. "David….Gerald…come on out here…Jack is here to see y'all" Sandra called out to the boys. Immediately, the two little boys, six year-old Gerald and four year-old David came running out from their room, hugging Jack around his legs from either side. "Come here boy" Jack said as he scooped little David up from the floor and carried him around; talking to him playfully. Then, he grabbed little Gerald and repeated the same little routine. "You takin' care of your momma, boy?...huh?....you takin' care of your momma?" Jack would repeat with each boy as he held them in his arm, carrying them around the room until he received a "yes" nod from them. "Hey….looka here….look what I got y'all" Jack said as he began rustling one of the three paper bags he brought in. "Look at that….a racin' car for you David….and here…looka' here…one for you Gerald" Jack said to the boys as he sat on the floor and began to open the packages the toys were in and demonstrate them to the boys. But, demonstrating a little too long and a little too much. "Look at that…vrrrroooommm!" Jack said as he ran the cars along the floor. "Oh, lord…here we go…three kids in the house, now" Sandra said with a light chuckle as she watched Jack playing with the toys before turning them over to the boys. "Okay….where is my package at?...I know it's in one of these bags" Sandra commented. "That one over there" Jack said as he pointed to one of the two paper grocery bags still sitting on the dinner table. Sandra walked over and peered into the bag before pulling out two six-packs of her favorite brand of beer. "Oohhh…Jack…thanks-a-lot….you always look out for me" Sandra said with gratitude before giving Jack a big hug. Indeed, the late afternoon into early-evening had turned into a party at Sandra's apartment; Jack played endlessly with the boys while Sandra prepared a chicken and rice dinner. They all ate. After dinner, Sandra sent the boys to their room to watch TV before bedtime. She and Jack sat in the living room and had their usual talk that was always punctuated with good-natured joking and laughter. Sandra and her boys were family to Jack. The oldest boy, Gerald was Coley's kid. Many times in the past, Coley, Jack and Sandra hung out and drank together. Sandra sipped on her beer but, Jack did not drink with her; explaining how he was sticking to his new-found, sober lifestyle. He gave Sandra a little money to tide her over as they sat and talked. "Okay, sista-in-law….I got to get goin'…I got to get up early for work tomorrow mornin' Jack finally said.

"Okay then, Jack….It was nice havin' you over….thanks for everything…I really appreciate it" Sandra said. "Next time I come over on Winthrop, I'll look for you" Sandra said. "Well…I don't hang around there too much anymore…you know…with me bein' in school and everything" Jack replied. "That ain't why you stayin' away" Sandra said. "What do you mean?" Jack asked as he furrowed his brow. "That girlfriend is what's keepin' you out of trouble" Sandra said with her instinctive wisdom. "How do you know that?" Jack asked. "Jack…you cain't fool me….you're in love…I can tell…don't forget…I know you…you tell me everything about yourself 'cause you know you can trust me…you just don't want nobody to know how much you really care for that woman" Sandra said confidently as she smiled with a knowing twinkle in her eyes. "Well…I'll be damned…let me get out of here….hahaha" Jack said with a hearty laugh as he walked out of the door. Sandra just laughed as Jack left. Jack was in a much better mood after leaving Sandra's place. Whenever he was around Sandra and her little boys, it seemed to lift his spirits tremendously. Being around them seemed to fill him with a special kind of joy that he could not describe. They seemed to give him so much and he loved them. That was why he gave to them as much as he could and didn't like to see them in need.

Jack arrived back at his room at the Y. He bumped around his room for a while before getting comfortable and going out to the bank of telephones in the hallway and calling Tina. He was feeling hopeful that she would answer. "Hello" Tina answered. An immediate sense of relief came over Jack. 'Hey, baby…how are you doin'?" Jack asked. "I'm alright, honey….what's going on?" Tina asked. "Nothin'….I called you last night…couldn't get you…called real late, too" Jack said. "Well, honey…remember I said I would be in pretty late…I was out with Vickie again after a very long teacher's meeting at the job….we had a few drinks like we always do….I came in and crashed right out…that's probably why you didn't get me" Tina explained. "Okay" Jack replied, not wanting to probe or complain; wanting to set a pleasant tone for their talk. "Hey, babe….I will call you tomorrow night and let you know what we're gonna do on Sunday afternoon…I don't have it quite planned out, yet…but…it will be really nice…I promise…I want you to have a good time"Jack said "Okay, honey…sounds good" Tina replied. "Hey…check it out…Coley, Shirley, Freddie B and Carmen want us to meet them at the Mystic Lounge Sunday night after we go out…how about it?" Jack continued excitedly. "Yea…sure…I'll go, Jack" Tina said. "Good, baby…we'll have a good time…I wanna' see you smilin" "Oh…that's very sweet, Jack" Tina said, before there was a pause of silence on the phone. Jack wasn't quite sure but, it sounded like her voice was cracking with a little emotion at the end of what she just said. "Hello…"

Jack said after the silence lasted a bit long. “I’m here, honey…””(cough)” “You alright, baby?” Jack asked. “I’m okay, honey…I’ll wait for your call tomorrow night…I’ll talk to you then….good night, honey” Tina said before she hung up. The end of the conversation left Jack with an odd feeling. He wondered what was wrong with Tina. Something wasn’t right. She sounded like she was about to cry. Jack was puzzled and alarmed. The puzzling thoughts and feeling lasted for a little while. But, just as before, they were going in circles. Jack realized he needed to snap out of this negative state. It was time to plan a happy little excursion for his outing with Tina on Sunday. He prepared to go to sleep. As he lay in his bed, he tried to think of his plans for Sunday; dinner at a nice restaurant; another carriage ride and a stroll---a movie; he turned these thoughts over-and over in his mind. But, intermittently, the nagging worry of what was going on with Tina would involuntarily pop into his mind; interrupting the pleasant, dreamy thoughts about his plans. It was annoying. He tried to fend the worry off; push it to the back of his mind. But, they persisted until he finally fell asleep.

Jack was awakened by the drizzle of rain from the dark sky pelting his window and an occasional thunderclap. He propped himself up on his elbows as he lie in bed; straining to read the clock-radio on the dresser that read “6:11am. He decided not to go back to sleep; but, to shower right away and go to the Village restaurant to buy a newspaper and have breakfast. He wanted to read the entertainment section of the paper to see what he might plan for his outing with Tina tomorrow. After showering and dressing, he left out and headed for the restaurant. He arrived and sat in his favorite spot. He gave his breakfast order and read his paper. He read about Jazz shows; what was playing at the movies; he ruled a movie out because it was too long of a spell of not talking and he hoped that the outing would involve enough talking. He wanted to get at the root of why Tina had changed lately. A carriage ride would certainly be part of their Sunday activities. Jack knew that Tina loved the sense of romance that the carriage ride provided. They would be huddled close and the long, slow ride would give him a chance to find out where her heart was. Indeed, Jack was at the point of no return in his feelings for Tina. He wanted desperately to return to the way things were. She was deep in his heart and all of the happiness he had ever hoped for could be had---or it could slip away. He planned to be as romantic and sweet to her as he could; to bring her back to her old self. Hopefully, he could spark her enthusiasm once again. Still, there was this mysteriously haunting feeling lurking in the recesses of his mind. He hoped against all hope that it was not real---just a figment. Jack checked the weather forecast for Sunday in the paper. It would be a sunny day---no rain, it read. The carriage ride could go forward and he also decided they would have dinner at a nice seafood restaurant called Oceanus just north of downtown in the Gold Coast area. It was popular for it's quiet, classy and romantic ambiance; the perfect place to set the mood he wanted. After Jack finished breakfast, he drifted into a suspended state of mind; somewhat like a hypnotic spell where he seemed to be delving into the future; to telepathically see into it to get a vision of things to come.

Jack sometimes had an occasional vague notion that he may have some kind of extrasensory perception. It had come about almost magically at times out on the streets. When he was down and out; when nothing was going his way and he was desperate; some strange force would suddenly turn things around in his favor. He couldn't explain or decipher this mystical force. But, he knew it was real---like something that was protecting him; that allowed him to survive out on the streets time-after-time. He snapped out of it. After he came to himself, he realized that he was still sitting at the restaurant table and his newspaper was spread out in front of him. He looked over at his empty breakfast plate that he had set aside. "Time to go to work" was the thought that suddenly popped into his mind and he took off.

Jack arrived at the gas station and the rain was still drizzling steadily. There would certainly be no wash or wax customers today. But, that was okay, he thought. He had a lot on his mind, anyway. He worked all day, pumping gas and selling cigarettes to the customers in his work-issue rain jacket; thinking all along about Tina and how he was going to romance her and capture her heart once again on their outing. During his shift, he called and made 7:30pm reservations for dinner at the Oceanus restaurant for tomorrow.

Finally, his shift ended and it was time to clock out. He suddenly realized it was Saturday evening. He had been thinking so much about his plans with Tina until he had forgotten that it would be another empty Saturday evening for him. He had not really been drinking for some time now. If he had been, he would never have to worry about what to do with himself on Saturday night. But, he knew all of his hopes and aspirations depended on him not living the way he used to---drinking and getting high as a way of life. He knew that he could not live that way anymore and be able to fulfill his dreams. But, only recently with the apprehension and doubt that had been raised about his relationship with Tina, had he began to feel a curious sense of peril about himself and his future. He began to realize that so much depended on his relationship with her. Jack could sense the subtle changes she had undergone and he could feel in his heart that she was not quite the same. It was all a bit unsettling. But, he had to forge ahead with a renewed sense of hope. He hoped he could change things himself by virtue of his talking with her on their Sunday outing;

Jack hopped into his car and drove off. He drove toward home. A mild feeling of melancholy tried to overtake him. But, he fended it off by thinking about how he would romance Tina and how exciting it would be. Still, he needed to find something to do on this rainy Saturday evening. He would stay in and he would check to see if his friend, The Weep was in his room today; hoping that the rain may have kept him off of the streets. He swerved his Cadillac into a space at the YMCA parking lot. After parking, he went inside and straight to The Weep's room on the third floor. He knocked on the door. "Weep....Weep" he called out. There was no answer but, all he could hear was muffled groaning. Jack beat on the door again even harder. "Weep....Weep...it's me...Jack" Jack called out once again. Jack could hear The Weep stirring and getting out of bed. But, he still did not answer. Jack knew that The Weep must be in bad shape and suffering a hangover. "Weep" Jack yelled out again. "I'm comin" he finally answered groggily.

Finally, the door creaked open slowly and behind it stood The Weep; red-eyed; puffy-faced; looking miserable. The bit of hair on his partially-bald head sticking up wildly. "Hey, Weep...what's the matter, man?...feelin' sick?" Jack asked. "Hell yea, Jack...go get me a drink...will ya?"" The Weep asked in a sorrowful tone. "Okay, bro'...I'll go right now....I see you hurtin'....vodka?" Jack asked. "Yea....and hurry up...okay?" The

Weep asked meekly. "Okay…be right back" Jack said before he took off. Jack got into his car and drove the couple of blocks to Montrose and bought a pint of vodka at the corner liquor store and came back. He knocked on The Weep's door and it popped open. Jack had barely begun handing the bottle wrapped in a brown paper bag to The Weep before he snatched it.He hurriedly cracked the top and began guzzling the vodka. Jack just watched still and silently as The Weep paused after bringing the bottle down from his lips; like someone who was receiving medical treatment; painfully enduring the process; but, knowing he had to have it. Jack sat in the chair of The Weep's room that was standard for every room in the Y. He was silent as he grabbed an old newspaper lying on the floor and began to read it without much concentration. But, just doing it to pass the time. The Weep sat on the edge of his bed quietly pacing his drinking; pausing momentarily in-between each swallow. Jack understood all too well what The Weep was going through; that desperate feeling of getting the drink that he needed so badly; a drink to vanquish the craziness in his mind and the deathly feeling of nervous trembling that wracked his body. It was common among the drinkers that Jack knew on the streets. But, he could tell from observing him that it was more pronounced in The Weep; perhaps, because he was older and had been drinking a lot more years than himself.

Finally, The Weep spoke. "Whoooweee…damn…humph….I think I'm straight now, Jack…I wasn't feelin' worth a damn 'fo' you knocked on my door…that was right on time…'preciate it, brotha'" he said with a sigh of relief. "You musta' got tore-down yesterday…huh?" Jack commented. "Aw, man…hell….I was out there drinkin' in the alley with Chump Boy, crazy-ass Vernon, Robert Lee and Sally" The Weep started. He continued to sip on the bottle of vodka as he launched into his story. "Yea, man…Chump-Boy and Vernon got their checks yesterday…they was spendin' real good…buyin' drinks all day long…I was gettin' high as hell just for bein' the runna'…anyway….Vernon and Chump-Boy got to fightin'….you know Vernon been in the crazy house...got that plate in his head from the war…and you already know Chump-Boy ain't got no damn sense…them fools got to scrappin' like two old goats…then, they went to chunkin' rocks up-and-down the alley at one another…hollin' back-and-forth talkin' 'bout they gonna bust each other's head…maaannn…I ain't never seen nothin' so funny in my life…then, Ella Mae come along and tried to talk to 'em to stop 'em from fightin'…she give ol' Vernon a li'l kiss on the cheek after she talked to him and asked him to stop it….he acted like a saint after that…sat down…didn't say another word…they didn't fight no more, neitha'…I asked Ella Mae, with her fine ass….damn…you done give him a li'l peck on the cheek just 'cause he fightin'….I'm gettin' ready to *kill* this som' bitch next to me…what do *I* get?…hahaha" Jack had just been sitting quietly watching and listening as his friend The Weep had transformed from a miserable soul to a high-spirited story-teller in a matter of minutes. Jack was glad to see him back to himself. The Weep continued on with his neighborhood stories; getting more-and-more animated; gesturing and using his characteristic voice inflections to tell his stories; cackling hysterically as he sipped on the bottle; seeming to feel better as he carried on. Jack stayed a while longer before he decided to go. "I'm gonna take off, Weep….got to call my girl" Jack said. He dug into his pocket and handed The Weep several bills. "That oughta keep the haints offa' you…I want you to get yourself somethin' to eat, too, Weep…don't just drink it all up…buy some food…alright?" Jack admonished good-naturedly. "Okay…I will….I will" The Weep promised. Jack walked one flight down the stairs to his room. He took a few minutes to get comfortable before going back into the hallway to call Tina.

"Hello…Jack?" Tina answered. "Yea..it's me" Jack said, a bit taken aback by the way Tina answered. "Hi, honey…how are you?" she greeted more cheerfully. Hi, baby….you gonna be ready for tomorrow?" Jack started. "Yes, honey…what you got planned?" Tina asked. "Well…I think you will really like it…first..we'll go on a carriage ride…I know you like that...right?" Jack said. "Oh, Jack…you know I love that…but, we usually do that on special occasions…is this a special occasion?" Tina asked. "Sweetie…the way I feel about you…every time we get together is a special occasion" Jack replied. "Ooooww, Jack…humm…that's really sweet" Tina responded. "And….we will also go to this very nice seafood restaurant called Oceanus…I never been there…but, I hear it's one of the best…I called and made us reservations" Jack said. "You did?..okay, honey…sounds really good…what time are we going to meet?" Tina asked. "Meet me at the Lawrence stop as close to four as you can…I'll be parked near the station and I will drive downtown from there…you can see my ride…okay, baby?" Jack said. "Okay, honey…I'm gonna go ahead and go to bed right now…I need to do laundry and clean up early tomorrow morning" Tina said. "Okay, baby…see you at Lawrence at four tomorrow…love you" Jack said. "Love you, too, honey…good night" Tina replied.

After they hung up, Jack was feeling so much better about their relationship. He had actually begun to think that all of his musings about Tina changing were, perhaps, unfounded; a figment of his imagination; or a feverish paranoia that was a remnant of his street life; when he suspected everything and everybody; trusting no one had been a constant frame of mind back then. But, he had broken new ground over the last several months. He regarded himself on new footing. He had learned from Tina to be more trusting; more loving; more relaxed. But, when he began to have a rare sense of mistrust for her, he had unconsciously slipped back into his combative, distrusting mode. Their conversation tonight seemed to have put all of that to rest. Things seemed to be back to the way they were. He was happy.

Finally, it was Sunday morning. Jack awakened with a new spirit. He rose out of bed and the sun was shining brilliantly through his window; there was a joyfulness in his heart. He could feel the rhythm of happiness dancing in his soul; an exciting energy that felt strong, vibrant and spiritual. Today, he was feeling his connection to Tina stronger than ever. He could sense the sweet taste and smell of her; her tender touch; her presence seemed to be all around him; he sang and hummed his favorite tunes as he showered in the second floor community shower down the hall from his room. He noticed how much calmer and relaxed he was. He had not felt this way in some time. Right now, life seemed simple and easy; unlike the confusing, complicated state of mind he had endured in recent weeks. It all seemed so surreal; giving himself so completely to another human being; trusting; doing things that were so unlike himself. It was a poetic feeling; like dreams; magic; beauty; a wonderful song. At the same time, it was a feeling that was stubborn; relentless; hopeful; believing; faithful; trusting. Either way, it had expanded his existence, making his life seem ever more significant.

It was a warm, sunny day so, after his shower, he dressed casually, putting on blue jean shorts that seemed to add to the sense of freedom he was feeling. He left out of his room and walked with a bouncing stride. He hopped into his car and drove to the bank on Lawrence Avenue a short distance away. He withdrew a sum of money to ensure that the special outing would go as planned. He decided to drive back to the strip of stores on Broadway and Wilson where he did most of his buying. He would pick up a few little things to enhance the occasion; a stylish pair of sunglasses; handkerchieves. He even stopped in a men's store to buy silk underwear. He walked along the Broadway strip; stopping at store windows to gaze at the displays; or darting inside another to see what was offered for sale. He went back to his parked car and put the few bags of things he bought inside the trunk. Today, Jack was not only feeling joyous, he was finally beginning to feel that he was winning the battle of life. Each time Tina said "I Love You" it made him feel important; that he mattered to someone and the world was not so bad a place. It also made him feel giving; generous and loving. It dissipated much of the wary feeling he had for the world around him.

He was striding along Broadway when he suddenly heard someone call out "Cool Breeze!....Cool Breeze!....over here!" Immediately, Jack knew who it was. He turned to look across the street at the Wilson L station entrance to see Tyrone and Calvin standing near it. Tyrone was the only person who called him "Cool Breeze" It was Tyrone's way of showing respect and fondness for Jack. Tyrone liked Jack because Jack seemed to treat him as an equal; unlike some of the other people in the streets who talked down to Tyrone and disrespected him and his brother. It was all very sad for the two brothers to experience; and sad for Jack to see. The people who showed no respect for them now were the same people who once feared them. "What's goin on, y'all?" Jack called out across the street from them. Jack made a beckoning motion to the brothers. They walked across the street toward Jack; Calvin almost getting hit by a car in the process. "Hey, Cool Breeze...how you doin' brotha'?" Tyrone greeted as he and Tyrone stepped up onto the curbside near Jack. "What y'all doin' man?" Jack greeted. "Nothin' Cool Breeze…we need somethin' brotha'….let us hold somethin'" Tyrone continued, with a hint of desperation in his voice. "Alright…hold on...let's step around the corner" Jack suggested as he gave the usual wary look around the streets to see if anyone might be observing. The three walked several yards to the alley at Clifton and Broadway across from the Boozery. "Here you go…that's the best I can do, now" Jack said as he gave aTyrone a five dollar bill. "Yea, Cool Breeze…man…you a life saver…thanks…we sho' 'nough 'preciate this…I ain't lyin" Tyrone said with a sense of relief and gratitude. "We just woke up…you know…we sleepin' back on Clifton…you know that buildin'" Tyrone continued. "Yea…I know" Jack responded to say he acknowledged their living situation. "What you been doin' Cool Breeze?…lookin' all fresh and everythang" Tyrone said, now able to turn his thoughts away from his desperate plight and sounding cheery. "Aw, man…I been stayin' off the strip…stayin' out of trouble" Jack said. It was an answer that was a non-answer. It was the way Street Gypsies spoke to one another when they could not afford to be direct. Jack could not say that he had a place to live and could take showers every day---not in the face of the two men's living situation. Jack's response was face-saving. Jack and the two brothers meandered slowly along the street; walking another block north; making small talk and having a laugh or two along the way. They came to stop at Leland and Broadway right in front of the Leland-side entrance to the huge Goldblatts store that stretched the entire block. "We goin' to get us a taste first, Cool Breeze…we'll check you later" Tyrone said to Jack before he and Calvin marched toward the Time-Out Lounge and Carry Out in the near distance.

Jack had only taken a couple of steps to go back south on Broadway to where he parked his car when two men burst out of the Goldblatt's door. "Hahaha....we did it, man…we cool now…hahaha" one said to the other as they laughed and walked near Jack. Jack recognized Hondo and Pee-Wee who were regulars around the streets. On occasion, they were seen hustling together. Jack could see that they were feeling good and in a goofy, silly kind of mood. He knew that they were drinkers who also loved to smoke weed. "Oh…hey, Hondo…look who we done run into, man…looka' here…hustlin' ass Jack!" Pee-Wee said as he stopped in his tracks with a wide smile and glazed-over eyes; looking at Jack in that fond, funny kind of way that Jack had come to know. "Hey, Pee-Wee…Hondo…what y'all doin' man?" Jack greeted. "Check it out, baby…let me holla' at you" Pee-Wee said as he and Hondo walked ahead of Jack. Pee-Wee turned back to Jack, making a beckoning wave of his hand for him to catch up to them. Jack made a few quick strides to catch up. "Hey looka here, Jack…you just the man we need…look in there" Pee-Wee said with a smug kind of devious pride as he took the long strides of the slender, six-foot-four man that he was. He handed Jack the large Goldblatts bag that he had in his hand. Jack did not understand just then why he should look into the bag. But, he looked just as Pee-Wee suggested. Jack could see a few pairs of blue jeans and several other items such as watches and sunglasses. Right away, Jack realized that they had just boosted the merchandise. "Go on…hold onto that…you can make yourself some money and sell it for us" Pee-Wee said. "I know you got plenty o' fences around here you can check out…right?" Hondo added. Immediately, Jack panicked. "Naw, man…I cain't do it right now…I got to go somewhere" Jack lied before handing the bag back to Pee-Wee who seemed as though he was feeling no pain as he shuffled his feet along the street with erractic, drunken strides and eyes that were red-tinted and glassy. "Hahaha…aw, nigga…you ain't goin' nowhere…go 'head on…take the bag…we know you can sell that shit in no time…we done seen you in action" Pee-Wee said as he pushed the bag back into Jack's hands, still smiling broadly. "Naw, Pee-Wee…I told you…I cain't do it, man" Jack said as he volleyed the bag back to Pee-Wee with his open palms. The bag fell to the ground. Jack got a little nervous; knowing they had just stolen these items from the Goldblatts store. He didn't know if the security inside the store would be rushing out any minute to arrest them. He also knew that there was the chance that the police in squad cars or plain detective cars were subject to stop and search them at any time on the streets just as they always did. "Damn, Jack…you done throwed our shit on the ground…the shit *is* hot, man…but, it ain't *that* damn hot…hahaha…"" Pee-Wee said as both men burst into wild, giddy laughter. Jack left the bag lying on the ground as he stepped away at a quick pace from the two men who seemed especially amused by his behavior. Their laughter faded behind him as he walked back south on Broadway.

Jack arrived back at his car and jumped in and sped away. Lately, it seemed that whenever he came around his old stomping ground, something happened to remind him of how much he had changed; reminding him that his former life was a rebuke to how he was trying to live today. It was an odd, conflicting circumstance. He had succeeded, so far in making the change. But, it seemed to have become increasingly harder to maintain as time went on. He realized that he could be drawn back into the madness with the slightest moment of weakness. He needed to be vigilant and resolute, he was telling himself as he drove back to the Y. It was encounters such as the one he just had with Pee-Wee and Hondo that filled him with fear. He envisioned all of his hopes and dreams being dashed in that moment.

By the time Jack arrived back at the YMCA, his thoughts had turned lighter, happier and back to his outing with Tina. He would take another shower before leaving. He would be dressed tastefully casual. He would wear his best cologne. But, most of all, his attitude would be positively romantic and charming. This would not be a contrived notion but, something that he truly felt in his heart. He would just let go of all of his manly instincts of pride and ego; and be as loving and generous as he could to his sweetheart; to hopefully, reverse any misgivings or second thoughts she might have about him. It was still a few hours away from the time he would leave. Jack went to the room of the YMCA janitor who was off work today but,who lived in the Y. He got the keys to the maintenance room to borrow the water hose. He took some car-cleaning things from his room out to his car in the YMCA parking lot. He cleaned up his car; giving it special attention and care. After he finished, he remembered that he had exams on Monday morning; and while he felt good about how much he had already studied, his mind was relaxed and clear enough that he could pass the time studying until it was time to go. Jack cracked his books and studied for nearly two hours without his mind straying. Finally, it was almost 3pm; he took his shower and dressed; being meticulous about every aspect of his appearance. He was feeling carefree. A warm excitement was rising inside. After checking his appearance, he took off.

Jack drove to the Lawrence station and parked on the Broadway side of the Uptown Bank. The nice dress watch he had recently bought read “3:42pm” He was a little early. He walked from his car the short distance to the Lawrence L station. As he entered, he paid a fare to go up to the platform because that was what he had always done to meet Tina. The station had come to take on meaning to Jack. It was where his happiest moments had taken place; the sweet anticipation of waiting for Tina to arrive at the station on the train; the joy of seeing her smiling face emerging from the train car; the warm embraces; the tender kisses that all happened right here. The station had come to symbolize the heavenly bliss he had been experiencing; and right now, it was especially poignant to be here to meet her yet again. He had loved her almost from the beginning. But, now his heart burned with passion and desire for her like never before. The sweet anticipation of waiting was now even sweeter. Jack checked his watch again after he had climbed the long stairs and was on the platform. "3:47pm" He peered northward to see the Argyle station in the distance. There was no train on the tracks. He waited. Several minutes passed before he finally saw the glaring light of a train. In a couple of minutes, it was pulling up to the Lawrence stop. Jack could feel a slight racing of his heart as he waited for the train to stop and the doors to open.

When the doors opened, several people got off and toward the end of the train, he could see Tina's familiar frame appear. She looked like she was stepping out of a dream. Jack watched her all the way until she walked up to him and put her arms around his neck and they kissed passionately. But, for Jack, the kiss seemed deeper, warmer and more heady than ever before. Her warm body soothingly pressed against his. "How's my baby?" Jack asked with a passionate whisper. "I'm fine, Honey…I missed you" Tina responded. "You *know* I missed you…it's hard only seein' you once-in-a-while" Jack said softly. "I know, honey…I know" was all Tina could say before they turned and walked toward the platform steps with an arm around each other's waist. Quietly, they walked down the stairs and stopped twice within a few seconds to have a short kiss; saying nothing, except with a momentary gaze into each other's eyes. They continued on, walking out into the bright sunshine glaring down onto Lawrence Avenue. It was calm and peaceful on the streets with the usual sparse pedestrian and vehicle traffic of Sunday afternoons. Jack was mindful of the vow he had made to himself about making the outing very special; and so, he began.

"Hey, baby…this is the first time you'll see my ride...I think you'll like it!" Jack said with a tone of excitement to initiate the outing with the spirited, pleasant tone he intended.

"Yea…okay…so where did you park it, honey?" Tina asked with the kind of genuine excitement that Jack had hoped for. "It's parked right around the corner up here on Broadway, in front of the bank" Jack said with a broad smile. "Okay" Tina said, smiling back and grabbing Jack's hand and holding it. She swung her arm with his as they held hands and she continued a bright smile toward Jack. The warmth of her smile struck Jack with such emotion that his mood seemed to brighten suddenly, immensely and magically. It was the mood and tone he had sought from her for weeks; that had that familiar vivacious sweetness he had been yearning for. His Tina had disappeared for a while and now, she was back. He felt the joy. "Yea…we've been takin' trains and buses all this time…now, we can ride, baby!" Jack said. "Yes, honey…that's right!" Tina responded with the same cheeriness. It wasn't long before they had finished walking the short block from the CTA train station to the corner of Lawrence and Broadway. Jack led Tina around the southeast corner where the Uptown bank stood. They walked south a short distance before Jack stopped and said "This is it…what do you think?" They stood in front of the gleaming gold-colored 1969 Cadillac Coupe DeVille. "Wow, Jack…it really looks good…real nice…you must have paid a pretty penny for it" Tina said. "Not really…it's an older car…older than it looks" Jack said. Jack walked over and opened the passenger-side door for Tina. She slid into the seat looking around the inside of the car with a pleased little smile on her face. Jack closed the door for her and walked over to the driver's side and hopped in. He moved with energy and excitement, smiling all the while. He cranked the car up and the smooth sound of the engine started. Jack pulled off and he turned right at Lawrence Avenue and drove eastward, passing The Corner. As he did so, he noticed Jabo, Larry and a couple of the other regulars gathered up near the poolroom. He smiled to himself as he looked at them in the rearview mirror. He drove on to Lake Shore Drive. "So…how do you like the ride, baby?" Jack asked Tina with an obvious sense of pride. "This is nice…nice to have privacy in the car…but, you know, Jack….I really didn't mind the L train or the bus…I really enjoyed it…watching people…being around people…but...yes…this is really nice….convenient" Tina commented.

"You're still my baby…right?" Jack said with a sincere look on his face as he reached over and placed his hand gently and dotingly over her's, studying her reaction closely. "Yes, honey…I am…I know I might seem a little different…but, I've been going through a few changes lately…no big deal…I just have to work it out myself…I don't want to go into it right now…okay, honey?…I just want to relax and have a good time today…just fun today…no serious stuff…okay?" Tina said as she turned her palm upward and squeezed Jack's hand assuringly. "Yea, baby…whatever you want…I'm gonna see to it that you have a good time" Jack said, flashing a happy smile at Tina. Tina didn't say anything. She could see that Jack was really happy to be with her; that he had really missed being with her. She rubbed the back of his neck perhaps, giving him some kind of assurance or soothing him because she knew he had suffered a bit from her absence. Soon, they arrived around Michigan Avenue; Jack drove around for a while to find parking. Finally, he found a place on Dearborn near Chicago Avenue. He parked.

After they got out of the car, they strolled casually along the streets in the bright sunshine. It was a warm and pleasant day. The atmosphere of people and cars around them was calm. They walked and talked. Jack kept the mood light by cracking a joke here and there; occasionally making a little tease at Tina to get a smile or laugh out of her and to draw her into the happy mood he was creating. He had tossed his suspicious nature aside; abandoned all worries. He would just be happy today, no matter what. They walked toward Michigan Avenue. Before they reached Pearson Street where the carriage rides started, they stopped at a fancy ice cream parlor. "Hey, baby…come on…let me treat you" Jack said as he suddenly detoured from their walk along Chicago Avenue near Rush Street. He walked over and opened the door to an ice cream parlor. Tina said nothing but, smiled and walked with a playfully swanky stride through the ice cream parlor door. It was a charming little shop. It was spacious inside with several booths and tables spread about. It had a somewhat gourmet menu of ice cream treats. Jack and Tina chirped cheerfully over the menu selections; seeming to be immersed in the fun of the outing and really getting into it. Finally, they made their choices and their talk remained lively and upbeat as they found a booth and sat down.

Right now, Jack really understood that this was, indeed what happiness was. His life had been void of anything he could really identify as real happiness. Mostly, it had been a struggle of dysfunctional emotions and misunderstandings with his immediate family. They never seemed to understand him; and he certainly couldn't understand them. Growing up, his father was boorish and treated him like a stranger. His street life was full of friends, associates and acquaintances; and while his friends and many of the people he knew on the streets mattered to him and he mattered to them, the life was never what he wanted to begin with. None of his relationships were as meaningful as what he had with Tina.

After they got their ice cream treats, they sat and relaxed to enjoy them; making little comments in-between about nothing serious. Jack took care to keep a light and carefree mood. When they were done, they played around by smearing little dabs of ice cream on each other's face and laughing heartily. They left the ice cream shop holding hands. Jack could see and sense a few people who gazed at them a little long; perhaps, unaccustomed at the sight of an interracial couple; Tina always seemed oblivious to them. By this time, it had become second-nature for Jack to ignore them. They walked the short distance to The Chicago Water Tower location with Chicago Avenue at the south and Pearson Street to the north. They walked past people lounging on benches near the Tower; continuing on to the corner of Michigan and Pearson where the horse and carriage rides lined up. They came upon a lone driver who had parked the carriage and seemed to be attending to the horse. He was dressed in the traditional riding gear that was so familiar to people in Chicago. He turned from his attending to the horse to notice Jack and Tina approaching and looking directly at him.

"We want to ride" Jack said to the man. "Sorry, folks…Elmira here has to go in to eat, rest and take her bath…she's been out riding for a good while, now" the man said. "You'll have to wait for the next rider who should be along in about ten minutes" he added. "Let's walk over and sit on a bench and wait there, Jack" Tina suggested. The two walked back the short distance to a bench and sat down. They hugged up on the bench for a moment. "We'll go for the long ride instead of the short ride today…okay, baby?" Jack said. "Oh, Jack…you don't have to spend so much…we can go for the regular ride" Tina advised. "No, baby…this is for you…I know how much you enjoy the carriage ride…it's cool…alright?" Jack responded. "Ooohh, Jack" Tina began. "No, baby…really..it's cool…don't worry about it" Jack insisted. "Alright…thanks, honey" Tina relented before giving Jack a hug and a quick kiss on the lips. "Oh..hey…here comes a carriage…let's go grab it" Tina said excitedly as she could see the carriage over Jack's shoulder, further back on Pearson street, approaching the starting area. The driver was a young woman who looked classic in the riding outfit as she slowly rode the carriage up to the starting area and stopped.

"Hello…you available?" Jack anxiously asked of the driver. "Yes…but, I will be breaking for about fifteen minutes…you can be next" she said. "Let's stroll around the block, Jack" Tina suggested. "Good idea" Jack responded. They began casually strolling north on Michigan Avenue, taking their time; hardly saying anything; just hugging and smiling. Soon, Jack noticed a lady across the street with a makeshift flower stand. "Wait right here" he said before he dashed across the streets, ducking a couple of cars. Tina was puzzled at what he was doing as she waited patiently, watching him across the street. Then, she realized what he was doing. "This is for you, Tina" Jack said with a warm smile after he returned and handed Tina a single red rose. "Very sweet, honey…thank you" Tina said with a smile that seemed to be curiously mixed with happiness and a tinge of sorrow. She gave Jack a warm, short kiss as she clutched the rose in her hand. They continued on, strolling slowly; holding hands. They enjoyed the view around them; looking at the big hotels and fancy shops along the avenue that was teeming with other people also enjoying the pleasant Sunday afternoon. They took a few minutes walking around the block before they came back to where the driver and carriage were stationed.

Jack negotiated the route with the driver and paid the fee. He helped Tina climb into the carriage before joining her. Tina was beaming as she sat in the carriage with Jack beside her. After a few moments of preparation with the horse and carriage, the driver climbed aboard. The carriage lurched forward as the horse began with the sound of hooves echoing on the pavement. They rode along snuggled up together. This was the time that Jack had planned to take to find out what was in Tina's heart for him. He had to know. "So..baby…you want us to be together…right?" Jack started. "Sure, Jack" Tina responded. "I know we said we didn't want to look too far ahead…that we would just enjoy what we have…but…I need to know am I in your future" Jack said, speaking almost in a whisper. "Jack…you *are* in my future as far as I can tell…but, we don't know how things are going to change…just like with my job…teaching includes a lot of preparation outside the classroom…I have a lot of students…so I had to cut our time down so that I could do all of that…please understand, honey" Tina said in the soft, sweet tone she always spoke to Jack when they were having these intimate lover's conversations. "You forgot, Jack…just fun today…no serious stuff" Tina said as she playfully grabbed Jack's chin and gave it an admonishing little squeeze. "Besides…remember…the kids are out of school next week for the summer" Tina added with a smile and a little gleam in her eye. A broad smile slowly spread over Jack's face as the inference of what she just said fully struck him. They hugged and smooched for a moment and giggled. Now, Jack was thinking that his little plan was foiled by what Tina said about "serious stuff" He had to stop asking her those questions. Still, he was encouraged by what she said about her students "being out for the summer" He decide now, that he could abandon any worries he had because things were back to the way they used to be. Now, here they were; snuggled up together; riding majestically on a romantic carriage ride through the Gold Coast area of Chicago. His mind was at ease; and so was his heart. He was feeling completely happy and carefree. Tina seemed blissful, as well. It was all so grand. For a kid from the projects who had fallen into a wretched way of life while trying to find his way, this was like paradise. He had all that he needed right here and right now, he wanted no more of the traipsing up-and-down the streets to fill the incessant void he once carried around with him; no more of the mindless, drunken nights and the empty, regretful mornings. He wanted no more of the desperate, perilous existence where he found himself risking his life to save it. Now, he had found purpose, meaning and perhaps---himself. The two lovers continued to ride on, cuddled up together in the carriage with Tina's head on Jack's shoulder, making small, simple lover's talk. "Tina…I've been wantin' to tell you how much you mean to me…but, I hesitated for a long time because I didn't know if you wanted us to stay together…but, I want you to know that I love you…very much" Jack finally said with all of the sincerity in his heart. Tina was silent for a while. Then, Jack could feel her body quivering as he held her in his arms. He could hear her faint moan as she buried her face into his shoulder. Jack was waiting for what seemed like an eternity for Tina's answer that he wanted to hear so much. "I love you, Jack" she finally whispered with a sniffle. Jack didn't know what to make of Tina's reaction to his words---but, her words in return were all he ever needed. From that point on, Tina would occasionally take Jack's hand and kiss it; then rub it gently. Jack, from time-to-time, would kiss Tina on her forehead. They continued to snuggle in blissful silence as the carriage rolled peacefully along. They started from Pearson street, at the west side of Michigan Avenue, crossing to the east side of it, going several blocks before turning just short of Lake Shore Drive and heading south for almost a mile; then, coming back north along Dearborn Street. Finally, they were back where they started. Jack tipped and thanked the driver. "How was the ride, baby?" Jack asked. "Ohhh, Jack..that was the best ride…I really enjoyed it…you're so good to me" Tina beamed up at Jack from where she was still snuggled up to him.

"You ready for dinner, baby?...it's almost time" Jack said after they got off of the carriage and were standing on the sidewalk. "Where is the place?" Tina asked. "Just up the street about four blocks" Jack replied. "Let's go…I'm starved…I don't have energy…let me ride on your back, Jack" Tina said, playfully feigning distress with the facial expression for good measure. "Okay…hop on" Jack said, smiling broadly before he turned his back to Tina and stood with his back bent slightly forward. Tina stuck her precious rose in her purse and slung it over her shoulder. "Wheeee!" Tina said before she hopped on Jack's back and he carried her up the street, weaving through the now lighter pedestrian traffic on the streets. Some passersby turned to look at the revelry they were creating with most smiling at their antics. Tina was smacking Jack on his butt and saying "gediyyup, Jack…I'm hungry…hurry up" laughing and giggling along the way. Jack carried her for an entire block before he let her down and they had a good laugh at the fun they were having. They walked the last bit of the way more subdued and civilized, with Jack's arm around her shoulders and her arm around his waist.

“Here we go” Jack said when the two finally arrived in front of the restaurant. “Oceanus” was emblazoned over the entrance. It had all the appearances of a classy establishment. As they approached it, they could see the diners through the windows looking relaxed and elegant; dining casually. They entered and gazed around at the peaceful atmosphere. “We have seven-thirty reservations…Rollins” Jack said to the woman at the reception area. “Okay…I see you here…you’re early…but, we can seat you in just a couple of minutes” the woman said. Jack continued to look around at the modest group of people dining at their tables. “Right this way, please” a different woman said before she led the couple to their table. Some of the diners looked up from their tables to gaze at the two as they walked through the dining area. “Here you are…enjoy” the lady said before giving them menus and leaving. “What do you think, baby?” Jack asked after they were seated. “Nice, Jack…you picked a nice place…you’re spending a lot of money today” Tina commented. “It’s okay, baby…this is what I want to do” Jack said assuringly. “Thanks, honey” Tina said as she reached over and squeezed Jack’s hand lying on the table. Jack didn’t say a word but, his look into her eyes told Tina all he wanted to say. Jack was feeling very good that his plan to enhance his standing with Tina seemed to be working. It was all only because he loved her sincerely and was hoping she felt the same. They ordered their food and dined casually and talked. Jack mostly talked about how school was going; how excited he was about his recent test scores and how hopeful he was feeling about school; perhaps, trying to impress upon Tina that he, indeed, had a future. Tina talked about her plans to get another apartment; her plans for her teaching career and so on. It all felt royal and regal to Jack to be sitting in this chic dining establishment with Tina; relaxing; enjoying the ambience; it all warmed his heart and he felt serene.

“You up for our little get-together tonight with Coley and the rest of ‘em?” Jack asked. “Yea…I think it would be nice…I really like your friends” Tina replied. “These are my most decent friends….some of my friends…I wouldn’t want you to meet” Jack said. “I know…’cause they’re so messed-up and crazy like you always tell me” Tina responded with a grin. “Yea…it’s true….I mean….I really like my friends…even the crazy ones….but…when you get to know people and you see ‘em every day….they don't seem so crazy….especially when you're high like I was most of the time" Jack said with a chuckle. "You may have been out there with them on the streets…but…you're different, Jack….I don't think you realize how different you are" Tina said earnestly. "Different?…I don't know how…I was in the same shape as them" Jack said. "But, Jack…are any of them trying to get off the streets or do better?" Tina asked. "Yea…some of 'em" Jack responded. "Who?" Tina asked. Jack paused for a moment but, could not think of a single soul outside of the group they would meet tonight, who fit his argument. "Well…they may not seem like they want to do better…but…I know some of 'em do" Jack argued. "Jaaacck….that's what I love about you…loyal to the end" Tina said with a sweet smile. They took their time dining for more than an hour, enjoying the well prepared seafood. "Time to make it to the Mystic Lounge" Jack said after they had finished their meals. "Okay…I'm ready…but, Jack…I don't want us to stay too long because of work tomorrow…let's leave by about eleven" Tina said. "Yea that's cool" Jack responded. "And we won't mess around too late tonight, either…I have a lot to do for my classes tomorrow" Tina said. "But…we *will* mess around" Jack said with a hint in his voice and the expression on his face.

They left Oceanus and walked several blocks back to where Jack had parked. Jack drove north toward Uptown. They arrived at the Mystic Lounge just after it had become dark. Jack parked nearby and they walked to the entrance. There was a large sign on a stand just outside the entrance door advertising an Afro-Cuban jazz group called Questo that was playing the weekend at the lounge. Jack paid their admission fees to the man at the door. When they entered, it had the same low-key atmosphere as before with the strategically arranged dim lighting that gave the place a certain cozy ambience. The evenly-spaced tables were filled with people buzzing with conversation inside the small lounge. The band was mingling off to one side in the small concaved area that served as a stage. They were tuning up for the next session. As Jack looked around, he could see the same element in the sophisticated crowd. It included some of the upper-echelon pimps and hustlers from the area. Others were middle-class working folk who were serious jazz fans; still others were local regulars trying to maintain an image; still, there was that other element of blacks and whites who mixed well together and included interracial couples. That was what Jack thought was so cool about the Mystic Lounge. It was not for people with hang-ups. He loved the free-spirited, open-minded atmosphere. “Can I get you a place to sit” a perky waitress asked Jack and Tina just inside the doorway “Uhh…we’re lookin’ for some friends already here…ohh…there they are” Jack said as he was looking around and suddenly spotted Freddy B and Carmen seated at a table in a far corner. Just as he spotted them, they spotted him and Jack could see Freddy B waving them over. He grabbed Tina’s hand and they walked on the perimeter of the mass of people at tables, passing by the bar section.

“Whaddya say, Cuda?” Jack called out as he came in front of the bar with the owner, Cuda Watson standing inside the counter by the cash register with two sultry waitresses working near him. “Oh…hey, young-blood…Jack…right?” Cuda said with his characteristically wide smile. He stepped over to the counter and reached his hand across it and shook Jack’s hand. “Glad you could come…we got a good Cuban band tonight…they’re really good, man…I think you’ll like ‘em” Cuda said in the high-spirited manner he always spoke. “Yea…I know you wouldn’t have ‘em here if they wasn’t good” Jack commented with a smile. “Hey…where’s my man, Coley?…he showin’ up tonight?” Cuda asked. “Yea…he should be here soon…we’re supposed meet up with him and Shirley tonight” Jack responded. “Okay…enjoy yourselves…okay?” Cuda said as Jack continued holding Tina’s hand, leading her toward the table where their friends were seated. “Hey, good people…what’s shakin’?” Freddy B greeted as he and Carmen rose from their seats as Jack and Tina arrived. They all hugged. “Girl…you look fabulous!” Carmen said to Tina. “It’s good to see you, Carmen…long time” Tina responded cheerfully. Everyone sat down and the happy chatter began. “Where is Coley?” Freddy B asked Jack. “Oh…he’s probably on colored-folks time” Jack answered. His words brought an immediate puzzled look on the faces of Freddy B and Carmen. “He probably is gonna be here a little later” Jack added, realizing that the couple may not be privy to the cultural concept. The two couples continued with their lively conversation; ordering drinks in-between; and of course, Jack was not drinking. It was not quite an hour before Coley and Shirley appeared. “Hey..hey, y’all” Coley greeted spiritedly with Shirley at his side. They were both dressed especially well, just as they were at the group's last gathering at the Mystic Lounge. "For a minute…I thought you wasn't gonna make it, Coley" Jack said as he stood up and they soul-shook. "I didn't know if I was gonna make it, either" Coley said wryly. "What do you mean?" Jack asked. "Ask Shirley" Coley said flatly as he motioned toward her and sat down. Shirley started. "I swear…I don't know what I'm gonna do with this man…I had my nice little dress laid out on the bed after my shower this evening. Then, here he comes after he took his…he done lotioned all up and then sat his naked butt down on my nice dress…got that ol' smelly lotion of his on my beautiful dress I was gonna wear here tonight…but…that's the way he is…don't look at what he's doin'…one day he's gonna sit down in a pile o' shit and then…" "It was an accident…that's enough…okay, baby…you made ya' point…let's party" Coley interrupted with a defensive tone. "Anyway…that's why we're just now gettin' here…I had to do a little fixin' on this dress so I could wear it tonight…sorry we're late" Shirley said. "Ain't no big deal…let me buy you two a drink…that ought to fix everything" Freddy B offered with a broad smile. "Cool…Courvoisier for me…double shot" Coley said without hesitation. "And what can I get for you, Shirley?" Freddy B asked politely. "I'll have a Heineken, Freddy B..thanks, dear" Shirley replied. "I like that dress you have on" Tina said to Shirley. "Thank you, baby…you really like it?" Shirley asked with a broad, pleasant smile. Shirley and Tina continued on with their talk and the whole group was soon immersed in lively conversation. They continued to talk and laugh through the night. They enjoyed the lively play of the band, as well. All the while, Jack was observing Tina; watching to see if she was really enjoying herself. She seemed completely engaged with laughter and jovial exchanges with everyone at the table. It warmed his heart because he wanted her to be in his world forever; a part of the group of people he considered his family. His concern tonight was for her to have a good time; and the longer he had been with her, the more he seemed to care. He was especially proud when Tina was complimented for one reason or another by the others around the table. Coley was his usual gregarious self. He was always the loudest; constantly laughing and joking; debating and arguing good-naturedly while drinking steadily. "Tina…let me tell you…if Jack is with you…he's with you all the way…I'm much older than him...but, he's my best friend....most of his friends are older cats…that's who he likes to hang with…you stick with him and he'll stick with you…believe me" Coley said. This was Coley's way of showing love toward his friend by talking him up. Finally, it was shortly past 11pm when Tina said "Jack…it's time for us to go, honey" "Okay" Jack replied before he announced to the group that they were leaving. "You hold onto that nice girl so she can keep that spell on you, boy" Shirley teased Jack as he and Tina were leaving. She always treated Jack like a nephew and that was the nature of their relationship. "Okay, aunt Shirley" Jack replied with a wide smile just as he always did whenever she was in that aunt-like mode. They all said their goodbyes before Tina and Jack took off, leaving the others inside the lounge still partying.

They got into the car and Jack drove up the North Shore, taking the local route toward Tina's place in Evanston. The mild evening air softly breezed through the open car windows as they cruised through the tranquil night. He looked over to see Tina sitting quietly in the passenger seat; scooted down just a bit with a hint of weariness. She only had a couple of drinks back at the lounge because of work tomorrow. But, she seemed alert. She reached over and they clasped hands and glanced at one another the way lovers do. Jack was riding a wave of pure serenity right now. He was feeling especially hopeful for their love affair with most all of his worries now cast aside. The evening had been all that he hoped. "How are you feelin' baby?" he asked. "A little tired…but, I'm okay" Tina answered easily. "You have a good time tonight?" Jack inquired. "I had a blast, honey…Shirley and Coley are a couple of nuts" Tina chuckled lightly. "Yea…my old buddy and my play aunt Shirley…they *are* somethin' else.....I'm real close to them and I know they can put away some liquor…they can be really funny when they get high" Jack said with a reminiscent gleam in his eye and a chuckle. They finally arrived in front of the apartment building where Tina lived. Jack parked and they walked up to the building entrance in the dark, peaceful surroundings.

Inside, they were quiet. Tina slowly undressed for bed. Jack did the same; taking off all except his underwear, then throwing on his robe that stayed hung in Tina's closet. As a matter of routine, he sat on the living room sofa until Tina finished in the bathroom. Then he would go in, shower and brush with his extra toothbrush that was also left there for his convenience. Usually, when Jack was done in the bathroom, he would go straight to the bedroom where Tina already was. "Come here, lover-man" she said, after Jack entered the bedroom; playfully holding out her arms as she lay on top of the bed spread wearing a lavender night-gown. Jack walked over to her and opened his robe before getting on the bed then, leaning over Tina. She enveloped him in her arms. They kissed long and passionately. "Let's just lay here for a while…hold me, honey…okay?" Tina said as they both laid on their side with Jack putting his left arm around her waist and snuggling up behind her. They began to talk; saying simple little things. Then, suddenly, after several minutes, Tina fell silent---she had fallen asleep. Jack was surprised as he raised his head up and leaned over to see that she was, indeed, asleep. He had hoped they could have their usual sensual session of lovemaking. But, he realized that it did not really matter to him. It occurred to him that he loved her to the point that sex was not as important as how they felt about one another. He had crossed into another realm of loving Tina----he was surprised at how it was affecting him. Jack went into her linen closet and took a light blanket. He gently covered Tina and got under the blanket next to her. He went to sleep. Finally, he awakened and looked at Tina's clock-radio on her night stand to see "5: 21am" He knew that Tina always arose at 6:30am without fail. She lay there still sound asleep. He got out of bed and quietly got dressed. He wrote her a note and left it on the night stand "Left so you could get some sleep. I will call you tonight. Love you--Jack". With that, he locked the apartment door from the inside and pulled it shut; then went out, got into his car and drove toward home.

As he drove along the North Shore, the faint light of dawn could be seen with the sun peeking over Lake Michigan. The majesty and serenity of it seemed to give Jack a sense of calm as he drove along. He began to wonder how he had come to do what he had just done at Tina's place; tucking her in bed and leaving because he wanted her to sleep, undisturbed by his presence. Somewhere he had crossed the line into a place he had never been. He couldn't remember ever doing anything like that for any other woman before; and if he had, it was insincere; all part of the game. He had carried the same cavalier attitude as his friends in the streets regarding encounters with women. But, somewhere in this affair, his heart had been touched with this notion of caring.

Jack finally arrived at the YMCA. After parking in the lot, he went to his room and went immediately to bed. He awakened a few of hours later. It was almost 9:30am. While he sat on the edge of the bed and his head cleared, he felt a light, warm feeling as he thought about the good time he had last night. Although there were questions that still loomed about his affair; he felt good about things right now. He remembered that today he would be taking his last mid-term exams. His first class was at 1:50 this afternoon. He got up and took his time showering before getting dressed. He walked to the Village restaurant and had breakfast. When he returned to his room, he still had plenty of time; so, he studied; brushing up for his two exams today. Soon, it was time to go and he took off.

He parked on Sheridan Road in front of The Center like he always did. With his book bag on his back, he bounced up the long stairs. There were a few students mingling and walking around the hall as Jack made his way to the student lounge. He was feeling especially happy today and his mind was clear. He was full of energy, as well. He didn't see any of his friends in the lounge. He walked in and sat down at a table. He cracked open his book and thumbed through it for a final brush-up before his class in about half-an-hour.

"Jack Sprat could eat no fat…his wife could eat no lean" Jack suddenly heard a distinct voice recite. He knew right away who it was before he even looked up from his book. He saw Billy standing in front of him. "What's goin' on, melon head?" Billy greeted as he and Jack soul-shook. "Ain't nothin' fool…what you up to?" Jack replied as Billy joined him at the table. "Exams this afternoon…huh?" Billy asked. "Yea, man…I'm ready to deal with it" Jack answered. "I just finished mine on campus…I came here to talk to Sam so he can call the campus and straighten out some financial aid stuff for me" Billy explained. "What else you been doin' besides studyin?" Billy inquired. "Nothin…went out with my girl last night" Jack said with a non-chalant air. "How long you been with her, now?" Billy inquired. "About nine months" Jack replied. "Must be gettin' serious after that long" Billy said, not knowing how much the comment really affected Jack. "Yea…I don't know about that…we been hangin' pretty good"

Jack replied, a little strained with the same air, attempting to mask how serious it really was for him. "Well, I'll tell you…that girl, Karen I've been seein'…the one I was with at the party…we are on-and-off…I can't afford to have no serious relationship right now…it's too demandin'…throws me off from my school work…I need to be able to focus on that right now…dig what I'm sayin?" Billy explained. "Yeaaa…I can dig it…but, we're cool…it ain't affectin' *my* studyin" Jack said a bit squeamishly, feeling that little twinge of guilt from what he just said. The two chatted for a while longer, cracking jokes and having fun chiding one another. The bell for the next class period rang and the two said their goodbyes. Billy going to see The Center manager, Sam and Jack was off for his Man and His Physical Environment class. As Jack headed for his class, the conversation he just had with Billy seemed to linger in the back of his mind. What Billy said about not wanting a serious relationship because he wanted to finish school seemed to stick with Jack. It struck him in such a way as to give him pause. He wondered for a moment if he was doing the right thing for himself. He certainly couldn't study very well recently when he was feeling disturbed by what was going on with Tina and their affair. He knew deep down that Billy's reasoning may have merit. But, he did not want to give up his relationship with Tina so that it would be easier to finish school. He found himself deeply ruminating on the matter even after he arrived at his Physical Environment class and sat down. He was half-listening while the professor was prepping the class before passing out the exams.

He snapped out of it when the student next to him passed him a copy of the exam. Jack was able to concentrate on the exam; being deliberate in answering each question. Finally, after about forty-five minutes of the hour-long exam, he was done. The professor had advised everyone that they could leave after their exams were done because there would be no time left and they would discuss the exam at the next class session after he graded them. Jack went back to the student lounge and sat down. There were only a couple of other students sitting around, quietly studying. A few minutes passed before Lupe appeared.

"Hi, Jack" she spoke as she approached him. "Hey, Lupe…how you doin'?" Jack greeted. "Ahhh….I'm alright" Lupe answered with a forlorn tone. Jack looked at her a little closer and he noticed the glum expression on her face. "What's goin' on?...you're lookin' all depressed and stuff" Jack inquired. "Me and Eddie broke up" Lupe said with the same sad tone. "Sorry to hear that, baby" Jack said, standing up from the table where he was sitting and rubbing Lupe's back gently, then, wrapping his arm around her shoulders and giving her an affectionate squeeze. "When did that happen?" Jack asked. "Saturday…we had been out and came back to his place because I had only been there once for a few minutes…I asked him could we go back to his place…he said "yes"…we went out to a club…danced…had a good time…got back to his place…his phone rang…I happen to answer it while he was in the bathroom…it was some girl…we were arguing about that phone call when a different girl called him…I walked out…I left" Lupe explained. "Damn…that ain't cool" Jack replied. "Here…sit down…relax…think about it this way…at least you found out about ol' boy before you got too involved…better to find him out now than later…right?" Jack reasoned, hoping to show Lupe the brighter side of her unhappy situation. "Uhh…I guess you're right, Jack…thanks for being my friend" Lupe relented before she stood up and gave Jack a hug. "I got to get goin', Lupe...got to take my last mid-term in a little while" Jack said before they parted.

Jack arrived at his Intro to Uptown class and he took that exam. He was done rather quickly as were most of the other students. The class had to remain for a short lecture after everyone completed their exams. Finally, the class was let out at 5pm. Jack felt a sense of relief that the last mid-term exam was over. He hung around in the student lounge for a while, hoping that some of his school friends would show up. But, no one did. They probably all left The Center as soon as their exams were completed, just as most all of the other students had done. Even though he was feeling good about everything right now, especially concerning Tina, Jack began to sense that lonely feeling creeping upon him again. It always felt a bit eerie. He was baffled by it. It always seemed to arise suddenly. It was annoying and nagging; making him feel odd. He felt compelled to find a way to dissipate it. He could not decide what he would do next; where he would go. He had tried his best to avoid visiting The Corner.

Finally, he decided to hop into his car and just drive. He decided to call Sandra to see what she was doing and perhaps visit with her and the kids. He was driving around when he stopped and called her at a pay phone just outside of Truman College. The phone just rang-and-rang. He was disappointed at not getting an answer. Then, he remembered that she was probably at church music practice where she attended rehearsals a couple of evenings during the week. After attempting the call to Sandra, Jack went back to his car and just sat quietly. He had parked on Clifton Street near Wilson next to the fire station. The car was facing south and he could see the front entrances of the college in the near distance on the other side of Wilson. Students were coming and going. He was also around the corner from the Wooden Nickle. He could see the usual smattering of drinkers lingering on the corner. They were always the same mix of characters who bore the unkept, loose appearance of chronic drinkers. There was always some kind of upheaval going on around the Wooden Nickle. Jack was looking at them sort of absent-mindedly; watching them pace back-and-forth as they drank. Now-and-then, he could hear their loud talk with occasional outbursts of laughter, yelling or arguing. Jack began to feel more odd at that moment. Those drunks, at least, did not seem worried about anything, he thought. Just then, he felt a pang of envy. He continued to sit quietly in the car, letting his mind drift. Then, he could see a familiar hulking figure with a cane turn the corner in the distance.

It was Hank who was walking in his direction. Jack had not seen him since his last haircut more than a month ago. Hank was walking past Jack's parked car when Jack spoke. "Hey, Hank!...Hank!" he called out through the opened car windows. Hank stopped directly across from the car and stooped his six-foot frame down to peer into the Cadillac. "Who that is?" Hank asked curiously before he took several steps closer and leaned his head close to the opened car window. "Hey…that's you, Jack?" he asked. "Damn right, it's me…open the door and sit your big ass down" Jack said in a tone of sarcastic familiarity. "Man…I don't know if I wanna sit down…who car this is?" Hank asked, scanning the inside of the car as he spoke. "Who you see drivin' it?…come on…open the door and sit down, fool" Jack admonished. "I ain't sittin' down in no stolen car" Hank said with a somewhat mystified expression on his face. "Maaaann….stop actin' scared…this car ain't stolen…it's mine…sho' 'nough…I ain't lyin' Hank" "Sho' 'nough…this your car?" Hank asked again. “Yea...get in” Jack replied. “Alright” Hank finally relented. “Damn, Hank what’s wrong with you?…actin’ all scary and stuff” Jack said, giving Hank one more sarcastic shot after he was seated in the passenger seat. “Man…I’m not actin’ scary…I know you’ll steal the sweetnin’ outa’ sugar…you might be done started stealin’ cars…how I’m s’posed to know” “Stop crackin’ on me…what you been doin’ man?” Jack started, glad to have someone to talk to. “I ain’t been doin’ nothin’ much…got me a little part time job in the parkin’ lot over at the Ravenswood Hospital…all I do is sit down and take tickets” Hank said. “Hey…how you get this fine car anyway, Jack?” Hank asked after his curiosity had been temporarily side-tracked by Jack’s question. “Hank…you know I’m a hustler…plus, I’m gettin’ a little bit of money from goin’ to school” “You lookin’ kinda sharp…you ain’t drunk, neitha...what happened?” Hank inquired. “I stopped drinkin’ Hank” Jack said proudly. “Oh...so, you just on dope now…huh?” Hank added. “Hell, naw, Hank…I stopped gettin’ high altogether!” Jack said as though he was announcing a big news flash. “I know you lyin’ now…and this car *must* be stole, too…I’m gettin’ outa’ here” Hank said as he turned his body in the seat and began trying to open the passenger-side door. “Hahaha” Jack started laughing as he grabbed Hank affectionately around his neck and held him while he continued to laugh. “Let me go, Jack…you ain’t gonna get me busted” Hank said as he squirmed a little bit. Jack continued to laugh. After Jack’s laughter subsided, he let go of Hank. “No shit…be cool, Hank...it’s the truth…I really have stopped gettin’ high all the time…look at me…cain’t you tell?” Jack asked. “Aw…okay…I believe you…you *do* look like you all cleaned up” Hank relented. They both calmed down and began to talk. They talked for a good while, having their usual good-natured session of debates and put-downs before Hank finally said. “I got to get to the crib…I’m hungry” “You wanna go to the Private Pie….get some pizza, Hank?….I’ll buy” Jack offered. “Damn right…you buyin’ then, I’m eatin’” Hank said with a gleeful chuckle. Jack drove off and turned right at Wilson to go only a couple of blocks to the Private Pie Pizza restaurant next to the Wilson Liquor store. They went inside and ordered a medium pizza and took it back to the car and ate it there. They sat in the car parked across from the Private Pie, talking about most everything; mostly, the neighborhood and the various characters who lived there. After a good while, Jack drove Hank back the few blocks to the apartment-hotel where he lived next to the Time Out bar.

Jack drove home to the YMCA. It was still early and he got comfortable in his room and watched television for a while. He was glad to have run into Hank because it saved him from being alone. He would be calling Tina later on to talk for the brief time they usually did on Monday evenings after being together on the weekend. Finally, he called her around 9pm. "Hello" Tina answered. "It's me, baby" Jack asked with a happy lilt in his voice. "Hi, honey" Tina said kind of flatly. The tone surprised Jack. It didn't sound so happy. "How you doin' baby?" Jack started. "I'm okay" Tina said with the same monotone flatness. "What's wrong…you alright?" Jack asked. "Yes…I'm okay" Tina responded. "How was work today…everything went okay?" Jack said, trying incite conversation from Tina. "It was a pretty good day with the kids" Tina replied. "You get my note this morning after I left?" Jack asked. "Yes, honey..thanks for being so thoughtful" Tina said. "No problem, baby" Jack replied.

"Jack…there's something I have to tell you…I will be leaving this weekend on a trip out of town" Tina said. A feeling of uneasiness suddenly struck Jack in his chest. "Ohh…what's goin' on?" Jack asked with pause. "Well…I really didn't know if I was going to be able to take this trip or not..but, this is the last week for the kids in school…the summer break starts next Monday…I put in for this a few weeks ago to be able to miss Monday and Tuesday because us teachers have to do some administrative stuff even though the kids won't be in school…my principal finally told me today that I could turn the work in early and skip being there early next week" Tina explained. "Okay…where are you goin'?…what are you gonna do on your trip?" Jack inquired as he could feel a mild sense of anxiousness attempting to come over him. "I'm going with Vickie to her hometown in Albany, New York…I really need this break…we'll be seeing some old college friends and have a little fun while we stay at her parents' place" Tina replied. "Ohh…wow..you never said nothin' about this to me" Jack said kind of dazed. "I'm sorry, honey…but, like I said…I really didn't know if I was going to be able to go…I wanted to wait to see if it was final before I told you" Tina said. "Okay…how long you stayin'?" Jack asked. "Three days…I will be back late on Tuesday next week…I'll be home around 10pm that night after my flight comes in…I'll be coming back alone…Vickie is staying there for the summer" Tina explained. "Okay" Jack replied, still dazed by the sudden revelation. "You'll be alright, honey…three days isn't that long…I'll be back before you know it" Tina encouraged. "Yea…I'll be cool…it's alright…I hope you have a good time…okay?" Jack said, trying to muster up a casual show of emotional strength. "Good…I can go and know that everything is okay with you…right?" Tina said. "Yea, baby…don't worry about nothin'…do your thing" Jack said with a little more acceptance. "Alright…we'll be taking a flight out Friday morning…so..we won't be able to talk that night…okay?" Tina added. "Yea, baby…sure" Jack replied. They talked a little while longer and even had a laugh before hanging up. After they hung up, Jack had come to feel okay about his sweetheart taking her trip and not making a big deal of it in his mind; He certainly would miss her for those few days. They were still together and that was all that mattered to him.

Jack arose that Tuesday morning and as soon as his head cleared, a thought suddenly hit him----why didn't Tina just tell him about her plans even though she didn't have a final answer yet? That struck Jack as kind of odd. But, he did not want to dwell on it because it would lead his thoughts into a place he did not want to go----Doubt. He wanted to stay in a good frame of mind---not wanting to torture himself with all of the same doubts he had been having recently. He didn't want to stir it back up. He seemed unable to let himself relax and just be happy. He could not figure out why he was this way. He was so used to problems and troubles until it had become a part of his thinking; a part of his behavior. He couldn't help himself. And so, once again, he found himself shutting out the unpleasant thoughts that seemed to have just popped into his head this morning. After sitting on the edge of his bed momentarily and negotiating with himself to be in a better mood, he shifted his thoughts to school. He had early classes today with the first one at 9:30am, a couple of hours away. He also had work at the gas station this afternoon. He took his usual morning shower and dressed before he was out of the door.

He barely made it to his Expository Writing class on time. The instructor, Professor Thomas Walker began speaking shortly after Jack was seated. He passed out the exams that had been taken last week. Jack received his test paper and saw that he got an "A" He was happy and felt very encouraged by his score. The instructor wrote a break-down of the scores on the blackboard; showing how many As, Bs, Cs and Ds were given out to the seventeen students in the class. He pointed out that there were only five As and the rest mostly Bs; a few Cs and only one D. He lectured afterward and set a date for the final exams in three weeks. After that class, Jack went straight to his Community Organization class. He received a B in that class from his exam.

Finally, class was let out at 12:20pm and he went out to have his usual lunch at Jakes. Jack was eating his lunch inside Jakes restaurant and looking out of the big window that faced Sheridan Road. In the distance, he could see several of the usual street crowd mingling on the little concrete island that the locals called "Pidgeon Square" It sat conspicuously where Sheridan Road, Broadway and Montrose streets met. The buses for each street stopped on either side of the Square. Jack could see some of the same people who were there almost a year ago when he was engaging in the same madness; wandering street characters scraping the bottom of existence. Throughout the day, they would converge on the triangular-shaped area that had a couple of planters in the middle of it and a few concrete stoops where they lounged; passing the entire day congregating with their fellows; coming and going like pidgeons; drinking and carousing; occasionally stirring up commotion and providing theatre for all observers. Jack could see their weary body language as he watched them languishing on the island. It was kind of surreal for him as he sat there watching them; how the visual reality crossed into metaphor---stranded on an island. It felt like he was there doing the same as them; watching himself from where he sat; he could feel himself moving about on Pidgeon Square; drunk; interacting with the others; talking loud; acting crazy; it was all so intimately familiar; yet, he wasn't there; who was he, really? Was he that person out there doing those things? Or was he the person that was sitting here right now; clear-headed; sane; civilized; someone with hope. The person he was now didn't want to go back to being the person he was then. He shuddered at the thought and came out of his daze. Jack finished his lunch and he prepared to go to work at the gas station. He seemed to have a renewed appreciation for the simple fact that he had such a job and that his life had become what it was. He hopped into his car and drove away.

He arrived at the gas station and Brad and Roberto were already there working. He parked his car in the same corner of the lot that he always did. Roberto met him and began to speak. “Hey, Jack…check me out, man…check my ride out” Roberto said excitedly as he led Jack to an older car parked on the opposite side of the gas station from Jack’s car. “Look…what do you think?” he said, smiling broadly. Jack took a quick moment to look over the beat-up 1965 Chevy Chevelle. “Yea, that’s cool, Roberto…is it runnin’?” Jack asked sarcastically. “Hell, yea it runs…it’s all paid for to, goddammit!” Roberto said gleefully and proudly. “That’s cool, man…real cool” Jack said before he turned away and walked energetically into the station. He walked through the EMPLOYEE ONLY door and was met by Brad sitting down at Gus’ desk and mulling over the shift inventory book. “Hey, Jack…just remembered…got somethin’ for you” Brad said in his usual straightforward manner. He stood up, reached into his front pocket and pulled out a roll of cash. He counted out most of it and handed Jack the small wad of bills. “That’s all the waxes from yesterday and today” Brad explained. “Damn” Jack replied as he took the wad of money and held it close to his face without counting. “We musta’ done pretty good…you already got yours…right?” he asked, a little surprised at the amount of money he was getting for just two days worth of car wax business. “Yea..I got mine…we had four regular customers and we did six waxes for Hardy’s on top of that..everybody that waxed got their split, too” Brad said. “Cool” Jack responded non-chalantly as he stuffed the bills into his wallet.

“When is that baby due, man?” Jack asked Brad. “Oh..in about a month…man…I’m spending plenty of money already...baby crib…trips to the doctor…everything…babies are expensive… but…more-and-more I’m looking forward to being a dad” Brad said with a smile. “You know what else, Jack…I’m really glad you came along…the extra cash from the washes and waxes have really helped out a lot…thanks” Brad said as he held his hand out for a conventional handshake. “Ain’t no thang, Brad…thank Don Hardy…we got lucky and got all of that business from him…that’s what’s really helpin’ out” Jack replied modestly as he shook Brad’s hand. “Yea, but…you know what else…I never said much but…you work really good around here, too…we've had a lot of guys come here and they didn't last" Brad said with sincerity. Jack was a little surprised at Brad's words but, he just paused and looked at him and finally said "Well…I do my best 'cause that's how I like to do things…I'm tryin' to survive, man…dig what I'm sayin'?" A wide smile began to spread over Brad's face before he said "Yea…I dig what you're saying" Jack started his shift and things seemed to go quickly. There were plenty of customers and Johnny showed up with the same truck driver to drop off a couple of cars from Don Hardy's to be washed and waxed. Johnny stayed a good while, kickin' it with Jack because Oscar, the truck driver went up the street to the restaurant to get something to eat. Jack worked fast to wash and wax the two cars. He seemed to be full of energy as he detailed the cars with his unique and thorough waxing techniques. Before he knew it, it was 6pm, the end of his four-hour shift. Johnny and the driver returned to pick up the two cars just as Jack was about to get into his car to go home. Jack and Johnny talked for a while before Jack got into his car.

He turned the ignition key but, the Cadillac did not start up. He tried it over-and-over several times---it still did not start. Johnny paused after he noticed that Jack's car was not starting. He walked over and began to commiserate with Jack over his car problems; making suggestions; looking under the hood at the engine as Jack tried to figure out what was wrong with his car. Roberto and Oscar, the tow-truck driver joined in to assist; but, they could not determine the problem. "Tell you what, Jack…just leave it here…call Don Hardy or Jim Richmond in the morning…tell them about the car not startin'…your battery is good…everything looks okay…even Oscar said he can't see what's wrong and he *is* a halfway decent mechanic…I would take it with us now on the this two-car tow truck…but, they would scream at us for bringin' a car to the dealership lot without permission…make that call…when they say okay…we'll pick it up tomorrow and take it back to the dealership…they'll check it out within the first thirty days…cool?" Johnny advised. "Yea…that's cool…it *was* drivin' real good for three weeks…I don't know what happened" Jack said, a bit bewildered. Johnny and Oscar drove off in the tow truck with the two waxed cars. Jack left his car keys with Brad and took the bus back home.

Jack called Tina after he settled into his room. Tina was finishing up some final details of administrative work for her classes that she had to submit before she left for her trip; so, they spoke briefly because of that. They said "I love you" to each other before hanging up.

Jack awakened Wednesday morning and called Don Hardy's car dealership early. He was told that Don would not be in until about 9:30am and Jim Richmond would be in shortly. It was not quite 9am. He showered and dressed then, called back. He got Jim Richmond. Jack explained that he had the car for only three weeks before it stalled on him yesterday; that he didn't know what was wrong; Jack speculated that it might be the starter but, he remembered Oscar, Don Hardy's tow-truck driver saying that he didn't think that was the problem. Jim Richmond knew of Jack and the gas station he worked at from the car wash and wax work he was doing for Don. Jim mentioned to Jack over the phone how happy Don was with the good work he was doing. He told Jack that they would tow his car in when they dropped off cars at the gas station for waxes today; that they would take a look at it and see what the problem was; how they would live up to their policy of keeping their customers happy. Jack was very happy to hear Jim's assurances and it eased his mind. After that was done, Jack remembered that his classes started late today.

He decided that he would go to school a little earlier today and hang around before his classes started; hopefully, to have a little fun with his school friends. But, first he would go to the Village restaurant and have breakfast. He was feeling good today even though his car had stopped on him and his girl would be gone on a trip in a couple of days. Still, any problems of this new life seemed pedestrian compared to the risky, uncertain existence he once lived. Jack was amazed at himself that he stayed sober as long as he had. But, he knew, too that it was all inspired by his love for Tina; by his desire to keep what he had with her; before, he had nothing but, his drinking and his friends---or the best that he could call friends. He knew that if he allowed them to take advantage of him, that they would. Your mettle was always tested in the streets. Jack was keenly aware that if anyone showed weakness in the streets, that they would be severely exploited. He walked the few blocks to the Village restaurant on Montrose Street. He bought a newspaper and took his time eating breakfast as he read. Afterward, he was hiking eastward toward school. It was mid-day and he took a certain route to avoid some of his old haunts along the way; certain places that he knew some of the street crowd would be hanging around during this time of day.

He finally arrived near school and it was almost two hours before his first class. He stopped at Jakes restaurant and used the pay phone to call the gas station. He got Brad and asked him did Don Hardy's tow truck pick up his car. Brad told him that they did. Jack called the dealership after that and they affirmed that they had his car but, to call back tomorrow morning because they would not get to it until late today. With his mind more at ease, he went into The Center. He strolled past a few students hanging around in the hallway, heading for the student lounge. There were several students spread about the large room. Jack took a seat next to the window that faced the back of the building where he could see over the top of the next building and out to Lake Shore drive in the distance. He took out a class book and began to study. Almost an hour passed before Billy finally walked into the room with his characteristically energetic stride. He spotted Jack immediately and walked right over.

"Brother Einstein…what's happ'nin' baby?" Billy greeted spiritedly, as they soul-shook. "Billy…hey, man?" Jack replied with a broad smile, glad to see his friend. "Ain't nothin'…how did you do on your mid-terms?" Billy asked. "Pretty good, man…one A and two B's so far…I'll find out about the last grade today" Jack said. "Man…you're doin' alright…ain't too many people can come right off the streets and pull that off…congratulations" Billy said with a sincere tone. "Yea…I'm tryin' my best…that's all" Jack replied modestly but, not showing how encouraging Billy's words really were. "Yea…I'm doin' okay…but…my ride stopped on me last night" Jack said with a little disappointment in his voice. "Damn…already?...them Caddys…they're expensive to keep up…what's wrong?" Billy asked. "Don't know, yet…but…the dealership I bought it from is the same people I do the car washes and waxes for…they picked it up today and they'll check it out for free…lucky for me the car stalled right on the gas station lot where I work" Jack said. "That's too bad, Jack…good luck with that…I got to get over to the campus…see you later…okay" Billy said before he grabbed his book bag and took off. There was still almost an hour before Jack's first class. He stayed in the student lounge and continued to read. Before long, his friend Marvin appeared.

"Hey, Jack…how are you ?" he greeted. "I'm cool, Marvin…haven't seen you in a while" Jack replied. "That's right…I was studying so hard for those mid-terms…it was like I went underground…it's like you're studying so much…you're shut-off from the world" Marvin said. "That's right…I felt the same way" Jack agreed. "I'm glad those are over…the finals will be in about three weeks" Marvin said. "Man…don't even remind me" Jack said with a little exasperation. The two talked for a good while longer and before they knew it, it was time for their 2pm classes. Jack was feeling relaxed in his Man and His Physical Environment class. The mid-terms had taken a little bit out of him but, he felt fine. He took notes during the class lecture. Before long, that class was over and he attended his Intro to Uptown class that was always a lot less formal than the other classes because it was designed to be flexible and adaptive to the current neighborhood issues of Uptown. He found that he had received a B on his mid-term in that class. There were light-hearted quips and jokes exchanged between the instructor and the students. Whenever Jack was in this class, it always seemed to dissipate any feelings of aloneness that he might have. He felt a part of something that was wholesome and positive. He always enjoyed the easy group banter and laughter in his Intro to Uptown class. Soon, it was 5pm; time for the class to end. Jack always felt a little twinge of a letdown whenever the class ended at 5pm; because now, he was faced with the question of where he would go aside from home. What would he do with his time. The structure in Jack's life seemed to give it just the kind of meaning and direction that he needed. But, these pockets of idle time where he didn't know quite what to do with himself always raised a curious feeling of fear and apprehension; an odd, precarious feeling accompanied it, as well. He walked back to the student lounge and there was no one there. He walked over to Sam and Glen's offices, and when he peeked in, he could see Sam with his jacket in his hand, preparing to leave. He wanted to stick around The Center for a while but, there was no one to talk to. He knew that the last child at the daycare center where Lupe was got picked up by their parents at 4:15pm each day without fail. So, he could not keep company with her because she was already gone. He finally left The Center. He could go home but, he dreaded sitting idly in his little room for a couple of hours before he called Tina. It always made him feel so very alone.

Finally, he had the compelling notion to go to the poolroom. He didn't think about it very much but, seemed to instinctively begin to walk in that direction. Along the way, he ran into some of the people he used to drink and hustle with. They noticed how clean his appearance was and how he seemed to carry himself in a suspiciously prosperous manner. This always drew them to him. But, Jack was clever enough to give them the perfect line of bullshit to tell them why he was in a hurry and had to move on to do something urgent. Before long, Jack was near The Corner. There, he knew that he would have to fend off his friends from engaging him in some kind of folly or to ante-up on something to drink. But, he was prepared. He planned to not stay very long; just long enough to dispel the feeling of aloneness. Finally, Jack was at Winthrop and Leland and he turned to go north the one block to Lawrence and Winthrop where the poolroom was. As he strolled along, he could feel a mild mix of emotions arising; he felt that same apprehension that he had been having since he stopped drinking and started college. Each time he headed for the corner, he felt a sense of guilt, as well. He knew that going there went against all that he was trying to do---that this was exactly where his hopes collided with his fears.

"Hey, Jack…what's goin' on, brotha'?" Coley greeted. Jabo and Larry greeted Jack, as well. There were the usual smiles and soul handshakes. Jack could also see Melvin, LV and Andrew shooting pool at a table toward the back. A curious surge of fear shot through Jack when he saw Melvin and Andrew. They were his friends and acquaintances but, their dope-fiend overtures were threatening to his new way of life. Their brand of hustling was mostly of the hardcore variety that was too risky for Jack. "Hey, Jack....I'll talk to you in a few minutes after I break LV over here" Melvin almost yelled from the table they were playing. That comment brought about the usual banter of bluster and bravado between Melvin and LV. Jack stayed in the area where Coley, Jabo and Larry were; joking with them and enjoying a few laughs. Melvin was engaged in his game for a good while before he finally waved Jack over. "Jack…let me holla' at you" Melvin said with a beckoning wave of his hand. Jack casually walked over, belying the reluctance that he was really feeling. "What you doin" right now, man?" Melvin asked. "I'm just killin' time before I go to my part-time gas station job…I'm fillin' in for another dude on the late shift tonight" Jack lied. "Damn…you still workin' and goin' to school….huh?" Melvin asked. "Yea" Jack answered. "You can't call in and tell 'em somethin' came up?" Melvin asked. "Naw, Melvin…they just called a couple of hours ago and asked me to fill in…I can't call them right back and say I can't come" Jack argued. "Okay…I can dig that but…check this out…let me tell you this…" Melvin started. And so, the overture that Jack expected began. Whenever he was fiending for a hit, Melvin would make these dramatic and sincere sounding pleas for Jack to join him in some kind of scheme he had devised to make a hustle. He had pulled off many a caper with Jack in the past. He knew from experience that Jack was one of the more clever hustlers around. He had seen him pull off amazing stunts and make hustling moves that he wouldn't have believed if he had not seen them for himself. He knew just how down and dirty a hustler Jack really was; that he was especially cunning. "…Listen…Andrew got a good setup for a sting…this Chinese shop up on Argyle sells electronics, watches and stuff…they always have only one person in the shop…we could keep 'em busy while you do the boostin'…it's real easy, Jack…I'm tellin' you" Melvin urged as he spoke to Jack privately in a corner of the poolroom. "Roaddog…you know I can't mess around like that…I'm in school and everything…I got to pass on that…dig" Jack tried to convince Melvin. "Don't be scared, man…you ain't gonna get busted…I promise you…on the real" Melvin pleaded with Jack. The two haggled for a few minutes longer before Melvin finally relented. Afterward, Melvin went back to the pool table where Andrew and LV were still shooting pool. Jack went back to mingling with Coley and the others. But, as Jack was a bit of a distance away from where Melvin, Andrew and LV were, he observed Melvin standing up close to Andrew. Andrew was holding his pool stick and leaning over a bit to listen to what Melvin was saying. He noticed that Melvin seemed to be whispering to Andrew. Jack instinctively knew what was going on. He knew all the angles and all of the games that hustlers played. He knew that boosting was never Andrew's game; that robbing was his preferred hustle that he did alone. Jack concluded that Andrew must have scoped the Chinese store out and told Melvin about it; that they schemed to have Jack go into the store with Melvin. Jack knew that Andrew would not be a part of any such hustle. They were hoping that Jack would do the boosting; then, he and Melvin would sell the merchandise and Melvin would get Andrew high for putting him up on the sting. These were the insidious games that were played not only on ordinary marks but, on other hustlers, as well. And so, this was the world that Jack had come to know in the streets; the subtle cons; the posturing; the gestures; the words and phrases theatrically spoken; Jack understood the game and his ability to decipher these coded cons in the streets was enigmatic. He said goodbye to all of his friends before leaving the poolroom.

When he arrived at the YMCA, it was just about the time he usually called Tina. He made himself comfortable in his room before calling. He wasn't hungry so, he would forego having dinner. "Jack?" Tina asked after Jack called and spoke. Jack could feel a vague annoyance by the way she answered. But, he immediately dismissed it; not really understanding or giving much thought to why the feeling had occurred. Yea..it's me, baby…what you doin'?" Jack greeted. "Nothing…just getting all of my stuff together for the trip" Tina responded. "How was school today?" Tina asked. "It was okay…got a B in my Intro to Uptown class" Jack said with a tone of pride and excitement. "That's really good, Jack…you're doing pretty good for a freshman, honey" Tina said. The comment seemed to give Jack a special feeling of encouragement. Their conversation was pleasant and Jack did not mention his car problems, preferring to skip any conversation bordering on the negative. They talked a little while longer before Tina said. "I need to get off the phone with you, honey because Vickie will be calling me right about now" Tina said. "Okay…I'll call you tomorrow night" Jack said before they said "I love you" and hung up.

It was Thursday morning and Jack arose early for his morning classes. He had showered and dressed and was out of the door by almost 8am. He was famished so, he went to the Village restaurant and had a hearty breakfast. Afterward, he went to a pay phone to call Don Hardy's dealership about his car. The manager of the repair shop at the dealership advised Jack to call back in the afternoon because they had not gotten to his car yet. Jack walked toward school after that. Just as before, he avoided passing by the liquor stores and bars. He knew the usual street characters would be hanging around and panhandling to get that early-morning eye-opener. Jack arrived at school shortly after 9am and headed for the student lounge. He did not see any of his friends so, he spent a little time studying. He attended his classes. Both instructors informed him that his finals would be on June 17th in two weeks. After the last class was over at 12:20pm, Jack went next door to Jakes to have lunch. After having his lunch, he used the pay phone inside the restaurant to call the dealership once again. He spoke to the repair shop manager again who told him that his car had some engine problems and advised him to come to the dealership to take a look. Jack began to feel a little anxious about what the repair manager said. He was hoping that this would not lead into him having to pay a lot of money for any repairs. He remembered being told that the dealership had a policy of repairing or exchanging a car that had certain kinds of repair problems within the first month. But, he did not remember the exact terms. He took the Montrose bus to Cicero before taking the Cicero bus south to Belmont. He finally arrived at the dealership lot and walked over to the repair garage. “See here…this engine would run okay for a little while but, there are some pretty bad valve problems that would run into a pretty big repair bill…but, engine problems inside of the first thirty days are covered by repair or exchange…you were lucky that this didn’t happen *after* thirty days…you would have been up the creek for sure…you just made it by a few days” the repair manager said as they both stood inside the repair shop looking at the engine of Jack’s car under the raised hood. The repair manager advised Jack to go over to the main offices and set an appointment with his salesman to discuss his options regarding his car problem. Jack walked over and asked for Don Hardy or Jim Richmond. Don was gone for the day and Jim was away from the lot on business. The secretary advised Jack to call back tomorrow morning.

It was almost 3pm when Jack got off the bus at Montrose and Broadway after leaving Don Hardy’s dealership. Once again, he was faced with idle time. He was near The Center so, he went back in. He went to the student lounge where a few students that he did not know were studying. He cracked open a book and began to do the same. After about an hour, he became a bit weary and stopped studying. He set his book down and just sat there letting his mind wander. He thought about Tina. He reminded himself that after tonight, he would not be talking to her for a few days. He was missing her already. He blocked out any thoughts of how he would spend three days not talking to his sweetheart. He knew he would be yearning for her the whole time she was gone. Jack came out of his daydreaming and looked around to see the student lounge was now completely empty. He looked at his watch. 4:37pm. Most all classes at The Center were done by 4pm on Tuesdays and Thursdays. What would he do now? He knew that Sandra was at church for music practice at this very hour. He could go to his little room at the YMCA but, he just couldn't stay there all evening. He would be too restless. He locked up his book bag in his locker and walked out of The Center. He began walking north on Sheridan Road. He told himself that he would not go to The Corner this time. But, he didn't know where else he would go or what he would do. As he approached Sunnyside, he could see in the distance at Wilson Avenue, familiar figures hanging around the corners and in front of the notorious Sheridan Liquors bar. He turned west onto Sunnyside and walked past the Salvation Army Center. He stopped at the corner of Broadway and looked up-and-down the street. He stood there kind of absent-mindedly.

"Jack!...Jack!" a voice suddenly called out that snapped him out his malaise. Jack looked around to see a car pulled over to the curb and stopped near the stop sign at the intersection. Right away, he began to smile as he recognized his friend and hustling partner, Cooper. He was driving a decent-looking older Buick. Jack would see him in the area only once-in-a-great while. Cooper was always moving around; living a loose and care-free life that was always on the edge. Cooper was the same kind of daring free-spirit as Jack. They had become good friends who seemed to connect in a spiritual kind of way. "What's the deal, Coop?…what you up to, man?" Jack greeted excitedly after he walked over and stood in front of Cooper sitting relaxed in the driver's seat. "Ain't nothin' brotha' Jack" Cooper replied very upbeat as they engaged in a vigorous soul handshake. "Nice ride, Coop…how did you get up on this one?" Jack asked, smiling as he looked the car over. "Aw..hey…this is my new girlfriend's ride…I'm stayin' with her up in Rogers Park" Cooper explained. "You're playin real hard, these days…huh?" Jack commented with a smile. "Well…since me and my old lady broke up…I ain't got no choice" Cooper responded. "What you doin' right now?" Cooper asked. "Nothin'" Jack replied. "Hop on in, then" Cooper offered. "Cool" Jack said before he slid into the passenger seat. The two sat in the car parked at the curb for a good while, catching up on what each had been doing lately. These get-togethers always had the lively cadence that brethren of the streets often shared; talking excitedly about their recent exploits while doing a little soul-bearing.

"Ride with me over here to the Arms, Jack…I got to pick up a little somethin'" Cooper asked before Jack agreed. Cooper pulled off. A few minutes later, Cooper parked his car in front of the Malden Arms. "Come on in with me….I'm goin' to get a six-and-six for me and my old lady" Cooper explained. Jack understood that Cooper was going to cop some T's and Blues—T-shirts and Blue-jeans, they were called on the streets. Fiends were always trying to get prescriptions for these pills because they were like gold. Out on the streets, they were being dealt like pure heroin. The ominous-looking building was so familiar to Jack. It had been his home several months ago before he met Tina. He and Cooper got out of the car and strolled up to the building. Immediately after stepping across the threshold of the entrance, the dark, dingy lobby with it's sinister aura sprang into reality. Jack looked around and not much had changed. He saw a few hardcore characters loitering about. "Hold on a minute, Jack…I'm gonna holla' at this stud…find out who got the pills" Cooper almost whispered to Jack. Cooper walked over to a dark-skinned man gazing toward the street through a lobby window. From a short distance away, Jack could faintly hear the exchange of voices between the two. Not long afterward, Cooper walked back over to Jack. "Apartment three-o-seven…come on….let's go" Cooper said before he and Jack took the stairs behind the clerk's office.

When they arrived on the third floor, Cooper found apartment 307 and banged on the door. A silent moment passed. Cooper knocked again. Still silence. A door popped open down the hall where they had passed. A wild-looking, stout man stepped partially out of his doorway and looked down the hallway at Jack and Cooper. They both turned to look back. The man just stood looking. After a moment passed, he went back into his apartment. Cooper began to knock again and a voice inside called out "Who is it?" "Joe Willie" Cooper replied before the door sprang open.

"Hurry up…come on in" a short, serious-looking man urged. Jack and Cooper both stepped inside. Right away, they looked around the dimly lit apartment to see a big, tall, powerful-looking man with a well-defined physique. His shirt was off and he was sweating profusely. He was standing in a corner with a needle stuck in his arm. There was another man sitting in a beat-up sofa chair not far from him. He had a shirt sleeve rolled up and a needle stuck in his arm, as well; his eyes drooping almost shut. "Who is that, Saheeve?" the droopy one asked, slurring his speech and seemingly unable to open his eyes to see. "I don't know who them marks is" Saheeve mumbled as he nursed the needle in his arm; gently touching and maneuvering it. He was struggling to be alert but, he seemed almost paralyzed; moving in slow motion. "I know one thing…if they ain't buyin' I'm throwin' they asses out" Saheeve added boldly. "Damn right" the other man chimed. "Y'all be cool…they customers" the man who opened the door interjected.

"What you need, bro?" the short man asked as he turned to Cooper. "Six-and-six" Cooper replied. "Jenny!...Jenny!" the man called out toward the bathroom door in the back of the apartment that was shut. Quickly, a fairly attractive white woman opened the bathroom door and peeked her head out. "What?" she asked. "Get me a six-and-six out of there....hurry up!" the man urged. The woman closed the bathroom door back and a short moment passed. Jack looked over at Saheeve. He remembered seeing him around when he lived in the Arms. He had heard of his reputation and had seen him in passing. Jack heard that he was a prominent member of the G-Royals; a well-known Southside gang; that he had spent some time in prison. But, he never had any occasion to speak to him. Right now, Saheeve was too immersed in his get-high ritual. "Jenny!...Jenny!...what the hell you doin' in there?…hurry up!" the short man called out again after a long moment had passed. "I have to wrap this shit up in some foil…give me a damn minute!" the woman shot back through the closed door. "Damn!...it don't take but a second" the man complained while the woman was still behind the shut bathroom door. Finally, she trotted out and handed him a couple of little packets wrapped in aluminum foil. The man took the packets and gave the woman an admonishing glare. "You slippin'…you know that, don't you?" the man commented as the woman walked away.

He turned to Cooper. "Eighteen dollars, man" he said. Cooper already had the money counted and ready. He handed it to him. Cooper took a moment to open the two little packets to check them. "Cool" he said after he wrapped them back up and stuffed them in his pocket. "Hold on, bro' before I let you out" The short man said before he peeked out of the peep hole then, opened the door and looked up-and-down the hallway. "Alright…come on, bro'…you can go" the man said after he pulled himself back inside and held the door open to let Jack and Cooper leave. Jack felt a bit odd at finding himself inside of the Arms after so long. But, he knew how to carry himself in this menacing environment. He was well aware that the scene that he had just witnessed in apartment 307 was being played out in many of the other apartments inside the Malden Arms. He and Cooper took the stairs again to go down. As they were strolling through the lobby, Cooper veered over to the same man he had spoken to when he first came into the lobby. From a short distance away, Jack could see Cooper hand something to the man. "Cool, brotha'…good lookin' out" Jack could hear the man say. "I promised him a coupla' dollars for lettin' me know where to cop…he gave me the password" Cooper explained to Jack as they continued walking out of the Arms.

Cooper drove back to Wilson Avenue. He parked in front of Wilson Liquors and went in while Jack stayed in the car. Cooper strolled back out of the liquor store with a bottle in a brown paper bag. "Where can we go to take off?" Cooper asked as he pulled the car away from the liquor store. "I ain't gonna do nothin' Coop…you go ahead" Jack said. "You don't wanna get high, man?…sho' 'nough?" Cooper asked. "I cain't do nothin'….I been straight for a while….ain't really been high for almost eight months" Jack commented. "You bullshittin'?" Cooper asked with genuine surprise. "Yea, man…no shit…I'm serious about this school thang…remember I told you when I first ran into you today that I wasn't gettin' high" Jack explained. "When we was talkin' earlier, I thought I heard you say somethin' about you stopped gettin' high…but…I thought I misunderstood you" Cooper said. "Naw…I still ain't messin' around" Jack assured. As he drove along, Cooper stared silently into space for a long moment; then, finally said. "Okay…I'm headin' for the crib, then…where you want me to drop you off?" "At the Y on Wilson" Jack replied. "Alright….cool" Cooper said before he drove Jack there.

It was past 7pm and Jack walked to the Village restaurant from there to get dinner. He ate it there and headed back home to his room at the YMCA. Jack made himself comfortable in his small room before he went out into the hallway to call Tina. "Hi, Honey" Tina answered after Jack greeted her on the phone. "All packed and ready to go…huh?" Jack commented, trying to sound upbeat but, feeling a bit glum. "Yea…my flight from O'hare will be taking off at 9:43 in the morning….Vickie will be here early…..she will drive us to the airport" Tina explained. "You *know* I'm gonna miss you" Jack said with a forlorn tone. "I know, honey….I'll miss you, too" Tina said. "It won't be long…I'll be back before you know it" she added, attempting to cheer Jack up. "I wish I could be with you tonight before you go" Jack said. "Well, honey…I don't know if Vickie would like to see us naked early in the morning…might be too much for her…you know…her not having a boyfriend right now….besides…you and I never get much sleep, anyway…I'm gonna need to sleep tonight…okay, honey?" Tina explained. "Yea…I can dig it" Jack replied reluctantly. They continued to talk, making small talk about other things. Jack dragged the conversation out, savoring their time on the phone. Finally, they said "I love you" and hung up.

Jack went back into his room and just laid across the bed. Lying there quietly; staring at the ceiling. His mind was blank and he felt numb. Already, he could begin to feel the loneliness descending upon him. Suddenly, the thought came to him---how had he ever lived before without Tina. His life before meeting her seemed a dull and vague blur in his mind that he could barely remember; nothing significant---an uneventful existence. Jack turned on his side and curled up almost in a fetal position and lay silently until he fell asleep.

Jack awakened Friday morning. As the grogginess cleared from his head, he suddenly remembered that Tina would be leaving today. He sat on the edge of his bed, allowing that realization to come fully to his conscious; a sense of emptiness soon followed as he continued to sit there. Finally, he realized that it was Friday morning and he looked over at his clock-radio. "7:14" He had just enough time to shower and catch the bus to work. Afterward, he made it to the bus stop and arrived at the gas station a little late.

"Hey, Jack" Brad greeted non-chalantly. "Que pasa, Roberto…what's happ-o-ning!'" Jack greeted Roberto cheerfully, jokingly patronizing him with a Spanish inflection of his words. This was how Jack sometimes joked around. "Hey, money-man" Roberto answered with the nick-name that he had given Jack. Before long, Jack found himself working non-stop with a steady stream of customers visiting the station. "Hey, Jack….you got a call" Brad called out from inside the station after a couple of hours. Jack was just finishing up with a customer. He wondered who this could possibly be that was calling him at the station. "Hello" Jack greeted after picking up the telephone at Gus' desk. "My man, Jack...hey, it's Johnny!" his new friend from Don Hardy's dealership answered. "Hey, bro….what's happ'nin?" Jack said. "Hey, man...I had to call you...they just got a sweet '69 Caddy Coupe in yesterday….I grabbed it and started detailin' it and puttin' some better tires on it….drove it around for a while…you better get on over here and get 'em to let you have this one to replace the old one" Johnny explained excitedly. "Oh, yea?…what kinda shape is it in?…how does it look?" Jack asked. "Why you think I'm callin' you about it?…it's sharp as hell, man….a pretty green…ain't got a scratch on it…engine purrin' like a kitten…low miles….I'm tellin'" you…get on over here!" Johnny continued excitedly. "I'm still workin'…I'll be off at noon" Jack explained. "Hey…we gettin' ready to come over with a couple wax jobs…you can ride back with me and Oscar" Johnny offered. "Cool…how long?" Jack asked. About an hour" Johnny replied. Jack was already planning to stop at Don Hardy's car lot after work to see about his car situation and getting a replacement for his broken-down ride. The news he had gotten from Johnny seemed to give him hope that perhaps, this could turn out okay. After another hour of work, the familiar big, two-car tow-truck with "Don Hardy Cadillac-Chevrolet" artfully etched on the doors rolled up onto the gas station lot.

"What's to ya' brotha', Jack?" Johnny greeted spiritedly, as the two shook hands. "I'm cool, Johnny…thanks for pullin' my coat about that ride, brotha'" Jack said. "Aw…no doubt…wait 'til you see it, man…it is sho' 'nough sweet....for real!" Johnny declared. "Let me help Oscar unload these two wax jobs for you"

Johnny said before he went back to the parked tow-truck and assisted Oscar, the driver with lowering the two cars to the ground. After they were done, Johnny strolled back over to Jack. "You wanna stay and do the wax jobs and I come back and pick you up in my ride?" Johnny offered. "Hell, naw…I'm givin' 'em to these studs I work with…I'm goin' back with you before somebody buys that ride out from under me!" Jack said with conviction and a chuckle. "The two laughed heartily. Brad and Roberto were pleased when Jack told them they could have the wax jobs to make money. Afterward, Jack jumped into the tow truck with Johnny and Oscar and rode off at his quitting time. The ride to Don Hardy's was filled with the lively chatter of youthful exuberance. The three had a good time talking game all the way there. After Oscar pulled the tow truck onto the dealership lot, Johnny began to coach Jack on a little strategy.

"Check this out, man…I parked the car where it's kind of hid….on the side of the repair garage…like I said before, I detailed it and put some good tires on it for you…now, I got to take the papers that came with it over to the secretary in the office buildin'….she will type up the information to put the car into inventory…if I sweet talk her a little bit…she'll put it in right away…you just walk around the lot for a little while…like you lookin' at rides…I'll give you the signal…then, you come into the office and talk to Jim or Don...tell 'em this is the ride you want for a replacement…Jim already knows the ride you bought is shot…dig?" Johnny advised. "Damn, Johnny…thanks…you looked out for a brotha' real tough…I sho' 'nough 'preciate it, too!" Jack said excitedly. "Let's go, then…I'll get the papers and run 'em over to the secretary…just be cool….everything is gonna work out real nice…watch for my signal!" Johnny said before he took off stepping lively across the lot. About fifteen minutes passed as Jack strolled around a small area of the lot. He kept glancing back at the office building in the near distance. Finally, he could see Johnny walk several yards out from the office entrance and wave at him. Immediately, Jack began walking toward the offices. Johnny met him at the door. "Don is here…wait 'til he gets through talkin' to that stud in his office then, go over and knock…I'll be workin' over at the garage" Johnny almost whispered to Jack. Jack paced back and forth in the same little area until he saw the man who was in Don Hardy's office leave.

"How ya' doin' Mr. Hardy" Jack spoke after he rapped on the open door of Don's office. "Well, hello there….Rollins….Jack Rollins…come on in, son" Don Hardy greeted cheerfully with a broad smile. "Have a seat…what can I do for you?" Don said. "Uhh…well…my car broke down a few days ago" Jack said modestly. "Ohh…ohh…well…did you get it towed to the lot so we can have a look at her?" Don asked. "Yessir…all of that's been done…your repair manager told me the engine is shot" Jack explained. "Sorry…sorry about that…but, you know about our thirty day policy on used cars…right?" Don started. "Yessir" Jack replied. "I'll be glad to replace it for you…with a car of equal value, of course" Don said. "Now…you can go out there and pick another one out that's about the same price and I'll personally give the okay…how's that?" Don Hardy offered as he reared back in his big chair in the grand style of the successful business man that he was, smiling all along. "Yessir…that's cool with me…I mean…I appreciate it" Jack said with a wide grin, trying to hold back the bursting satisfaction just underneath. The rest of the transaction was a blur of paper-work. There were back-and-forth exchanges over the phone between Don and the sales manager who handled inventory because they had not had time to price the car. Don barked at the sales manager to price the car the same as the one Jack bought. Jack was sitting in Don's office while all of this was going on. He was getting a first-hand view of how a powerful business man like Don Hardy operated. Before Jack knew it, the deal was done. He was standing there out on the dealership lot with an envelope of papers he had signed in his hand. He was standing in front of the gleaming automobile with Johnny standing next to him. "Hahaha…told ya' brotha', Jack!…check you out…you hooked up now, baby!…sweet ain't it!" Johnny was saying. Jack snapped out his daze---momentarily spellbound as he stared at the automobile. The car was nicer than the one that he had lost to a bad engine. "Aw…yea…haha…it *is* sharp, ain't it?" Jack finally responded to Johnny's excited chatter. "Johnny…thanks, man…you my guy for stickin' ya' neck out and doin' all of this to get me a nice ride outa these people" Jack said with sincere gratitude. "No doubt, brotha' Jack…ain't no thang!...let's go for a spin" Johnny suggested.

With that, they jumped in the car and Jack drove several miles south on Cicero Avenue to get a feel for the car. Then, he drove back to the dealership lot. He and Johnny hung around the car talking for a good while before Jack said he was leaving. Jack told Johnny all about his girl being out of town and how he had no plans for the weekend. Johnny asked Jack if he wanted to go disco-clubbing and checking out the ladies that night. Jack agreed because he had nothing else to do. They parted with a soul handshake. "Meet you around 9:30 at the Crossover tonight!" Johnny yelled as Jack pulled off the lot in his newly acquired ride.

It was a few hours away before Jack would be meeting Johnny at the Crossover Disco Lounge located at Lincoln and Peterson Avenues. Jack went home to shower and change clothes. He was thinking that Johnny's offer to hang out was right on time. He needed a distraction to keep him from dwelling on Tina or being tempted to visit The Corner. Johnny had already mentioned in his conversations that he smoked a little weed and was not much of a drinker. Jack was glad of that because he did not like the peer pressure of being with someone who was a drinker like his friends on The Corner. He didn't smoke weed, anyway so, that would not bother him. After his shower, Jack laid out a set of his nicer party clothes that he had not worn in some time. He dressed and went out to the Village restaurant before it closed and had dinner. He left the restaurant just before it closed. When he got back to his car, it was not quite 8pm; much more time than he needed to drive to the Crossover Disco and meet Johnny at 9:30. Jack just sat there in his car parked a few doors from the restaurant. He laid his head back in the driver's seat and tried to relax; but, as he did so, his mind began to spin involuntarily, it seemed, with thoughts of Tina; how he was missing her and the subconscious worries that loomed in the back of his mind about what the future might bring for them. He nodded off momentarily. He had that wild dream again about him and Tina riding in his car and being chased by another car with a man yelling out Tina's name. Jack snapped out of the hazy dream with a snatch of his breath. It seemed to have a haunting effect. He was feeling a little crazy before the haze lifted.

He immediately cranked up his car and drove to the Crossover Disco. It was still early so, he was able to find a parking spot on the same street about a half-block from the club entrance. As he sat in his car, Jack could hear the lively music emanating from the club. There was a smattering of people spread about; up-and-down the street on this clear and balmy night; some standing out on the side-walk; others lingering around and sitting on their cars with their party friends. They were all people around Jack's age. There was lively chatter and laughter all around the club perimeter. This was a club that had a mostly Latino following because some of the nearby neighborhoods were Hispanic. But, like most clubs around the city, there was a mix of all kinds of people who just wanted to have a good time. Jack looked at his watch and it was a little past 9pm.

He sat quietly in his car watching the people walking past, heading for the club, There was the usual party atmosphere. Occasionally, he noticed a foxy lady or two who cast a discerning eye toward him and his sleek automobile. Before long, Johnny surprised Jack, pulling up alongside his parked car. "Hey, brotha' Jack!" Johnny called out from his impressive ride as he stopped even with Jack's car. "Hey, fool…what's the deal!" Jack replied, suddenly having his spirits lifted by the appearance of someone he knew. "What do you think?...nice set, Huh?" Johnny commented from the short distance as he peered inside of Jack's car. "Yeah…pretty cool" Jack responded. "I'll kick it with you soon as I park" Johnny said before he pulled off. Johnny had to park further down the street and walked back to Jack's ride. He hopped into the front passenger seat and they kicked it for a while; keeping an eye on the crowd converging on the club. They made comments about the more attractive females in the crowd. "Look at that, man…fine Black chicks, hot Spanish chicks, Snow chicks…Asian chicks…all kinda chicks, …damn!" Johnny said excitedly. "I haven't seen this many fine women at any of the other clubs" Jack commented. "Just right for players like us…huh?" Johnny commented, with a tone of bravado. "Yea" Jack responded modestly, not really feeling like a player. Nonetheless, he was ready for a night of fun to dispel the void he was feeling. He was trying to get in tune with the feeling of merriment and excitement in the air; generated by the popular tunes pulsating over the club audio system. "Let's hang out here for a few…let the club get full of women…then, make our move" Johnny suggested. The two sat in Jack's car a little while longer before they finally entered the club.

Right away, Johnny was into his game plan. “I’m makin’ my move on that sweet thang over there, Jack…holla at you later” Johnny said before he casually strolled over to a young woman accompanied by two others. From across the room, Jack could see Johnny talking to her; smiling and gesturing the whole time. It was just a short time later before he saw them go onto the disco floor and begin to dance. Throughout the night, Johnny was mingling and mixing; approaching every unescorted, attractive woman he could; spreading himself around; dancing and talking; Jack was doing the same; albeit, at a slower pace. Mostly, Jack was forcing himself to have a good time. He could feel the absence of Tina. It had been quite some time since he had gone out for a good time without her by his side. He danced and ordered sodas from the bar; trying to lose himself in the party atmosphere. From time-to-time throughout the night, Johnny would find Jack and report the fun he was having with various women. Before long, it had gotten late into the night. Johnny found Jack again and with a fairly attractive, caramel-complexioned young lady at his side, announced. “I’m droppin’ her off at home” The two soul shook and parted for the night. Jack left the club alone.

As he drove through the dark maze of night lights and traffic, the party feeling he had at the club seemed to fall away from him like a dead weight. It uncovered the somber mood underneath. He seemed to be driving home with a sense of emptiness. His mind was blank; he was surprised at the slight numbness he was feeling. He never imagined that a woman could get so deep into his soul; that it would have this kind of effect on him. Sometimes, he felt like a prisoner to the feeling; bound to it like he was to his skin; unable to escape from the uncertainty that had arisen. It was the overriding sense of hope that he derived from his love for Tina that seemed to buoy him above those nagging clouds of doubt. He went home and went to bed.

Saturday morning arrived and Jack arose with the same solemn feeling he had gone to bed with. He was fully aware of having a full shift of work today at the gas station. He awakened in plenty of time to shower, dress and be on his way. He arrived at the station. He greeted Roberto and Brad before starting work. He went about his duties mechanically. He felt fine except for the nagging thought about what would he do this evening when work was done. His visits to The Corner had proven to be too uncertain and risky. Now, just as he had been afraid to be sober when he was drinking, he could sense the creeping fear of getting high, as well. He knew himself; that if he drank and drank too much, he would want drugs and chasing them would disrupt all of the good he had achieved. This was the reason he drank very little or not at all. There was also the frightful thought of being alone the entire evening. All of this was a bit overwhelming and daunting to Jack. These little fears were playing havoc in his mind; like little ghosts, they would jump up and send a phantom little shock of fear through him then, quickly disappear; and when they did, he would feel as though he had physically reacted to a scare; but, the feeling was purely mental----all in his head.

Finally, Johnny arrived with Oscar driving the Don Hardy tow truck. They dropped off two cars for wax jobs just before the noon hour. Jack could sense a strange sigh of relief. He could kick it with Johnny and not have to be alone with his thoughts. Johnny was very animated; laughing and joking about his good time at the Crossover Disco Club last night; doing a little bragging and talking in the spirited language so-called players liked to use. Jack went along with Johnny's happy mood. It was plain to see from his conversation that he had a good time last night. Listening to him carry on, Jack was feeling a little odd. His experience at the club did not seem to match Johnny's joyful reminiscing. He felt a bit of envy, as well because Johnny was drinking last night and he was not; envious because he seemed so happy and carefree. Usually, Johnny's spirited talk would lift Jack but, he could not shake the odd feeling. "Yeah, Jack…that girl I dropped off last night…we goin' out tonight to The Machine" Johnny announced with a wide smile. Jack endured Johnny's happy chatter for a while longer before Johnny hopped back in the tow truck and they drove off. Jack continued his shift and his somber mood. He washed and waxed both of the cars that were dropped off. As he worked on, Jack could feel a creeping little fear growing inside. The approaching end of his shift was giving him a certain uneasiness. What would he do when he got off work? He was turning this over-and-over in his mind; trying to stave off the impending loneliness. He knew that Sandra would be at music practice at the church for the better part of the evening. He knew that if he visited Annie on Clifton, that it would involve drinking;

that if he went to The Corner, it would include getting high; that keeping company with almost any of the people he knew in the area would involve some drinking or getting high as a part of being in their company. He felt stuck; trapped; lost; isolated. The feeling of pressure was becoming annoying. How was he going to get through the evening? In the recent past, when he did hang around his friends on The Corner without drinking, he could do it for short periods of time before he went home and called Tina. Talking to her on the telephone those nights seemed to defuse the pent-up feelings he would have from trying to stay sober. Right now, he was feeling less secure than before about going to The Corner. All of these little thoughts and feelings seemed to culminate into that sense of doing a high-wire act; treading ever-so-carefully by walking that fine line; trying hard to keep from falling out of his pattern of sobriety. Jack continued to wait on customers at the gas station; losing himself in his work while he tried to cut off those nagging thoughts. As he was pumping gas for a customer, he happened to look up to see the big clock behind the cashier counter inside the station. 4pm. It sent one of those little phantom shocks of fear through him. It was almost time to get off work. A half hour more. Finally, it was 4:30pm. At the end of his work shifts, Jack usually had a feeling of joy; of uplifting. He was confused by the curious sense of dread that came over him all at once. He took his time washing up and taking off his work coveralls.

When he was finally seated in his car, he just sat there. His mind was blank. He couldn't think of anything; least of all, anywhere to go. "What's the matter?…car won't start?" Roberto asked as he stood in front of Jack with an expression of concern. Jack snapped out of his haze. "Oh..oh…naw…I'm cool" he replied before he cranked the car up and pulled away. As he was driving, he decided to go to the one place he *could* go---to his room at the YMCA. Jack took a shower. He bumped around his room, taking his time straightening things up. He turned on the television. He sat there absent-mindedly and watched one television show after another. It was 9pm; too early to go to bed. He wasn't sleepy. He felt he couldn't watch any more television in his room. It was boring him out of his mind. The loneliness had become even more pronounced. The deafening silence. The deadness he felt inside. Wearing the sweat outfit that he used to lounge around his room, he sprang up from his bed and went into his dresser drawer, grabbed his keys and locked his door before walking downstairs.

He went into the community area in the lobby and sat in one of the lounge chairs. There was a smattering of residents already there, engrossed in a classic western movie on the community TV. Jack sat there and watched along with them. Being there around them gave him a mild feeling of relief; even though he had no real interest in the movie. It was a much smaller crowd than on the weekday evenings. Most of the other men who lived in the YMCA probably had somewhere to go on the weekends; something to do. They were out having a good time somewhere, he surmised. He looked around at the others sitting there. Lonely souls just like him. It brought a twinge of pain and melancholy to think that he was, at least for now, the same as them; nowhere to go on a Saturday night. He couldn't even visit with his friend, The Weep on the next floor above his room because he was surely out drinking in the streets right now.

Finally, Jack went back upstairs. He got into bed. He laid there for more than an hour with his eyes open and not feeling sleepy. He sat up in the bed. He turned on the lamp sitting on the dresser. He looked at the clock on the dresser. 11:19pm. He sat back down on the edge of his bed, staring blankly at the walls for a long moment. Time seemed to be standing still. His spirit was stagnant; he began to have a mild sensation of suffocating. He thought about dressing and going out to get into his car to go somewhere. Anywhere; and then, his thinking was cut off right there. He couldn't think of anything beyond that. He abandoned the idea. Finally, he turned on the television and laid in the bed. He wasn't watching it. He just let it drone on-and-on, using the sound to keep himself company. He eventually fell asleep. He was awakened by the noisy static of the blank television screen. It was still dark. 5:09am his clock-radio read when he looked at it. He turned the television off, laid his head back down and closed his eyes. He fell asleep again.

Jack awakened slowly. His head cleared and a spurt of happiness popped into his mind; then suddenly, he remembered his condition. He was alone. Tina was not around. It was Sunday; the loneliest day of the week. And when he remembered all of this, his mood became poisoned with gloom; and dread followed.

It was the very beginning of the day. He had to contemplate how he would get through it. The urge to forget about all of his goals and aspirations came to mind. Why didn't he just go out, drink and forget about everything? It would be easier than this. But, he knew he didn't want to do that. He had not given up hope. The notion was vanquished when he thought about Tina. He had to endure and maintain what he had. He just needed to get through the next two days. Jack threw on his robe and grabbed his shower stuff. He went out into the hall to the community shower and took a shower; drawing it out as long as he could. He came back to his room and sat on the edge of the bed. His mind wandered as he was trying to think of something to do to fill the day. He began to strategize. Finally, he thought that he could go to the gas station and hang around with Brad and Roberto for a while. He would act casual and non-chalant; behave as though he just happened to be in the vicinity and was stopping by. But, if he stayed too long on his off day, his co-workers would wonder why, he thought. He felt a little odd thinking about doing this stupid stuff. But, he had to do whatever he needed to do to keep from falling back into his old habits. He dressed and his hunger told him what to do next.

He took off toward the Village Restaurant. He bought a Sunday paper before he had breakfast. The restaurant had a good crowd on this Sunday morning; so, he could eat his breakfast and read the Sunday paper for a long while without being noticed. He was still reading long after he had finished breakfast. Finally, he looked around and the restaurant was almost empty. Jack knew the ebb and flow of the restaurant customers throughout the week. He practically lived there at breakfast time. He knew, too that on Sunday afternoons, very few people came in for lunch. People were usually out-and-about in the afternoon; going to church or engaging in other activities. When Flo, the waitress he had come to know so well asked "Can I take your plate?" Jack knew it was time to go. He paid and left his usual tip before leaving.

"Didn't think I'd see you here on a Sunday, Jack" Brad greeted with a surprised expression after Jack parked his car on the gas station lot and got out. "What brings you to the job on a Sunday?" Roberto asked shortly afterward when he came out of the washroom on the side of the station building. "I had to stop over at the parts store on Belmont" Jack lied immediately with a false cheerfulness. Jack chatted with them for a while; making small talk while things were slow. He told Brad that he wanted to wash and wax his car and that was the main reason he stopped by. Jack went into the back room and gathered up some of the supplies that they all used for the wash and wax business. He washed his car and took a good while putting wax on it. He lingered around the station for more than an hour longer; letting the wax dry so that he could buff later was a perfect excuse to hang around longer. When he finally finished buffing his car, Jack knew that he was out of excuses. "Hey..."I'll see y'all tomorrow" he said with the same fake cheerfulness before he drove away.

As Jack drove along, the sky went from partly cloudy to sunny. It was becoming a beautiful day. But, his mood did not change with it. Sunny days had always filled him with exuberance--but, not today. He could have endured this day better if it had stayed more overcast. The sun seemed to be mocking him----it's a sunny day---sunny always means happy---what will you do now? The subliminal message seemed to be saying. Jack drove to the lakefront at Wilson Avenue. He parked in the drive facing the lake. He sat in his car and all he could think about was Tina---what was she doing?---was she thinking of him? How would she greet him when she returned? These questions swirled around in his mind. He was besieged by these constant thoughts tugging at his heart; mercilessly torturing him in his solitude. He realized that his peace-of-mind was steadily slipping away.

Why was he doing this? Isolating and punishing himself---and then, he remembered. His mood shifted when he thought about what his life had been before he met Tina. How it had changed since. She had invaded his dark, wretched world and set it aglow with love, happiness, serenity and peace. Surely, she had been sent by god as his salvation; replacing the ache of sorrow and loneliness deep in his heart; filling it with love. He thought of the blissful moments they had shared; that he cherished so much; that he played over-and-over in his mind; giving him comfort. He could visualize her soft, pretty face and her smiling eyes when they sat across from one another during those times they had dined out. He could feel the warmth of her spirit; hear the echo of her ultra-sweet, feminine voice in his head; her cheerful chatter and laughter, filling him with delight. He could feel her tender touch and their heated, passionate lovemaking that released him from everything earthbound. She had given him the hope and courage to stop drinking and to go to college. He may not have had the strength or the will to do it on his own. It was their divine connection that had inspired it all, he realized. Now---he could endure. He had been rejuvenated by that shift in his thinking.

Finally, he got out of his car and walked and walked along the lake shore. He passed time walking and observing all of the people around him. Relaxing; playing volleyball; rubbing lotion on one another; lying on beach blankets in the sun. The walk and the peaceful surroundings had a calming effect. Jack's day continued in the same way. He took a long nap in his car. He read the Sunday paper again. It was late afternoon when he drove from the lakefront and out of the area. He found a coffee shop and sat in it for almost an hour, sipping coffee. Finally, he stopped and called Sandra on a pay telephone. It was shortly past 5pm and he knew she was out of church and probably at home.

Jack felt a sigh of relief when Sandra answered the phone. She told him to "come on by" Jack stopped at a store outside of the Uptown area and bought her a six-pack. He almost always brought her something when he visited her. When he arrived, she greeted him happily with her usual warm hug. They sat, talked and watched television for a couple of hours. The visit allowed Jack to loosen up and feel a sense of relief and calm. But, he wouldn't even let his good friend, Sandra know just how alone he had been. He left Sandra's place and went home. His time with her seemed to settle his mind a bit more. Another long day into night had passed. It was not long before he was able to fall asleep.

Monday morning. When Jack awakened, he was feeling hopeful. He had school today and he did not have to be alone. He felt an enormous sense of relief that the weekend was over. He had never felt so alone before. The depths of it had been frightening. He had always carried this notion around with him that he didn't need anyone; that he could live alone because no one seemed to care. He had been living like an orphaned scoundrel; maintaining a stoic veneer and being deeply distrustful toward most people. But, now that he had Tina in his life, all of that had changed. The gloomy weekend had been full of yearning. Now, somehow, the malaise he had been feeling had lifted. He felt so much better about making it through the next two days. Tina's flight would land late tomorrow night. He felt excited about his plan to call her after 10pm when she said she would be home. He turned his attention to the day ahead. He didn't have classes until this afternoon. So, he showered, dressed and went out to the Village restaurant for his ritual of having breakfast and reading the newspaper. He returned to his room. He was feeling more relaxed and his mind seemed uncluttered and free of worry. So, he was able to study for two hours for his upcoming final exams next week. Things seemed to be turning back to normal. But, of course, they would not be until his sweetheart returned and they were together again. Jack finished studying.

He wasn't hungry so, he skipped lunch and took off toward The Center; arriving almost an hour before the start of his class. He felt happy to be back in the familiar setting as he plopped himself down in one of the cushy student lounge sofa-chairs. He sat and soaked in the atmosphere; feeling a more profound sense of gratitude that he was there. He looked around to see a few students spread about the room having lunch. None were his friends but, he felt connected to them. He remembered how odd and out-of-place he felt when he first came to The Center; how he continued to have that feeling for a while. But, somewhere along the way, and he could not say when, he had began to feel as though he belonged. The people there made him feel welcomed. They had encouraged, mentored and nurtured him. Sam, Barbara, Glen---all of them had validated him. He had come to feel connected and to care about them more as time passed.

Finally, he saw Lupe dragging in; towing her usual assortment of purses, book bags and the like with her. "Hey, Jack…how are you?" She greeted cheerfully" "I'm cool…how are you doin'?" Jack responded. "Getting ready for these finals next week…and for summer break…I can't wait!" Lupe declared before she plopped down in a nearby chair. "So, how do you like your first semester in college?" Lupe asked. "It's been real cool…I like it" Jack replied with a smile. They chatted for only a few minutes before Marvin appeared. "Hey, Lupe….Jack" he greeted. "Hey, Marvin" they both replied at the same time. "You guys ready for the finals next week?" Marvin asked. "I am *never* ready…even after I study my brains out….I just get so uptight taking those exams…but, I end up doing better that I thought" Lupe said. Billy entered the lounge next with his characteristic high-energy strut. "People…people…what's the deal" he spoke out very loose and carefree before he sat his book bag down on the floor next to where he sat. “All y’all here and classes don’t kick off for another half-hour” Billy muttered as he glanced at his watch. Soon, the entire group was chattering away about this-and-that. Jack fell quiet for a moment and just looked at them. A warm feeling of fellowship came over him and he realized that he liked these people very much; just as he did many of the people he knew in the streets. It felt good to be sitting among them; talking; exchanging ideas; to hear their happy voices. This seemed to be the manner in which Jack connected with people. When he came to know them and could feel their spirit, he would begin to feel something in his heart for them. These connections seemed to fill an unknown void within him and gave him a special feeling of joy. “Hey y’all…anybody want a coffee or a coke out of the machines?…I’m buyin’” Jack suddenly offered. “Thanks, Jack…I’ll have a Coke…Lupe called out after a moment passed to allow Jack’s offer to register. “Big-money, Jack…Cadillac drivin’….money spendin’….sharp dressin’…..hook me up with one o’ them Cokes, baby” Billy said, going into a street character imitation that was part of his joking arsenal. “Can I get a coffee, Jack?” Marvin asked politely. “Most certainly…you can have two coffees if you want, Marvin” Jack offered, kind of half-jokingly. Jack found himself enjoying the sudden turn of attention after he made his offer. He made the offer earnestly; not intending this as a result; but, enjoying it, nonetheless. “Thanks, Jack…I’m glad you have some money, because I don’t have *any”* Marvin commented with a smile. “Hey, Jack…how do you manage to have money and a nice car while most of us are struggling?” Lupe asked good-naturedly. “Oh---from my job…tips” Jack replied plain and simple. “*Tips*?” Marvin asked with a tone of disbelief. “*Tips*?” Lupe repeated. “Tips” Jack answered. A moment of silent confusion passed. Jack stood at the coffee and Coke machines, putting in money and retrieving the coffee and sodas that each of them wanted; carefully handing them out, almost like a waiter. Afterward, they all sat around, happily chirping away and laughing.

Finally, it was time for classes and everyone said their goodbyes before taking off. Jack went to his classes in a good mood. He was attentive in taking notes as the instructor in his Man and His Physical environment class prepared the students for the final exam next week. He went to his Intro to Uptown class and it was the same thing. When the last class ended, Jack went out and jumped into his car, drove to the Village Restaurant and had dinner. The evening was approaching and he was beginning to think about tomorrow. A feeling of anticipation was beginning to build. Just one more day before he could talk to his sweetheart. The time without her had been grueling. But, he had survived. He had never missed anyone before; never needed anyone; never loved anyone like this. This was all so new and strange to him; and it seemed to consume his entire being; to occupy every fiber of him. After dinner, he drove home and settled comfortably into his room; he studied a short while before relaxing and watching TV. He went to bed peacefully, looking forward to tomorrow.

Jack awakened and went through his usual routine to prepare for early classes today. His first class was at 9:30am. So, he was at the Village Restaurant shortly past 8am. He read his paper and had breakfast before taking off toward The Center. He was feeling especially cheerful. He could hardly wait to call late tonight and hear Tina's sweet voice again. He felt a growing excitement inside. He had a four-hour shift at the gas station after classes. So, he had the better part of a day to keep himself occupied until that time came. Classes seemed to go fast with all of the note-taking in preparation for the final exams. After the last class, Jack had lunch at Jakes before driving to work.

He arrived at the gas station feeling upbeat; laughing and joking with Gus and Roberto as he started his shift. There was a lone car left at the station earlier by Johnny and Oscar for a wash and wax. Jack started on it after the customer traffic died down. He seemed to be full of energy; singing to himself as he performed his duties and washed and waxed. He felt carefree and much happier than he was during his somber weekend. He stayed busy the whole shift. Finally, there was less than an hour before Jack's quitting time. He tried to contain himself when he noticed the big station clock was at about 5:20pm. It felt strange to experience this maddening anticipation. What was wrong with him? Is this the way this is supposed to feel? questions came from deep in his mind. It felt awkward; like an ill-fitting garment; like something he was not supposed to feel. These thoughts and feelings seemed to dominate his conscience. Why didn't he have any control over them? That was where the awkwardness came from----he had no control. He felt a kind of helplessness. Still, his love for Tina seemed hopeful---undaunted. Something he felt he could never give up. He was completely submerged in it---hopelessly committed. When the station clock read 6pm, Jack was already in the back room taking off his work coveralls and cleaning up. The day had passed peacefully. He was looking forward to tonight when he expected that he could feel completely happy once again.

When Jack drove off the gas station lot, the feeling of excitement he already had seemed to be quietly growing. He could only think of the blissful moment when Tina's sweet voice pierced his senses. Only a few hours until then. Before Tina, nothing seemed to matter so much; but, now everything mattered. At this moment, Jack's mood was light and he felt good--good enough to go where his instincts always guided him----to The Corner. What harm could it do? he told himself. Sure, he could not afford to hang around all the time. But, he would go there to hang around for just a little while; be with his friends and have a little fun before he went home. Jack drove that way and when he arrived at Lawrence and Winthrop, turned south onto Winthrop and parked in the next block south of the poolroom where the Tower apartment building stood. He walked back toward The Corner and when he arrived, he stopped on the southeast corner where Frances Tavern stood. He could see across the street through the big picture window into the poolroom. The bright lights from inside illuminated everything. He saw only a few of the regulars that he usually saw shooting pool. But, none of his crowd. Not Coley or Jabo or Larry or any of them. He was hungry so, he decided to go into the A&W restaurant next door to the poolroom to get something to eat.

When he walked inside, he found Motic and Jabo sitting side-by-side on stools. Motic was eating and Jabo seemed to be just keeping him company. "Hey young-blood…what's happ'nin' ….man?….you missed everythang" Motic said. "Hey Motic…Jabo" Jack greeted. "What happened?....what you talkin' about?" Jack asked. "Man…the po'lice come 'round the poolroom and started searchin' every nigga' standin' 'round outside...lucky me 'n' Jabo was sittin' inside…anyway, Lenny was out there gettin' searched with the rest of 'em and I'll be damned if that fool didn't break and run…got away, too…they lookin' for his ass…detective cars been drivin' up-and-down the streets…all in the alleys for 'bout an hour now….you know…he sells dope…he musta' been dirty…prob'ly why he broke and ran…if they *do* catch him, all they can do is charge him with runnin' 'stead o' possession…you *know* he done got rid of his dope by now…yessir…it's sho' 'nough hot around here right now" Motic said. "Yea...everybody that was here is stayin' away….them detectives prob'ly mad as hell 'cause Lenny got away" Jabo added. "Hell, yea…I 'spect anybody who looks *anything* like Lenny might get locked up today…much gas and time them detectives usin' up lookin' for Lenny's ass" Motic chuckled. "But, tell the truth, Motic…Lenny was flyin' wasn't he?" Jabo said with a broad smile and about to burst with laughter. "Maaann…who you tellin'…me 'n' you was sittin' inside, lookin' out the window watchin' all of 'em get searched…next thang I know….I heard a detective yell "Halt!...or I'll shot!....sheeiiit…he might as well saved his l'il breath….Lenny was gone!...I seen a streak go past the window" Motic joked. "Damn right…he prob'ly in Detroit by now…hahaha" Jabo said as he and Motic both laughed out loud. The two continued for a while with that line of joking; drawing as much fun out of the incident as they could; laughing hysterically with one crack after another. Jack couldn't help but to laugh along with them at their ridiculously funny jokes. Jack chatted with his fences, the owners John and his wife, Marcie as he ordered a burger and fries. In the time he had known them, Jack had sold them plenty of good merchandise. They had become part of his street corner family.

Jack gave Jabo enough money to buy himself a drink. Motic volunteered to accompany Jabo to Saxony Liquors to buy the drink while Jack ate his meal inside of the A&W restaurant. When the two came back to the restaurant, Jack was finishing his meal. They all walked together down to the next block on Winthrop. They stood out on the sidewalk in front of the Tower building having their usual lively conversation in the evening twilight. And so, this was what seemed to compel Jack to come to The Corner all the time; these free-spirited associations full of fun and laughter; being with people like himself. He loved their rebellious spirit that seemed to coincide with his own; where he was absolved from being imperfect; a little crazy and non-conforming; where he found complete acceptance. Jack was having a good time with them. He stayed as long as he could before he finally forced himself to say “I got to get goin’ y’all” But, the conversation carried on a little longer after that with a few more jokes and laughs before Jack finally left.

It was past 9pm when Jack arrived at his room. He got comfortable and felt very relaxed. He turned on the television and was lying across his bed before he fell asleep. He awakened, surprised that he had fallen asleep. When his head finally cleared and he saw the time to be 10:40pm. He immediately thought to make his call to Tina. He opened his dresser-drawer where he kept a ceramic bowl full of change. He hurriedly picked out dimes and quarters before he rushed out of his room and went the short distance down the second-floor hallway to the bank of public telephones. He felt excited as he dialed her number. He was very happy that the lonely time that he suffered through had passed and the glorious moment he waited for had finally arrived.

“Hello” Tina answered. “Hey, baby!...it’s me..how was the trip?…everything go okay?” Jack said with an excited, joyous tone. “Jack… yes, everything went fine” Tina responded. “You had a good time, huh?” Jack said with a big smile in his voice. “Yes…yes, I did” Tina answered. Then, there was a long pause. “So, tell me about it” Jack asked with the same excitement. “Jack… honey…I have to tell you something….I don’t know how to tell you this…” Tina started. “Tell me what?…what’s happenin?’” Jack asked with pause. “Jack…I can’t be with you anymore” Tina said. Jack was struck with dread and fear when he heard those words. His chest tightened up and his mind began to spin. He closed his eyes and tried to compose himself. Certainly, he could not be hearing this. This was not happening. “Wha..what do you mean, baby?…what’s wrong?… what’s goin’ on?” Jack stammered. “Jack…I don’t know how to say this…I met this black guy in my sophomore year in college….almost two years ago. …we started dating…you know what I told you already about how I was attracted.. anyway, when we dated, we really hit it off…I fell for him real hard…his name is Randall…he was very nice to me…I was crazy about him….but, he dumped me …we were together about eight months when that happened…his family has money…they’re not rich but, they are well-off…his dad is some kind of entertainment executive….anyway…I was devastated…heart-broken…I tried my best to forget about him…I was so lonely and sad when we split up…it was hard…finally, he transferred away from the college where we met…where I graduated from when you and I met…he went to a college in Pennsylvania…he finished school a couple of semesters ahead of me….three months ago, he came back into town to see his folks…he's been staying with them and calling me…he's been begging me the whole time to get back together…telling me he made a big mistake…that he really does love me" Tina explained.

"But, baby…why didn't you tell me about him when we first met?" Jack asked with a bit of desperation in his voice. "Jack, please don't be upset with me…this is hard enough.." Tina said, beginning to sob. A long pause ensued while Tina cried. Jack just listened with exasperation as a world of emotion flooded his entire being. "I never said anything about him to you because I thought he was behind me…I didn't mention him because I was trying to forget him…I thought we would never see each other or be together again…when he came back and started calling me…I was able to resist him for a while and kept him away but, he finally got to me…you have to understand, Jack…I got weak and I gave in…he came out to Albany with Jason, his friend because Jason told him I was going out there with Vickie…he came with Jason because we all used to hang out together…then, when he started begging me again…that's when I let him back in…I'm sorry, Jack…I'm really sorry…I couldn't help it…he was my first love…do you remember how you felt about *your* first love?…" Tina continued to sob. Jack could feel his entire world crashing around him. His heart dropped. He was feeling more pain that he had ever know. His mind was swirling with confusion. "Tina…*you* were my first love…" he said weakly with unmistakable sadness in his voice coming across to Tina. She felt it and she knew he loved her; knew how deep his love for her was; how deeply hurt he was. "Jack, I am so sorry…I'm sorry I did this to you..I know you love me…and I loved you…but, Randall came first…my love was deep for him…it's been all stirred back up…those old feelings…I'm sorry I hurt you" Tina continued to sob. "But…Tina…Tina…you told me you loved me" Jack said, his voice cracking with emotion. "I know, Jack…I know…I felt that I did…I thought I did…but…I guess I never really got Randall out of my heart…I guess I was fooling myself….I was looking for someone to help me forget him but, replace him at the same time…I'm sorry, Jack...I…"" (sob) Tina continued to cry and plead. "I cain't believe this, baby…all of a sudden…you're puttin' me down…I thought we had somethin' good…I thought you loved me like I love you" Jack said with heart-wrenched anguish. This painful, emotional talk went on late into the night. Through it all, Jack was feeling a helplessness that he had never known. He felt sick in his mind and his body and all the way to the core of his soul. How was he going to live without this woman who had come to mean everything to him? Who had brightened his life and gave it meaning and inspiration. As the time on the clock turned to one…two..three o'clock in the morning, Jack poured his heart out to Tina; telling her how much he loved her; how she had saved him from himself. Tina mostly listened courteously; knowing how much pain Jack was in; knowing he needed to say what he was saying to her; to get it all out; and even though he was hurting so much; there was not a single word of blame for Tina; not one word said in anger or resentment. They knew each other; knew each other's spirit and soul; knew each others hopes and desires; they weren't just lovers—they were friends. And so, Jack knew from all the time he had shared with Tina; from knowing her intimately; knowing who she was and what she was all about----he knew that she would never hurt him intentionally. He knew that it was not a part of her makeup. He understood that if she could have prevented from hurting him in this way, that she would. She was trapped; caught between her past and her future; between two difficult choices. There was no way that she could bring herself to fake all of the affection and the sweet words she had said to Jack in their time together; all of her smiles and hugs and giving herself completely to Jack in their passionate lovemaking. It was all sincere; heartfelt; real----it was not even a question for Jack. But, there was heartache, nonetheless. Tina was able to regain herself enough to tell Jack that she told Randall about him right away. She told him that she was already in a good relationship. How she had fended him off for more than two months. She spoke of how hard it was to turn away a man she had deep feelings for. She told of how difficult it was for her to not say anything to Jack about Randall's occasional calls. How she asked him not to call her too often. How she felt more-and-more trapped as her old feelings for him began to return. How she had feelings for Jack and how close she was to giving him her heart completely. Everything Tina said made sense to Jack's mind. But, his heart did not want to hear it. Underneath the maddening feelings of hurt and sorrow, Jack was hoping, still, that somehow, someway he and Tina could stay together; that she would come to her senses and reject the man who had broken her heart; that this was all a mistake. He had pleaded his case throughout the night. But, there was no change of heart on Tina's part. All night, she had explained in every way she could why things had to be this way. How she could not turn back to their love affair.

"Jack…it's 3:30 in the morning…I need to get up at 6:30 for work…I have to go" Tina finally said wearily. "Baby…can I call you again?" Jack asked with a somber tone. "Sure…you can call me…I told Randall that it was going to take some time before I stopped being with you…that I didn't want to just break it off with you just like that…I told him it might take a couple of weeks…I know it's hard for you, too, Jack...and I *do* have special feelings for you" Tina said. "Okay…okay" Jack replied soft and weakly before they said good night. And so, Jack was suffering the very first real heart-break of his young life. It all made sense now; the suspicious notions that he began to have about Tina; the anonymous phone calls at her apartment; the changes in her behavior. All of that had come painfully to light for Jack. But, there was nothing he could do. He could not bring himself to be angry with her. He understood. He loved her. And now, his aloneness had, indeed, become loneliness.

He thought back to all of the times he had spoken to men in the streets; confessing those stories of lost love. He remembered their voices sounding so monotone with a tinge of sadness; the emptiness in their souls coming through the sound of their voices; the ghostly, far away look in their eyes as they spoke. They seemed to become like zombies when they told their tales of loss. It was as if they had died just when their loss was realized. Back then, Jack had become curious about this phenomenon; grown men sounding helpless. He was mystified by it because he knew nothing about it. And now he understood; he knew intimately because now, he had become one of them. He remembered when he listened to those men, he would internally scoff at their words and their sentiments. It all sounded kind of weak to him; not something a real man would experience. But, now Jack realized---It was just a matter of time before his turn came. Perhaps, this was an experience that every man who desired women would come to know---a passage into true manhood.

Jack fell asleep out of sheer weariness. He was emotionally, and it seemed, physically exhausted. He finally awoke in a daze and could not remember anything through the haziness in his head. He sat up in bed in for a long time in a groggy state. It felt like a hangover. Finally, his head became clear and he realized what had happened last night. And when he did, he wished that he could go back to sleep for a thousand years. Because the heartache began again; the racing of his heart; the fear that came with it but, then, as he began to think and move forward, there was a sense of acceptance that began to sink in. Tina was leaving him for reasons she seemed compelled. He had beseeched her throughout the night; he remembered, it had done no good. She had been adamant about why she had to end their affair. And after that moment of recollection, his mood became somber and his spirit was flat. There was the heavy feeling of emptiness. He looked at his clock-radio on the dresser. 12:08pm. He felt fearful to be alone so, he decided to go to his afternoon classes today to dispel the maddening loneliness. He fought the weighty, lethargic feeling to gather himself to take a shower. His mind was in a suspended state; as if in disbelief; wandering; hazy. Finally, he found himself dressed and ready to leave for his 2pm class.

He drove to The Center in the same dispirited condition. He felt completely disheveled inside; and the feeling was so strong until, Jack knew that it must be showing on his face and in his body language. He didn't feel like himself. The feeling was strange; eerie. After parking, Jack carried himself up the long stairs to The Center. He wanted to talk to people. But, he did not want to talk about Tina or, what happened. He wanted to shut it out of his mind. But, of course he could not. He needed an outlet; relief. Something to help him take his mind off of the chaos going on in his head and his heart. He was a little early for his first class so, he went into the student lounge. He saw a few students sitting around mingling but, none of his friends. And just then, he could not decide if he was happy or disappointed. He wanted to see them because their companionship would offer him the relief and distraction he needed so desperately; but, at the same time, he did not want them to detect the condition he was in. The indecision made him wonder was he thinking right. Finally, it was time for his Man and His Physical Environment class. As he sat in the class, the instructor was talking away and the other students were taking a flurry of notes for next week's final exam. Jack was trying to take notes and keep up but, he was missing bits-and-pieces of the lecture material. His mind would wander off momentarily; and when he came back to try to focus, he had missed parts of the notes he should have taken. His thinking seemed muddled and sluggish, as well. He also had this continuing feeling of being a little sick. There was a knot in his gut that would not go away. Finally, the class was over and it seemed as though he had been there for several hours instead of an hour-and-a-half. As he was walking down the hallway among other students during the intermediate class-changing period, he felt that he could not attend his last class. He did not seem motivated and his energy seemed to be sapped. As he was about to turn to walk down the long stairway outside to the streets, his friend, Billy popped into view at the top of the stairs, coming into The Center.

"Einstein…what's goin' on, baby!" Billy greeted Jack spiritedly, as soon as he saw him. "Hey, Billy" Jack forced out. "What you doin', man?…where you goin'? Billy asked. "I ain't feelin' too good…stomach ache" Jack half-lied. "I'm goin' home, man" he added. ""Stomach ache?...come on, man..a soldier don't get sick with no stomach ache…you too hard for that, brotha'…stomach ache?…you sound like a little kid…my tummy hurt…hahaha!" Billy began to tease. "Naw, man…straight up…I start gettin' it last night…I thought I could make it to my classes today but, it's still botherin' me" Jack explained kind of anxiously. "Alright…alright…I dig where you comin' from…you eat anything this mornin'?" Billy asked. "Naw" Jack responded. "Well, come on…let's get some o' that poison Jake got downstairs…that'll straighten you right up…stop the stomach ache" Billy said with his usual self-assured cockiness. "Okay" Jack agreed. Just then, Marvin and Lupe were coming up the stairs, as well. "Hey, Billy…hey, Jack" Marvin greeted them. "Hey, guys" Lupe said. "Yea, Billy…that's a good idea…I'll meet you down there…hey, y'all" Jack said with the same anxiousness before he dashed down the stairs past Lupe and Marvin. Jack walked a few doors south to Jake's restaurant on the corner. A few people were ordering lunch and Jack went straight to a table and wearily sat down. He waited and after a short moment, Billy appeared, and strolled inside the restaurant and joined Jack at the table. "Relax, man…you gonna be alright…you just need some grub…that's all" Billy said calmly. "I'm hungry…you ready to order?" Billy asked before he turned and looked at the menu posted on the wall above the ordering counter. "Yea…I'm gonna get a chicken sandwich with fries" Jack said. "You order…here's my money" Jack said as he reached into his pocket and gave Billy the money. He didn't want to order for himself because he felt too uncomfortable. Finally, not long after Billy ordered, their food was ready. Right away, Billy was wolfing his food down. "Eat up, man…it'll do you good" Billy said almost dotingly as Jack seemed to be moving in slow motion, preparing to eat his food. Billy was chattering away in his usual lively manner about his classes and the upcoming final exams. Jack was eating very slowly as he quietly listened. Before he was halfway done eating, Jack began to feel tired and sleepy. "Billy, I got to go home, man…I'm tired as hell…I didn't sleep much at all last night" Jack said. "Go on upstairs and stretch out in one of them sofa-chairs in the lounge…I have done it many a day" Billy suggested. "Naw, man…I better get home before I'm too tired to drive" Jack said. "Alright, brotha-man…go on and get some rest…talk to you later" Billy said as they both stood up and soul-shook before Jack took off.

Jack was on Montrose at Clark street, heading west to the YMCA. He was suddenly startled from the loud sound of the car horn behind him. His eyes sprang open and he jumped after nodding out at the red light that was now green. Jack pulled off and struggled to keep his eyes open. A short distance later, he parked his car in the YMCA lot and dragged himself inside to his room where he immediately undressed and passed out in his bed.

Jack awakened and looked at his clock-radio. 8:49pm. He sat up. His head began to clear and he felt a lot better. He had some wild dreams, he remembered. But, all he could remember was it was about Tina and strange, conflicted feelings. He decided to call her. He went through the same routine of going into his dresser-drawer and grabbing a handful of change from the ceramic bowl inside. He walked out into the lobby and called. "Hello" Tina answered. "It's me, babe" Jack answered. "You okay, Jack?" Tina asked sweetly. "Not really but, good as I could expect" Jack answered as honestly as he could. “I know…I understand” Tina answered sympathetically with perhaps, a tinge of guilt. “It’s okay, baby...I understand what you’re goin’ through…but, I can’t deny, it still hurts” Jack said. “I know, honey and I wish I could change things…but, I can’t… you know that by now…I explained it all to you” Tina said. “I know, baby but, it was a surprise and it’s gonna take some time for me to get used to this…not havin’ you in my life” Jack said with the same tone of disappointment that he had all last night over the phone. “Well, I’m still not with Randall, yet…I told him that I couldn’t really be with him yet because I have to make some kind of peace with you, first…I need to give you time to adjust to this because I know it must be very hard on you…I’ve gotten to know you very well, Jack and I care too much about you to cut this off without trying to make it easier on you…I know you care for me very much..(sob)” Tina said before she began to sob again. Jack let her sob for a moment or two before he spoke. “I’m sorry, baby…it’s okay…I see that it’s hard on you, too” Jack said. “…and, besides, I need this time, too to get myself together…I’m scared, Jack…to be honest, I am really scared…even though I *do* love Randall very much and I decided to be with him instead of you…I’m afraid he might do the same thing again…he has said over-and-over how he will never do that again…dump me like he did before…he swears up-and-down that he would never do it…he says he realized that he couldn’t find anyone else like me…that’s what he said” Tina confessed and continued to sob. “You know *I* would never dump you, sweetheart…*never!”* Jack said emphatically. “I know, Jack and I don’t know why I want to trust him again but, my heart is telling me to” Tina said, continuing to sob. “Baby…I really, really wish you would change your mind…I don’t know how you decided to pick him over me, either…especially after what he did to you” Jack said. “I know, Jack…but, honey…this is really hard for me…I never planned for things to turn out this way” Tina said in a pleading tone that seemed to be begging for understanding. “Okay…I’m sorry…I didn’t mean to press you but, you know how I’m feelin’ right now, Tina” Jack said. Jack stopped talking and let Tina’s sobbing subside. “Jack…we can get together on Sunday…you can come over” Tina suddenly offered after composing herself. “Really?…what about Randall?” Jack asked. “I already told you I’m not with him, yet…he knows that” Tina said. “So…we can be together like old times?” Jack asked. “I know what you mean…yes” Tina said. “But, remember, Jack…it won’t mean anything except it’s my way of saying goodbye to you...don’t let it get your hopes up…don’t get the wrong idea…okay?” Tina added. “Yea..okay…alright…I guess I don’t have much choice...but, I wish it really *was* like old times” Jack said with a hint of resignation and hope all at once. “I know, Jack…call me Friday night…alright?” Tina asked. “Okay” Jack replied before they hung up.

Jack was still out of sorts. Not quite himself. There was a constant current of anxiety underneath the more pronounced feelings of fear and dread that were already making him crazy. He was constantly trying to psyche himself to be calm and think and behave naturally. He was already in the stage of trying to accept this situation that had once been unthinkable to him. Still, the fear and dread came from him thinking about what would happen to him when he and Tina had parted for good. Because of her, he had come to know the pristine world of clear-headed sanity and civility---to experience a taste of the peaceful, mainstream life that he once knew before moving to Uptown. During his time, with her he had never been so happy in his life. But, now, his heart palpitated with the fear and anxiety of returning to that wretched life of mindless drunkenness----the dope-chasing insanity and chaos that he would retain by default. Right now, he was still with Tina; and although he understood that she was leaving, his undying love for her had him holding onto the slimmest of hopes. Jack lay in the bed thinking into the night about the whole situation. His thoughts went around-and-around in circles until he fell back asleep.

Jack awakened and it was nearing 8am. He had early classes today and he needed to get moving. But, he just sat on the edge of the bed; and as soon as his head cleared, the incessant thoughts began. The ache in his heart had his mind churning with thoughts about Tina; about what may have gone wrong; of what he may not have done right; or what he should have done that he didn’t do. It was a burdensome state of mind. And whenever he was alone, these thoughts would race through his mind. He sluggishly showered and dressed. He left as soon as he could and after he parked on Sheridan Road across from The Center, he walked over to Jakes and had breakfast. It was 9:15am when he finished and walked the few doors north to The Center. He went straight to his writing class that started at 9:30am. The instructor began right away to lecture for the final exam on Tuesday next week. Jack took notes in-between his drifting thoughts. He tried to stay focused on the lecture. But, he could not shut those thoughts off. Finally, the class was over. Ten minutes later, Jack was in his Community Organization class. He had the same subdued mood as he took notes; and while those thoughts were turning over-and-over in his mind, he was beginning to have more acceptance, as well. The reality of Tina leaving him had turned his world upside-down. He was anxious; down-hearted. But, he had to face the fact and right now, he had to muster all of the emotional strength he could to endure the heartache.

At the same time, he was thinking about her offer to be together once again. It allowed a ray of hope to creep into his thoughts. He was hoping that when they got together on Sunday; when they had their time together, that she would be reminded of how sweet it all had been; of how much he really loved her; how they were so right for one another. It was his last bit of hope and he vowed to himself to do all that he could to sway her. Jack's last class was over and he was alone again. He did not want to leave The Center. So, he went to the student lounge and stayed. He tried to study as best he could while students came and went. His friends appeared from time-to-time. Billy came into the lounge and he and Jack had a long session of hanging out; talking; laughing and joking before Billy left for his class on campus. Jack went back to studying and, after a while, Marvin came into the lounge. Jack stopped studying and they had a pleasant conversation, as well before Marvin left for class.

It was now late afternoon and Jack's hanging out in the student lounge was serving it's purpose. It was the distraction he needed. Being around people was allowing him to focus on something else and keep his mind from dwelling on his painful reality. Jack noticed the clock in the lounge read 4:07pm. He remembered that Lupe would be at the Daycare Center down the hall until 5pm. He locked up his book bag and walked in that direction. As he headed that way, he told himself that he would keep her company. But, he really knew better. "Hi, Jack...what brings you in here?" Lupe greeted with a broad smile. "Aw, nothin'...I'm done with all my classes...figured I'd stop by to see what's goin' on with you" Jack said. "Come on over here and sit down…stay a while" Lupe offered, pleased that Jack was paying her a visit. The two sat for a while, yakking away before the last parent came to pick up the last child. "Well…Jack..thanks for stopping by and keeping me company…you can stop by anytime…okay?" Lupe said before she and Jack walked out of the empty Center and down the long stairs to the streets outside. They said their goodbyes before Lupe strolled toward Montrose, a short distance away, to head home.

Jack was still standing in the same spot when he snapped out of a mindless state where his thoughts had drifted into a blank haze. He was standing there alone, not knowing where he would go. He did not want to go home and be alone in his room where he knew he would be tortured by his obsessive thoughts. Besides, it was a beautiful, sunny day near the beginning of summer; certainly not a day to stay indoors. He jumped in his car and instinctively began to drive toward Lawrence and Winthrop. He drove to the block just south of The Corner where the Tower building stood. As he was parking, he could see in the near-distance, a group of the neighborhood regulars gathered around the northwest corner of Winthrop and Leland. He got out of his car and decided to walk toward them. He could see some sitting on steps and others standing on the sidewalk on the Winthrop-side of the Leland building that housed the Leland Baptist church. There was Robert Lee, Ella, Anita, Bow-tie, Mae, Mr. Jackson and "Old Man Dave" As usual, there was drinking. "Old Man Dave" and Mr. Jackson were sitting near the others in folding chairs that Mr. Jackson kept in his garage. They were drinking cans of beer from a six-pack inside of a paper bag sitting on the sidewalk nearby. Ella and Mae were sitting on the steps along with Bow-tie. Robert Lee and Anita were standing on the sidewalk talking to the others. This was the usual ritual that passed the time many a summer day in the forty-seven-hundred block of North Winthrop.

"Hey, y'all" Jack greeted them all. "Hey, young fella" Mr. Jackson greeted. "Old Man Dave" nodded his head. "Hi, Jack" Anita and Ella both responded. "Hey, good buddy…want a taste?" Bow-tie said as he held a pint bottle of whiskey and made an offering motion toward Jack. "I'm cool, Bow-tie…thanks, anyway" Jack answered, even though he was very tempted. "I'll have another hit if you don't mind" Robert Lee said as he walked from where he stood out near the curb up to Bow-tie sitting on the steps, holding out a plastic drinking cup. "Damn, Robert Lee…you drinkin' faster than me and I bought this stuff!" Bow-tie complained mildly before he let out a light chuckle. "I'll buy next time…my money is real funny, right now" Robert Lee excused himself. "Alright..here you go" Bow-tie relented as he poured some of the whiskey in the outstretched cup. "Dressin' real nice, Jack…what you been doin?" Anita asked kind of curious and sweetly. Nothin' much'" Jack replied, wanting to stay low-key and not wanting to give out any hints of prosperity. "Yea, Jack…you don't come around too much anymore…where you stayin' at, now?" Ella asked. "I stay where The Weep stays" Jack answered. "Awww…okay" Ella said.

"Robert Lee…there ya' boy is down there…he done got his check…better check him out 'fo somebody gets to him" Bow-tie commented as he leaned out from where he sat on the steps and peered north up the block. Jack turned to look behind him and could see Crazy Vernon leaning against a parked car not far up the block, looking wild-eyed. He had been drinking and seemed to be pretty high. "Don't listen to Bow-tie, Robert Lee…you go down there fuckin' with that man, he might stab the shit outa' your ass" the feisty older woman, Mae warned half-seriously. "I knooww…you don't have to worry about me goin' down there messin' with his ass…I might be broke but, I ain't no damn fool…I *know* what he might do" Robert Lee chimed. Crazy Vernon had a plate in his head from being wounded in the Korean War. He lived alone in a single room apartment in the building that stood in front of the parked car he was leaning on. He was very quiet and seemed like a very nice person when he was sober. But, when he drank, he transformed into a completely different person; seemingly losing his mind and being in a different world; occasionally becoming violent. "You know, that's a goddamn shame, he gets a two-hundred-fifty dollar-a-month crazy check…plus, he gets an army pension check" Bow-tie commented. "Yea, he gets more than any one of us" Mae said. "I oughta go down there and talk to him" Anita, one of the more desirable women in the neighborhood said; openly expressing her thoughts about some easy money. "I know he likes women…but, he too crazy to understand what's goin' on" Ella said. The group continued for a while, making comments about Crazy Vernon with anxious thoughts of clipping him for his money lurking in the back of their minds. Jack stayed for a good while, enjoying their banter and laughter as he remained low-key; making only occasional comments. Jack hung around as long as he could before he finally said goodbye to everyone and went home. When he got home, he watched the little TV in his room until he fell asleep.

Friday morning. Jack arose mindful of his early morning four-hour shift at the gas station today. He came fully conscious with the same pensive mood. Right away, he could feel the aching void in his heart begin. In the back of his mind, he could sense the faint urge to drink emerging; flashing on-and-off like a blinking light. There was also the ambiguous feeling of anticipation for how his tryst with Tina would play out. It would be perhaps, his last rendezvous with her. But, he didn't know quite how to feel about it. He was looking forward to it with a sense of joy and dread all at once. Through the stream of thought that dwelled on her, he gathered himself to forge ahead into his routine of showering, dressing and going out to the Village Restaurant for breakfast. He was sitting at his favorite dining table inside the restaurant when he found himself coming out of another hazy day dream that was so deeply introspective that, he momentarily forgot where he was. He snapped out of it and jumped into his car to drive to work.

After Jack arrived and parked on the gas station lot, he met Gus walking off the lot to go to lunch. Roberto rushed out to wait on a customer at the pump as Jack was coming into the station. Brad was inside working the cash register. "Hey, Jack…guess what?…the baby is born!" Brad gushed excitedly. "No kiddin'?...boy or girl?" Jack asked. "A boy, man!...she had him yesterday around four in the afternoon" Brad continued in the same happy, excited tone. "Congratulations, my man" Jack said. "Hey…tell you what…I'll buy pizza and beer for lunch to celebrate...okay?" Jack offered. "Alright…that's real cool of you…thanks!" Brad said with a broad smile on his face. Jack was happy for Brad. But, he wondered why the offer to buy beer along with the pizza had rolled so easily off of his tongue. At the same time, he felt a little envy for Brad's happy situation because he would have been very happy for it to be his situation with Tina. But, it wasn't and he had been slowly accepting the inevitable loss of the woman he had come to love so deeply. Jack ordered the pizza and beer over the phone before he began working.

He made a mistake on the first customer and pumped more gas than was asked for and he had to tell Brad about the mistake so he could account for it on tonight's check-out when he added up the shift sales. As his shift continued, his friend, Johnny stopped by with a girl in his car. She was a different girl from the ones he had seen him with at the Crossover Disco. Johnny sat in his car as he spoke to Jack. He told Jack he was off work today. He introduced Jack to the attractive woman sitting in the front passenger seat. Johnny was talking a little more politely than he usually did. But, he seemed to speak with those same cocky undertones in his voice that seemed to be coded in the inflection of his words. Jack had come to know enough about his friend to know that it was all a show for the woman in his company. Johnny spoke of how he and his date were going out for a good time later that night before he drove off the lot. Jack was beginning to get the odd feeling that everyone seemed to be happy except him. The pizza and beer was delivered a short time later and everyone ate and drank. Without much thought, Jack drank a beer from the six-pack. The little alarm inside of him that went off when he drank that last beer, went off again. The deviation did not seem to have the same reaction from him this time. There was no guilt or worry. It just didn't seem to matter anymore. Before long, his shift was over. When Jack was in the back room taking off his coveralls and preparing to leave, he could feel that his workday had not been as joyful as it had in the past. For some reason, it seemed more like drudgery.

After he was ready to leave, he realized that he had no plans for what he would do with his free time this Friday afternoon. He remembered Sandra and that there was a good chance that she would be home so, he called her. "Jack..I'm glad you called…come on by" she said with a happy tone in her voice. Jack was relieved because he did not feel like going to The Corner or hanging around The Center because he just wasn't in the mood. He just wanted to be somewhere quiet where he didn't have to pretend that he was so happy and making a lot of conversation and trying to make someone else feel good by entertaining them. He could just be himself with Sandra because they were good friends who were like family. He asked Sandra what could he pick up at the grocery store for dinner and she told him. On his way, he stopped at one of the grocery stores just outside of Uptown and bought a pot roast and potatoes and a package of macaroni and cheese.

"Glad you came, Jack..the boys love it when you stop by" Sandra said with a broad smile as she greeted Jack at her apartment door. He was holding a big grocery bag in one arm and a six-pack of Sandra's favorite brand of beer in the other hand. "They oughta' be glad to see me 'cause look what I got!" Jack announced as he sat the grocery bag down and quickly reached in and pulled out a mess of little kiddy candies and toys, holding them in both hands. "Alright..where them little rascals at?…Gerald…David…where you at!" Jack called out toward the back of the apartment where the boys were. "Come on out, David, Gerald…Jack is here!" Sandra called out to them, as well. The boys came rushing out like they always did, hugging Jack around his legs. "Hey, boy…hey little Dave…look what I got you!" Jack said to the boys excitedly as he held the two hands full of little toy gadgets and packages of kiddy candies up to their faces. The boys began their excited, delighted outbursts, giggling and laughing as Jack made a fuss over the items with them; intentionally revving up the excitement level of the boys. "Okay, now…boys…you know you can't have all this stuff at once…let them play with the toys while I cook dinner and then, they can have a little candy after dinner…I'm gonna put all of this candy up for now" Sandra said as she stepped in and gathered up the candy from them. The two boys looked disappointed as she scooped up the several little packages of candies. "I'll put this up for you…okay?....you can have some after dinner…alright?" she promised them. The boys shook their heads in agreement and went back to playing with Jack and the toys. Jack got lost in playing with the boys as Sandra began preparing dinner. Sandra never said much to Jack when he was playing with the kids. She knew that afterward, she and Jack would have their usual fun-filled conversation like always. She could see that when he spent time with them, that he seemed to have tireless energy; that he seemed to enjoy them so much. She knew how much Jack loved her boys and how he was always trying to make them happy. She also knew that the boys made Jack very happy, too. She knew that, even though Jack had been a thief and a dope user and had committed numerous scandalous acts in the streets that, he was only trying to survive and that he really had a good heart and she could count on him.

Finally, dinner was ready and they all sat at the table. Sandra said grace and they ate together. Jack could feel the lifting of his sagging spirits when he looked around the table at the happy little faces of the two boys and the humble, quiet joy that he could see on their mother's face. She would beam when she looked at her boys and could see the happiness on their faces. She would look at Jack with a sincere expression of appreciation. She didn't have to say anything. Jack was well aware of all the struggles that she endured in her daily life and how she appreciated his friendship. After dinner, Sandra and Jack sat on the sofa and talked while the boys played on the floor with their toys.

"So, how is everything with your girlfriend?" Sandra asked. Jack looked at Sandra with a sorrowful expression and paused for a long moment. "We broke up" he finally let out. "I could tell that somethin' wasn't quite right with you today, Jack…I kinda thought it might have somethin' to do with your girl" Sandra said. "You did…huh?" Jack replied. Jack proceeded to tell Sandra the whole story of his very first heartbreak. Sandra was one of the few people around Uptown that Jack could be completely honest with. Even though he kept a valiant front and did not want to reveal how vulnerable he was, he knew he couldn't hide his unhappiness from her. So, they sat there for another hour, or so as he told her the entire story. She expressed her sympathies to him. But, Jack didn't like this idea of anyone feeling pity for him. His hardened street psyche would not allow him to entertain any notions of weakness. But, there he was, feeling as helpless, weak and down-hearted as he had ever been. "So, that's it…but, I don't want to talk about it anymore" Jack said after they had discussed the issue at length. "Okay…I know how you feel, Jack…I remember how it felt when me and Coley broke up" Sandra said. The two talked about other things and even had a few more laughs. Jack left Sandra with some money and she gave him a big hug before he finally took off for home.

It was a bright, sunny Saturday morning and Jack had a full shift at the gas station today. He got up early and went through his usual routine. Showering, dressing and having breakfast at The Village Restaurant. The sunshiny day seemed to be of little consolation to him. He arrived at work and his mind had been mostly blank before he came into the same cloudy, pre-occupied state-of-mind; a deeply pensive mood where he was wondering just what was happening to him; uncertain about how to feel and think about it. He felt all jumbled inside; anxious. It felt like a sickness that wouldn't go away. Being with the woman he loved for the very last time. He was happy with the idea of being with her. But, he didn't want it to happen because it would have to end. He even thought about not being with her at all; but, his heart spoke differently. His desire for her was too compelling. He had to be with her to experience the joy and sorrow all at once. He would be speaking to her on the phone tonight. What would he say? What would they talk about? It was all so strange and awkward. Jack went about his duties quietly and half-heartedly; not being as talkative as he usually was. Johnny came by in the Don Hardy tow truck with Oscar, the driver to drop off a couple of wash-and-wax jobs. He lingered for a while, talking to Jack. The conversation served as a momentary distraction and relief for Jack. He started washing one of the cars; but, then, he decided to give it away to Brad to wax. He told Brad that he probably could use the money for the new baby and all. But, it was self-serving, as well because Jack's spirit just wasn't into doing the job himself. The shift dragged on and Jack was not as sharp as he usually was; having a couple of miscommunications with the customers because he wasn't listening closely enough; getting a cigarette and a gas order wrong and having to take time to straighten them out. Finally, quitting time came at 4:30pm and Jack was in the backroom taking off his coverall uniform. He was deeply immersed in thought; trying to play out in his mind what he would say to Tina on the phone tonight; what he could say to bring her back to him. But, she had been adamant; steadfast; and at the same time, expressing her fear and apprehension about a future with the other man. It did not stand to reason that he would lose her to these circumstances; or to lose her at all. He had done all that a lover could do; given all of his devotion; all of his heart. The harsh reality was profoundly disturbing. He was feeling the torture and agony that seemed like a spiritual death.

He hopped into his car and drove toward home. He stopped at The Village and had dinner. He sat there lost in thought between cups of coffee long after he had finished his meal. Finally, he left and drove the short distance to the YMCA. In his room, he got comfortable and tried to relax. But, the coffee had him a bit wound up. He tried to study for his exams next week. But, he could do so for only a short while. He looked at his clock and it was near 7pm. He would be calling Tina soon and his mind was turning over-and- over what his attitude would be; how he would respond; what to say. But, there seemed nothing fitting to say or do for this awkward situation. He gave up on rehearsing anything in his mind---let it go just as he had to let her go; all seemed to be lost after their meeting tomorrow, anyway. There was nothing to salvage except memories. Jack felt a fluttering in his chest as he finally decided to make the call; grabbing a handful of change from his ceramic bowl inside of his top dresser drawer and going out to the bank of telephones down the hallway.

"Hi, Jack…how are you?" Tina asked very calmly. The inflection in her voice and the more formal way she spoke gave Jack a hint of the distance she was establishing between them. "I'm alright…how are you?" Jack responded with a somber tone. "So…are you ready for our last get-together?" she asked with a slight nervousness in her voice. "Yea…I guess so..uhh..I don't know, baby…I don't know if I'm ready or not…this is kind of crazy...I don't know why we're gettin' together if we're not gonna see each other anymore" Jack said. "Well…would you rather just forget about the whole thing and just say goodbye right now?" Tina asked. "Uuuhh…naw…I didn't mean it that way…what I'm sayin' is…uhh…I want us to get together tomorrow…you want to do this?" Jack asked. "Yes, Jack…I would feel a whole lot better if we *did* get together tomorrow…at my place…just like we always did" Tina said, sounding very certain of what she was saying. "But, I have one condition, Jack…let's not talk very much…I just want us to go out…have dinner…come back to my place and just make love" Tina said. Jack didn't understand at all. Why did she want things to be that way? He remembered that, in the past on the many nights they had been out and came back and lay in her bed, how she liked to talk late into the night. That was what seemed so important to her and what she enjoyed. But, now not talking? Just making love? He didn't understand where she was coming from. But, since he had come to love her the way he did, being with her was what he desired more than anything in the world. And if they could not be together in their hearts then, being together physically would have to do. "Okay…if that's what you want…it's okay with me…not much talk" Jack relented. "Okay…come over early, like about four…that way we can go out to dinner and have plenty of time left to be together…alright?" Tina said. "Okay, baby" Jack replied. They talked a little longer, having a polite, impassive and short conversation before hanging up. Jack lay awake in the bed for a long time pondering and meditating; his emotions vacillating between desire, dread and a loss of hope. He finally fell asleep from the mental exhaustion.

Jack awakened to a quiet Sunday morning. He stirred and looked over at his clock-radio to see 10:39am. When his head cleared, the same gloomy mood descended upon him like a trap. It seemed like a prison to his thoughts and emotions; a prison that felt eternal and from which he could not escape. He sat up on the edge of the bed, his posture slumping and his head hanging down as he searched his mind for bearing. Today was a day like no other day in his life. He would be with Tina and then---it would be over. The thought started that same flashing light in the back of his mind. Now, the urge to drink was stronger than ever. The flashing light had grown into a neon sign. He had until the late afternoon before he would be seeing her. He needed relief so, he lay back in bed and closed his eyes and hoped to fall back to sleep. After a while, he did. Finally, he awakened again. He was surprised that he had slept as long when he opened his eyes and looked to see his clock-radio read 1:47pm. His heart began to palpitate and he could feel a bit of anxiousness welling up inside. His thoughts were, he wished that he could suspend time and his get-together with Tina; and therefore, postpone the finality of his heartbreak. But, reality had set in, and he needed to go forward. He moved lethargically about his room, gathering himself for his shower. As he did, he began to think about the time he had been with Tina; how happy it all had been; the happy days when they cracked jokes, horsed around and teased each other; the delightful outings to dinner and the Jazz shows; the walks around downtown Chicago; the carriage rides and the ice cream shops; the joyful escapades on the city buses and trains; the meetings at the Lawrence Avenue L station; the get-togethers on holidays; the gatherings with his friends and with Tina's friends; the many wonderful, relaxed, carefree, happy nights they lay in her bed and talked forever about everything, allowing their souls to connect; how wherever they were together seemed like the center of the universe. It had all been so glorious; it had been paradise. And now, he was losing it all; losing his lover and his friend; his family. He shut the thoughts off because he was beginning to feel too emotional. He steadied himself mentally and emotionally and he carried on and took his shower. He was zombie-like as he moved about his little room, grooming, dressing and preparing to drive to Tina's place in Evanston.

Finally, he was ready and it was time to leave. As he drove along, he was feeling a world of emotions and the drive felt like a death-march. He arrived in front of Tina's apartment building shortly before 4pm. He paused a long time after he parked and cut the engine off. He looked across the street at the familiar building that had come to symbolize so much to him. It was perhaps, the last time he would be here. He moved slowly and apprehensively as he locked his car doors and began to walk across the street toward the building. He opened the entrance door and walked into the pristine vestibule with the neat, bronze-colored, metal mailboxes on one side and the bank of door bells on the other. He walked over and pressed the one that read "T. Newberry" A moment of silence passed. He raised his hand to press it again and the locked inner door buzzed that familiar sound that triggered the happy little feeling he knew so well from all of his previous visits there. He turned to grab the door handle, pulling the door open and walking through it as the buzzer rang. He walked the same path that he had so many times before down the hallway to her apartment door. He stopped and stood in front of it and the door slowly swung open.

Behind it stood Tina. She looked especially well-groomed and neat. She had light makeup on and she was wearing one of her favorite dresses that was sexy and revealed her nice figure. Jack's heart skipped a beat as soon as he saw her. She looked angelic. All of the love that was in his heart for her seemed to rush to the surface. It was so intense until it seemed to burn inside of him. "Hi, Jack…come on in, honey" Tina said with almost a doting lilt to her words. Jack tried to speak but, the words got caught on the lump in his throat. So, he just nodded nervously and mumbled "Hey" "Come on inside…sit down" She said with the same sweet, caring tone. Jack walked over and sat on the sofa in the living room. Her nice little apartment used to feel like a second home to Jack. But, now it seemed so eerily strange. Jack looked all around at the place that was so familiar, until it felt as though he once lived there. He didn't live there but, the little apartment lived in him---in his heart. "I'm going to get you a glass of your favorite juice, honey… cranberry-apple…okay?" Tina offered and walked straight toward the back to her little kitchen. She returned with a tall, fancy glass. "Here you go, honey…I put just a couple of ice cubes in it just like you like it" she said and gave Jack a sweet smile that held a hint of sorrow. "Thanks, baby" he said, feeling a little more uplifted. After she sat the drink on a coaster on the cocktail table in front of him, she sat next to Jack and just looked at him. He took a sip of the juice and sat it back down. She kept looking at Jack and reached over and ran her hands gently through his bushy hair. She did it several times more, slow and gently. Then, she moved her hand down and caressed his back, again ever-so-gentle and lovingly. There was silence the whole time. "School okay?" she asked as she continued to rub his back. "Yea" Jack uttered, turning to her and nodding his head as he spoke. Then, she stopped rubbing his back and re-positioned herself by placing her right knee up on the sofa and anchoring her left foot to the floor. She moved closer to Jack and put her finger under his chin and moved her face close to his and, as she did so, the expression on her face turned passionate before she closed her eyes and pressed her lips to his. Jack responded and the kiss became erotic. It lasted for a long moment before Tina tore away and spoke. "Uh..Jack..let's save this for later...I'm sorry, honey…is that okay?" She said as she was breathing heavily and straightening herself. Jack almost got lost in the heated moment and just responded by nodding his head and trying to catch his breath.

"We can go to the restaurant on Sherman for dinner…is that okay with you, honey?" She asked. "Yea, that's cool" Jack answered. "I need to go to the bathroom and finish getting ready…I won't be long…okay?" Tina said. "Okay" Jack answered. Tina went into the back and Jack sat there quietly. She finally returned and they left the apartment and got into Jack's car. They drove the short distance to the restaurant. It was a bit early for dinner at the popular local restaurant. So, there was not much of a crowd. The Sunday crowd was much lighter, anyway because most families cooked on Sunday in this peaceful, more upscale part of town. After they were seated in the restaurant, it was just as Tina had requested---there was not much talk between them; just things like "What are you ordering?" "Nice day today, huh?" and "Your dress looks nice" Each expression an attempt to cut into the somber mood. But, nothing deeper or emotionally charged. The arrangement seemed to be working perfectly for Jack because he didn't have anything to say and he didn't want to say anything, either. Not talking much seemed to be keeping his emotions in check. When their food arrived, the two sat and ate quietly. They continued to make small talk with long periods of silence in-between; talking about other people and other things that did not center on themselves. "Let's get back, honey" Tina finally said after they were done eating and the silence between them had become deafening. It was shortly past 6pm when they arrived back at Tina's apartment.

"Go ahead and get ready, Jack…I'll be getting ready in the bathroom" Tina said after they were inside. Jack went into the bedroom and stripped down to his shorts. He lay in the bed straight with his head on a pillow and his legs together and his hands folded on top of his stomach. He had positioned himself that way unconsciously. But, the positioning seemed to have a certain foreboding that struck him oddly just at that moment. He was feeling an array of emotions, as well. He felt a bit somber; excited; anxiety; dread; desire. He lay there almost incandescent before the moment of truth and passion would arrive. Tina suddenly appeared in the bedroom doorway. She paused there for a short moment wearing nothing but a bottom slip. Her firm young breasts standing at attention; her shapely body giving classic feminine form to the slip. Jack just stared at her. The sight of her curvaceous form prompted a strong arousal within him; his desire announcing itself from his groin. Tina started walking slowly toward the bed. When she was near him,she placed a hand gently on Jack's right shoulder as she had done so many times before. Jack knew what it meant and he slid over just to the left-of-center of the bed before Tina slid into the bed next to him. She lay her upper body across his chest until her face was inches away from his. They began to kiss as both of Jack's hands began to caress the middle of her back and then slid down to grab her luscious, well-defined buttocks in each hand; squeezing them hungrily. Her familiar, soft, deep kiss tasted sweeter than it ever had before; deeper and hotter.

The maddening kiss drove them both into insane desire. Jack gently flipped Tina over on her back before he greedily snatched her half-slip off and then rolled onto his upper back, raising his legs and quickly snatching his shorts off and tossing both garments out of the bed to the floor. It was only a short moment later that the flood of passion was unleashed and the gyrating motion of lovemaking began; the guttural sounds; the moaning; the driving rhythm playing a strong, steady tempo on the bed; the contrasting hues of their flesh intertwined into a work of art. They reached paradise almost simultaneously before Jack crumbled to the bed. They both lay there breathing deeply for a while before the breathing subsided into gentle, easy resting. Not a word had been spoken. They both lay there still. Jack held Tina from behind and would occasionally kiss her in the crook of her neck. They lay there resting for long periods of time before the passion would stir again. Tina took a trip to the bathroom and when she returned, Jack ravished her in front of the dresser; then later on the living room sofa; in front of the kitchen cabinets from behind. There were times when he stroked her ferociously; perhaps, subconsciously revenging the inner pain; or was it to give all of the love he had for her that he would never be able to show? There seemed to be a measure of healing for Jack with each pounding stroke. In-between, she would initiate sessions by mounting him as he lay on his back. This went on-and-on throughout the evening with long periods of holding in-between. Still, they had not said much to each other, except to say they were going to the bathroom or asking the other to move to a certain position. Finally, it was late into the evening---almost 10pm.

"You want something to eat, Jack?...I feel a little hungry" Tina said after she raised up while they were both lying quiet and motionless in the bed. "Yea...okay" Jack responded from a haziness as he propped himself up on an elbow. Tina put on her robe and Jack wore the one that he kept in Tina's closet. They went to the kitchen and Jack sat at the table as Tina went into her refrigerator and cabinets, calling out to Jack what was there to eat. After Jack told her what he wanted, Tina fixed up a snack for them both. They sat at the kitchen table and ate. Tina began to talk. "Jack...I want you to stay the night, then drop me off at the train station in the morning...would you please do that for me?"

she asked. “Yea…I’ll do it” Jack responded passively as he ate. “And another thing…you plan to take your finals…right?” she added. “Yea…why?” Jack asked. “I want you to call me Tuesday night after your last exam and tell me how you did…it’s important to me to know…I know you’ll do okay…I just want you to call and tell me” Tina said. “Alright…I will” Jack answered with the same subdued tone. “But, then…I’ll be with Randall the next day….you understand…you remember what I told you” Tina said a little uneasy. Tina could see the strong emotion begin to show on Jack’s face. He seemed to grimace and press his lips before he shook his head in the affirmative. Tina rose from the table and walked over and took the empty plate from in front of Jack. She threw the few dishes they had used into the sink and began to wash them as she kept turning to look back at Jack as he sat quietly at the table. She knew that her last statement to him had triggered the kind of emotion within him that she was trying to avoid. She seemed to be monitoring him; being mindful of his emotional state. She washed the dishes quickly and then hugged Jack from behind as he sat at the kitchen table. She began to kiss and caress him; pulling off his robe before throwing off hers. They went at it again; having another powerful session right there in the kitchen. They went back to bed and rested. They had one more round of lovemaking before they fell asleep.

Jack suddenly awakened to see Tina walking toward the bathroom, she turned back to him just as he was raising his head from the bed. “Time to get ready, honey..I’ll shower real quick then, you can go in” she said to Jack as she walked toward the bathroom. Jack awakened to an empty, somber mood. This was it---the end. His heart would finish breaking today. He had one last, intense period of being with his sweetheart and now, he had to surrender all claims to her. His heart was feeling so heavy after he sat up in the bed until, he felt that he would just tip over and die. The feeling of loneliness had already begun. The dead, cold reality was heart-wrenching. He was struggling to hold all of his trembling emotions inside. He sat quietly in the living room with his robe on. About twenty minutes passed before Tina came out of the bathroom. “It’s all yours, honey…I’m done” she said. Jack wanted to hurry up and drop Tina off and get this over with because the heartache was becoming unbearable. He grabbed his clothes from the bedroom and rushed into the bathroom. His usual routine on a Monday morning at Tina's place was to just wash up and not take a shower; and this was what he was doing. But, when he went through the routine, he was so out of sorts, he couldn't hold himself steady as he tried to wash up. He was anxious and a bit shaky. At the same time, that blinking light in the back of his mind had come to the fore and was flashing quickly. The urge was stronger than ever. His mood became dark. Finally, they were both ready. The two shared one last, deep, passionate kiss just inside the door; caressing each other gently for a long moment before they finally went outside of the apartment door and Tina locked it. They were quiet as they walked outside to the street and got into Jack's car.

Just as Jack was checking his rearview mirrors, he could see a man park his car almost a block behind him. He was a young black man with a medium-brown complexion. He saw the man finish parking and walk away from his car. There was something about the man that struck Jack in a curious way. Jack began to pay him closer attention as he crossed the street to walk to the other side where Tina's apartment building was. Jack watched as he crossed the grassy median that divided the southbound side of the boulevard from the northbound. He was almost across the streets to the other side when he turned to notice Jack's car. He stopped and began to gaze curiously. Then, Jack could see him turn and begin to take slow steps in the direction of his parked car, still peering as if he was trying to see inside of the car. Suddenly, the realization came to Jack and he quickly cranked the engine up and the noise of the engine roared. He quickly flipped the radio on as he continued to be fixated on the male figure now, about a half-block behind his car. Jack whipped the Cadillac out of the parking space and pulled away from the curb. He could see the man raise his hand into the air and open his mouth as if he were calling out. Then, Jack could see him break into a trot, still moving his mouth as if to call out full-throated again; the noise of the engine and radio inside the car drowning him out. He faded into the distance behind. Tina was completely unaware of that development. "This shouldn't take long…there will be a little morning traffic but, the station's not that far…we'll be there not much more than five minutes" Tina said. Jack turned to her and gazed longingly and forced a smile through the somber expression etched on his face. "Thank you, honey…thanks for last night…thanks for everything…I'm sorry" Tina said, her voice going from upbeat and tailing off with a hint of sorrow at the end. She grabbed Jack's free hand and squeezed it gently. She held it for a long moment before he had to use it to make a turn. There was silence from there. Jack reached the elevated tracks at the Davis Street train station. He pulled over to the curb on the station side of the street out of the stream of traffic where Tina could get out safely. Tina gave Jack a quick kiss on the lips before she paused to look at him for a moment. "Don't forget to call me Tuesday night" she said before she weaved her way through the rush of people traffic streaming into the station.

Jack drove off and the sense of separation and loss flooded his conscience. He was alone. He stared blankly straight ahead as he drove toward home; feeling confounded; empty; defeated. He had endured the brutal, savage streets littered with miscreants and fraught with mayhem. He had always found a way to rise above his circumstances; slip by; get away. He had always managed to survive. But, this whole thing about love was new and strange to him; perplexing; disarming. It had been the most profound experience of his young life. Tina had appeared in his life as an unwitting savior; and more than that, had reversed his fortunes with love and inspiration. Now, she had abandoned him; cast him back to the vicious pavement where she had found him. The thought of anger never occurred to Jack; because he knew Tina so well. He knew her heart. He knew that it was not in her to undermine his dignity; to intentionally hurt. Even when she let him go, she had done so caringly; graciously; giving him all that she could of herself without giving her heart. Jack knew that, even though he did not have her heart, that he had a place in it. And for that, she would be forever enshrined in his.

Jack arrived at the YMCA and after parking in the lot, dragged himself up to his room. He undressed and immediately plopped into his bed for his usual Monday morning nap after leaving Tina's place. But, it would be usual no more. This would be the last time. He was exhausted from the marathon lovemaking and his spirit was weary from the emotional trauma; the melancholy running deeply to the core of his soul; clouding his mood like an impending storm. He passed out in the bed.

He awakened. The brightness of daylight shone through the lone window in his room as he stirred, squinted his eyes and groaned. He could barely see through his bleary eyes. "11:34am" the clock-radio read. He stretched and yawned as his head cleared from the grogginess. He laid his head back down and just lay there; staring vacantly into the ceiling; and as he did so, he became more conscious. Momentarily, the same gloominess enveloped him; reminding him of the morbid reality that his existence had become. He could sense the dead emptiness inside. At the same time that flashing light was raging in his head. The urge to take a drink was so powerful until he felt that he needed to run out and buy one right away. After lying there for a long while, his thoughts turned to the day ahead. He stirred and prepared to shower. After showering, he moved sluggishly as he dried off and put on his robe. He returned to his room and stood in front of his dresser mirror. A gloomy expression stared back at him. It struck him as the same expression he would have on the rare occasions when he was sick as a child; and he felt the same way inside, as well.

Finally, he was ready and it was time to go to school for two of his final exams today. As he drove along, he realized that he was driving through his old haunts instead of the evasive route he had been taking since he had started school. He was driving along Wilson Avenue when he spotted the Wilson Liquor store coming into view. He pulled over and parked in front of it. He cut the engine off and sat there for a moment. He took a deep breath. He looked over at the store seemingly contemplating. Then, he hurriedly cranked the car up and drove away. He arrived on Sheridan Road a short time later and parked. He looked at his watch to see that it was five minutes before his Man and His Physical Environment class would begin. He dashed up the long stairwell to the second level. He was in the classroom a moment later. He was trying to pay attention as the teacher was giving exam instructions.

The exam started and Jack tried to concentrate; doing well for stretches of time before his mind would drift and he forced himself back to reality. Finally, the exam was over. It was quiet in class as some students had finished and brought their test papers and placed them on the teacher's desk. They returned to their desk and sat quietly. Jack looked up from his exam and he could see that half of the class had completed their exams. He was almost done. He finished and placed his test paper on the teacher's desk just as the others had done. When the last student to finish had handed their test paper to the teacher, the teacher announced "Okay, everyone..all of you who wish to know their grades today, stick around…I should be done grading in about fifteen minutes" Jack sat anxiously. He looked at the big clock high up on the wall behind the teacher's desk near the doorway. There was just enough time for the instructor to finish grading the papers and for him to get to his next class on time. Finally, the instructor was done grading.

"Okay…Anderson…Coffield.." he began as he called out names of the students on each graded test paper. Finally, Jack was called toward the end. The teacher handed him his test paper. A ninety-one. "Not bad" he thought before he dashed off to his next class. The same routine ensued. But, there seemed to be less pressure. The Intro to Uptown class had been the most fun and the easier of all of Jack's classes. It was more a class for civic awareness and it seemed to have served that purpose for him. The exam was a mix of questions on in-class discussions and part essay. Jack was done early with the test. The instructor graded papers quickly after the last student was done. "Jack received a ninety-five. He suspected that most of the students received a similar grade. Jack was looking at his test paper as he held it in his hand. After the grade, registered, he realized that school was almost over. One more day. Most of the students left out and some stayed and mingled inside the classroom. The Center was empty and quiet, as it usually was at around 5pm when Jack was leaving his Intro to Uptown class on Mondays and Wednesdays. But, today held a certain finality.

Jack could not see into his future from this point. It was clouded with uncertainty. He jumped into his car and drove toward The Corner. It was a pleasantly mild and sunny day. Jack arrived at The Corner. He drove past the poolroom after making a left turn onto Winthrop Street. He parked just south of the poolroom near the Tower building. When he passed the poolroom, he saw that there was a good crowd hanging around inside and outside of it. He could also sense that same old excitement in the air; the excitement and anticipation that came with the warmer weather each year; the season of Street Gypsy insanity. After Jack got out of his car, he began to walk back north one block to the poolroom. In the distance, he could see many of the local regulars spread out around each corner of the intersection. Some hanging outside the poolroom; others hanging on the northeast corner across from it; still, others hanging on the southwest corner around Frances' Tavern; and Fuzzy and Woody's crowd hanging on the E-Z-GO gas station lot on the southwest corner. These gatherings were a stage for all of the Street Gypsy theatrics. There was always the usual dose of clever lies; bragging; posturing; debates; joking and the echoing laughter. In-between was the more serious business of hustling. Hustlers came and went; most made a stop in the poolroom to sell their stolen merchandise or to sell their dope; or to run whatever game they were running. This was also where bonds were made between brethren of the streets. Constant drinking was the fuel that kept these gatherings lively. This was all so familiar to Jack.

As he walked toward The Corner, he was feeling a bit of ambiguity. He felt as though he was suspended between two worlds; the peaceful, joyous life that he had been living and the crazy, hapless world of Street Gypsies. He had not left one and he had not yet returned to the other. But, he knew. For a time, he had been comfortably nestled in the bosom of heightened self-esteem; of belonging somewhere and to someone. But, fate had been cruel and fickle. He knew. He knew that this was where he would be when the summer sun beamed down from the sky during the hottest times of the year. He would be out here submerged in the folly and foolishness---the madness. And yet, he could not avoid the inevitable. He had nowhere else to go; no one else to talk to; no Tina; no school. Yes, there were his so-called friends in the streets. They sustained him to a certain degree; but, all of those bonds never reached beyond the pavement they stood on. Jack knew. He had no illusions about this life; the Street Gypsy life.

Jack approached his group of friends standing just outside of the poolroom on the Winthrop side. His breakup with Tina had been very trying and he was still in the emotional throes if it. But, he had vowed to himself that he would not be one of those men in the streets that he heard tell their stories. He would keep his sorrows to himself. "Hey, looka here…my main man, Jack…ain't seen you in a while, brotha'….what's hap'nin'?" his good friend, Coley greeted, smiling broadly before they engaged in the customary soul handshake. "Hey, Jack…Jack…hey, bro' Jabo, Larry and Skip all greeted, as they all congregated on the same area of the sidewalk. “Fellas…Fellas…what’s the deal” Jack greeted in the same lively manner he always did. Jack was surprised to hear his words come out with such vigor and spirit. It didn’t quite match the way he was feeling. But, he suddenly had that same familiar uplifted feeling that he always had when he met up with his friends on The Corner. His troubles seemed to diminish. “What’s goin’ on with you, Jack?…how’s your girl?” Coley asked. “She’s cool” Jack responded matter-of-factly. “What’s been goin’ on around here?” Jack asked to change the subject and move on to another topic. “Maaann…you see what’s goin’ on…everybody is out…niggas already actin’ a fool…dig” Coley said in his characteristically fun-loving manner and smiling broadly. Jack and Coley continued to talk, catching up on the latest developments. Jack never said a thing about his breakup with Tina; pretending that everything was still going along swimmingly.

“Skippa’…what you up to, baby?” Jack later turned to Skip to kick off the usual lively round of banter that they always engaged in and that seemed to bring a few laughs. “Man…listen…I don’t know whether to shit or go blind…po’lice been settin’ up decoys in the dope spots lately…I been wantin’ to cop from my regulars…but, I already heard that some people tried to cop from ‘em and got busted…I’m scared to cop right now…scared to get a little bump from my regular spots, anyway…I been ridin’ the bus up north to get my stuff…but, I don’t like messin’ around up that way” Skip said plaintively. After Skip’s comment, the banter began and the joking and laughter filled the balmy air around the intersection. “Jack…you drinkin’?” Coley asked. “Yea…I’m drinkin’” Jack responded without hesitation. “Walk with me down to Saxony’s, then?...I’m gonna buy us a taste” Coley said. Street-corner bullshitting always involved a trip to the liquor store. They left the group and walked the one block distance. At Saxony’s, Coley ordered a six pack of beer and a pint of Hennessey. Jack was standing next to him in front of the counter when Coley pulled out a large roll of cash and peeled of a bill to pay. “Damn, Coley…you got a hell ‘uva knot there…hustlin’ been good lately…huh?” Jack commented, clearly impressed but, not surprised. “Hell, yea…I’ve been rollin’ pretty good lately” Coley bragged before they laughed and slapped five. “I’ll tell you all about my hustle later on” Coley said with a gleeful smile. Jack knew how clever and resourceful his friend was and this was the kind of money Coley would have from time-to-time. There were highs and lows in the hustling game out on the streets. Hustlers lived for these times when they had done well; when they could brag and walk and talk with that cool, rhythmic swagger.

Jack and Coley decided to walk further up the street, going to Dover Street a couple of blocks away where they could get away from the group and talk privately. They found a concrete stoop to sit on in the middle of the block just south of Lawrence Avenue. They sat, drank and talked. Jack drank a beer then, another; and as he did so, he could sense the little twinge of angst and sorrow deep inside for his surrender to the drink. But, it was fleeting because, as soon as he felt a little buzz, the old feeling of not caring returned. Coley offered Jack some of the Hennessey. Jack took a single shot and stopped at that. He was thinking about when he would be talking to Tina on the telephone tomorrow evening; how he wanted to save himself one more day for that; to tell her how well he had done on his final exams. The two sat on the stoop for more than an hour drinking and talking before Jack forced himself to say that he was leaving. He went home with a lighter feeling from the camaraderie and the bit of drinking he had done.

It was Tuesday morning. Jack was up early. He had slept well perhaps, somewhat sedated by the drinking he had done. He was grateful that he did not drink very much. He had awakened with the same aura of melancholy that seemed surprisingly muted. He had been with his friends yesterday and that may have brought a little relief; even though he was suffering through this heartache, at least it was not compounded by being alone, as well. He was able to shower and dress without the sluggishness he felt yesterday. He had time to go to The Village Restaurant and have breakfast.

Afterward, he drove toward school. When he arrived, he stopped in the student lounge to see if any of his school friends were there. He didn't see any of them; only a couple of students he didn't know who were studying. The Center was fairly empty because most of the students had already taken their final exams. Jack arrived early to his favorite class, Expository Writing. The same routine took place with the teacher saying that the completed exams would be graded in-class and each student could know their grade before leaving. When Jack got his grade, he had gotten an A on the essay exam. He was very pleased that he would be able to tell Tina. He went on to his Community Organization class. The exam went okay and he had gotten a good grade there, as well. But, as soon as Jack walked out of the classroom, a creeping fear coursed through him. It was his last exam. School was out for the summer. Attending college classes at The Center had been so meaningful for him. It had given him so much hope; gave him a good feeling about himself; given him the self-esteem that he could be somebody; that he didn't have to be in the streets living that crazy life. But, now, it seemed that an ominous cloud was building. His inspiration was gone and so, it seemed, his will to go on without it. Just at that moment, a strong desire to drink emerged. But, Jack had his four-hour shift at the gas station today. He had just enough time to have lunch and then head to work. Work was just the distraction he needed right now to prevent him from buying a drink and going out of his mind like he wanted to do. It would take him to the evening when he could talk to Tina sane and sober.

Jack arrived at work. As he went about his duties, he was thinking about tonight when he would be speaking to Tina on the phone. He didn't know what he would say or how he would feel when they talked. In his mind, he had accepted that she was gone from his life. They had been heart-to-heart; soul-to-soul. There was a time when their love seemed invincible. It had lifted his spirits to the heavens; but, an unforgiving fate had left him crestfallen; and now, here he was---at love's last episode.

He went about his work almost in a catatonic state. He struggled to keep himself focused on his tasks. There were already two cars on the gas station lot left by Don Hardys for wax jobs. He kept busy with work and was able to finish both jobs by staying for a while after his shift. Somehow, he didn't mind staying longer; hoping to put off his destiny. Finally, it was time to go. Jack drove toward home and stopped off at the Village restaurant for dinner. He ordered dinner and sat for a long time eating it; mulling over the food and eating very slowly; being deeply pre-occupied the whole time. "Food okay" a voice suddenly spoke out, breaking his meditation. Jack looked up to see Flo, the waitress' familiar face staring at him with a concerned expression. "Oh…uuh…yea, the food is good" Jack said lazily.

"Hahaha…the way you were looking, I thought maybe you didn't like the taste of your dinner" Flo said with a light chuckle and a smile. "Naw…everything is good" Jack reiterated. Jack looked up at the diner clock and it was 7:51---almost closing time. He paid for his dinner with his usual tip. He slowly rose from his seat and walked out.

He drove the couple of blocks to the YMCA. He entered his room and took time to get comfortable. He sat on the edge of his bed. He sat still and quiet for a good while. He was trying to find his mood but, his thoughts and emotions were blank---paralyzed. Finally, he came to himself and walked over to his dresser and opened the top drawer. He scooped out a handful of change and walked out of the room. As he walked toward the bank of telephones in the hallway, he began to have that stark feeling that was accompanied by a mild palpitation. He picked up the telephone and shoved in a coin and dialed the telephone number that he knew as well as his own name.

"Hello" Tina's sweet, feminine voice came over the phone. "Hey…it's me" Jack said a little nervously. Hi, Jack…you called…I was hoping you would…I was thinking that you might say to hell with calling me" Tina said. "Naw…I said I would…you know how I feel about you" Jack said somberly. "I'm glad you did…how did your finals go?" she asked. "Pretty good..I got two A's and two B's" Jack said with pride. The sense of pride he was feeling carried much more than that. Deep in his subconscience, he wanted the knowledge that Tina had about his grades to say to her that he was indeed, a worthy person; that he had substance; that he could be a good person. Because deep in his mind, her rejection of him had set off those same notions of unworthiness within him; the sense of worthlessness that his father seemed to have instilled in him; the idea that no one cared about him. Those same emotions were triggered even though he knew better about Tina; that she was an honest, loving person who was genuine.

For Tina, she wanted to send the message to Jack that, even though she had decided to be with her former lover, that Jack mattered to her and that she cared about him and that she held him in the highest esteem. "Jack, that is terrific…I am very happy for you…keep it up when you go back in the fall" Tina encouraged. But, Jack knew better about that prospect, as well. "Yea" was his reply. “Jack…I wanted to say something to you…just like I said before…you really mean a lot to me…I felt so ashamed…I felt like a big phony when I told you that I was leaving you for Randall…I knew how hurt you would be…I thought about it for a long time…it was very hard on me to try to tell you…I cried a lot… I felt trapped between the man I had loved so much and the man I was falling in love with…I hope you understand…I hope you can forgive me” Tina said, as she tried to control her emotions. Jack paused a long time before responding; knowing instinctively how Tina was feeling just then; that she was struggling to control her feelings. “It’s alright, baby…it’s alright…I understand” Jack said dotingly. “That’s why I wanted us to have that time together…to make crazy love…I wanted to have something for us both to remember…and it was all I could give you” Tina said with a cracking voice. “Jack paused for a long moment once again. “Tina…baby…you gave me way more than you might think…I had some good times with you…you kept me off the streets…I went to school…I couldna’ done it without you…I learned how to be…uhh…more like a normal person when I was with you...all of that meant a lot to me” Jack finally said. “I’m not mad at you…it does hurt a lot…I admit…but, that’s the way things go sometimes” Jack added. “Thank you, honey…it means a lot to me for you to say that” Tina responded with a hint of relief. They talked for a very long time after that; mostly reminiscing. They had been on the phone almost two hours before Tina finally said “I have to get to bed for work tomorrow, Jack” “Okay, baby…if you ever need me…call me…you know…if things don’t work out” Jack said. “I will, honey…I will” Tina responded. “Good-bye” “Good-bye”

CHAPTER 6
THE STREET GYPSIES ENDING

Jack awakened slowly that morning. When he came to full awareness, he realized that it was not only a new day but, a new life for him, as well. Everything good that had filled his life before was gone. It felt as though he was at the center of a vast emptiness. There was a heavy, hollow feeling with it. All meaning had been drained. All purpose in his life had been canceled. And yet, he felt no sense of betrayal; no feelings of anger. Even though he felt a tremendous sense of loss, he had chalked it up to an unexpected, wonderful happiness in his life being subtracted and he had broken even. But, such reasoning and intellectual acceptance could not erase the pain. He felt as though he was in a state of convalescence; a sickly condition. He understood all too well what remained. He needed relief. The bright sunshine lit up the window and filled his lonely little room with brightness. The world outside and life was beckoning unto him. Jack knew what was ahead of him. He leaped up from the edge of his bed and prepared to take a shower. When he was done, he dressed and went into his dresser drawer and took out his bank book. He locked his door and rushed out of the YMCA to the parking lot and jumped into his car. He drove to the bank on Lawrence Avenue. He went in and withdrew a large sum of money. He drove back to the YMCA. He went to the clerk's desk in the lobby. His rent was twenty-four dollars-a-week. Jack was a bit anxious as the clerk took quite a while to record the six months of rent that Jack was paying in advance. Jack felt a lot better when it was done. He went up to his room and put away his receipt. Immediately, he went back out, got into his car and drove to the

Village Restaurant. There, he had breakfast and drove straight to The Corner afterward.

With the warm weather and bright sunshine, The Corner was teeming with the usual crowd of misfits. There were all kinds of activity around the intersection. Hustlers were hustling and drinkers were drinking. People buying drugs and weed in the nearby courtway came and went. The same old crowd was spread about the intersection doing the same things they always did. Further down the block, the residents from the Tower building were hanging out around the Winthrop-Leland end of the block and, of course, drinking with their friends and neighbors. New characters that Jack had never seen before popped up on the scene from time-to-time. Jack hung out with Coley, Jabo, Larry, Skip and his other friends. He bought drinks and laughed and joked along with all of them. He finally had to tell Coley and his other friends about his breakup with Tina. By the time he did, he was good and high and the confession did not have the emotional, hurtful sting that it would had he been sober. Jack's carousing went on into the night. It went on the same way the next day. He went to work at the gas station on Friday and Saturday that week.

When he got off work, he was back at The Corner each evening. But, he never drove his car there; leaving it in the YMCA parking lot because he knew he would be drinking every day; and also because he did not want to have to fend people off from asking him favors to drive them here and there. The next week, he called in sick on Tuesday. When his next work day came on the following Friday, he was out on the streets getting high. He never called in and never went back to the gas station to work again. Weeks passed by and Jack found himself hanging out on The Corner most every day. Over time, his appearance began to slip. He didn't seem to take the care in grooming himself that he once did. Before long, he was engaging in all of the same madness; getting involved in a few risky schemes. One of them backfired and Jack got into a round of fisticuffs with one of the local regulars, as a result; all the while telling his friends and trying to convince himself that he would return to school in the fall. His affair with Tina and his stint in school were all he had to feel good about these days. But, that had all been in the past. Now, the harsh realities of the streets had come back into his life full force. The pavement he was standing on each day may as well have been quicksand for the way the streets were engulfing Jack and all of his dreams and aspirations.

There was one incident where he was hanging out near the Aragon Ballroom on a weekday afternoon. He and his good friend Coley were sharing a drink. Jack was trying to sell some sunglasses he had stolen from a local store while he was there buying liquor. He saw the opportunity was ripe and compulsively lifted a half-dozen pairs. When he tried to offer a passing pedestrian out on the streets a pair for sale, the well-dressed man waved him off and said that he was late for work and did not have time. Jack, uncharacteristically, went into a rage; calling the man a "mark" and a "square" and deriding his working life. Jack even walked behind the startled man, hurling insults; leaving his friend, Coley standing half-way down the block, wondering what got into Jack. After Jack was done yelling those insults, he broke down with frustrated, drunken tears that came out of nowhere. For some reason, the incident triggered a crazy state of mixed emotions within him. His friend Coley had to run behind him and warn Jack not to do what he was doing and to calm down. Jack hurriedly wiped the tears away before his friend caught up to him to see his face. He continued to drink and soon, he was getting high on T's and Blues again. The happy life and the love he once shared with Tina faded into the past underneath all of the drinking. Still, he could not forget her. He occasionally had moments when he comforted himself with those sweet memories.

"Coop…what's goin' on, my brotha" Jack called out, happy to see his old friend approaching The Corner. Jack was standing on the Winthrop-side of the poolroom, drinking with Jabo. None of the other regulars were around. It was late afternoon on a balmy and partly cloudy weekday. "Hey…my man, Jack" Cooper greeted before they shook hands. It was the same spirited encounter that the two good friends always had; all smiles and laughter. "What's been happ'nin' with you, Jack?" Cooper asked. "Short stakes, bad breaks right now" Jack said. "How's everything with that snow girl of yours?" Cooper added. Jack began to shake his head negatively without saying anything; borrowing time to control his emotions. "Ahhh…we broke up, man…her old boyfriend came back into the picture and stole her back…another black dude…I guess she musta' been real crazy about him" Jack sighed. "That's too bad, man….but, that's the way it goes sometimes" Cooper offered with sincere sentiment. "What you been up to?" Jack asked. "Believe it or not…I got the same kinda' problem…you know the chick I told you that I been stayin' with in Rogers Park…well….she broke bad on me…we was gettin' high offa' heroin and T's and Blues ever since I started stayin' with her…but, now she done turned into such a fiend, she goes over to cop for us at the dope man's house and ends up stayin' a couple of hours instead of coppin' and comin' right back like she was doin' at first…I think she's doin' the dope man for some extras" Cooper explained. "Damn, man…that don't sound too good" Jack commented. "Yea..and we been arguin' all the time' about that shit…she kicked me out the other night…I need to find me another woman to live with" Cooper said with a bit of frustration in his voice.

"Hey…you wanna get up on some tops and bottoms?" Cooper asked. "I don't care" Jack replied without hesitation, sounding very game. "Uh-oh…I guess I'll see you cats later" Jabo said as soon as Jack agreed to Cooper's proposal. With that, Jabo walked further up the street on Winthrop toward the apartment building across from 4848 where he lived. Jabo was well aware of the new synthetic high that consisted of two prescription pills and had been all the rage amongst dope fiends the last couple of years. But, he was an old heroin addict who didn't like these new-fangled ways of getting high that he regarded as very dangerous. "Let's go on over to the Arms and get us a six-and-six Cooper suggested. "Aw, man…Coop…a six-and-six?" Jack asked hesitantly. "Yea…six-and-six is cool, ain't it?" Cooper asked rather matter-of-fact. "I was thinkin' more like a four-and-four" Jack said. "I'll tell you what...we can buy the four-and-four together and I'll buy the extra two-and-two on my own....cool?" Cooper offered. "Yea…that's straight" Jack agreed. "Only thing is…where are we gonna get high?" Cooper wondered. "And where are we gonna get some outfits from, too?" Jack added. "Don't worry about that…I got two on me" Cooper said. From there, the two jumped into Cooper's car and rode the short distance to the Malden Arms.

In not much more than a few minutes, Cooper was parking in front of the building. "Let's ask the dope-man about somewhere to get high in the buildin'" Cooper suggested as the two walked up the stairwell inside the Malden Arms toward the third floor. They were going to apartment 307 where Cooper copped once before when Jack had accompanied him. When they arrived at apartment 307, Cooper knocked on the door. No answer. Cooper knocked on the door again and the door finally swung open. “Yes…can I help you?” a man probably in his sixties answered as he stood inside the door. Cooper and Jack were taken aback to see this older man in the apartment that had been occupied about a month ago by the short dope man that everyone called “Flukie” “Uh…you live here?” Cooper asked in a puzzled tone. “Hahaha…yes, I *do*” the older gentleman said with a light chuckle. “What happened to the dude that was livin’ here before?” Cooper asked with a furrowed brow. “Oh…he moved down-stairs there into 201…for a long time, he wanted to get an apartment with windows facing the streets…looks like he finally got it…then, I moved in here ‘cause it’s more quiet on this floor, now” the older man explained. “Oh…okay…sorry to bother you…201 you said…right?” Cooper asked as he and Jack backed away from the apartment door. “201…the apartment down in the corner to your left” the man called out. “Okay…thanks” Cooper said as the two started down the hallway toward the front stairwell. They reached the corner apartment and Cooper knocked on the door.

“Who is it?” a familiar voice called out from inside the apartment. “It’s Cooper” Cooper replied. “Naw, man…what’s the password?” the voice asked. “I don’t know the password…hey, man…I copped from you before” Cooper said with a little exasperation building in his tone. Cooper and Jack could see the little peep-hole in the middle of the door turn dark before the door swung open. “Yea…I remember you, bro’…come on in” the man said. He was the same lean, muscular, short fellow everyone called “Flukie” that Cooper had copped from before. Cooper and Jack slowly stepped inside of the apartment. There were a couple of other men sitting at a dining table playing a card game. There was a gun lying on the table between them. “What you need, brotha’?” Flukie asked. “Six-and-six” Cooper replied. “He don’t owe nothin’ does he?” one of the men sitting at the table said without taking his attention away from his card game. “He don’t owe nothin’…I know the ones that owe” Flukie assured. “Be cool for a minute, bro’…I’ll be right back” Flukie said before he walked toward the back to the bedroom. A long moment passed as Jack and Cooper waited a little uncomfortably. They watched and listened to the two men trade blustery comments as they played their card game. Flukie returned from the bedroom and stood in front of Cooper. "Twenty-four, bro" he said. Cooper quickly went into his pocket and pulled out some folded bills and handed them to Flukie. After Flukie finished counting the bills, he handed Cooper the same little packet of aluminum foil as before. Cooper opened the packet right away and paused as he visually counted the contents.

"Cool…hey…anywhere we can get high in the buildin'?...you know anybody who will let us get high at their spot for a few dollars?" Cooper asked. "Uh…tell you what…hey, Mack…you still got them keys for 205?" Flukie asked one of the men playing cards. "Yea…what's happ'nin'?" one of the men responded without turning his head and staying focused on the card game. "Let me get 'em" Flukie asked. The man went into his pockets and tossed the keys across the room. Flukie caught them in the air. "Hold on" Flukie said before he opened the front door and peeked up-and-down the hallway. "Alright, bro'…follow me" he said before locking the door of apartment 201. Jack and Cooper followed him down the hall to another apartment. "This is our apartment but, it's empty…give me five dollars and you can use it" Flukie offered. "Five dollars?...kinda steep, ain't it?" Cooper asked. "Well…forget about it, then" Flukie smirked before he turned to walk back down the hallway. "Wait, wait…hold on…Jack…give me two dollars" Cooper asked anxiously. Cooper dug into his pocket and feverishly pulled out three dollars. Jack handed him two more and he handed all of the bills to Flukie. "Alright, then" Flukie said with a tone of smug satisfaction. He took the bills and walked a few feet past the two men, unlocked the door and pushed it slightly open. "When you get done…clean your shit up and lock the door from the inside…we don't want these hypes comin' in here fuckin' up our spot…dig me?" "If you don't do it, I'm gonna charge you five dollars the next time you cop from me…understand?" Flukie said firmly. He spoke in the same hardcore manner as most dope dealers. "Yea…no problem…we'll clean up and lock the door when we finish" Cooper assured. "Cool" Flukie said before he turned and walked back toward apartment 201.

Jack and Cooper entered the apartment. It had a Murphy bed, an old dresser and sofa-chair inside. It had one window that faced the side wall of the next building. "Let's get this party started!" Cooper said gleefully as he pulled all of his get-high gear out of the leg of his sock where he kept it. He unwrapped a small plastic bag and pulled out two syringes. He took out one of those aluminum soda bottle caps that had the little piece of paper liner pulled out. "I'll crush the pills up if you get the water, Jack" Cooper offered as he pulled the aluminum foiled packet of pills out. He spread all of the paraphernalia out on the dresser. Jack took one of the syringes and went into the bathroom and turned on the water in the face bowl. He took the needle part of the syringe off. He cupped his hand under the running water and stuck the tube of the syringe flush into his palm. He pulled the plunger of the syringe up, drawing water into the tube. When he was done with that, Jack walked back to the dresser and shot the tube of water into the aluminum soda cap. Cooper was crushing the blue and orange pills together on a piece of cardboard that lie on the dresser. When he was done, he took an ID card out of his wallet and scrapped all of the powder up into a little pile on the cardboard. He moved the cardboard over next to the bottle cap of water and turned it upward and let the powdery substance pour into the water. After the powder dissolved, it turned the water into a lime-green color. Cooper and Jack paused and gazed at the little aluminum bottle cap full of green water as though it were a wonderful creation. A fiendish delight danced in their eyes. "Yessir…party-time, now!" Cooper said excitedly and rubbed his palms together very fast. Cooper hovered over the dresser with all of the paraphernalia spread out and the little bottle cap with it's green, liquid gold sitting off to one side. He grabbed a syringe and took the needle off before he stuck the tub of the syringe gently and carefully into the little bottle cap and drew up about a half-tube of the green liquid. Afterward, he placed the needle part back onto the syringe and pushed the plunger inward until a small, thin little stream shot through the needle. Cooper then stepped aside as he picked up the other syringe and handed it to Jack. Cooper took off his belt and looped it around his left arm and pulled all the slack and wrapped the belt around once again. He stepped away from the dresser. Meanwhile, Jack was performing the same action as Cooper; drawing up an equal amount of the green water into the syringe. Jack also duplicating the act of looping his belt around his left arm. The two fell silent as each concentrated on carefully aiming the needle into their arms. Each man had drifted almost to opposite ends of the room to find a comfortable space. Perhaps, trying to isolate themselves to achieve greater concentration. And so, this was the ritual that was performed by fiends every day all over Uptown; and all over the city and into other states and other cities.

This was the manner in which fiends tried to make their dead, crusty souls feel something; to rise up and resurrect themselves temporarily from a spiritual death; a death that occurred long ago; to sprinkle the false fragrance of getting high onto the stench of death that wafted mysteriously in the air about them. They were the living dead; the walking dead; making reality into fantasy; skewing all perceptions and realism; creating a reason to exist. "Finally got a hit" Jack mumbled from where he stood near a window on one end of the room.

"Still tryin'" Cooper murmured as he sat on the edge of the bare mattress bed and continued to maneuver the needle in his arm. Jack let go of the end of the belt that was clinched in his teeth as he held the belt in place like a tourniquet. He continued to manipulate the needle in his arm; carefully measuring each increment of the green liquid he pushed in; pausing for long periods in-between before pushing the plunger further inward. Jack began to feel the soothing high surging slowly into his bloodstream. It reached a point where he was feeling that familiar sense of levitation. "Hey, Coop…how you makin' out over there?" Jack asked, as his speech had become slightly slurred, "I finally got it" Cooper replied before he moved his left elbow outward to unloosen the belt around the arm with the needle in it. Jack was feeling the high envelope him. His eyes closed and he could see colors and feel a quiet humming inside his body; a floating sensation; then, a kaleidoscope of eerie visuals. This was the T's and Blues experience. The two men sat like zombies on opposite ends of the room for a very long spell of time; each man in his own world. Jack was seated on the floor under the window. Cooper was sitting on the edge of the bed, leaned over to one side on an elbow that was dug into the mattress like a stake. He was frozen in one position like a mannequin. Finally, Cooper came out of his nod. "Jack…damn, man..my high wore off" Cooper said, as he began to stir. "Ahhh" Jack murmured, still feeling his. "I'm gonna go ahead and drop this other two-and-two" Cooper said.

Jack remained in the same spot and in the same state as he nodded back out. He could faintly hear Cooper stirring about near the dresser; hear him take a trip to the bathroom and return. Jack's eyes slowly opened and momentarily he could make out a blurry vision of Cooper sitting on the edge of the bed, hunched over the needle in his arm. Jack drifted back into his dreamy world. He could hear Cooper tapping the needle with a finger and making an occasional grunting sound. "You cool?" Jack tried to call out across the room to his friend. But, he could barely get the words out; even though he could hear himself say the words, they were probably inaudible to Cooper. Finally, Cooper stopped tussling with the needle and he apparently had achieved his objective. "I'm cool, now" he said out loud. Jack continued with his eyes closed; drifting in-and-out of reality.

Suddenly, Jack was shaken by a loud thud. He was startled by the sound as his eyes popped open. He looked over to see Cooper on the floor with his body convulsing violently. Cooper's eyes were rolling around in his head and he was foaming at the mouth. He was making involuntary guttural sounds as his body seemed to stiffen as it continued to shake uncontrollably. He had lost consciousness. Jack sprang up from where he sat. Instinctively, he went into his back pocket and took out his afro comb. He tried to grab Cooper's jaw to hold it steady so that he could shove the plastic comb into his mouth to prevent him from swallowing his tongue. But, the violent convulsing made it difficult. Finally, Jack was able to hold Cooper's mouth steady by pinning his body down to the floor with his weight. He shoved the comb into Cooper's mouth, flattening his tongue. Jack kept his weight on Cooper to hold him in place; keeping his hand on the comb to steady it. Cooper's body continued to shake for a short spell longer before it relaxed and the convulsion stopped. "Coop…Coop" Jack called out in anguish. "Coop.." he said again painfully. Cooper lie there snoring as if asleep. Jack was engulfed with a sense of sorrow and guilt. He bit his lower lip as he rubbed his friends head while he lie still. Jack kept checking Cooper's breathing and pulse. They were okay. He paced back-and-forth, anxiously trying to think of what else to do. Jack had seen this occur a couple of times before. Every T's and Blues fiend knew that this was part of the risk of getting high. That it could happen to anybody anytime they got high off of this stuff. It was more likely to happen if you got greedy. Jack stayed in the empty apartment for almost another hour as Cooper slowly came back to consciousness. Cooper finally sat up and stared blankly at Jack for ten minutes or so.

"Where are we at?" Cooper finally said, still not seeming to have his bearings. "You went out, man" Jack said plainly. Jack knew that fiends did not like to hear that news because most felt as though they were invincible; that a seizure could not happen to them. "I went out?...I had a seizure?" Cooper asked, still in a daze. "Yea…you had one" Jack said soft and resignedly. "How you feel?" Jack asked. "I feel a little spaced-out…but, I feel okay, though…I feel alright" Cooper said like a punch-drunk fighter who was recovering from a knock-out. Finally, they prepared to leave the vacant apartment. Jack cleaned up the mess and locked the door from the inside. The two walked down the hallway to the stairwell with Jack staying close to Cooper and monitoring him closely. Cooper was slowly coming back to himself, although, still slightly groggy. The two men sat in Cooper's car talking for a good while. There were long spells where each man fell silent, nodded out then, opened their eyes with full consciousness.

"I'm straight, now, Jack…I'm gonna' drive home" Cooper finally announced. "You sure you're okay?" Jack asked with concern. "I'm cool…I'll drop you off…where you wanna go?" Cooper asked. "Drop me off at The Corner" Jack said. Cooper dropped Jack off before driving away. Jack was still a bit shaken from the experience of seeing his friend, who had always seemed so invincible to him, have a seizure.

In the following days and weeks, it weighed on his mind. Jack decided that he would stop getting high on T's and Blues. He began getting high on heroin again. That meant that he was now getting involved with the dope-fiend crowd of Melvin, LV and Andrew. A couple of times, Jack bought heroin. He recruited LV on one occasion to go and cop the dope because he didn't know where to go. On another occasion, he paid for the heroin that he had Melvin cop for him. Both times, he got them high by sharing half of the dope. Each time, LV and Melvin behaved like the true fiends they were; being greedy at the cooker. Jack suspected, too that on those occasions, each man probably stole a little bit of the heroin that he bought all by himself. Finally, late one evening, when Jack was hanging around the poolroom, drinking and carousing as he usually did, he got a craving for heroin. He decided this time, that he would go to the dope spot and cop himself; that way, he would spend only enough for one instead of two. None of his friends were around the poolroom late that weekday evening.

So, Jack went to the dope spot a few blocks north on Kenmore where he had seen Melvin go to buy heroin once before. He went into the courtway building. He went into the entrance he had seen Melvin go. He knew to go to the second floor to the first apartment off the stairwell. A lone light bulb at the far opposite end lit the dark vestibule as he entered it. He was about to walk up the stairs when a man suddenly popped out from one side of the staircase. "What's goin' on, bro?…you gonna cop?" the man asked Jack. He was a big, dark-skinned man with a hardened expression on his face. "Hey, guy…naw, I ain't coppin'…goin' upstairs to my folks place" Jack answered, knowing exactly what the deal was. "You a motherfuckin' lie…get your hands up, punk?" the man said, as he produced a gun and pointed it low in his hand at Jack. "Aw, man…come on, bro…why it gota be like that?" Jack began to plead as he raised his hands in the air. "Give it up, nigga'…you know what's happ'nin'" the man said very sinister and forcefully. "Hey, man..I…" Jack started before he was struck by the man with the gun squarely on the temple of his head. A flash shot through Jack's eyes and momentarily blinded him. The pain was excrutiating. "Give me what you got before I bust a cap in your ass, fool!" The man demanded very sternly. Jack continued to hold the left side of his head with his left hand while he went into his pocket with his right. He leaned against the vestibule wall grimacing with his eyes closed, trying to hold himself upright. Jack handed the man all of the bills that were in his pocket. The man snatched the bills from Jack's hand. "Now, get the fuck outa' here, bitch!" the man snarled before he kicked Jack in the seat of his pants.

Jack stumbled out of the entrance door holding his hand to the temple of his head. He continued stumbling out on the dark streets, still holding his head and suffering the pain. Soon, he arrived at the corner of Ainslie and Kenmore and passed a few people congregating on the corner. They gazed at Jack as he walked hurriedly past them, still holding the side of his head. Jack continued to walk along the dark streets while the side of his head throbbed with pain. He walked south on Broadway to avoid people on the residential streets. He did not want to run into people he knew who would ask what happened to him. He continued on south of Lawrence Avenue. He stopped at the Time-Out Lounge on Leland near Clifton Street and bought himself a drink to help the aching pain he was feeling in his head. He continued on from there to the YMCA. After entering his room, he took a face towel and ran cold water on it to press to his sore head. He put on his pajamas and lie on the bed nursing his throbbing head with the cold towel and sipping on the pint bottle of wine. He finished half the bottle before he fell asleep.

After a couple of days, the pain and soreness in his head went away. Jack was back to his carousing ways; completely immersed in the Street Gypsy life; hustling out on the streets; running a scam now and then. He tried not to draw any money out of his bank account. He made a little money here-and-there from his hustles to keep from doing that. Occasionally, when he made a big enough hustle, he would pay another week or two of rent. As time went on, Jack became a little more crazy and a bit more daring in his exploits. Soon, he was hanging out with the very element he had been trying to avoid when he was with Tina and attending college---Melvin and his crowd of get-high associates.

It was late-morning on a bright and sunny Saturday. There was a laziness in the warm air. There was also that sense of adventure and excitement. The young day carried a freshness with it that seemed to buoy one's spirit. On these mornings, the Street Gypsy crowd was slow to appear on the scene; having spent themselves from Friday night's episode of madness. Most were not seen until sometime during the afternoon. Some taking the time to sleep off their wild night. Others never even going to sleep but, carrying their recklessness through the night, past sunrise and into the new day. Li'l Murphy was standing just outside the playground on the south end of the 4848 building that was recessed a good distance from the Winthrop street sidewalk. The bright morning sun beamed down on him as he bounced a rubber ball off of the side of the building. Occasionally, he stopped to take a sip from the forty-ounce bottle of malt liquor that he had sitting on the concrete ground near the playground fence. L'il Murphy just made twenty-one a month ago. He was very pleased with the fact that he could buy liquor all on his own. He flaunted the privilege whenever he could. He was a short, energetic fellow who wanted to hang with the big boys; always hanging around them and trying to act older than he was. He sold weed for his uncle and sometimes for himself. He wanted to be a big-time hustler. He was always doing things out on the streets to build a reputation.

Jack was standing on The Corner just outside of the poolroom. It wasn't open, yet. He had awakened from a wild Friday night. He felt better than he did most mornings because he only drank beer for most of last night with beer-drinkers like "Old Man Dave, Mr. Jackson and Bow-tie; laughing with them as he listened to their crazy stories, gossip and jokes until late into the night. Last night had been more subdued because he hung around the Leland-Winthrop intersection with those old-timers after all of his other friends disappeared from The Corner. After a late-morning breakfast at The Village Restaurant, he walked all the way from there to The Corner, as he usually did; leaving his car in the YMCA parking lot. Jack's life was gradually reverting back to the way it had been. With each passing day, his existence became a little more depraved. The decent life that he was once inspired to live had faltered and failed. Now, he had dismissed his good conscience and all of the virtues that came with it. He had come to embrace the Street Gypsy life completely and with passionate rebellion. His associations and all of his activities in the streets only masked the loneliness deep down in his soul. This morning, he was looking for his friends who were probably still recovering from last night. As he stood on The Corner, he looked up the street one way then, down the street the other way. People were stirring about. But, he did not see anyone he knew.

Suddenly, he could hear a faint, recurring thud further up the street. Jack was curious so, he walked slowly up the street to see where the sound was coming from. After he passed the long wall of the Aragon, he came upon the playground just north of it. He could see in the distance across the wide-open space, L'il Murphy bouncing a rubber ball against the 4848 high-rise building; playing by himself. Immediately, Jack could feel the little sensation of relief that he always felt when he was alone and found any of his friends out on the streets. As soon as L'il Murphy saw Jack, he stopped bouncing the ball and held it in his hand as he put his other hand high into the air, making an enthusiastic, beckoning wave and yelling out "Jaaacckk!" Jack casually strolled toward L'il Murphy. "What you doin' man?" Jack asked rather blasé. "Nothin'…just out here messin' around…drinkin' a brew" L'il Murphy responded. "You love them forties, don't you L'il Murph?...you runnin' down to Saxony every chance you get…Murph…they ain't gonna run outa' liquor….don't worry about it" Jack teased. "Hey, man…I just felt a little thirsty…gettin' hot out here" L'il Murphy said, trying to justify his early-in-the-day drinking. "What's been happ'nin' around this way?" Jack asked just to make conversation. "Nothin' man…but, I got that fire weed…it's real good, too" Li'l Murphy boasted. "That's cool…but, I ain't lookin' for no weed right now" Jack responded. "If you run into anybody who's lookin'….send 'em my way" L'il Murphy urged. "Fa' sho" Jack replied. Jack and L'il Murphy had a lively conversation for another fifteen minutes or so before they saw Jabo suddenly appear, standing in the near distance on the sidewalk straight ahead of them.

"Jabooo!" L'il Murphy yelled out in his characteristic manner. Jabo walked slowly toward the two men. "Hey, y'all…what you cats up to?" Jabo greeted. "Got that good weed, Jabo" L'il Murphy announced with an enticing inflection. "L'il Murphy…you know I don't buy weed…I'll smoke it if you givin' out samples" Jabo chuckled. "Sorry, Jabo…hustler like me cain't go out like that" L'il Murphy said very sprightly. "Jack…let me holla' at you for a minute" Jabo said with a more serious tone as he touched Jack's elbow with his hand, indicating that he wanted to speak to him privately. "Excuse us for a minute, L'il Murphy…this is on the personal tip" Jabo turned to L'il Murphy to explain and excuse. Jack reacted by walking with Jabo a short distance away.

"Jack…I need your help, man" Jabo began. "What's happ'nin'?" Jack inquired as he paused to listen intently. "Listen...Puddin' ain't feelin too well right now…she needs to see her doctor so she can get another prescription for her blood-pressure medicine…she's been missin' takin' it for a few days…her doctor is up on Bryn Mawr…we already called and made an appointment for her…she's too sick to walk that far and we ain't got the money for a cab….can you help us out?" Jabo asked in almost a whisper. "No doubt, Jabo..I can drive you up there and back…but, I got to walk back home to get my car…can she wait that long?" Jack asked. "That shouldn't take too long…how long before you get back?" Jabo asked. "No more than a half-hour" Jack surmised. "That's cool, Jack…I'll wait 'til you get back…you know me and Puddin' sho 'nough appreciate it, too" Jabo said with sincere gratitude. "I'm on my way" Jack said. "Cool…thanks" Jabo said as Jack began to walk away. "L'il Murphy…I'll be back in a little while…got to make a run" Jack explained. "I'll still be here" Li'l Murphy replied. Jack always responded positively to Jabo and Puddin' for anything they might need. Jack felt very close to them. He loved them and there was a great amount of affection and trust between Jack and the older couple. They were like family and looked out for each other when they could; sharing whatever they had to offer to one another. There were a number of friends all over Uptown that Jack had these kinds of relationships with. Jack loved people; especially those he called his friends; those friends were usually the simple people on the streets who didn't have very much but, were full of personality and spirit; good people with good hearts that Jack seemed to gravitate to. Jack had this very protective nature about himself. He cared and worried about his friends. Jack walked briskly as he went west on Lawrence Avenue, then turned south onto Ashland Avenue before turning right on Wilson Avenue to walk a couple of blocks to the YMCA. He went into his room and retrieved his car keys. He always kept cash in his dresser drawer and he took a little extra cash from there before leaving right back out. He hopped into his car, drove back and parked it on Winthrop Street near the playground. As he was getting out of his car, Jack could see that Puddin' was already there waiting with Jabo and L'il Murphy as she sat at the bottom of the sliding board inside the playground. Jack started toward them and stopped just outside the playground fence. Jabo and Puddin' came out to meet him. "Yea, Jack…Puddin's doctor office is right there at the corner of Bryn Mawr and Winthrop" Jabo said as they all walked back to Jack's car and got in.

Jack drove north and arrived at the location in a short time. Puddin' went in to see her doctor as Jack and Jabo waited outside the office on the sidewalk. They walked up the street to a liquor store and Jack bought a half-pint of vodka for Jabo. He took a little swig himself. They came back and waited inside the office until Puddin' was done. Jack drove them to the pharmacy to fill her prescription. "Jack..you know I sho' 'nough appreciate you doin' this for me" Puddin' said with a mix of relief and sincere gratitude in her voice. "Anytime, Puddin'…you know I cain't let you down, especially when you ain't feelin' well" Jack replied. Everyone seemed a lot more loose after the anxious situation had passed. They laughed and joked in the car as Jack drove back toward The Corner. "Can you drop us off at the crib?…we just gonna take it easy…I'm gonna stay in with Puddin' until she is feelin' better" Jabo said. "Yea...no doubt" Jack replied as he made a left turn off of Broadway onto Ainslie and turned right onto Winthrop which was a one-way street going south. He parked in front of their apartment building that was across the street from the 4848 high-rise. "Here you go Puddin'" Jack said as he reached back and handed her a ten-dollar bill before she got out of the back seat. "Ohhh, Jack…thank you so much…bless your heart…I could sho' 'nough use this, too…I'll pay you back" Puddin' gushed with a smile. "You ain't got to pay me back…that's a birthday present" Jack responded. "But, my birthday passed in April already" Puddin' said with a hint of a puzzled tone. "Naw..that's an early birthday present for next year" Jack responded, smiling with a twinkle in his eye at Puddin' and Jabo. "Boy…you somethin' else…thank you" Puddin' chuckled as she and Jabo got out of the car smiling. That moment was Jack's reward. Jack always got a kick out of these pleasant little surprises that he would occasionally spring on some of his dearest friends. He drove onward a short distance down the block and parked back in the same spot across from the playground.

As he did so, he looked across the street into the playground to see Melvin, Andrew and LV hanging out with L'il Murphy. He got out of his car and began to walk over. When Jack was with Tina and was going to school, he had avoided Melvin and that whole crew because he had hopes and aspirations. But now, since his spectacular decline from civility, he had once again come to accept them and this crazy Street Gypsy life. He had already gotten high on heroin with them a few weeks ago on a couple of occasions; paying the bigger portion of the dope bill because the others were short. It was a small price to pay to keep from going to cop himself and risk getting robbed again. He had also been hanging out with them on The Corner recently; drinking with them and going on a hustling escapade now-and-then with Melvin just like they used to do. They were all heroin fiends and the slickest hustlers around. They knew every angle; every scheme; every mind game to play; the overlay-for-the-underplay; playing both-ends-against the middle; the pigeon drop and every other nefarious game that could be played. They were extremely clever; ruthlessly deceptive; rarely getting busted for their hustling activities. Melvin and Andrew had wives and kids so, it was important that they maintained a civilized façade. LV hung around with them occasionally but, liked to be by himself most of the time. “Hey, y’all” Jack greeted as he went from man-to-man with a soul handshake.

“What y’all doin’?” Jack asked with the standard street greeting. “We tryin’ to give L’il Murphy some game…teach him how to play the ladies…he got a lot to learn” “LV started as he looked at L’il Murphy with a sly, teasing grin. “Hey, man..I know how to deal with these women…I don’t need nobody to teach me *nothin*’” L’il Murphy said defiantly. “But, on the real, L’il Murph…didn’t I see you last night with that ugly girl that lives on the fourth floor?...you was givin’ her free weed wasn’t you?” Andrew said with a serious tone and a straight face. “Aw, hell naw!....come on, now!...I was *not* with her and givin’ her free weed…she was buyin’…she just a customer, man…I got a lot of female customers” L’il Murphy shot back emphatically with the same defensive tone. “I was standin’ right there..I didn’t see her give you no money” Andrew continued calmly with his teasing ruse. “She paid me, man..I ain’t lyin’…you know you seen her pay me…come on, now!” L’il Murphy said as he continued his defense. All of the men let out a little chuckle at the same time after getting that animated rise out of L’il Murphy. They moved on to another topic and stopped teasing L’il Murphy. Jack and all of them talked for a good while before a bunch of kids appeared and began to play in the playground. The men all moved together over to the 4848 building and sat in a favorite spot; the long ledge that was a wall to the underground, open-air parking lot that was ground-level. Most days, someone was sitting on these ledges that conveniently faced the streets and were along the path where people walked into and out of the building.

“Hey. Andrew…it’s almost time to go see that mark, ain’t it?…what time you got, Jack?” Melvin said with a hint of urgency. “Twelve-thirty” Jack replied, after glancing at his watch. “Yea…we better get on up there…if we get there too late, we might miss him" Andrew replied. "Jack…do us a favor, man…can you run us up around Broadway and Diversey?" Melvin asked. Jack didn't like using his car as a taxi for every little thing that came up out on the streets for various people. But, he would do it occasionally if it didn't inconvenience him. He never let anyone take advantage of him in that way; especially his dope-fiend pals. They probably knew better than most not to ask Jack these favors. They were all aware and a little wary of one another because there were so many mind games being played by each on the other. Each man was always conscious of the fact that the others were fiends; and fiends didn't care if you were their friend or not. They would play on you if you let them and if it would result in them getting high. These men were at the point that they had stopped even trying to scheme on one another because each was so guarded and wary of the others. This was the way it was in the esoteric world of Street Gypsies. "What Street around Broadway and Diversey?" Jack asked. "Uh..what street is that, Andrew?" Melvin asked. "Surf" Andrew replied. "How long you gonna be?" Jack asked. "We just gonna run up to his crib for a few minutes and come right back down…you know we hustlin' man…this will be real quick…no bullshit, Jack" Melvin assured. "Okay…I'll wait on you fifteen minutes…I'm gone after that…remember that" Jack said sternly. "I'm stayin' here" LV said. "Let's go..we got to get up there before one" Melvin urged. The three men got into Jack's car and as he began to drive, the sky was beginning to cloud up. As Jack drove along, Melvin gave out a few details of their hustle. "Yea, Jack…this stud is a mark we run into up on Lincoln Avenue in a bar one night…he was high as hell, wasn't he, Andrew?" Melvin said.

"Yea" Andrew replied. "Yea..we got to kickin' it with him and he told us he works in the jewelry shop on Halsted" Melvin continued. "He was so high…he started tellin' us about how he got a stash of jewelry he stole from there" Andrew added. "Yea..and he got it hid at his mother's house…but, he is lookin' for a safe fence for the jewelry" Melvin said. "How is he stealin' jewelry and still workin' there?" Jack asked curiously. "The books, man...he keeps the books as well as bein' a salesman" Andrew said. "Yea…he cookin' the books to hide what he stole" Melvin said. "He told us the owner is an old stud who trusts him a lot because he's been workin' for him three years with no problems…but, the mark say he is gonna quit pretty soon if he can sell all of this jewelry he's got" Andrew said. "So, what y'all goin' up there to see him for?" Jack asked. "Well..we talked him into lettin' us fence a couple of pieces and if we do that without no problem, we will put him in touch with our fence so he can sell directly to him without us" Melvin said. "He is takin' a chance givin' y'all some jewelry to fence" Jack surmised. "Yea, he *is* takin' a chance but, he ain't got nobody else he can trust…if he tries to sell to any of his friends or people in the bars, they might trace it back to him because the crowd he hangs around are mostly honest, square motherfuckers who might tell…he wouldn't dare tell them he is stealin'…he knows we're hustlers so, we ain't gonna tell nothin'" Melvin explained. "So how is he gonna pay y'all for doin' all of this for him?" Jack asked. "He supposed to give us a couple of pieces to sell right now" Andrew said. "Yea…and he is gonna kick us back some money from that once we sell it" Melvin added. "Awww…I get the picture" Jack said with a lazy, sly smile" They all burst into sinister laughter.

The Cadillac cruised south along the local route of Broadway; passing the specialty boutiques and shops along the way; stopping at almost every light. The sunshine had disappeared and the sky had gotten a bit darker. Finally, they reached Surf Street and Jack turned onto it. "Don't go too far…find a parkin' spot somewhere around here, Jack" Melvin advised as Jack slowed the car down to almost a stop. Jack parked at the end of the block behind the last car on one side of the one-way street that ran east-west. The end of the car stuck out slightly into the crosswalk of the intersection. The area was a bit dense with cars parked on the streets; most were later models. It was an upscale area that seemed to have a hint of affluence with well maintained buildings and cleaner streets. The smattering of people walking around seemed to carry an air of sophistication. "Jack…we're gonna take care of this business as soon as we can…wait for us, now" Melvin said. "Just remember what I said about takin' too long" Jack reminded them. Melvin and Andrew scrambled out of the car and began walking at a hurried pace directly across to the opposite side of the street. Jack watched them disappear around the corner to the next street that ran north and south. Jack reared back in the driver's seat and rested his head. He looked up at the sky to see rolling, darker clouds mix in with the gray ones as the sky became ominously darker. Jack nodded out and closed his eyes for a little while. He snapped out of it. He looked at his watch. 1:14pm. He sat and continued to wait. Another moment passed. He looked at his watch again. 1:21pm. Jack began to feel a little anxious. But, he continued to wait. He just sat there a bit absent-mindedly as another moment passed. He was about to look at his watch again when he suddenly saw Melvin and Andrew appear, coming back around the same corner. They were almost trotting and looking a bit wild-eyed. Jack could sense by their pace and facial expressions that something was amiss. When the two came within a few yards of the car they began to run. Each of them snatched a rear door open on both sides of the car and hopped in.

"Jack…take off, man…take off!" Melvin said with a tone of desperation. "What the fuck is goin' on man?…take off for what?…what's goin on!" Jack demanded with a confused and disturbed tone. "Jack…just take off, man…take off…somethin' didn't go right…we'll tell you about it later, man….let's get the fuck outa' here!" Andrew urged with the same desperation. Jack backed the car up into the crosswalk and as he cut the wheels to pull out, a man and a woman came running toward the car. They seemed to come out of nowhere. Jack looked across at them coming toward him. They were across the street running hurriedly toward the car. "Stop!…stop!" they were yelling. Jack floored the gas pedal and almost side-swiped a double parked as he wrestled to maintain control of the car. He looked in the rearview mirror to see Melvin and Andrew scooted down in the back seat. He could also see the strange man and woman running behind the car but, fading quickly in the distance behind the car. "Andrew..why you do that shit?…everything was cool…you shoulda' left that shit alone!...we already made our hustle…damn!" Melvin admonished Andrew. "Man…I couldn't help it…it was right there… anyway…it's too late to talk about it…let's just get as far away from here as we can!" Andrew reasoned with a heightened anxiety. Jack was confused and angry and feeling as desperate as they were to get away from what ever happened. "What the fuck y'all do, man!" Jack shouted angrily. "We'll tell you all about it later, Jack…let's go, man!" Melvin urged anxiously. Jack came to Sheridan Road and turned right to head south. He came to a traffic light at Diversey. Several cars were in front of him stopped at the red light. The sound of thunder rumbled in the air as everything had turned darker. It wasn't much longer before the light turned green as the succession of cars in front of Jack's pulled off ever so slowly. Jack was still arguing with the two; barely watching his driving as he argued angrily. Jack's mind raced with confusion and anxiety. He knew that whatever happened back there with Melvin and Andrew, now involved the police. Jack took the route through the park, continuing south and passing the huge statue that stood at the corner of Diversey Parkway. He drove fast and a short time later, reached Fullerton Avenue, a street that ran east-west. "Jack, it would be better if you turn left and take Lake Shore Drive" Andrew suggested. All of the men were feeling that same anxiety and desperation as Jack made the turn. He took the ramp onto Lake Shore Drive. Melvin and Andrew kept looking anxiously behind the car through the rear window. "Hey, man…I think we're cool, now…come off at the next exit" Andrew suggested with a sigh of relief. Jack slowed the speed a little as he came upon the LaSalle Street exit at Lincoln Park. He slowed more as he came onto the exit ramp.

Suddenly sirens began to blast in the near distance behind the car. Jack looked in the darkness of the rearview mirror to see several plain cars with the blue flashing lights, mixed in with the other traffic and coming onto the exit ramp behind him. Ahead, were several other plain and Chicago Police cars blocking the exit as they had come onto it against the grain of oncoming traffic. Several had parked on the edges of the grass and others were all around the exit ramp, surrounding Jack's car. Jack's heart dropped as the police vehicles had suddenly appeared out of nowhere. They had Jack's car blocked off from each direction. Jack pulled the car over to the side, stopped and just stared blankly into space over the steering wheel and through the windshield as his heart raced insanely. The policemen in each car jumped out and aimed hand guns, rifles and pumps at Jack's car. "Everybody get out of the car with your hands up!...right now!!...get out!!…get out of the car with your hands up!...hurry up!!" the police yelled. Each man got out and stood with their hands in the air at the center of a sea of police cars and policemen with drawn guns. Thunder crackled loudly across the dark sky and the rain started pouring down.

www.ingramcontent.com/pod-product-compliance
Lightning Source LLC
Chambersburg PA
CBHW030823310726
48980CB00006B/609/J

* 9 7 8 0 6 1 5 1 4 2 0 5 0 *